SHERLOCK BONES

AND THE

SEA-CREATURE
FEATURE

BONES

AND THE

SEA-CREATURE
FEATURE

RENÉE TREML

HOUGHTON MIFFLIN HARCOURT

Boston   New York

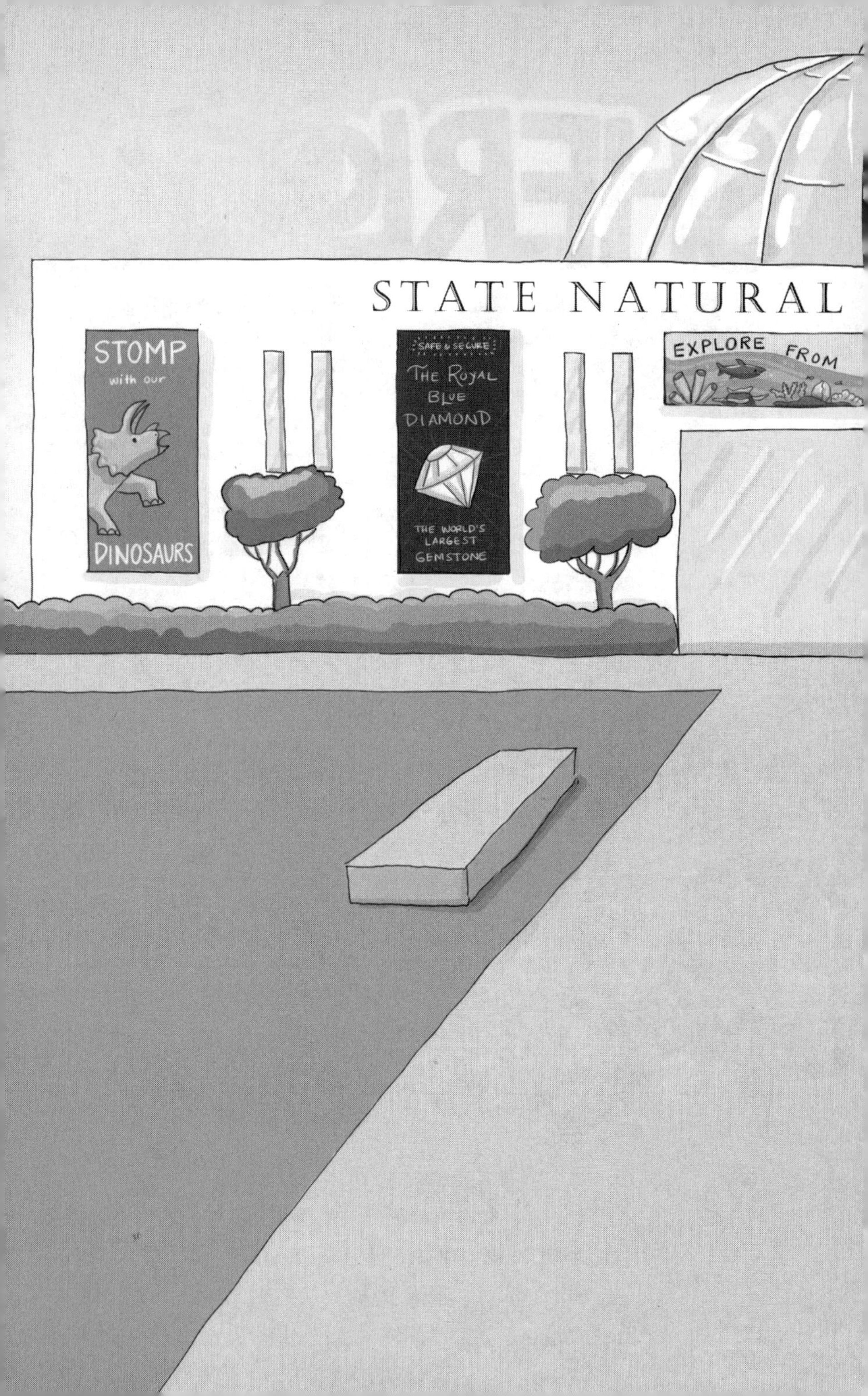
STATE NATURAL
STOMP with our DINOSAURS
SAFE & SECURE
THE ROYAL BLUE DIAMOND
THE WORLD'S LARGEST GEMSTONE
EXPLORE FROM

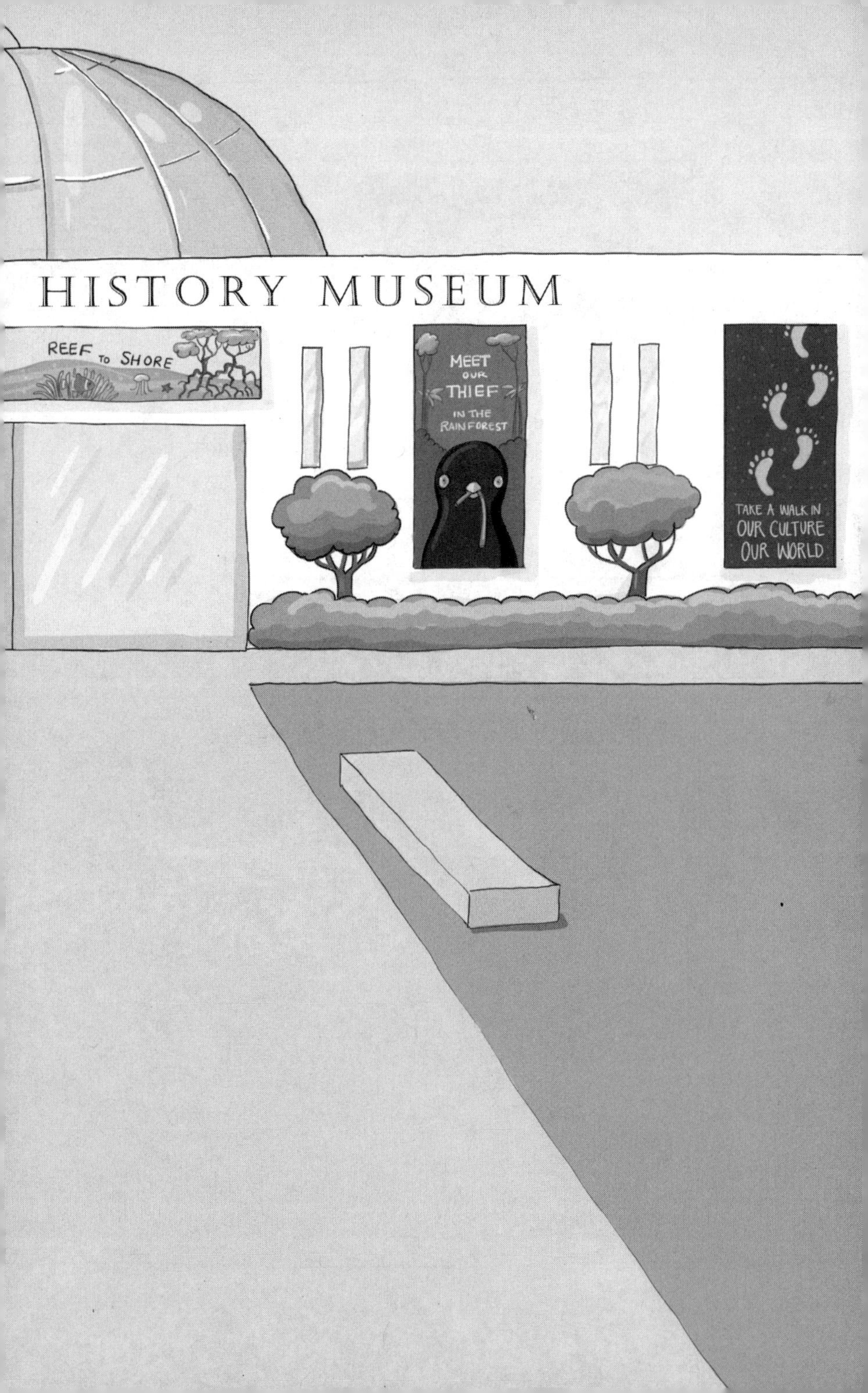

HISTORY MUSEUM
REEF TO SHORE
MEET OUR THIEF IN THE RAINFOREST
TAKE A WALK IN OUR CULTURE OUR WORLD

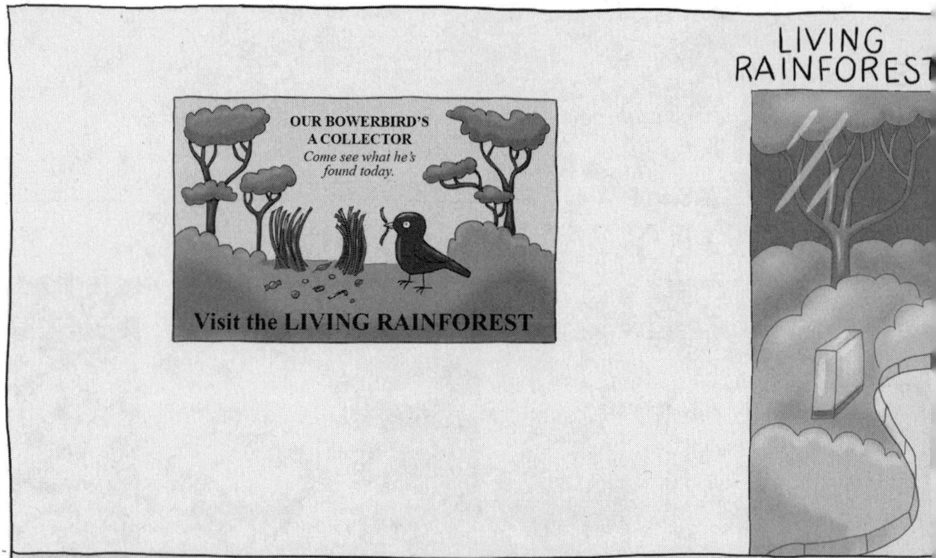
OUR BOWERBIRD'S
A COLLECTOR
Come see what he's
found today.
Visit the LIVING RAINFOREST
LIVING
RAINFOREST

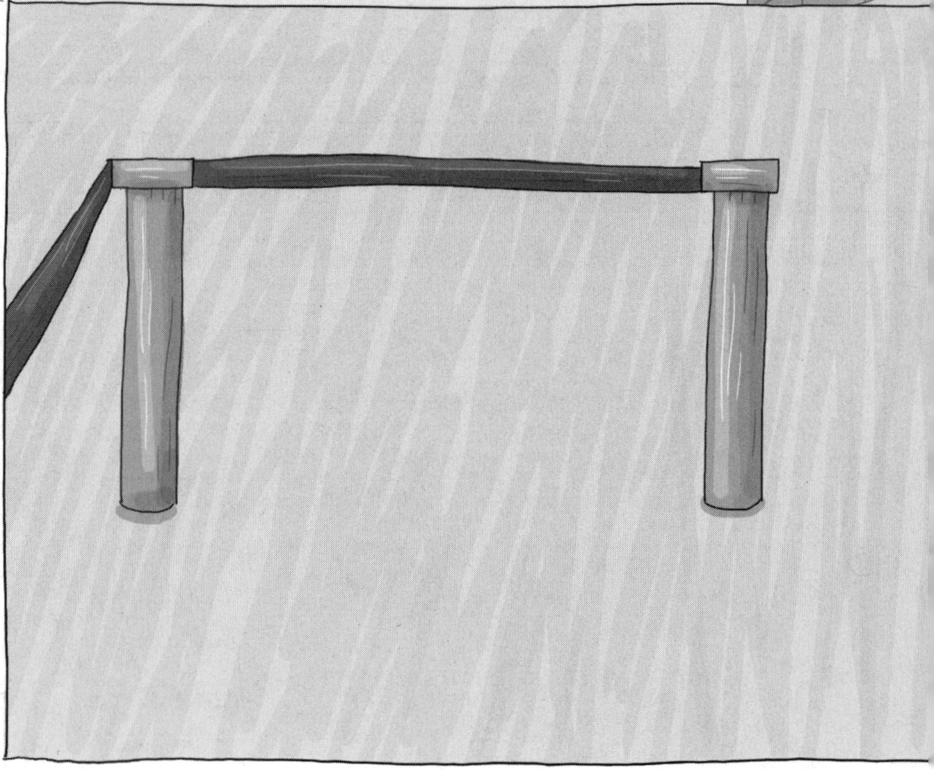

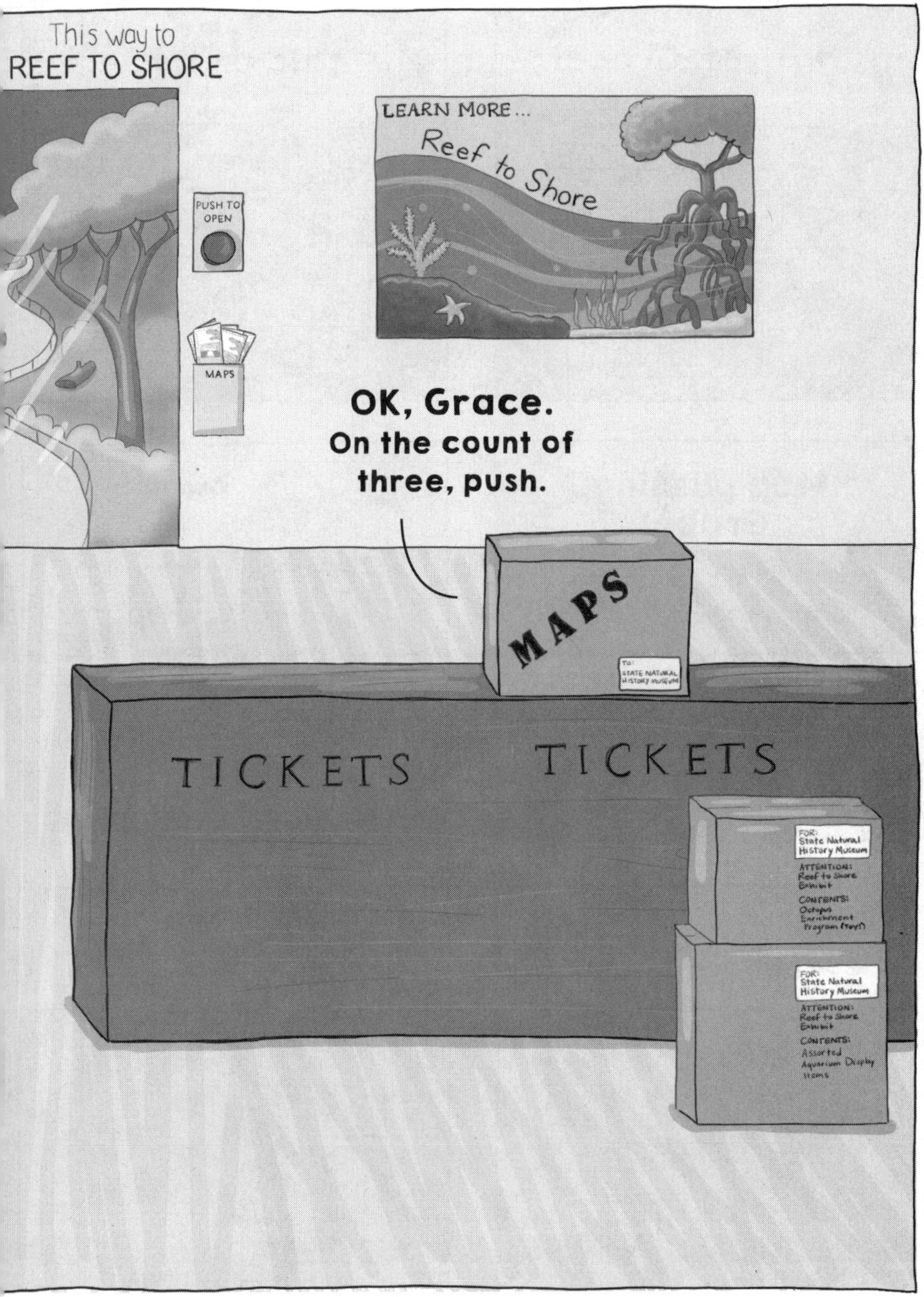
This way to
REEF TO SHORE
PUSH TO OPEN
MAPS
LEARN MORE...
Reef to Shore
OK, Grace.
On the count of three, push.
MAPS
TO:
STATE NATURAL HISTORY MUSEUM
TICKETS
TICKETS
FOR:
State Natural History Museum
ATTENTION:
Reef to Shore Exhibit
CONTENTS:
Octopus Enrichment Program (toys)
FOR:
State Natural History Museum
ATTENTION:
Reef to Shore Exhibit
CONTENTS:
Assorted Aquarium Display items

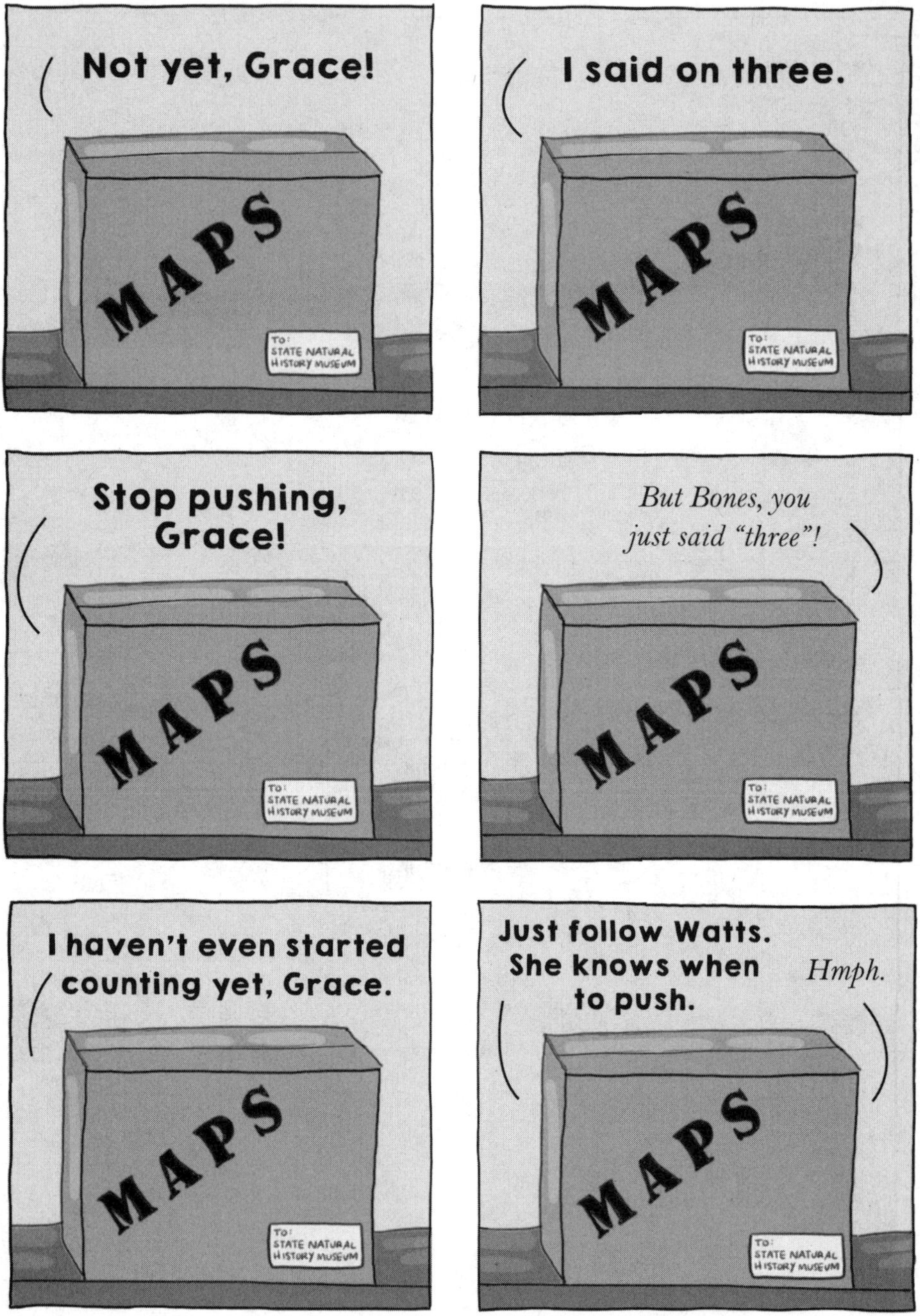
Not yet, Grace!
MAPS
TO: STATE NATURAL HISTORY MUSEUM
I said on three.
MAPS
TO: STATE NATURAL HISTORY MUSEUM
Stop pushing, Grace!
MAPS
TO: STATE NATURAL HISTORY MUSEUM
But Bones, you just said "three"!
MAPS
TO: STATE NATURAL HISTORY MUSEUM
I haven't even started counting yet, Grace.
MAPS
TO: STATE NATURAL HISTORY MUSEUM
Just follow Watts. She knows when to push.
Hmph.
MAPS
TO: STATE NATURAL HISTORY MUSEUM

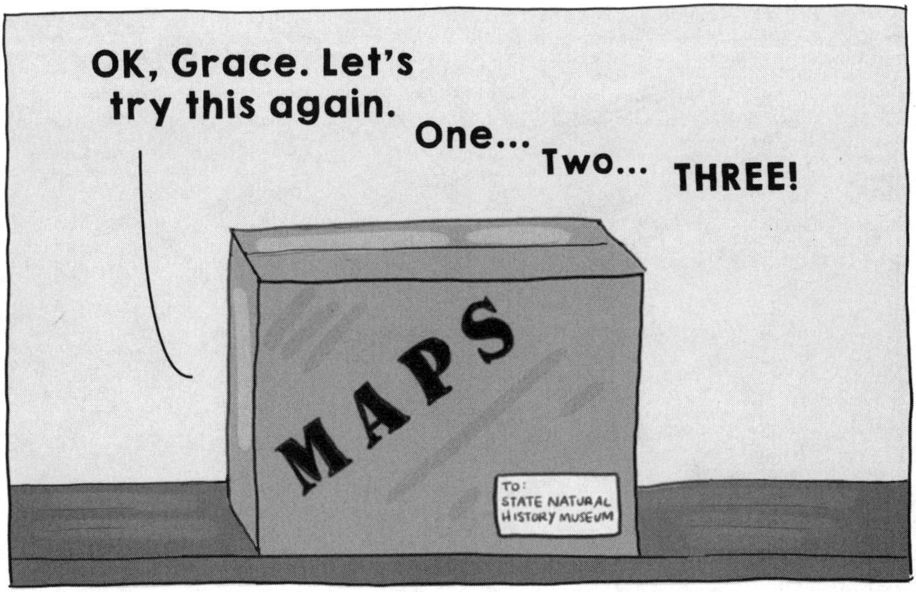
OK, Grace. Let's try this again.
One...
Two...
THREE!
MAPS
TO:
STATE NATURAL
HISTORY MUSEUM

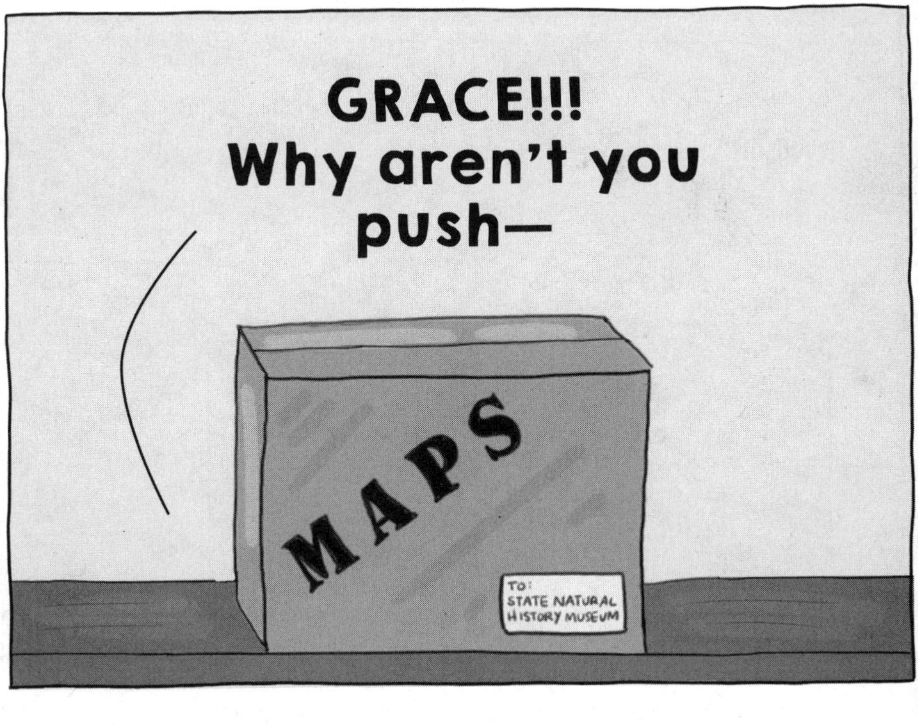
GRACE!!!
Why aren't you push—
MAPS
TO:
STATE NATURAL
HISTORY MUSEUM

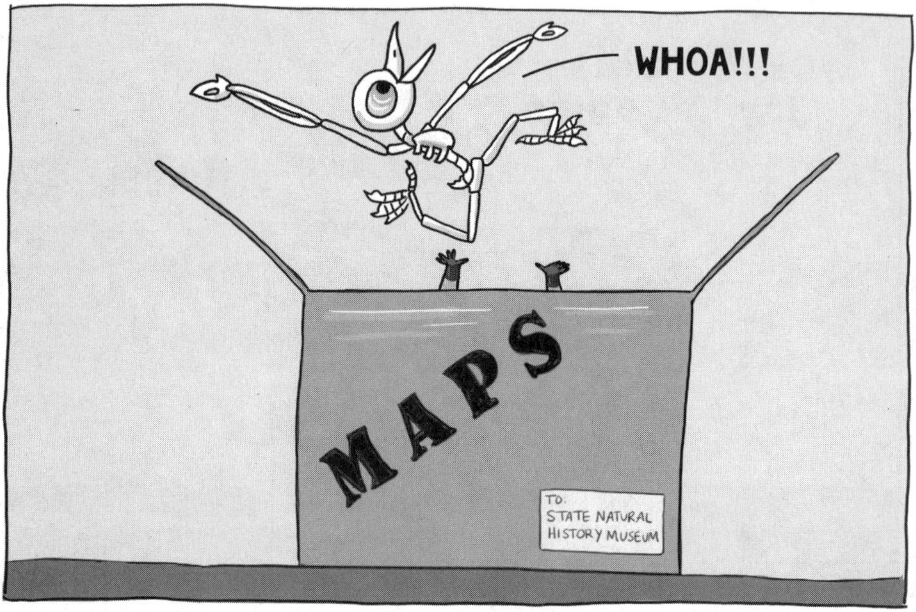
WHOA!!!
MAPS
TO:
STATE NATURAL
HISTORY MUSEUM

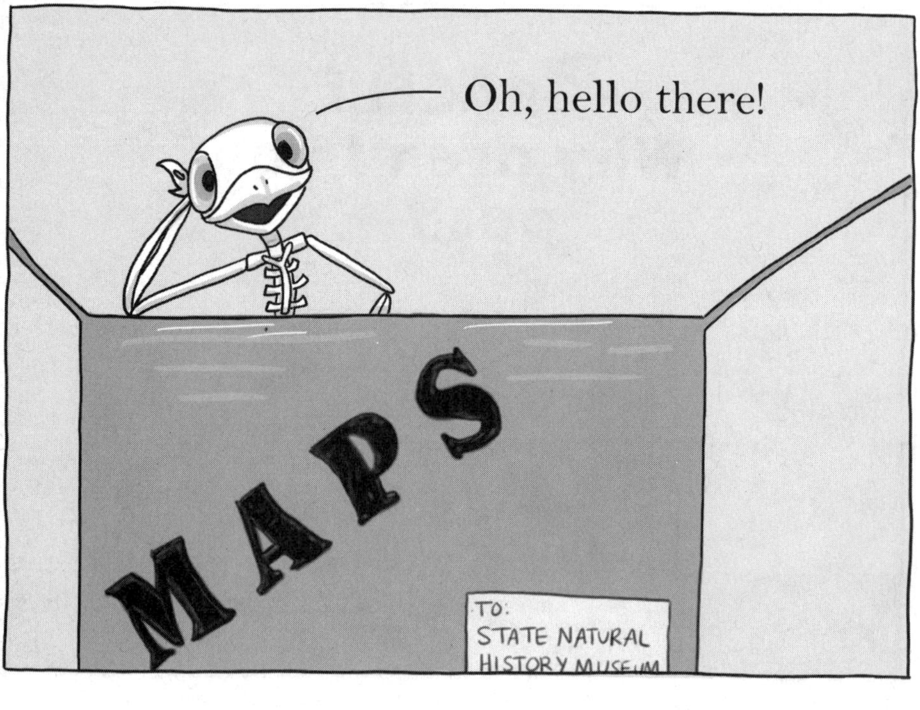
Oh, hello there!
MAPS
TO:
STATE NATURAL

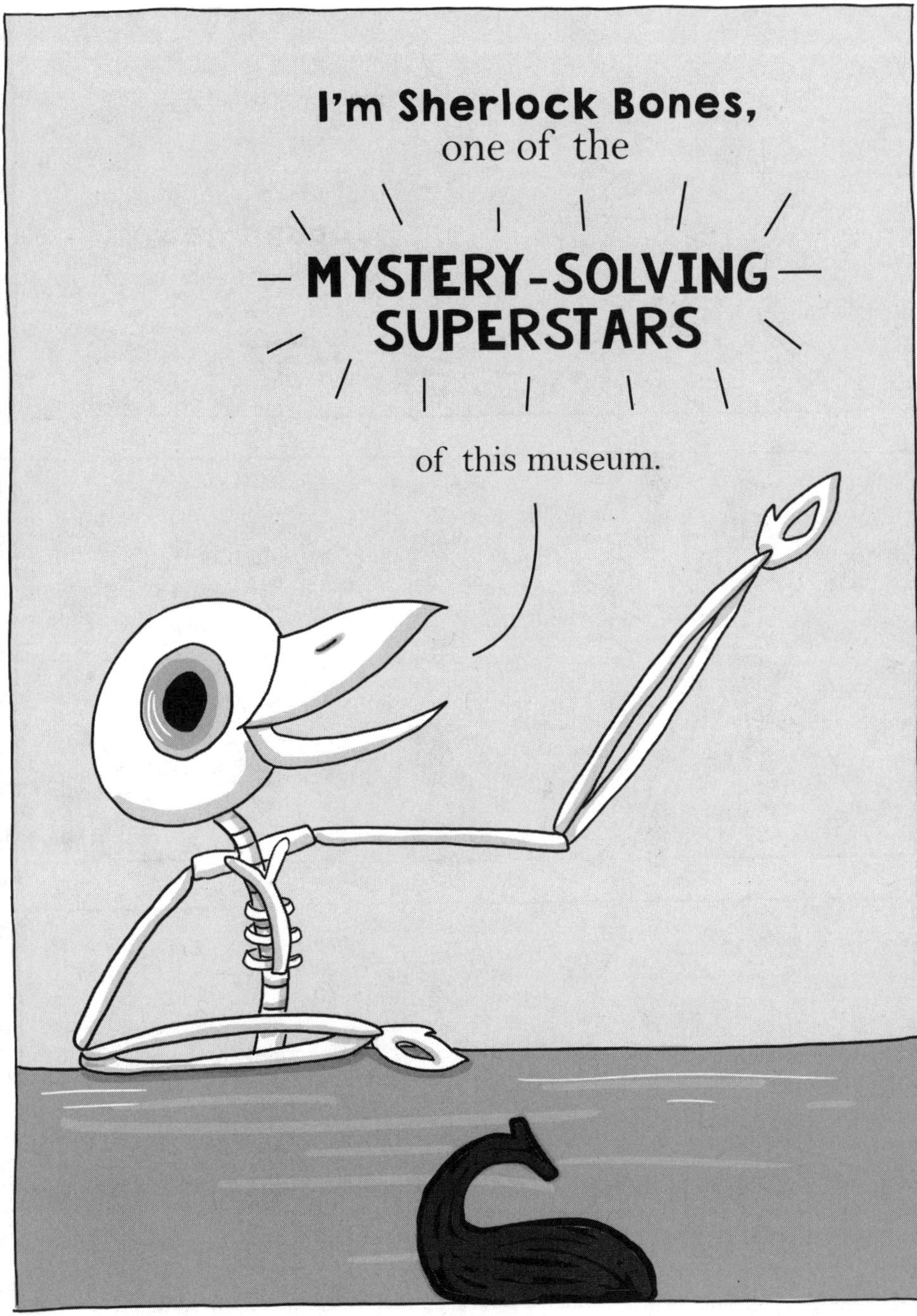
I'm Sherlock Bones,
one of the
MYSTERY-SOLVING
SUPERSTARS
of this museum.

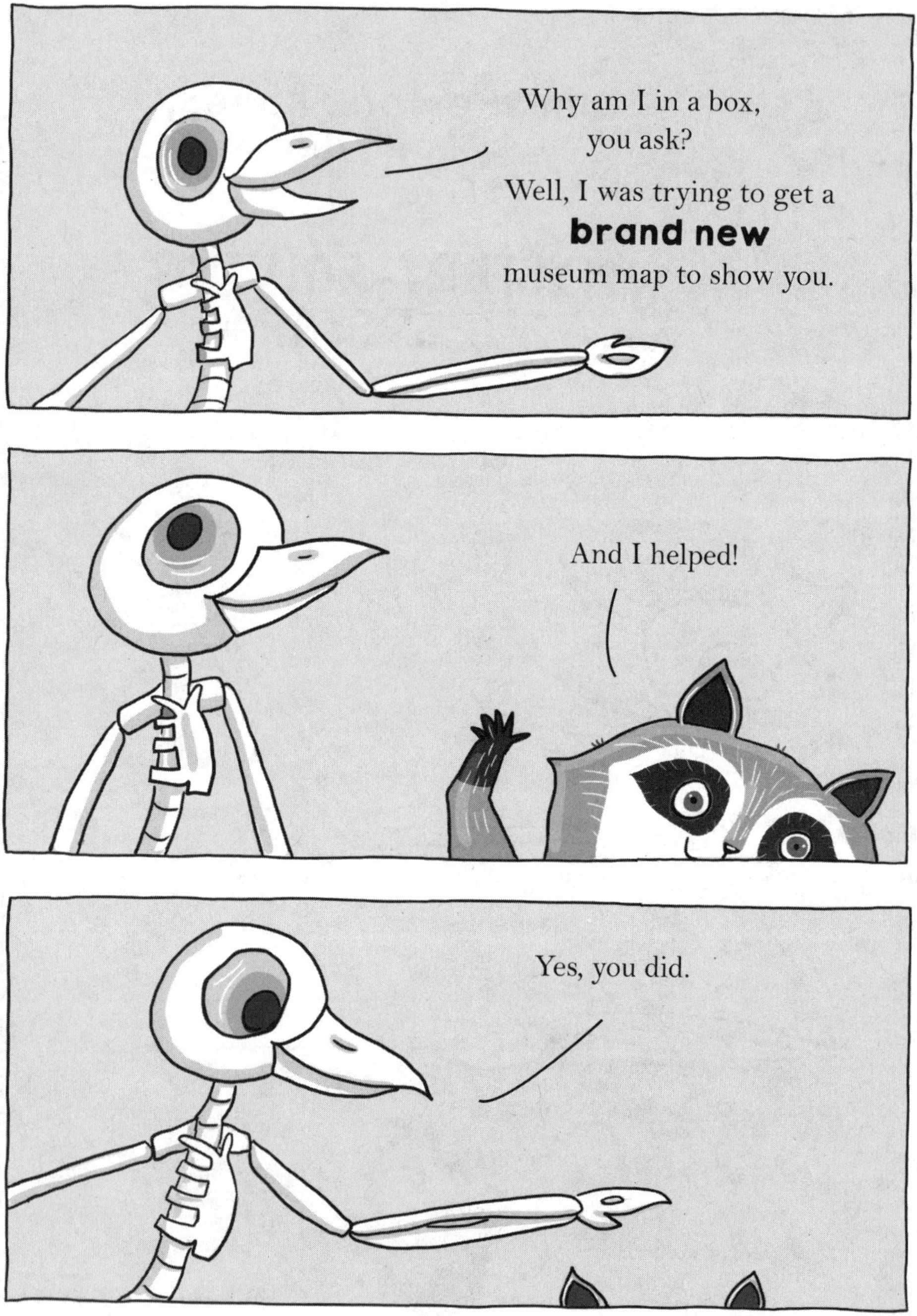
Why am I in a box, you ask?
Well, I was trying to get a **brand new** museum map to show you.
And I helped!
Yes, you did.

And by *helped* she means getting us stuck in this box.

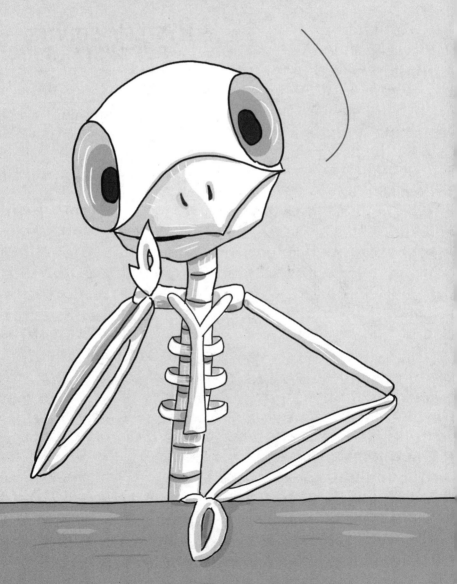

Allow me to start again...

I'm Sherlock Bones,
one of the

MYSTERY-SOLVING SUPERSTARS

of this museum.

And these are my
trusty partners...

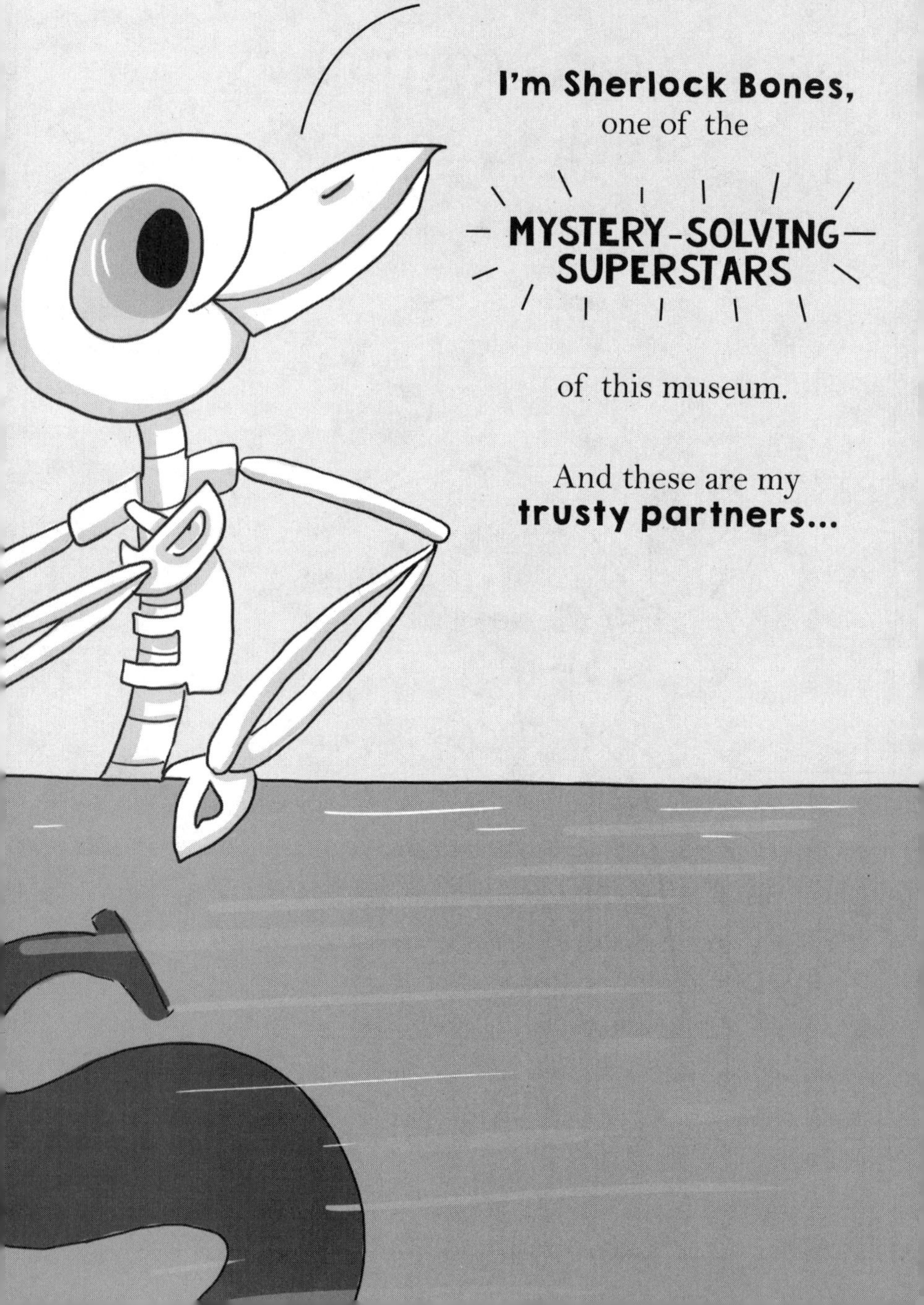

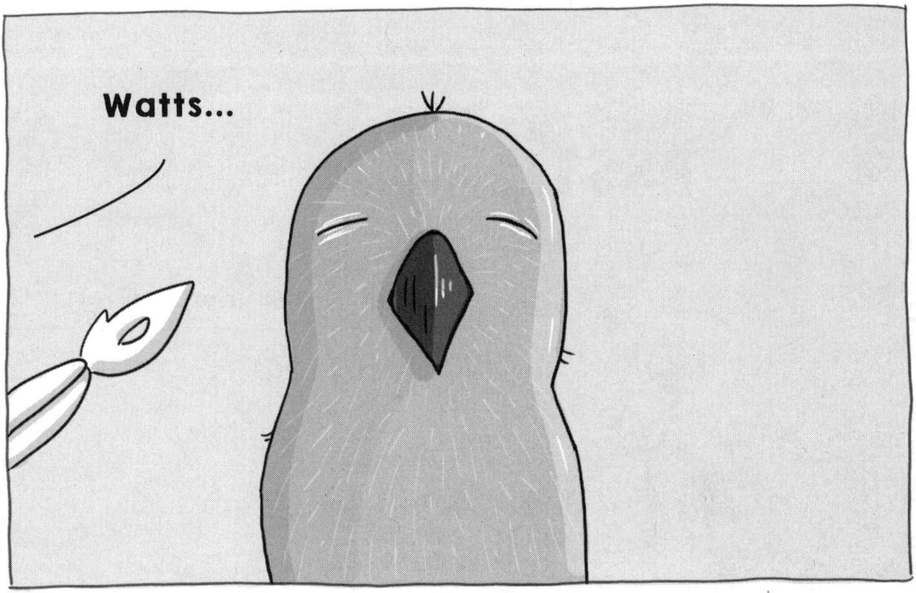
Watts...

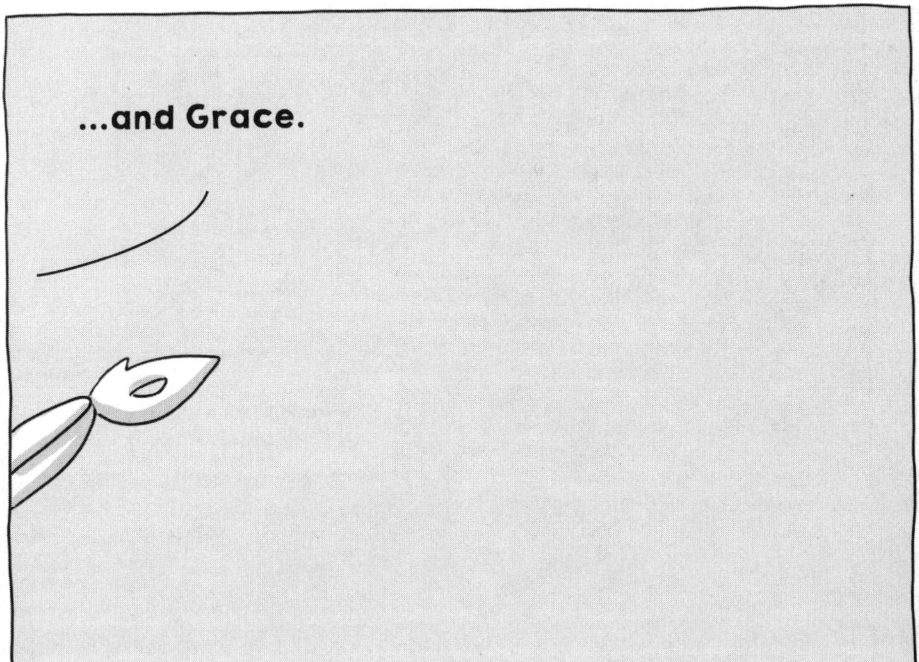
...and Grace.

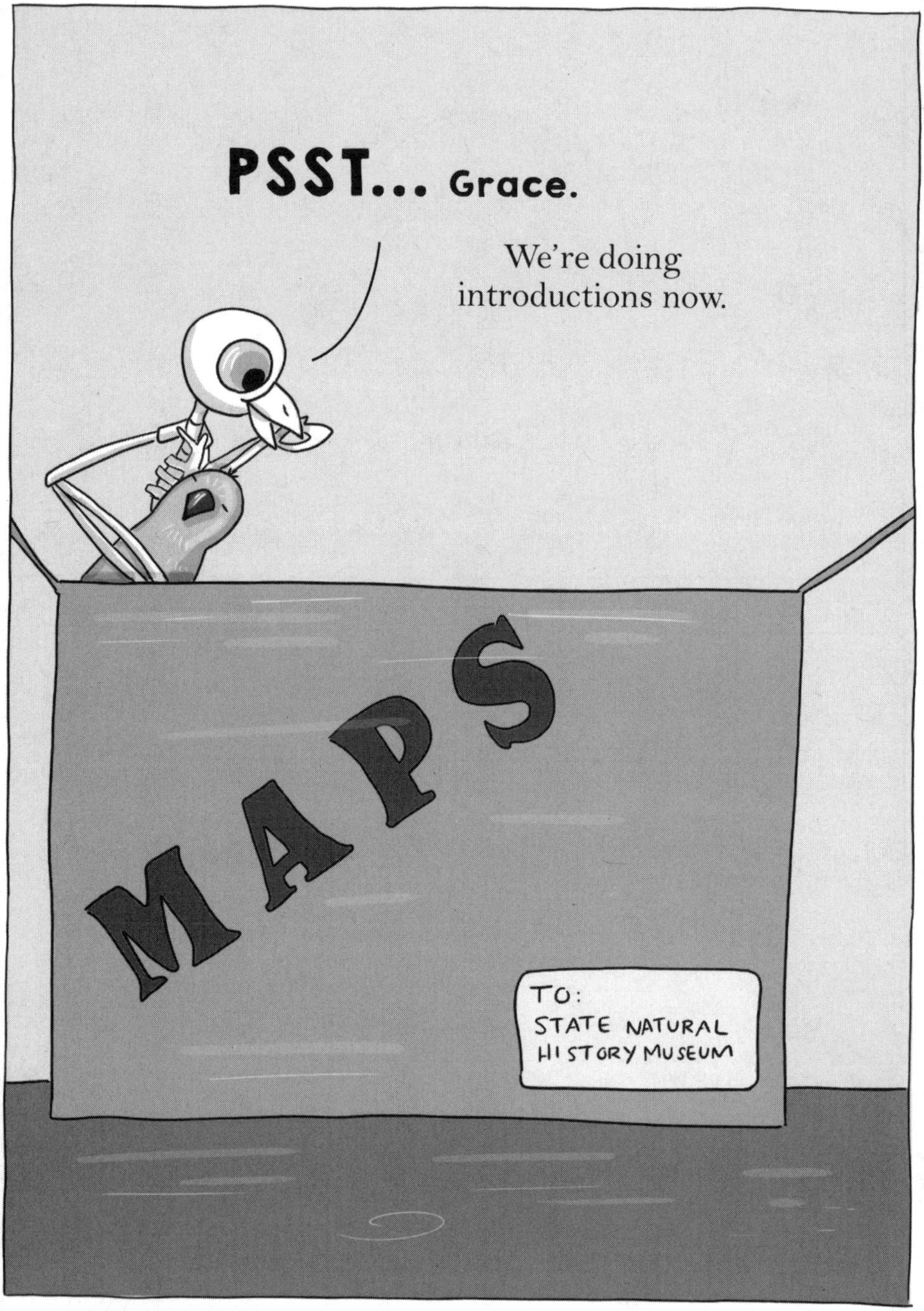
PSST... Grace.
We're doing introductions now.
MAPS
TO:
STATE NATURAL HISTORY MUSEUM

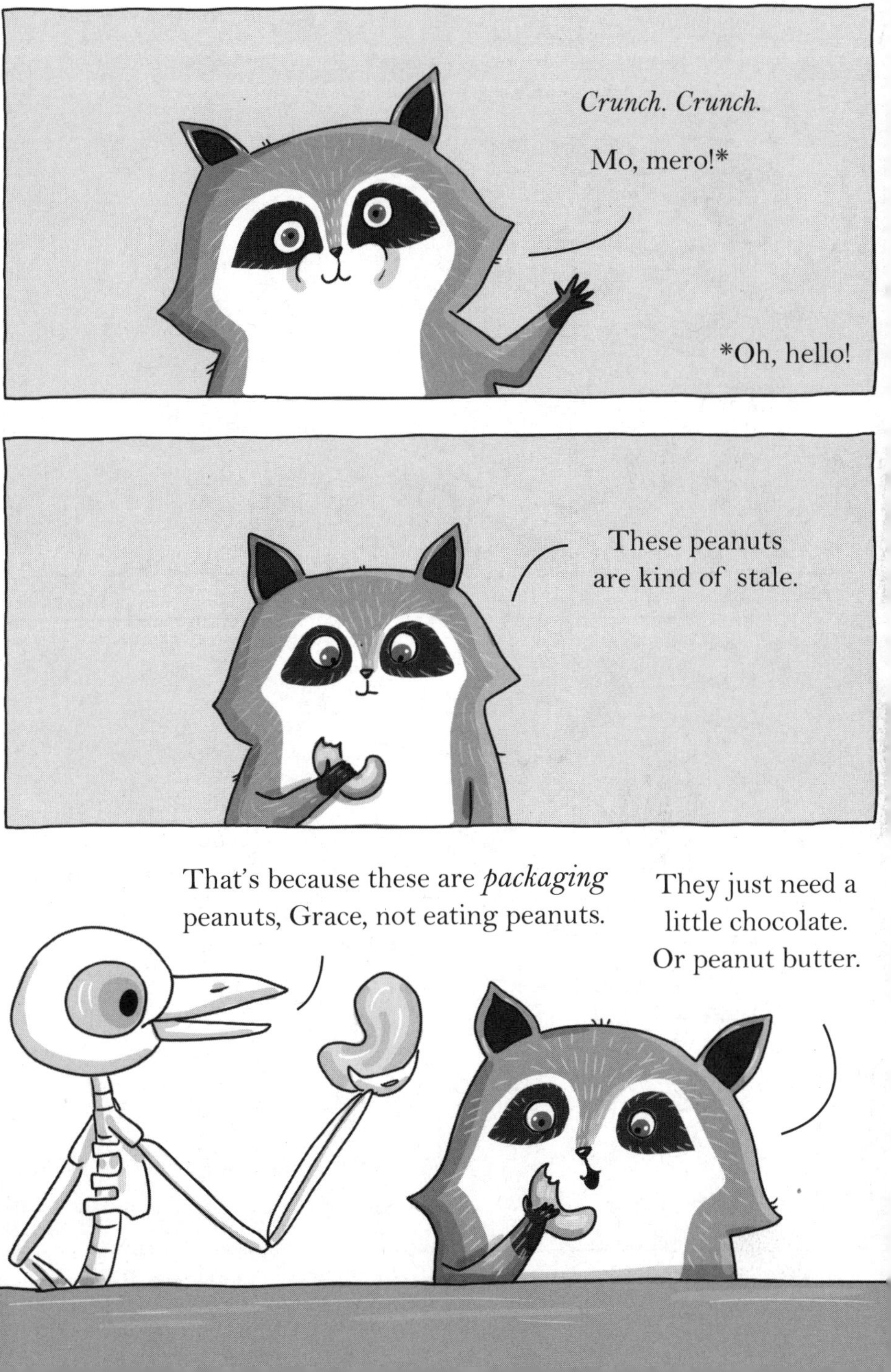
Crunch. Crunch.
Mo, mero!*
*Oh, hello!
These peanuts are kind of stale.
That's because these are *packaging* peanuts, Grace, not eating peanuts.
They just need a little chocolate. Or peanut butter.

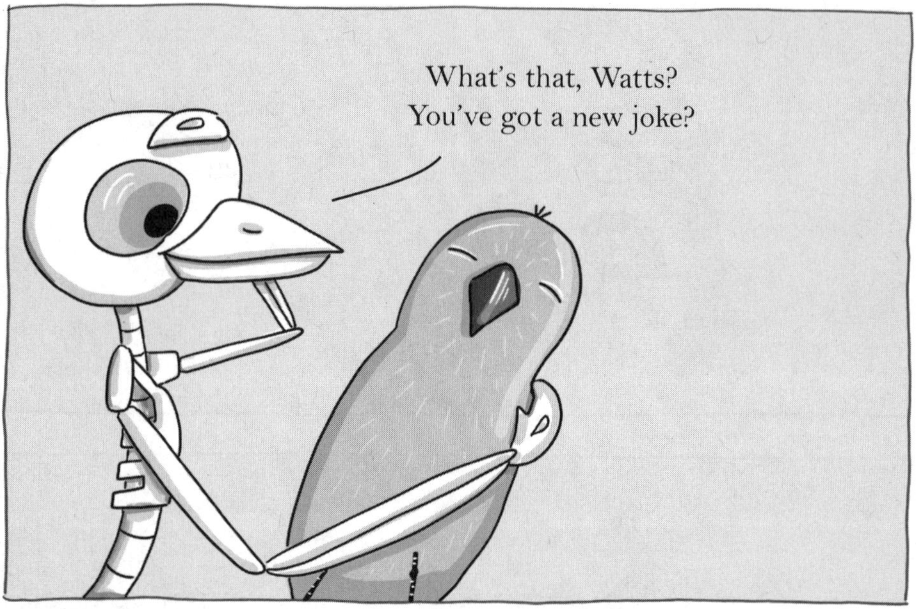
What's that, Watts?
You've got a new joke?

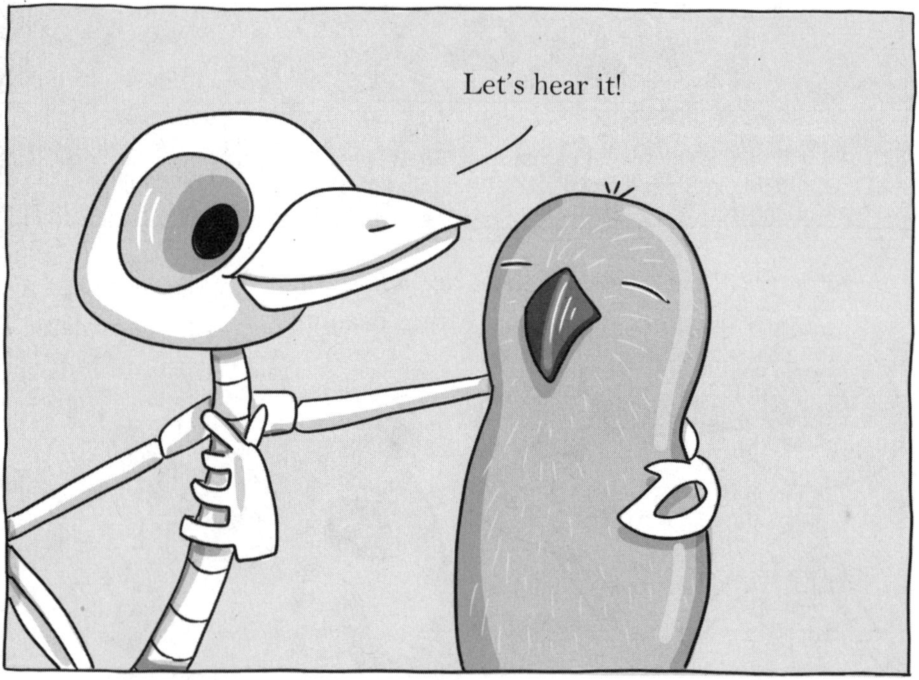
Let's hear it!

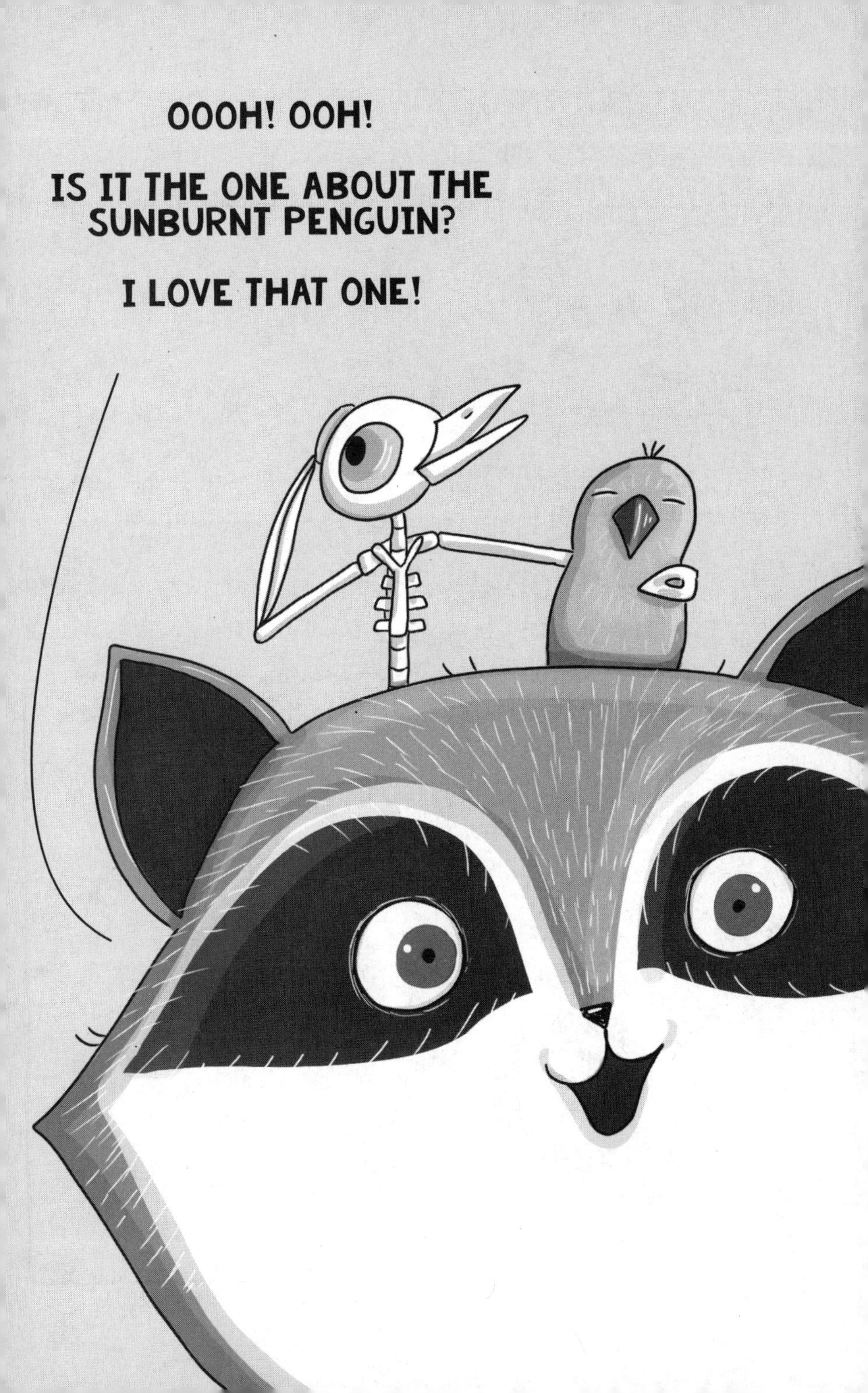
OOOH! OOH!
IS IT THE ONE ABOUT THE SUNBURNT PENGUIN?
I LOVE THAT ONE!

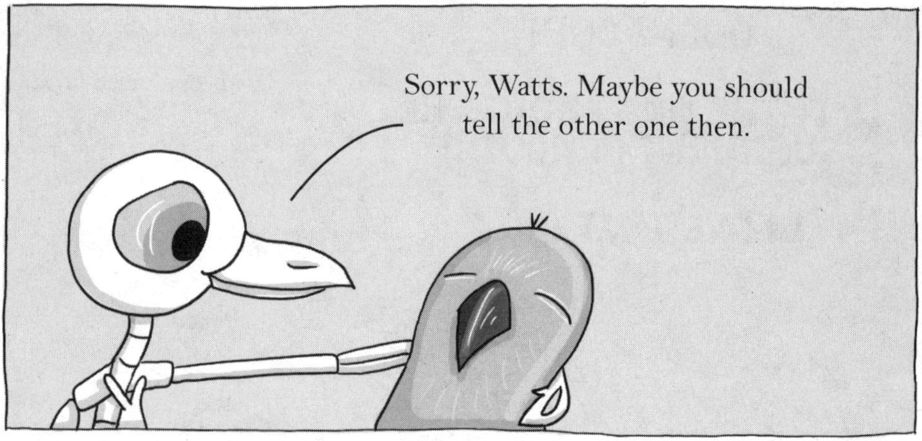
Sorry, Watts. Maybe you should tell the other one then.

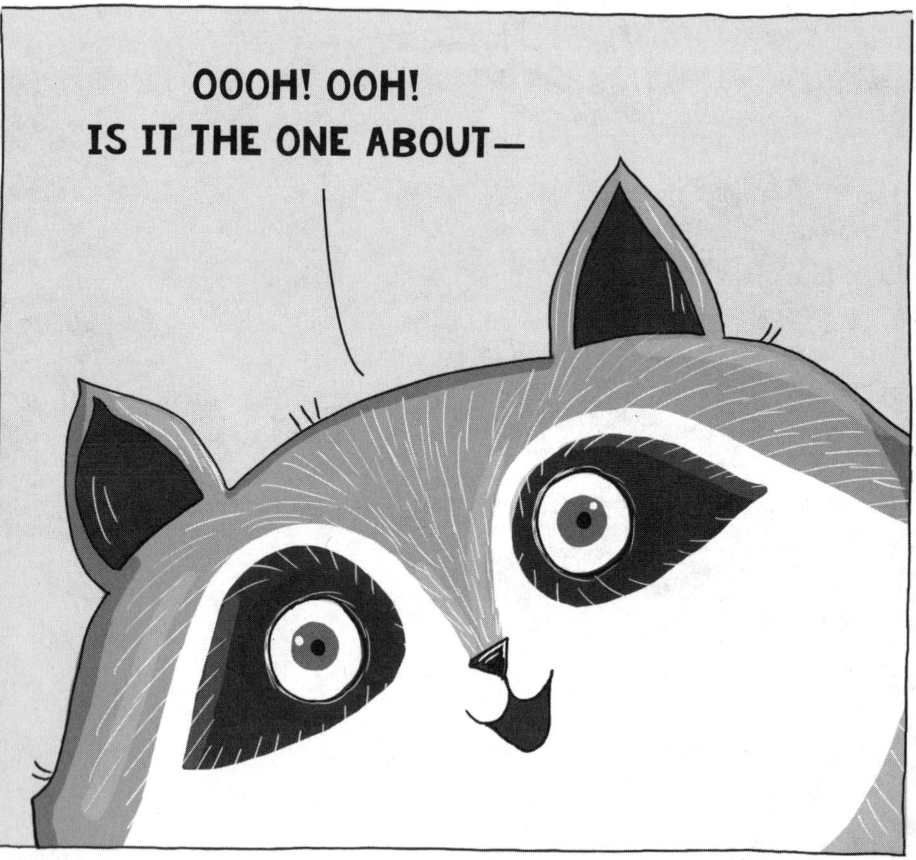
OOOH! OOH!
IS IT THE ONE ABOUT—

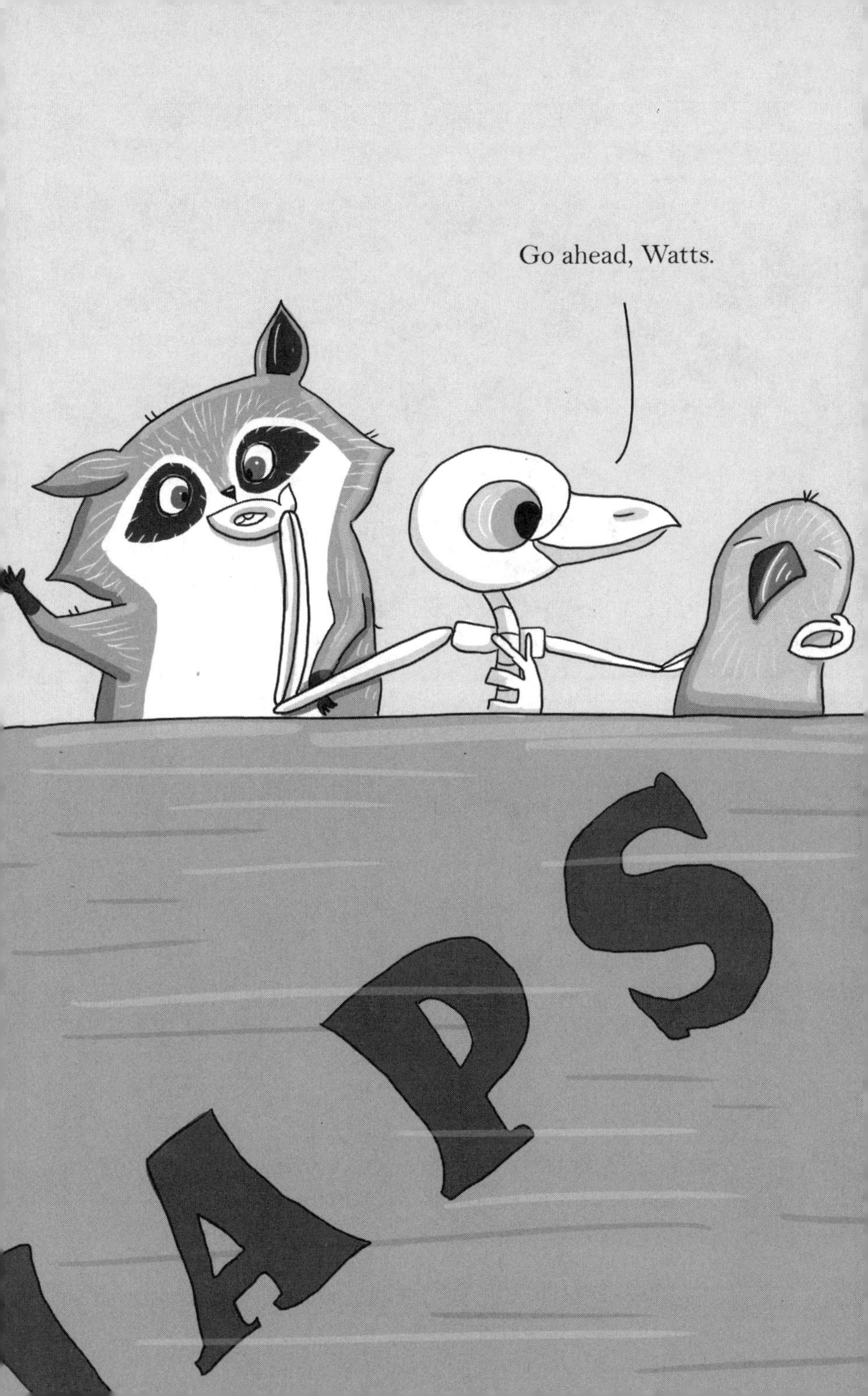
Go ahead, Watts.
APS

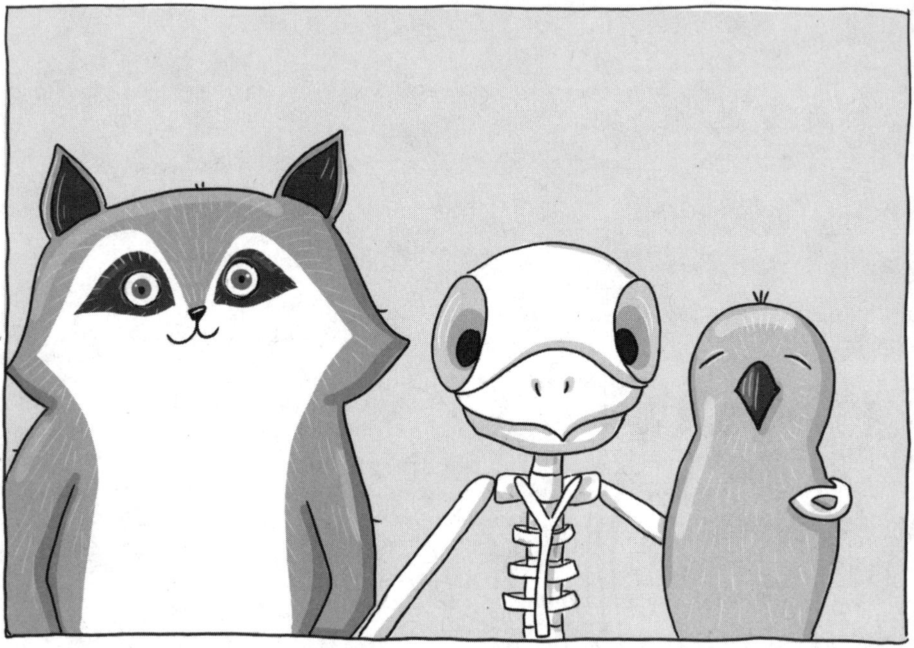

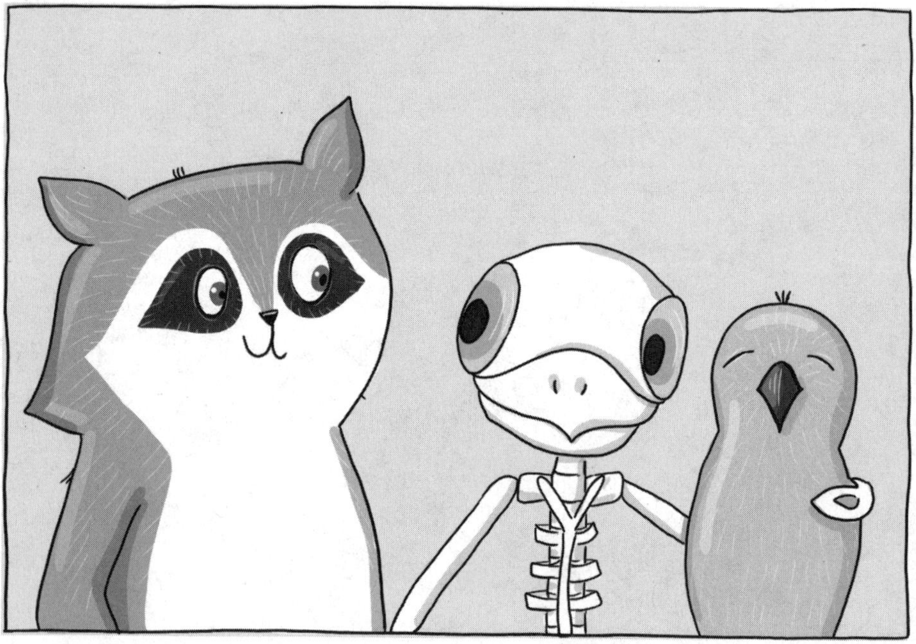

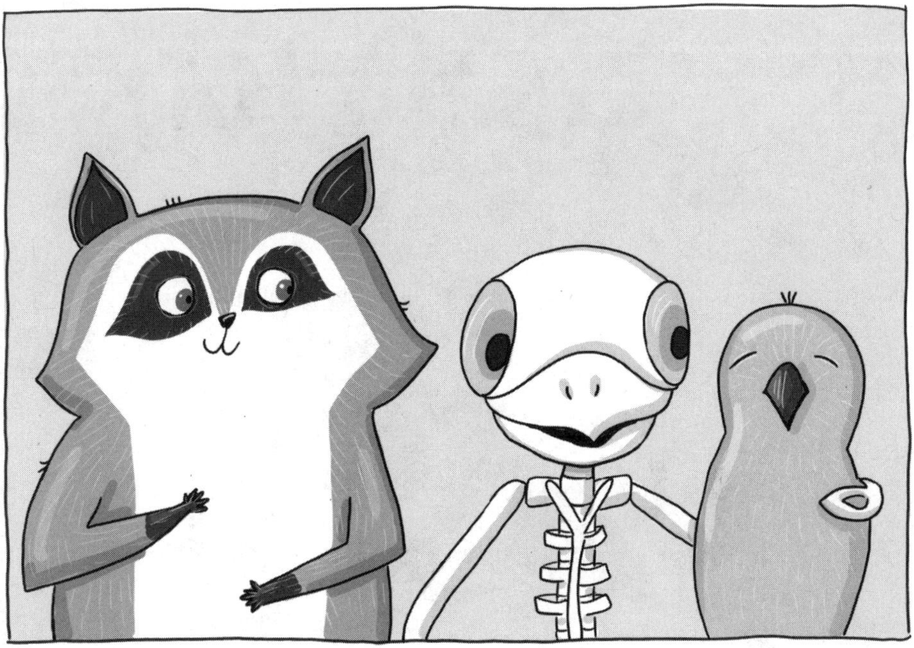

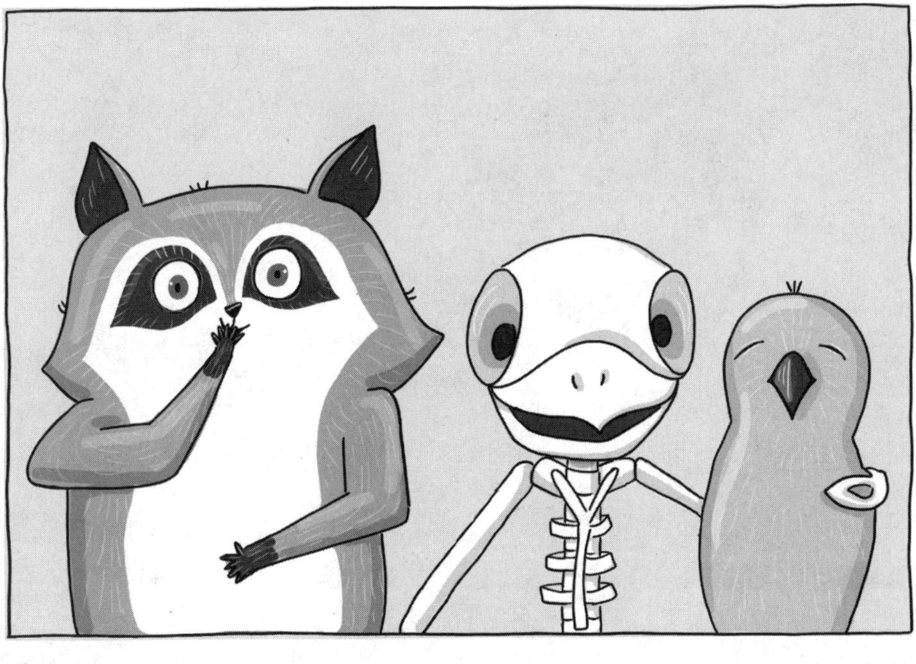

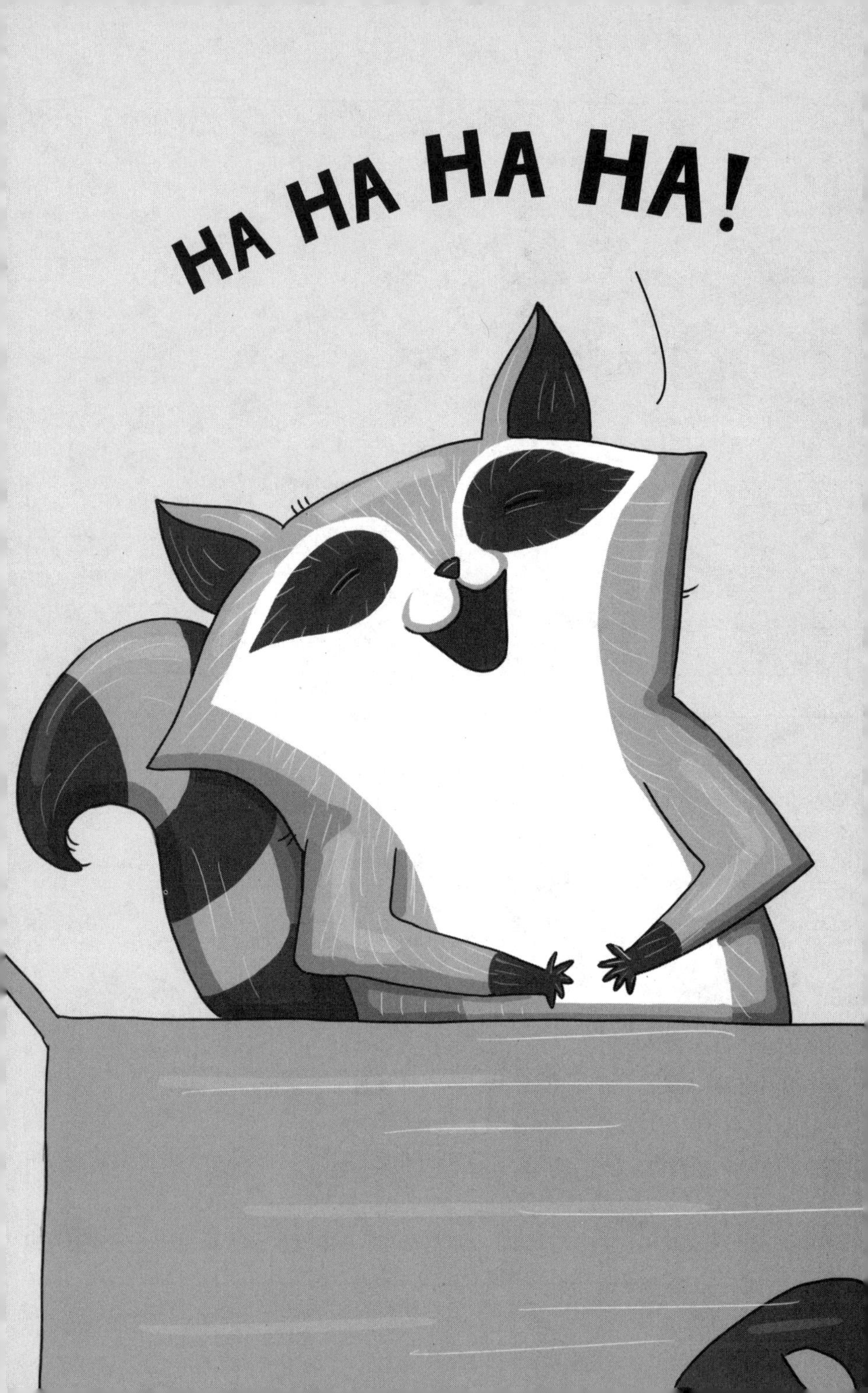
HA HA HA HA!

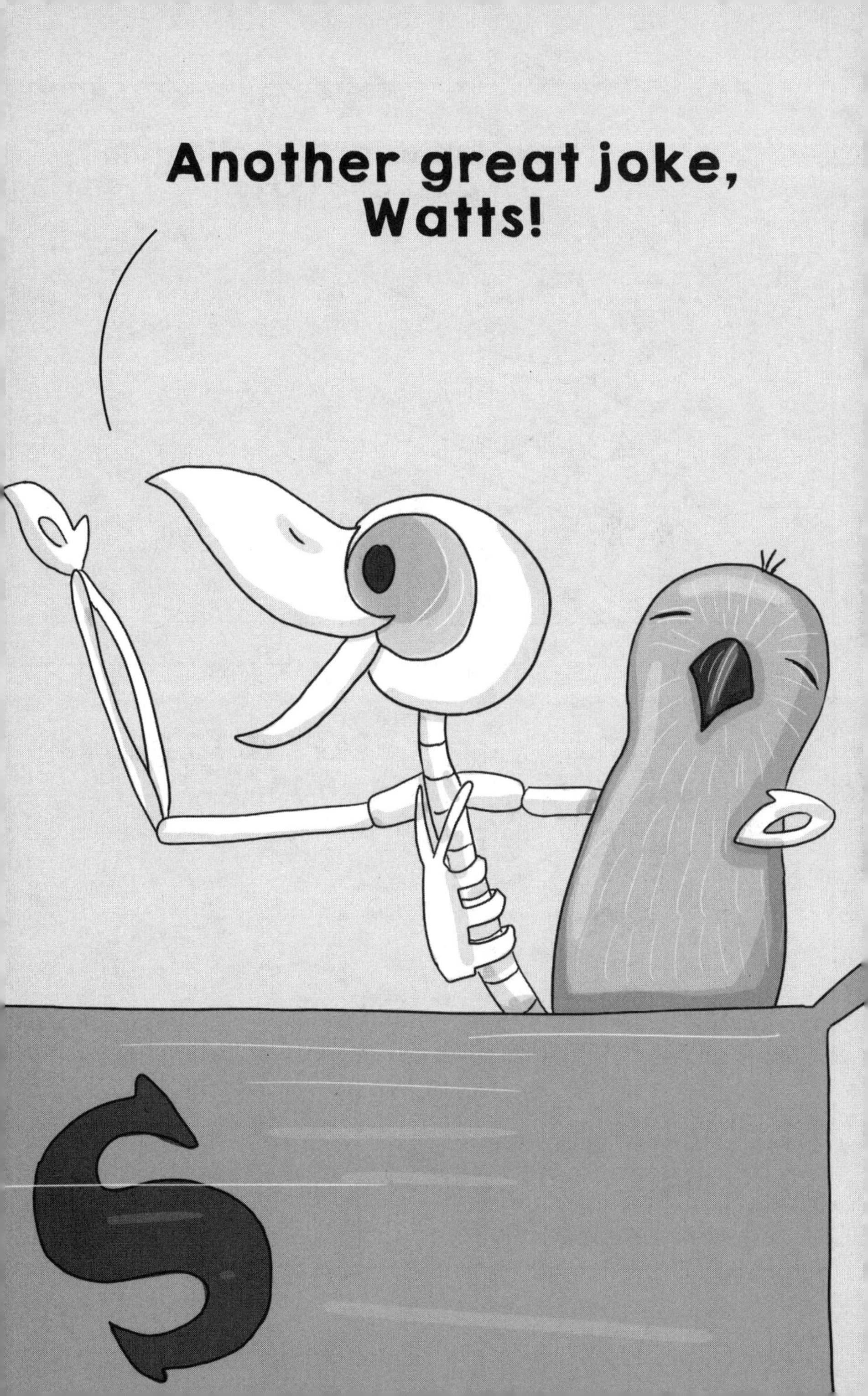
Another great joke, Watts!

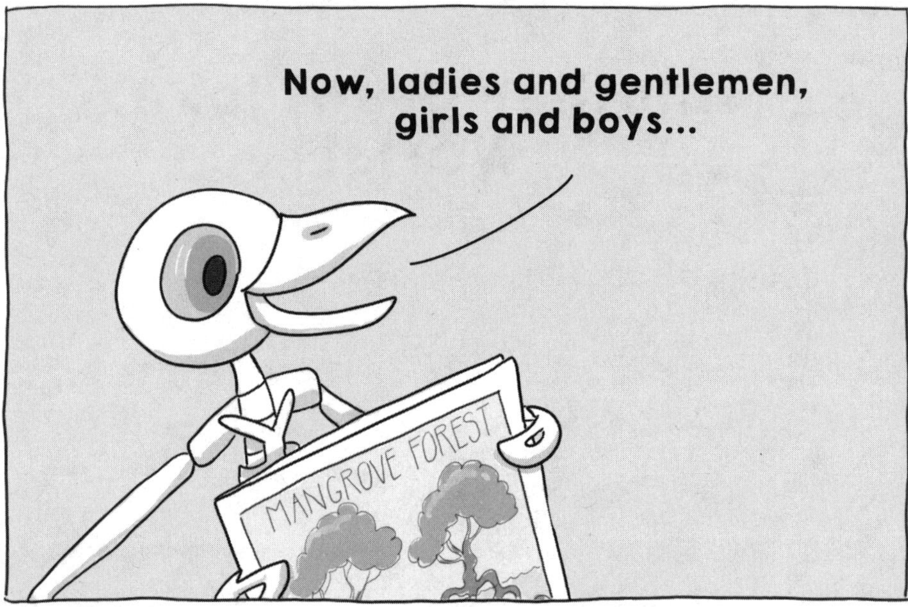
Now, ladies and gentlemen, girls and boys...
MANGROVE FOREST

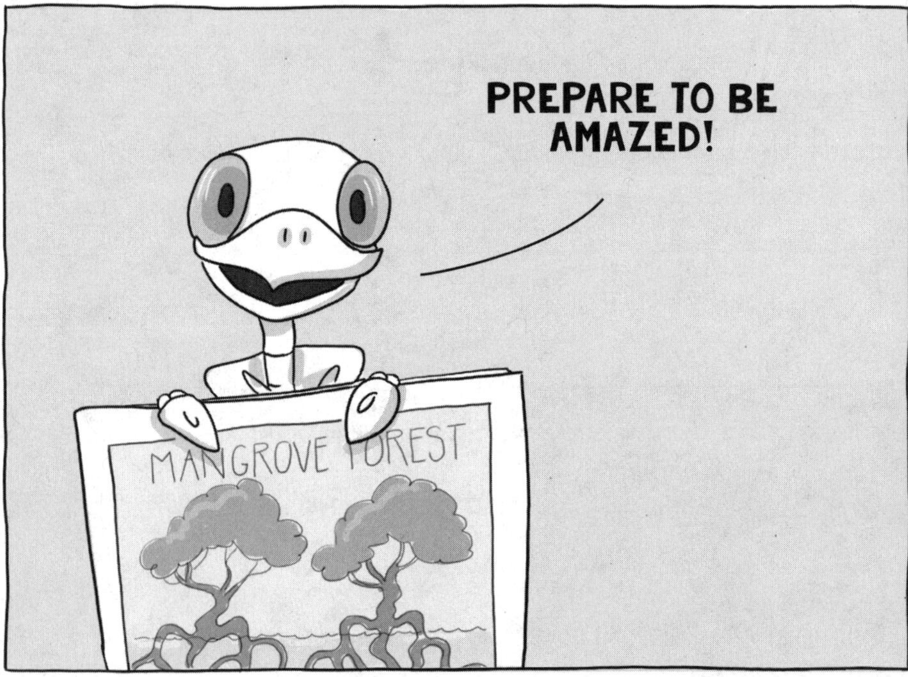
PREPARE TO BE AMAZED!
MANGROVE FOREST

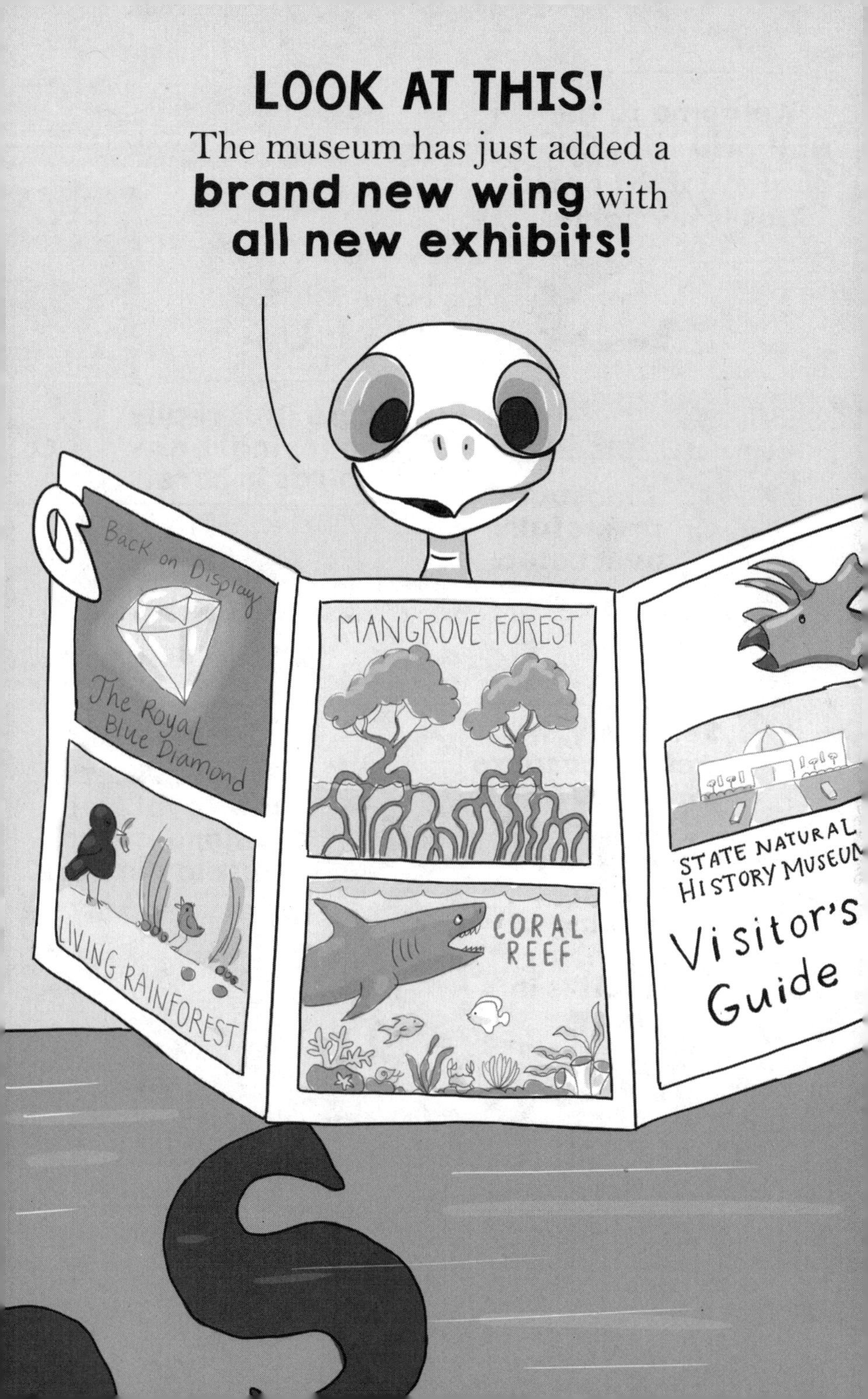
LOOK AT THIS!
The museum has just added a **brand new wing** with **all new exhibits!**
Back on Display
The Royal Blue Diamond
LIVING RAINFOREST
MANGROVE FOREST
CORAL REEF
STATE NATURAL HISTORY MUSEUM
Visitor's Guide

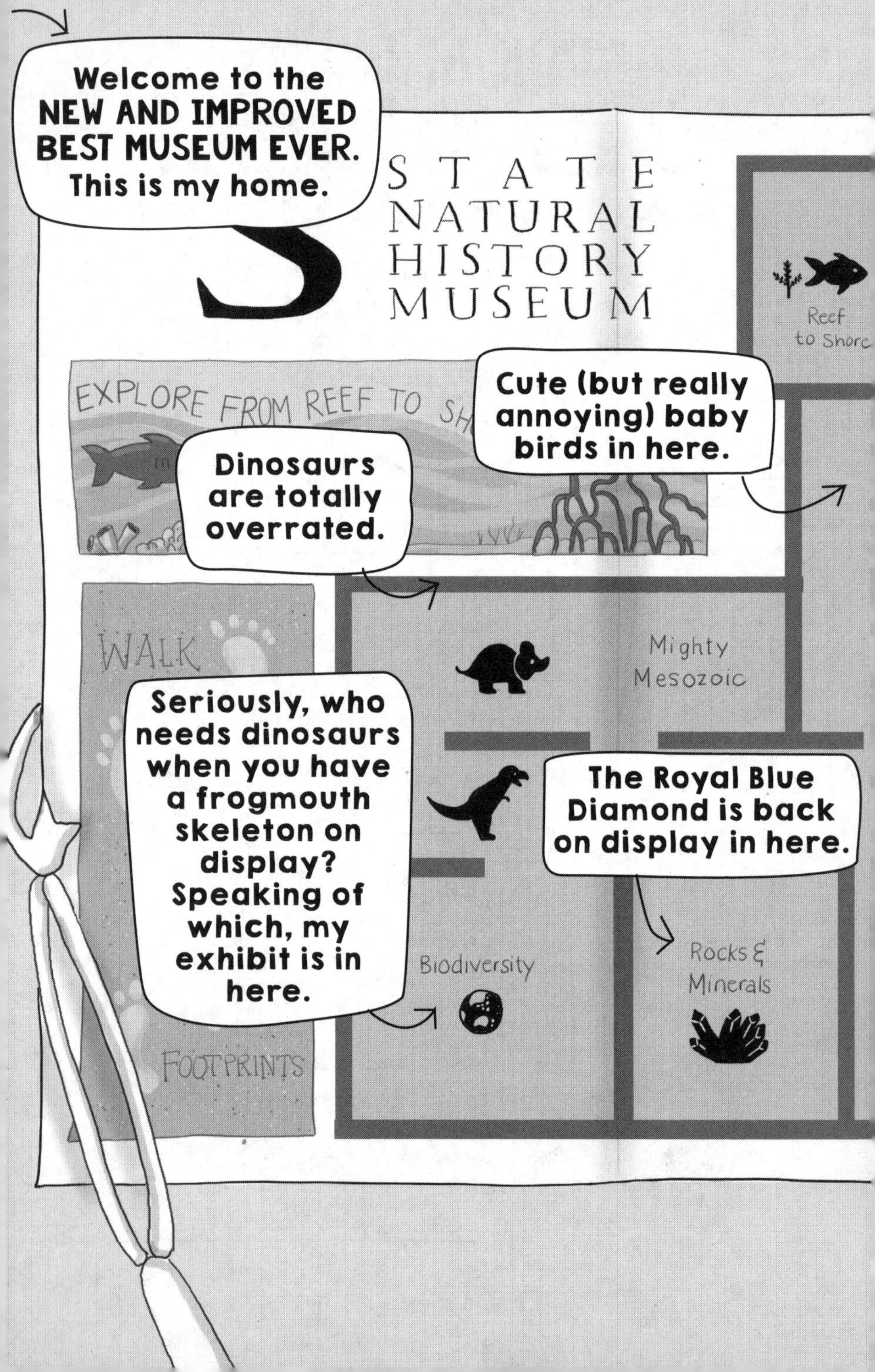

Welcome to the NEW AND IMPROVED BEST MUSEUM EVER. This is my home.
STATE NATURAL HISTORY MUSEUM
Reef to Shore
EXPLORE FROM REEF TO SH
Cute (but really annoying) baby birds in here.
Dinosaurs are totally overrated.
WALK
Mighty Mesozoic
Seriously, who needs dinosaurs when you have a frogmouth skeleton on display? Speaking of which, my exhibit is in here.
The Royal Blue Diamond is back on display in here.
Biodiversity
Rocks & Minerals
FOOTPRINTS

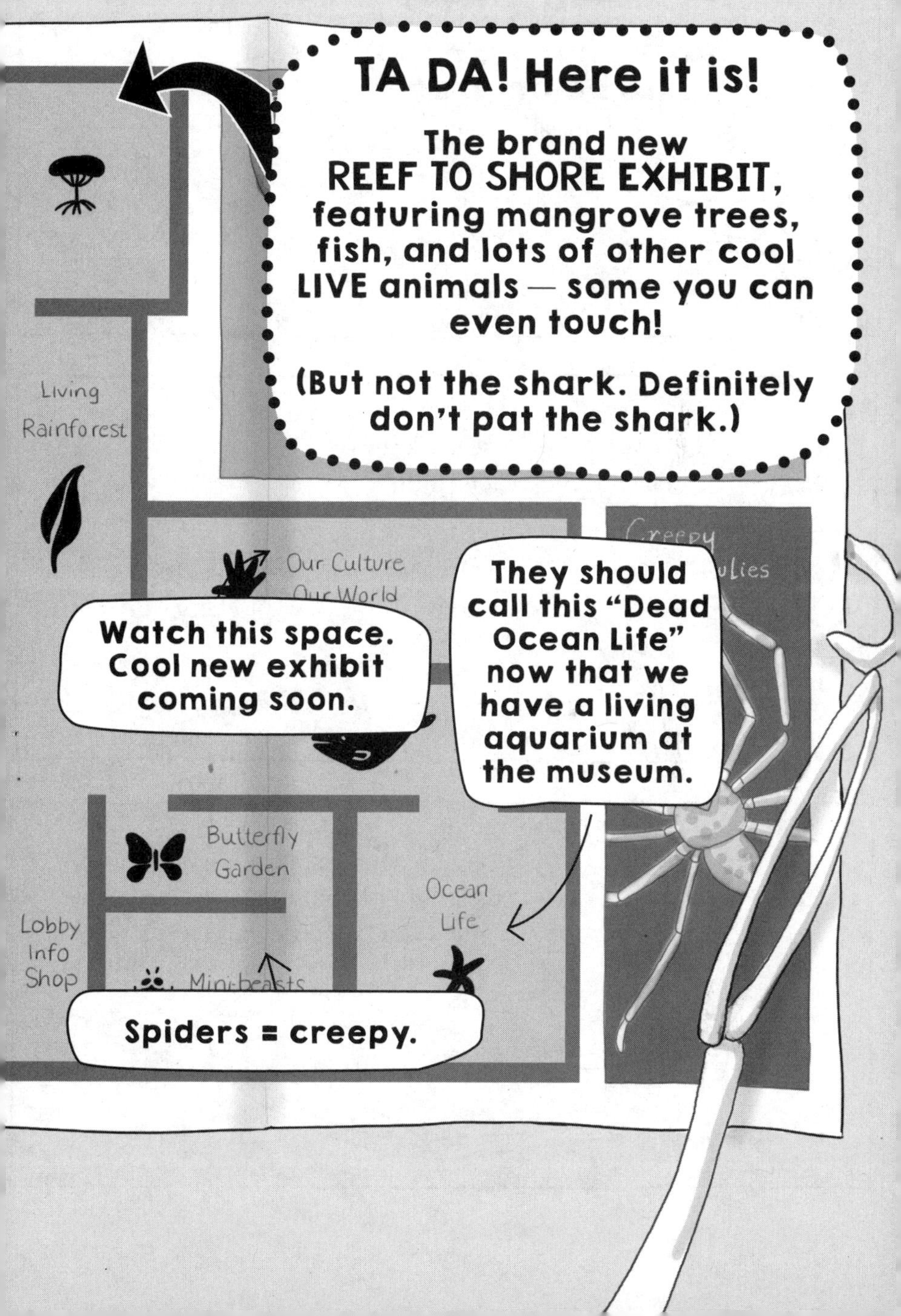
TA DA! Here it is!
The brand new REEF TO SHORE EXHIBIT, featuring mangrove trees, fish, and lots of other cool LIVE animals — some you can even touch!
(But not the shark. Definitely don't pat the shark.)
Living Rainforest
Our Culture
Watch this space. Cool new exhibit coming soon.
They should call this "Dead Ocean Life" now that we have a living aquarium at the museum.
Butterfly Garden
Ocean Life
Lobby Info Shop
Spiders = creepy.

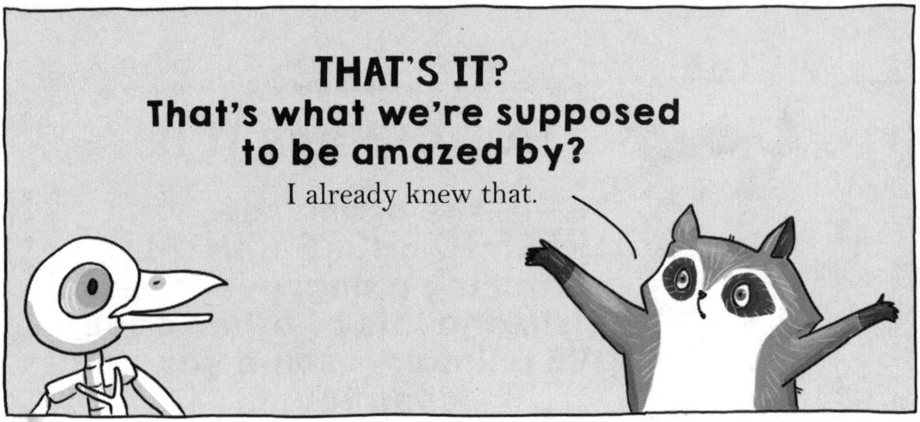
THAT'S IT?
That's what we're supposed to be amazed by?
I already knew that.

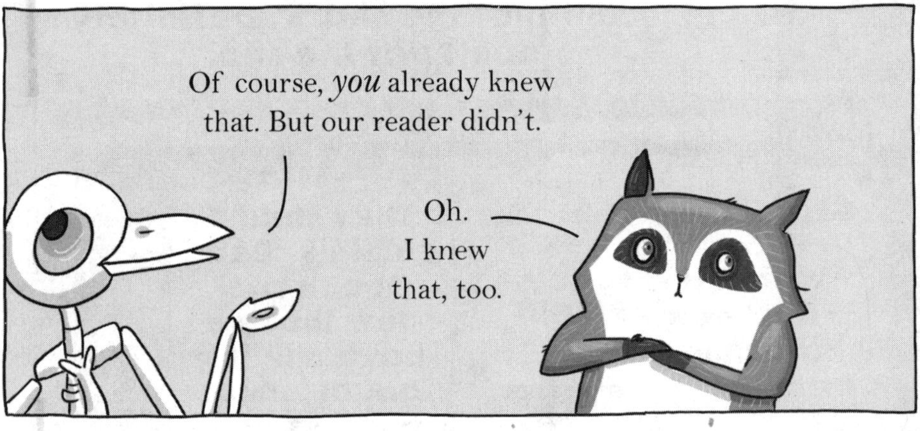
Of course, *you* already knew that. But our reader didn't.
Oh. I knew that, too.

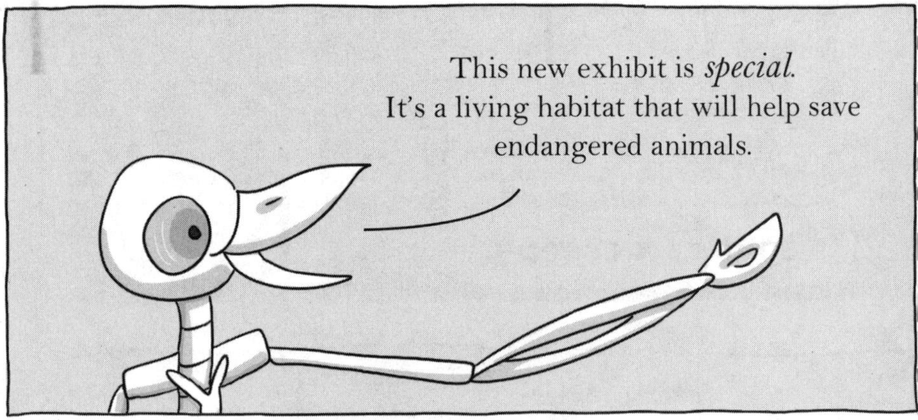
This new exhibit is *special.* It's a living habitat that will help save endangered animals.

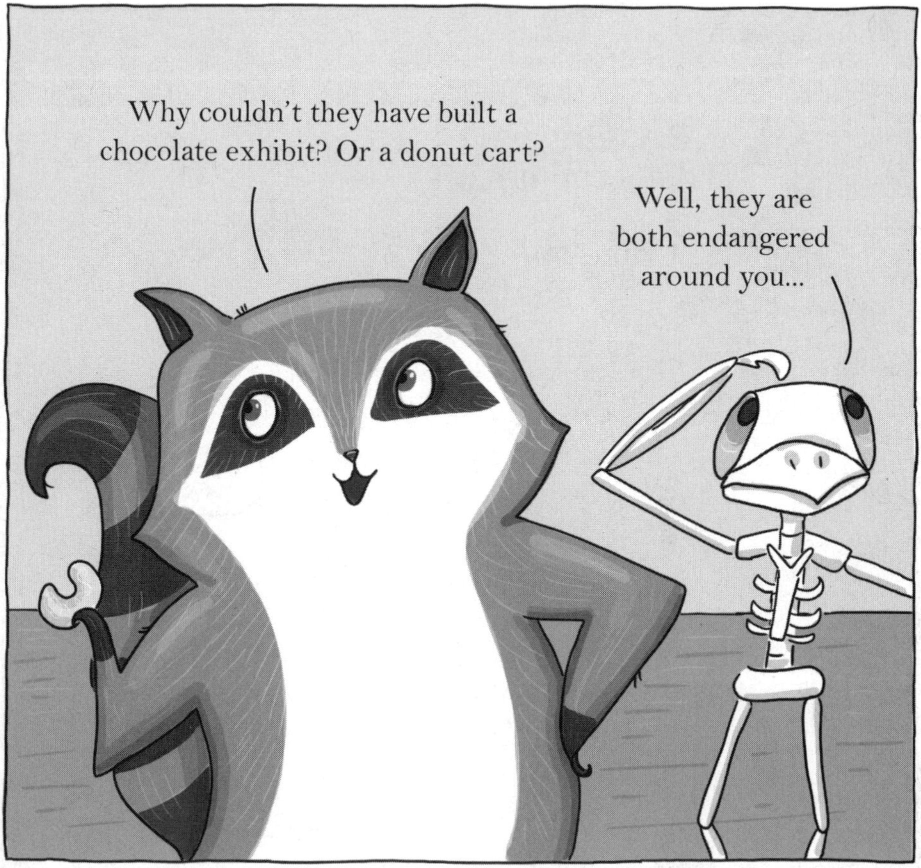
Why couldn't they have built a chocolate exhibit? Or a donut cart?
Well, they are both endangered around you...

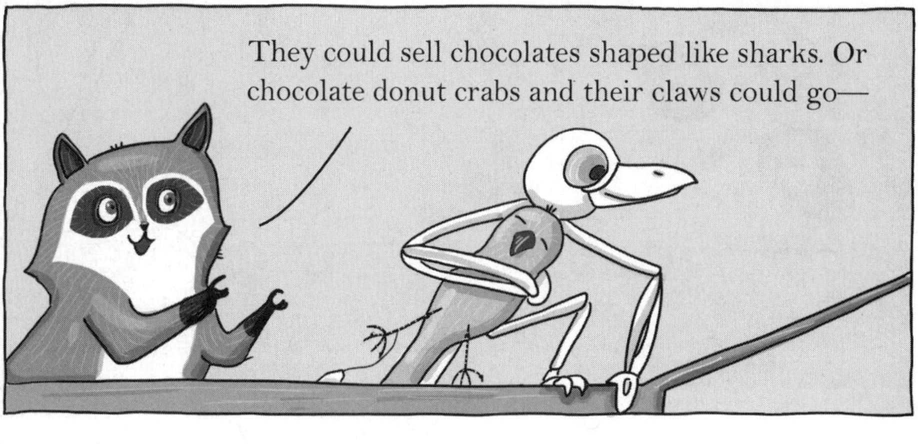
They could sell chocolates shaped like sharks. Or chocolate donut crabs and their claws could go—

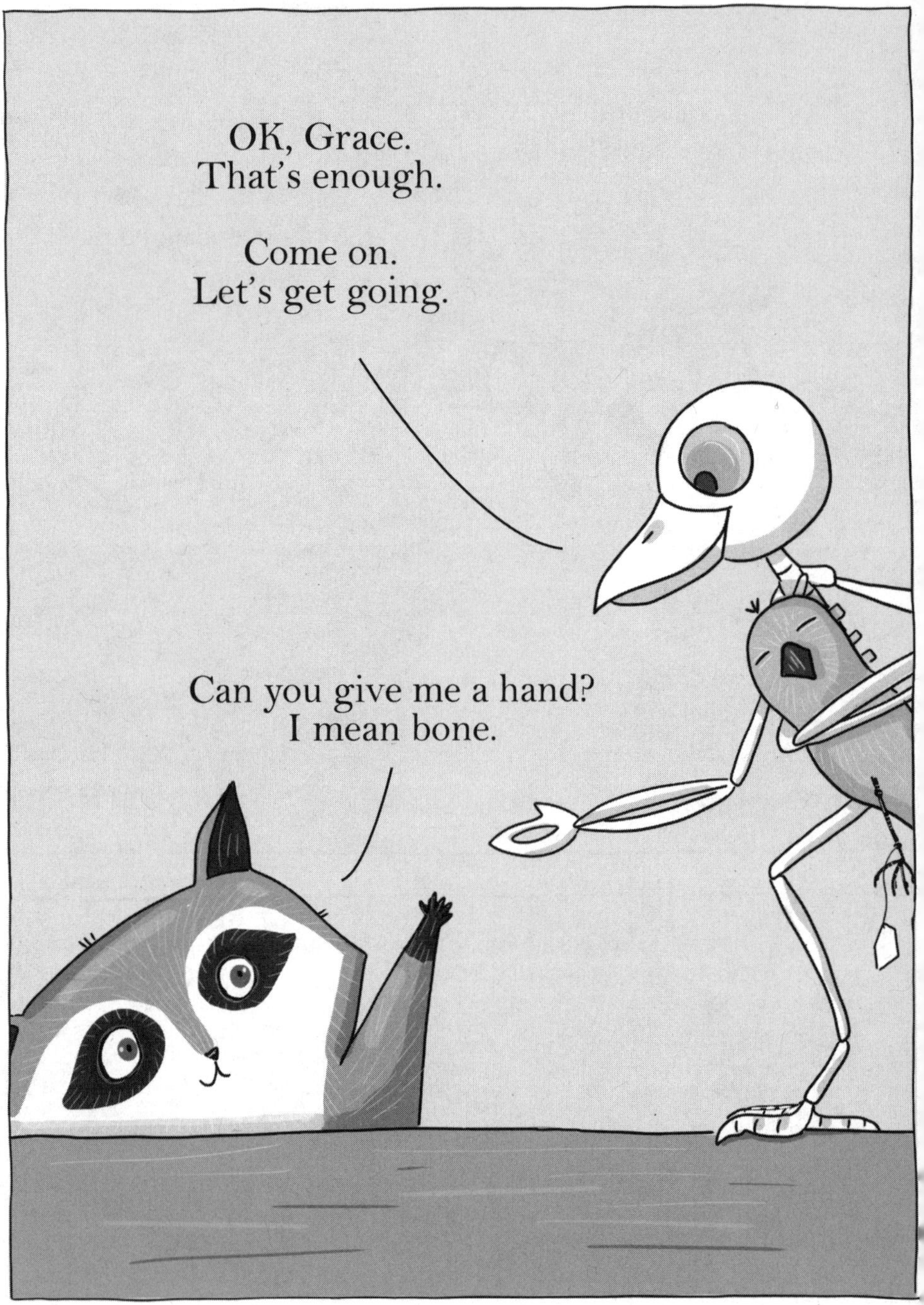
OK, Grace.
That's enough.
Come on.
Let's get going.
Can you give me a hand?
I mean bone.

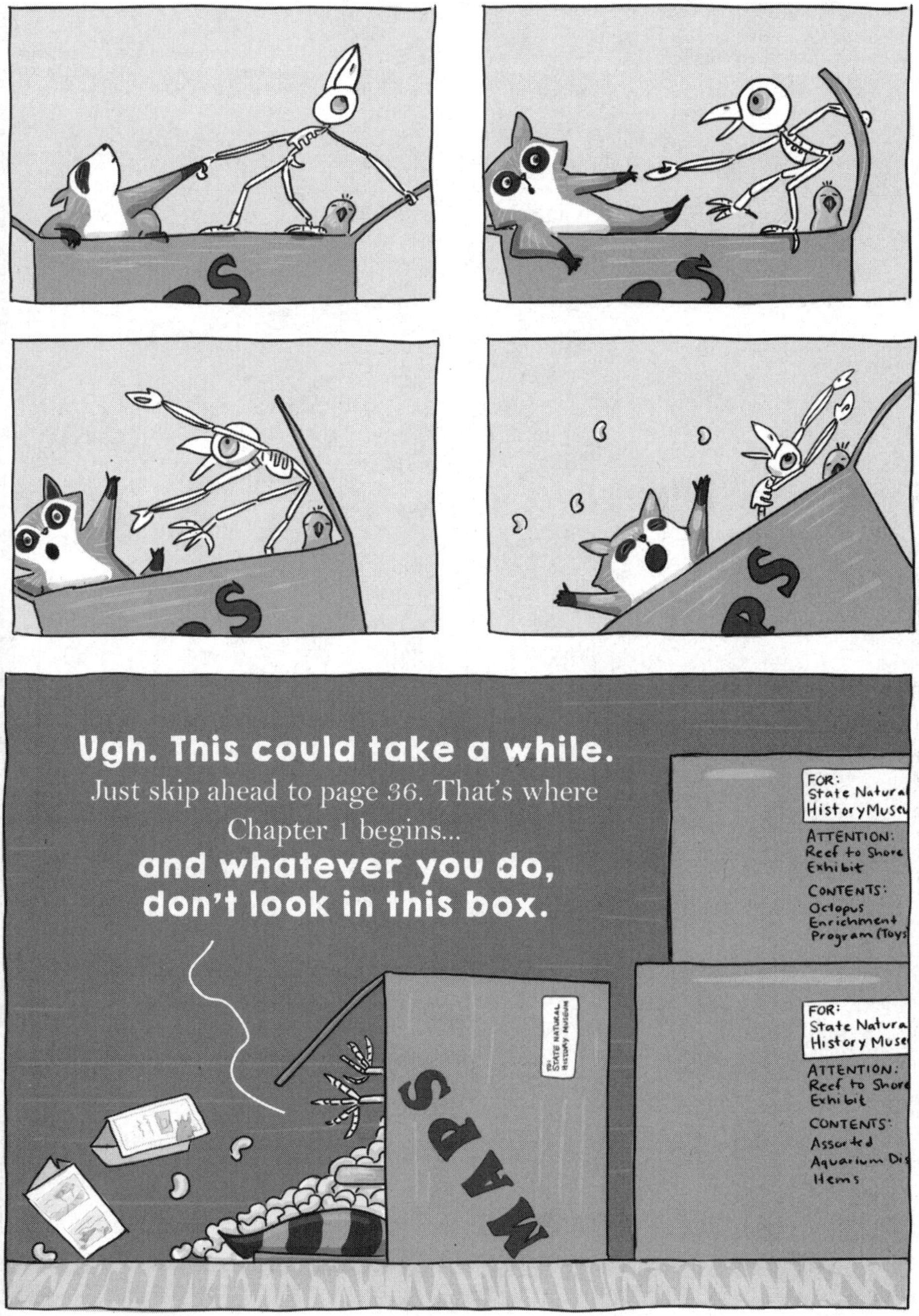

Ugh. This could take a while.
Just skip ahead to page 36. That's where Chapter 1 begins...
and whatever you do, don't look in this box.
SPAM
TO: STATE NATURAL HISTORY MUSEUM
FOR: State Natural HistoryMuse
ATTENTION: Reef to Shore Exhibit
CONTENTS: Octopus Enrichment Program (Toys
FOR: State Natura History Muse
ATTENTION: Reef to Shore Exhibit
CONTENTS: Assorted Aquarium Di Items

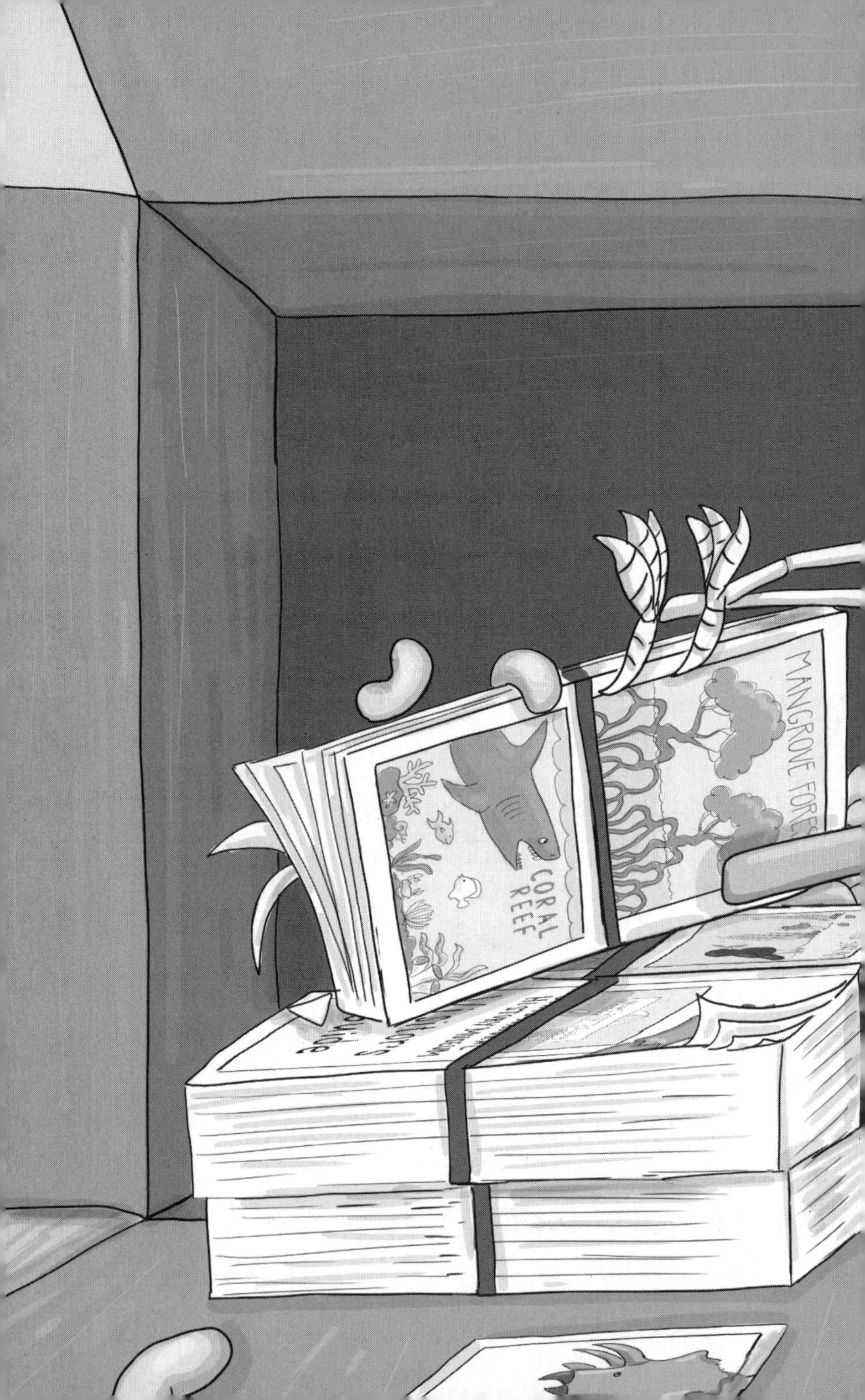
MANGROVE FORES
CORAL REEF

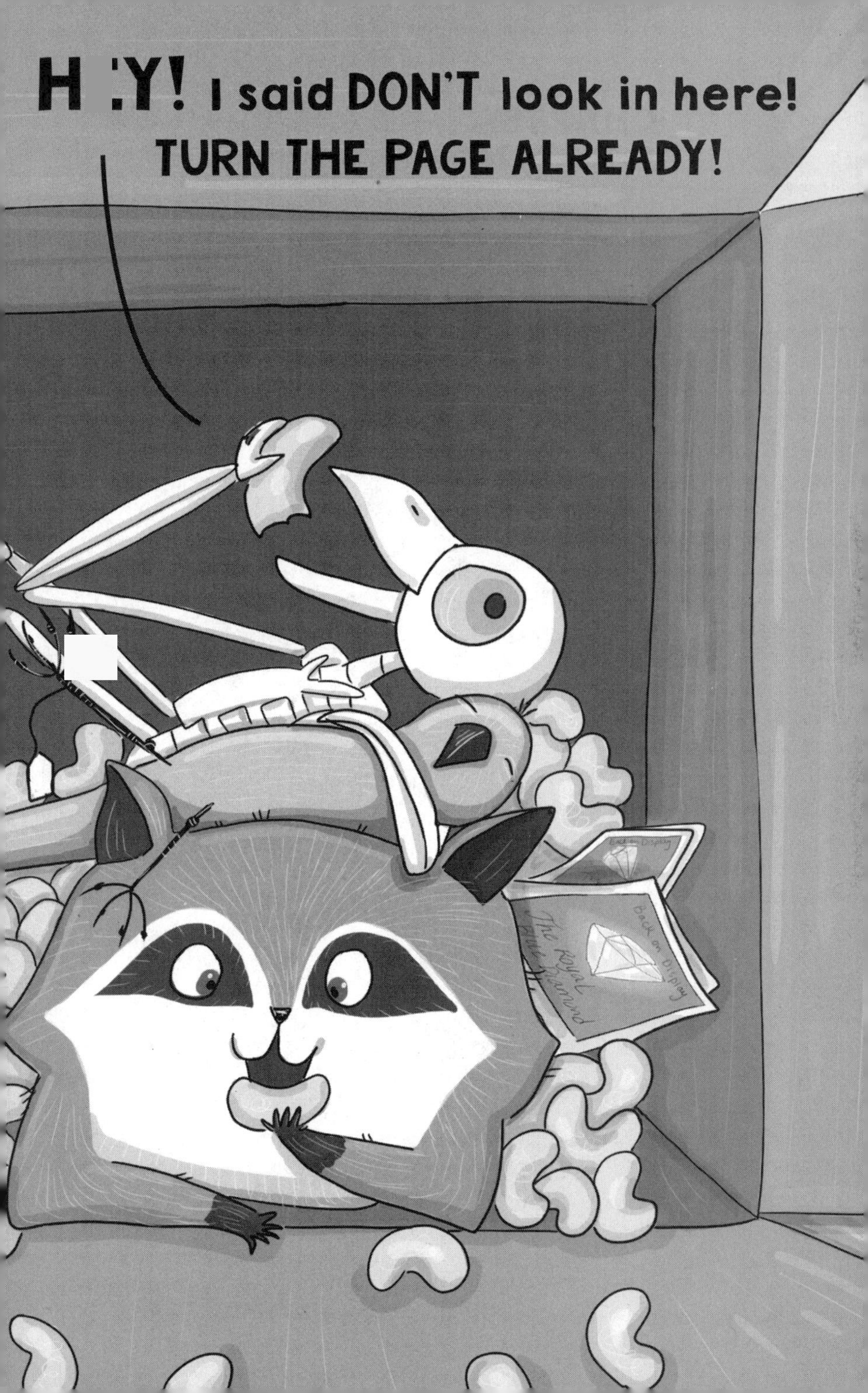
HEY! I said DON'T look in here!
TURN THE PAGE ALREADY!

CHAPTER 1
Fright Club

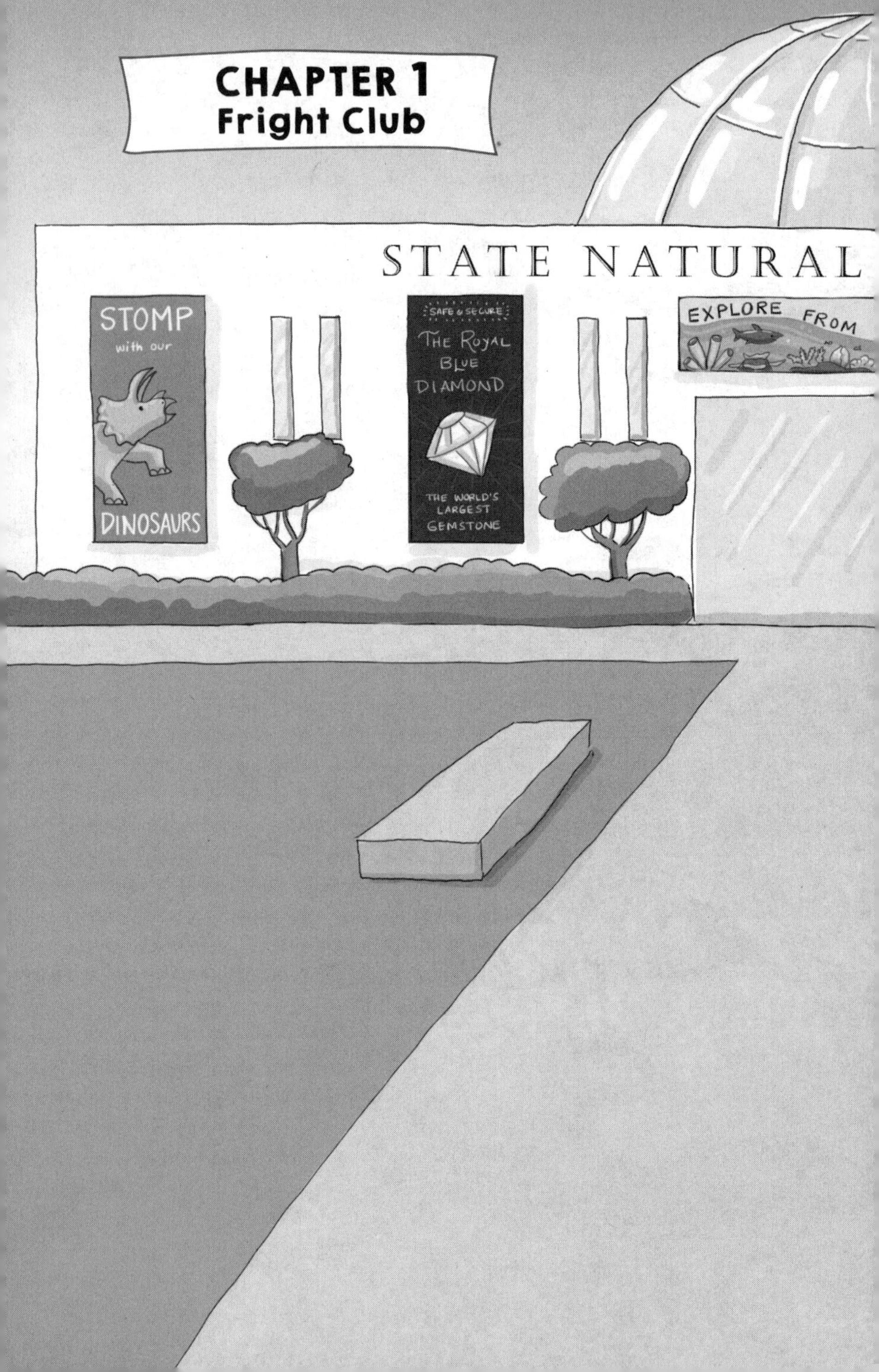
STATE NATURAL
STOMP
with our
DINOSAURS
SAFE & SECURE
THE ROYAL
BLUE
DIAMOND
THE WORLD'S
LARGEST
GEMSTONE
EXPLORE FROM

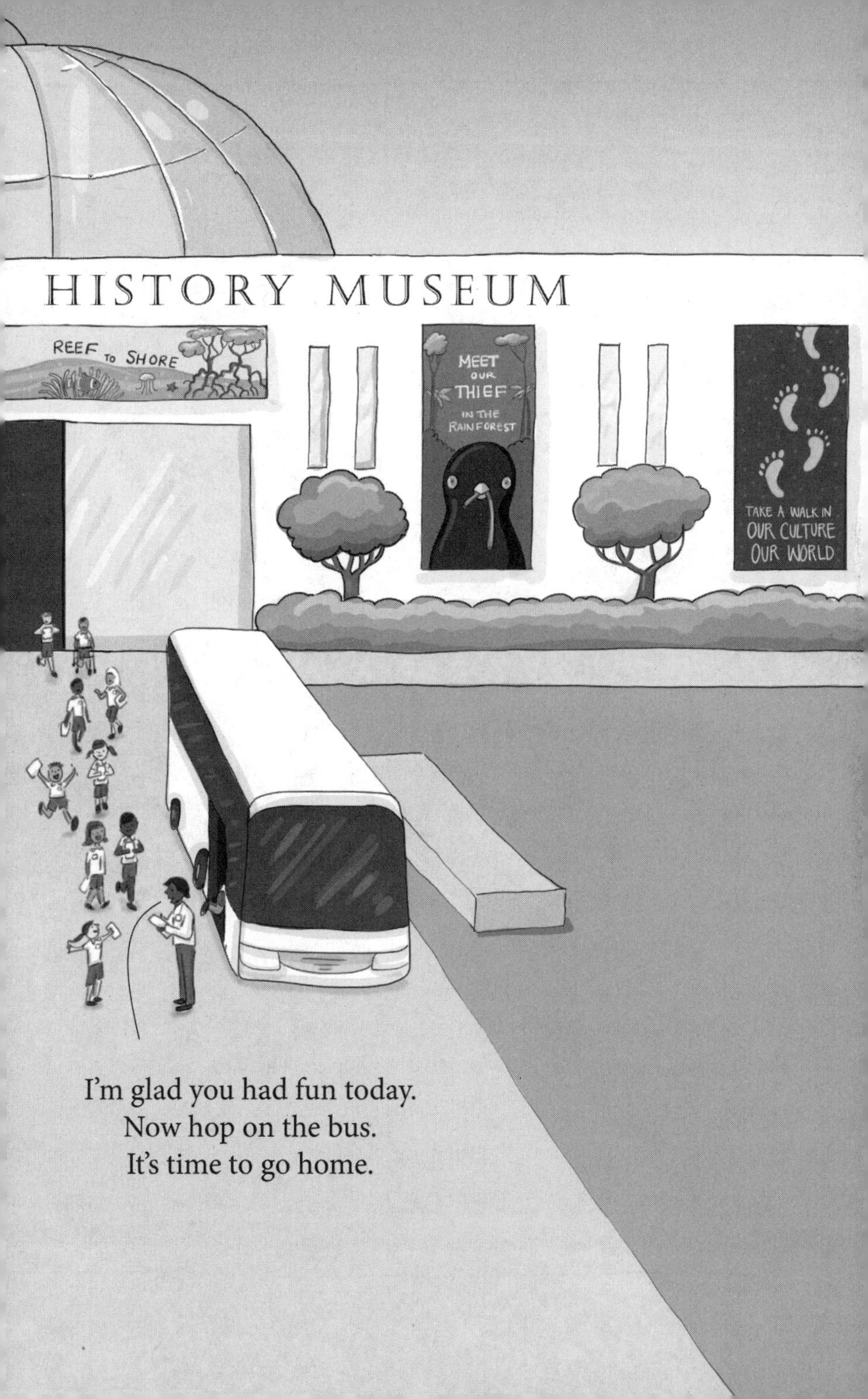
HISTORY MUSEUM
REEF TO SHORE
MEET OUR THIEF IN THE RAINFOREST
TAKE A WALK IN OUR CULTURE OUR WORLD

I'm glad you had fun today.
Now hop on the bus.
It's time to go home.

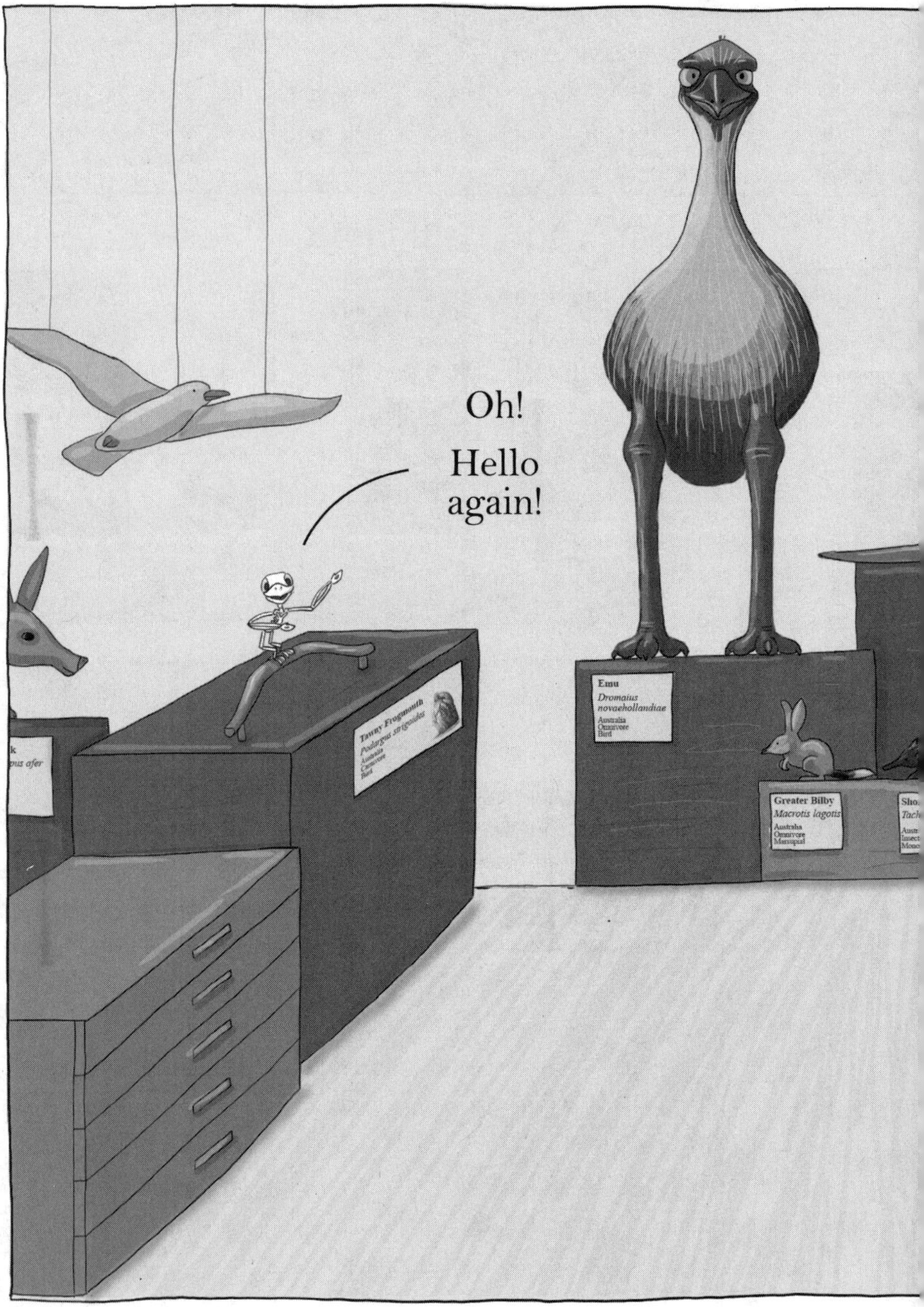
Oh!
Hello again!
Tawny Frogmouth
Podargus strigoides
Emu
Dromaius novaehollandiae
Australia
Omnivore
Bird
Greater Bilby
Macrotis lagotis
Australia
Omnivore
Marsupial

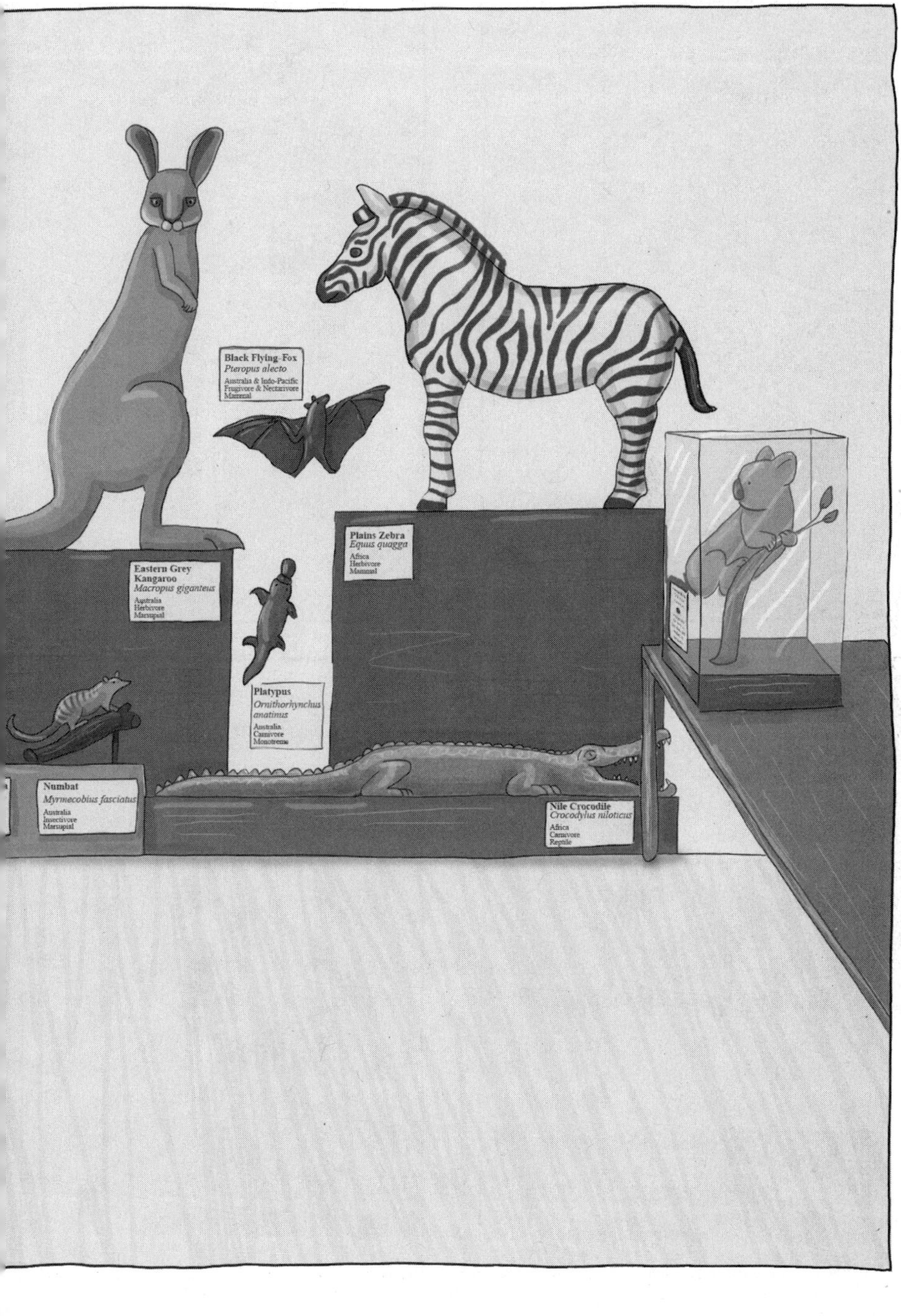
Black Flying-Fox
Pteropus alecto
Australia & Indo-Pacific
Frugivore & Nectarivore
Mammal
Eastern Grey Kangaroo
Macropus giganteus
Australia
Herbivore
Marsupial
Plains Zebra
Equus quagga
Africa
Herbivore
Mammal
Platypus
Ornithorhynchus anatinus
Australia
Carnivore
Monotreme
Numbat
Myrmecobius fasciatus
Australia
Insectivore
Marsupial
Nile Crocodile
Crocodylus niloticus
Africa
Carnivore
Reptile

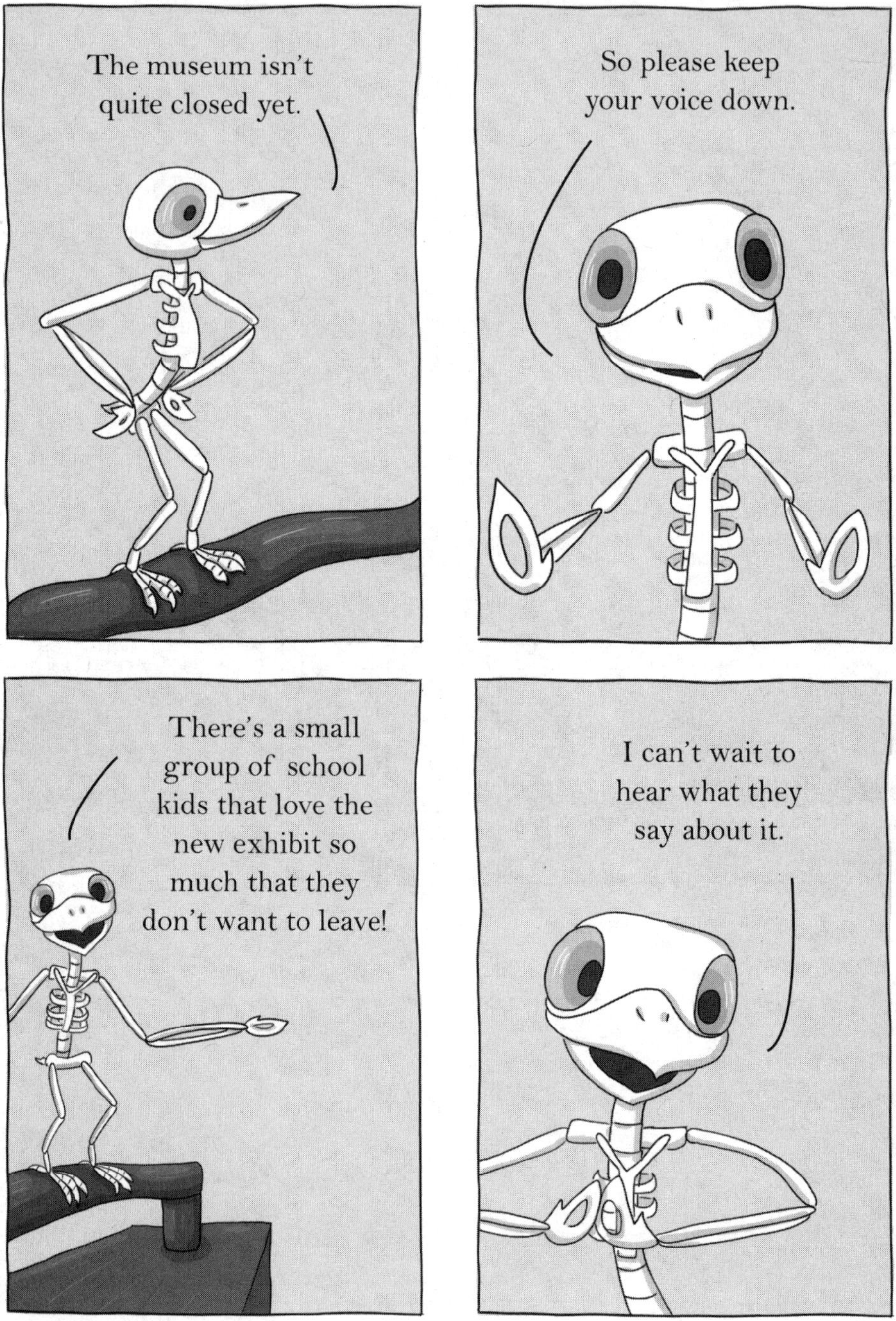
The museum isn't quite closed yet.
So please keep your voice down.
There's a small group of school kids that love the new exhibit so much that they don't want to leave!
I can't wait to hear what they say about it.

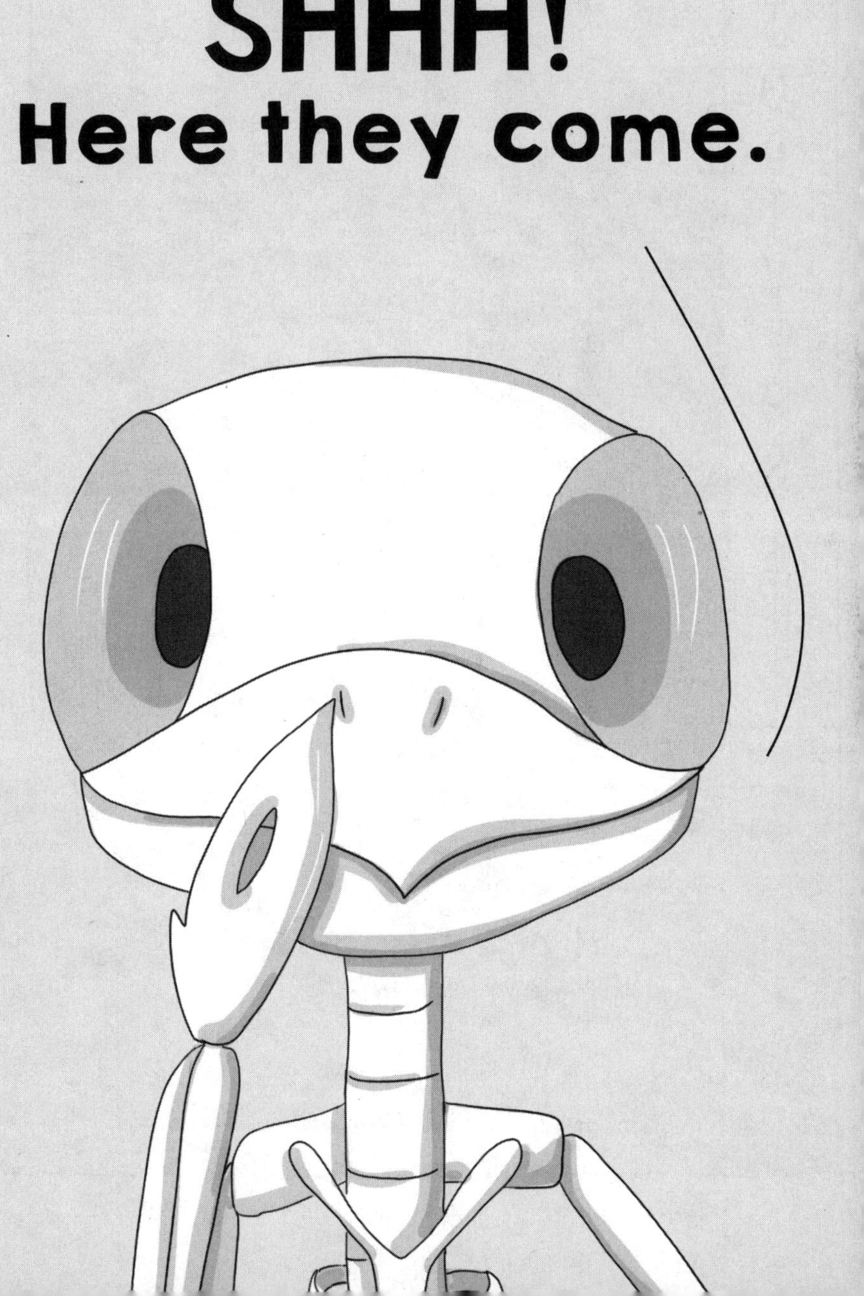
SHHH!
Here they come.

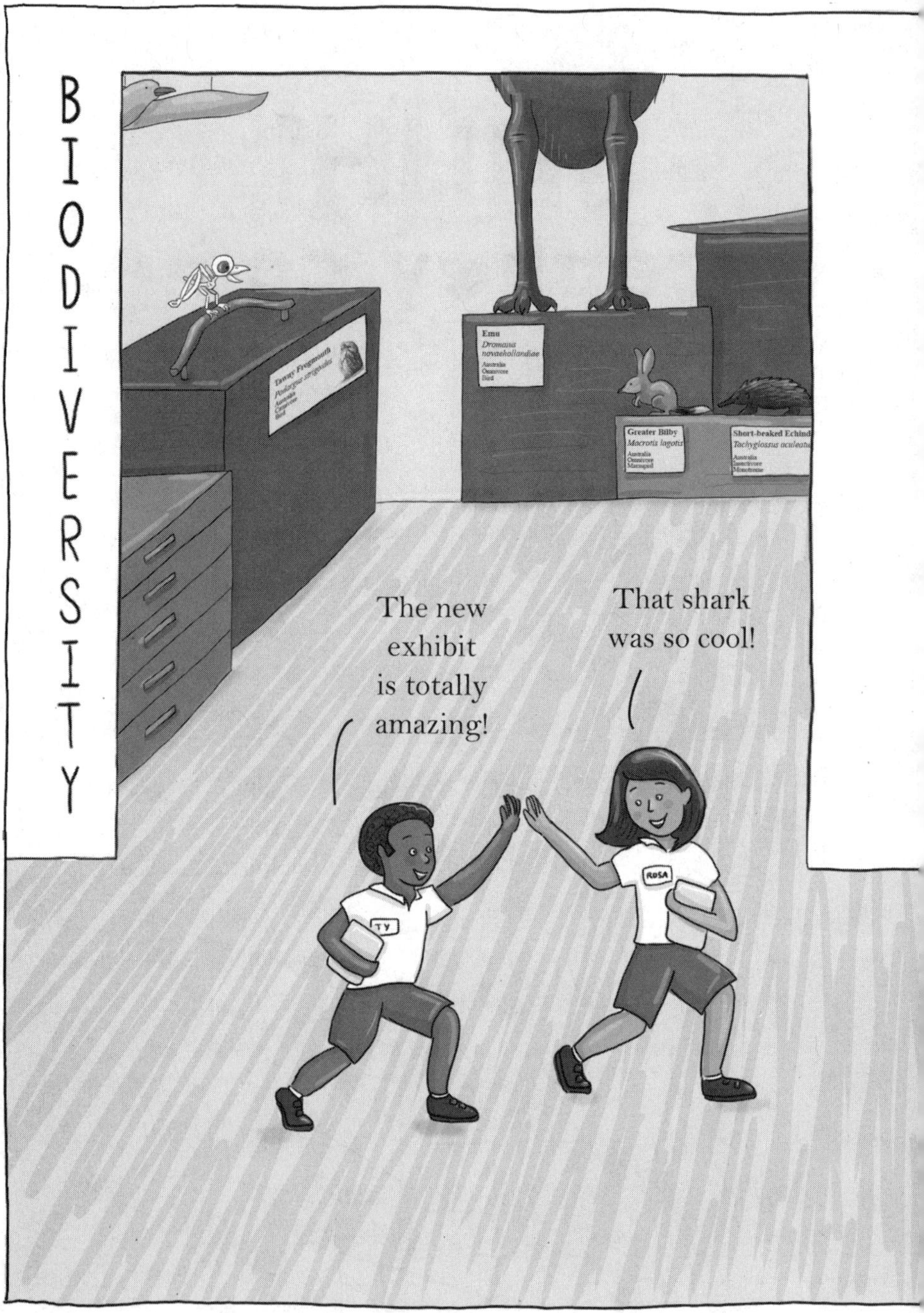
BIODIVERSITY
Emu
Dromaius novaehollandiae
Greater Bilby
Macrotis lagotis
The new exhibit is totally amazing!
That shark was so cool!

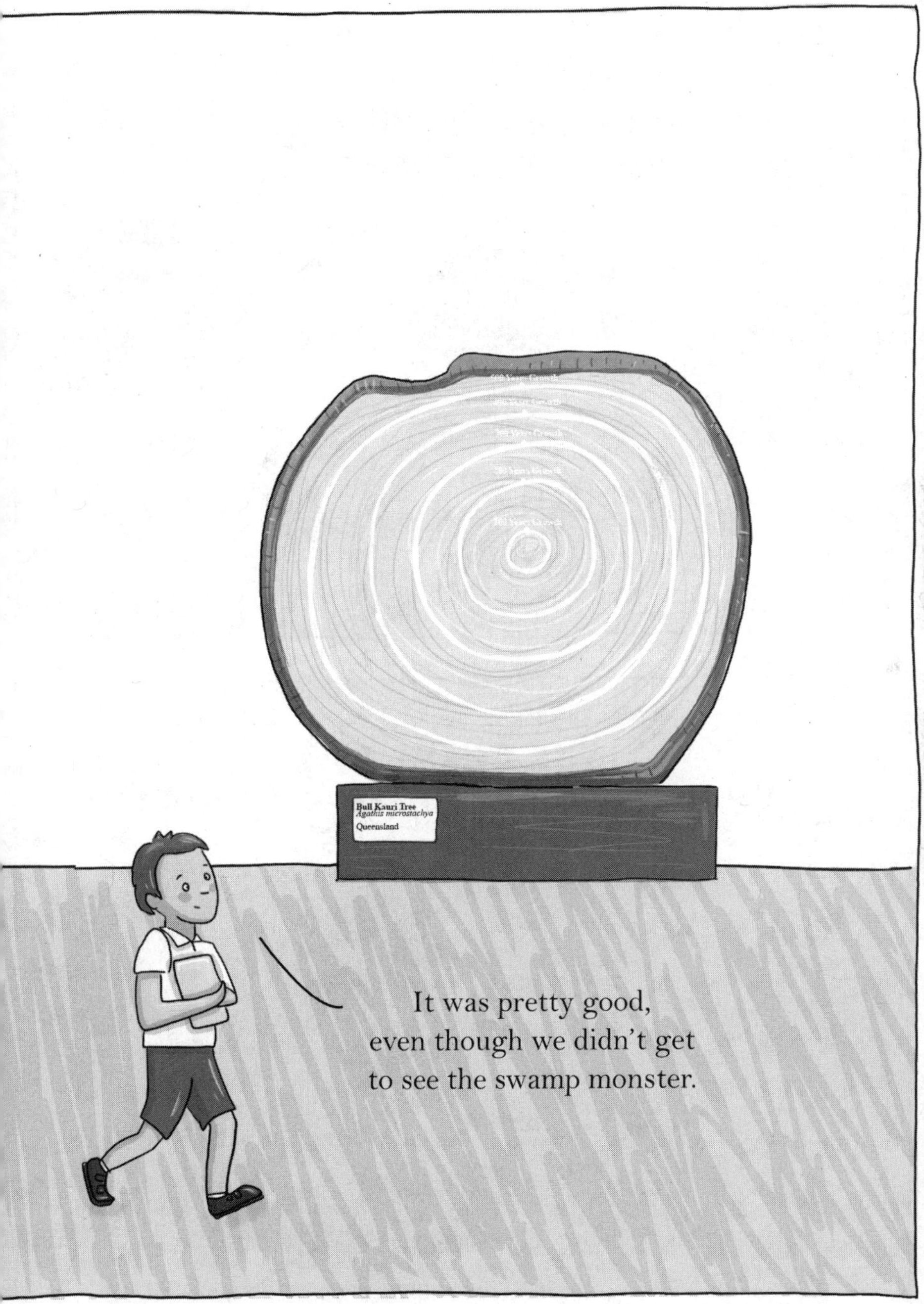
Bull Kauri Tree
Agathis microstachya
Queensland
It was pretty good,
even though we didn't get
to see the swamp monster.

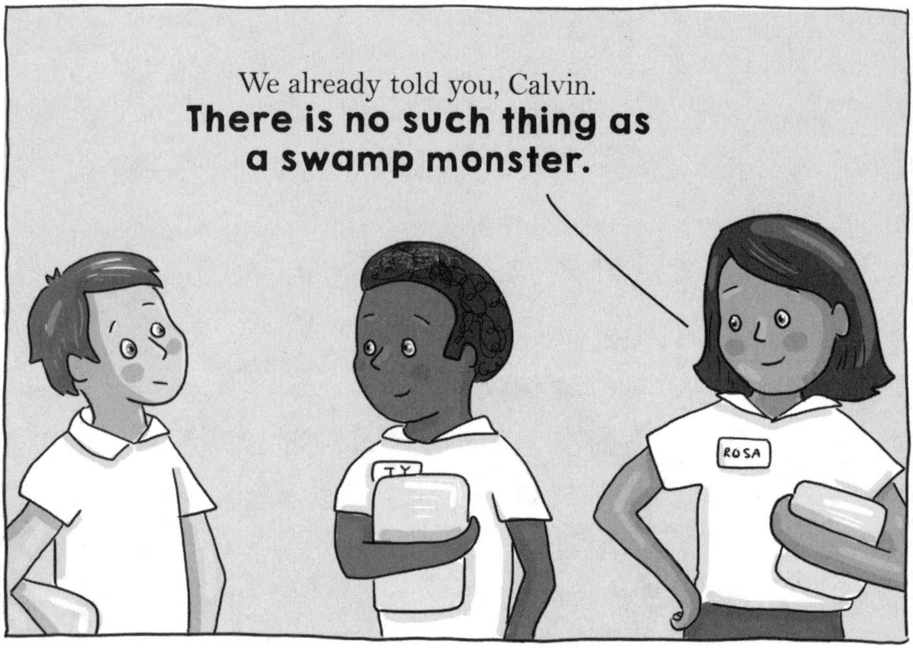
We already told you, Calvin.
There is no such thing as a swamp monster.
TY
ROSA

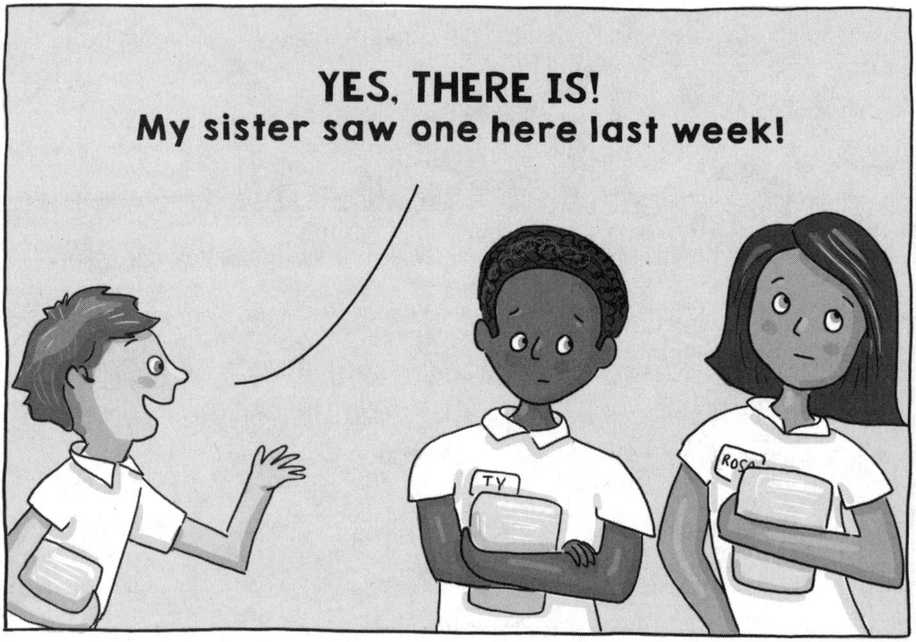
YES, THERE IS!
My sister saw one here last week!
TY
ROSA

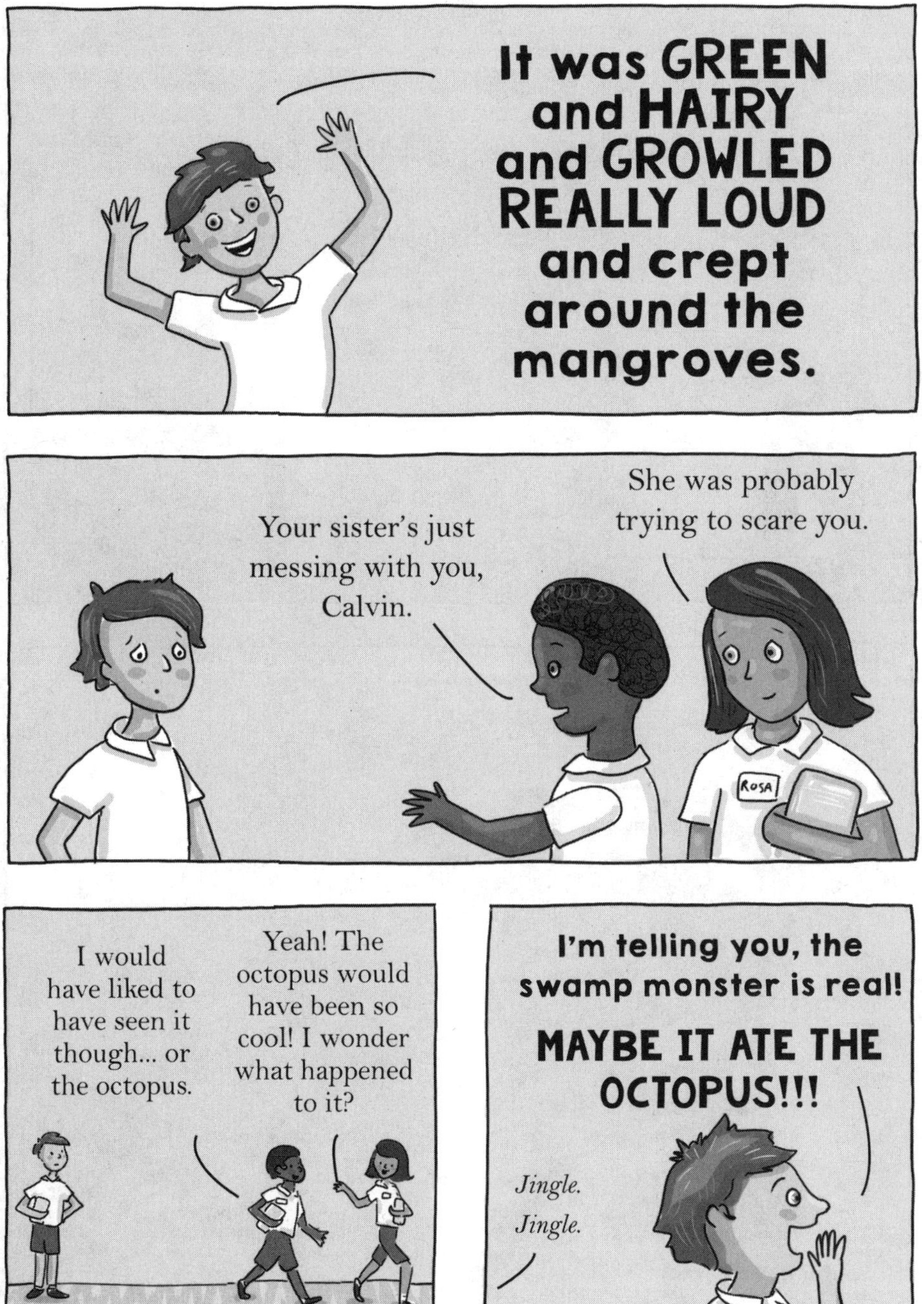

It was GREEN and HAIRY and GROWLED REALLY LOUD and crept around the mangroves.
Your sister's just messing with you, Calvin.
She was probably trying to scare you.
I would have liked to have seen it though... or the octopus.
Yeah! The octopus would have been so cool! I wonder what happened to it?
I'm telling you, the swamp monster is real!
MAYBE IT ATE THE OCTOPUS!!!
Jingle.
Jingle.
ROSA

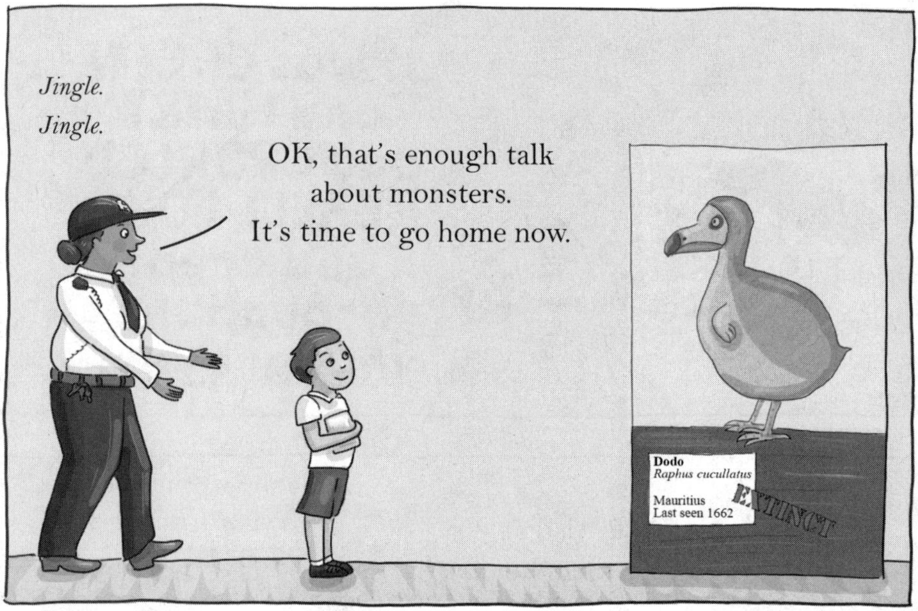
Jingle.
Jingle.
OK, that's enough talk about monsters. It's time to go home now.
Dodo
Raphus cucullatus
Mauritius
Last seen 1662
EXTINCT

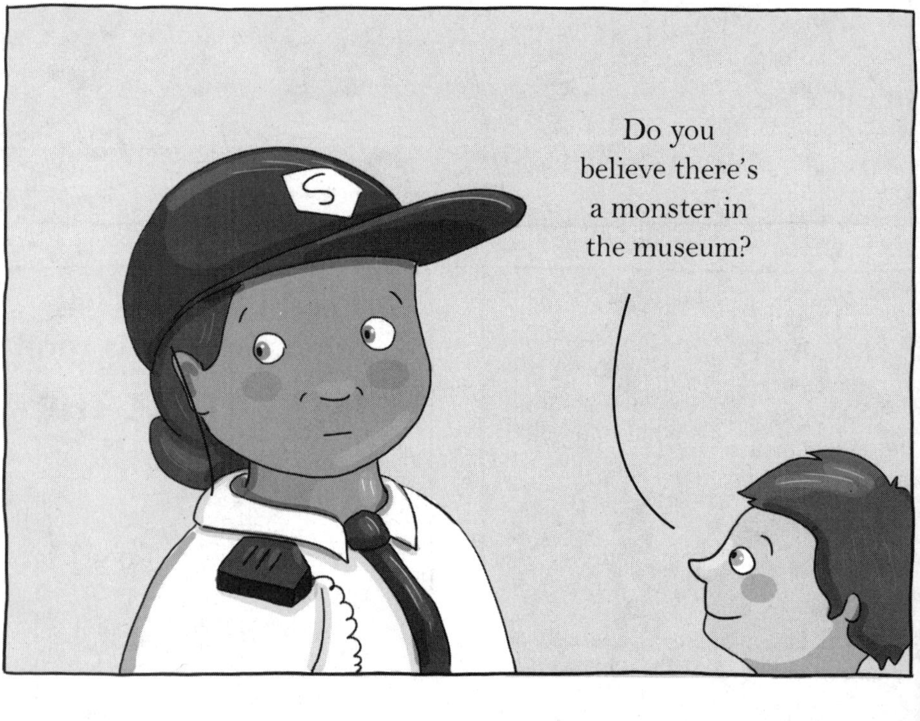
Do you believe there's a monster in the museum?

OH, LOOK!

The rest of your class is already on the bus.

Better hurry!

The museum is about to close.

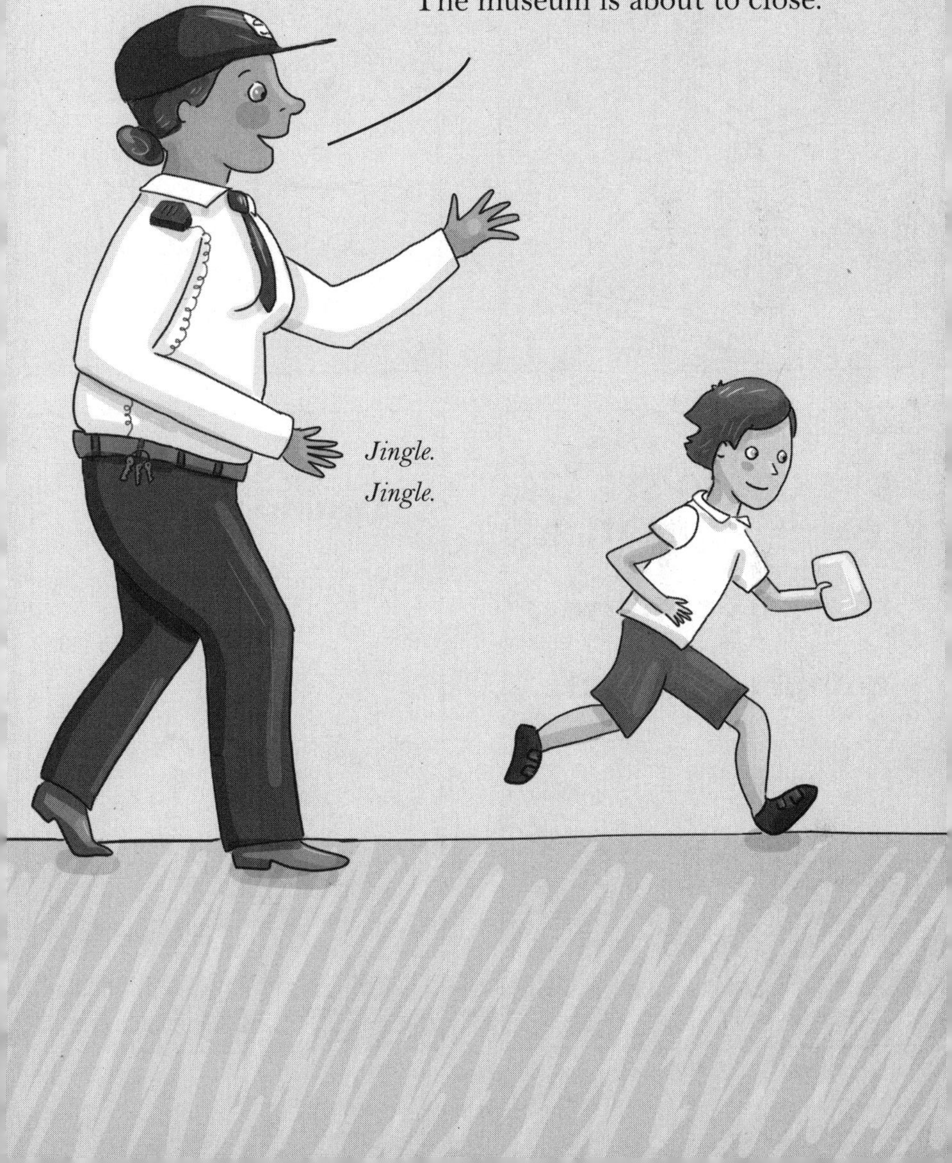
Jingle.
Jingle.

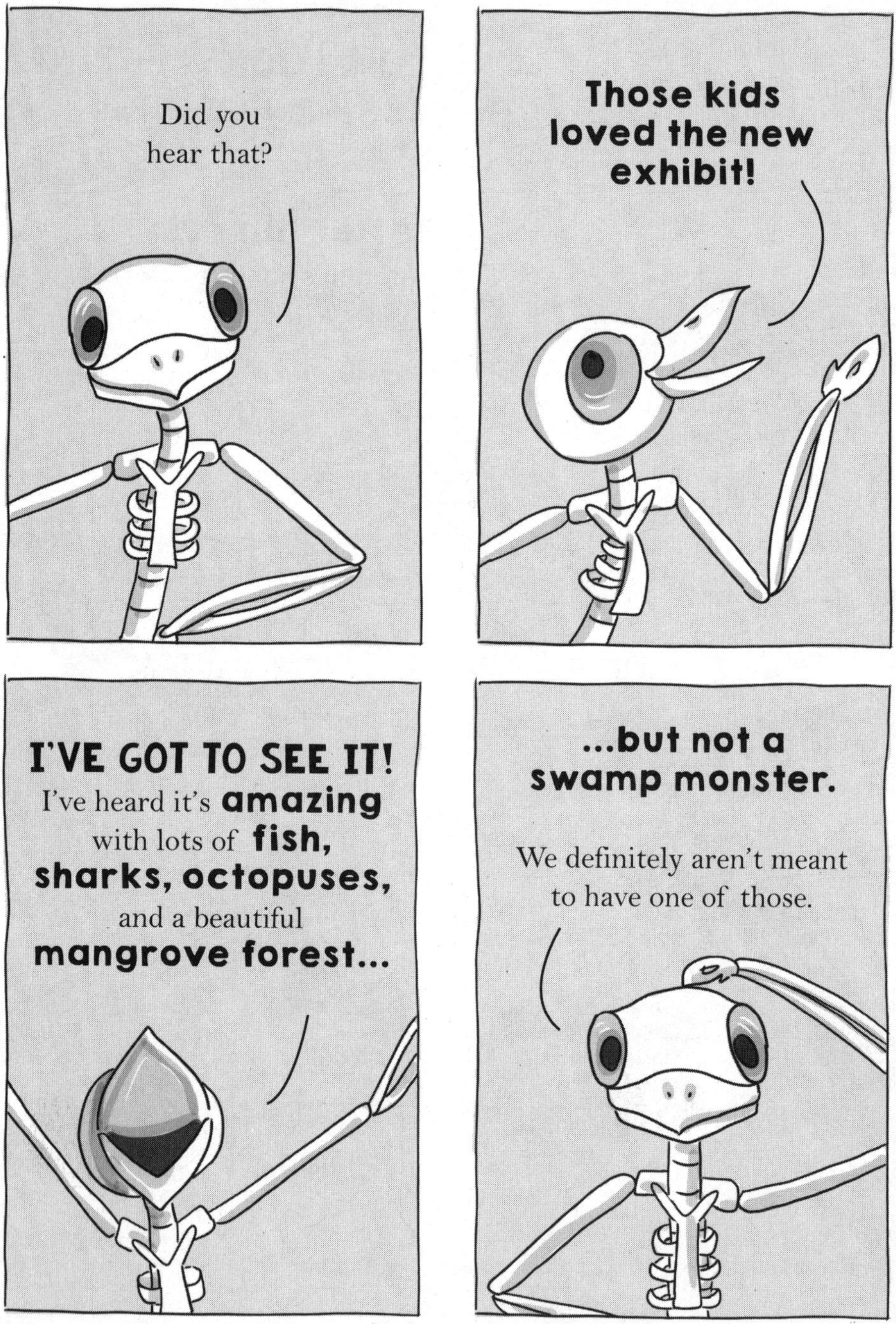
Did you hear that?
Those kids loved the new exhibit!
I'VE GOT TO SEE IT! I've heard it's amazing with lots of fish, sharks, octopuses, and a beautiful mangrove forest...
...but not a swamp monster.
We definitely aren't meant to have one of those.

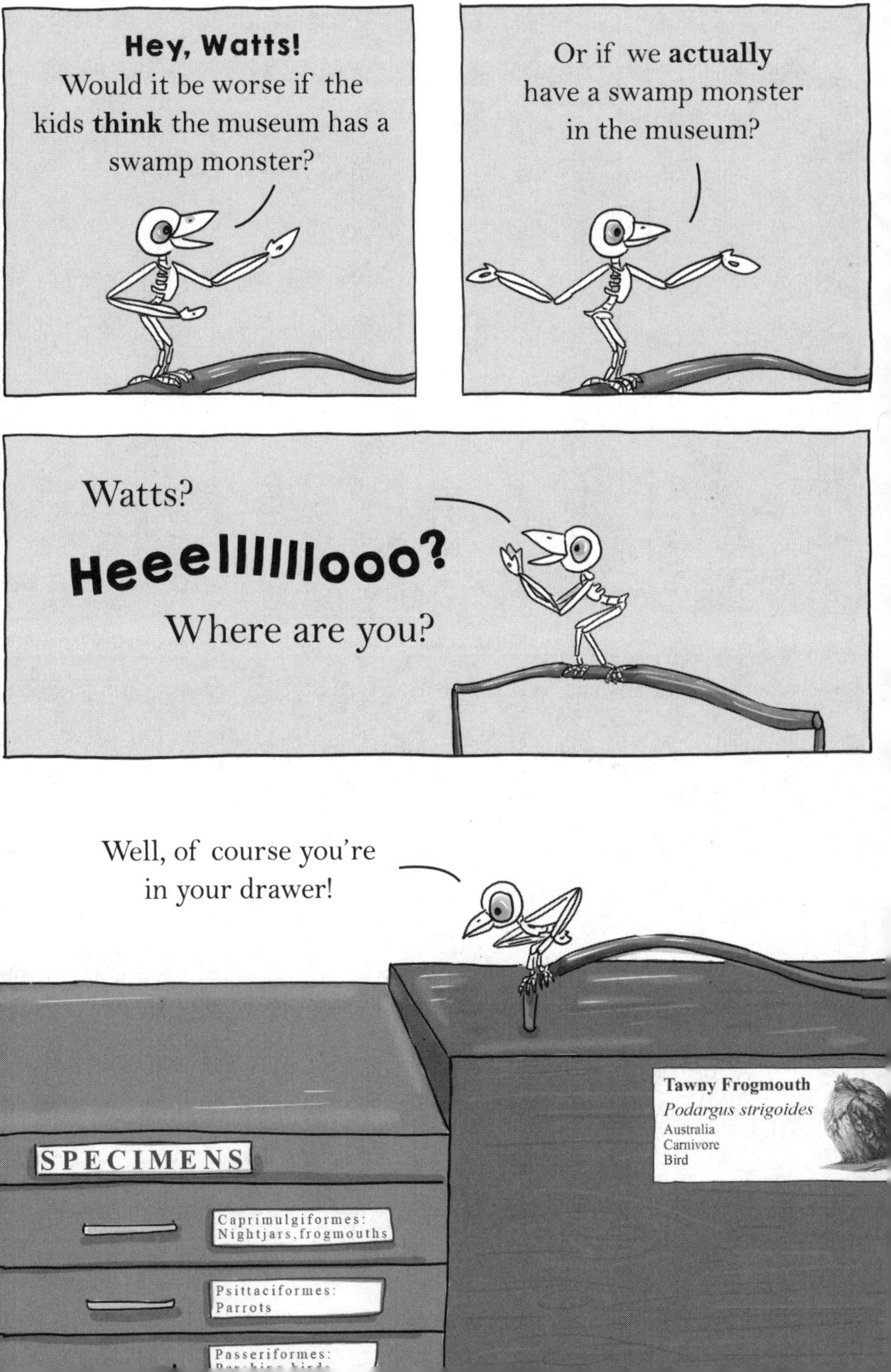
Hey, Watts!
Would it be worse if the kids think the museum has a swamp monster?
Or if we actually have a swamp monster in the museum?
Watts?
Heeellllllooo?
Where are you?
Well, of course you're in your drawer!
SPECIMENS
Caprimulgiformes: Nightjars, frogmouths
Psittaciformes: Parrots
Passeriformes:
Tawny Frogmouth
Podargus strigoides
Australia
Carnivore
Bird

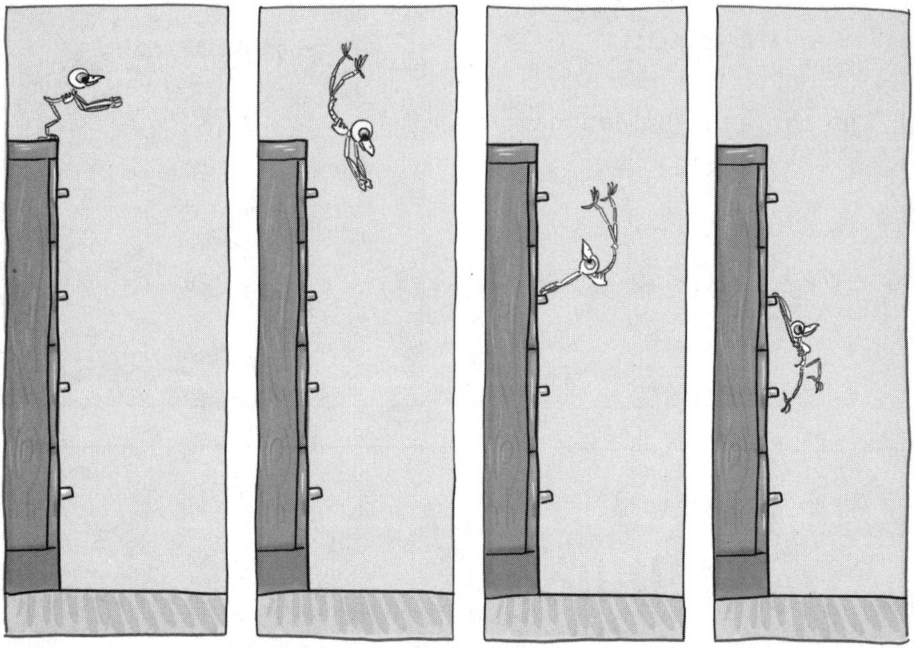

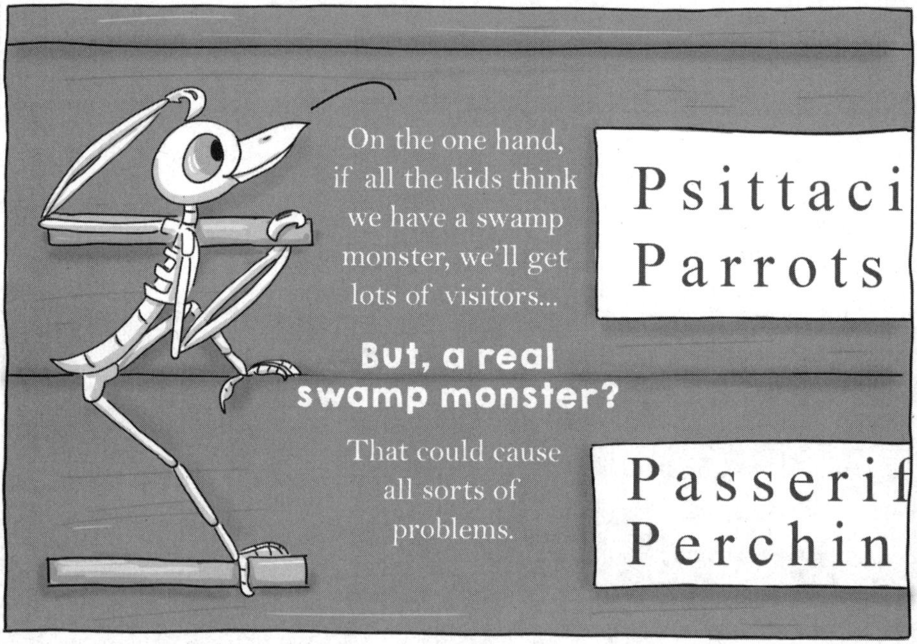

On the one hand, if all the kids think we have a swamp monster, we'll get lots of visitors...
But, a real swamp monster?
That could cause all sorts of problems.
Psittaci
Parrots
Passerif
Perchin

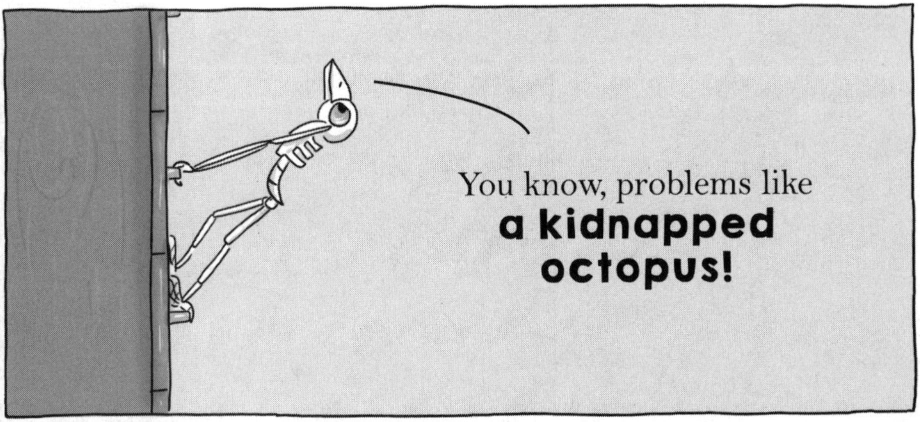
You know, problems like
a kidnapped octopus!

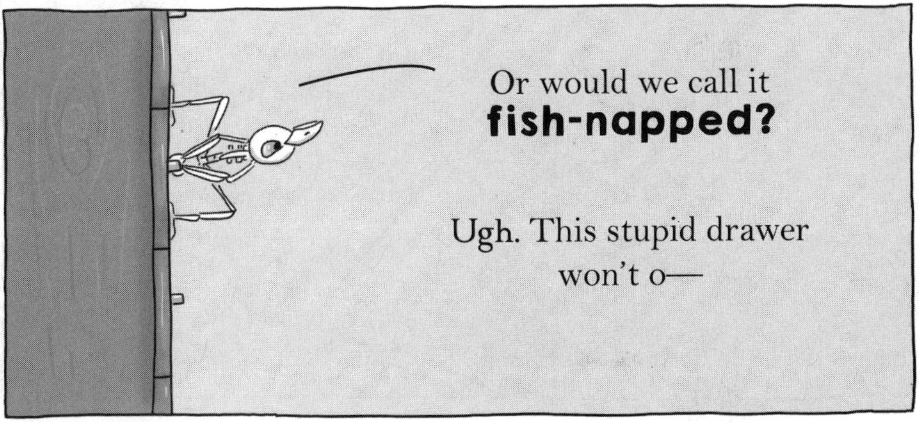
Or would we call it
fish-napped?
Ugh. This stupid drawer
won't o—

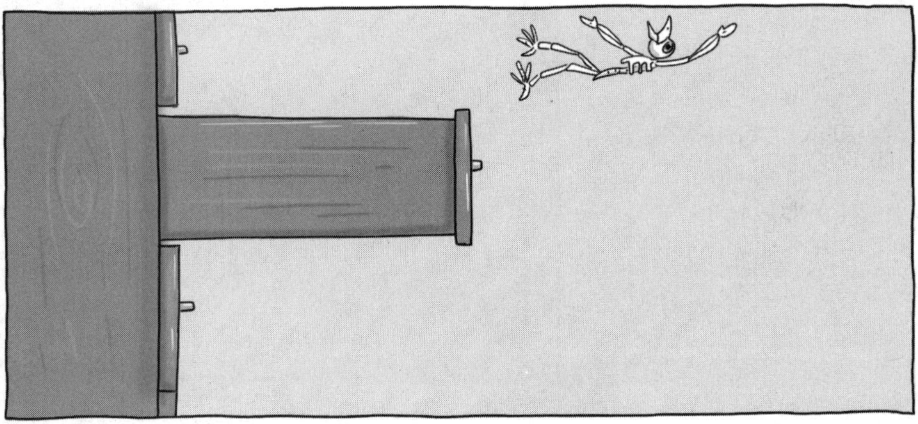

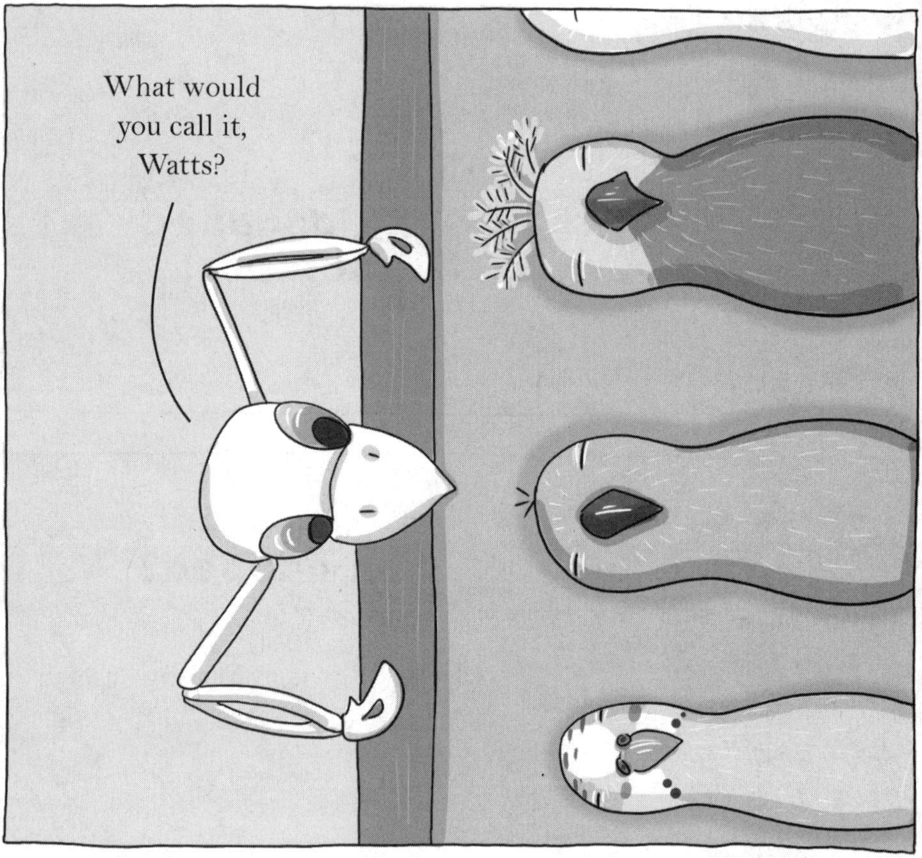
What would you call it, Watts?

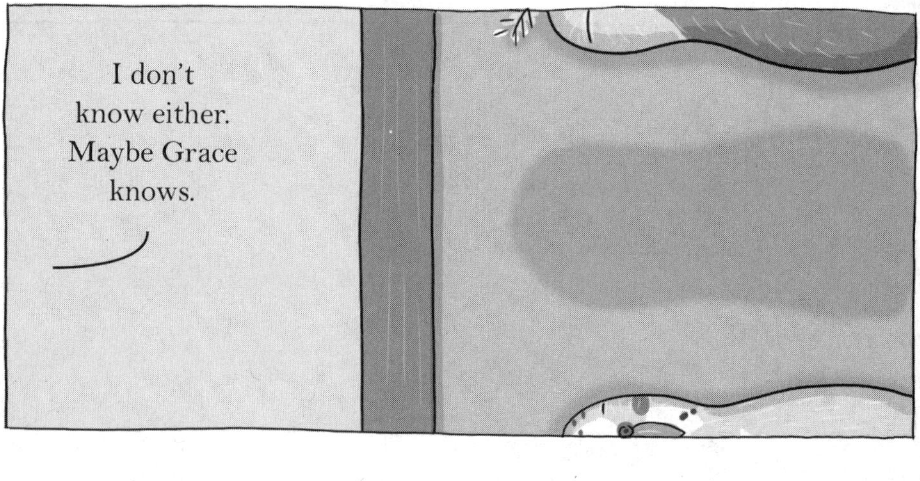
I don't know either. Maybe Grace knows.

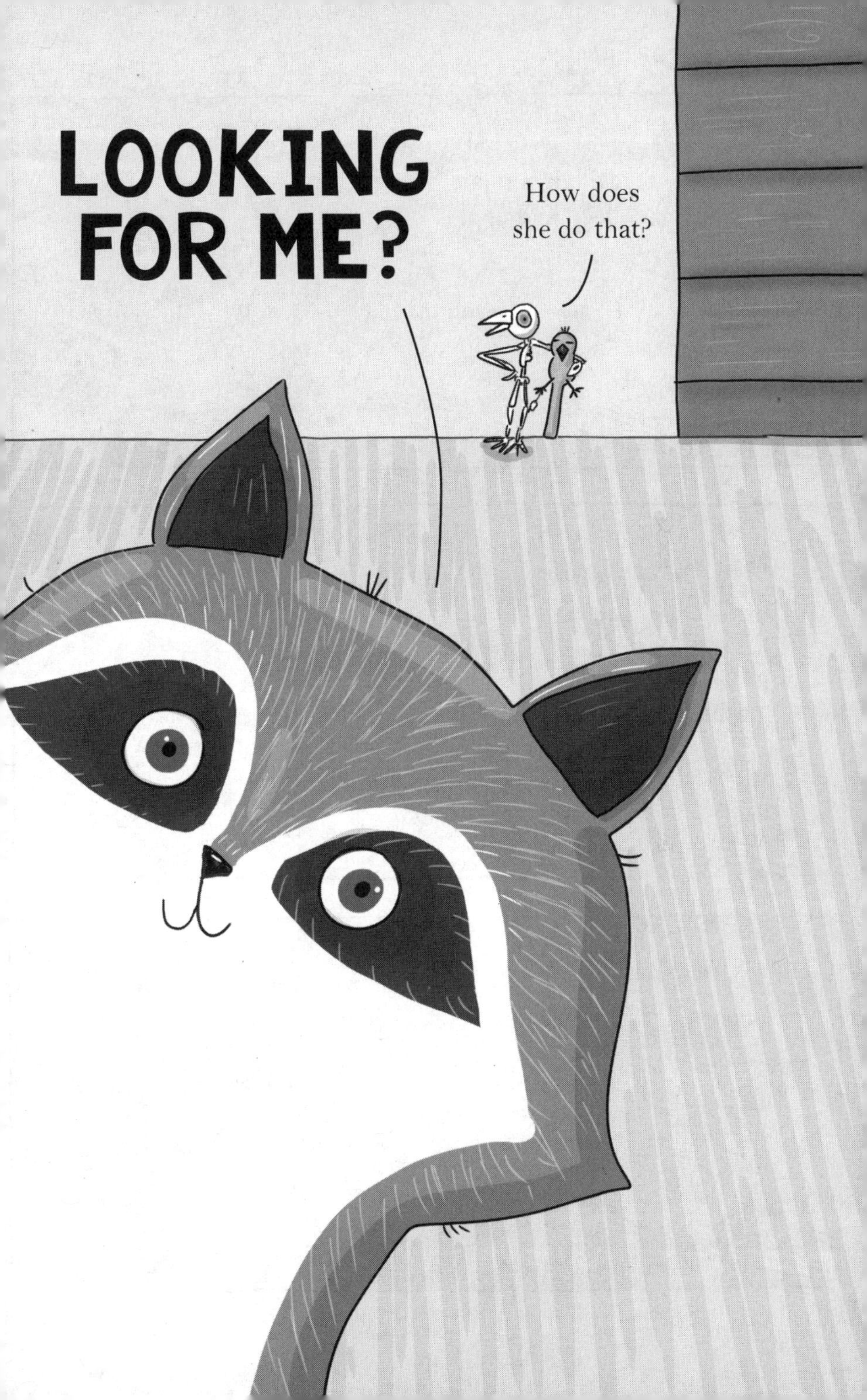
LOOKING FOR ME?
How does she do that?

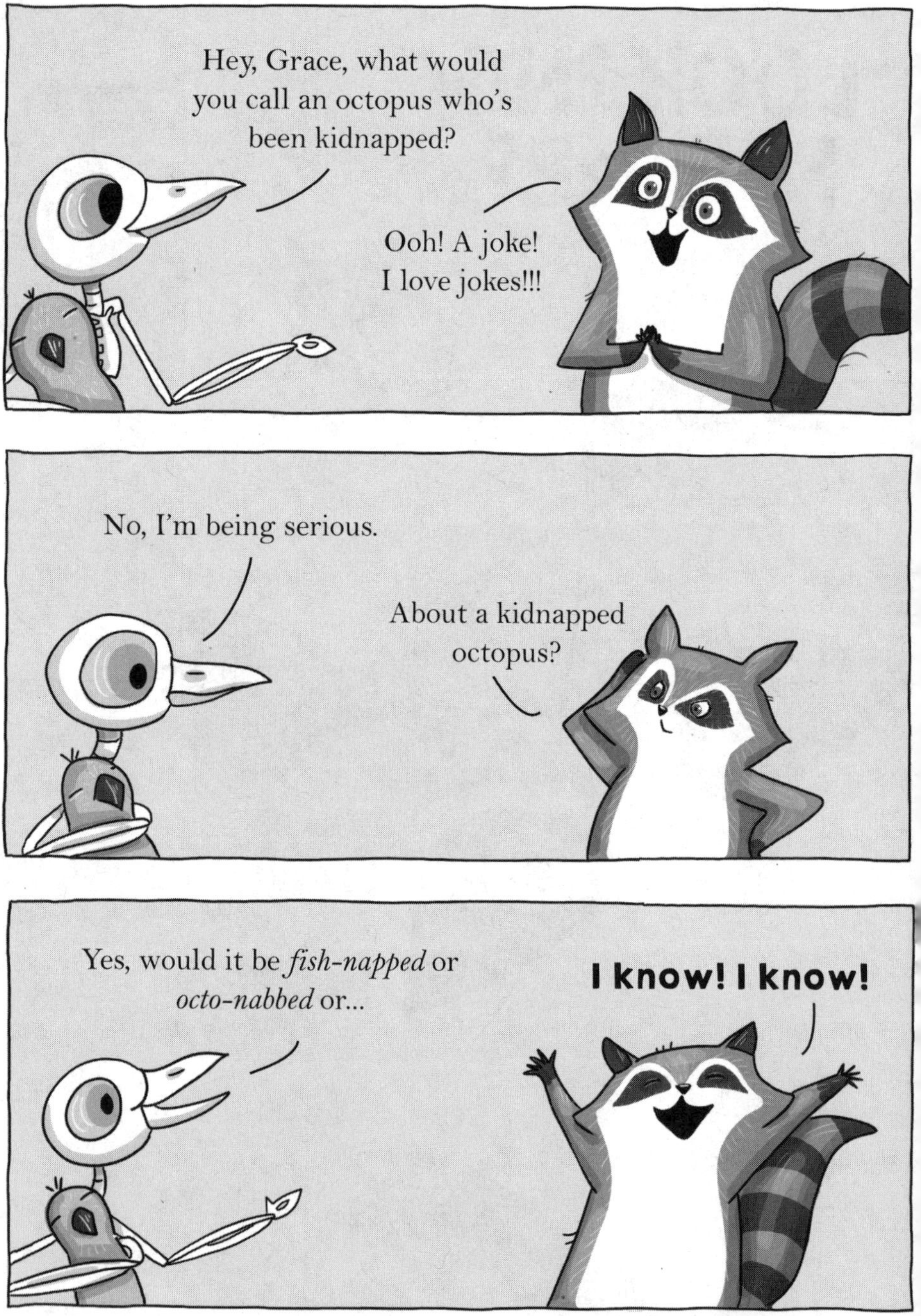
Hey, Grace, what would you call an octopus who's been kidnapped?
Ooh! A joke! I love jokes!!!
No, I'm being serious.
About a kidnapped octopus?
Yes, would it be *fish-napped* or *octo-nabbed* or...
I know! I know!

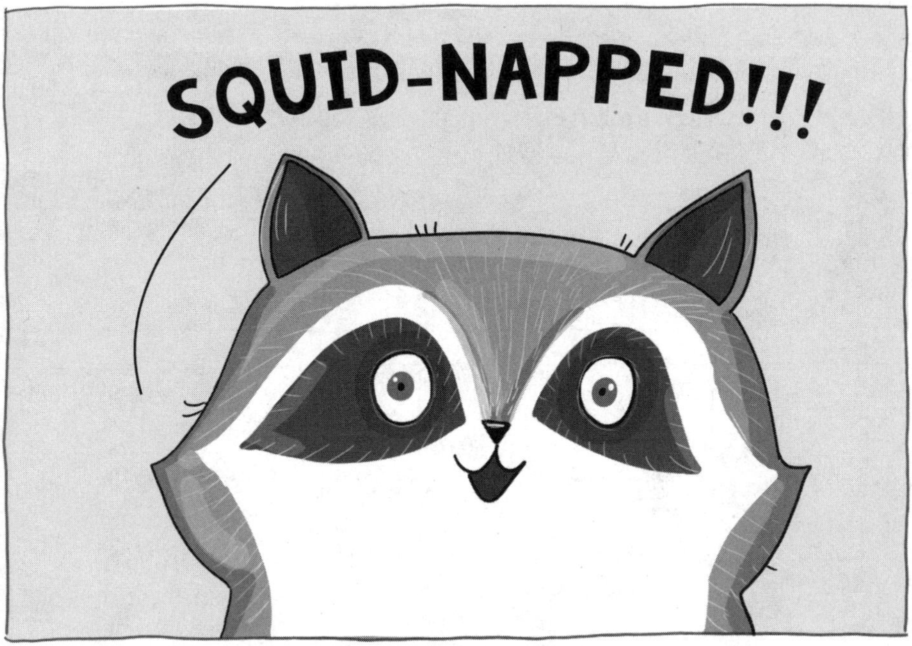
SQUID-NAPPED!!!

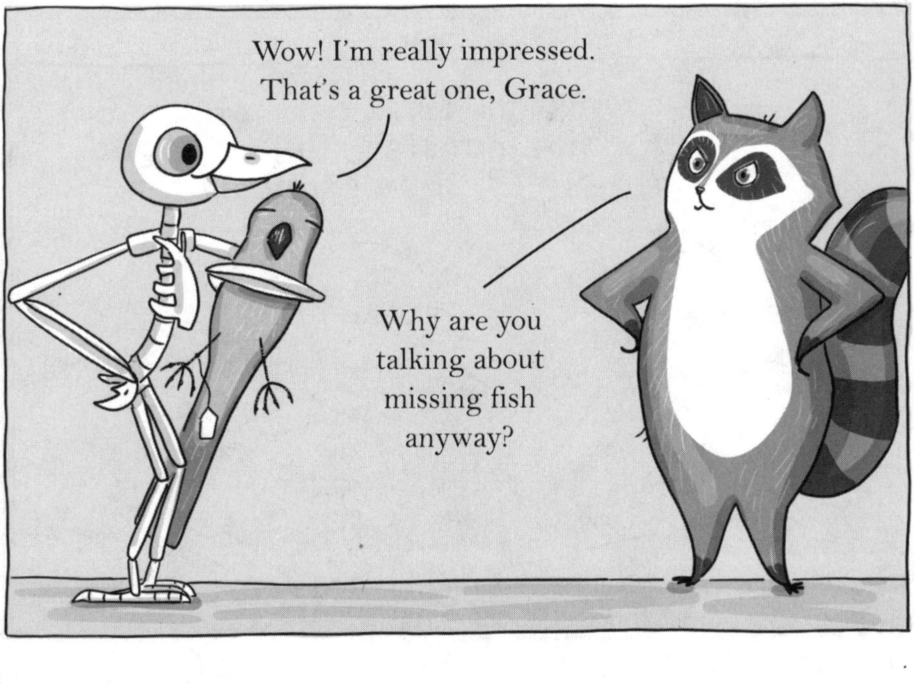
Wow! I'm really impressed. That's a great one, Grace.
Why are you talking about missing fish anyway?

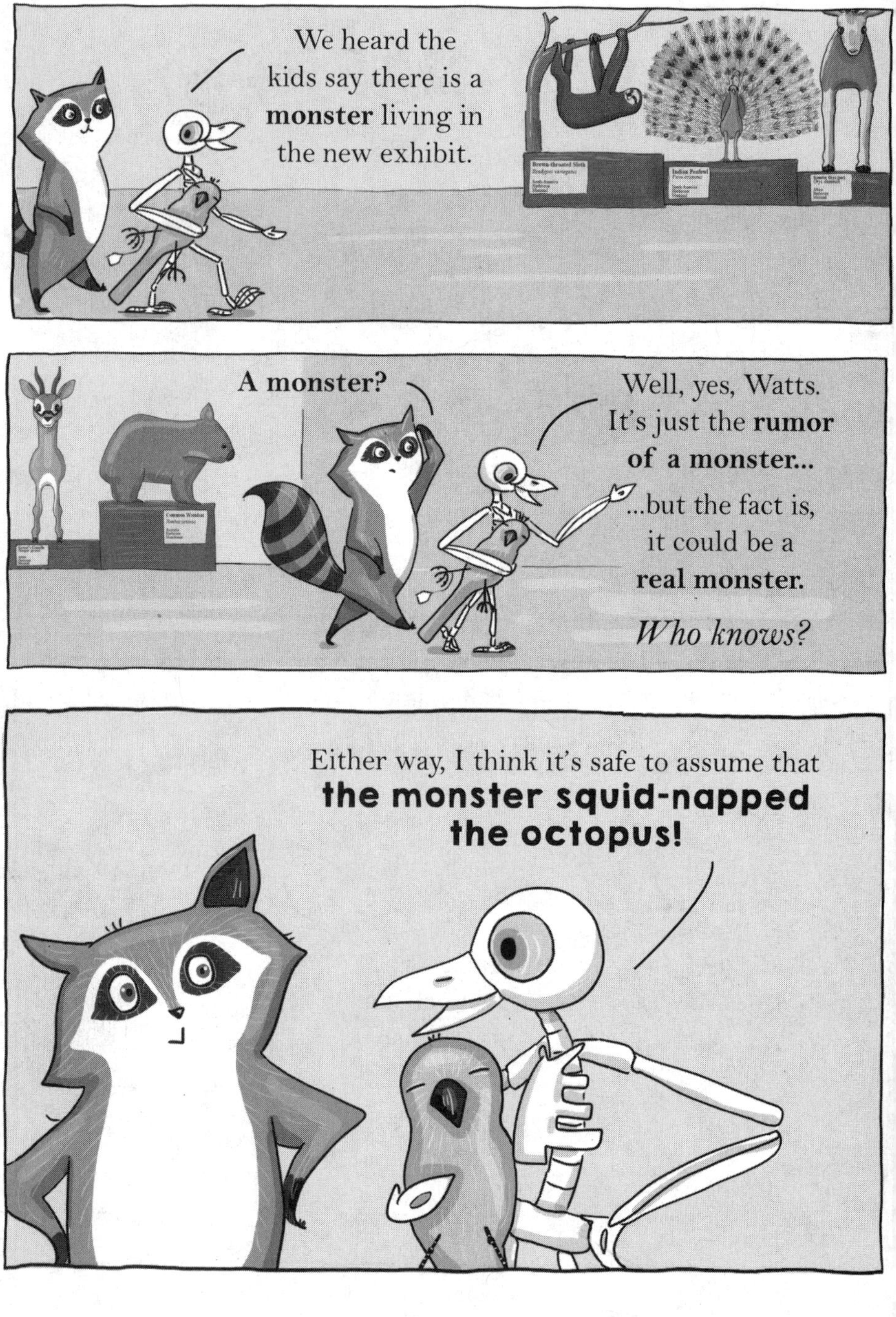

We heard the kids say there is a **monster** living in the new exhibit.
A monster?
Well, yes, Watts. It's just the **rumor of a monster...**
...but the fact is, it could be a **real monster.**
Who knows?
Either way, I think it's safe to assume that **the monster squid-napped the octopus!**

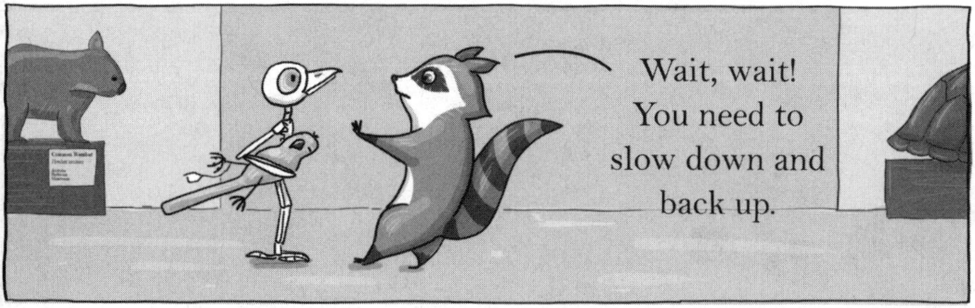
Wait, wait! You need to slow down and back up.

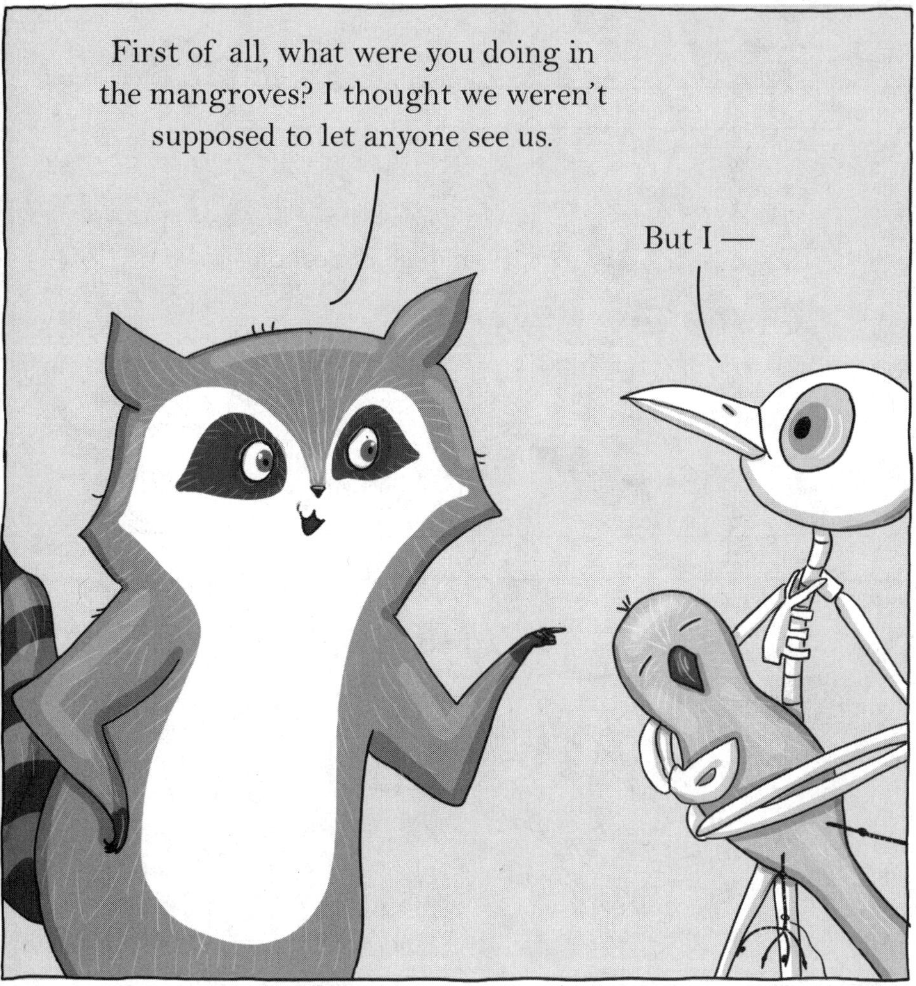
First of all, what were you doing in the mangroves? I thought we weren't supposed to let anyone see us.
But I —

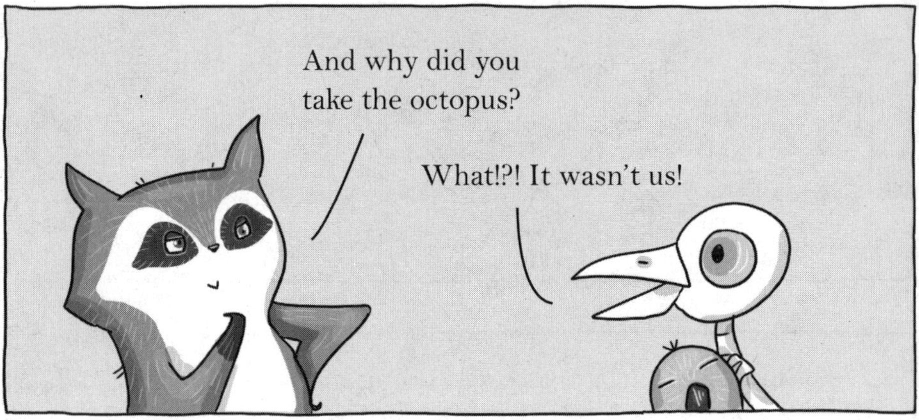
And why did you take the octopus?
What!?! It wasn't us!

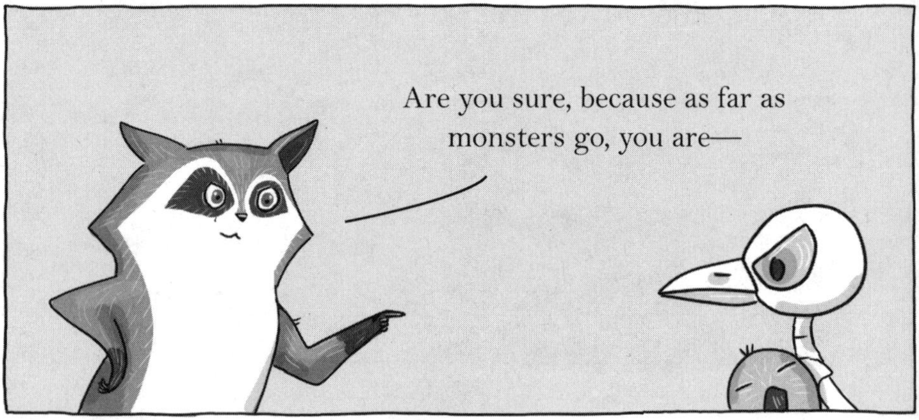
Are you sure, because as far as monsters go, you are—

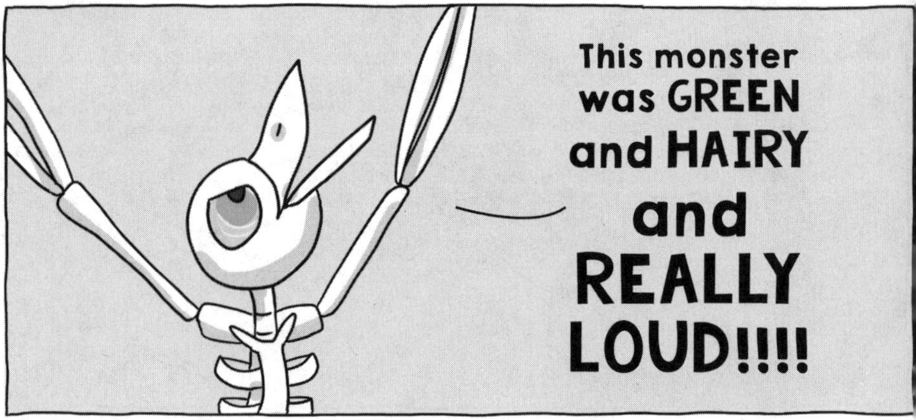
This monster was GREEN and HAIRY and REALLY LOUD!!!!

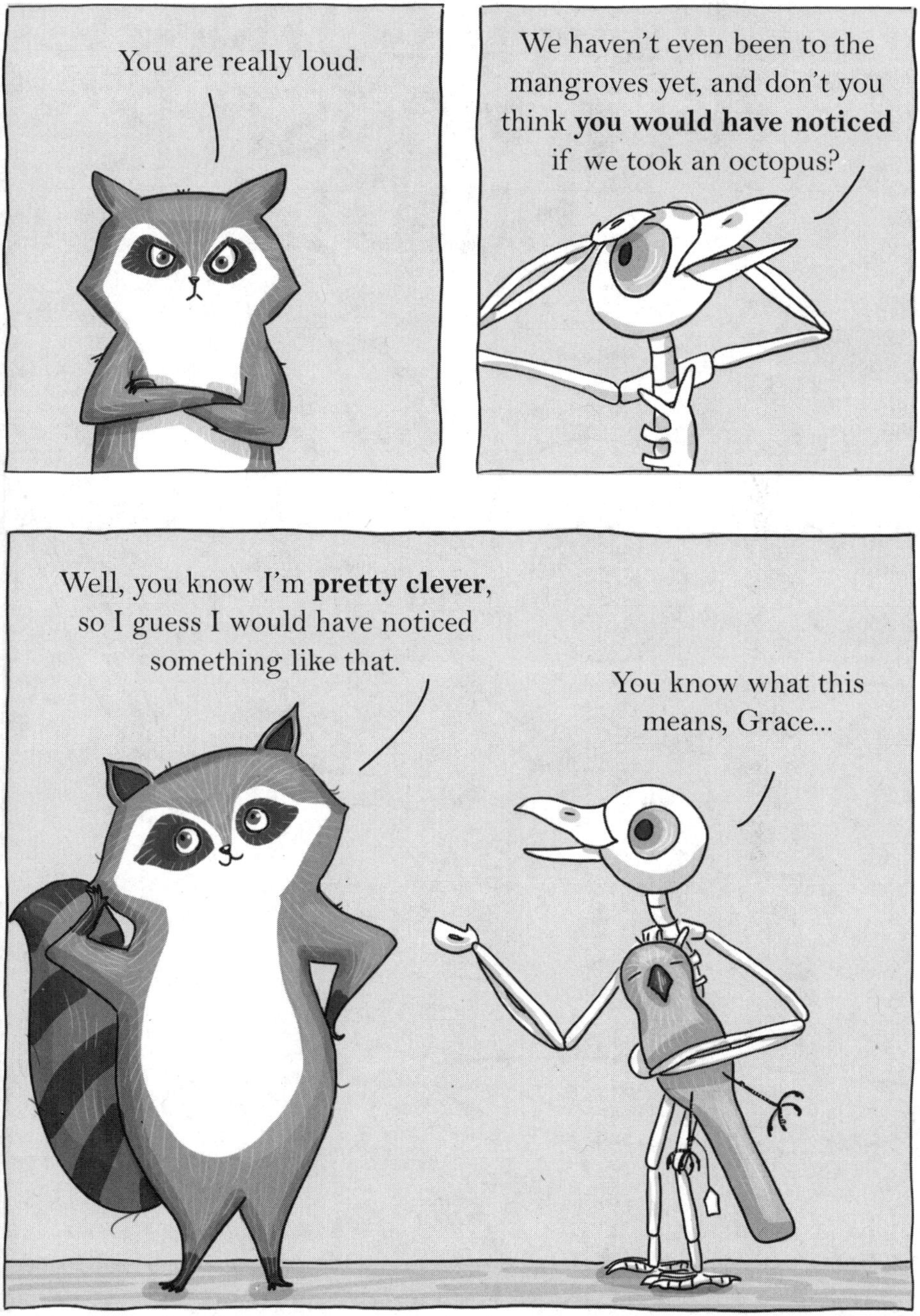
You are really loud.
We haven't even been to the mangroves yet, and don't you think **you would have noticed** if we took an octopus?
Well, you know I'm **pretty clever**, so I guess I would have noticed something like that.
You know what this means, Grace...

WE'RE GOING ON A MONSTER HUNT!

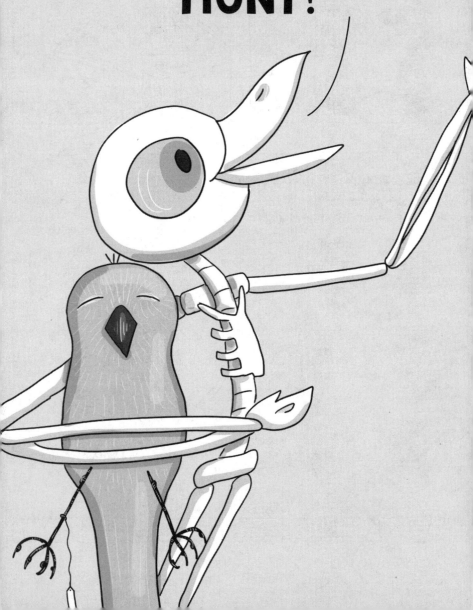

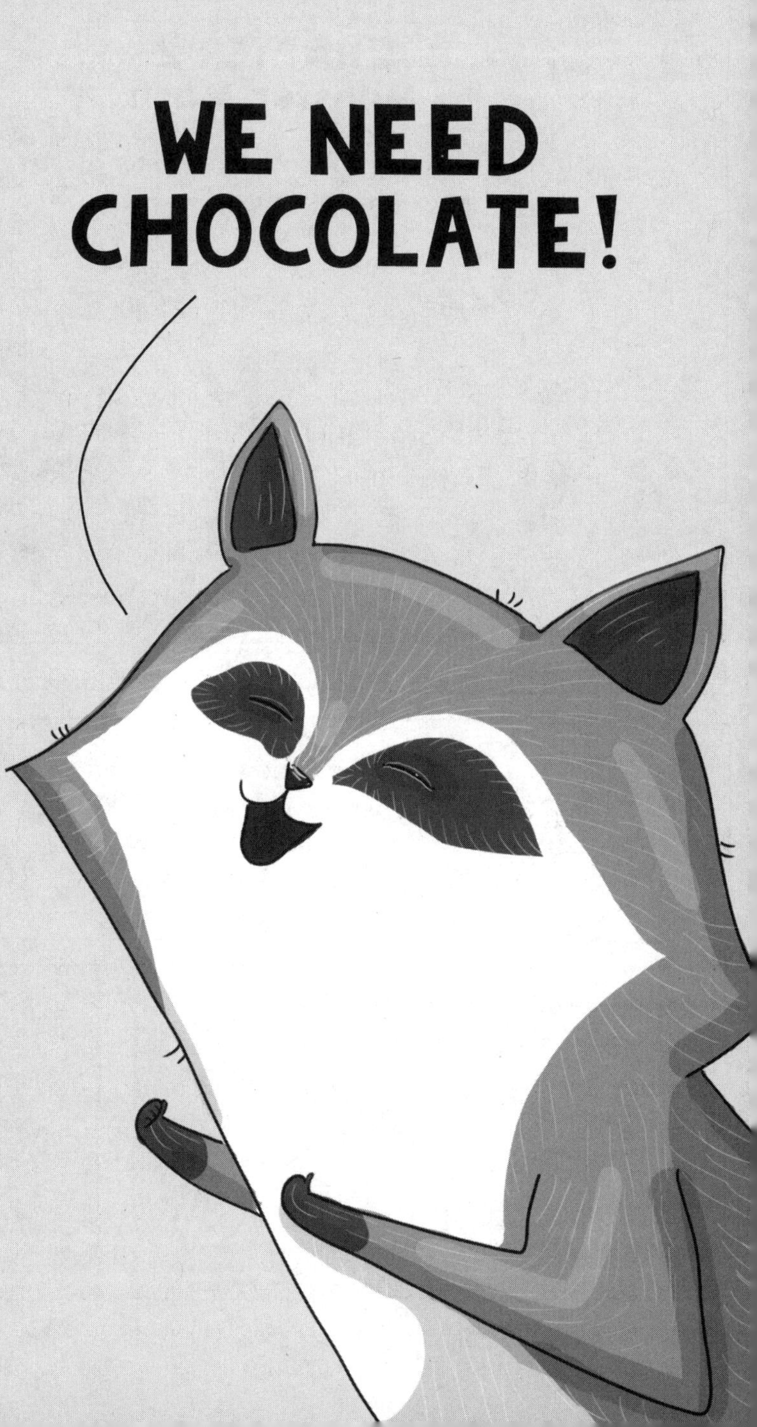
WE NEED CHOCOLATE!

CHAPTER 2
Monster Mash

So are we solving the swamp monster mystery or the missing octopus mystery?

We can solve them both.

You know what we need to catch a monster?

Strength?

Brains?

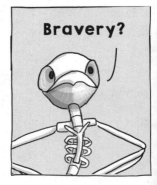

Bravery?

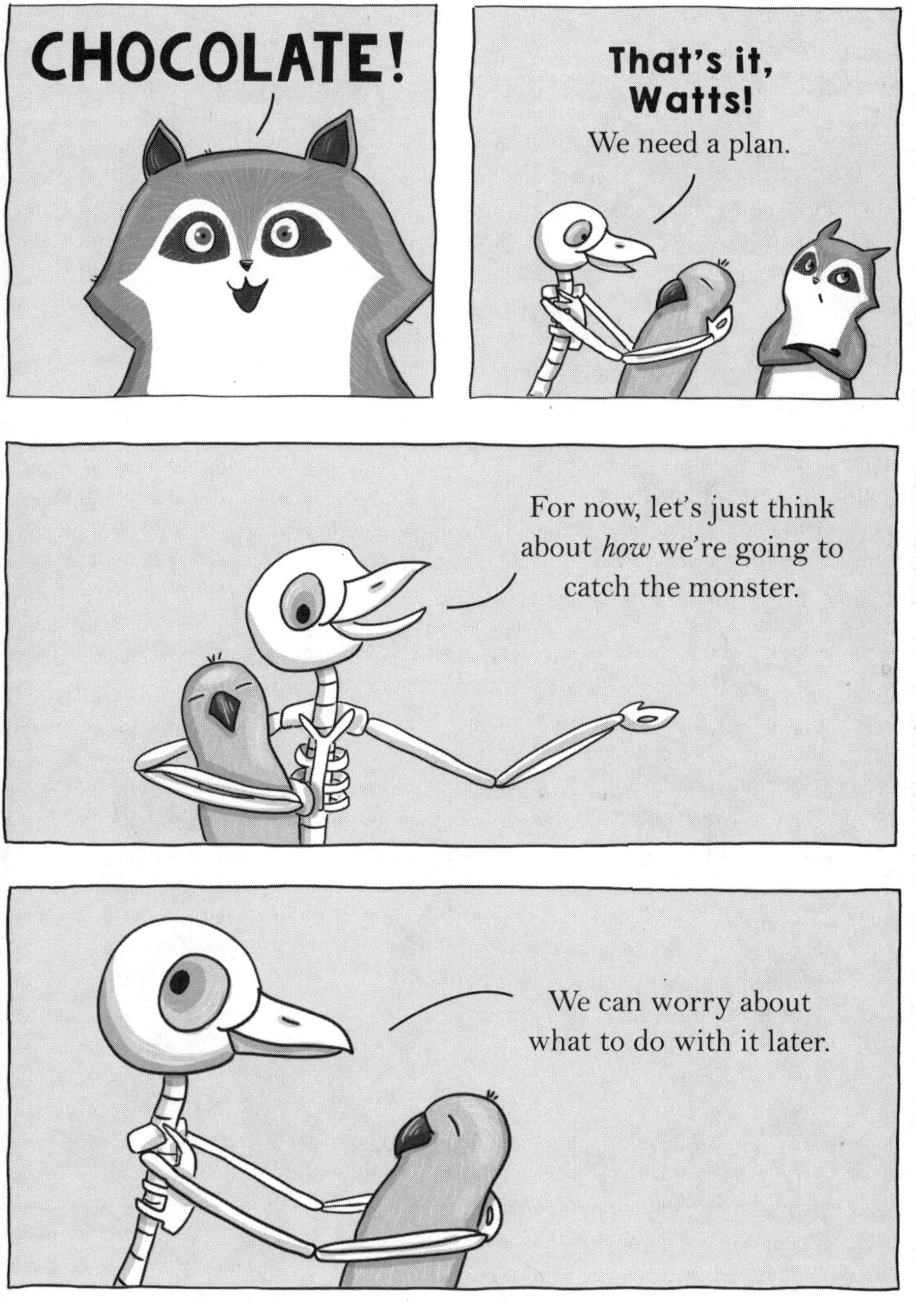
CHOCOLATE!
That's it, Watts!
We need a plan.
For now, let's just think about *how* we're going to catch the monster.
We can worry about what to do with it later.

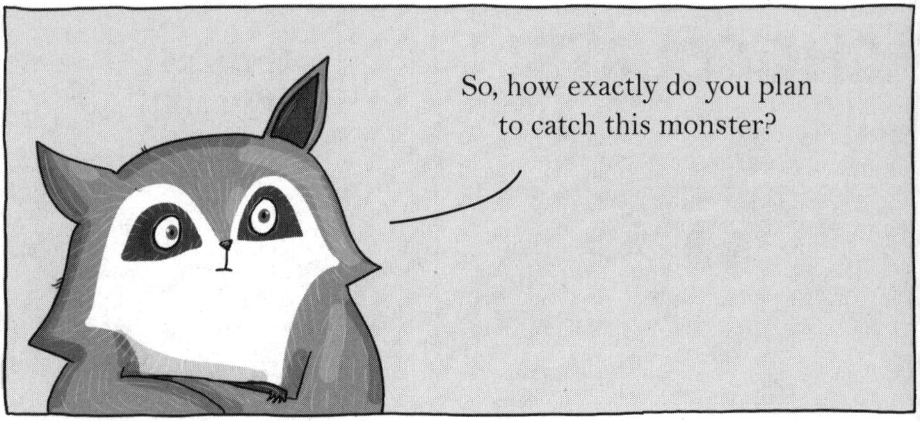
So, how exactly do you plan to catch this monster?

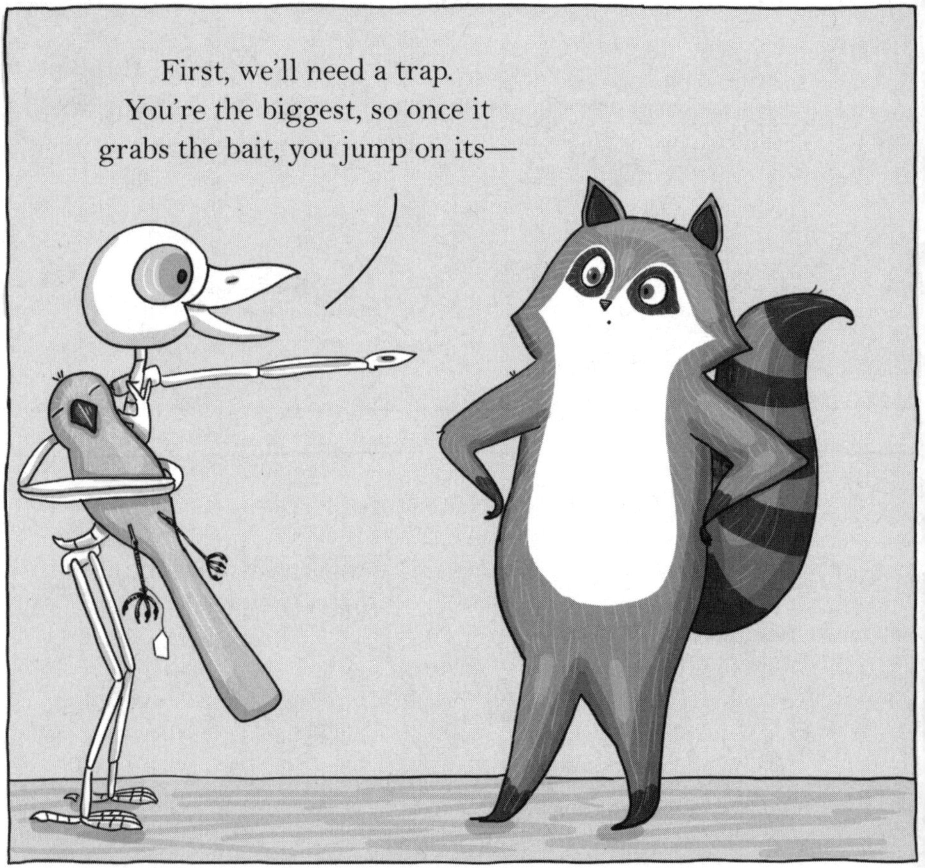
First, we'll need a trap. You're the biggest, so once it grabs the bait, you jump on its—

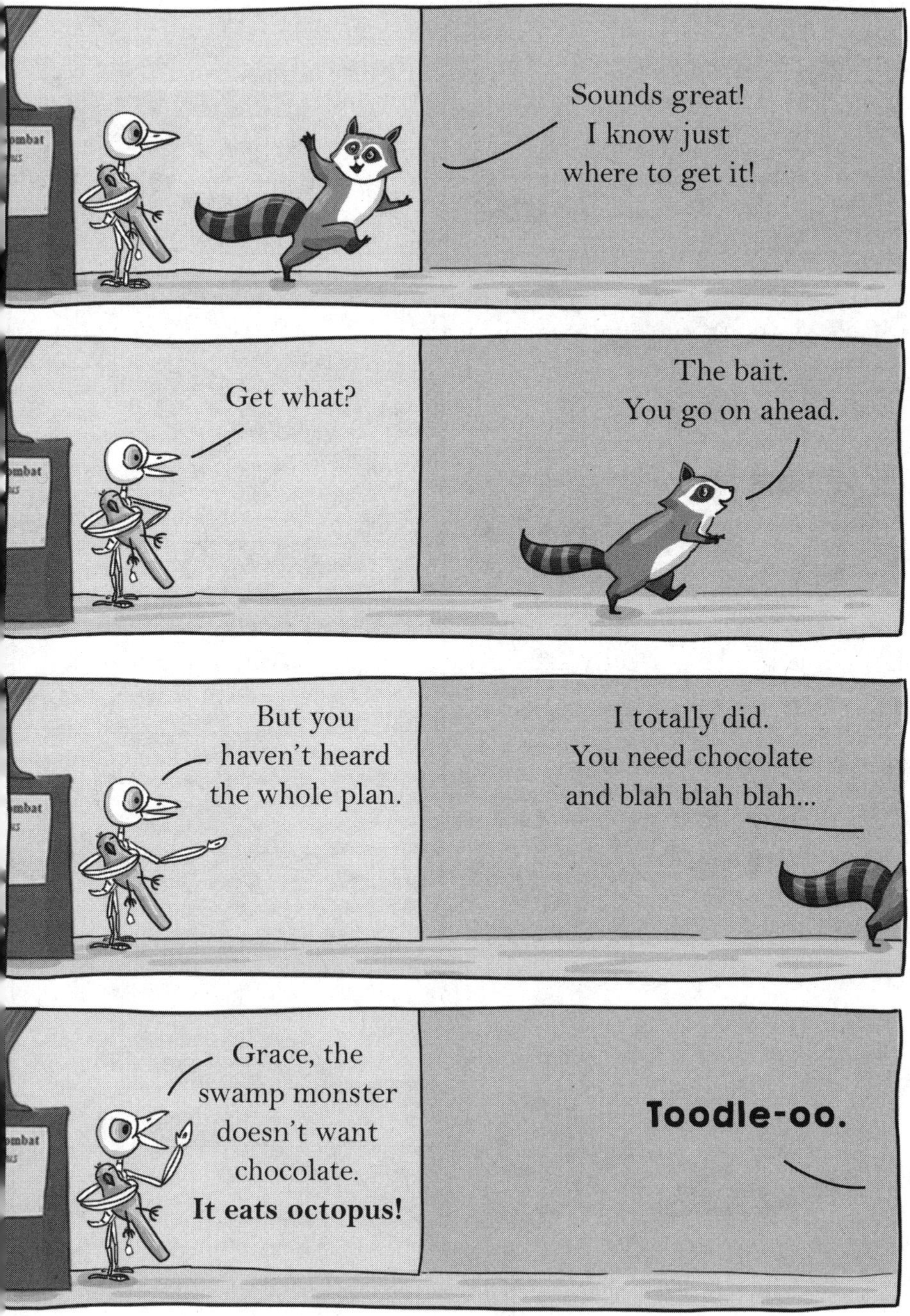
Sounds great! I know just where to get it!
Get what?
The bait. You go on ahead.
But you haven't heard the whole plan.
I totally did. You need chocolate and blah blah blah...
Grace, the swamp monster doesn't want chocolate. **It eats octopus!**
Toodle-oo.

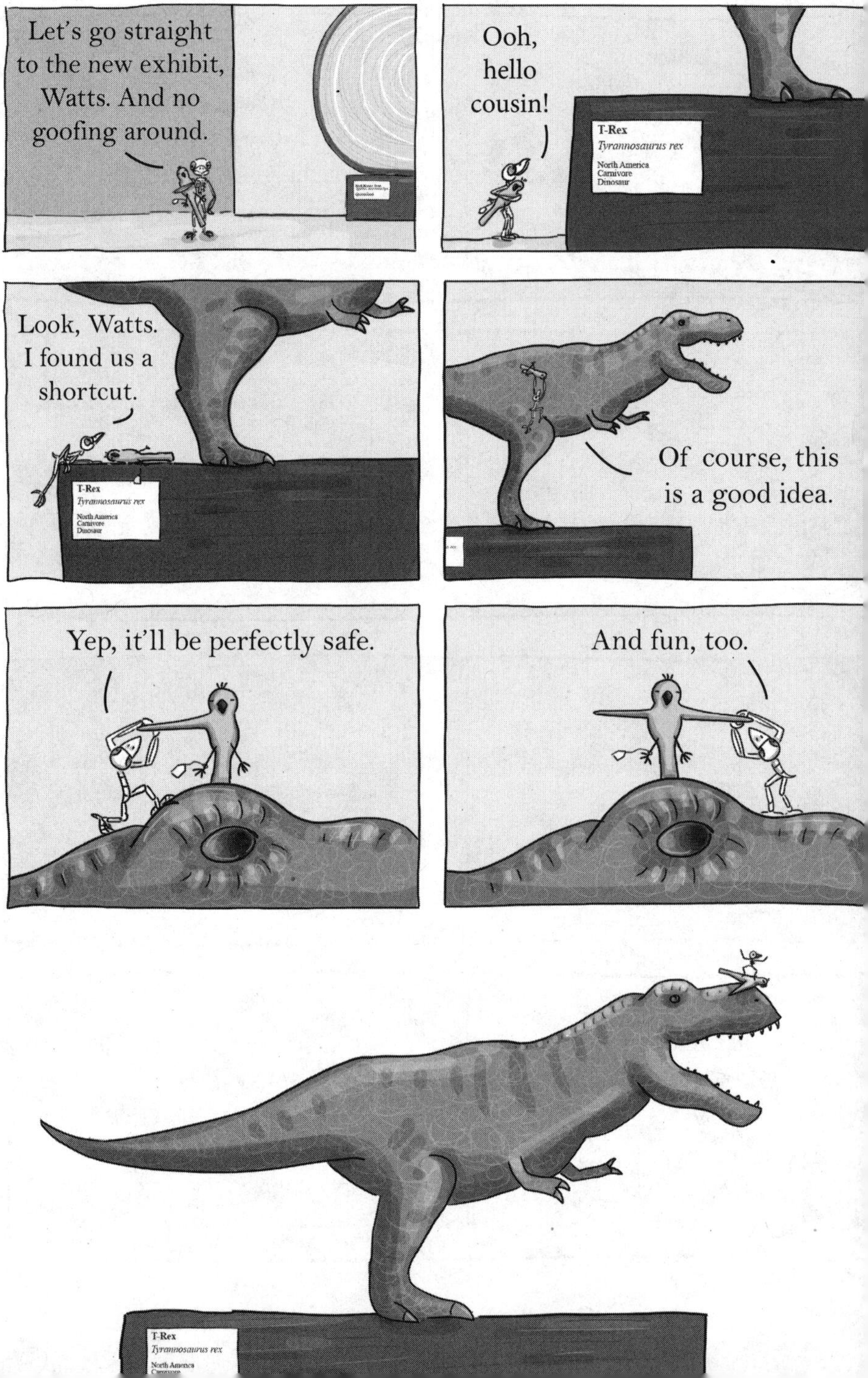
Let's go straight to the new exhibit, Watts. And no goofing around.
Ooh, hello cousin!
T-Rex
Tyrannosaurus rex
North America
Carnivore
Dinosaur
Look, Watts. I found us a shortcut.
T-Rex
Tyrannosaurus rex
North America
Carnivore
Dinosaur
Of course, this is a good idea.
Yep, it'll be perfectly safe.
And fun, too.
T-Rex
Tyrannosaurus rex
North America

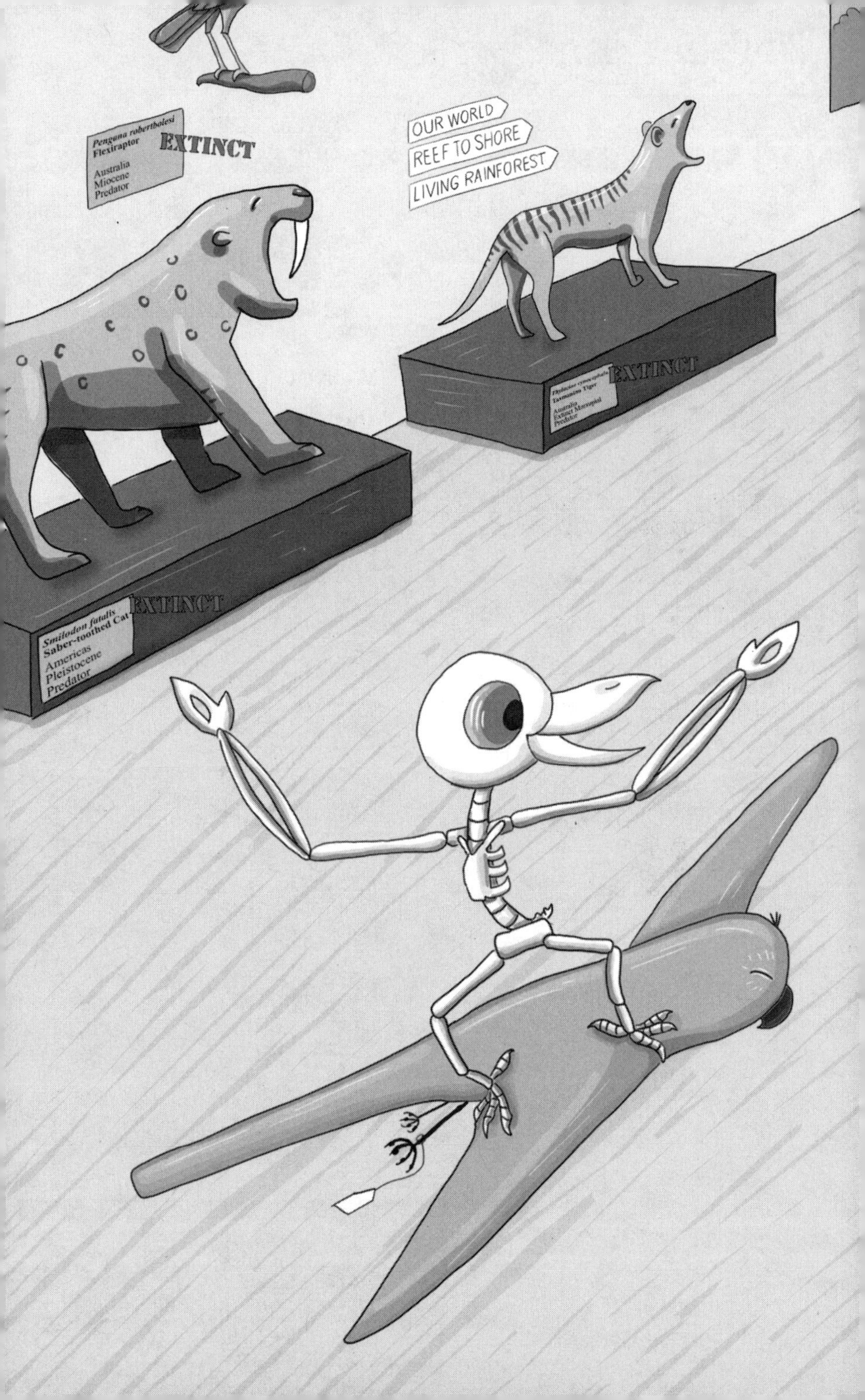

Pengana robertbolesi
Flexiraptor
Australia
Miocene
Predator
EXTINCT
OUR WORLD
REEF TO SHORE
LIVING RAINFOREST
EXTINCT
Smilodon fatalis
Saber-toothed Cat
Americas
Pleistocene
Predator
EXTINCT

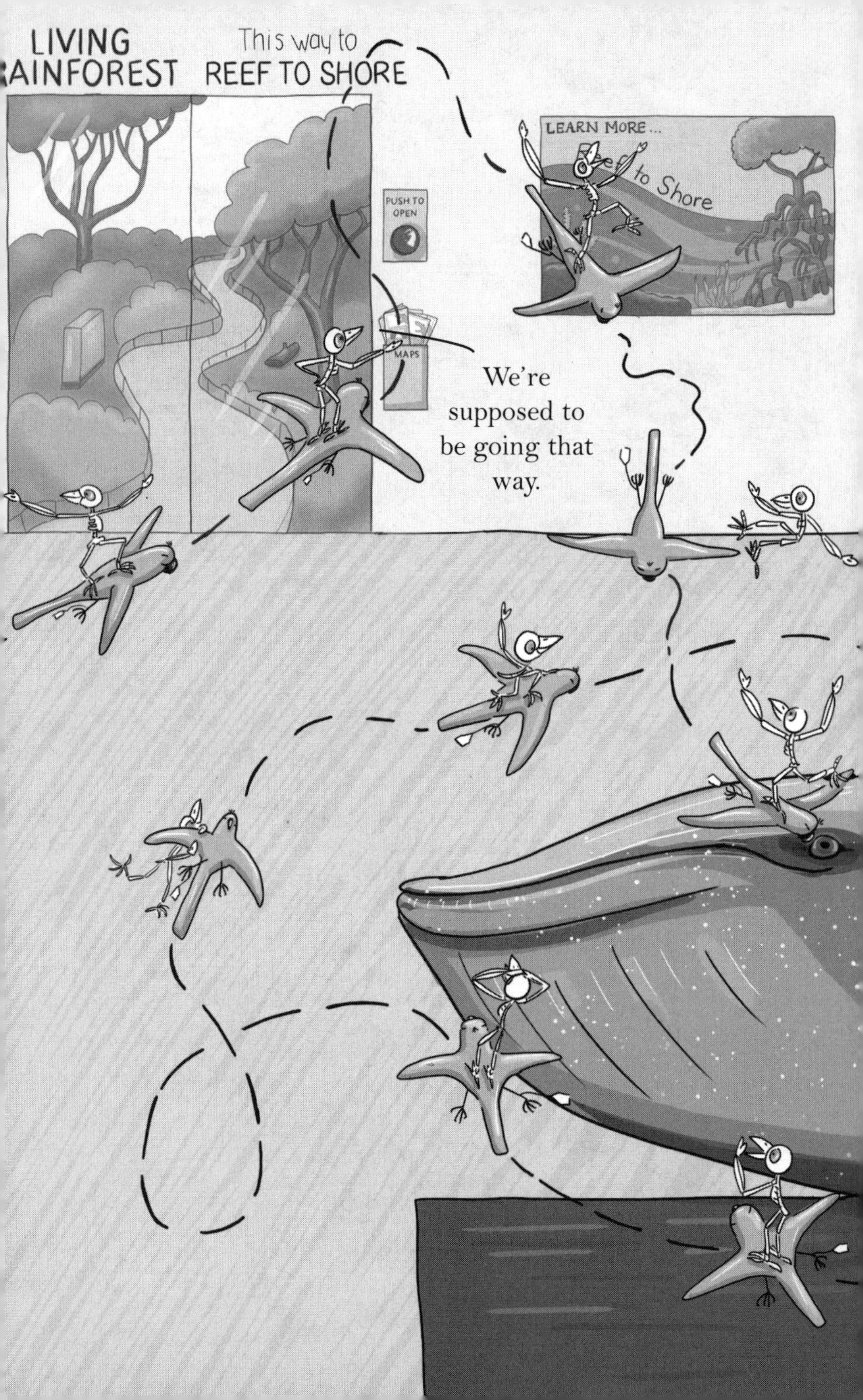
LIVING
RAINFOREST
This way to
REEF TO SHORE
PUSH TO OPEN
MAPS
LEARN MORE...
to Shore
We're supposed to be going that way.

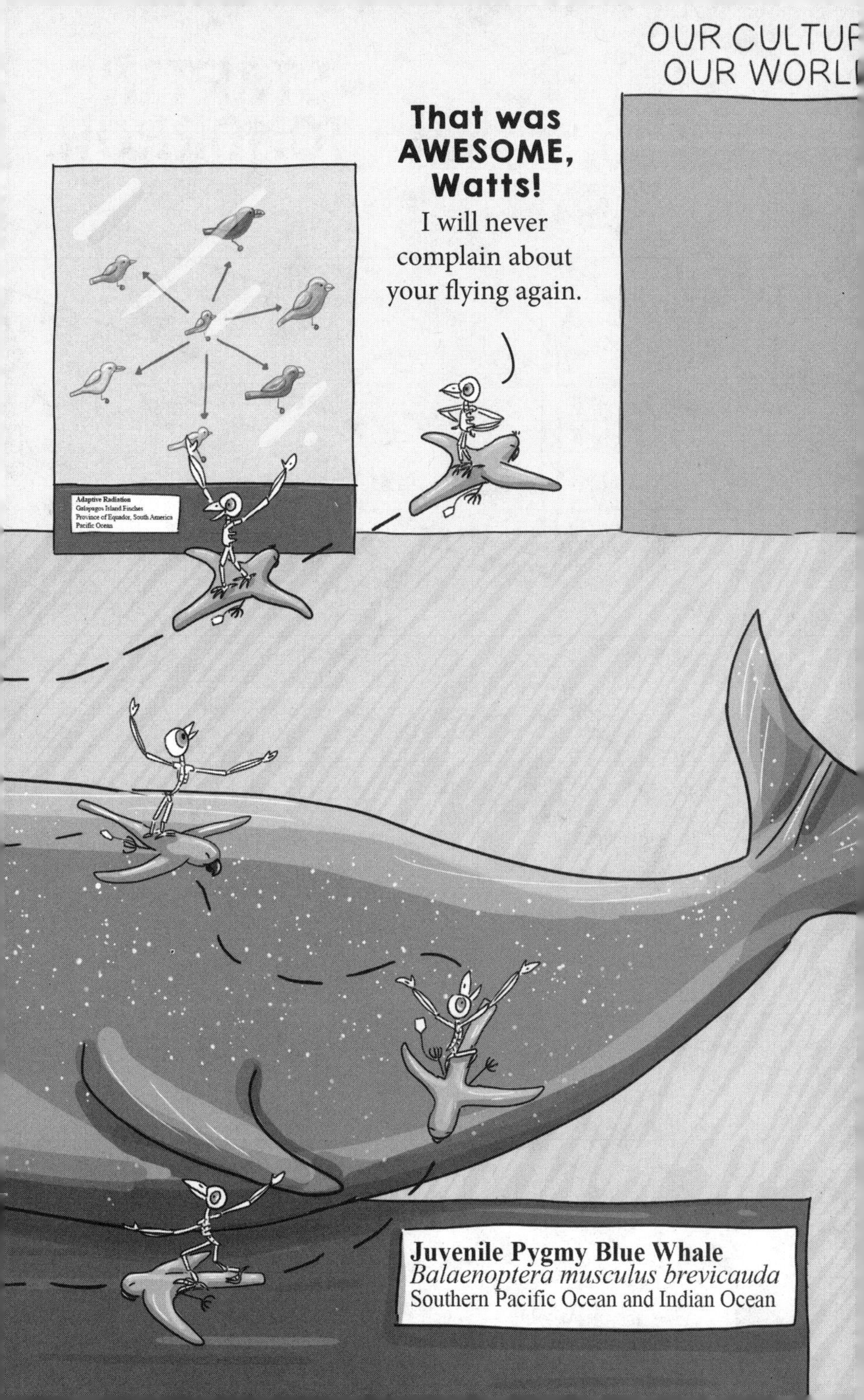

OUR CULTUR
OUR WORLI
That was AWESOME, Watts! I will never complain about your flying again.
Adaptive Radiation
Galapagos Island Finches
Province of Equador, South America
Pacific Ocean
Juvenile Pygmy Blue Whale
Balaenoptera musculus brevicauda
Southern Pacific Ocean and Indian Ocean

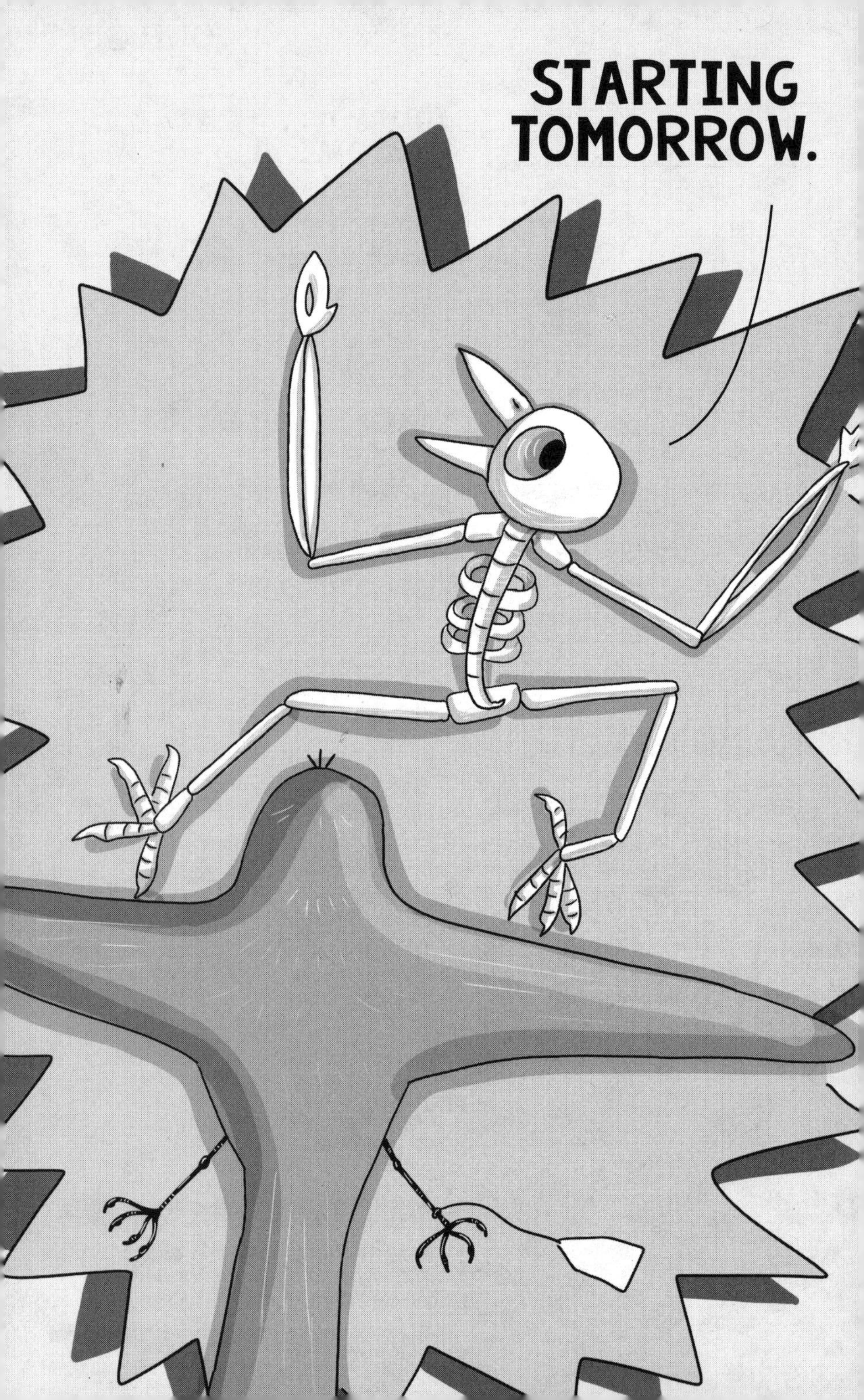
STARTING
TOMORROW.

CRYPTOZOOLOGY

Who are Cryptozoologists?
Cryptozoologists are people who try to find evidence of the existence of monsters and other creatures that are recorded in folklore. Cryptozoology is considered a pseudoscience as it does not follow the scientific method.

What is a Cryptid?
A cryptid is a term used for any animal or creature that has not been proven to exist by scientists.

What do Cryptozoologists do?
Cryptozoologists search for things like footprints, photos, videos, bones, fur, or hair for DNA that will prove a creature exists.

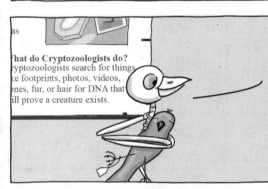

You know, Watts, all around the world people have different monster legends.

as

What do Cryptozoologists do?
Cryptozoologists search for things like footprints, photos, videos, bones, fur, or hair for DNA that will prove a creature exists.

Some people research monsters for a living. They are called cryptozoologists.

Yes, I think it's a cool word too.

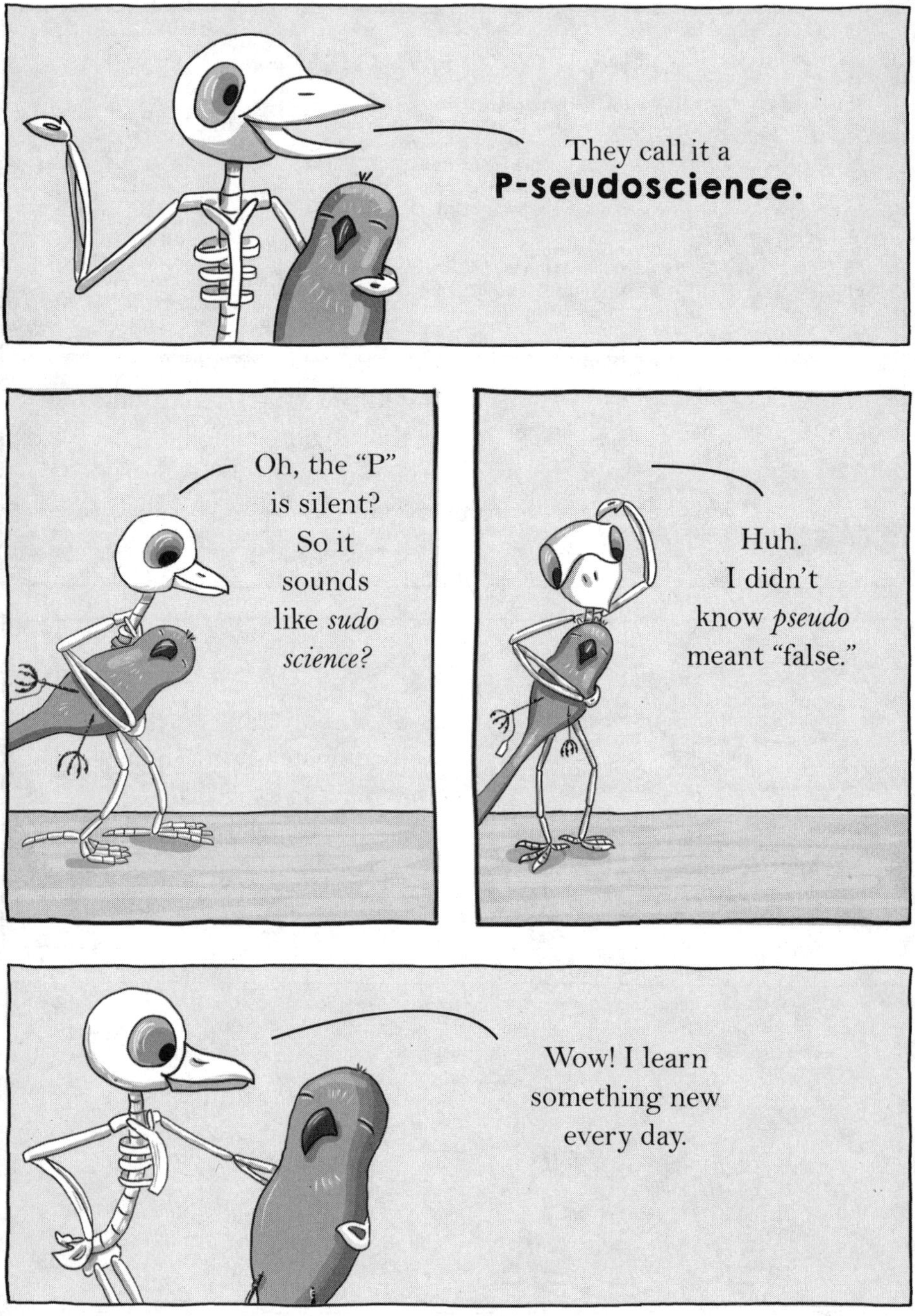
They call it a
P-seudoscience.
Oh, the "P" is silent? So it sounds like *sudo science?*
Huh. I didn't know *pseudo* meant "false."
Wow! I learn something new every day.

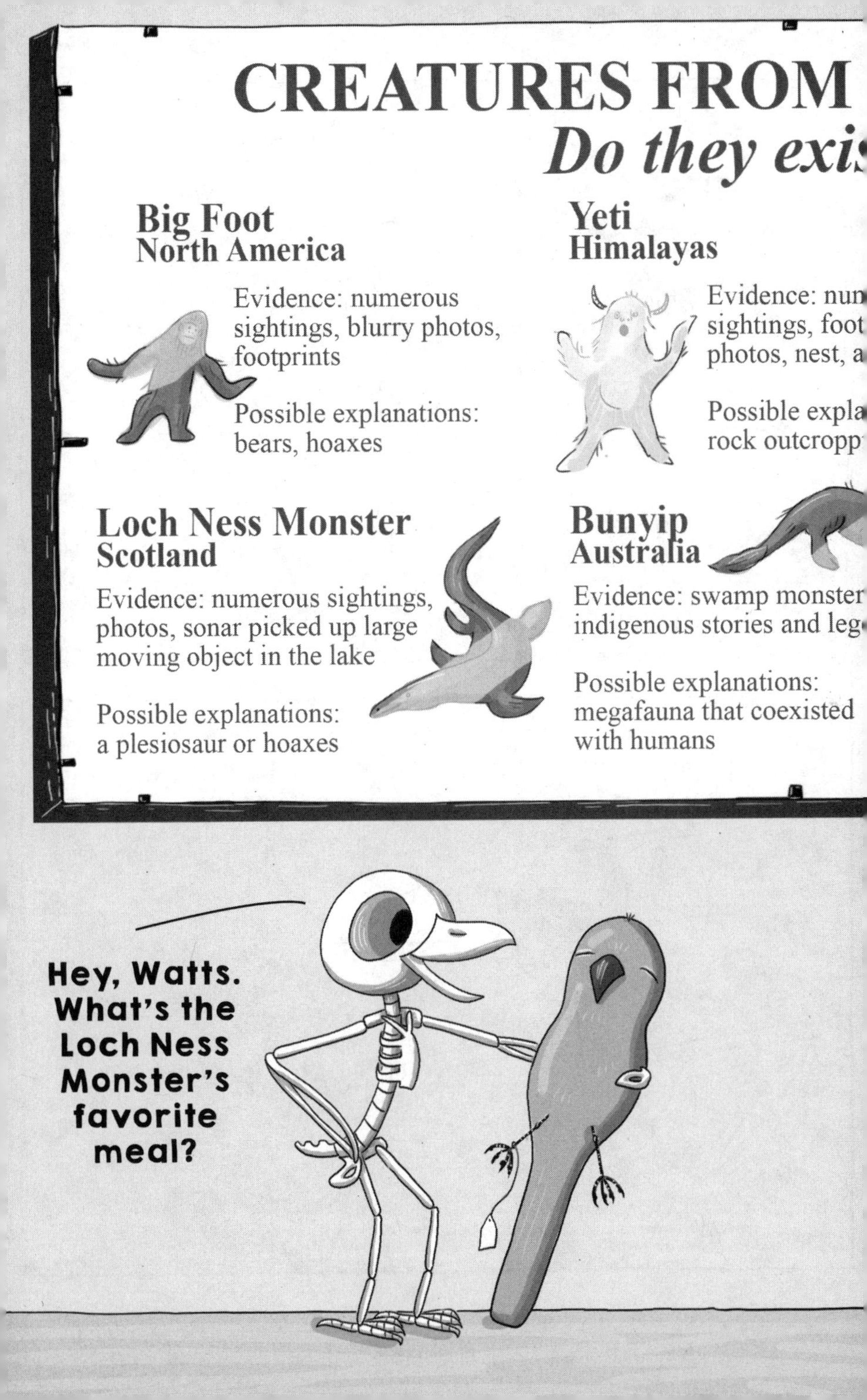

CREATURES FROM
Do they exis

Big Foot
North America

Evidence: numerous sightings, blurry photos, footprints

Possible explanations: bears, hoaxes

Yeti
Himalayas

Evidence: num sightings, foot photos, nest, a

Possible expla rock outcropp

Loch Ness Monster
Scotland

Evidence: numerous sightings, photos, sonar picked up large moving object in the lake

Possible explanations: a plesiosaur or hoaxes

Bunyip
Australia

Evidence: swamp monster indigenous stories and leg

Possible explanations: megafauna that coexisted with humans

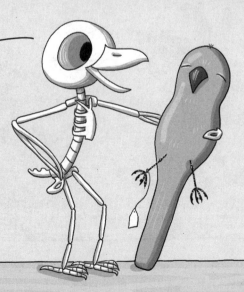

Hey, Watts. What's the Loch Ness Monster's favorite meal?

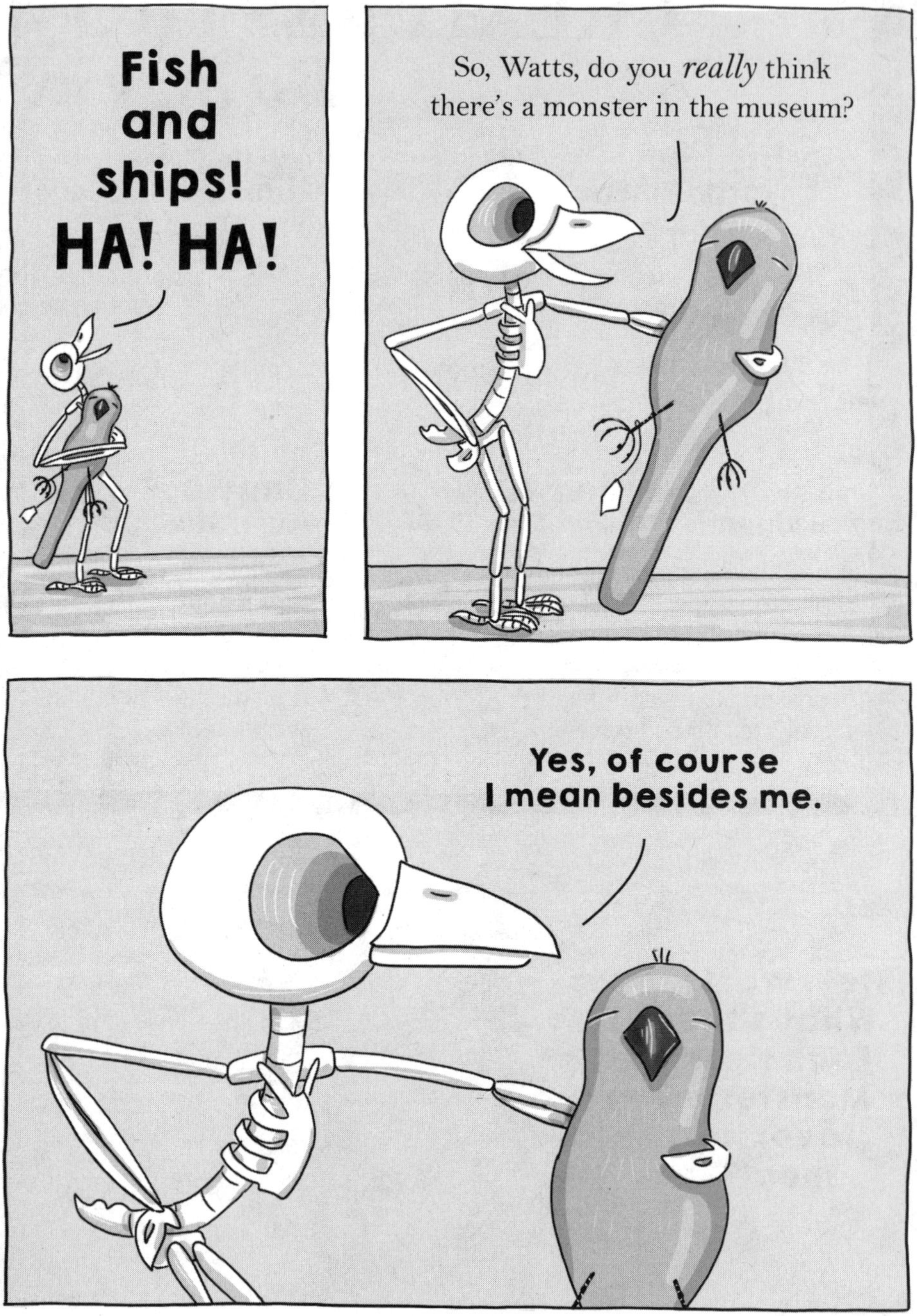
Fish and ships! HA! HA!
So, Watts, do you *really* think there's a monster in the museum?
Yes, of course I mean besides me.

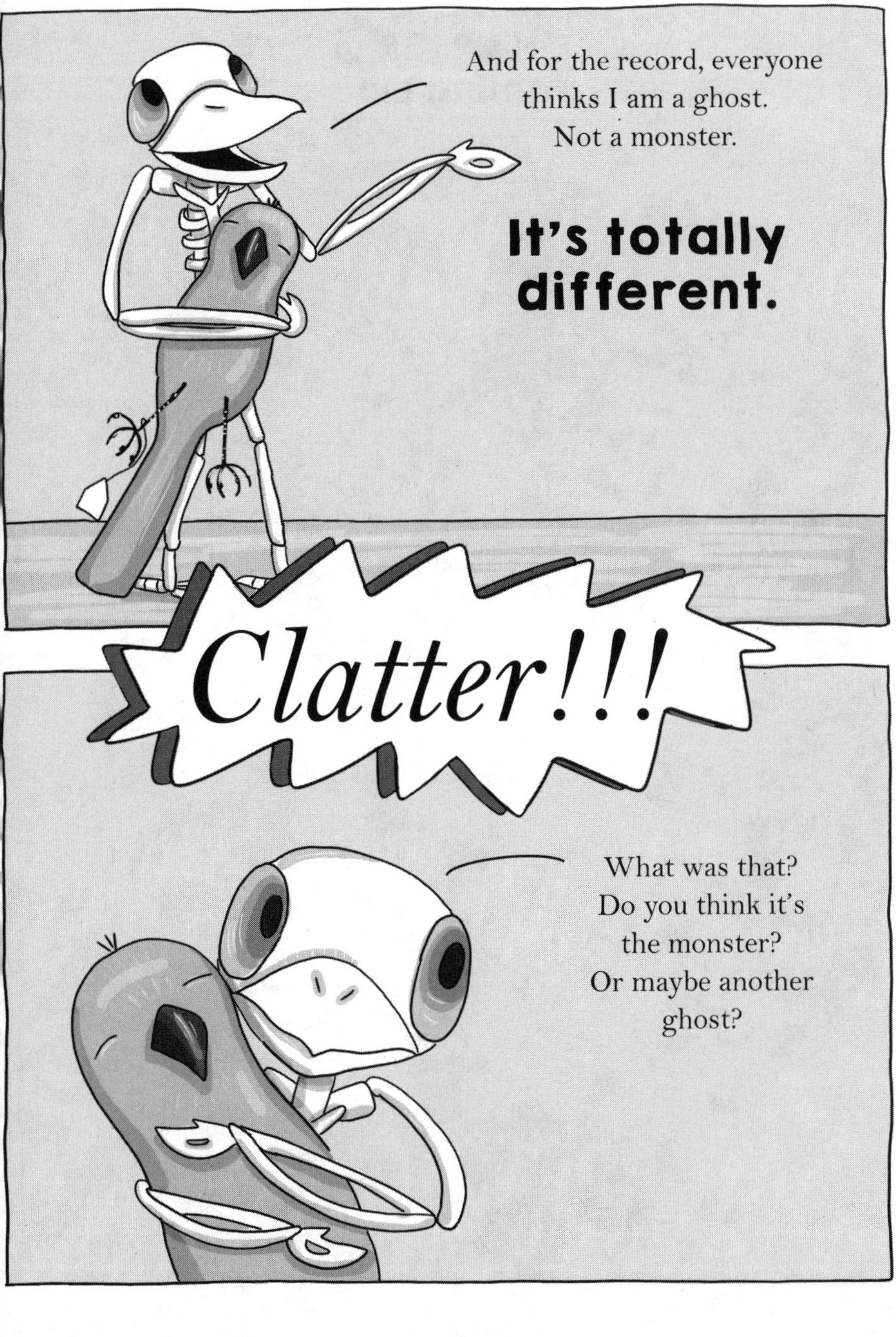
And for the record, everyone thinks I am a ghost. Not a monster.
It's totally different.
Clatter!!!
What was that? Do you think it's the monster? Or maybe another ghost?

CHAPTER 3
Feeling Blue

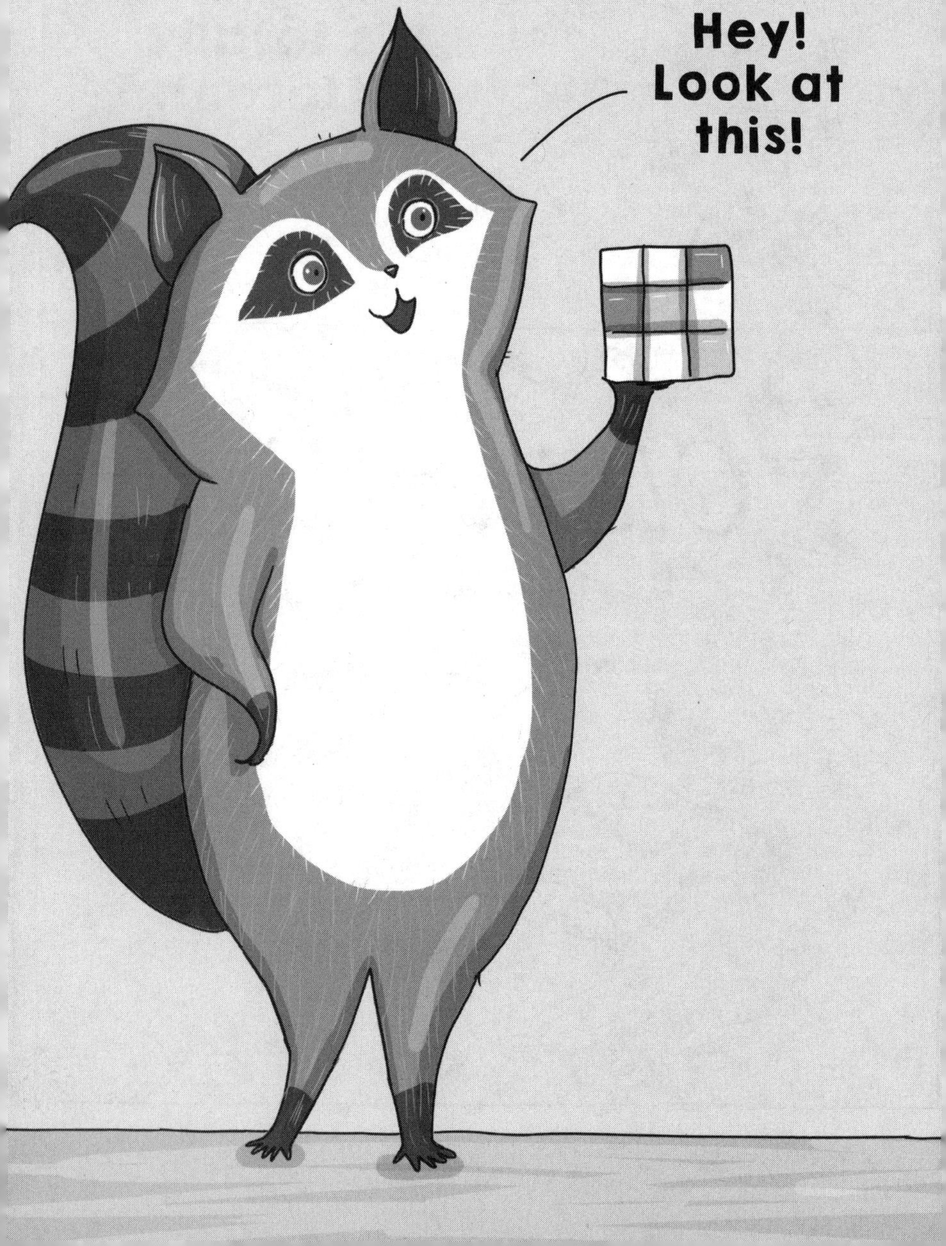
Hey!
Look at
this!

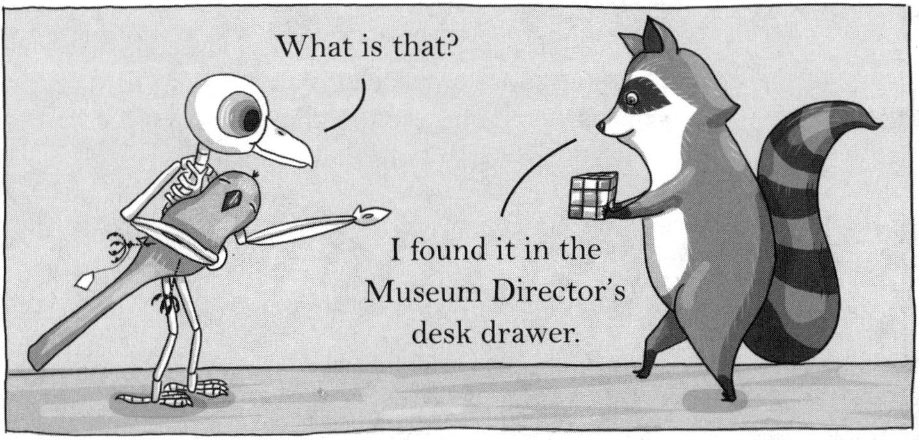
What is that?
I found it in the Museum Director's desk drawer.

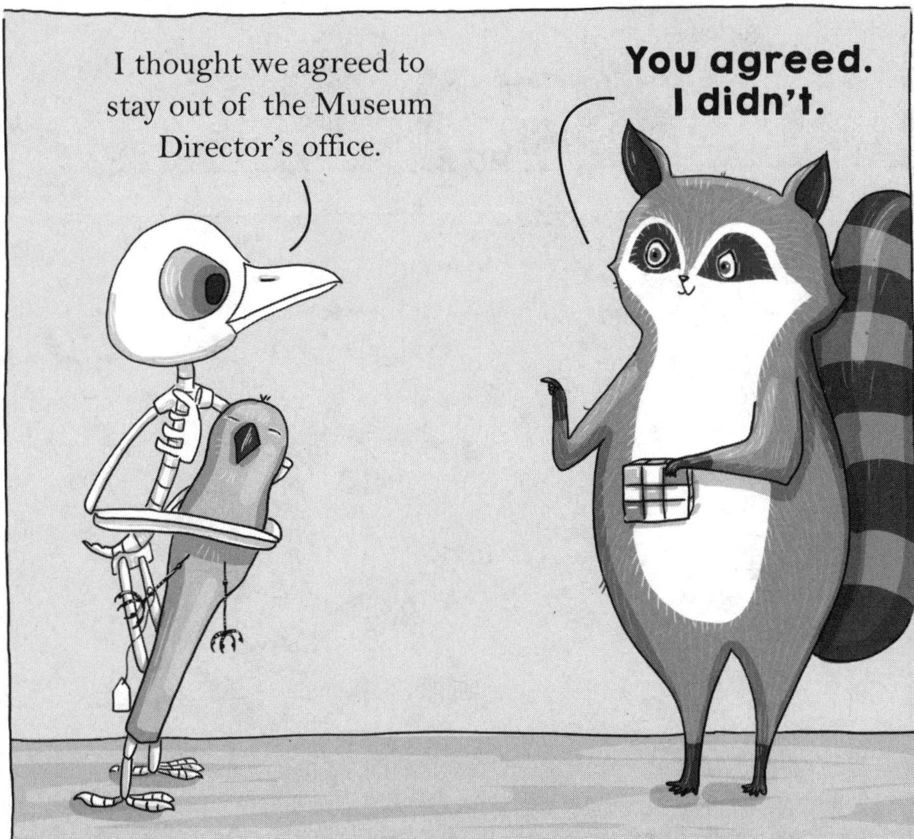
I thought we agreed to stay out of the Museum Director's office.
You agreed. I didn't.

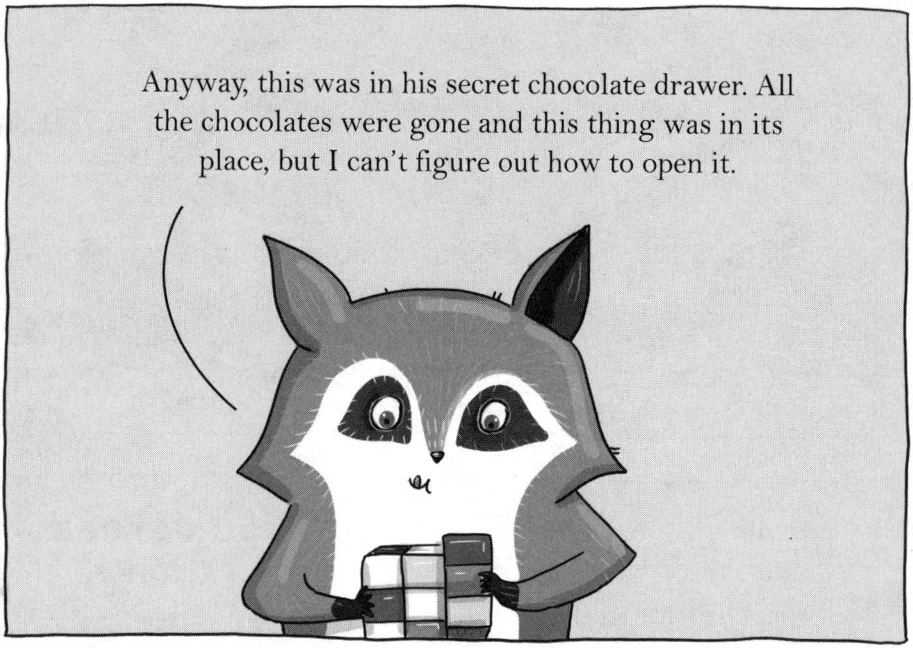
Anyway, this was in his secret chocolate drawer. All the chocolates were gone and this thing was in its place, but I can't figure out how to open it.

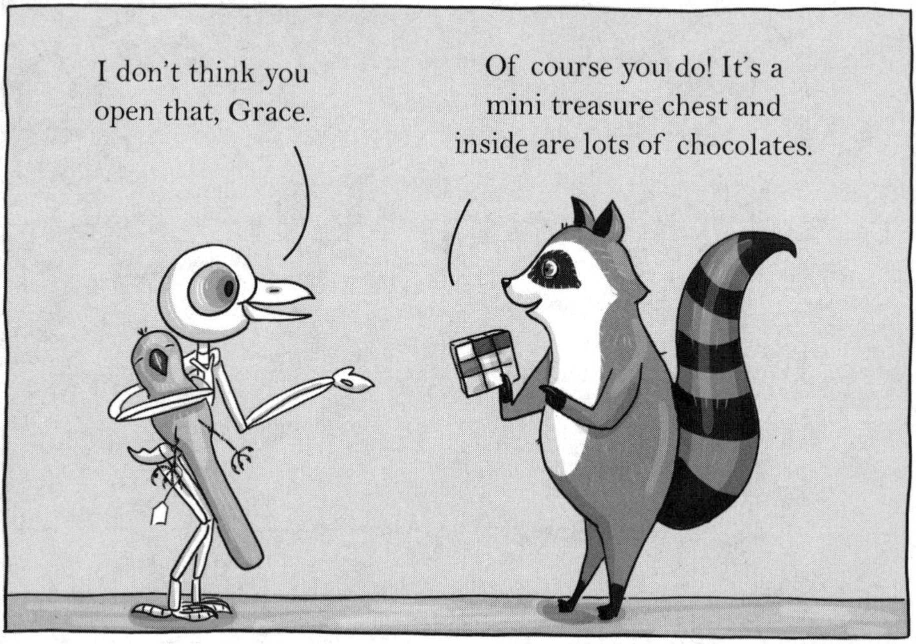
I don't think you open that, Grace.
Of course you do! It's a mini treasure chest and inside are lots of chocolates.

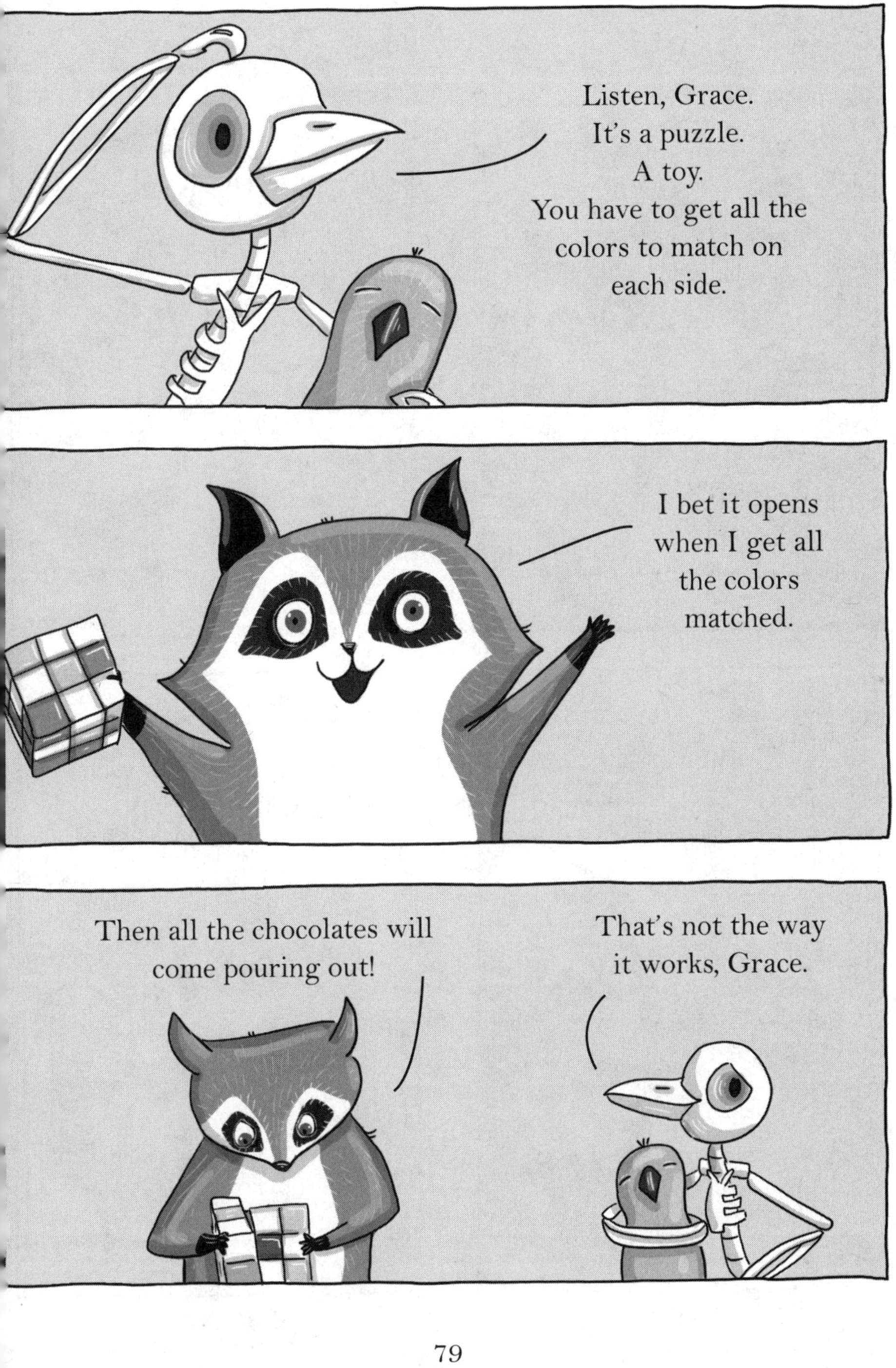
Listen, Grace.
It's a puzzle.
A toy.
You have to get all the colors to match on each side.
I bet it opens when I get all the colors matched.
Then all the chocolates will come pouring out!
That's not the way it works, Grace.

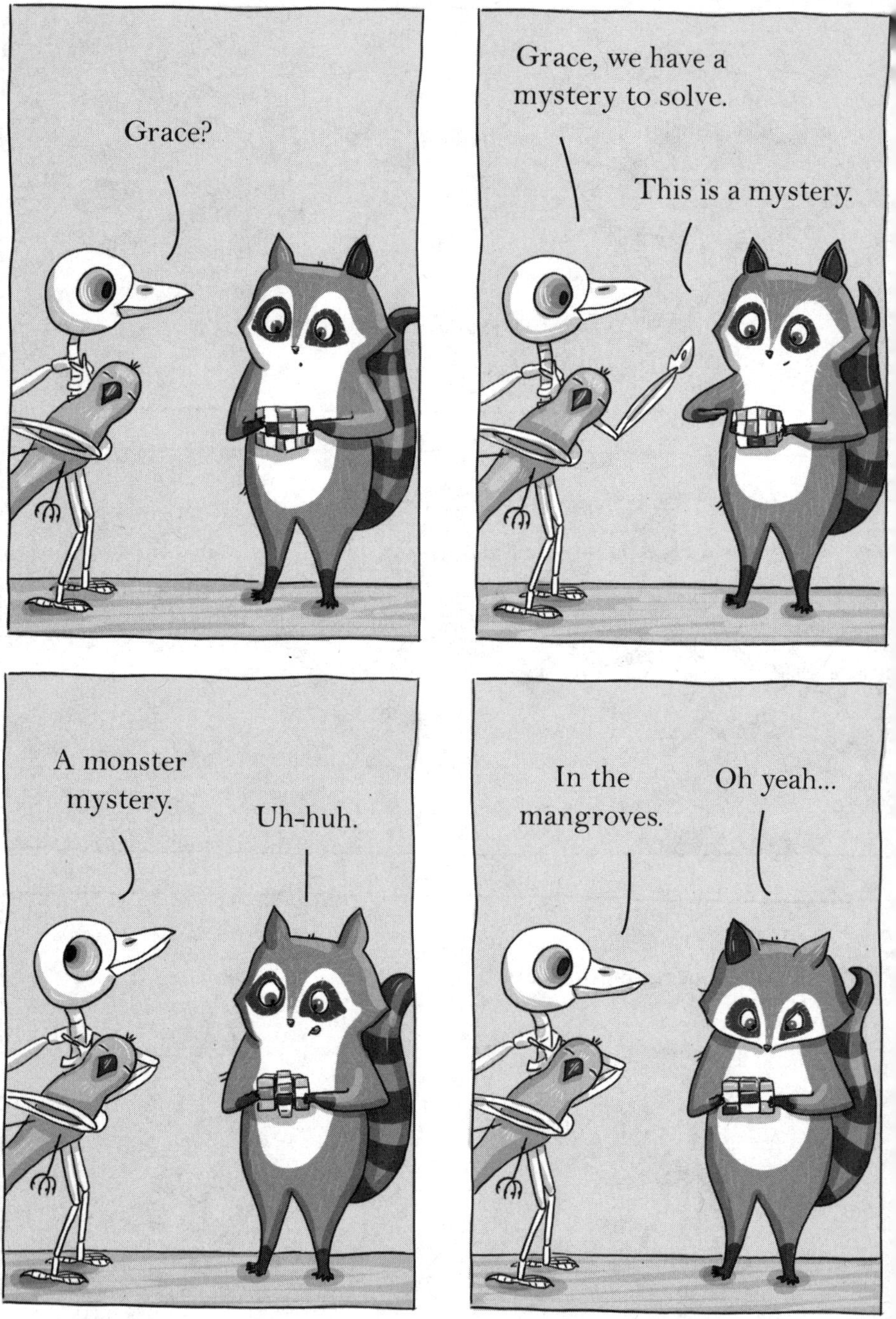
Grace?
Grace, we have a mystery to solve.
This is a mystery.
A monster mystery.
Uh-huh.
In the mangroves.
Oh yeah...

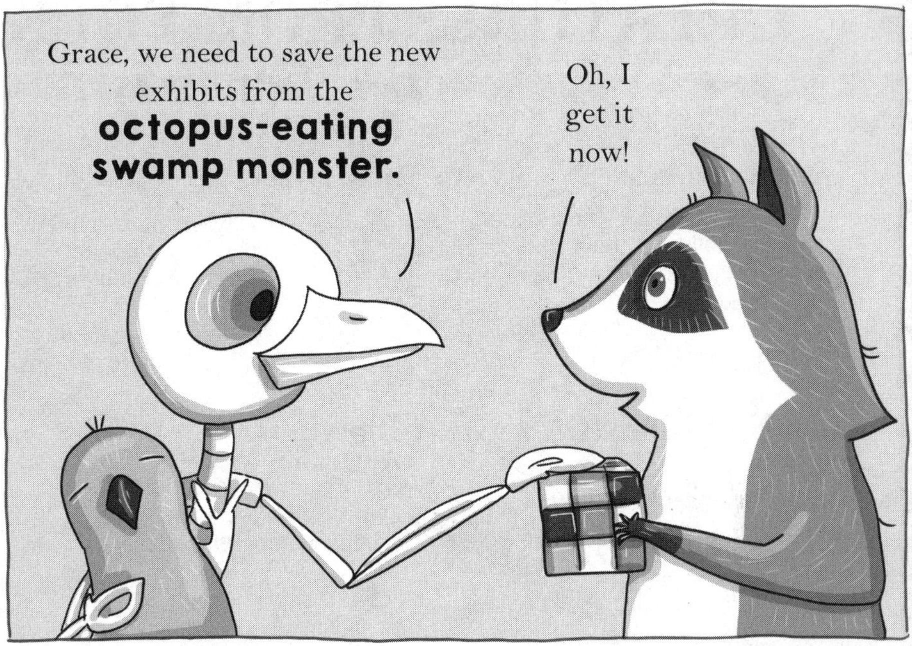
Grace, we need to save the new exhibits from the
octopus-eating swamp monster.
Oh, I get it now!

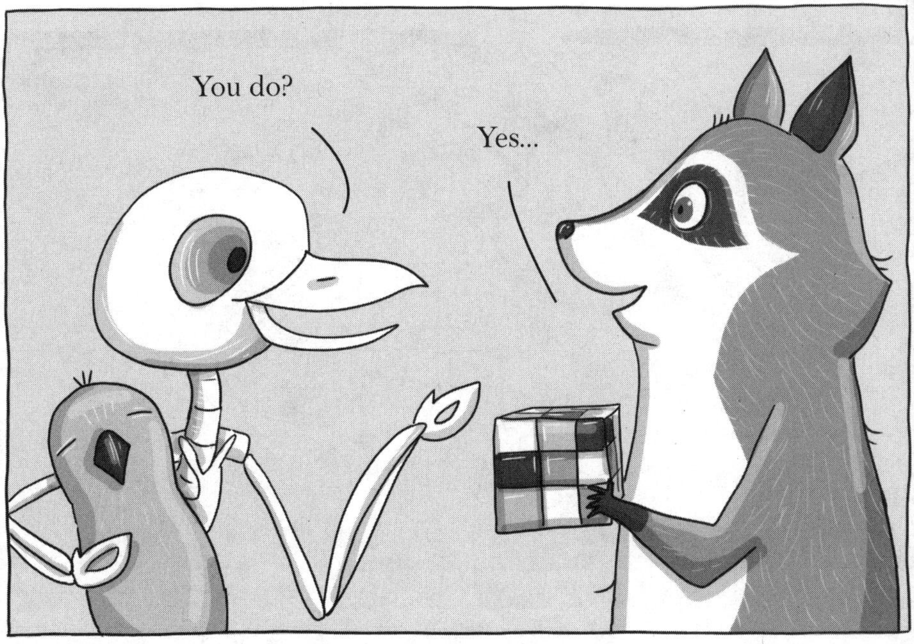
You do?
Yes...

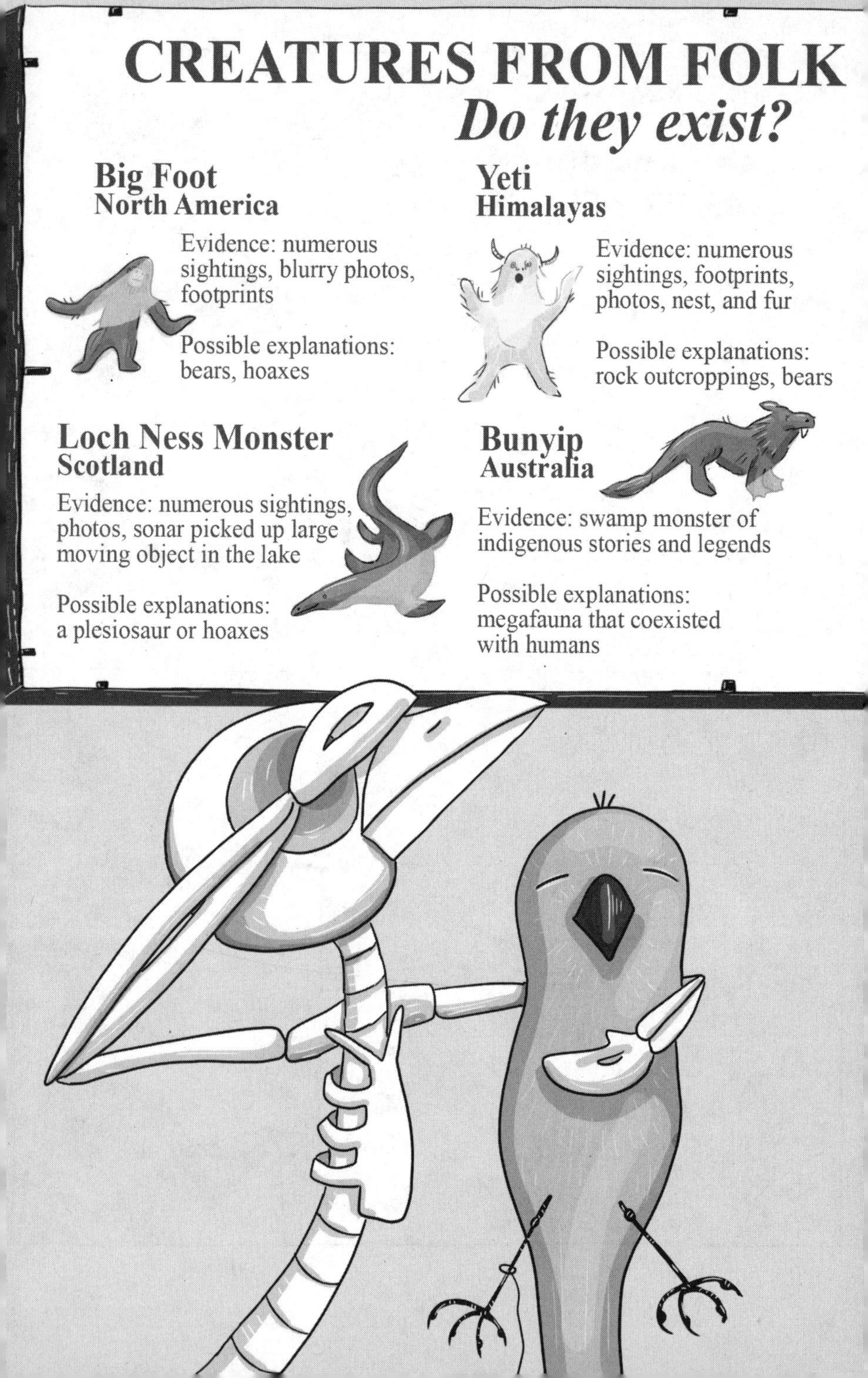

CREATURES FROM FOLK
Do they exist?

Big Foot
North America

Evidence: numerous sightings, blurry photos, footprints

Possible explanations: bears, hoaxes

Yeti
Himalayas

Evidence: numerous sightings, footprints, photos, nest, and fur

Possible explanations: rock outcroppings, bears

Loch Ness Monster
Scotland

Evidence: numerous sightings, photos, sonar picked up large moving object in the lake

Possible explanations: a plesiosaur or hoaxes

Bunyip
Australia

Evidence: swamp monster of indigenous stories and legends

Possible explanations: megafauna that coexisted with humans

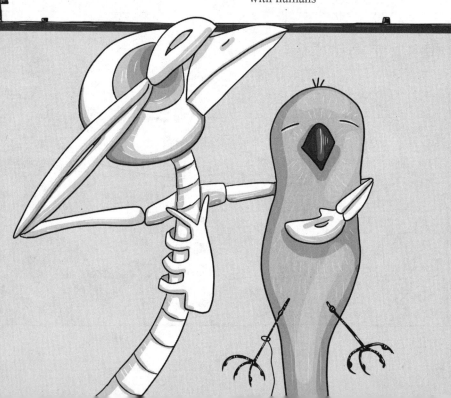

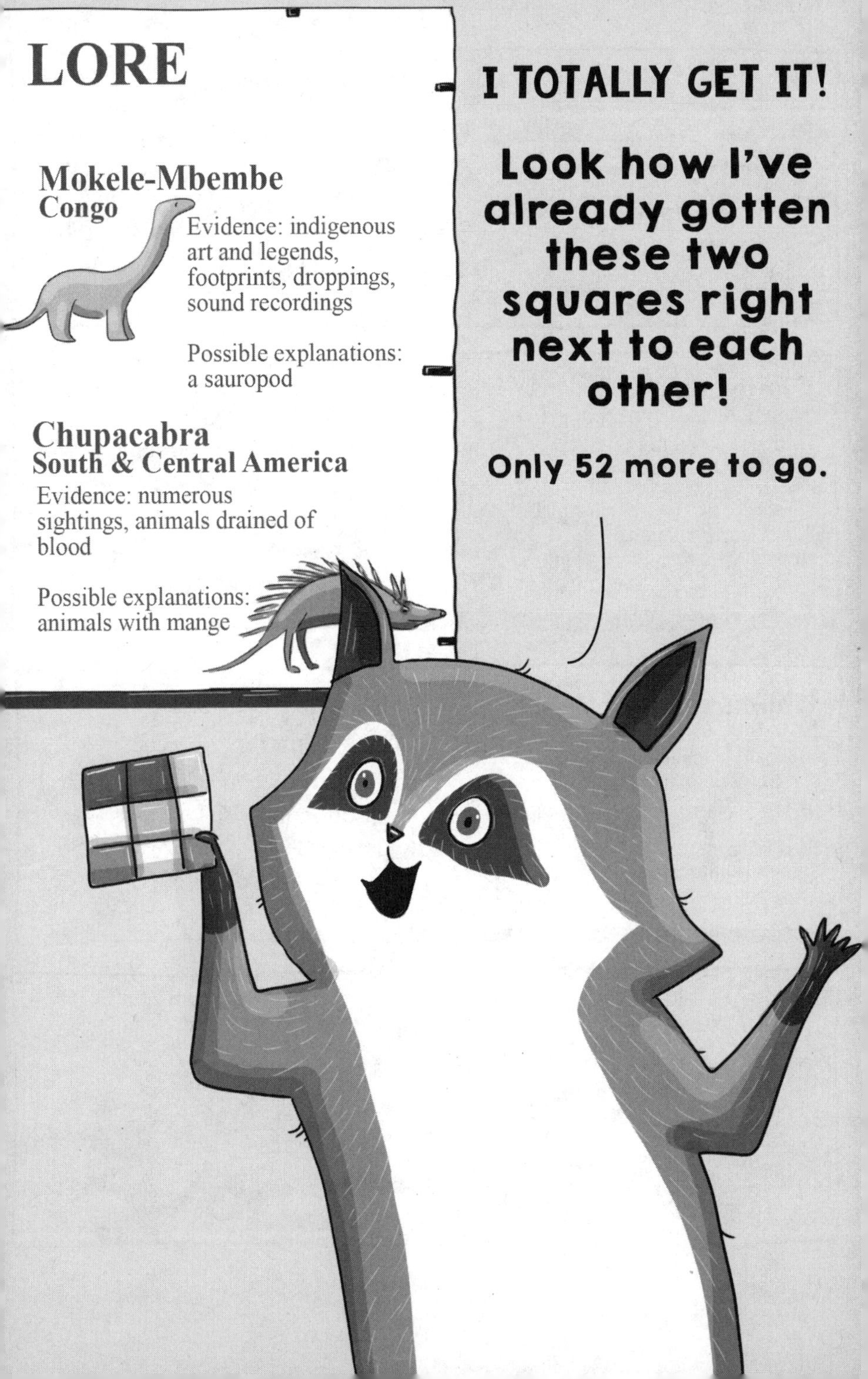

LORE
Mokele-Mbembe
Congo
Evidence: indigenous art and legends, footprints, droppings, sound recordings
Possible explanations: a sauropod
Chupacabra
South & Central America
Evidence: numerous sightings, animals drained of blood
Possible explanations: animals with mange
I TOTALLY GET IT!
Look how I've already gotten these two squares right next to each other!
Only 52 more to go.

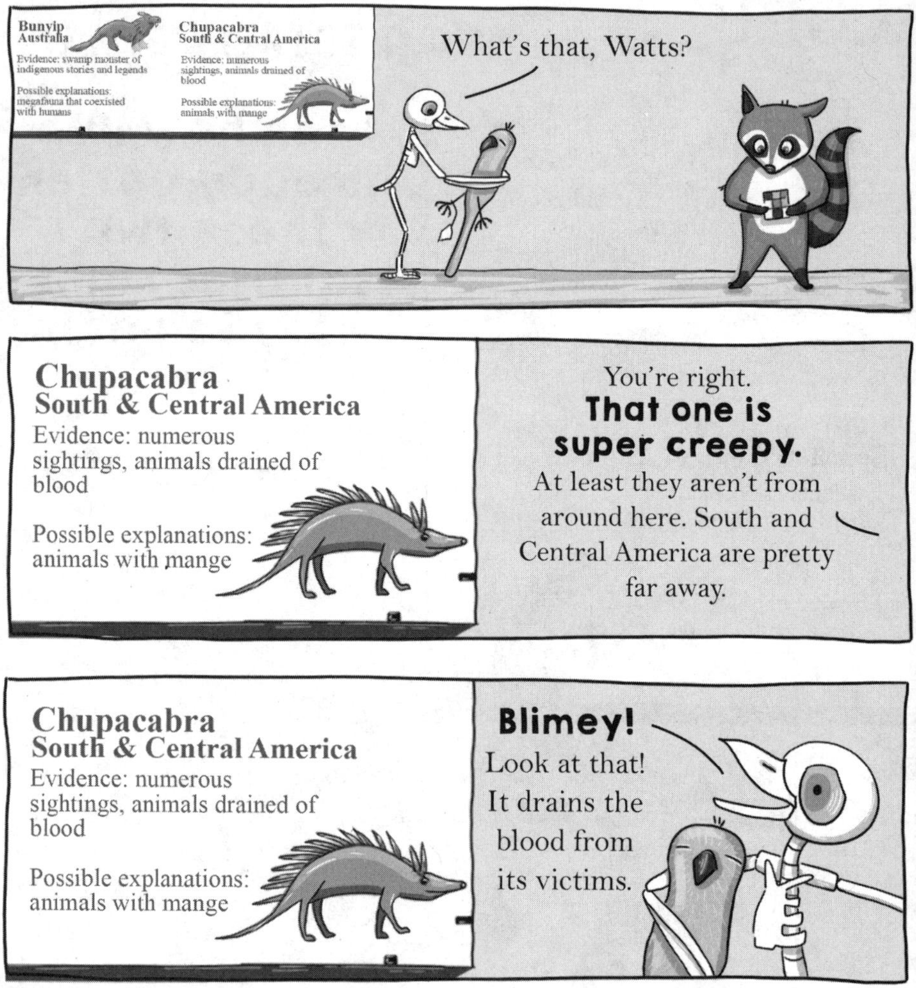
Bunyip
Australia
Evidence: swamp monster of indigenous stories and legends
Possible explanations: megafauna that coexisted with humans
Chupacabra
South & Central America
Evidence: numerous sightings, animals drained of blood
Possible explanations: animals with mange
What's that, Watts?
Chupacabra
South & Central America
Evidence: numerous sightings, animals drained of blood
Possible explanations: animals with mange
You're right. **That one is super creepy.** At least they aren't from around here. South and Central America are pretty far away.
Chupacabra
South & Central America
Evidence: numerous sightings, animals drained of blood
Possible explanations: animals with mange
Blimey! Look at that! It drains the blood from its victims.
Grace, did you hear that?
Mmm...

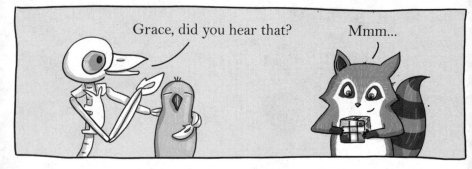

Wooo... wooo...

creepy and scary...

blood-sucking monsters.

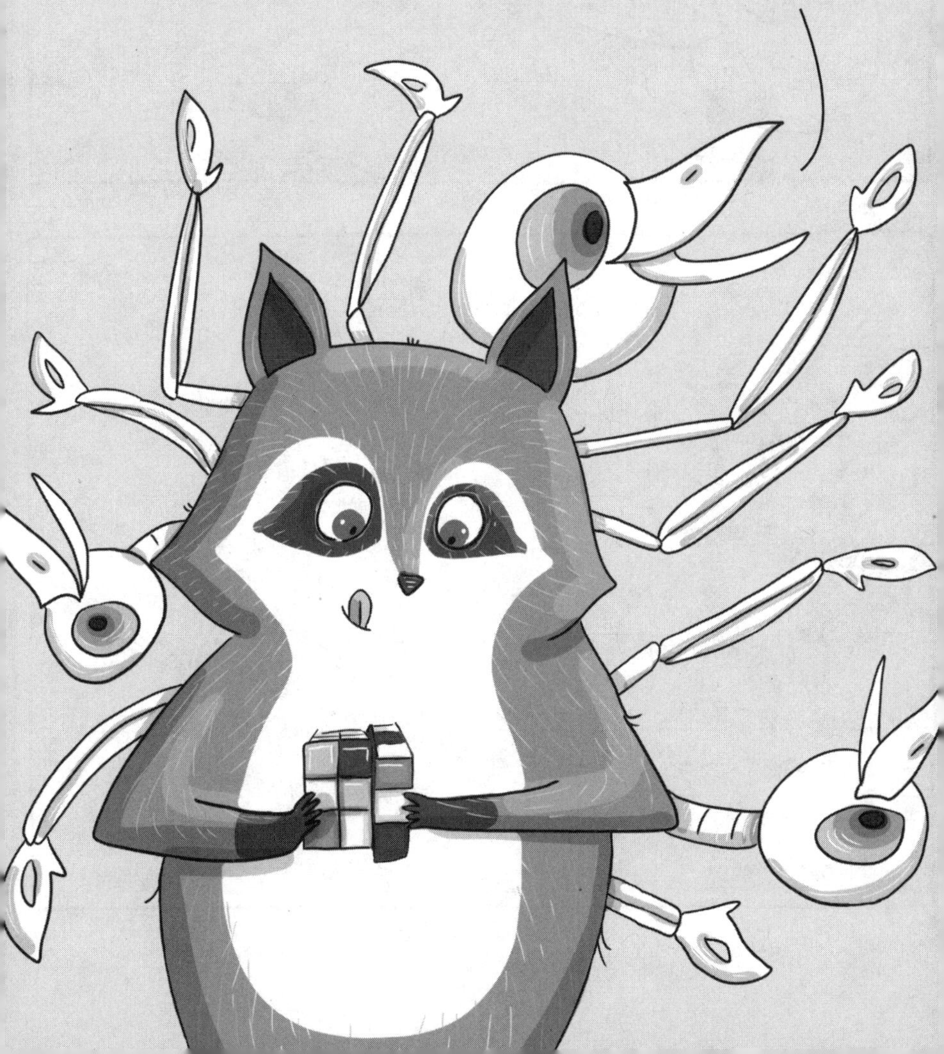

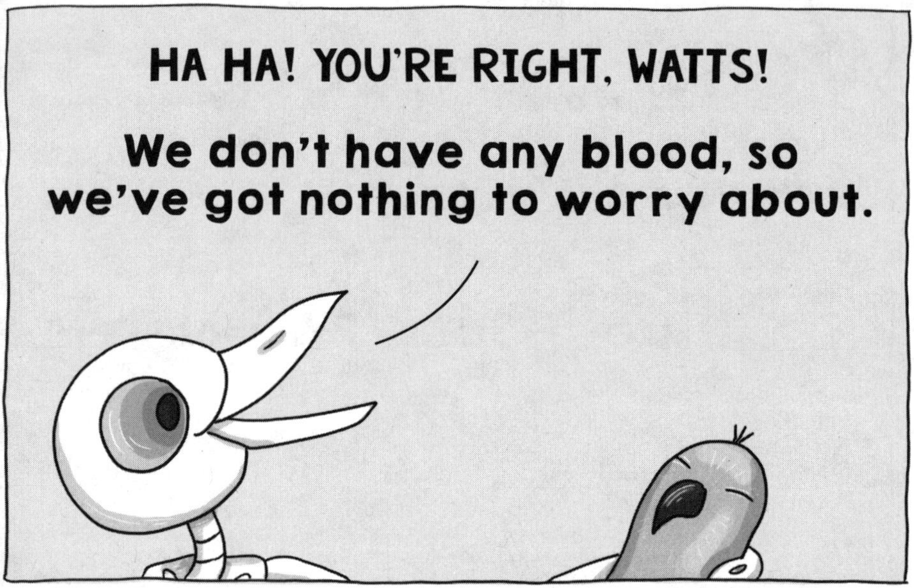
HA HA! YOU'RE RIGHT, WATTS!
We don't have any blood, so we've got nothing to worry about.

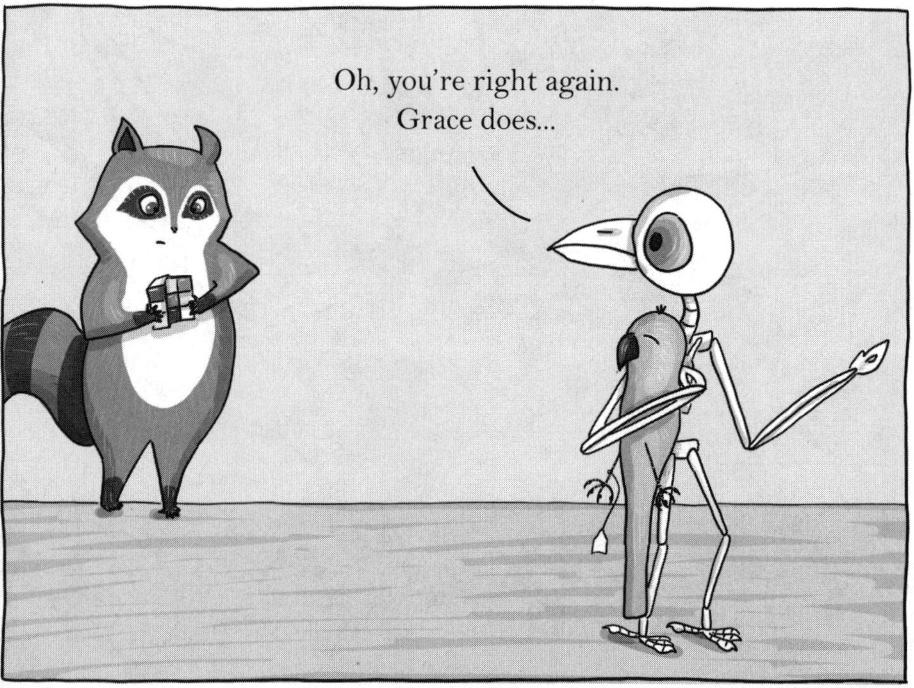
Oh, you're right again. Grace does...

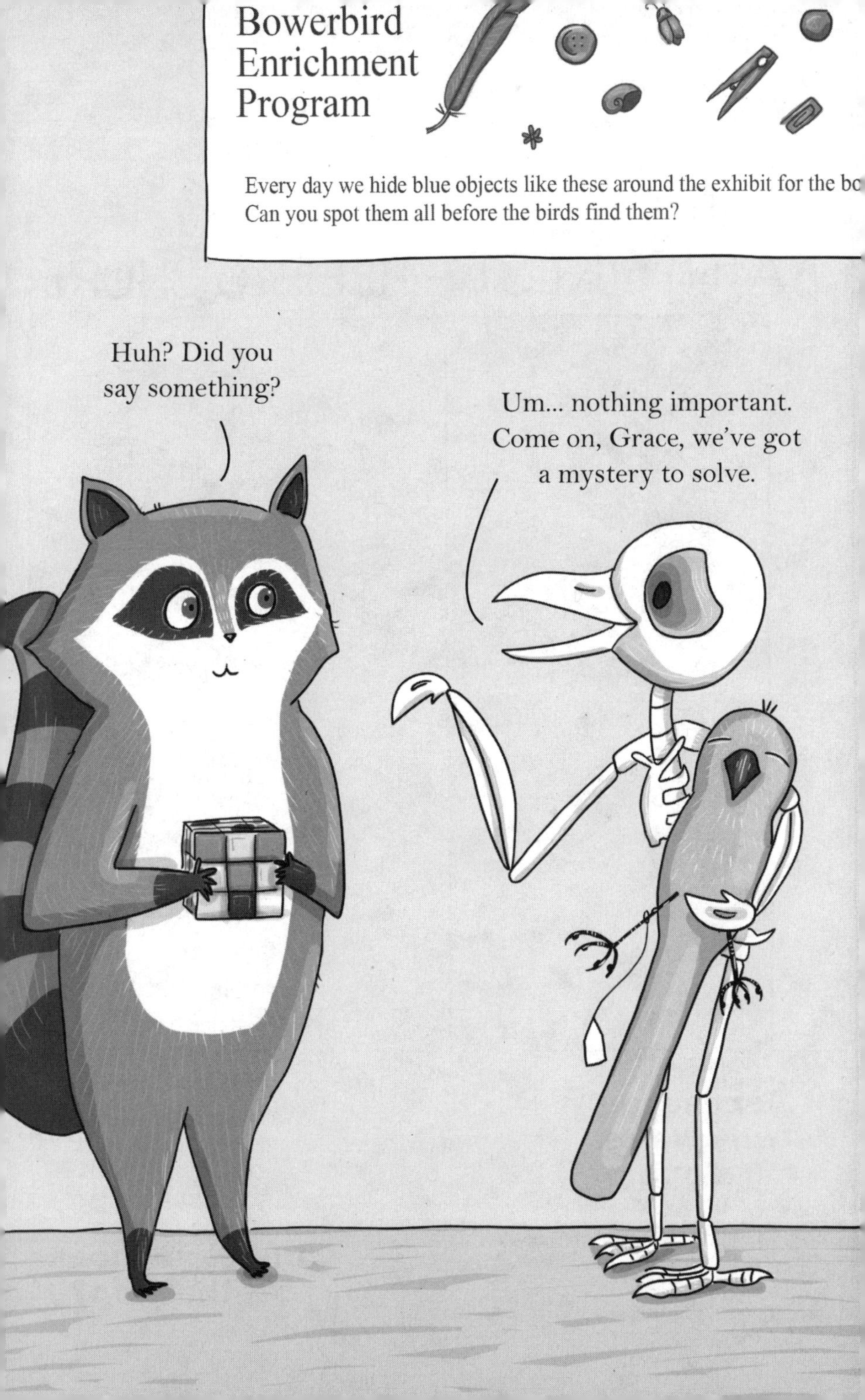
Bowerbird Enrichment Program
Every day we hide blue objects like these around the exhibit for the bo
Can you spot them all before the birds find them?
Huh? Did you say something?
Um... nothing important. Come on, Grace, we've got a mystery to solve.

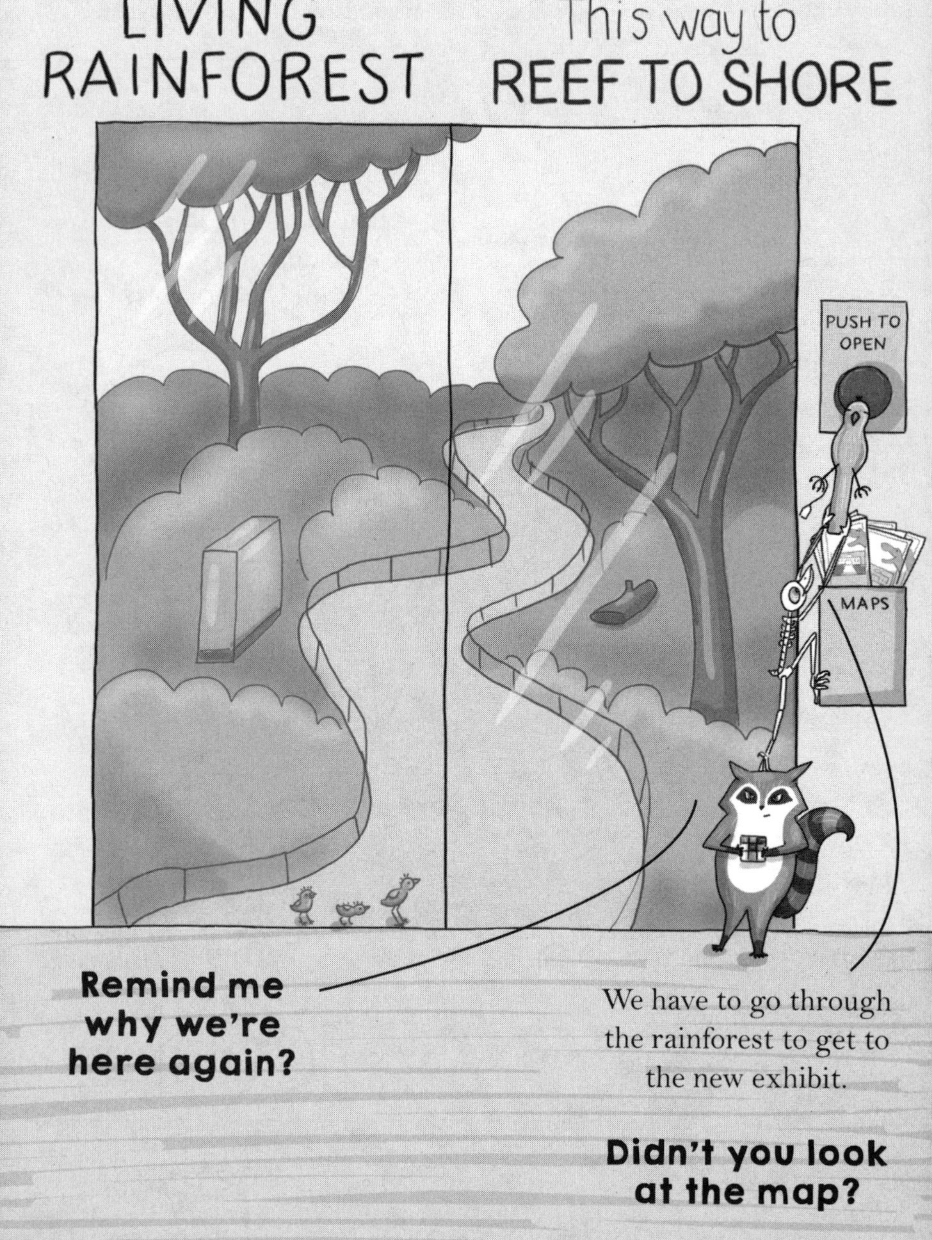
LIVING RAINFOREST
This way to REEF TO SHORE
PUSH TO OPEN
MAPS
Remind me why we're here again?
We have to go through the rainforest to get to the new exhibit.
Didn't you look at the map?

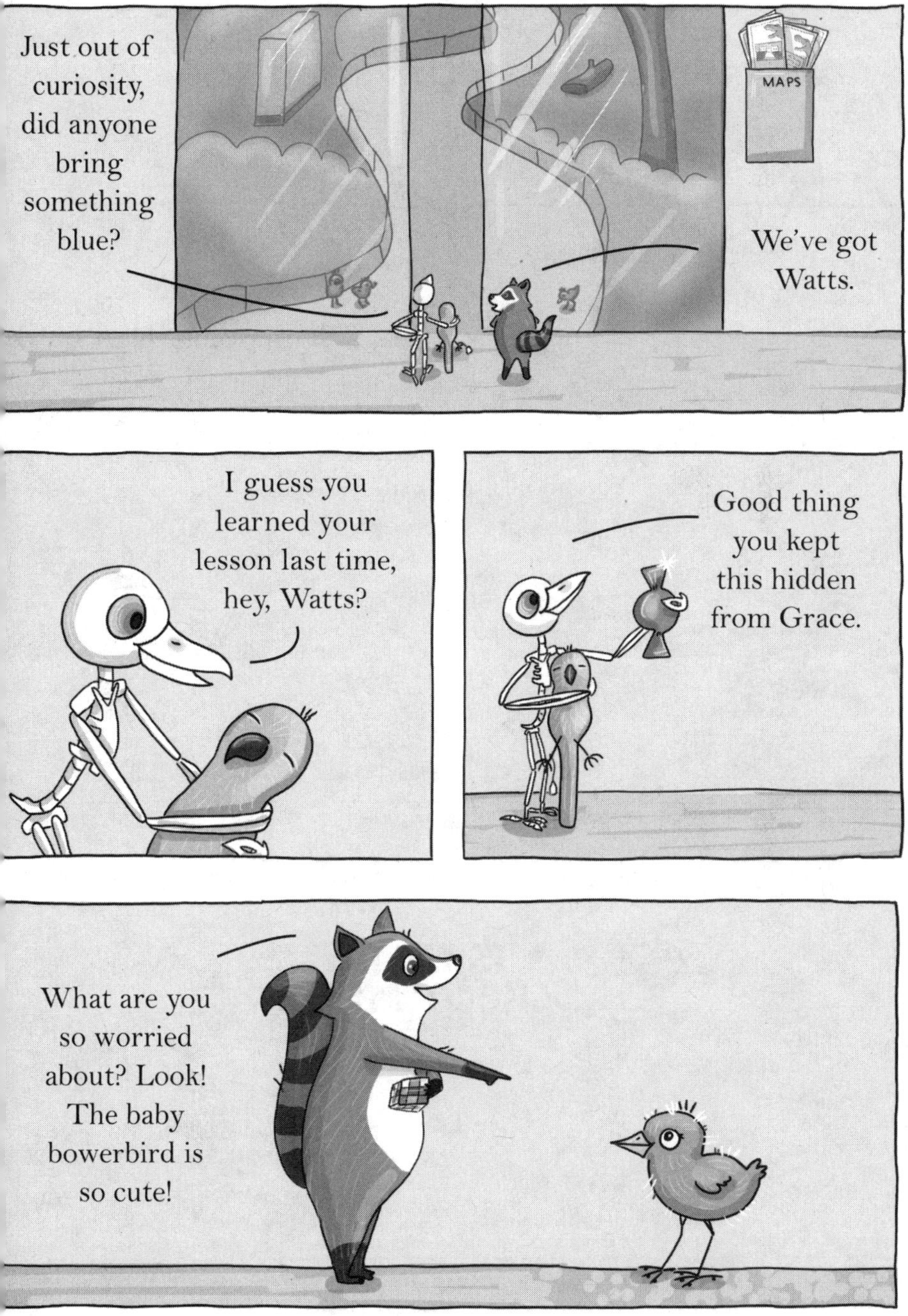
Just out of curiosity, did anyone bring something blue?
MAPS
We've got Watts.
I guess you learned your lesson last time, hey, Watts?
Good thing you kept this hidden from Grace.
What are you so worried about? Look! The baby bowerbird is so cute!

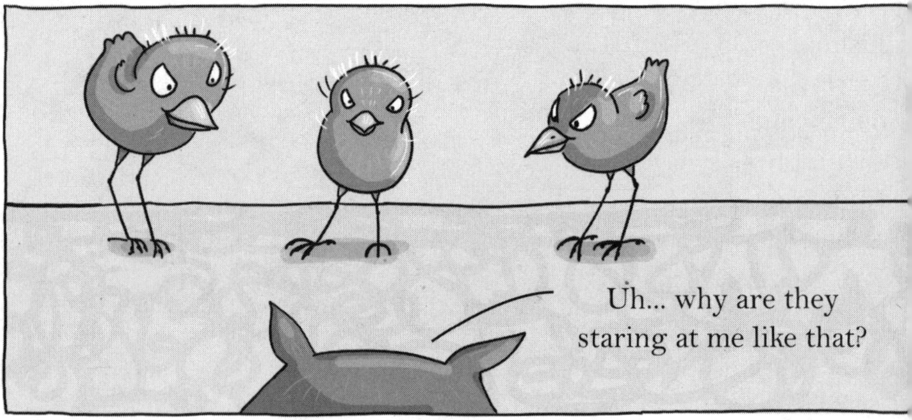
Uh... why are they
staring at me like that?

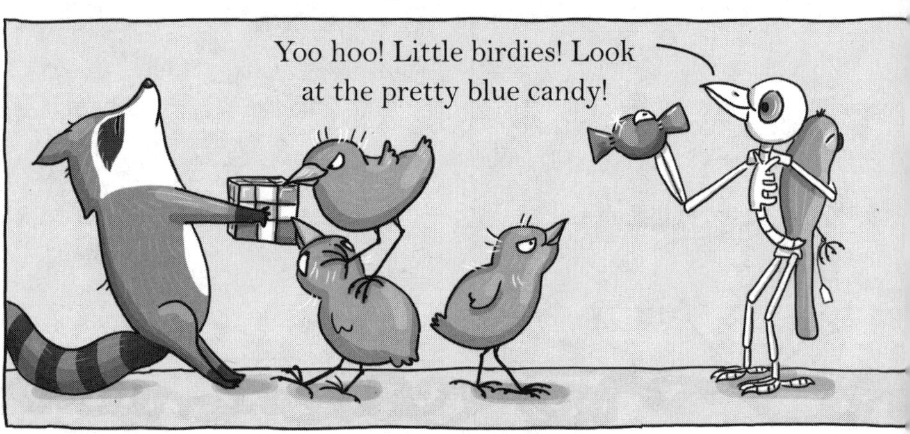
Yoo hoo! Little birdies! Look
at the pretty blue candy!

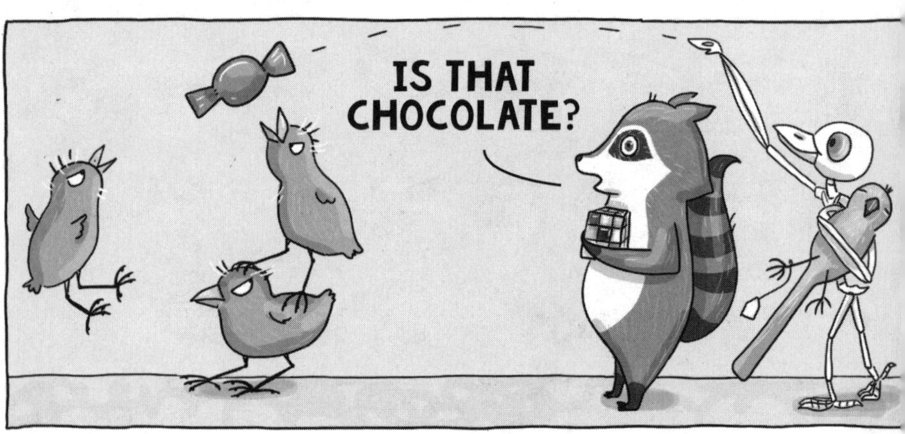
IS THAT
CHOCOLATE?

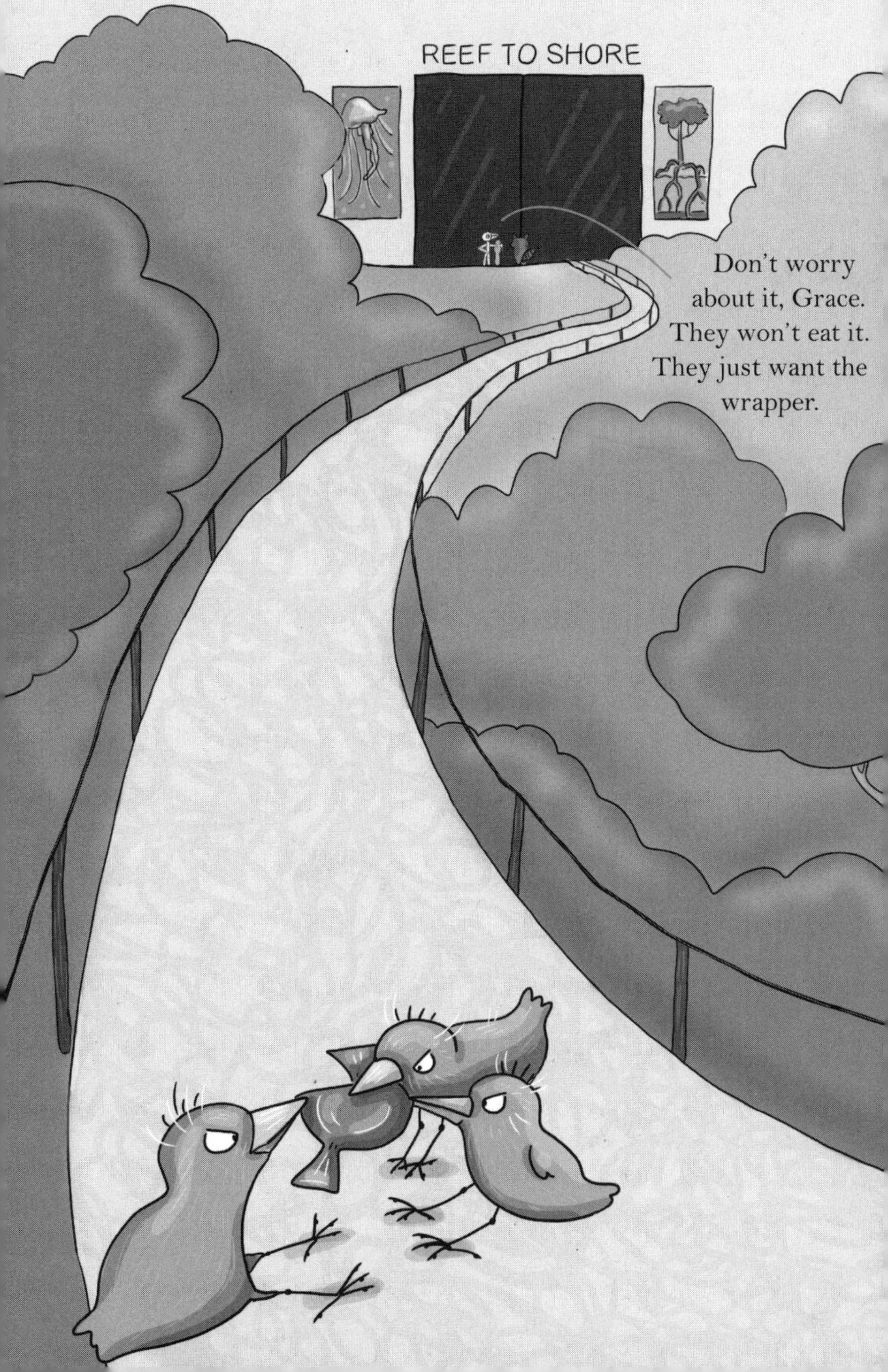
REEF TO SHORE

Don't worry about it, Grace. They won't eat it. They just want the wrapper.

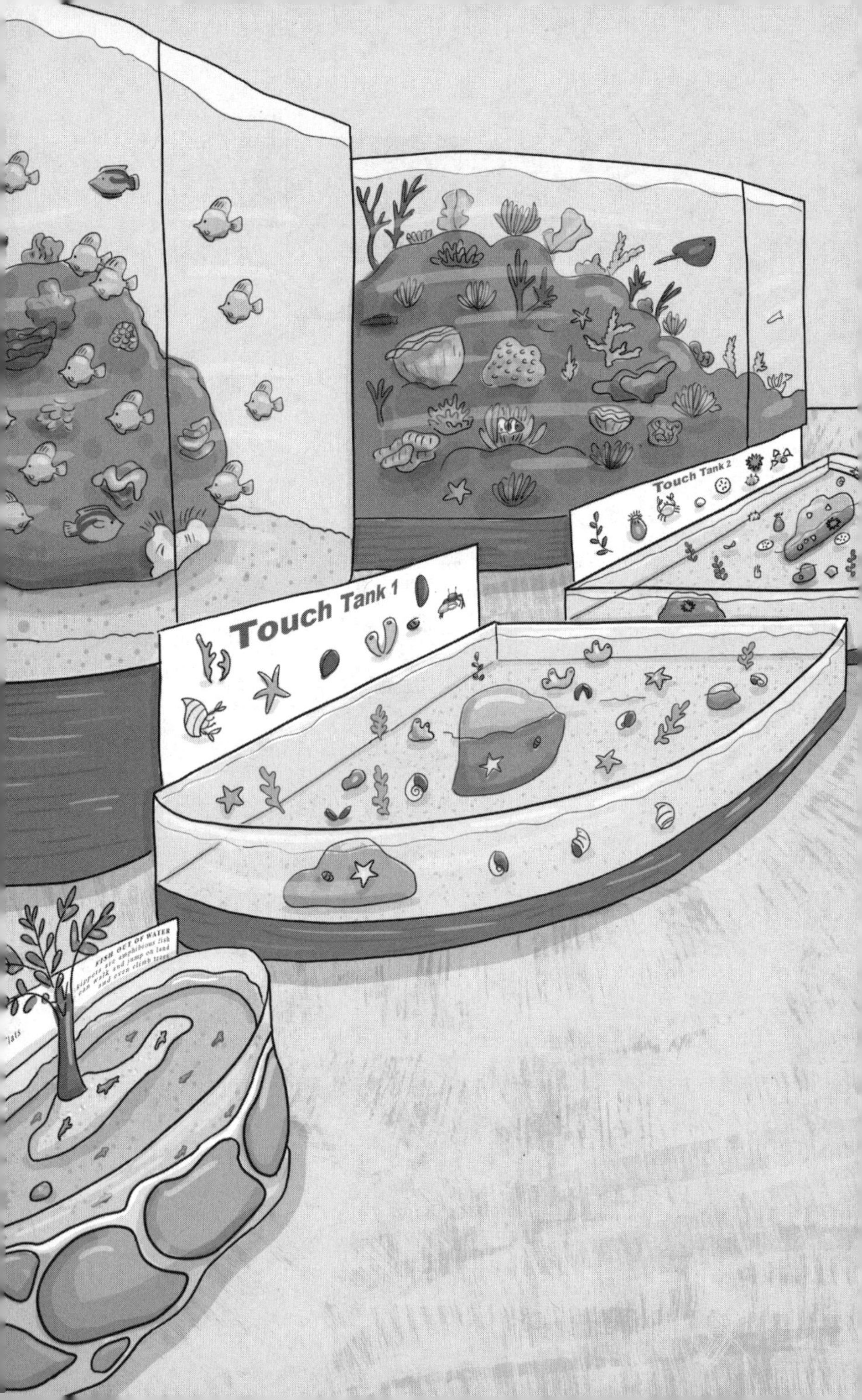

Touch Tank 2
Touch Tank 1
FISH OUT OF WATER
kippers are amphibious fish
can walk and jump on land
and even climb trees

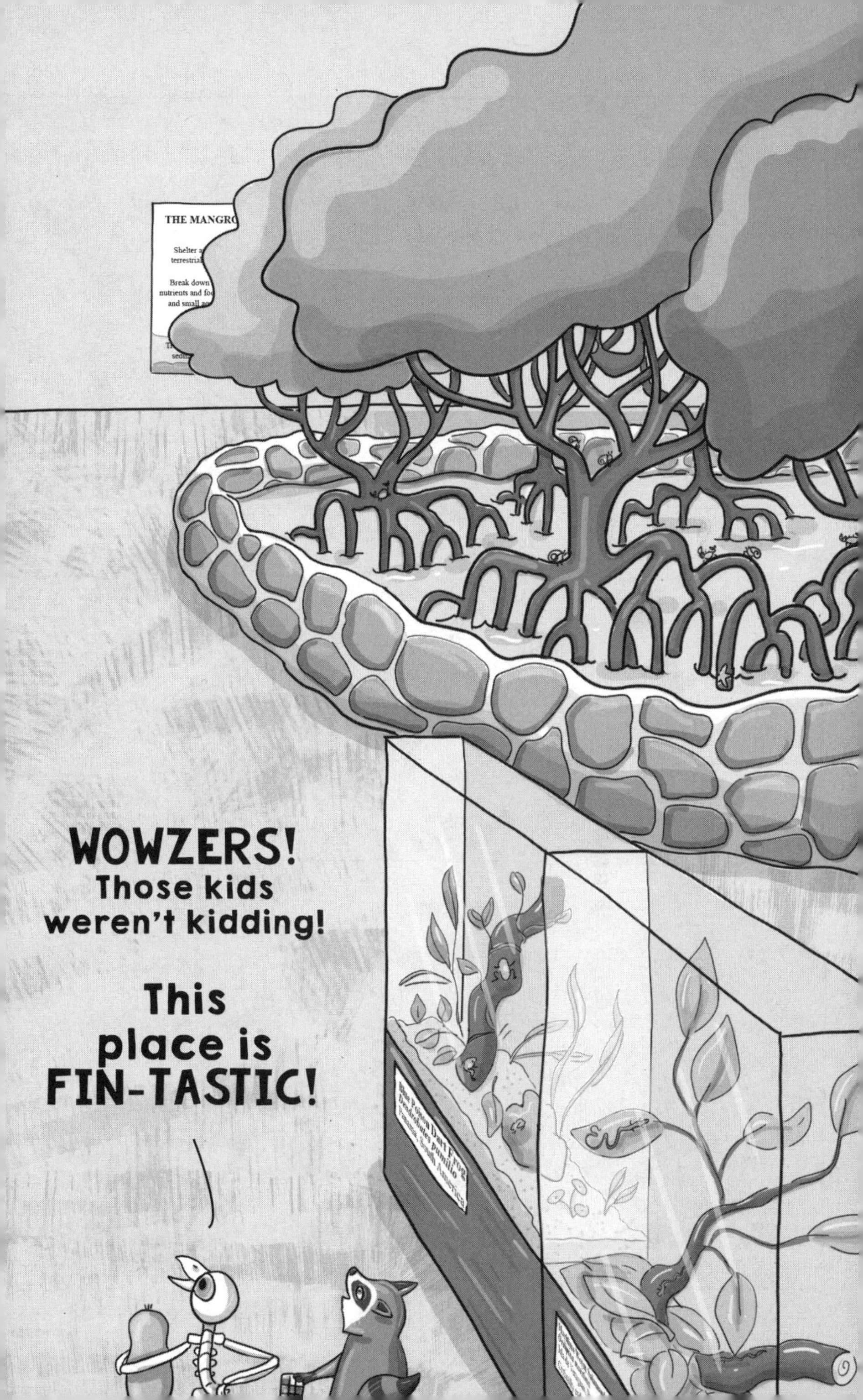
WOWZERS!
Those kids weren't kidding!
This place is FIN-TASTIC!
Blue Poison Dart Frog
Dendrobates pumilio
Panama, South America

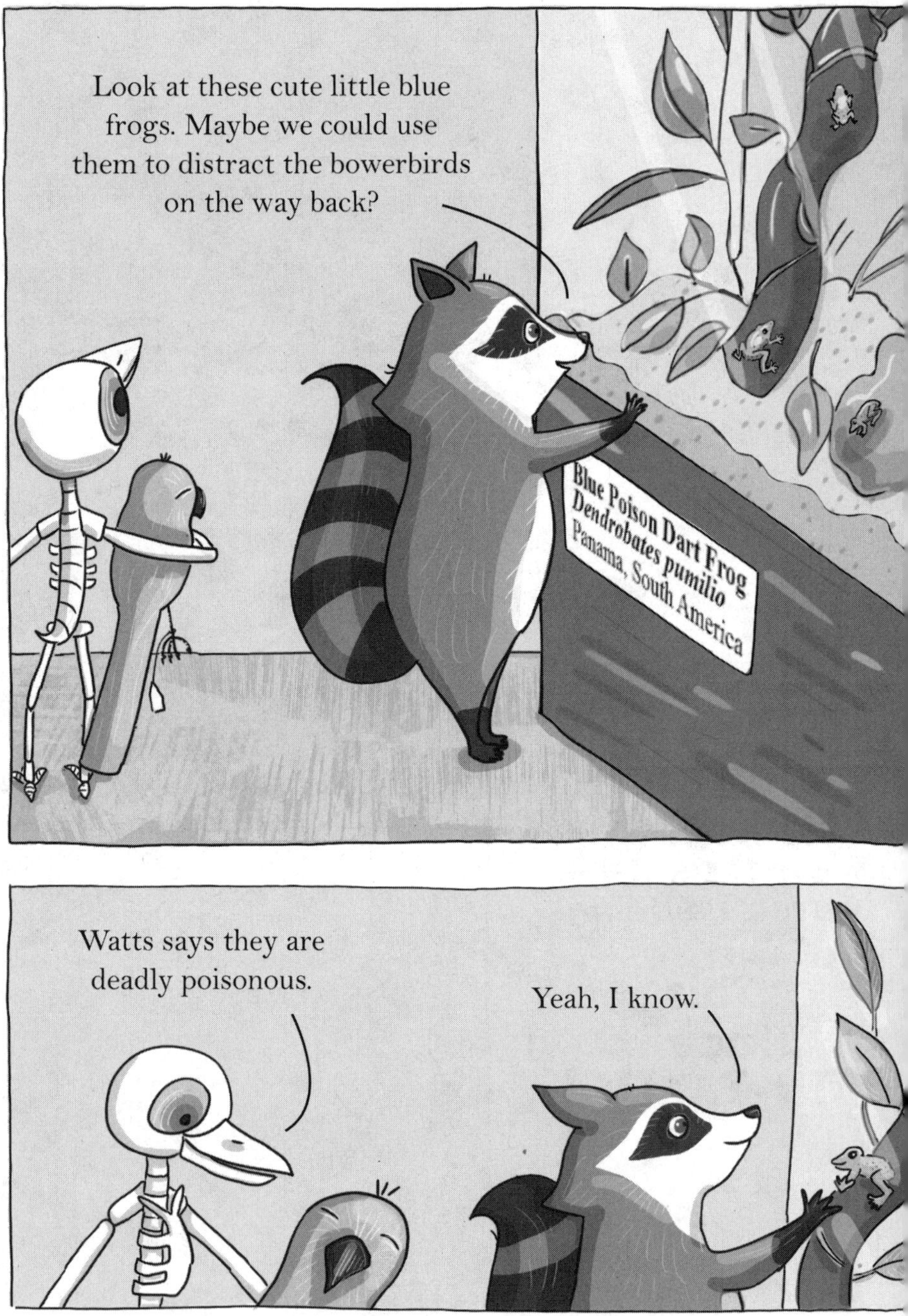
Look at these cute little blue frogs. Maybe we could use them to distract the bowerbirds on the way back?
Blue Poison Dart Frog
Dendrobates pumilio
Panama, South America
Watts says they are deadly poisonous.
Yeah, I know.

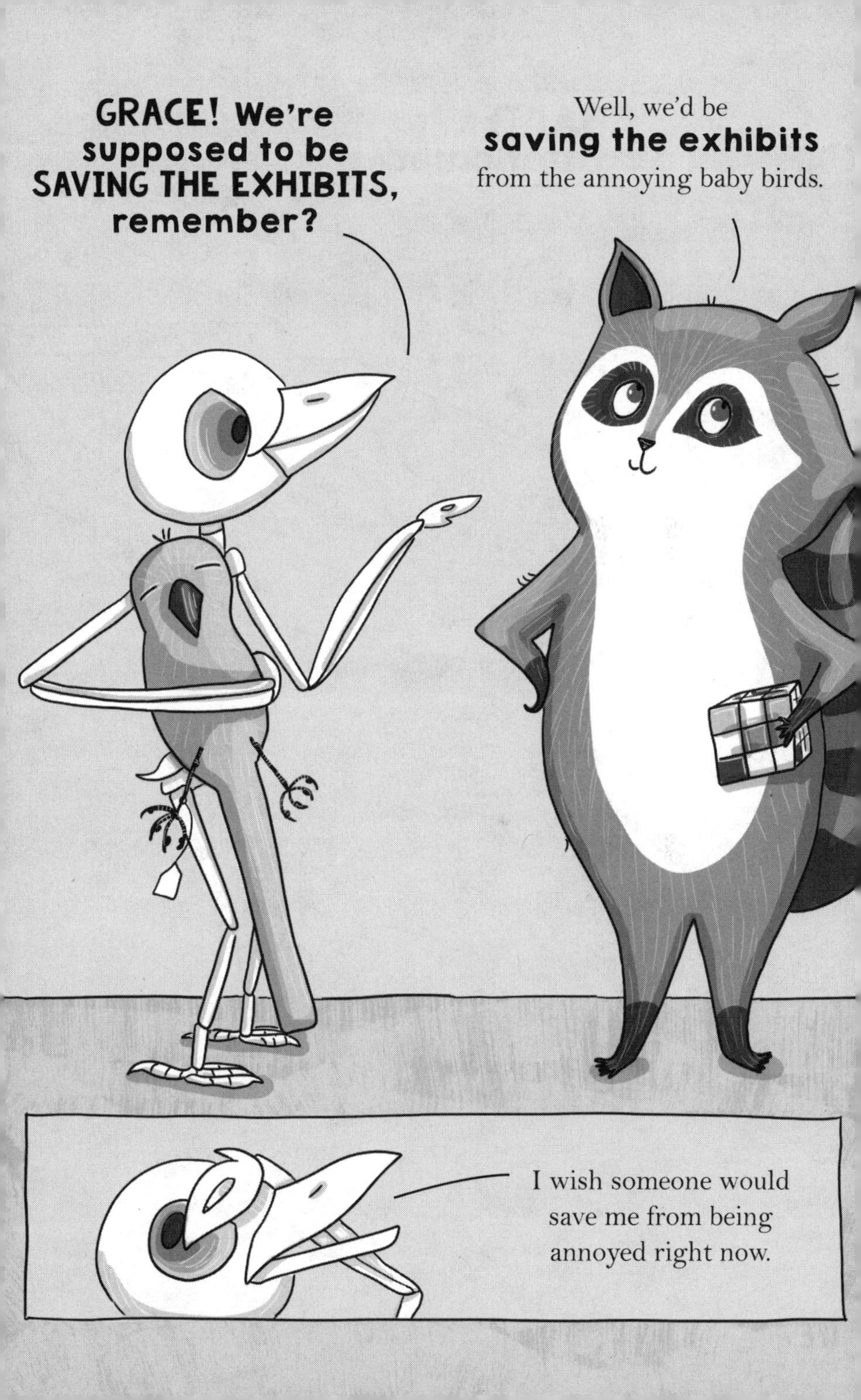
GRACE! We're supposed to be SAVING THE EXHIBITS, remember?
Well, we'd be saving the exhibits from the annoying baby birds.
I wish someone would save me from being annoyed right now.

CHAPTER 4
So-fish-ticated

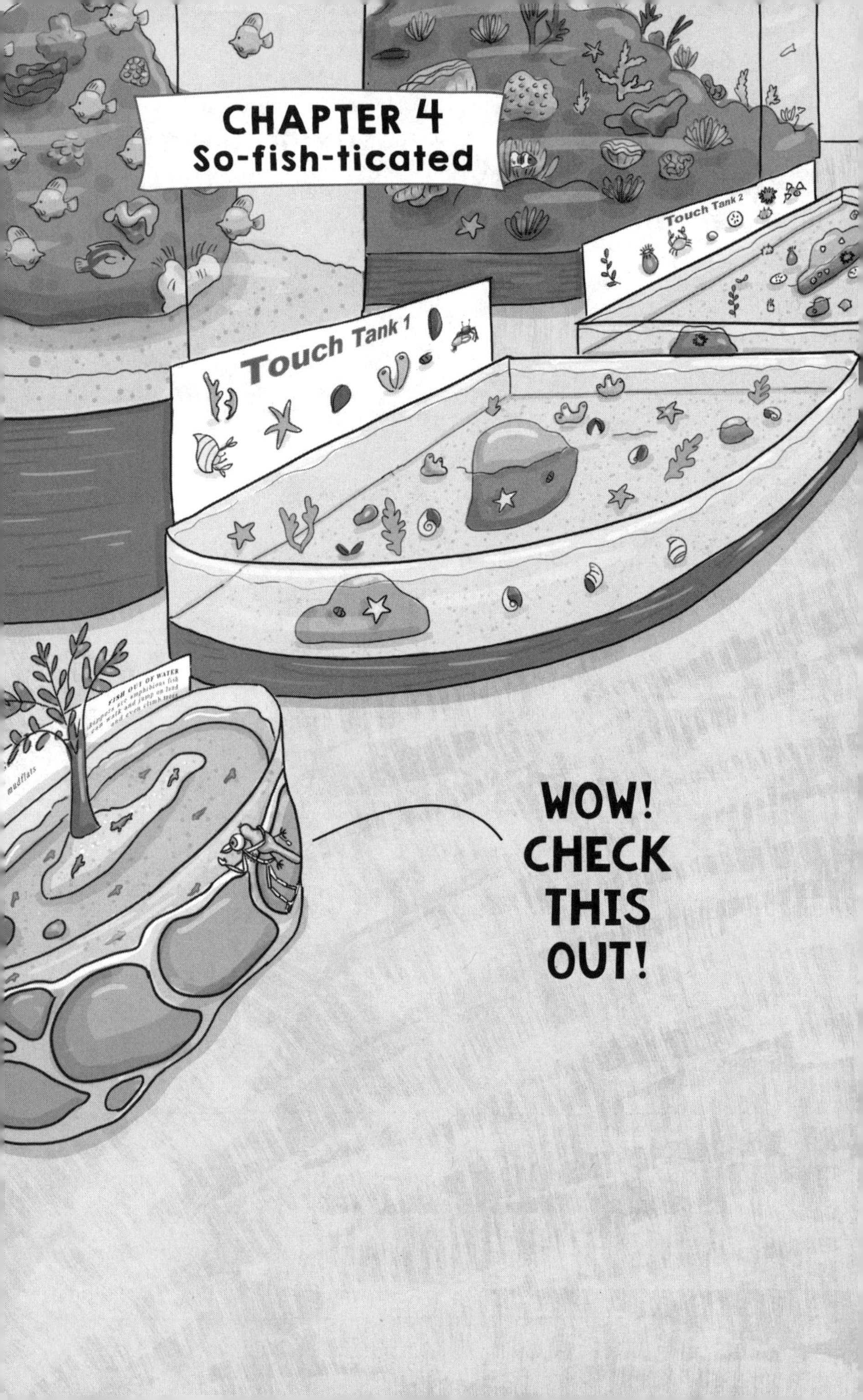
Touch Tank 1
Touch Tank 2
FISH OUT OF WATER
can walk and jump on land
and even climb trees
mudflats
WOW! CHECK THIS OUT!

These fish are walking on land!

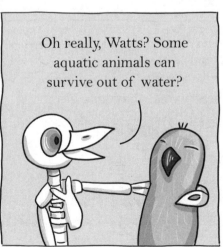

Oh really, Watts? Some aquatic animals can survive out of water?

But how? I thought all fish had to breathe underwater?

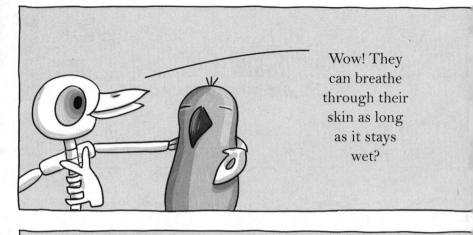

Wow! They can breathe through their skin as long as it stays wet?

That's just like some amphibians.

Oh, you know, frogs and salamanders...

Now stop distracting me, Watts. We need to investigate the mangroves before we do anything else.

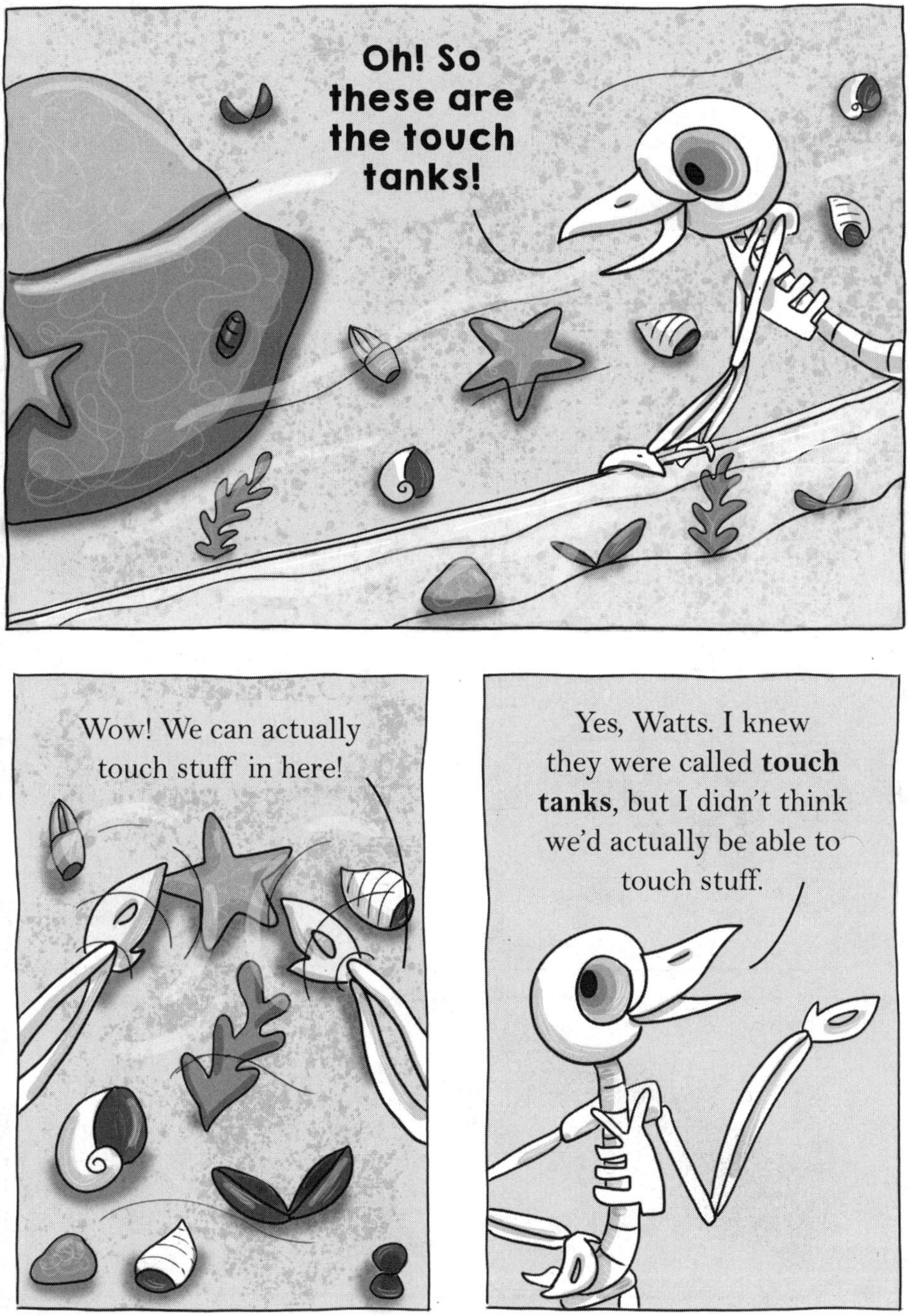
Oh! So these are the touch tanks!
Wow! We can actually touch stuff in here!
Yes, Watts. I knew they were called **touch tanks**, but I didn't think we'd actually be able to touch stuff.

Last week, one
of the kids got
pinched by a crab!

That's right, Watts!
I bet that made her
really crabby.

I hope she didn't
pull a mussel.

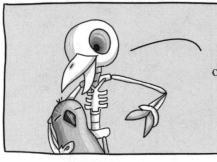

Do you think they had to
call a **clam-bulance?**

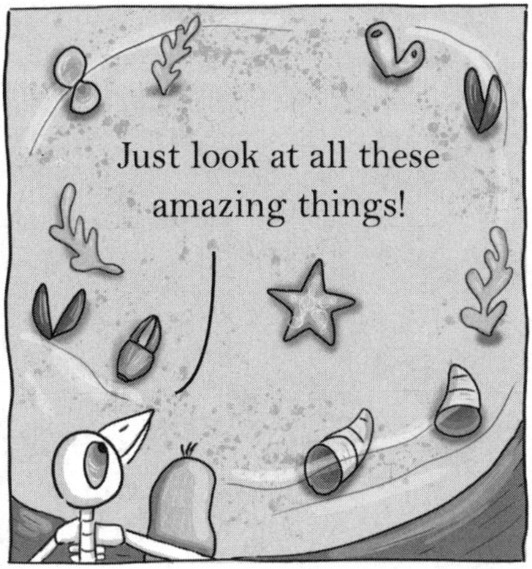
Just look at all these amazing things!

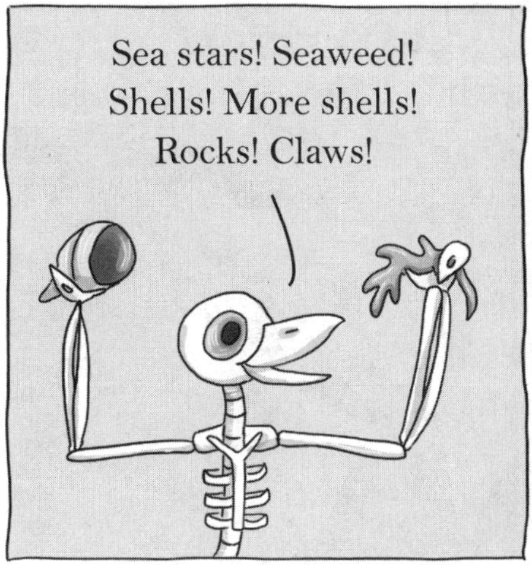
Sea stars! Seaweed! Shells! More shells! Rocks! Claws!

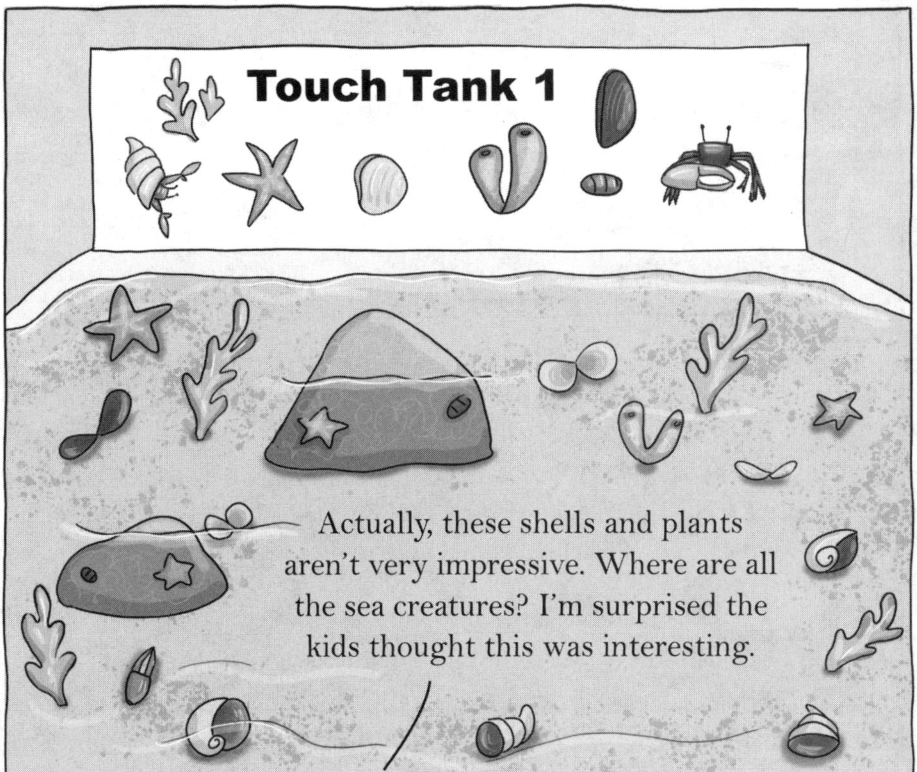
Touch Tank 1
Actually, these shells and plants aren't very impressive. Where are all the sea creatures? I'm surprised the kids thought this was interesting.

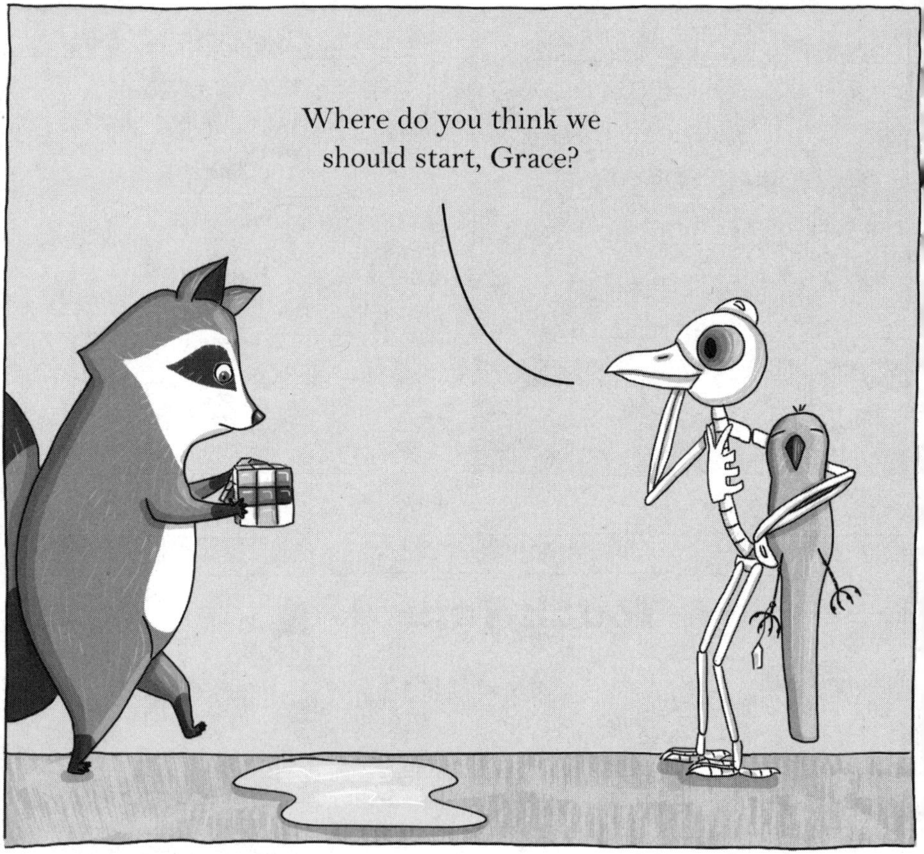
Where do you think we should start, Grace?

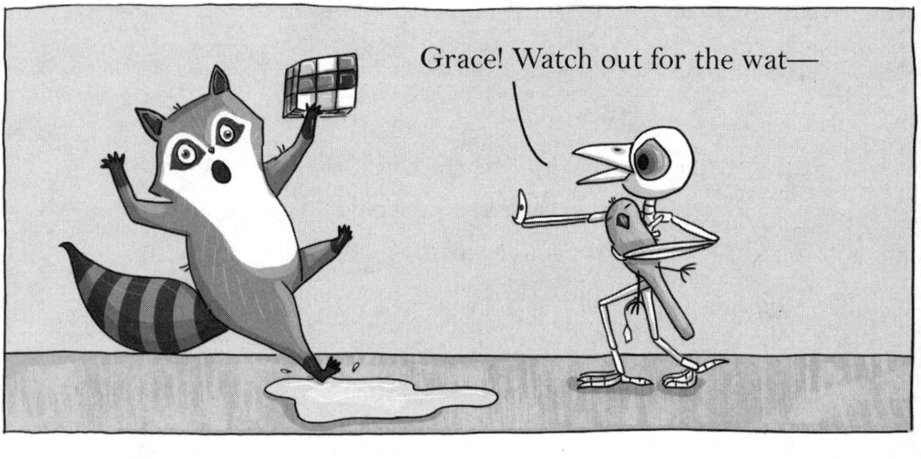
Grace! Watch out for the wat—

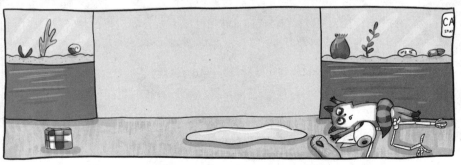

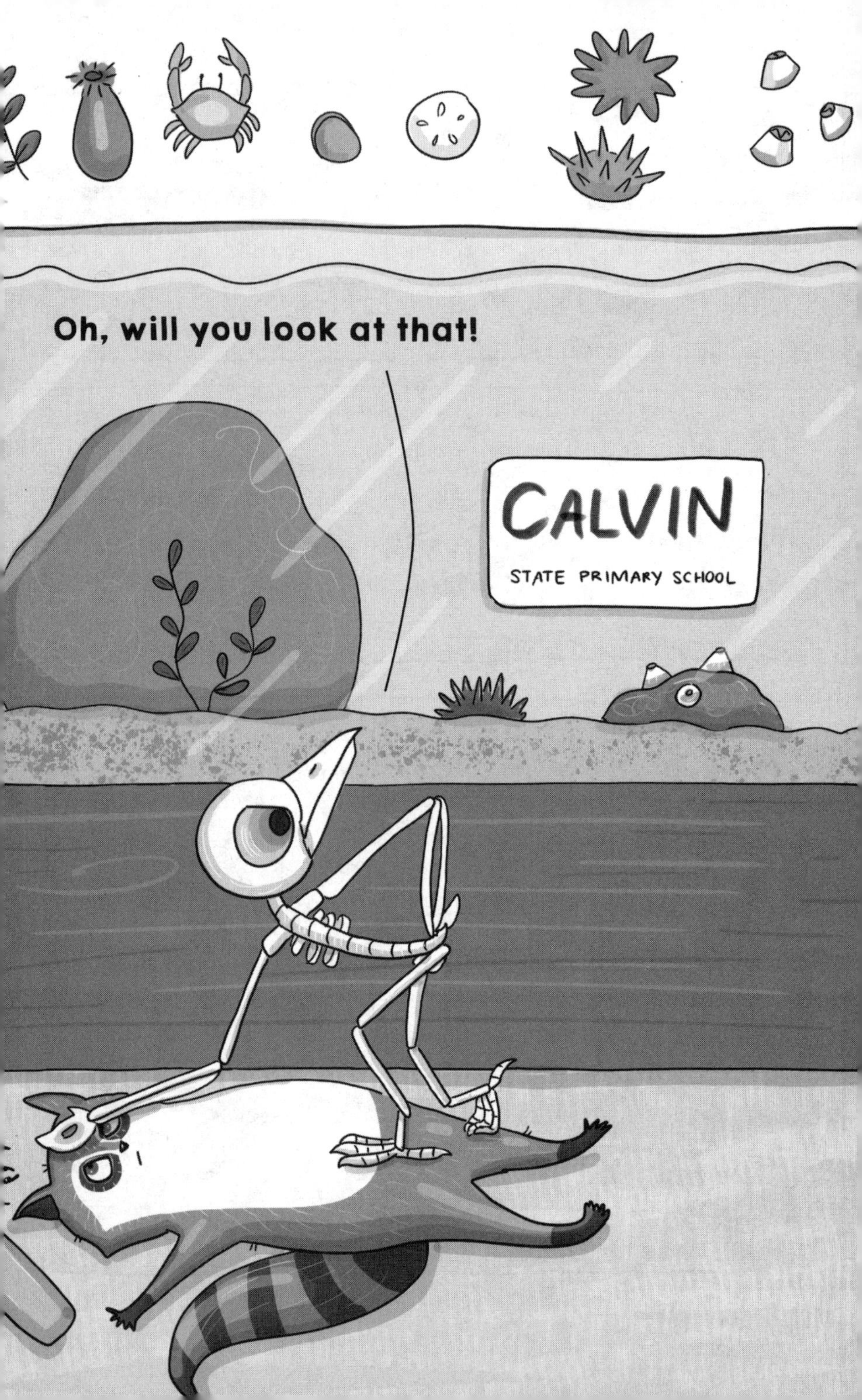
Oh, will you look at that!
CALVIN
STATE PRIMARY SCHOOL

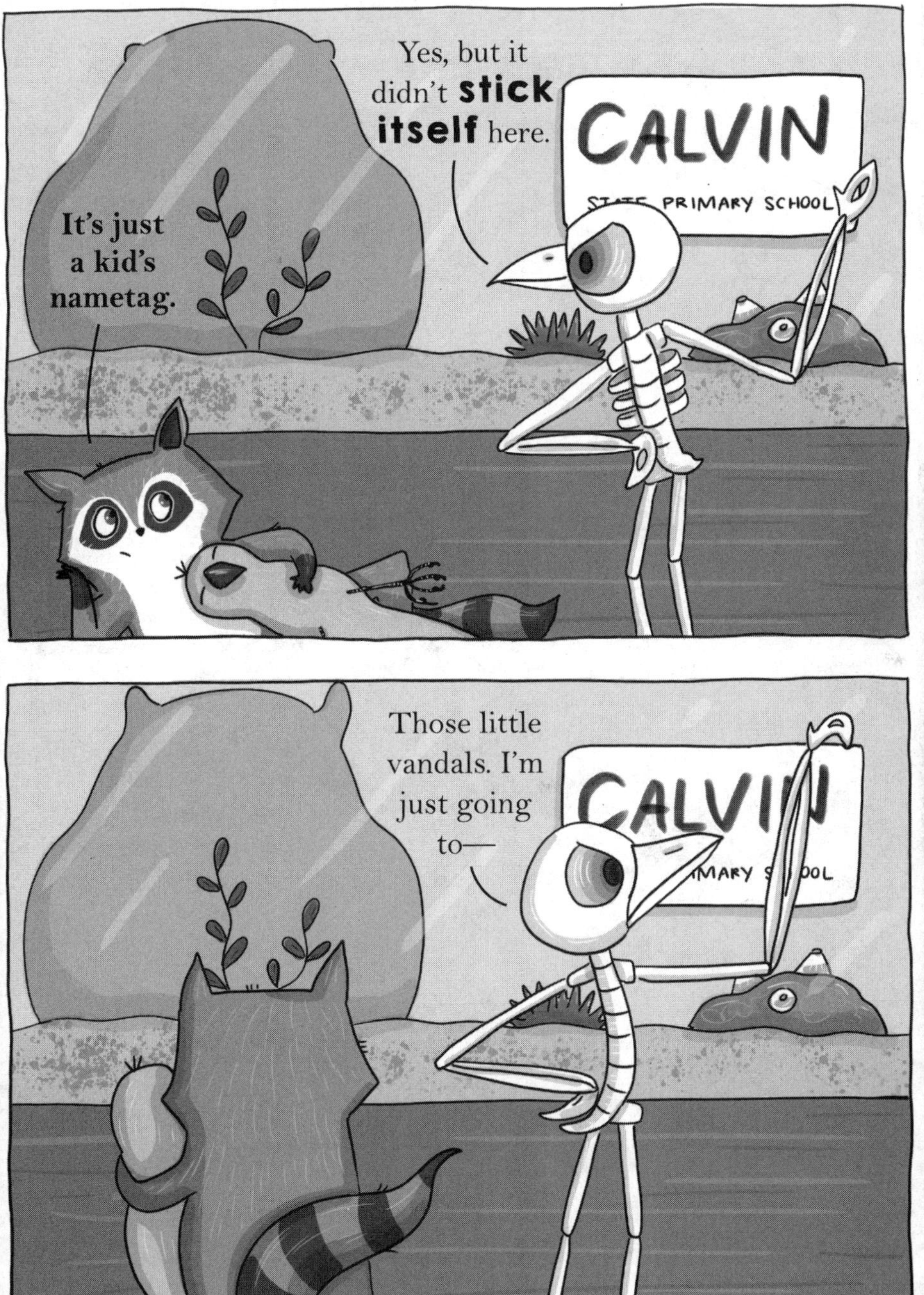
It's just a kid's nametag.
Yes, but it didn't **stick itself** here.
CALVIN
PRIMARY SCHOOL
Those little vandals. I'm just going to—

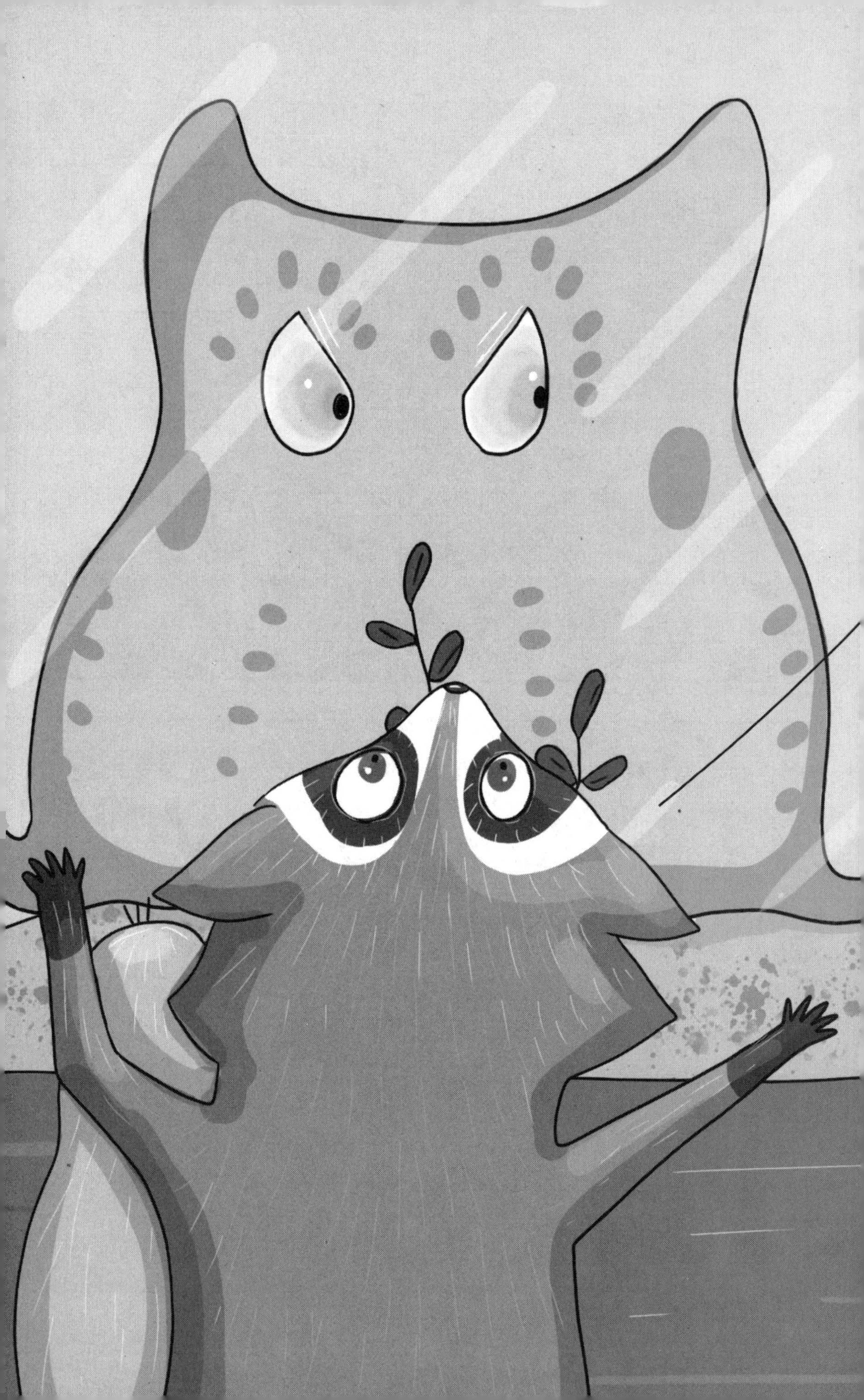

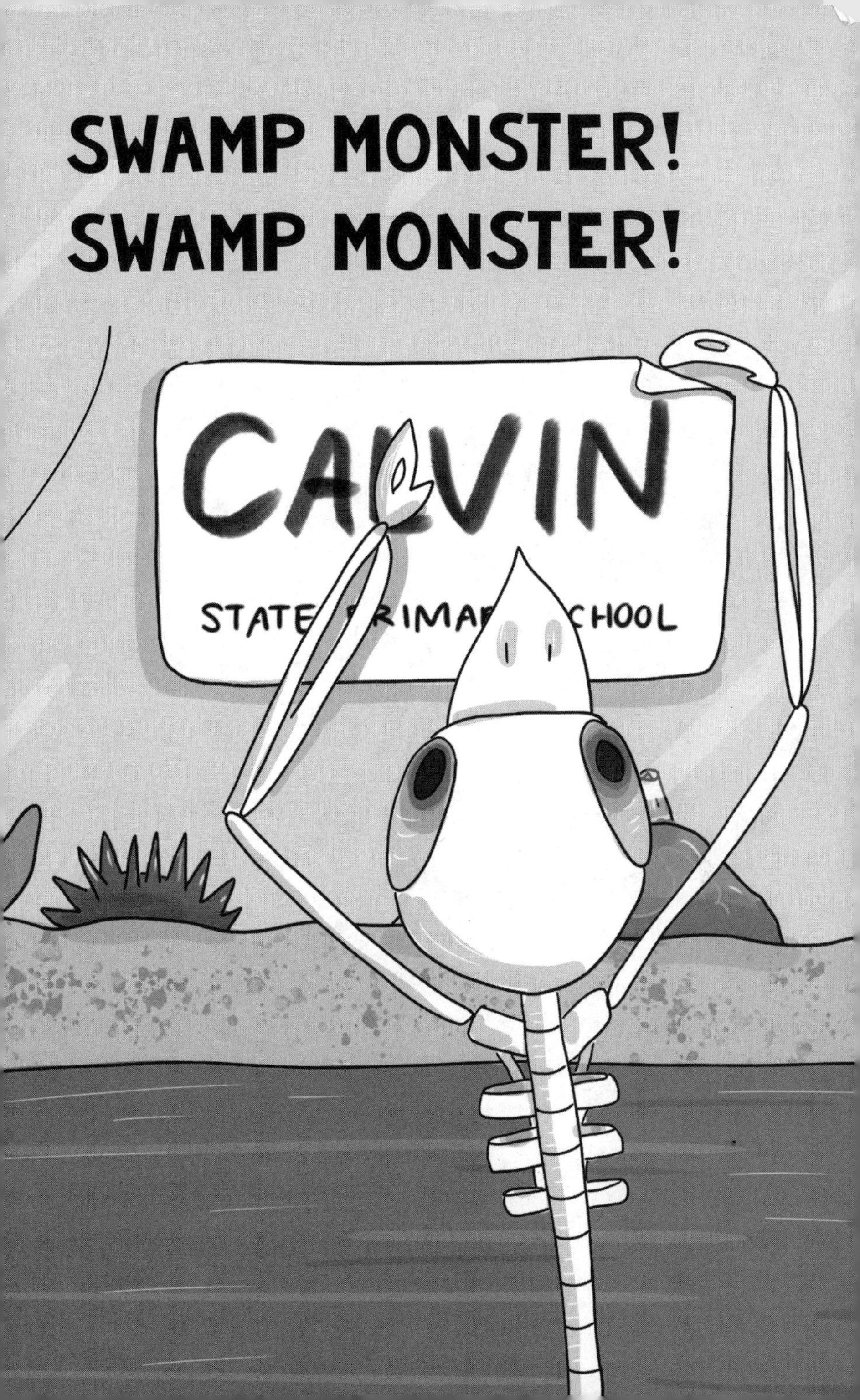
SWAMP MONSTER!
SWAMP MONSTER!

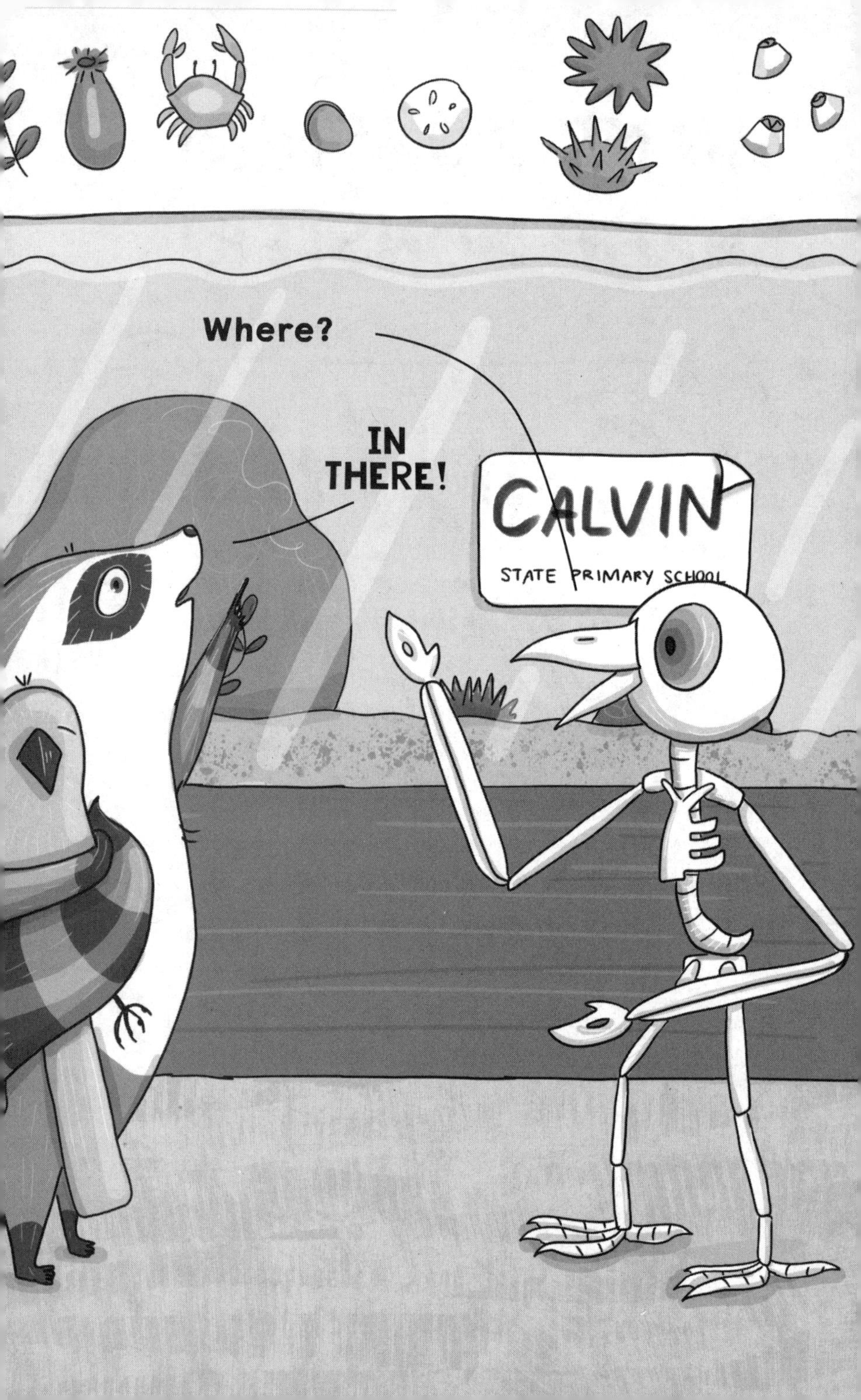
Where?
IN THERE!
CALVIN
STATE PRIMARY SCHOOL

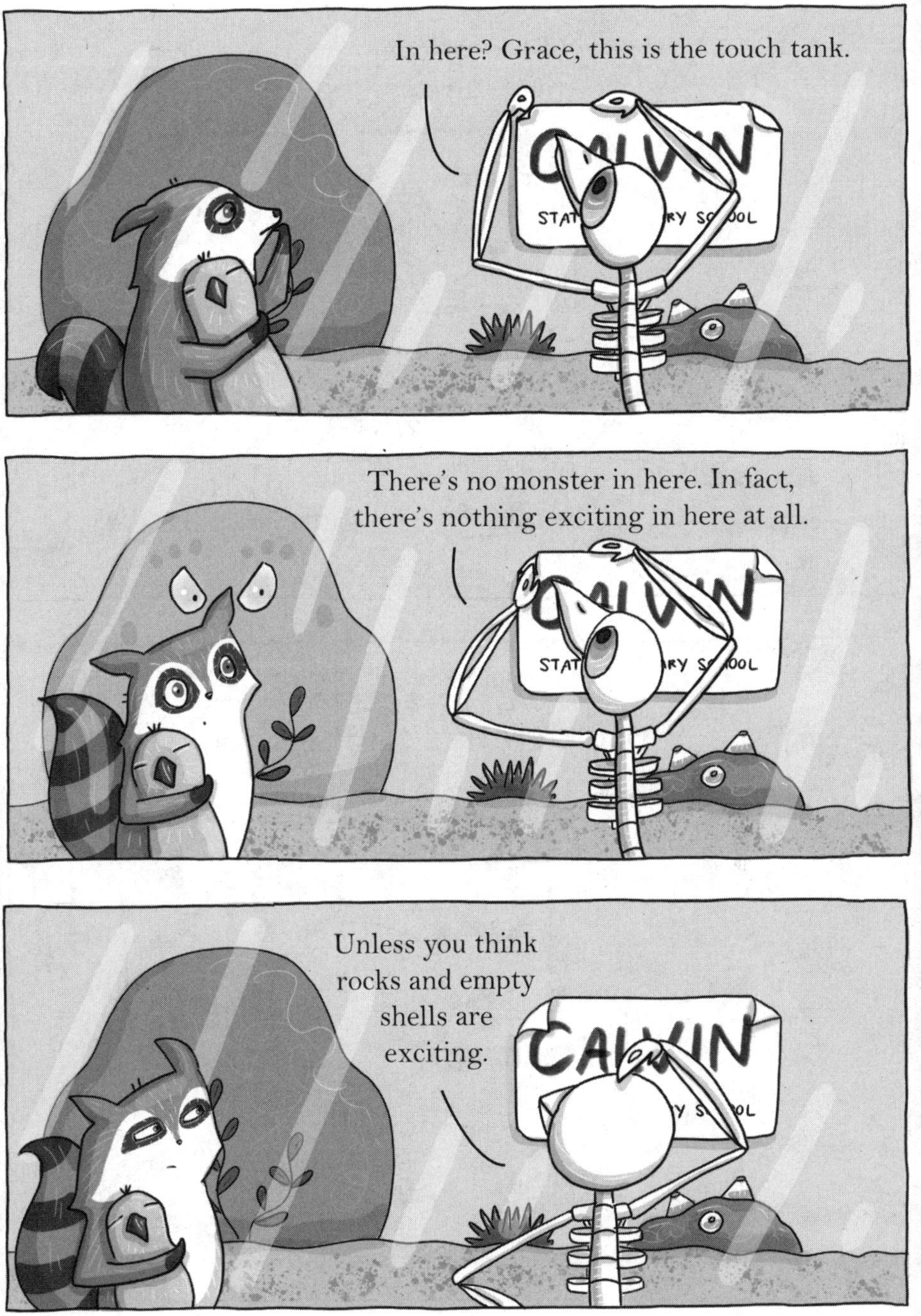
In here? Grace, this is the touch tank.
There's no monster in here. In fact, there's nothing exciting in here at all.
Unless you think rocks and empty shells are exciting.

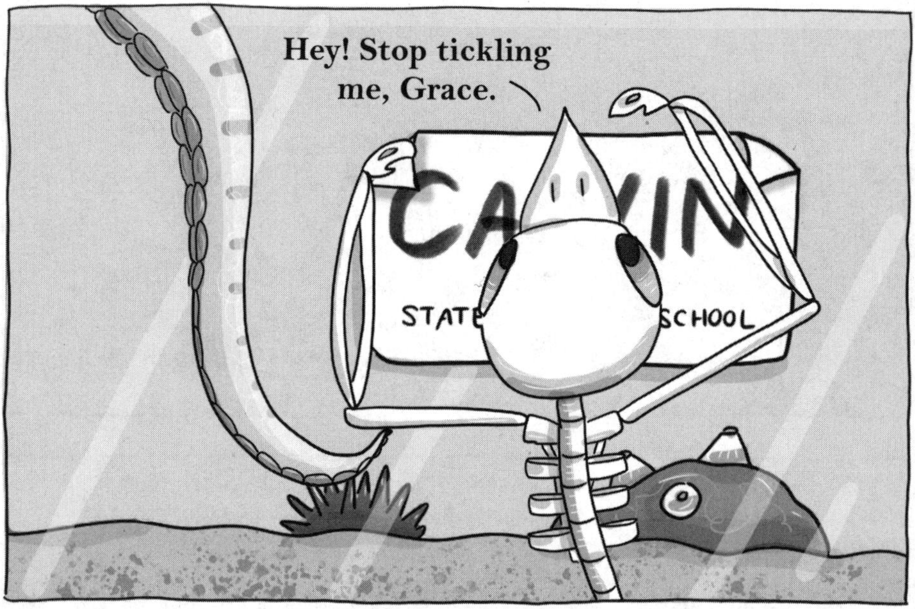
Hey! Stop tickling me, Grace.
STATE
SCHOOL

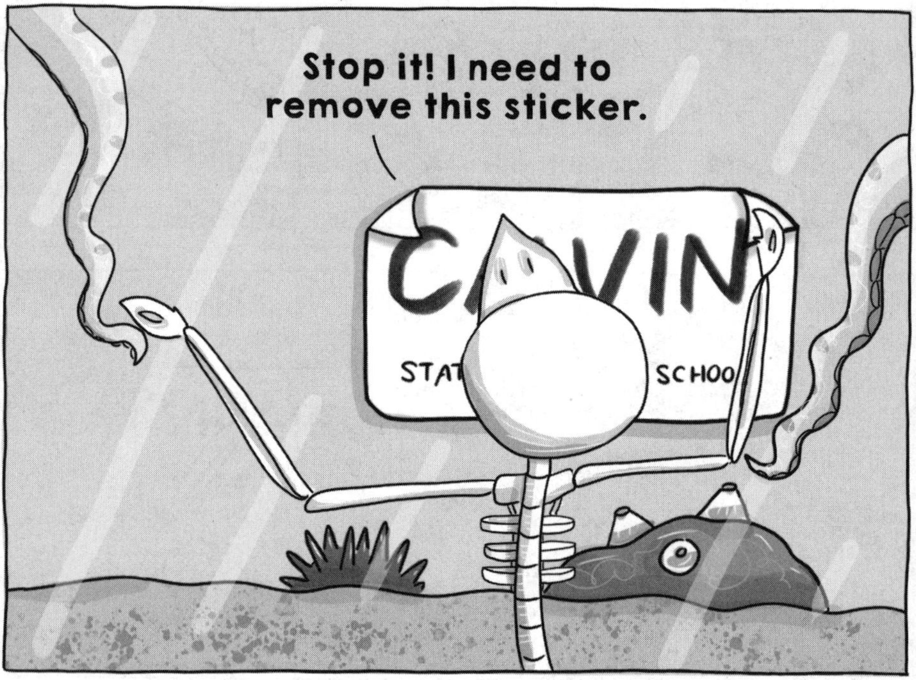
Stop it! I need to remove this sticker.
STAT
SCHOO

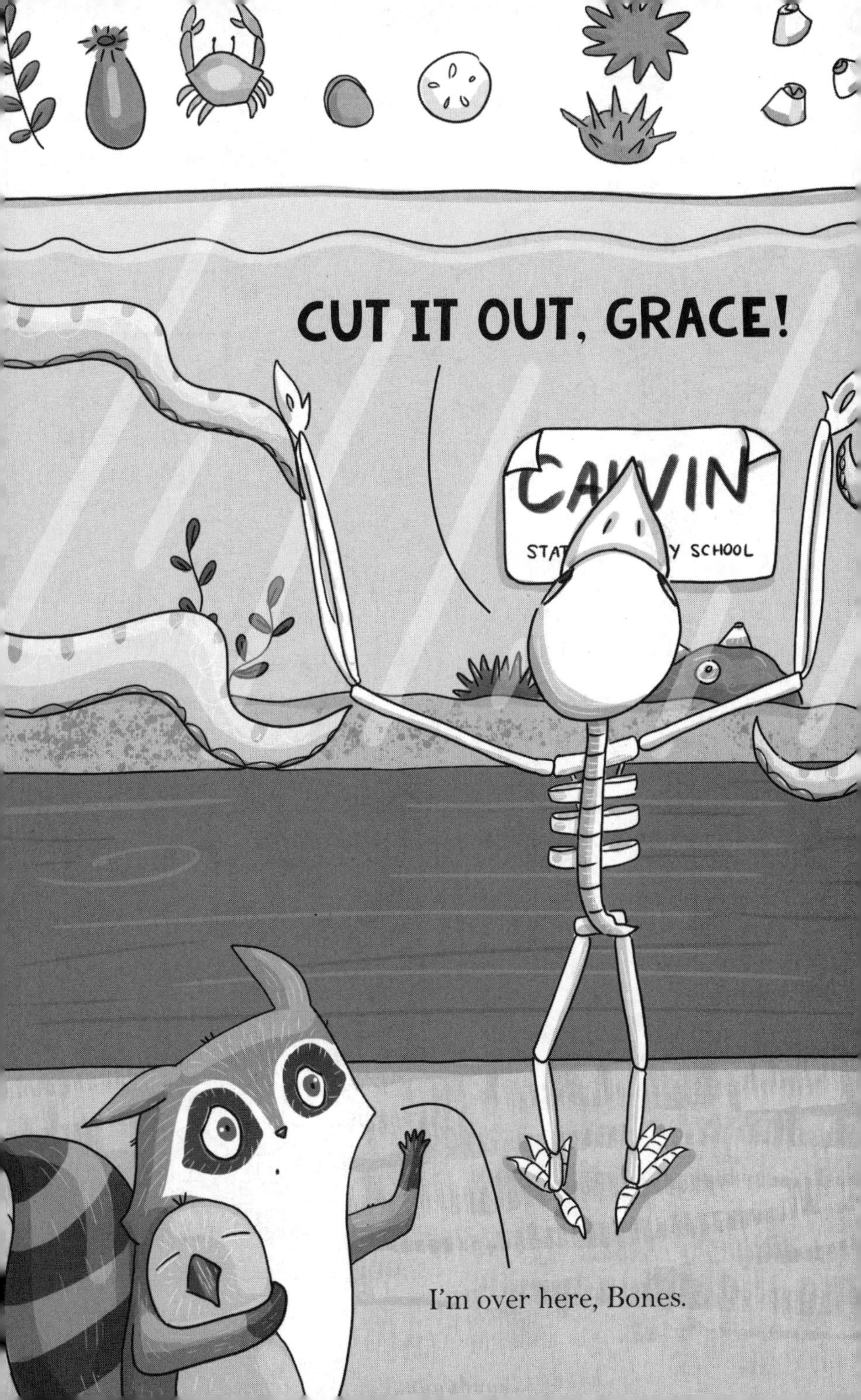
CUT IT OUT, GRACE!
I'm over here, Bones.

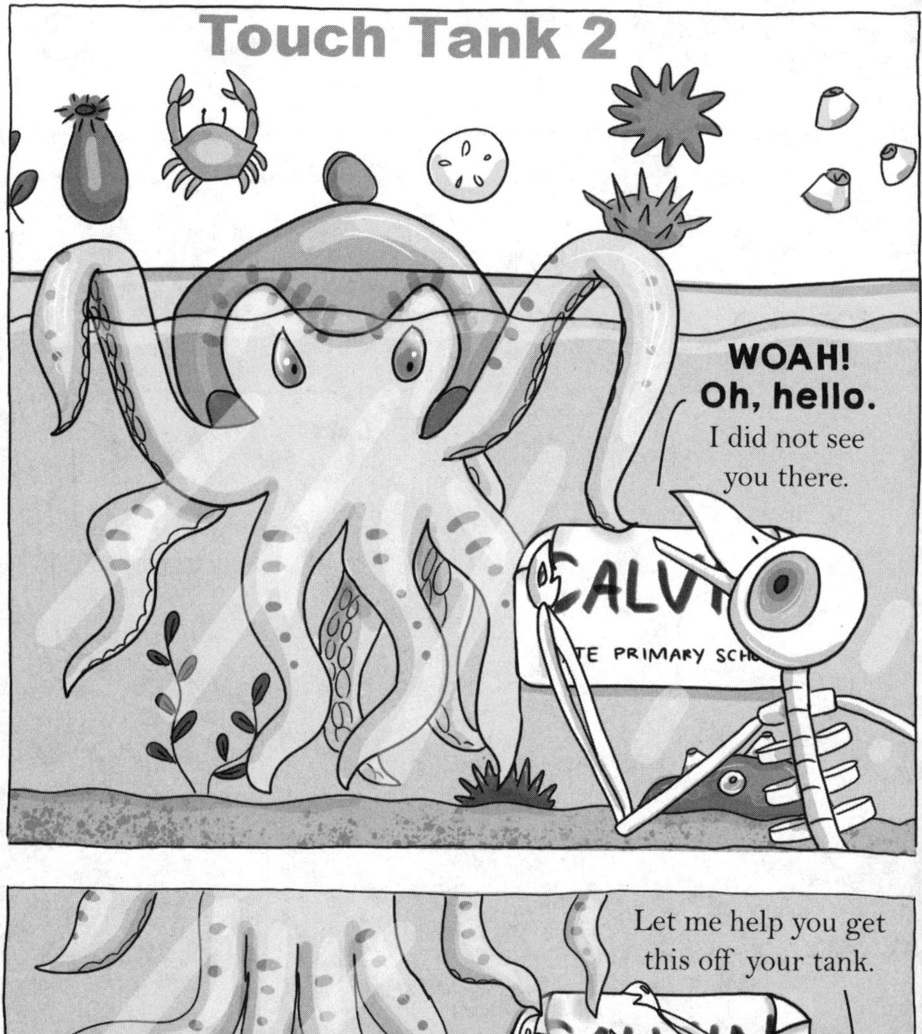
Touch Tank 2
WOAH!
Oh, hello.
I did not see you there.
CALVI
TE PRIMARY SCH

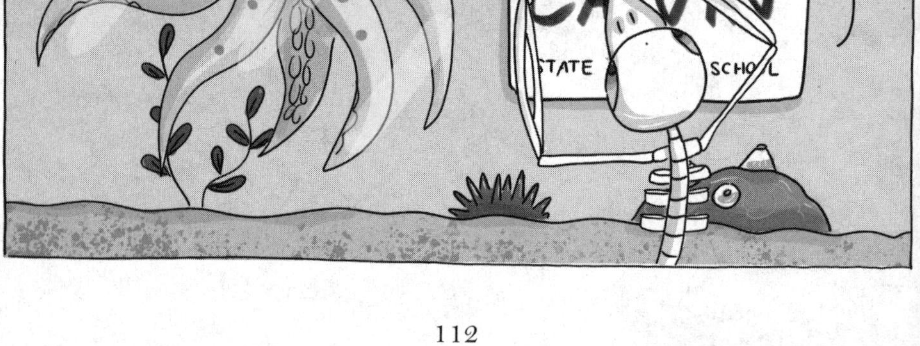
Let me help you get this off your tank.
CALVIN
STATE
SCHOL

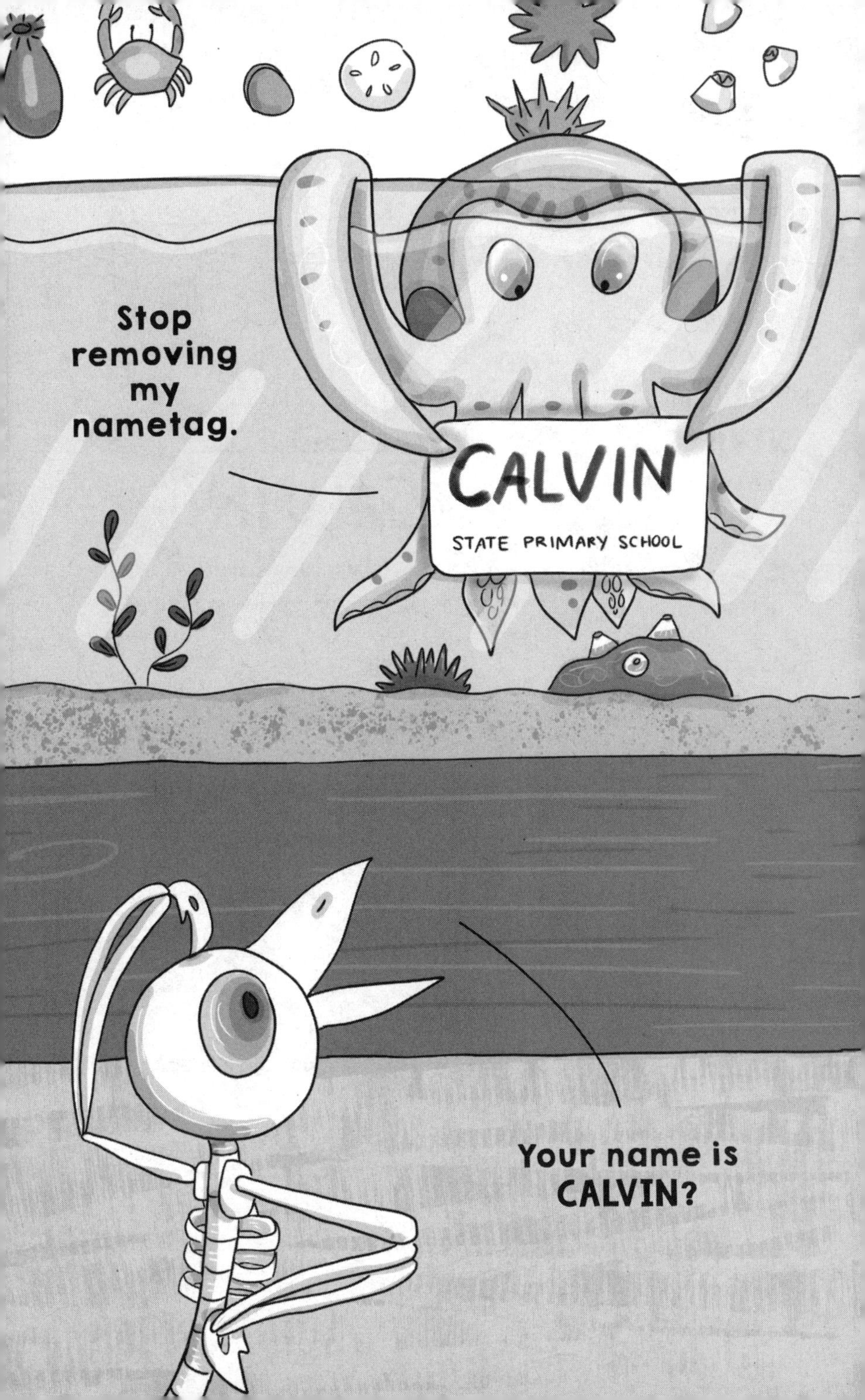
Stop removing my nametag.
CALVIN
STATE PRIMARY SCHOOL
Your name is CALVIN?

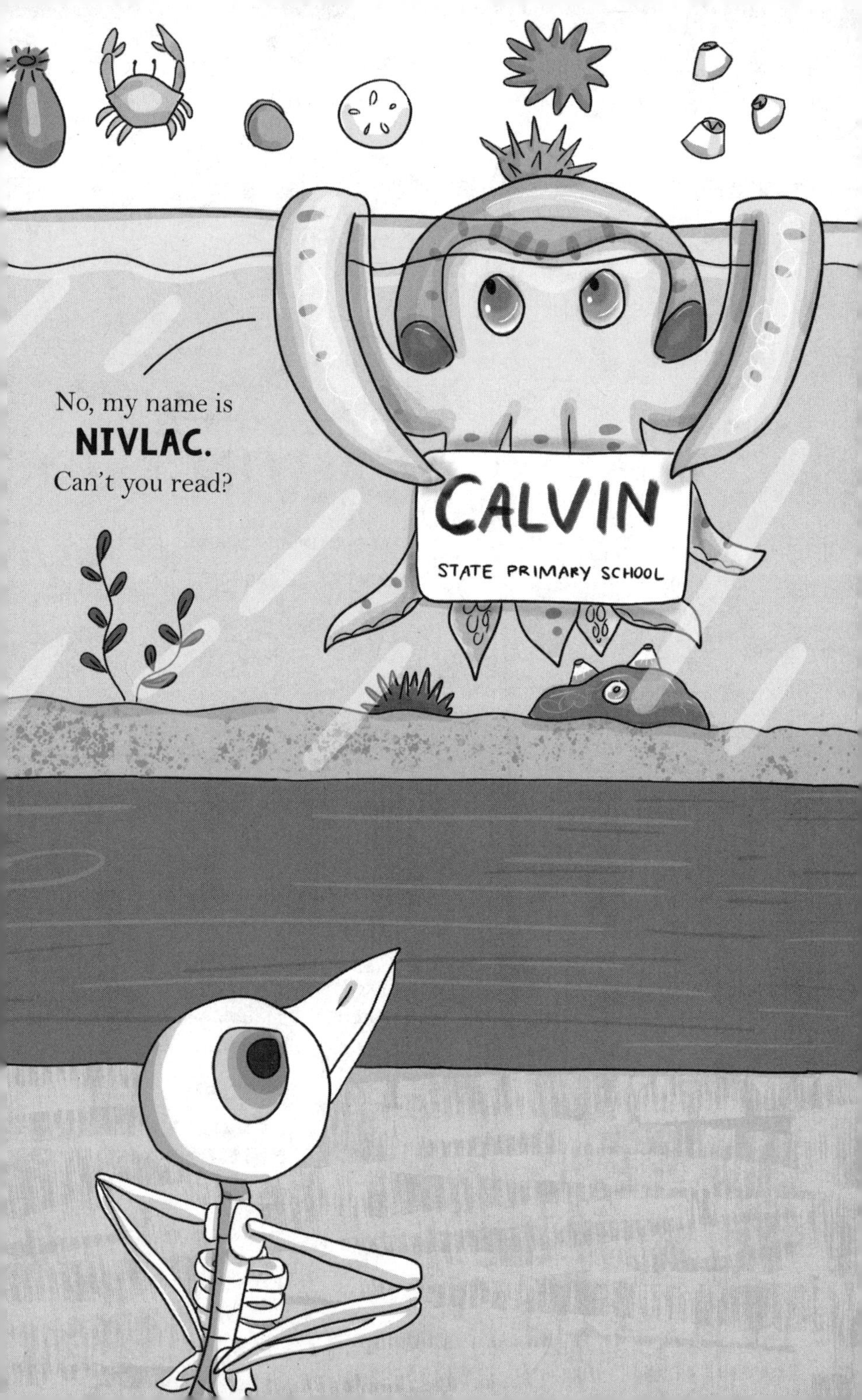
No, my name is **NIVLAC.** Can't you read?
CALVIN
STATE PRIMARY SCHOOL

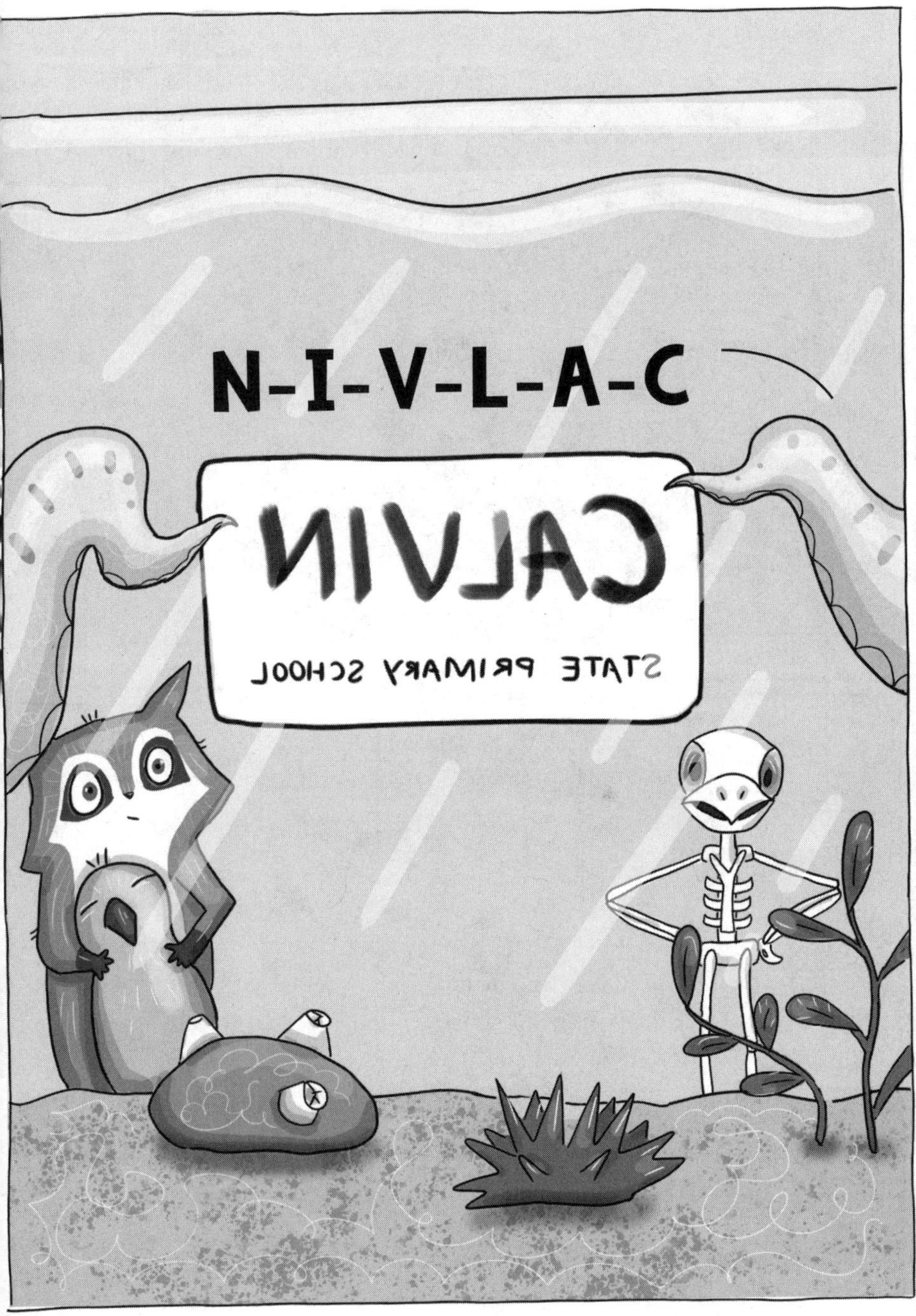
N-I-V-L-A-C
CALVIN
STATE PRIMARY SCHOOL

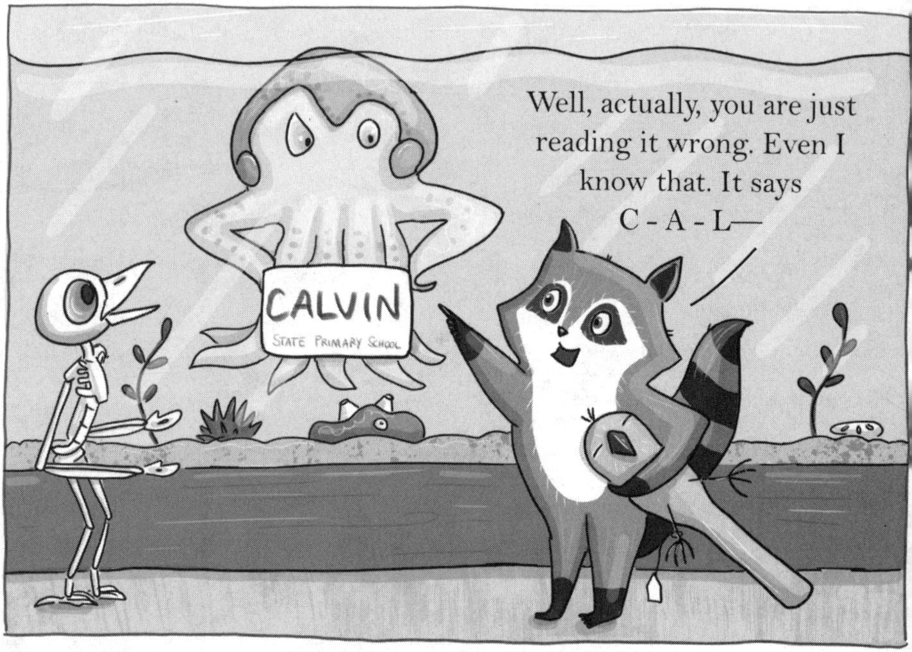
Well, actually, you are just reading it wrong. Even I know that. It says C - A - L—
CALVIN
STATE PRIMARY SCHOOL

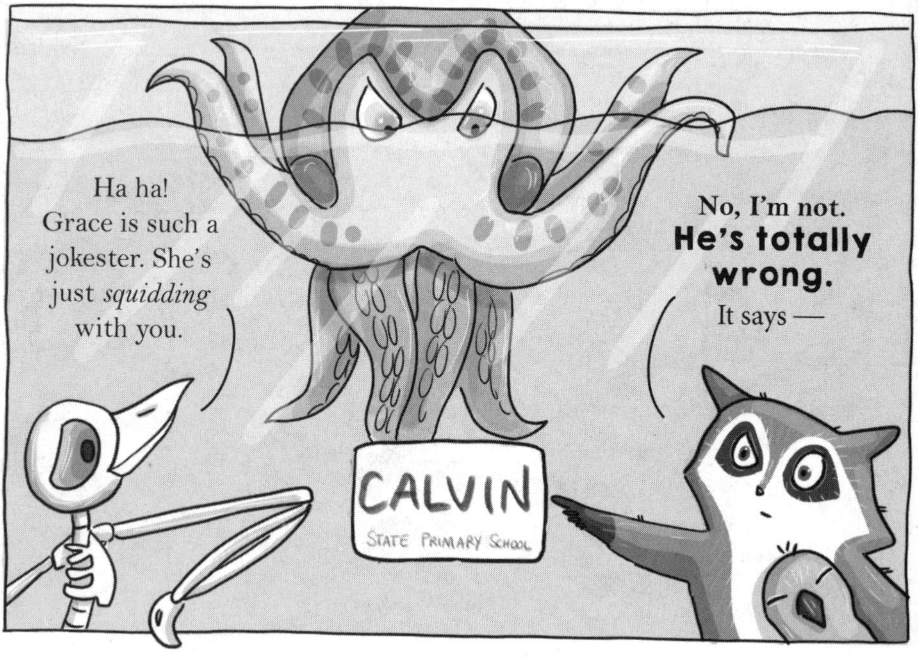
Ha ha! Grace is such a jokester. She's just *squidding* with you.
No, I'm not. **He's totally wrong.** It says —
CALVIN
STATE PRIMARY SCHOOL

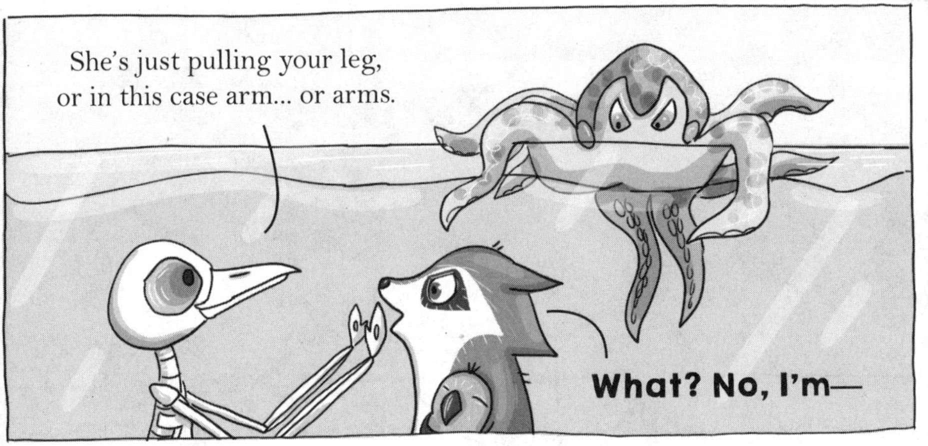
She's just pulling your leg, or in this case arm... or arms.
What? No, I'm—

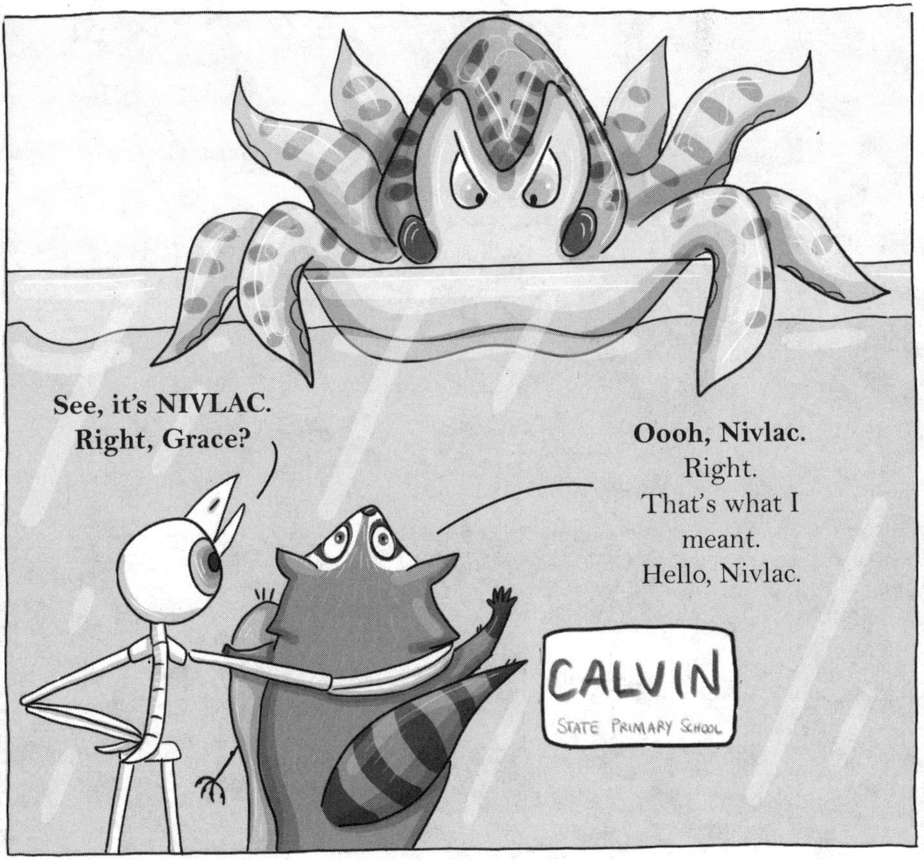
See, it's NIVLAC. Right, Grace?
Oooh, Nivlac. Right. That's what I meant. Hello, Nivlac.
CALVIN
STATE PRIMARY SCHOOL

Touch Tank 2

CALVIN
STATE PRIMARY SCHOOL

Nice to meet you,
Nivlac.
I'm Sherlock Bones.
You've already met
Grace and that's Watts.

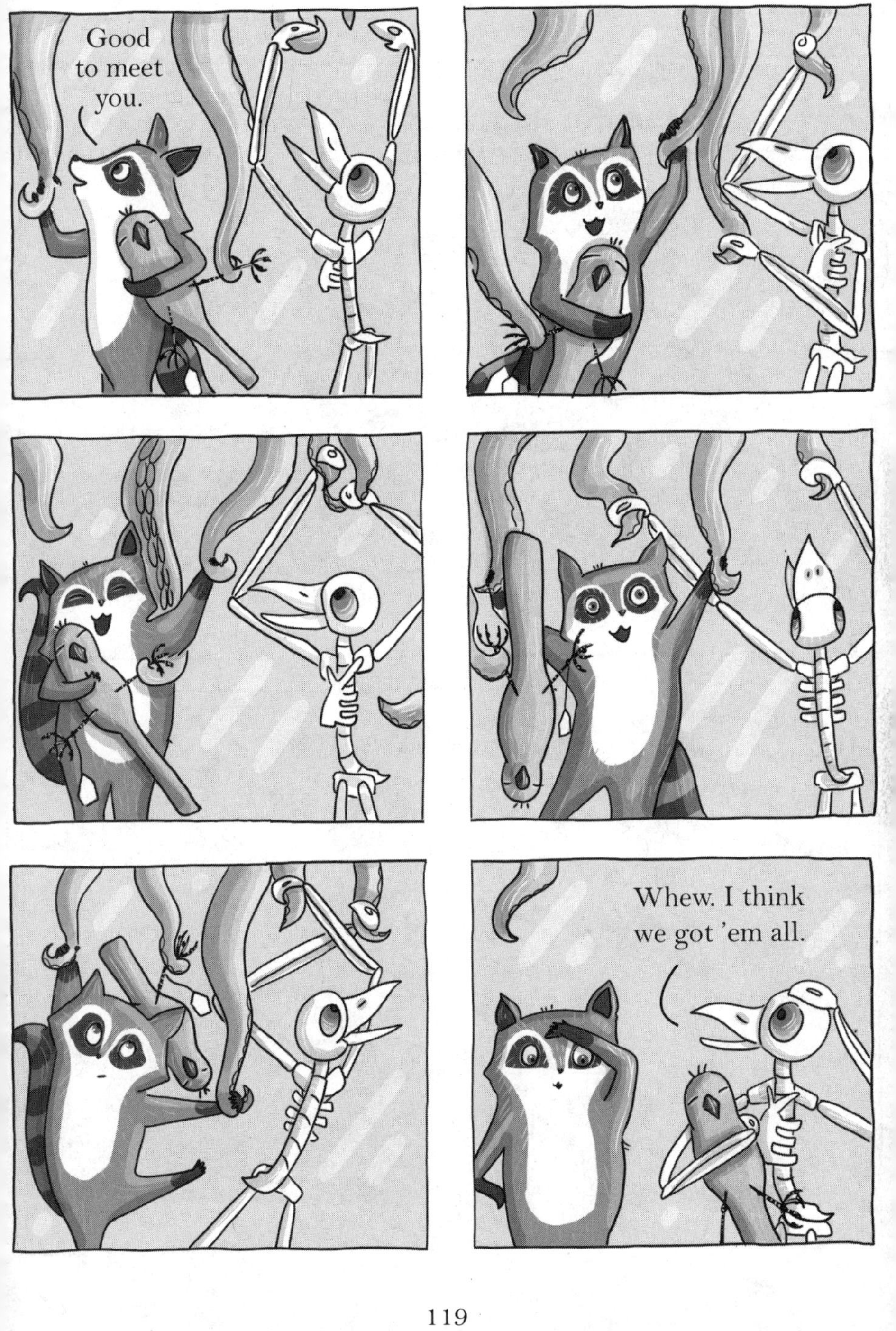
Good to meet you.
Whew. I think we got 'em all.

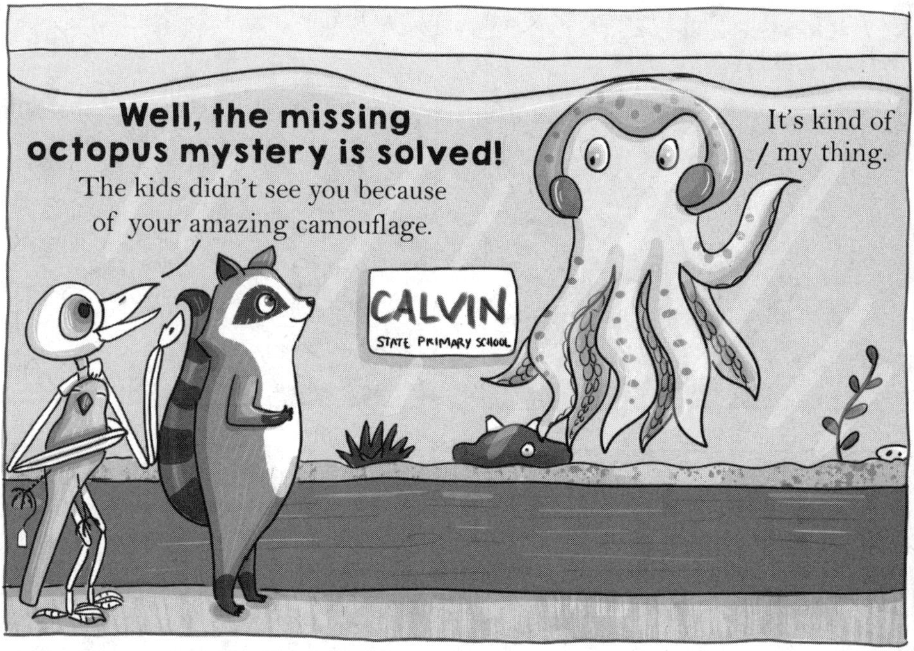
Well, the missing octopus mystery is solved!
The kids didn't see you because of your amazing camouflage.
CALVIN
STATE PRIMARY SCHOOL
It's kind of my thing.

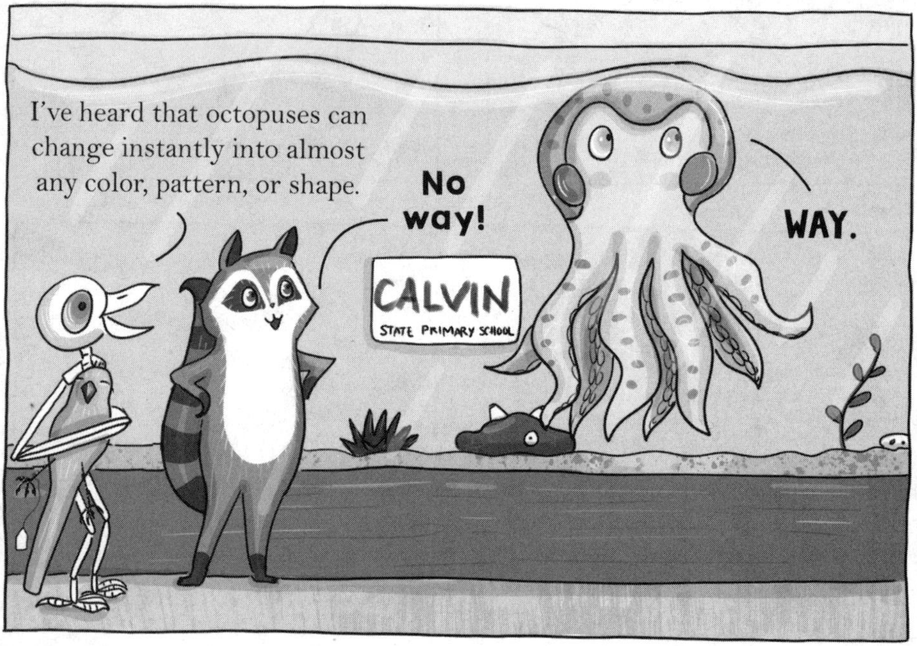
I've heard that octopuses can change instantly into almost any color, pattern, or shape.
No way!
CALVIN
STATE PRIMARY SCHOOL
WAY.

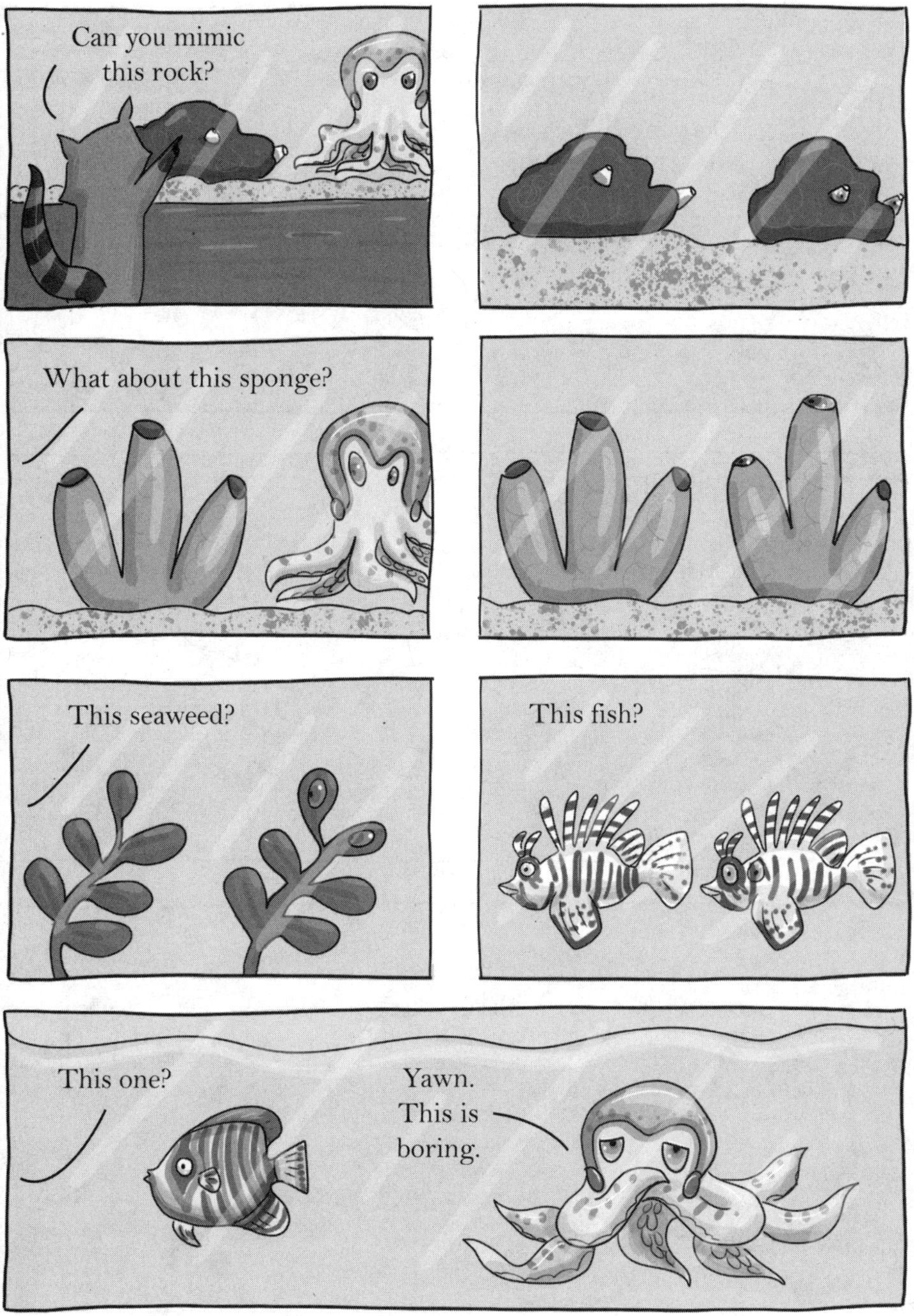
Can you mimic this rock?
What about this sponge?
This seaweed?
This fish?
This one?
Yawn. This is boring.

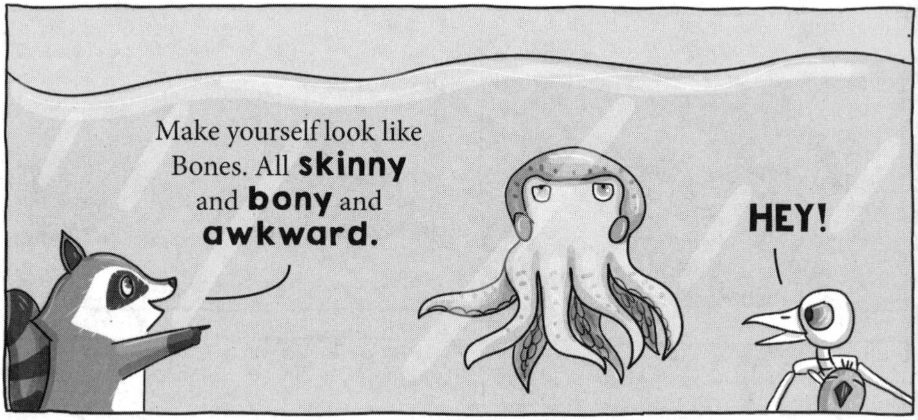
Make yourself look like Bones. All **skinny** and **bony** and **awkward.**
HEY!

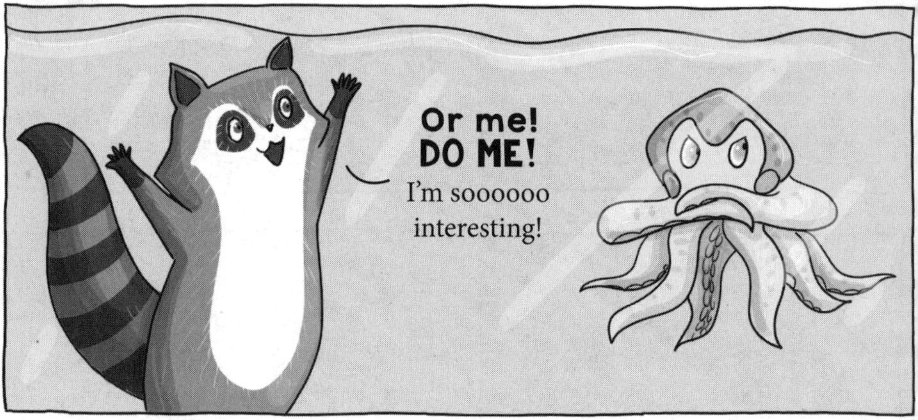
Or me! DO ME! I'm soooooo interesting!

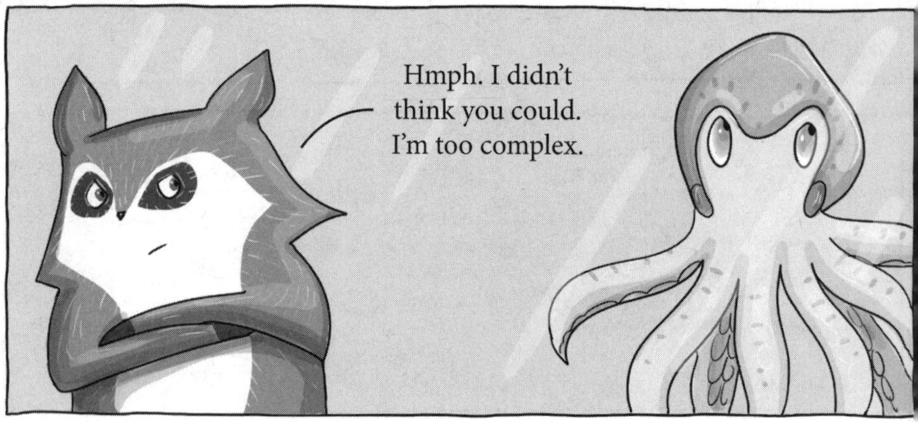
Hmph. I didn't think you could. I'm too complex.

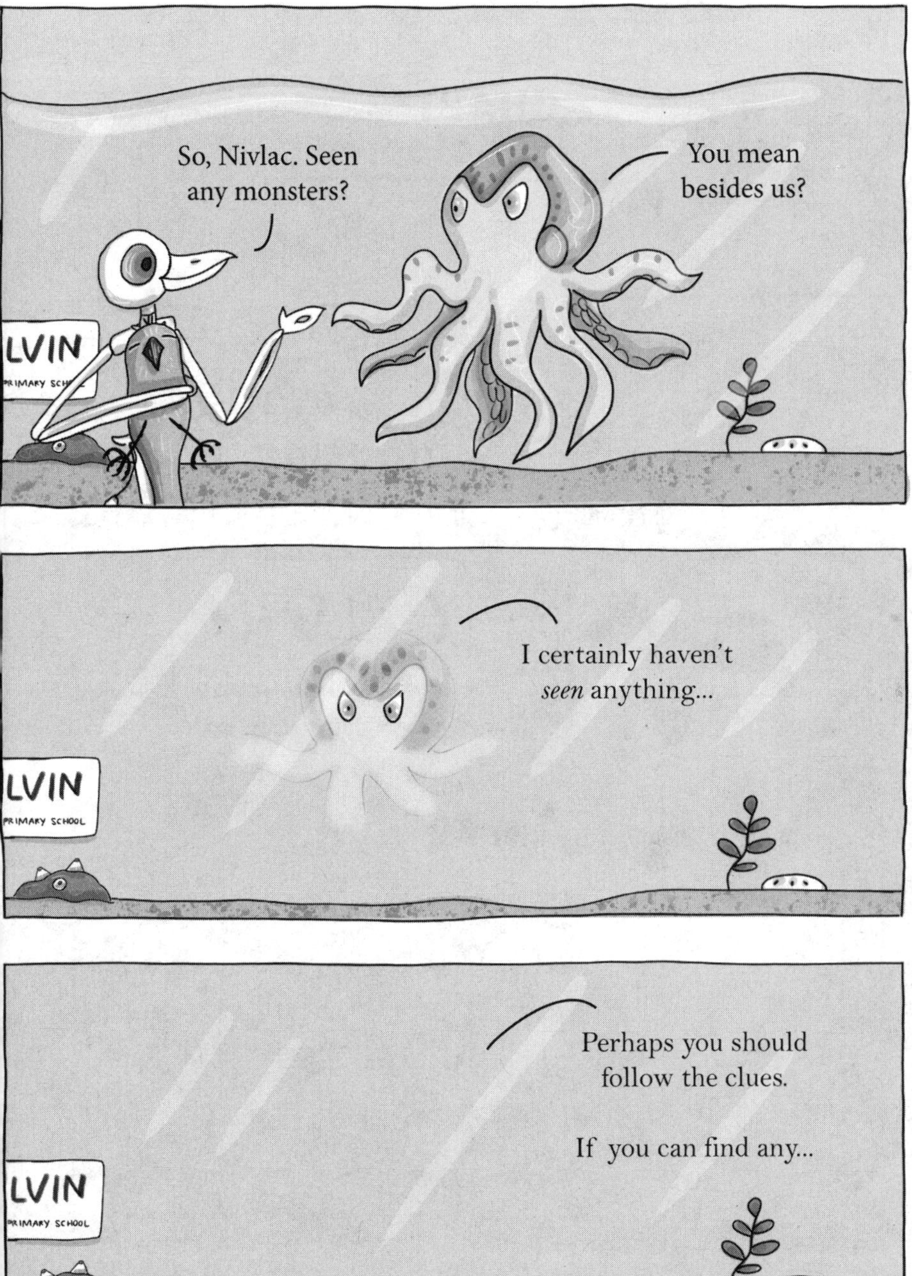

So, Nivlac. Seen any monsters?
You mean besides us?
LVIN
I certainly haven't *seen* anything...
LVIN
PRIMARY SCHOOL
Perhaps you should follow the clues.
If you can find any...
LVIN
PRIMARY SCHOOL

Touch Tank 2

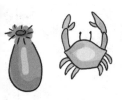

CHAPTER 5
Un-octopied

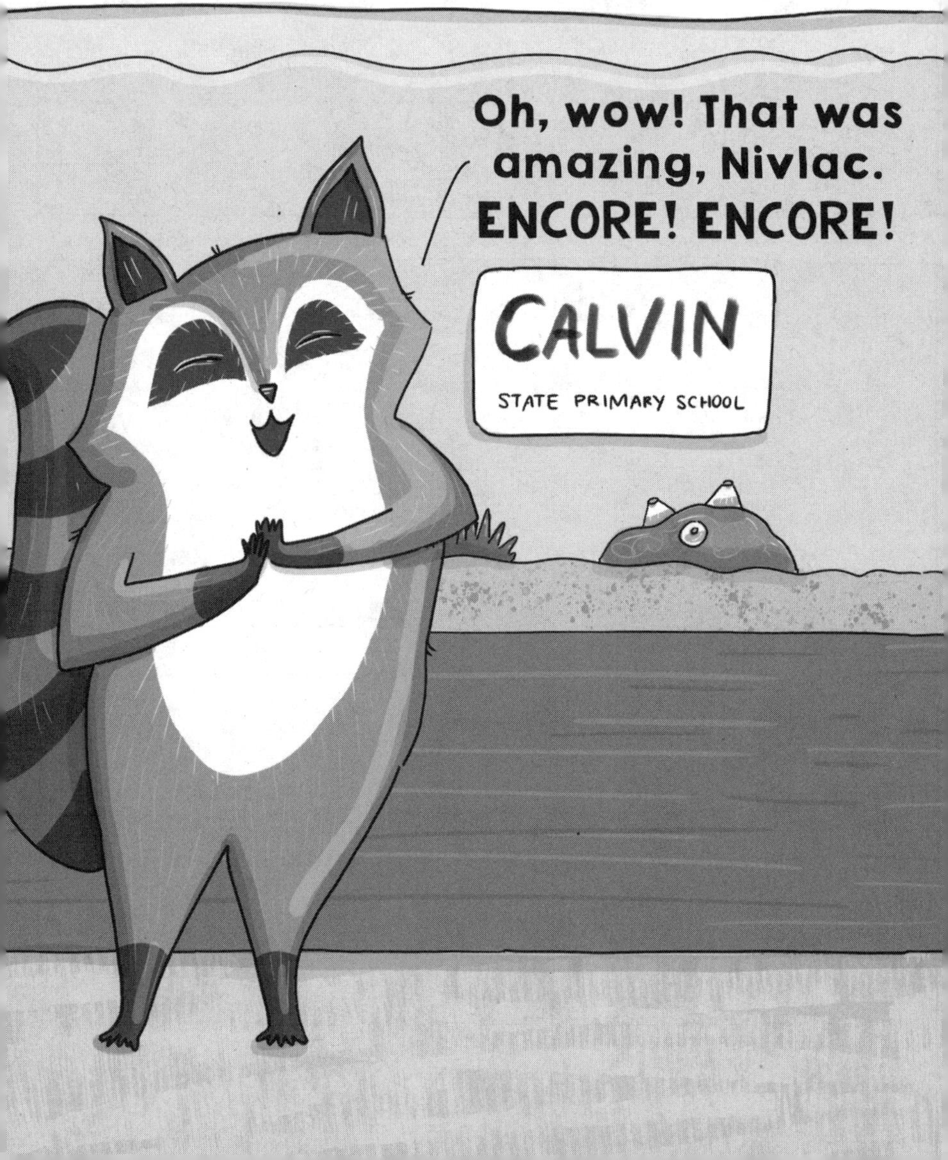
Oh, wow! That was amazing, Nivlac. ENCORE! ENCORE!
CALVIN
STATE PRIMARY SCHOOL

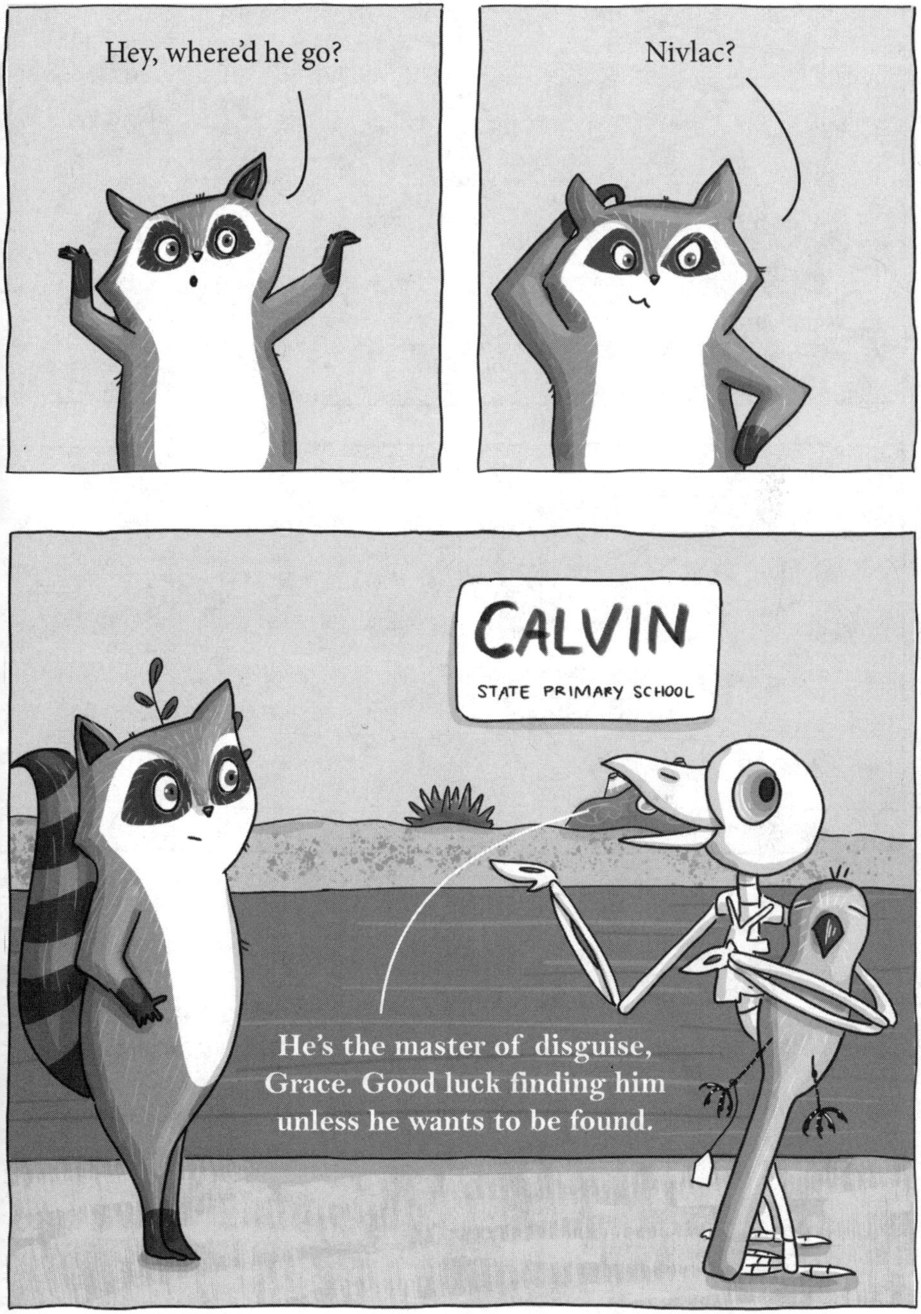
Hey, where'd he go?
Nivlac?
CALVIN
STATE PRIMARY SCHOOL
He's the master of disguise, Grace. Good luck finding him unless he wants to be found.

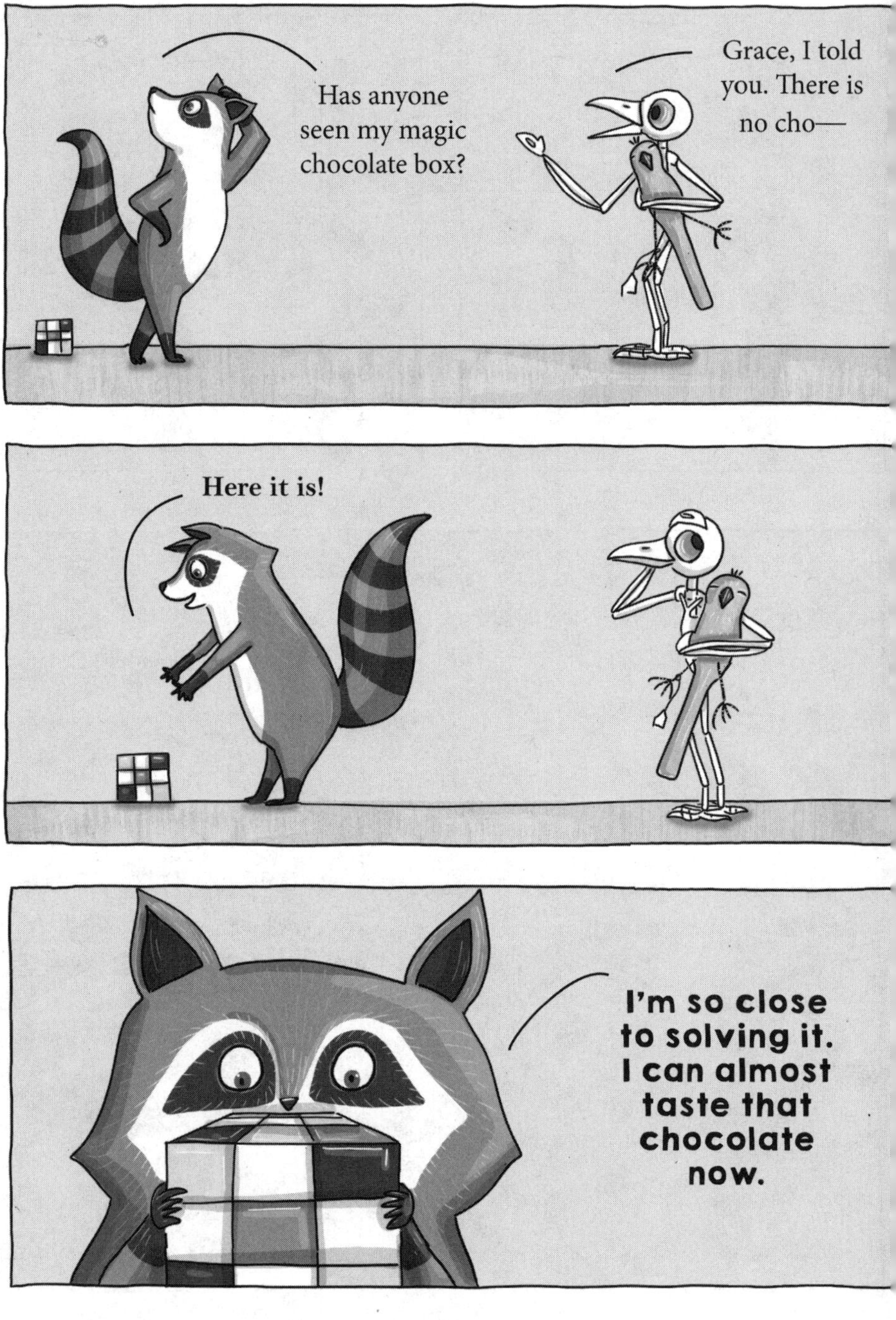
Has anyone seen my magic chocolate box?
Grace, I told you. There is no cho—
Here it is!
I'm so close to solving it. I can almost taste that chocolate now.

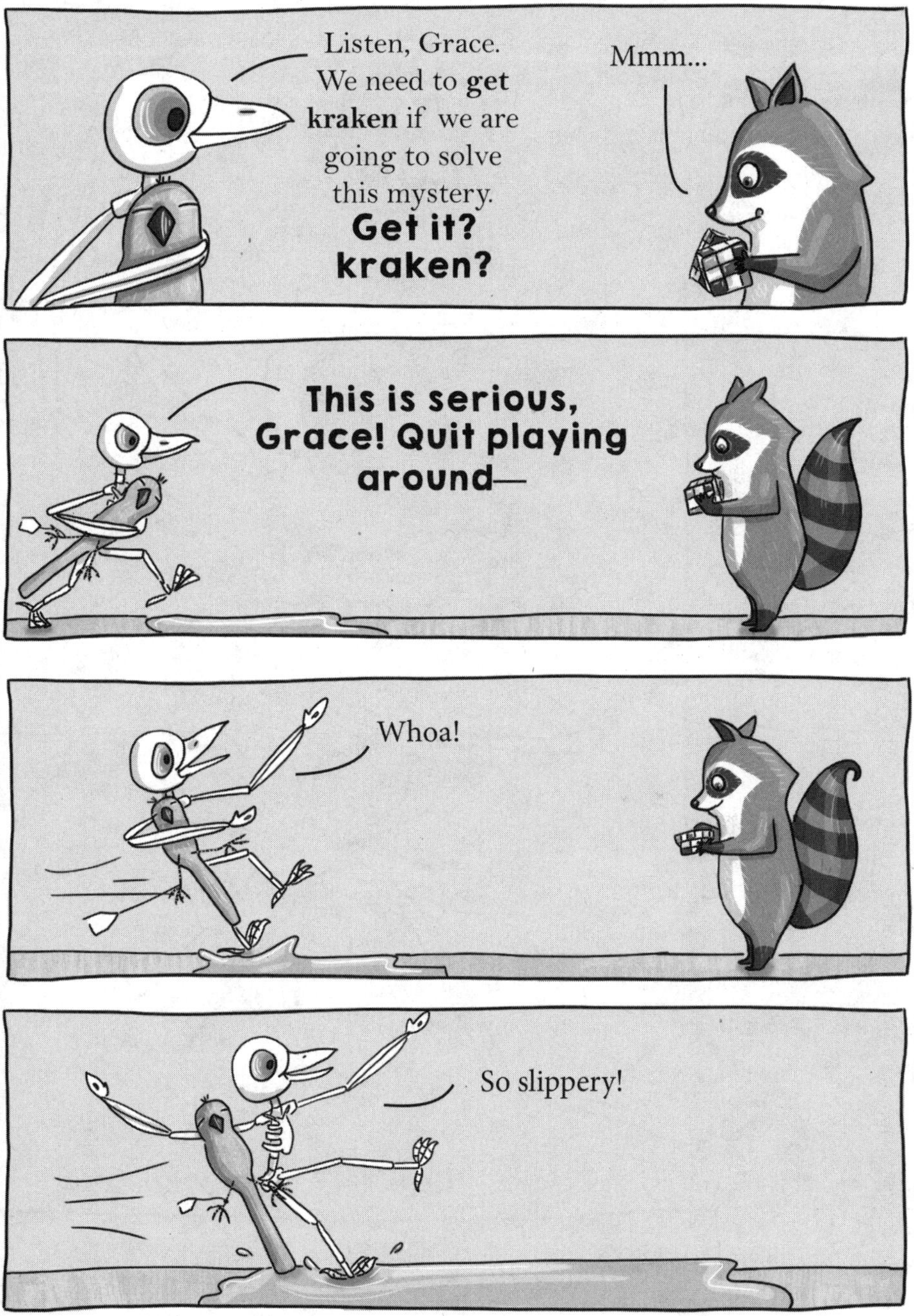
Listen, Grace. We need to **get kraken** if we are going to solve this mystery. **Get it? kraken?**
Mmm...
This is serious, Grace! Quit playing around—
Whoa!
So slippery!

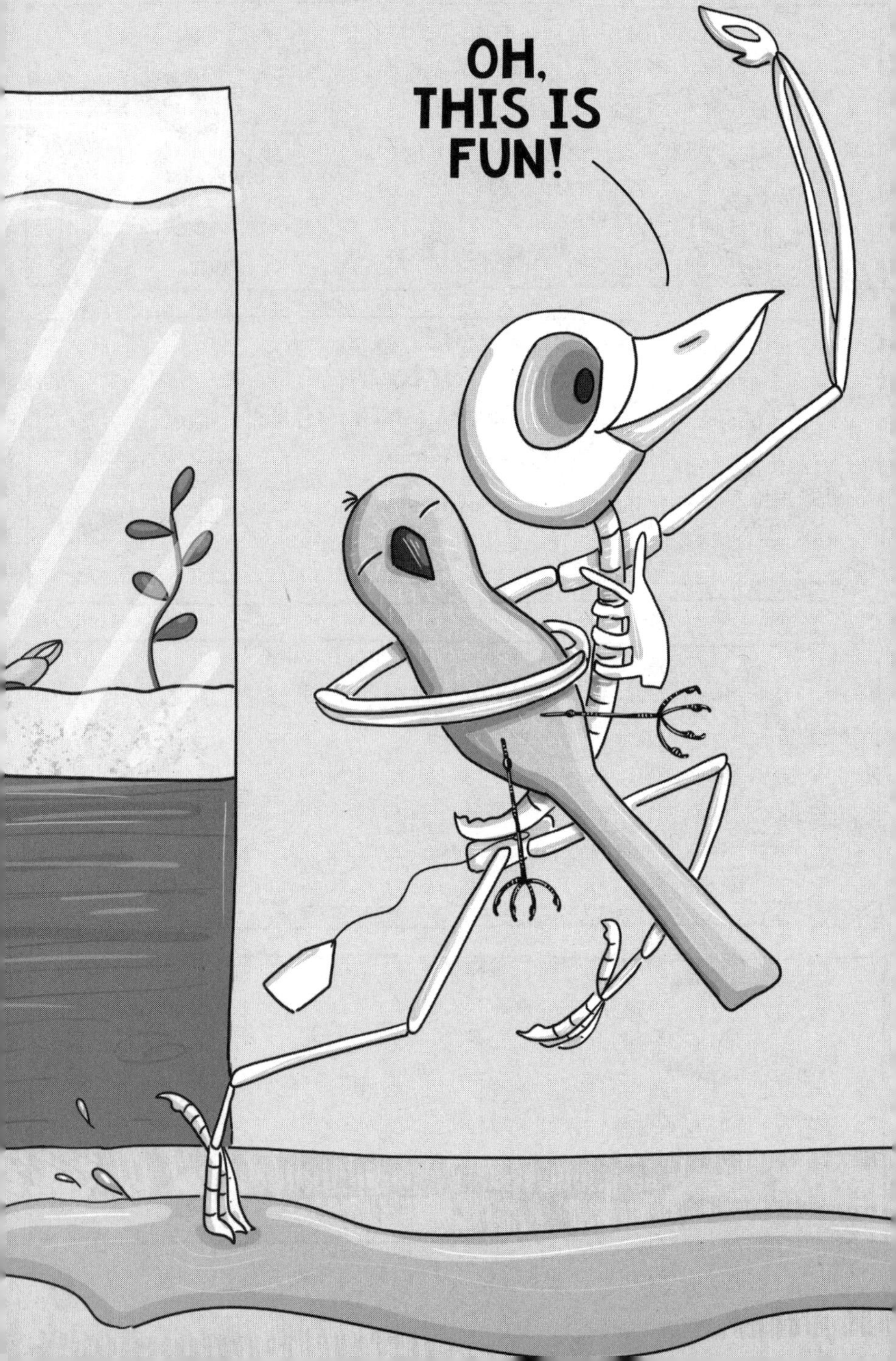
OH, THIS IS FUN!

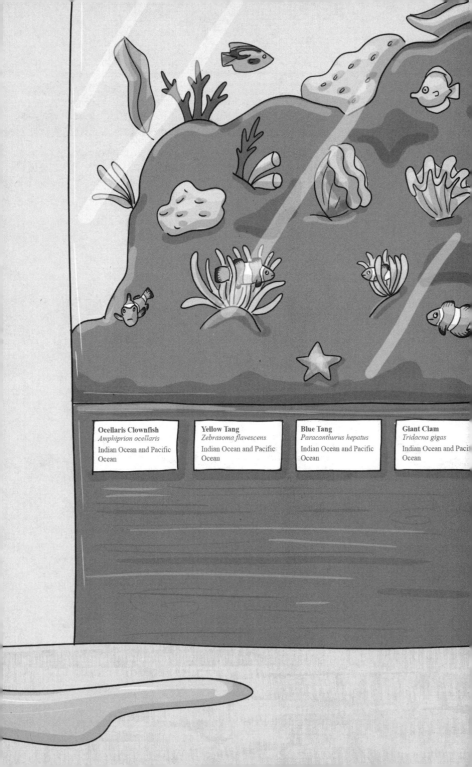

Ocellaris Clownfish
Amphiprion ocellaris
Indian Ocean and Pacific Ocean

Yellow Tang
Zebrasoma flavescens
Indian Ocean and Pacific Ocean

Blue Tang
Paracanthurus hepatus
Indian Ocean and Pacific Ocean

Giant Clam
Tridacna gigas
Indian Ocean and Pacific Ocean

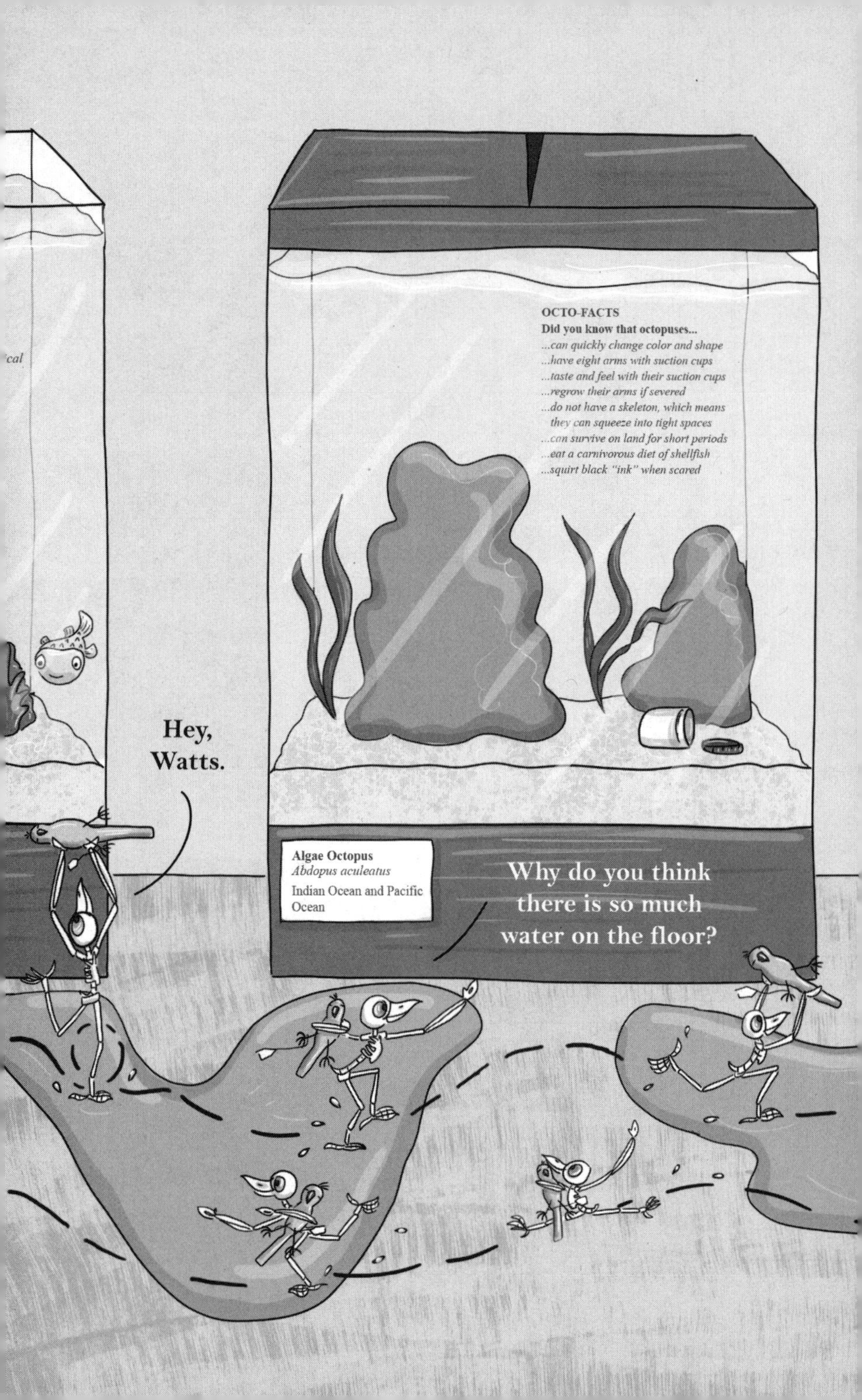

cal
OCTO-FACTS
Did you know that octopuses...
...can quickly change color and shape
...have eight arms with suction cups
...taste and feel with their suction cups
...regrow their arms if severed
...do not have a skeleton, which means they can squeeze into tight spaces
...can survive on land for short periods
...eat a carnivorous diet of shellfish
...squirt black "ink" when scared
Hey, Watts.
Algae Octopus
Abdopus aculeatus
Indian Ocean and Pacific Ocean
Why do you think there is so much water on the floor?

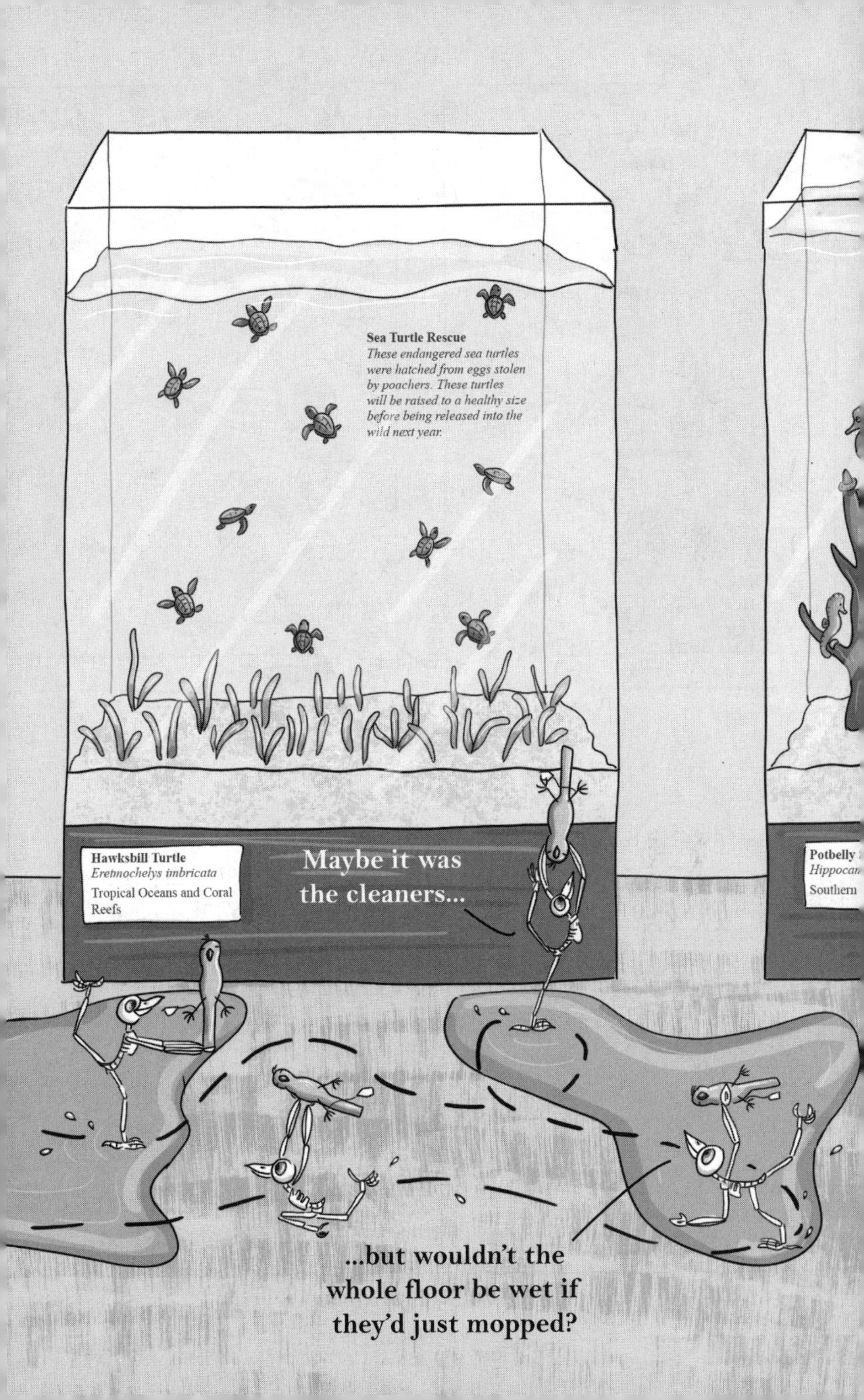
Sea Turtle Rescue
These endangered sea turtles were hatched from eggs stolen by poachers. These turtles will be raised to a healthy size before being released into the wild next year.
Hawksbill Turtle
Eretmochelys imbricata
Tropical Oceans and Coral Reefs
Potbelly
Maybe it was the cleaners...
...but wouldn't the whole floor be wet if they'd just mopped?

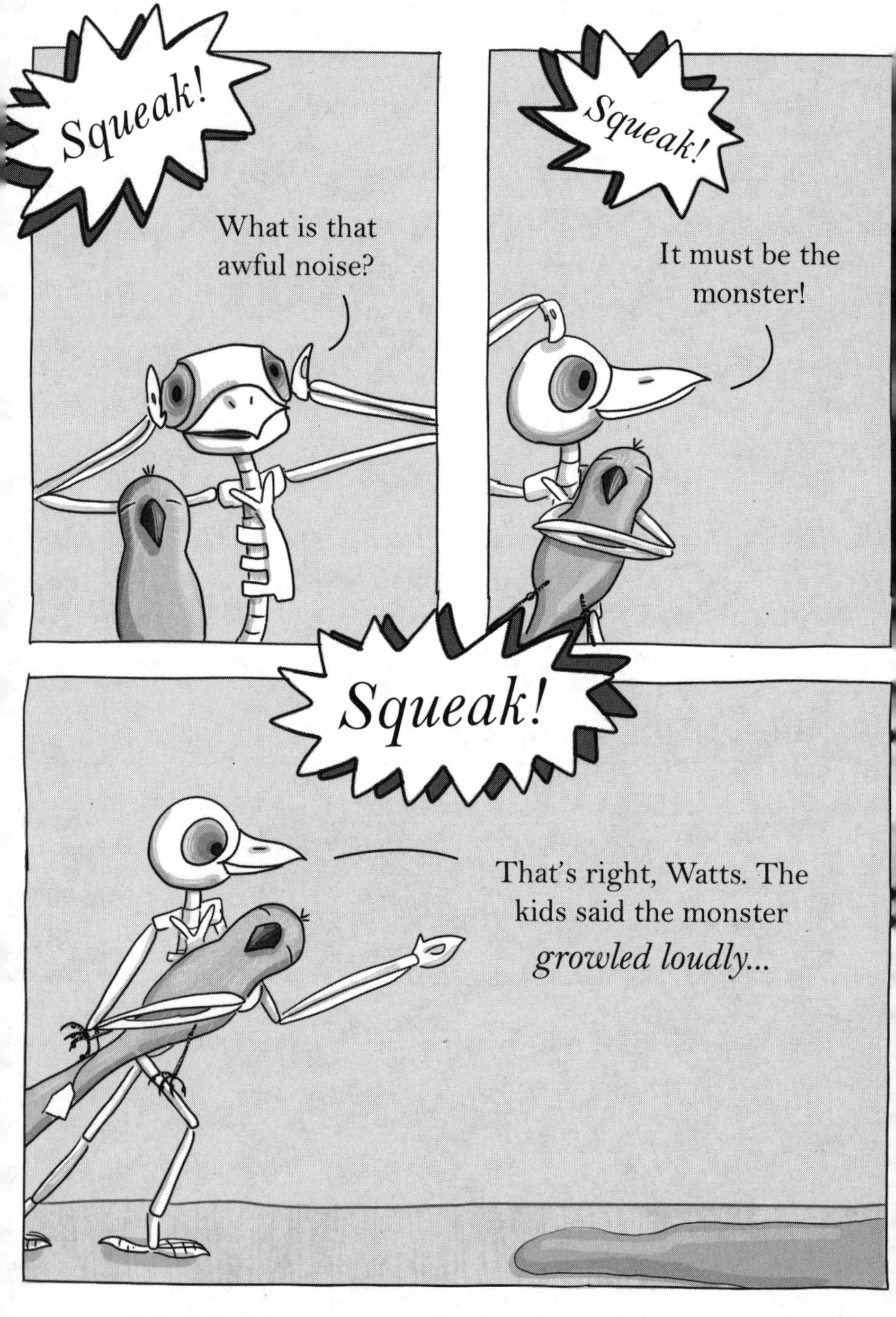
Squeak!
What is that awful noise?
Squeak!
It must be the monster!
Squeak!
That's right, Watts. The kids said the monster *growled loudly...*

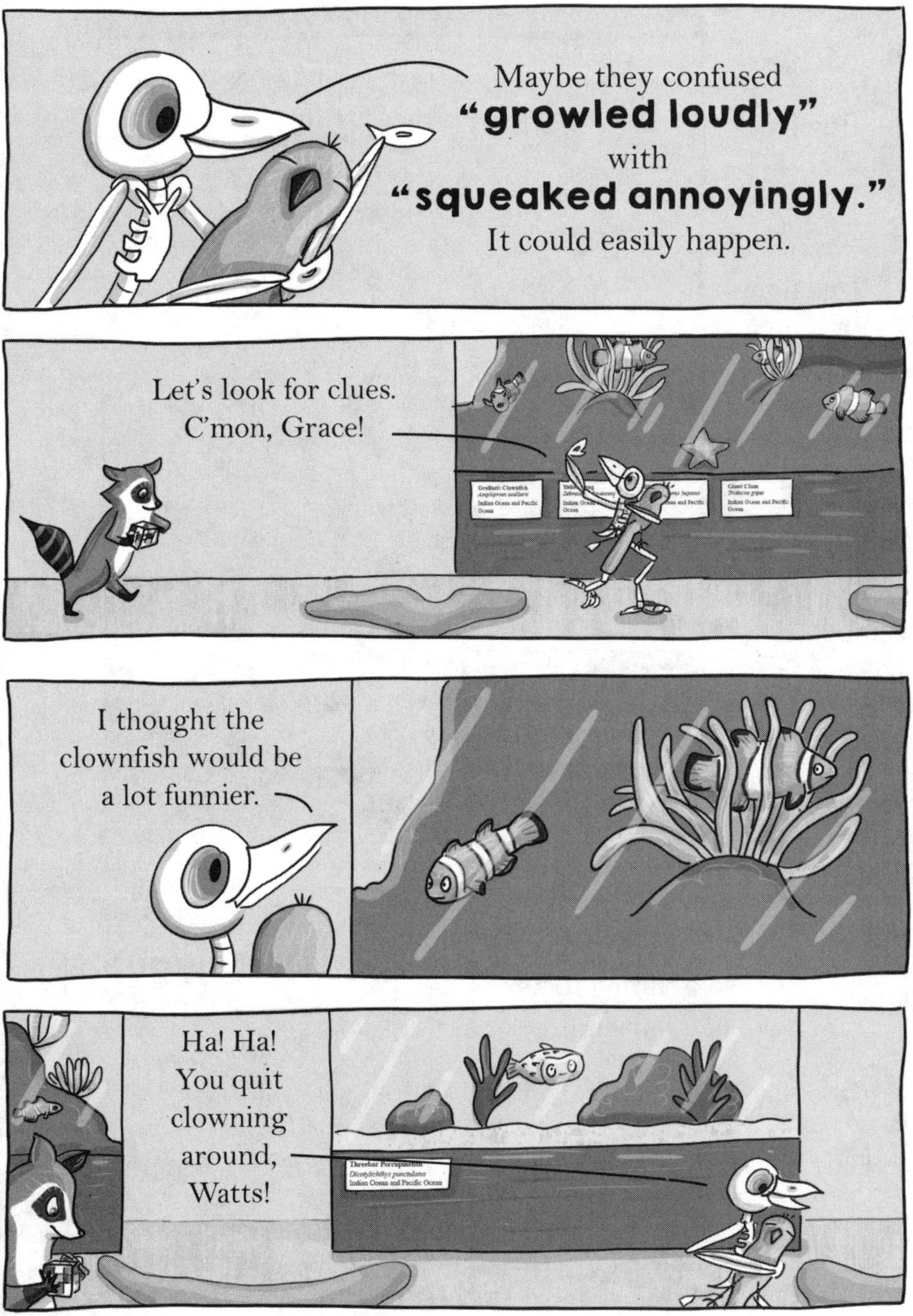
Maybe they confused **"growled loudly"** with **"squeaked annoyingly."** It could easily happen.
Let's look for clues. C'mon, Grace!
I thought the clownfish would be a lot funnier.
Ha! Ha! You quit clowning around, Watts!

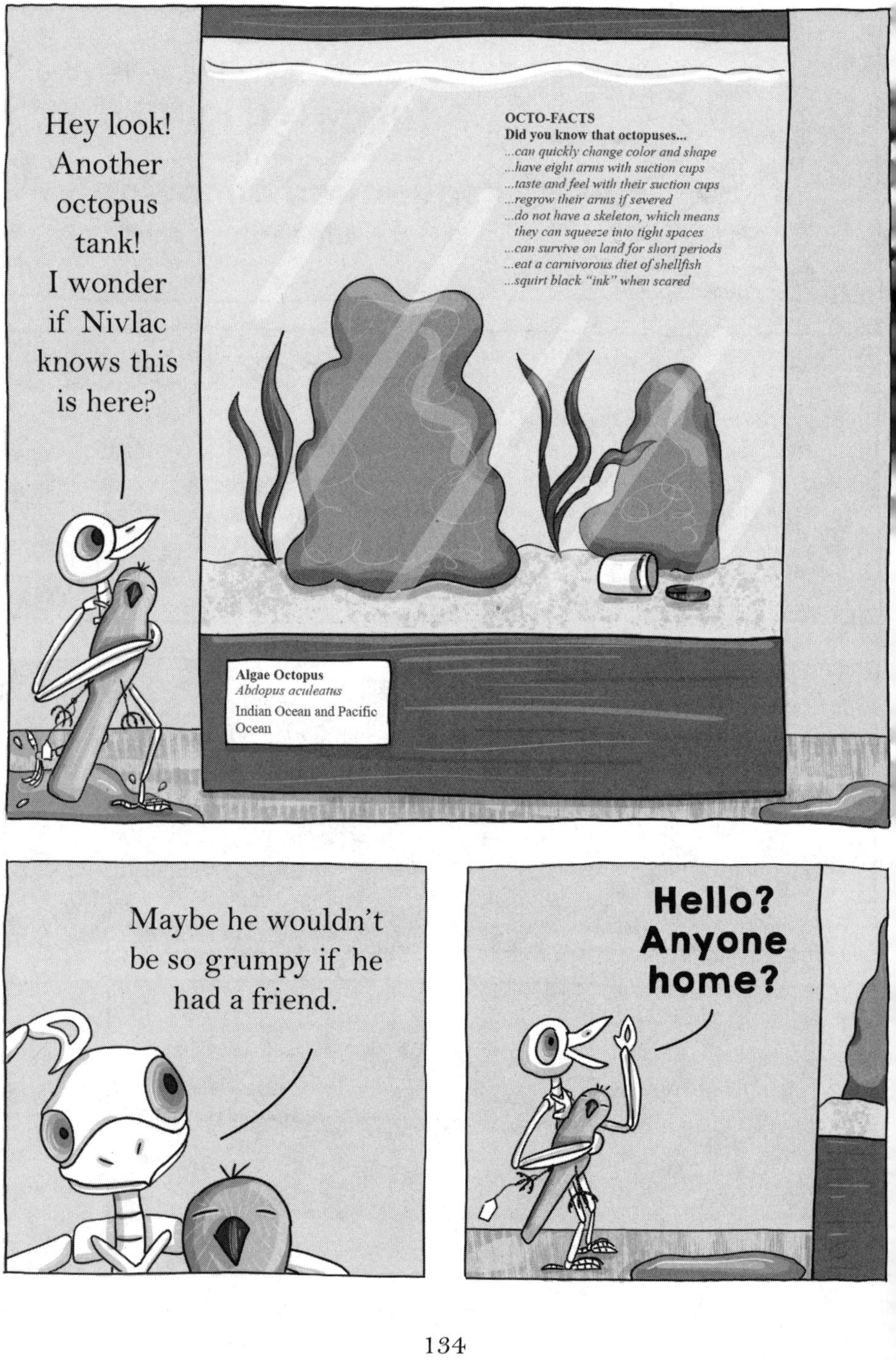
Hey look! Another octopus tank! I wonder if Nivlac knows this is here?
OCTO-FACTS
Did you know that octopuses...
...can quickly change color and shape
...have eight arms with suction cups
...taste and feel with their suction cups
...regrow their arms if severed
...do not have a skeleton, which means they can squeeze into tight spaces
...can survive on land for short periods
...eat a carnivorous diet of shellfish
...squirt black "ink" when scared
Algae Octopus
Abdopus aculeatus
Indian Ocean and Pacific Ocean
Maybe he wouldn't be so grumpy if he had a friend.
Hello? Anyone home?

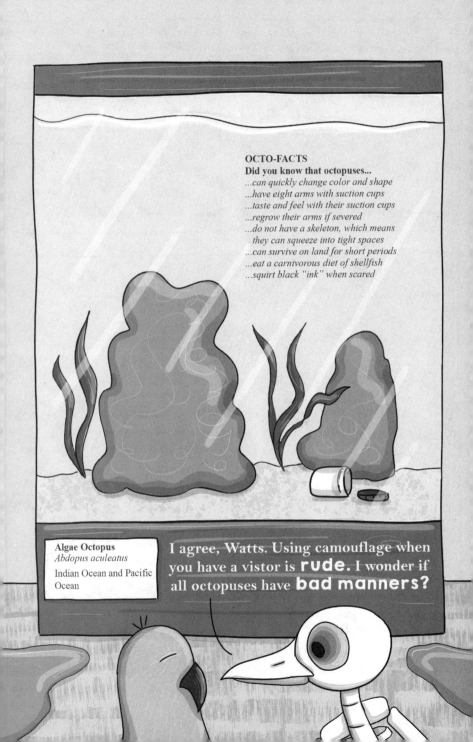

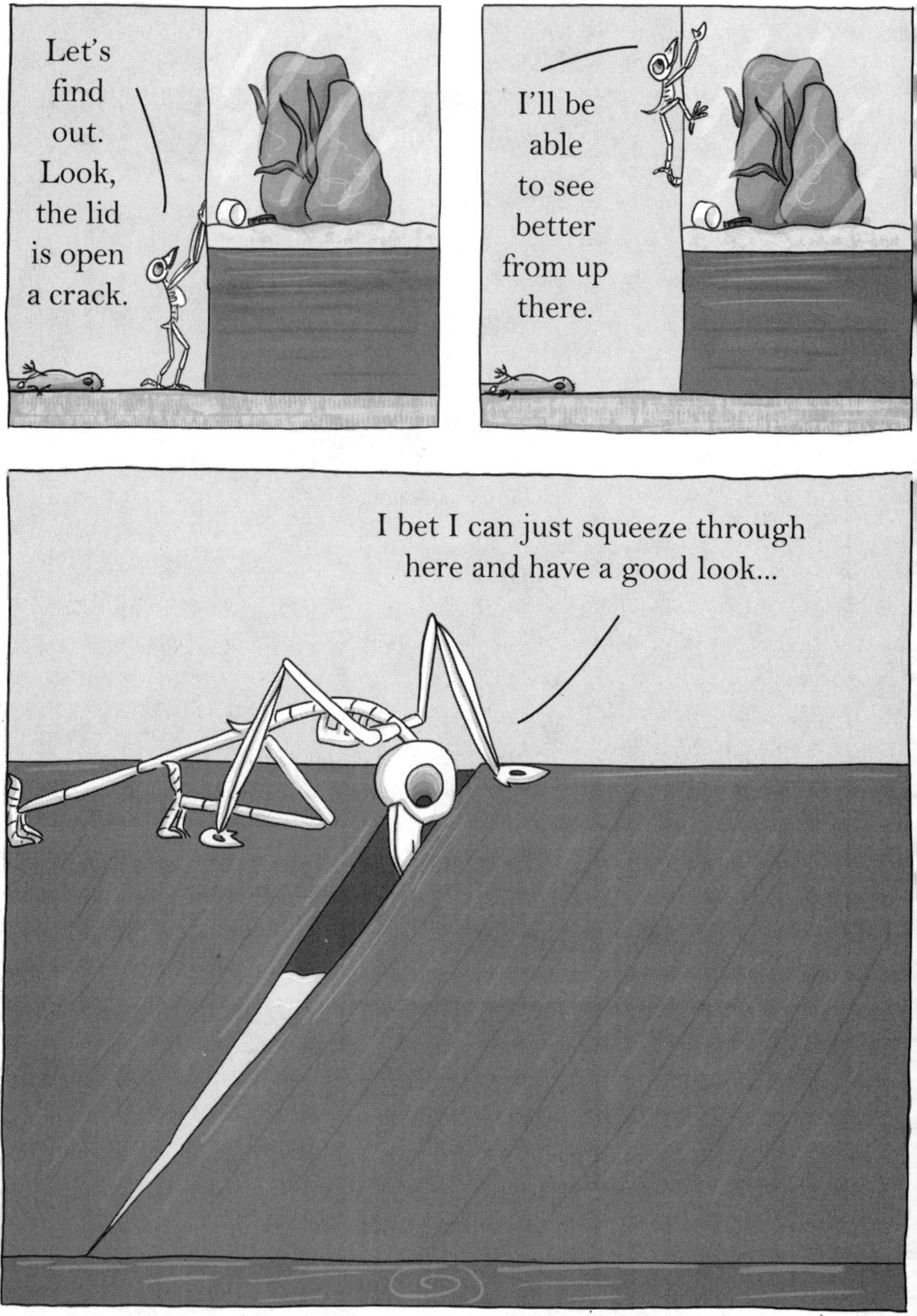
Let's find out. Look, the lid is open a crack.
I'll be able to see better from up there.
I bet I can just squeeze through here and have a good look...

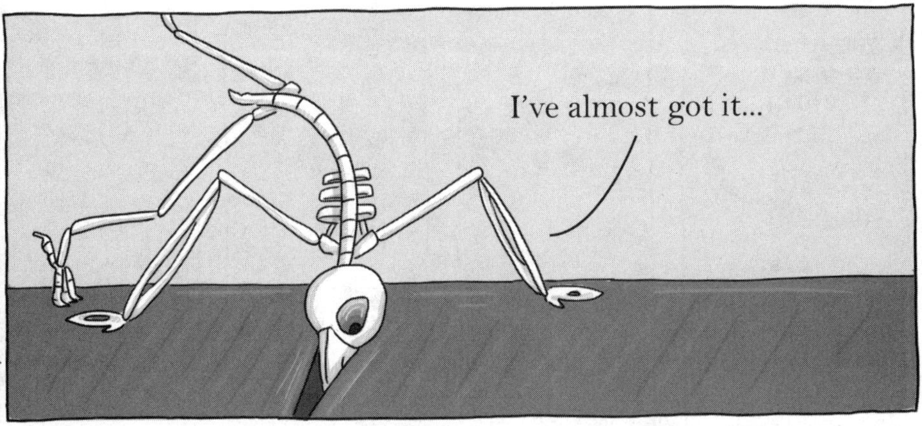
I've almost got it...

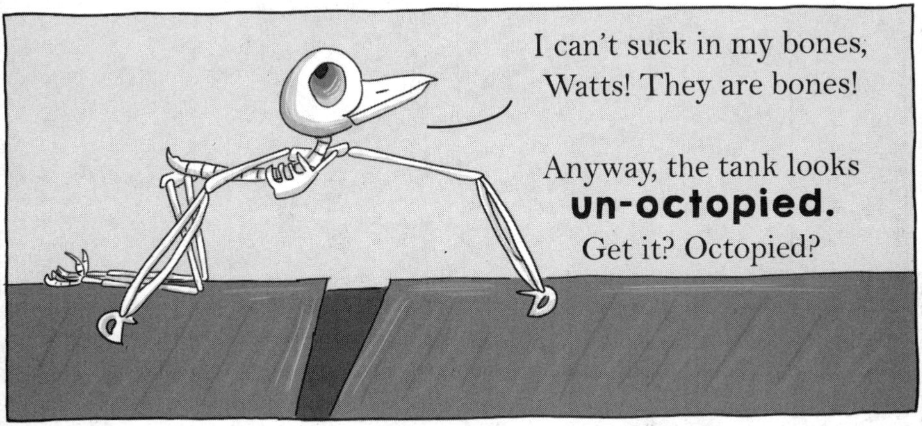
I can't suck in my bones, Watts! They are bones!
Anyway, the tank looks **un-octopied.** Get it? Octopied?

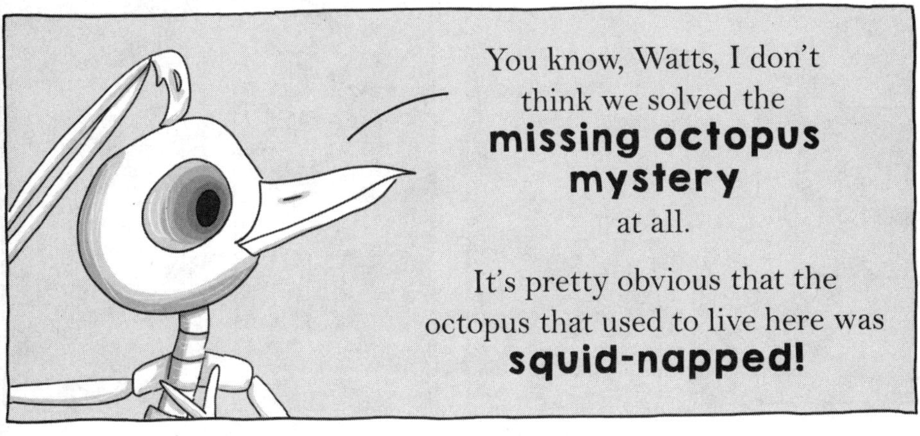
You know, Watts, I don't think we solved the **missing octopus mystery** at all.
It's pretty obvious that the octopus that used to live here was **squid-napped!**

We need to warn Nivlac!

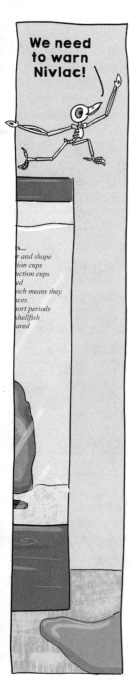

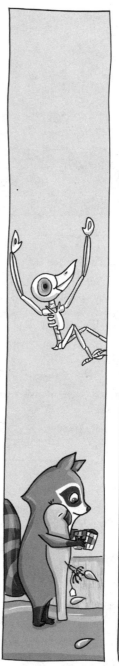

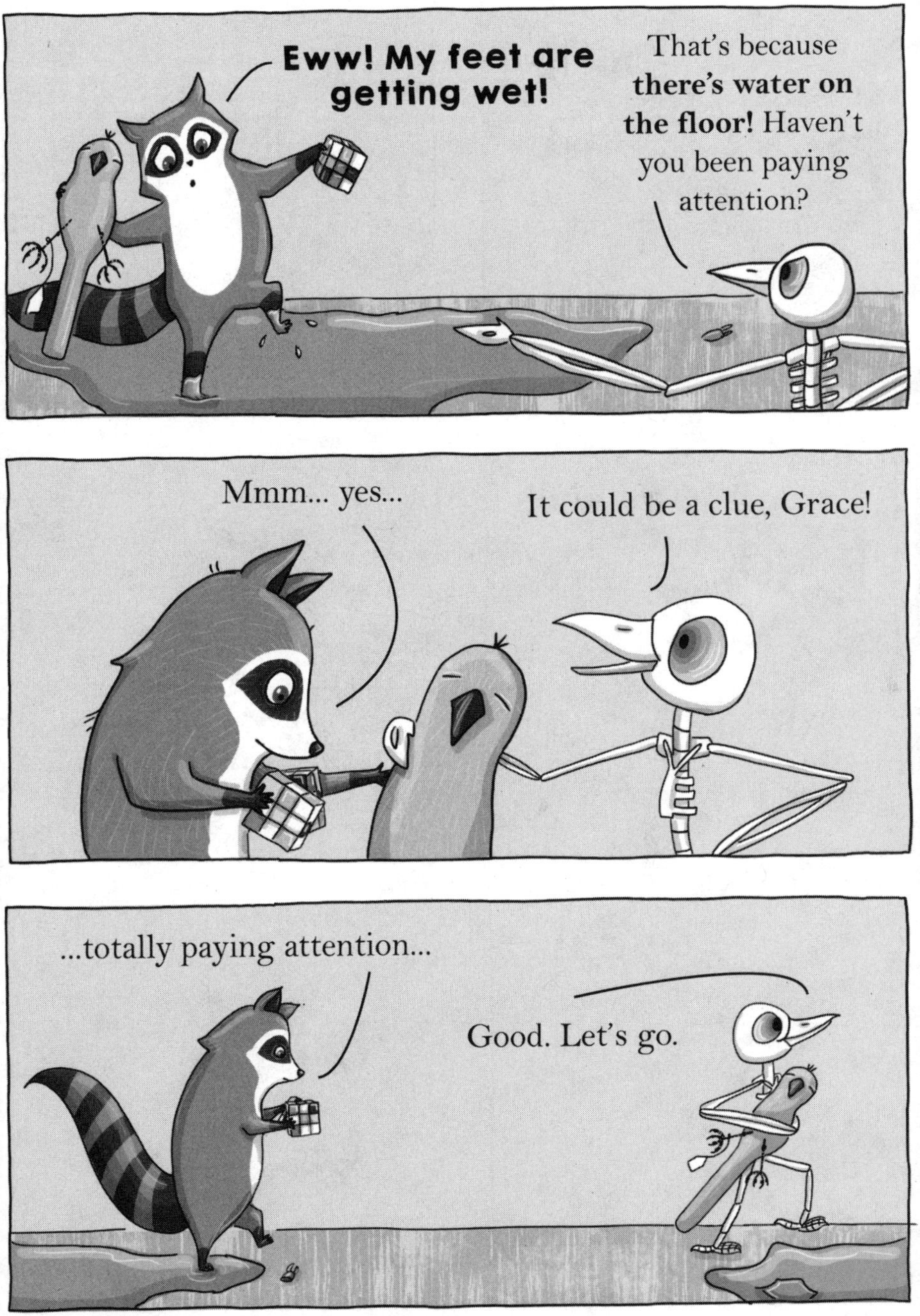
Eww! My feet are getting wet!
That's because **there's water on the floor!** Haven't you been paying attention?
Mmm... yes...
It could be a clue, Grace!
...totally paying attention...
Good. Let's go.

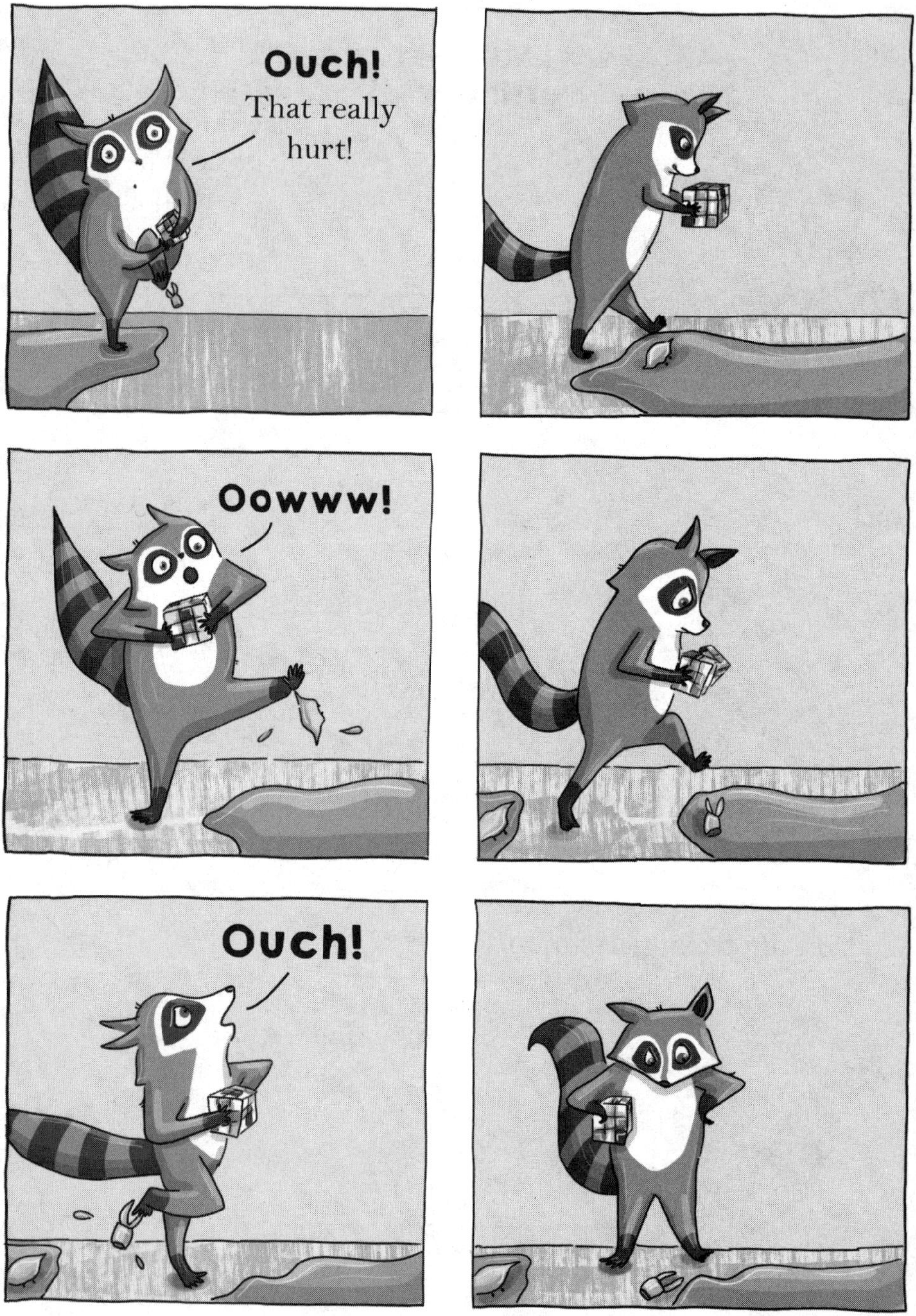
Ouch! That really hurt!
Oowww!
Ouch!

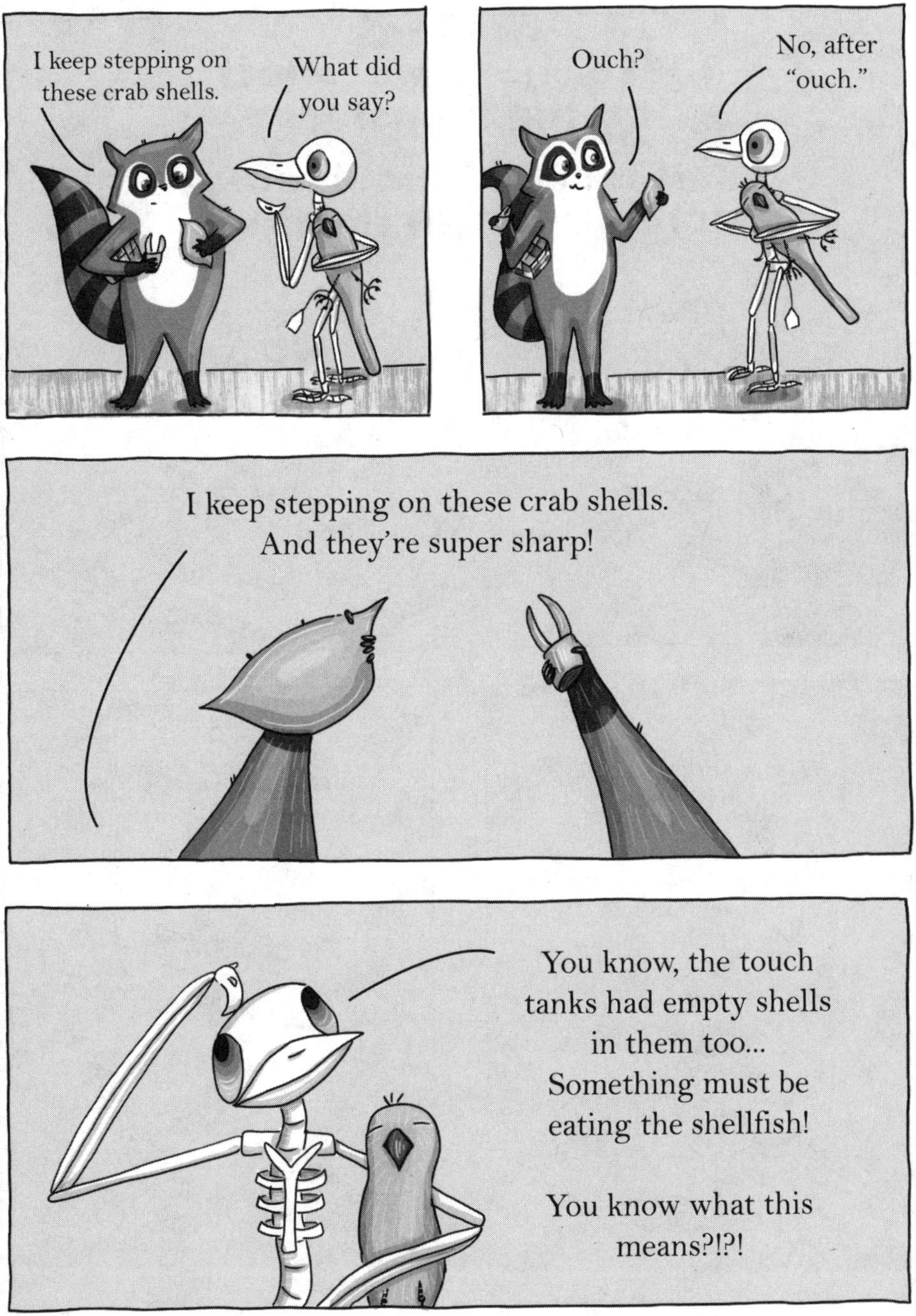
I keep stepping on these crab shells.
What did you say?
Ouch?
No, after "ouch."
I keep stepping on these crab shells. And they're super sharp!
You know, the touch tanks had empty shells in them too... Something must be eating the shellfish!
You know what this means?!?!

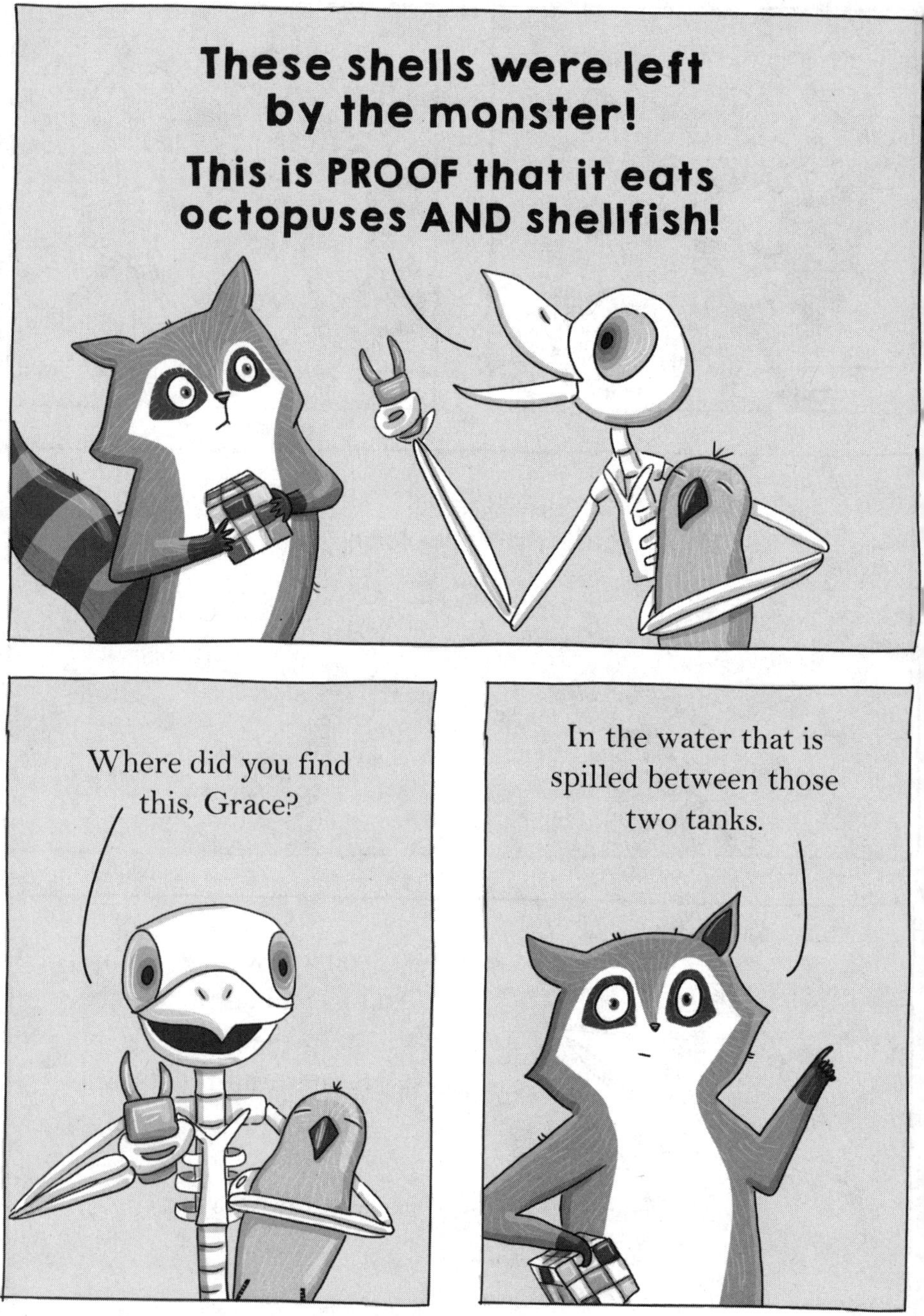
These shells were left by the monster!
This is PROOF that it eats octopuses AND shellfish!
Where did you find this, Grace?
In the water that is spilled between those two tanks.

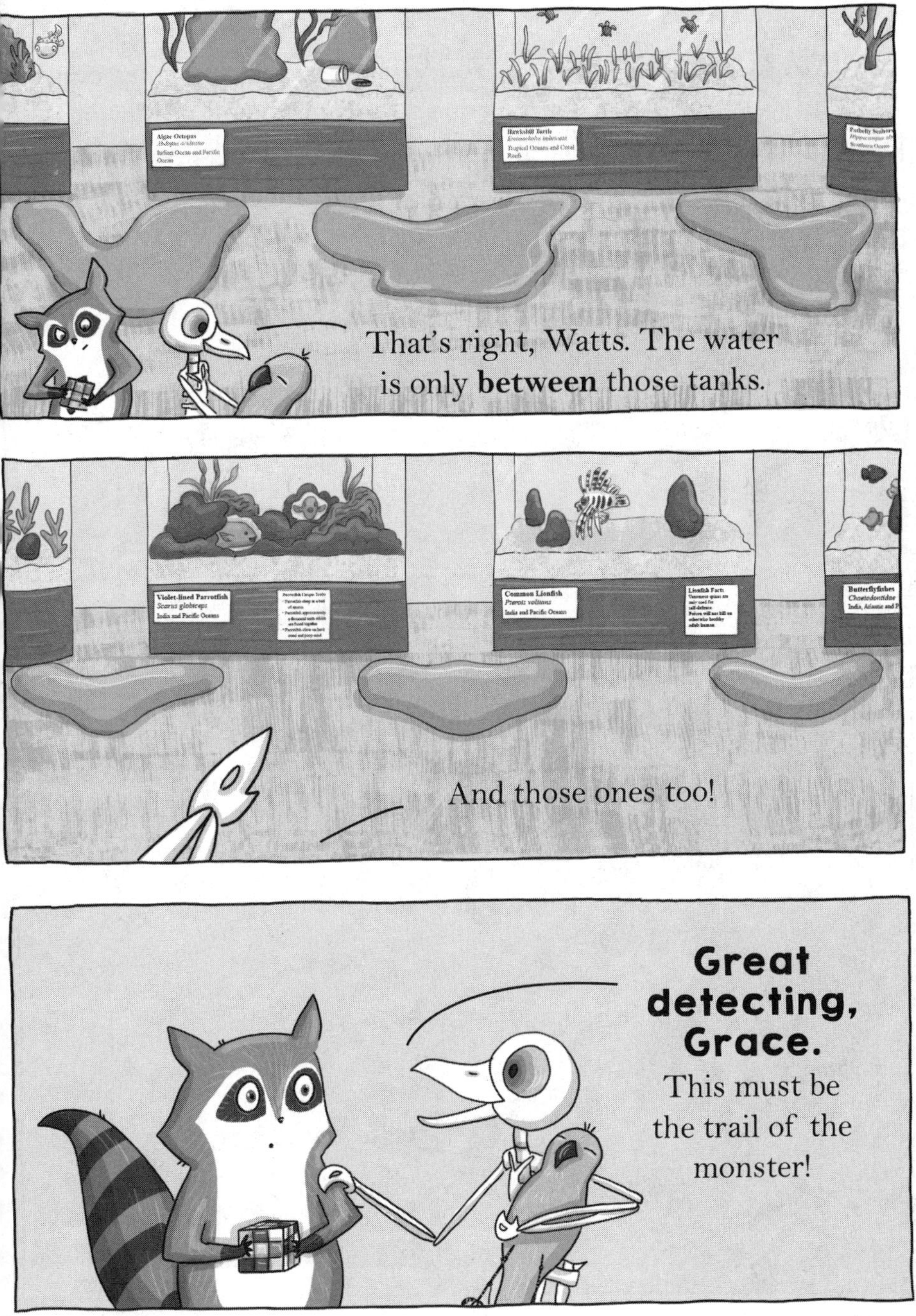
That's right, Watts. The water is only **between** those tanks.
And those ones too!
Great detecting, Grace. This must be the trail of the monster!

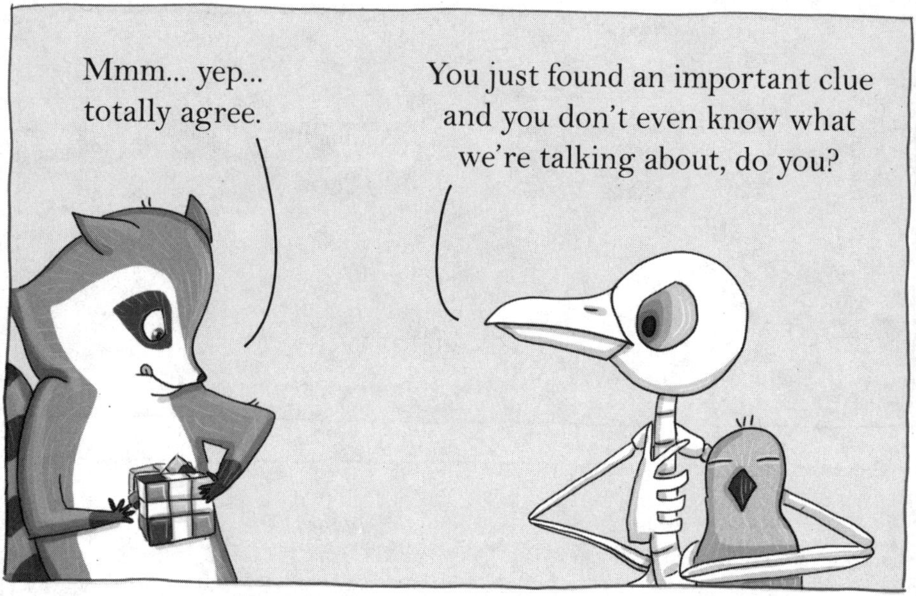
Mmm... yep...
totally agree.
You just found an important clue and you don't even know what we're talking about, do you?

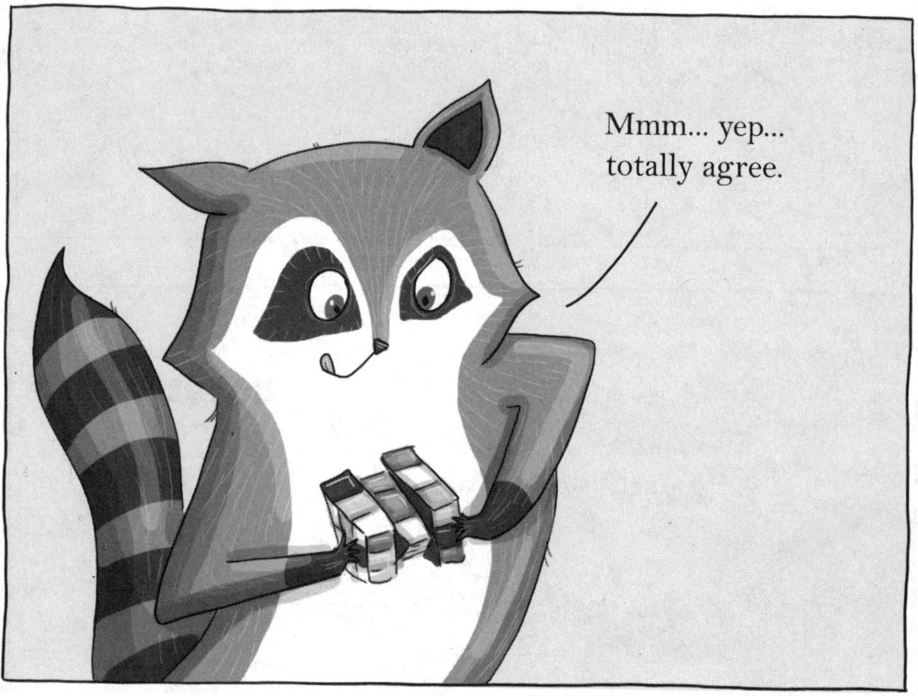
Mmm... yep...
totally agree.

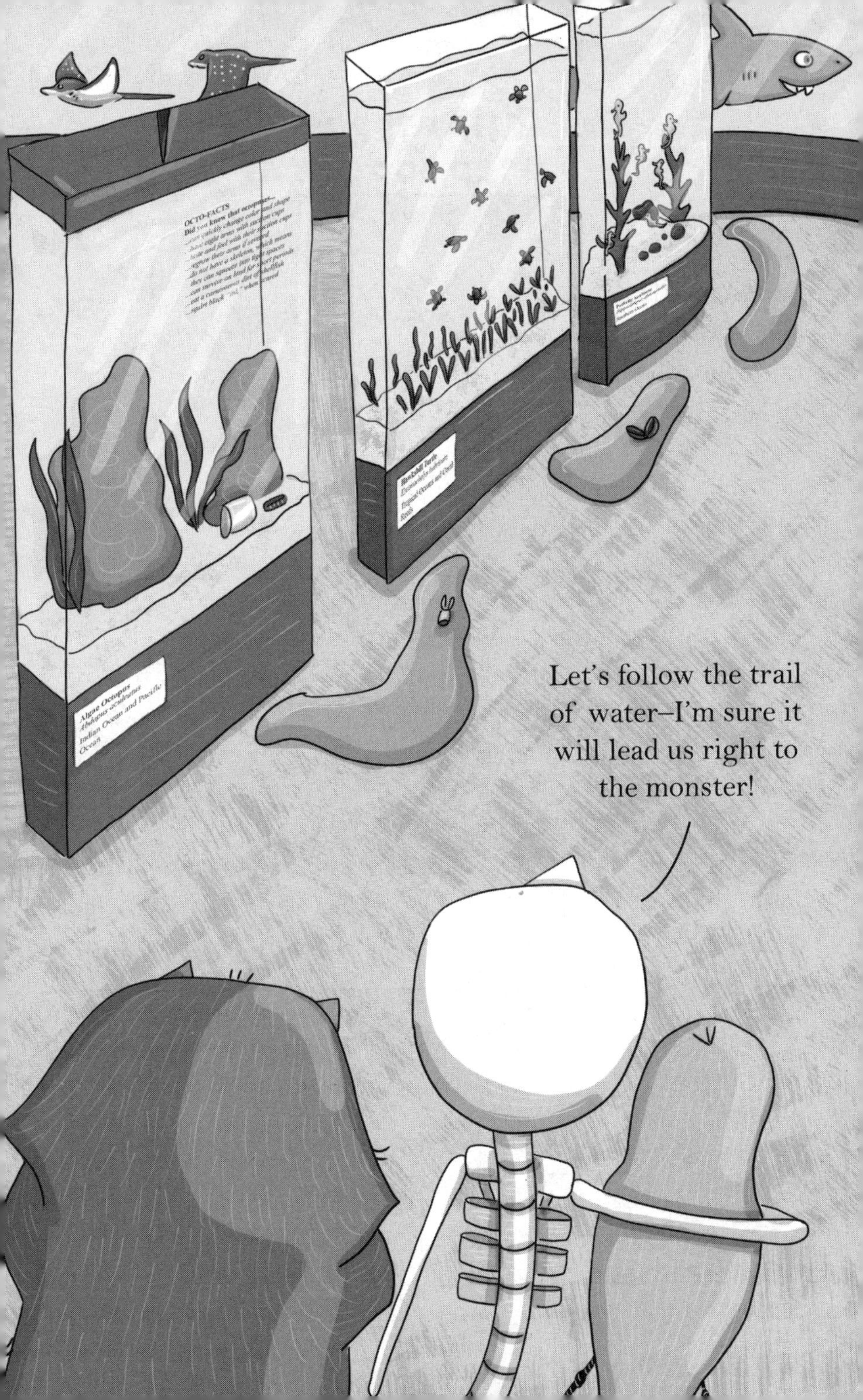
Let's follow the trail of water–I'm sure it will lead us right to the monster!

CHAPTER 6
Deep Boo Sea

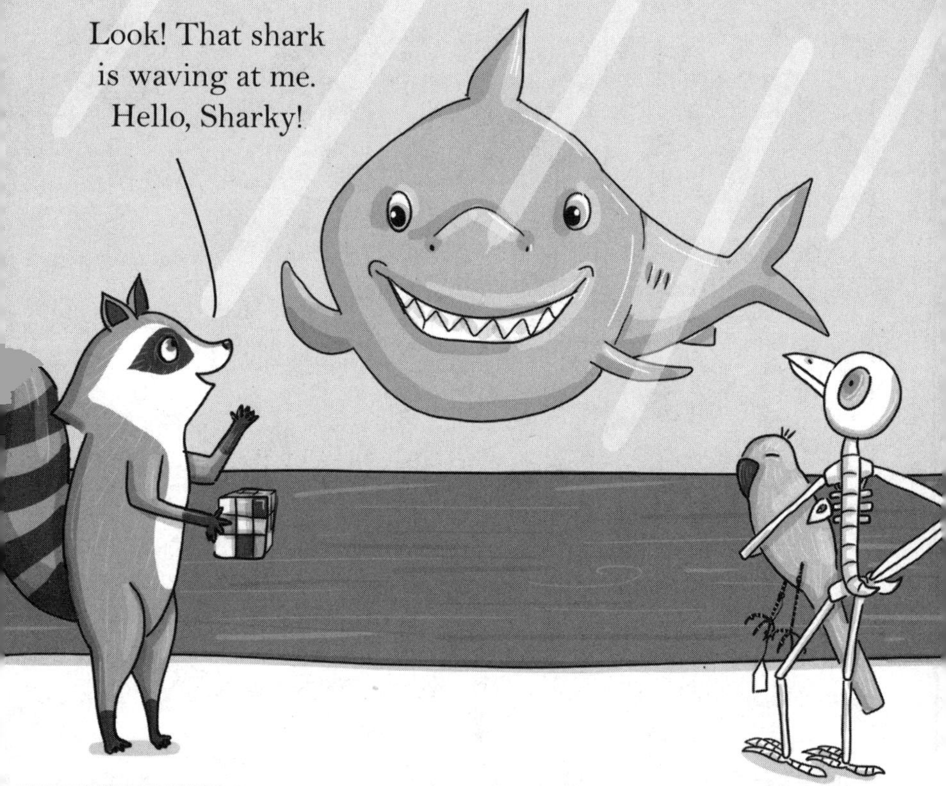

Look! That shark is waving at me. Hello, Sharky!

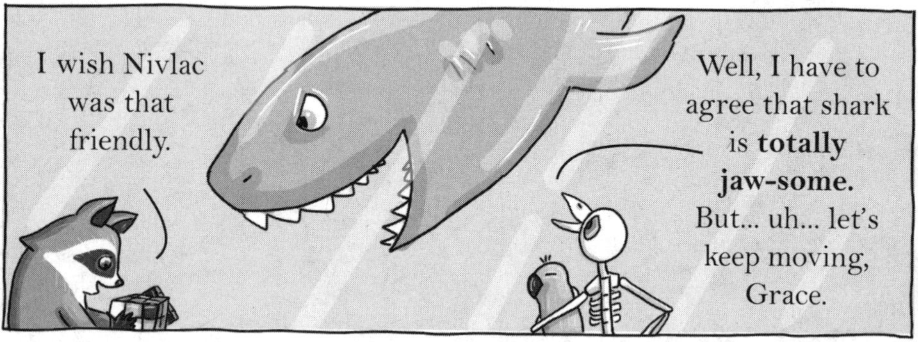

I wish Nivlac was that friendly.
Well, I have to agree that shark is **totally jaw-some.** But... uh... let's keep moving, Grace.

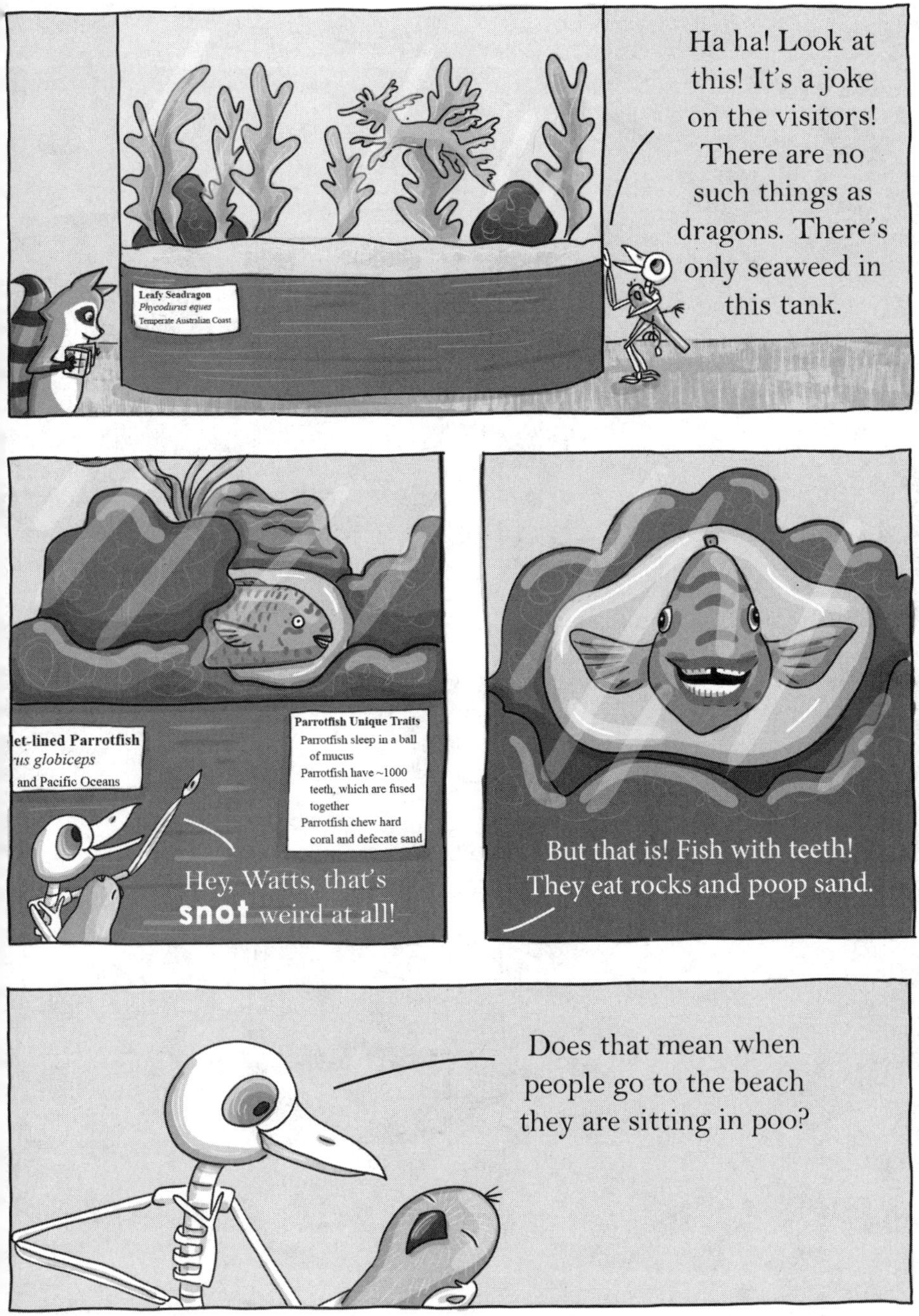
Ha ha! Look at this! It's a joke on the visitors! There are no such things as dragons. There's only seaweed in this tank.
Leafy Seadragon
Phycodurus eques
Temperate Australian Coast
et-lined Parrotfish
us globiceps
and Pacific Oceans
Parrotfish Unique Traits
Parrotfish sleep in a ball of mucus
Parrotfish have ~1000 teeth, which are fused together
Parrotfish chew hard coral and defecate sand
Hey, Watts, that's **snot** weird at all!
But that is! Fish with teeth! They eat rocks and poop sand.
Does that mean when people go to the beach they are sitting in poo?

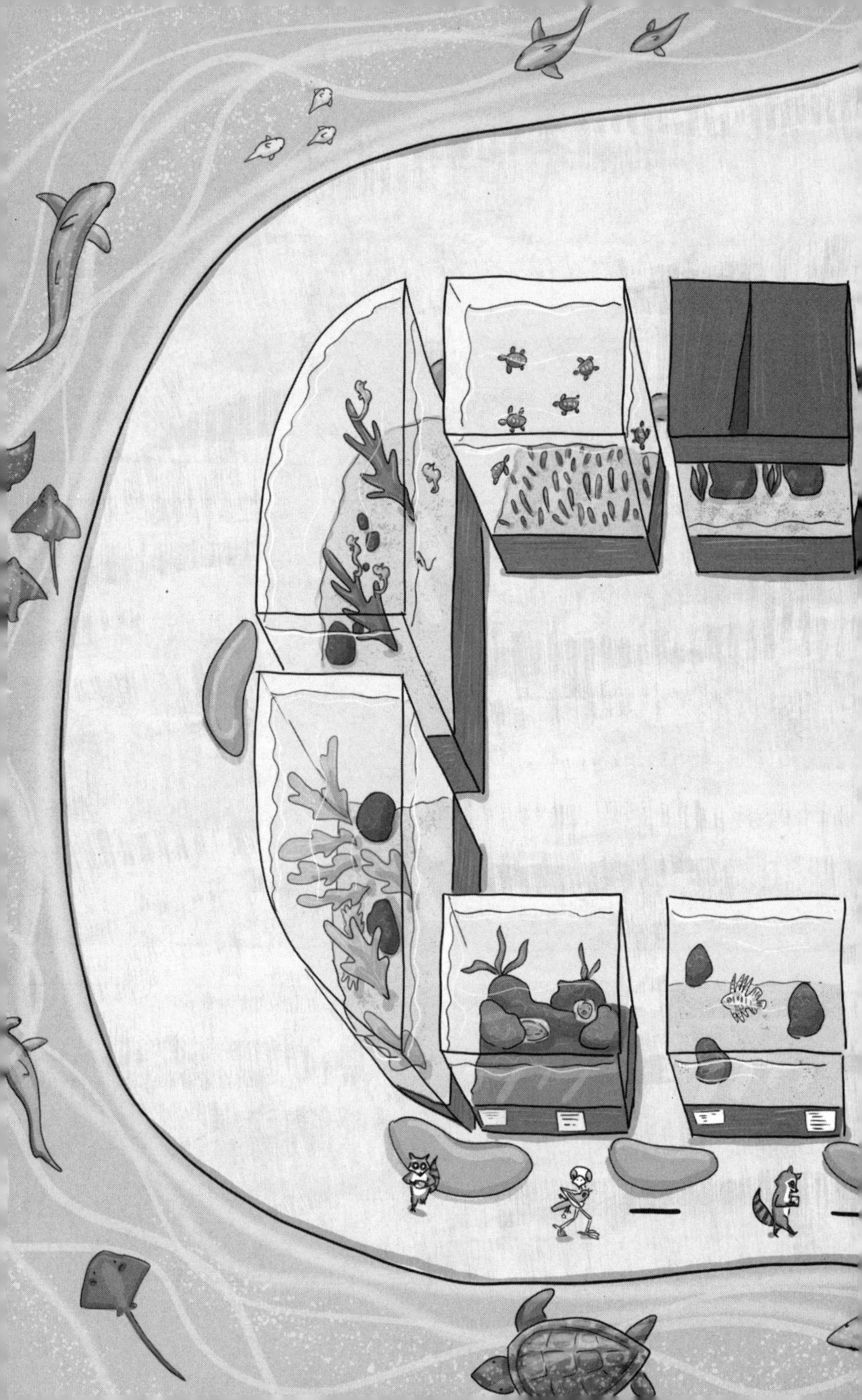

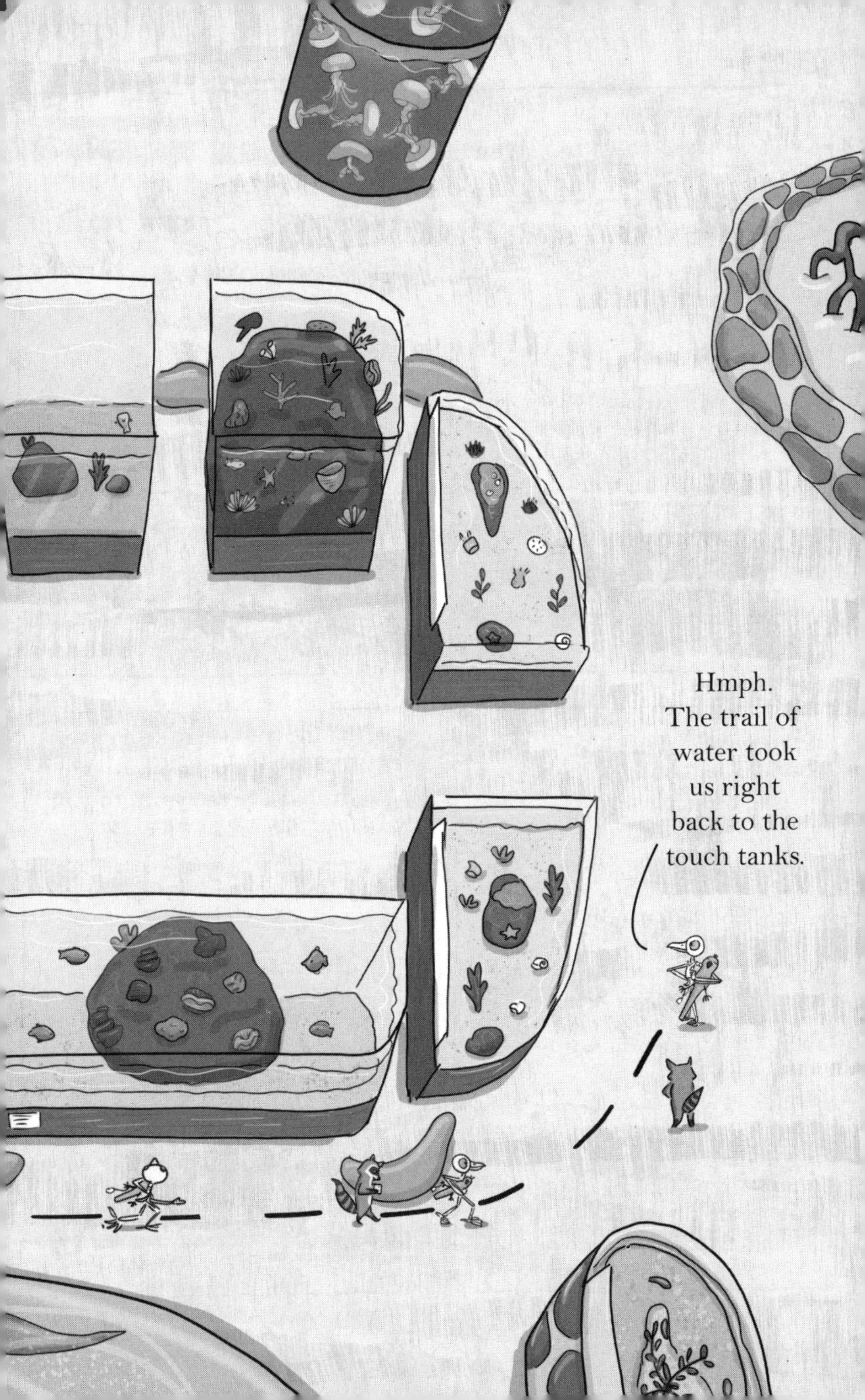
Hmph. The trail of water took us right back to the touch tanks.

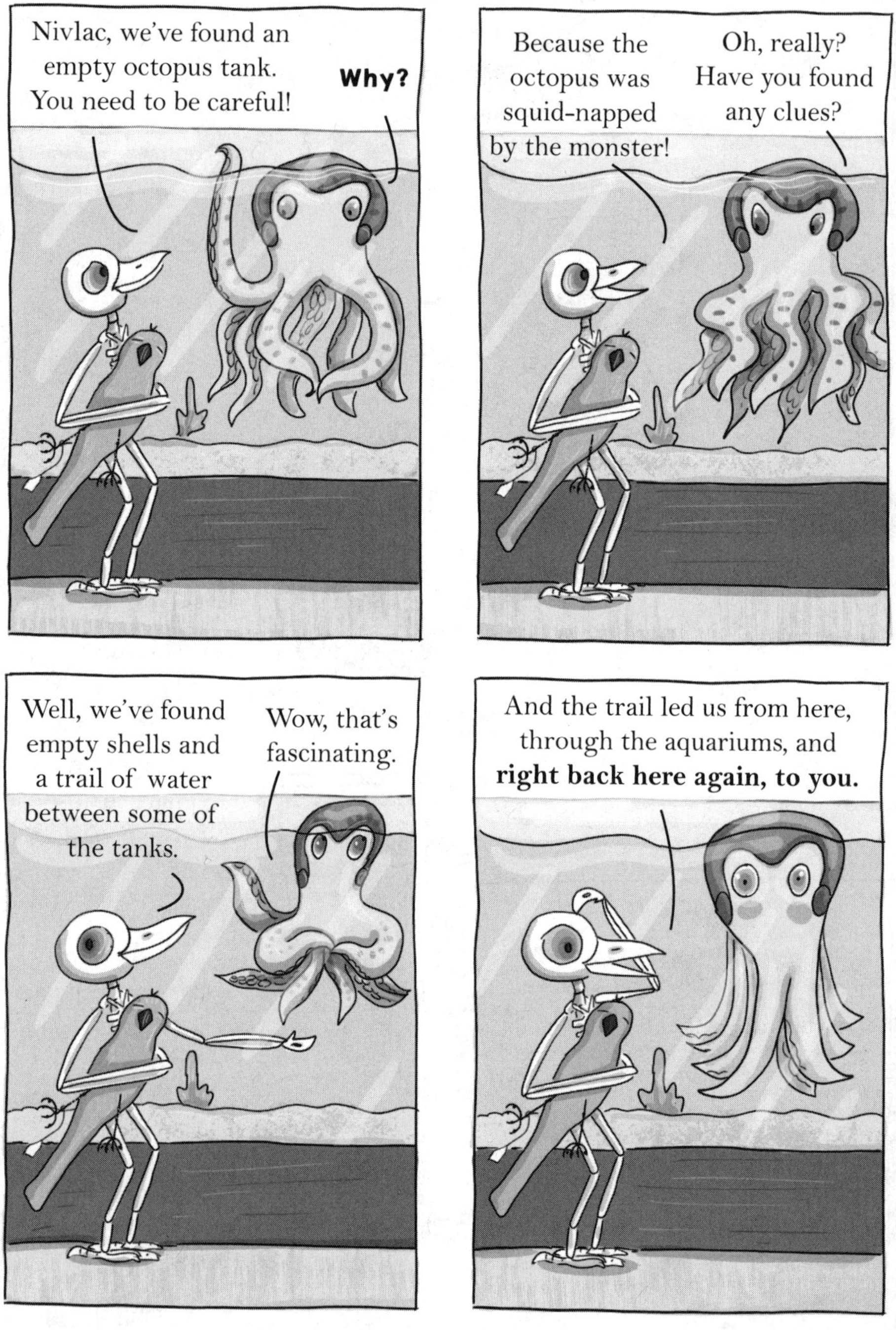
Nivlac, we've found an empty octopus tank. You need to be careful!
Why?
Because the octopus was squid-napped by the monster!
Oh, really? Have you found any clues?
Well, we've found empty shells and a trail of water between some of the tanks.
Wow, that's fascinating.
And the trail led us from here, through the aquariums, and **right back here again, to you.**

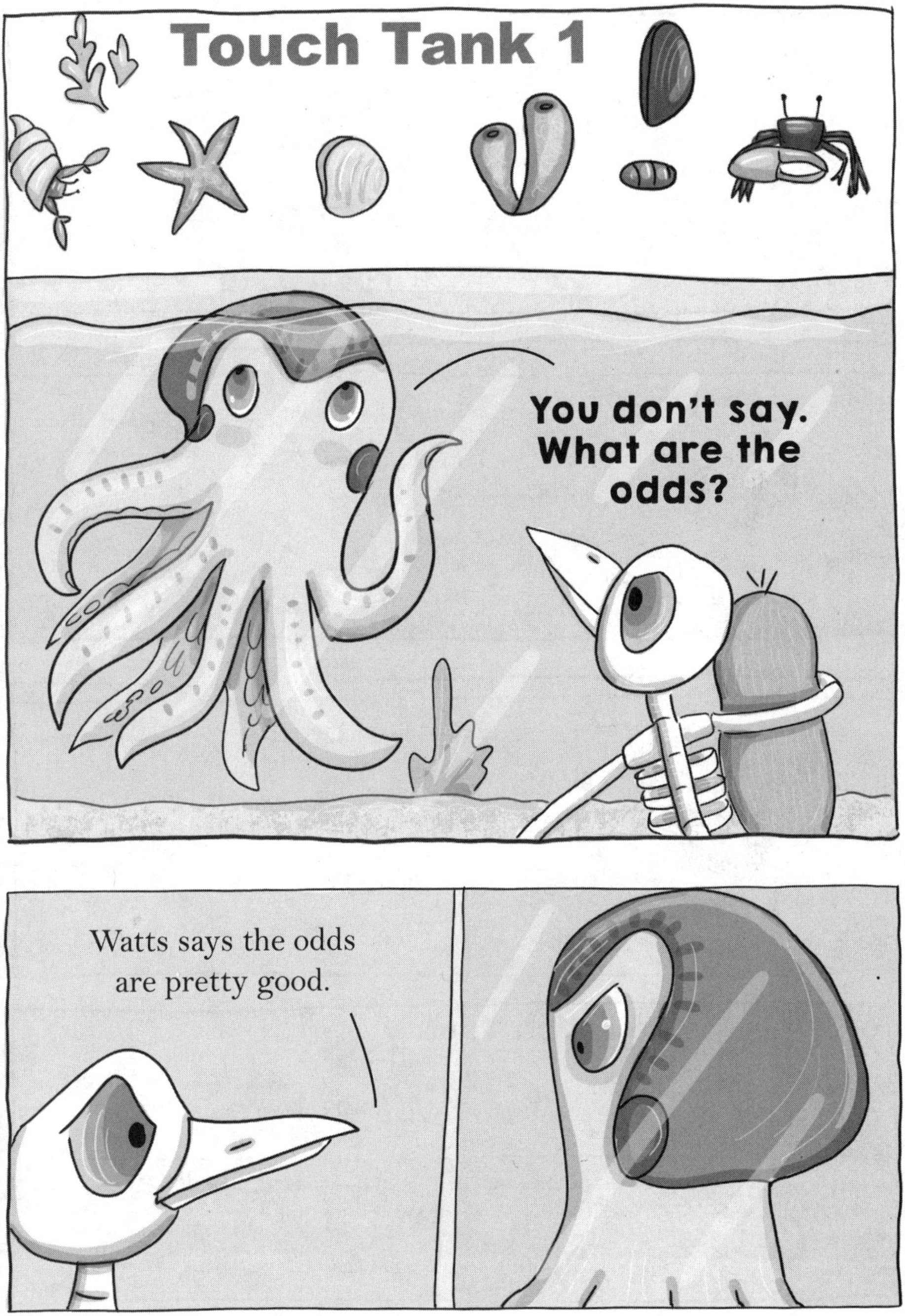
Touch Tank 1
You don't say. What are the odds?
Watts says the odds are pretty good.

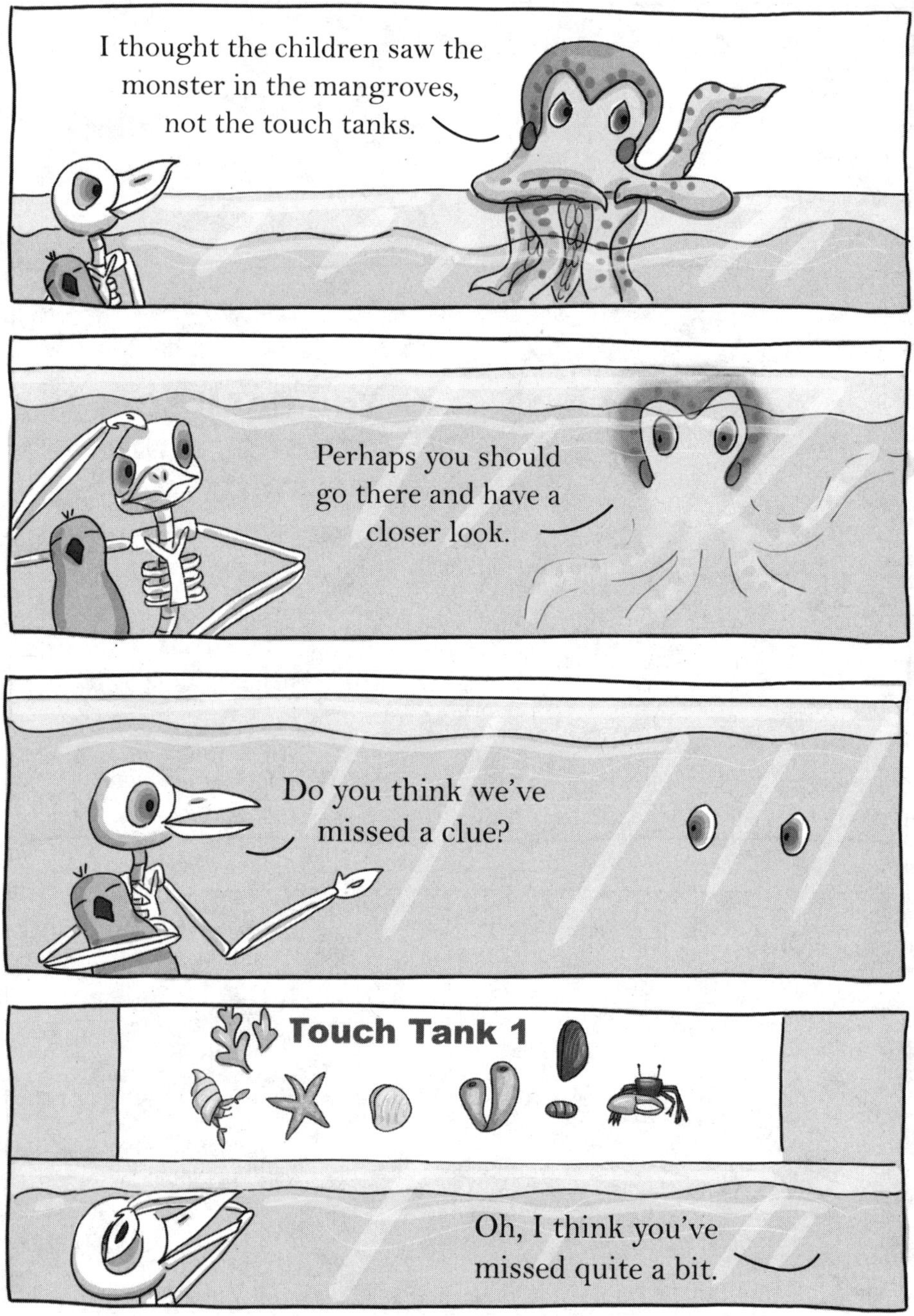
I thought the children saw the monster in the mangroves, not the touch tanks.
Perhaps you should go there and have a closer look.
Do you think we've missed a clue?
Touch Tank 1
Oh, I think you've missed quite a bit.

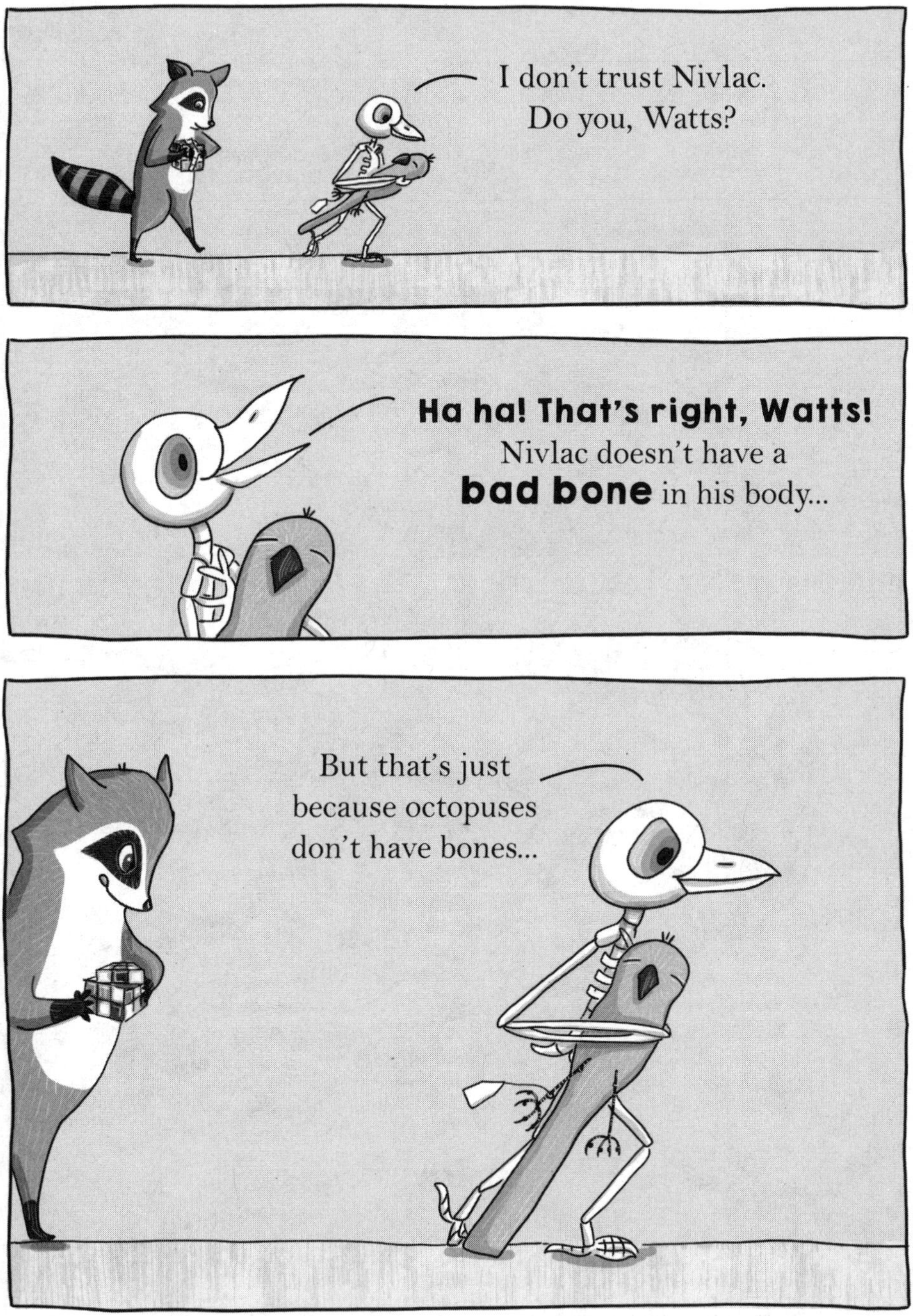
I don't trust Nivlac. Do you, Watts?
Ha ha! That's right, Watts! Nivlac doesn't have a bad bone in his body...
But that's just because octopuses don't have bones...

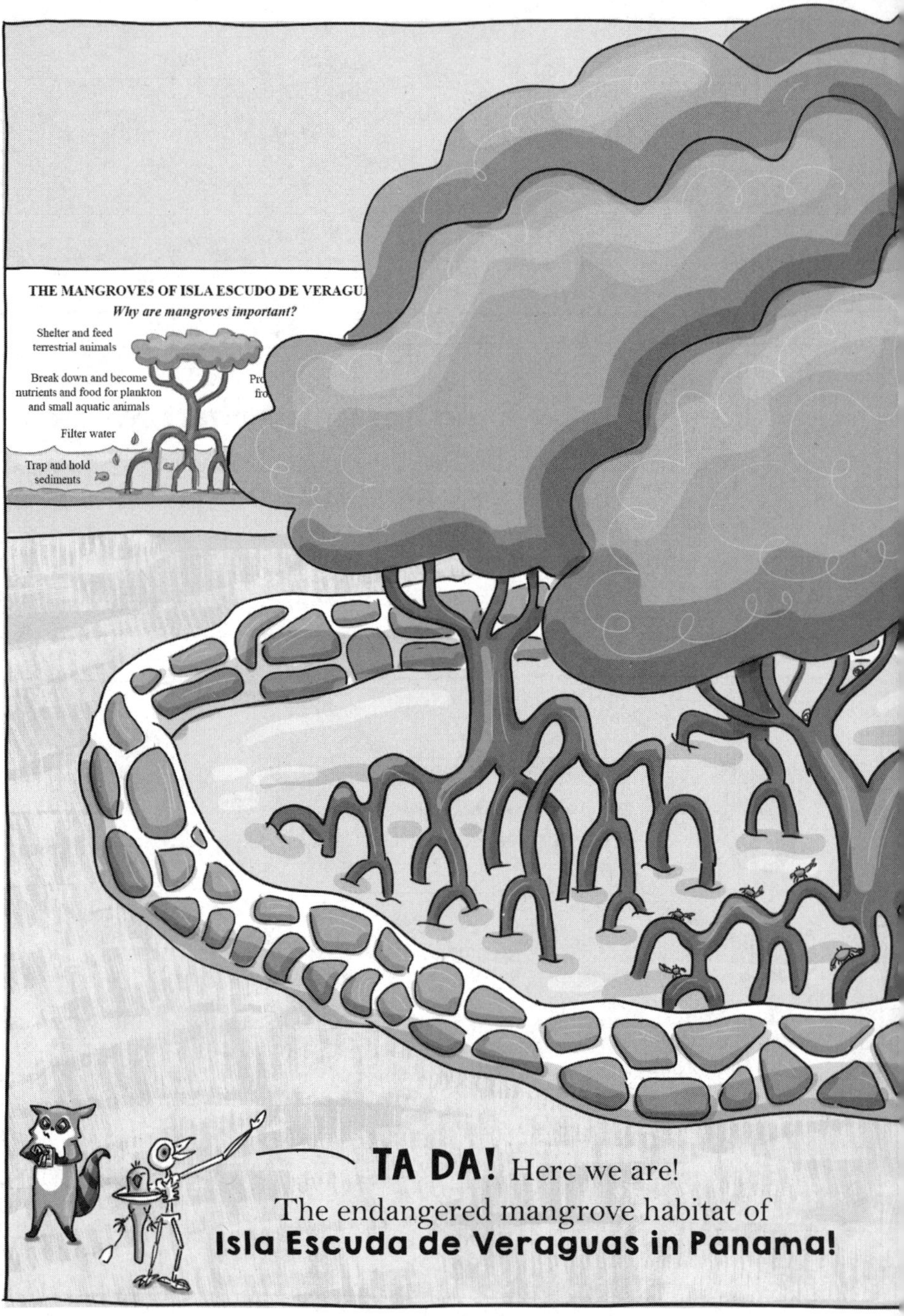

THE MANGROVES OF ISLA ESCUDO DE VERAGU
Why are mangroves important?
Shelter and feed terrestrial animals
Break down and become nutrients and food for plankton and small aquatic animals
Filter water
Trap and hold sediments
TA DA! Here we are!
The endangered mangrove habitat of
Isla Escuda de Veraguas in Panama!

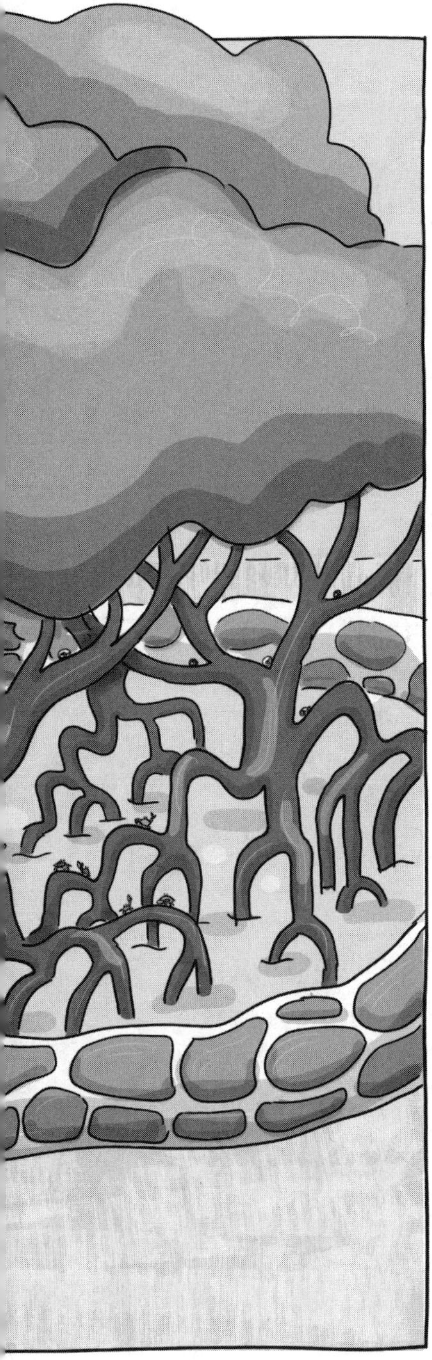

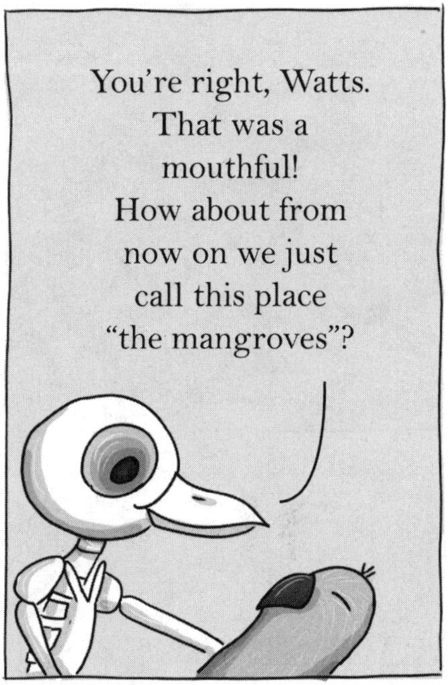
You're right, Watts. That was a mouthful! How about from now on we just call this place "the mangroves"?

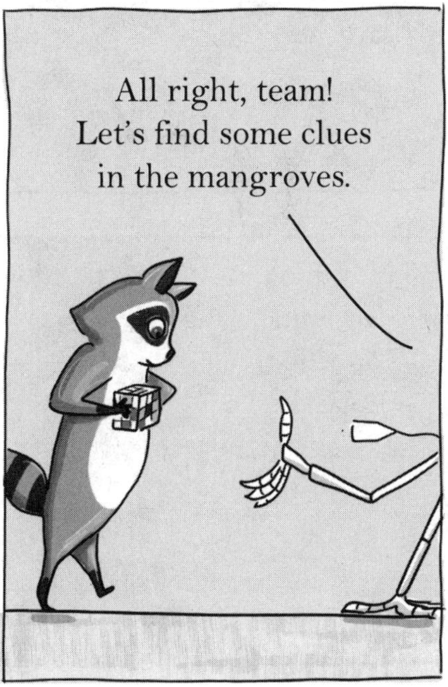
All right, team! Let's find some clues in the mangroves.

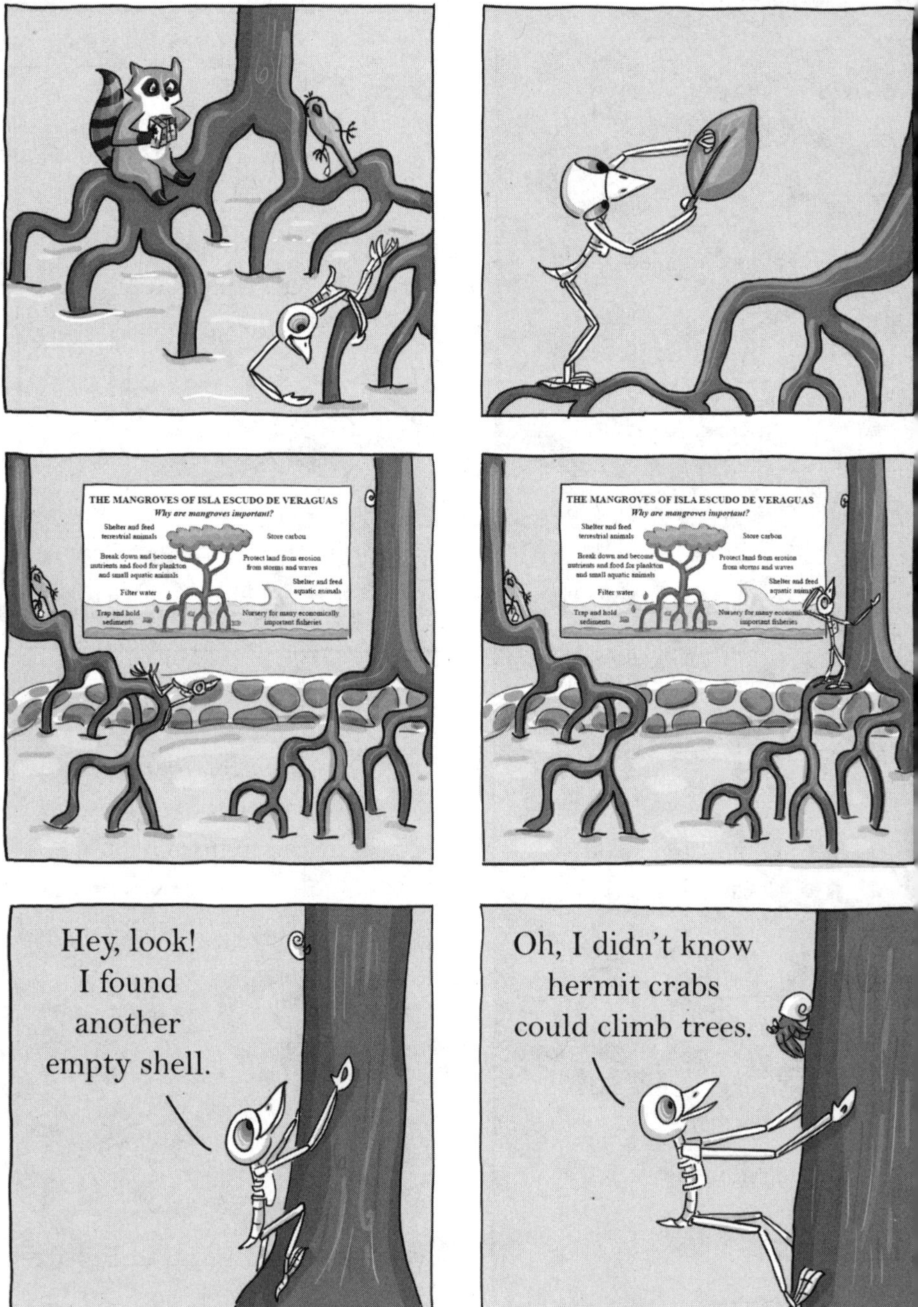
THE MANGROVES OF ISLA ESCUDO DE VERAGUAS
Why are mangroves important?
Shelter and feed terrestrial animals
Store carbon
Break down and become nutrients and food for plankton and small aquatic animals
Protect land from erosion from storms and waves
Shelter and feed aquatic animals
Filter water
Trap and hold sediments
Nursery for many economically important fisheries
Hey, look! I found another empty shell.
Oh, I didn't know hermit crabs could climb trees.

Hello!

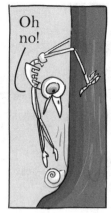

Oh no!

I can't look!

OH NO! I've killed the hermit crab.

Poor little dead hermit crab.

Wow! Would you look at that? It's OK!

There you go. You can join your sisters and brothers... and tons of cousins... My, you have a big family!

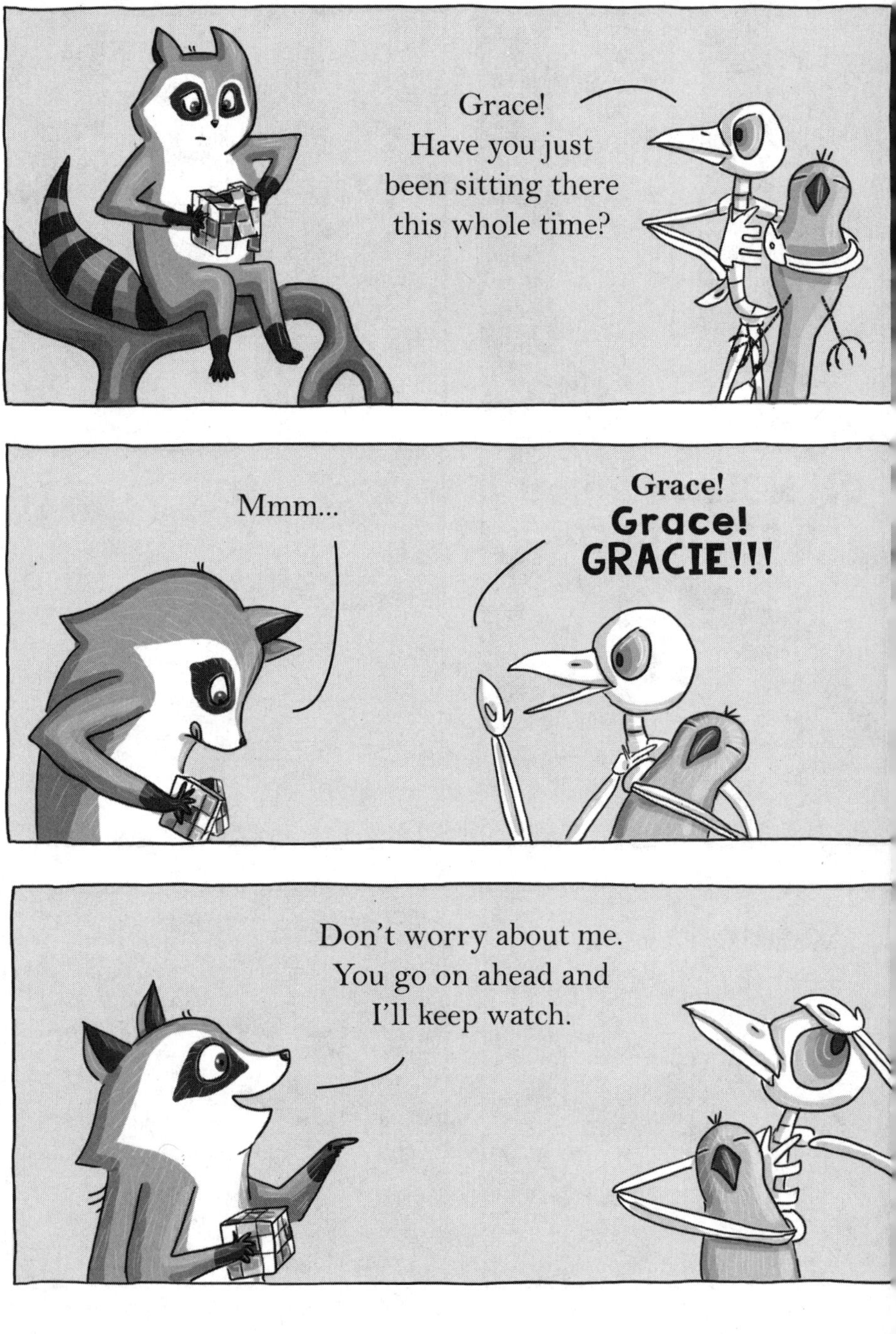
Grace!
Have you just
been sitting there
this whole time?
Mmm...
Grace!
Grace!
GRACIE!!!
Don't worry about me.
You go on ahead and
I'll keep watch.

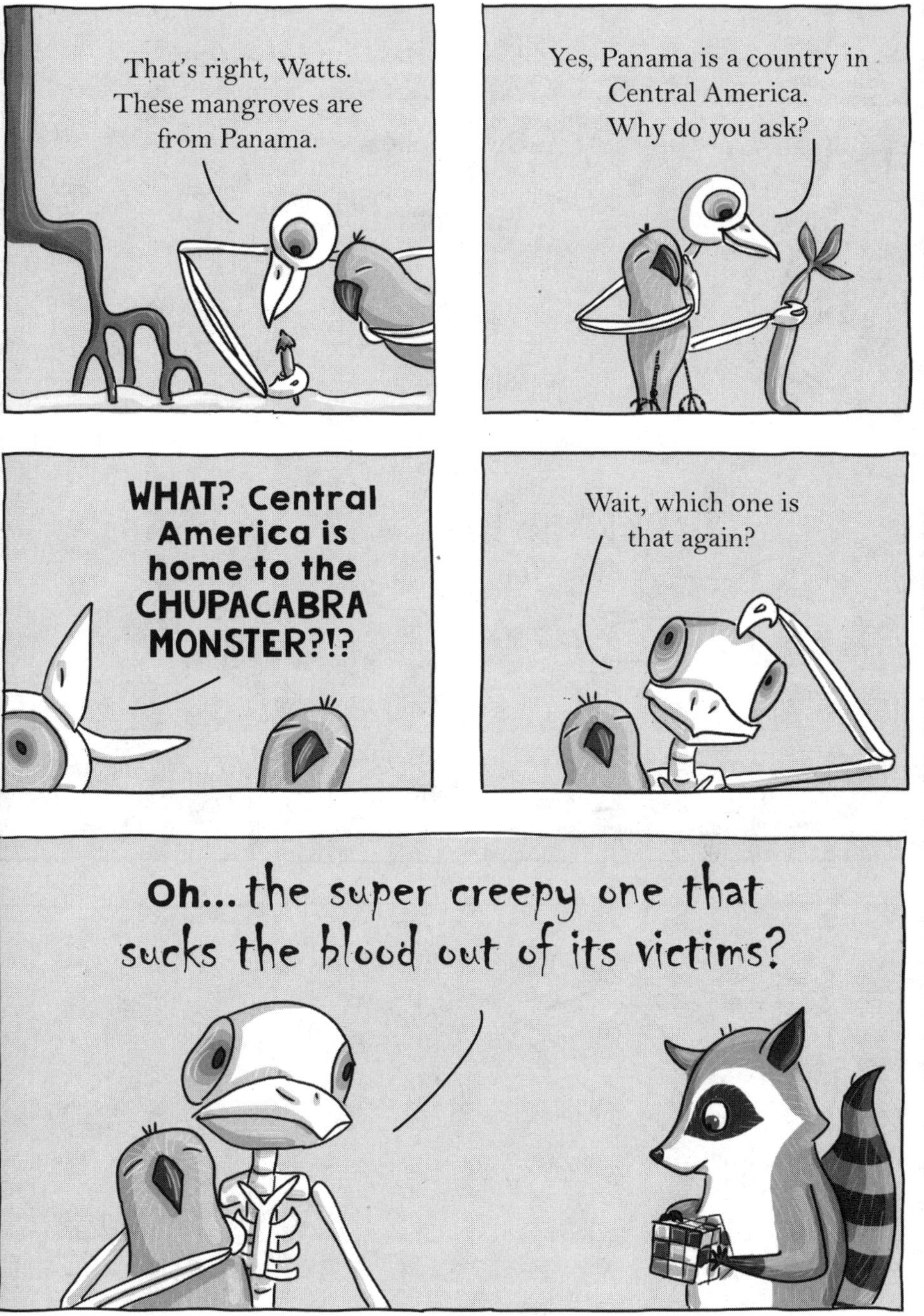
That's right, Watts. These mangroves are from Panama.
Yes, Panama is a country in Central America. Why do you ask?
WHAT? Central America is home to the CHUPACABRA MONSTER?!?
Wait, which one is that again?
Oh... the super creepy one that sucks the blood out of its victims?

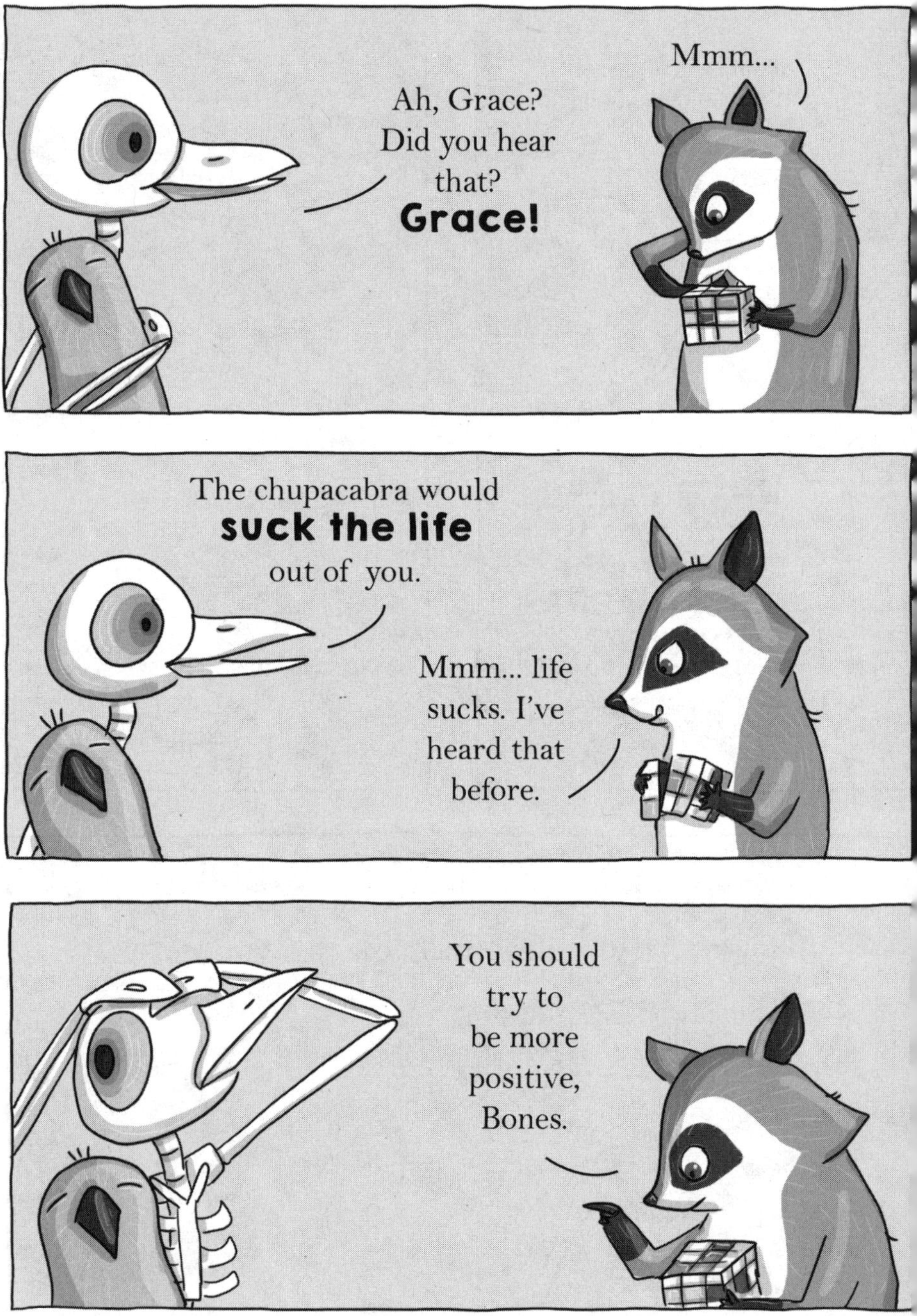
Ah, Grace? Did you hear that? **Grace!**
Mmm...
The chupacabra would **suck the life** out of you.
Mmm... life sucks. I've heard that before.
You should try to be more positive, Bones.

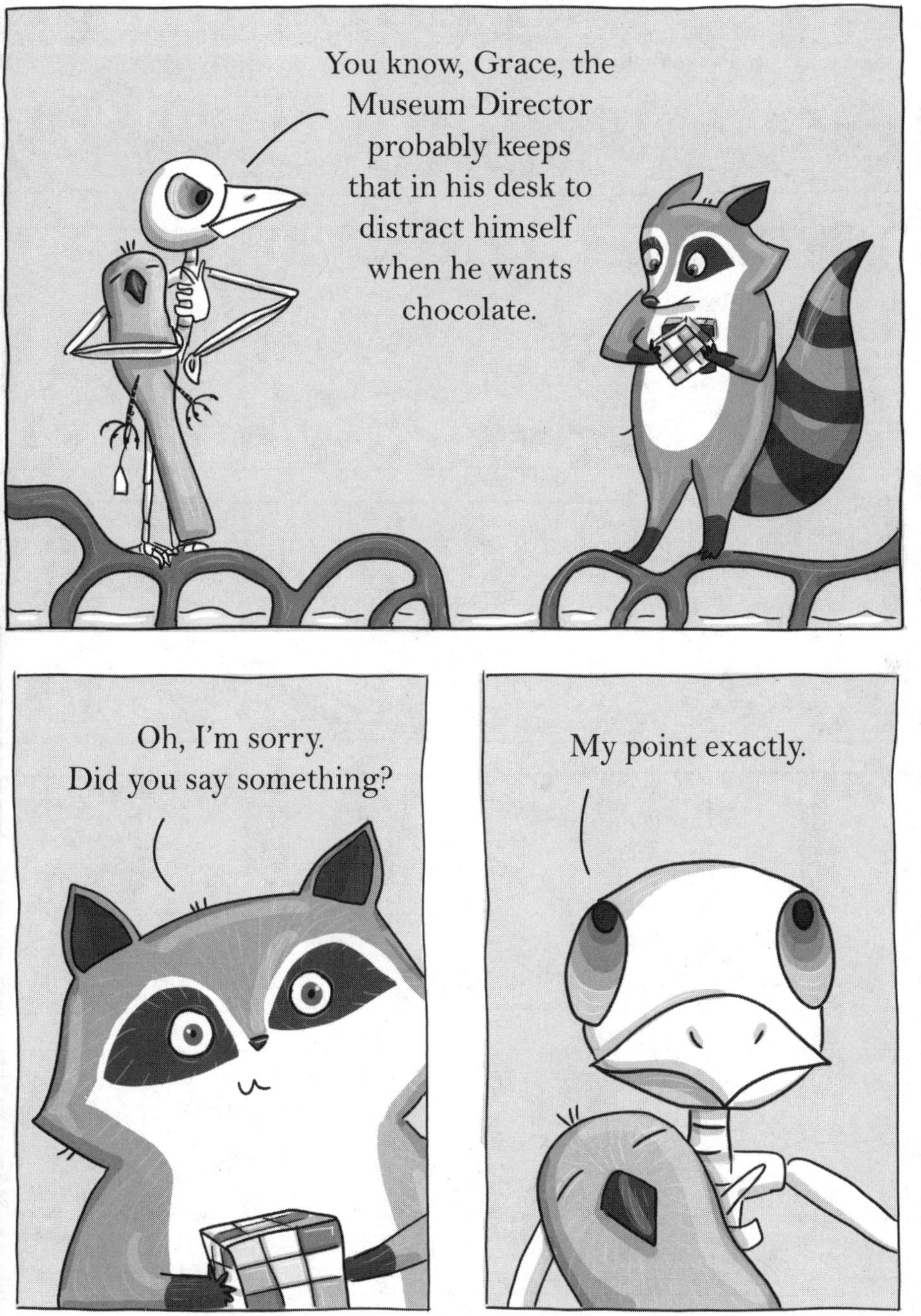
You know, Grace, the Museum Director probably keeps that in his desk to distract himself when he wants chocolate.
Oh, I'm sorry. Did you say something?
My point exactly.

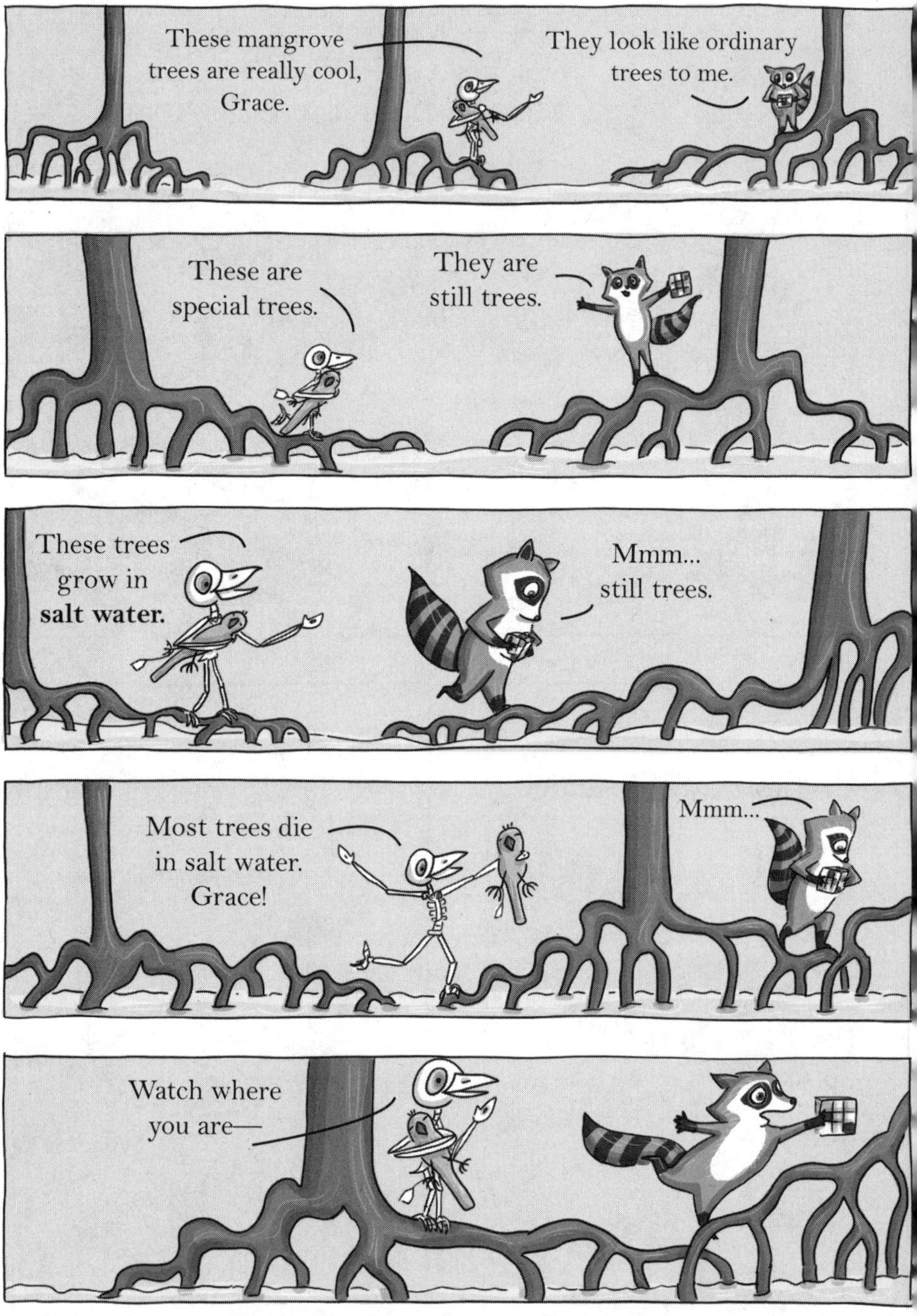
These mangrove trees are really cool, Grace.
They look like ordinary trees to me.
These are special trees.
They are still trees.
These trees grow in **salt water.**
Mmm... still trees.
Most trees die in salt water. Grace!
Mmm...
Watch where you are—

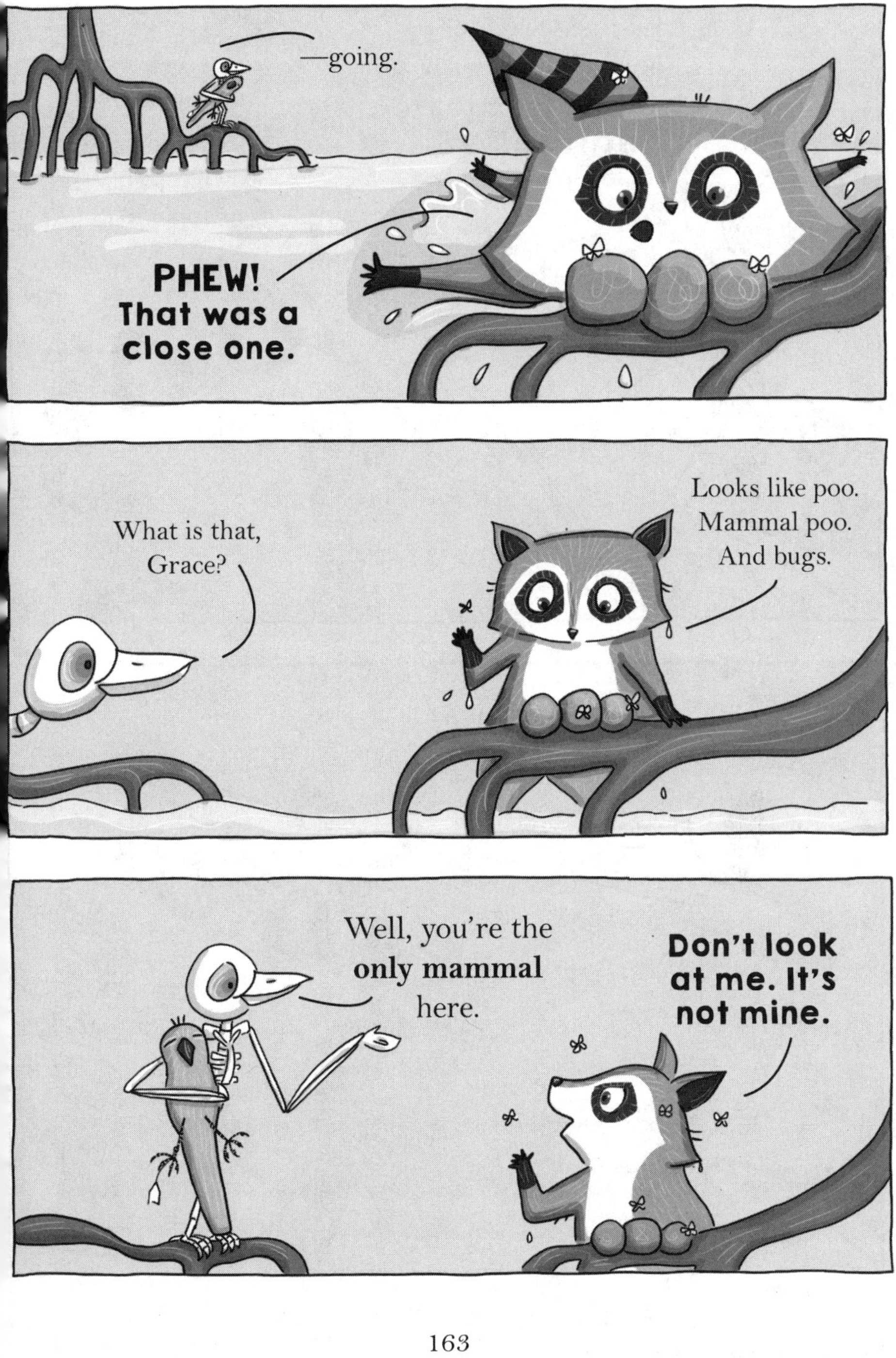

—going.
PHEW! That was a close one.
What is that, Grace?
Looks like poo. Mammal poo. And bugs.
Well, you're the **only mammal** here.
Don't look at me. It's not mine.

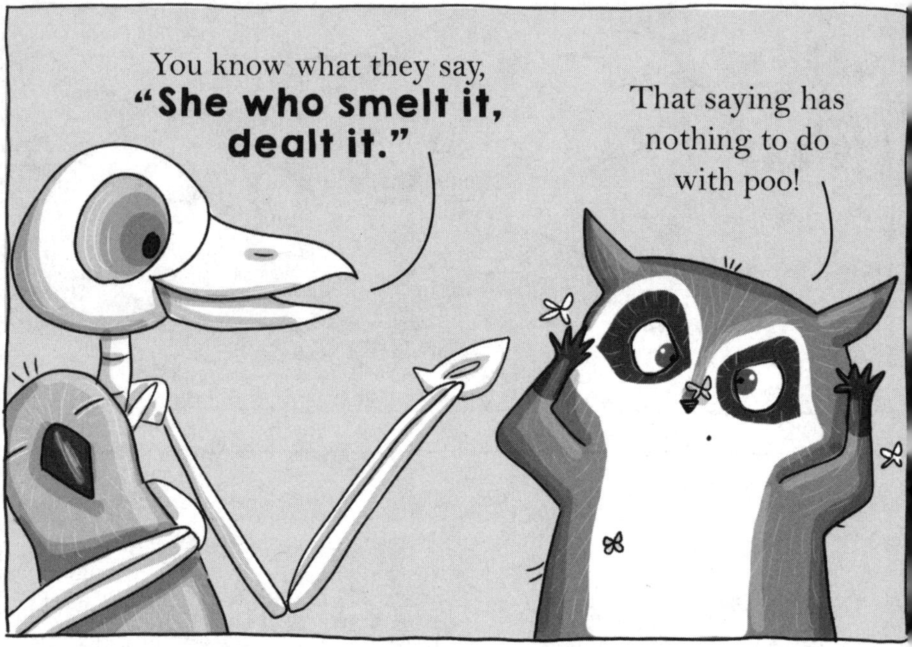
You know what they say, **"She who smelt it, dealt it."**
That saying has nothing to do with poo!

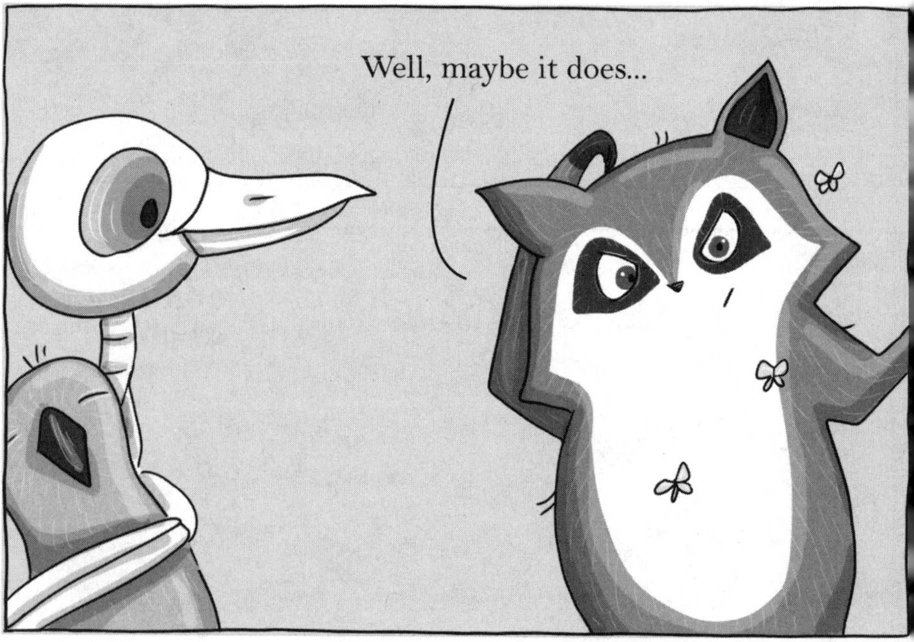
Well, maybe it does...

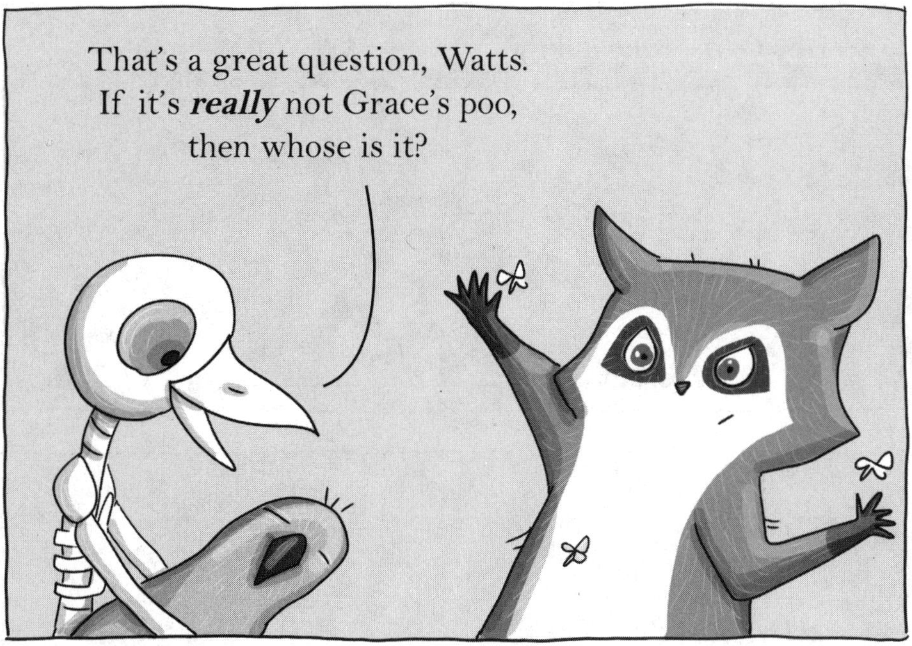
That's a great question, Watts. If it's ***really*** not Grace's poo, then whose is it?

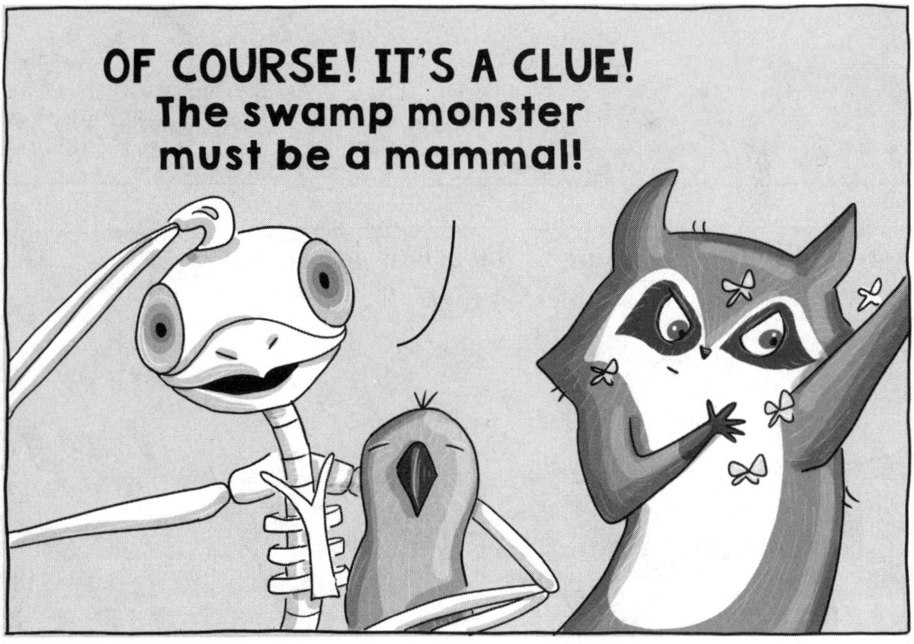
OF COURSE! IT'S A CLUE!
The swamp monster must be a mammal!

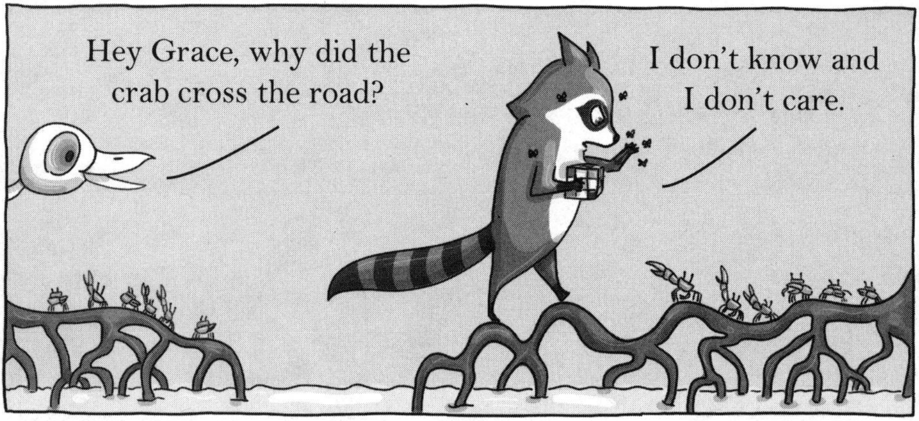
Hey Grace, why did the crab cross the road?
I don't know and I don't care.

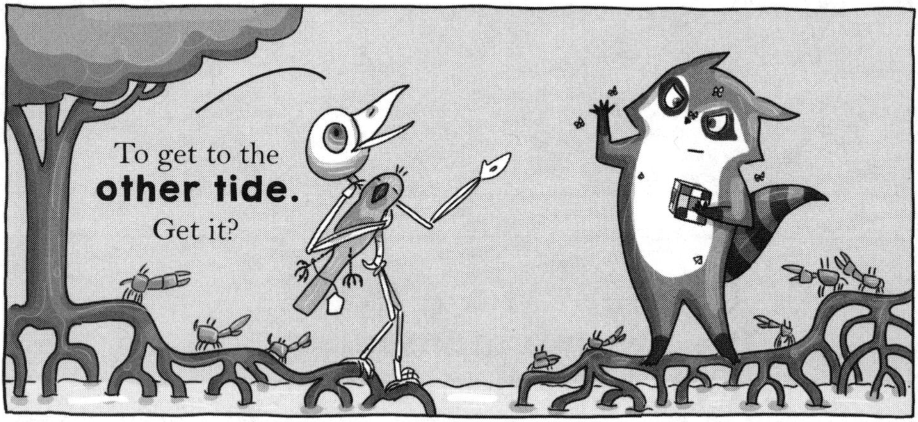
To get to the **other tide.** Get it?

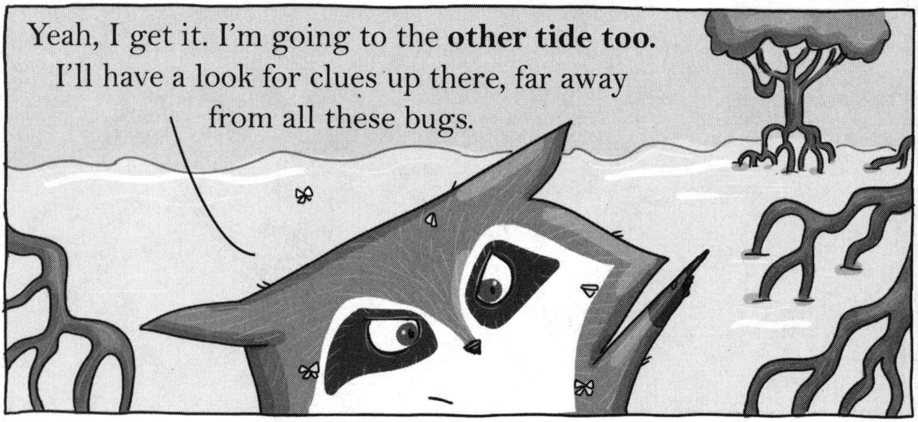
Yeah, I get it. I'm going to the **other tide too.** I'll have a look for clues up there, far away from all these bugs.

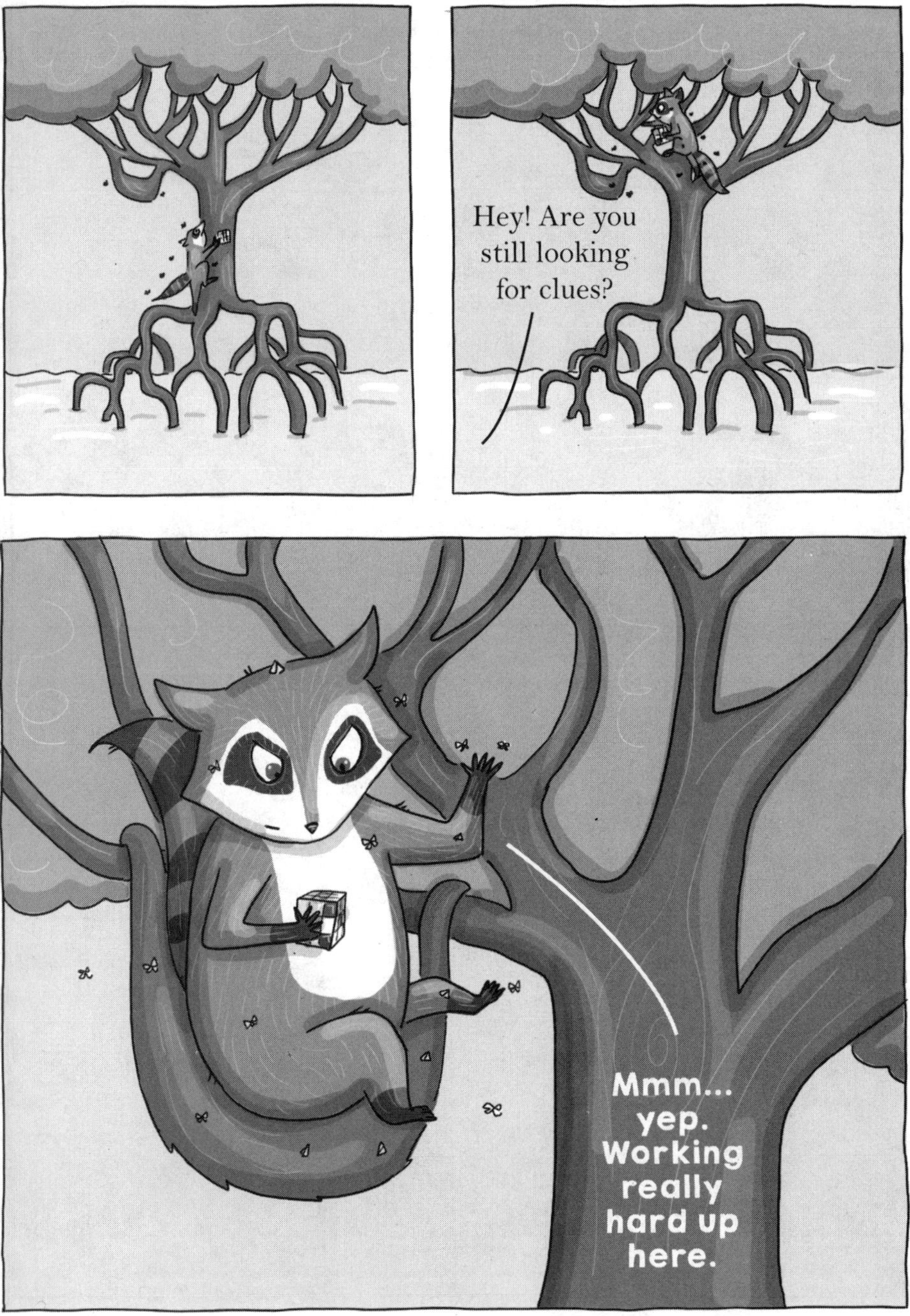
Hey! Are you still looking for clues?
Mmm... yep. Working really hard up here.

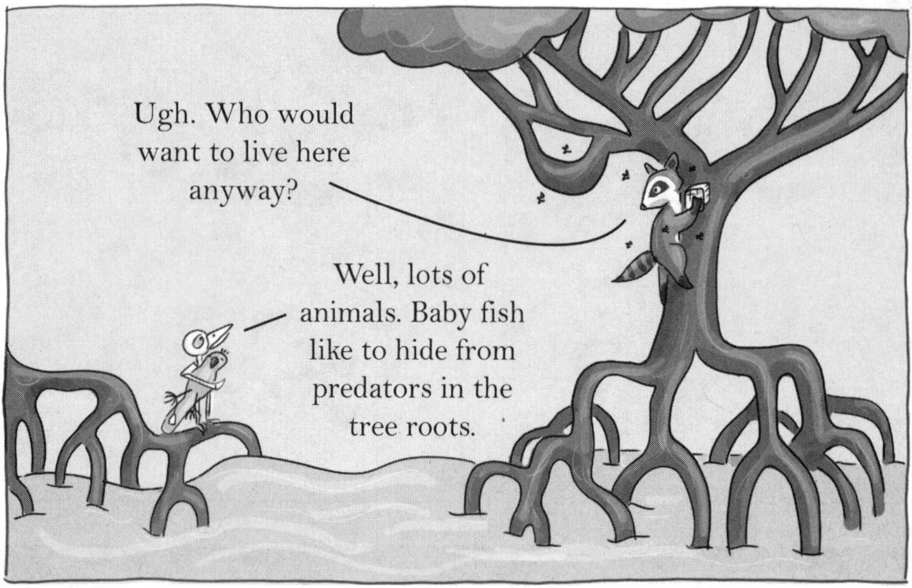
Ugh. Who would want to live here anyway?
Well, lots of animals. Baby fish like to hide from predators in the tree roots.

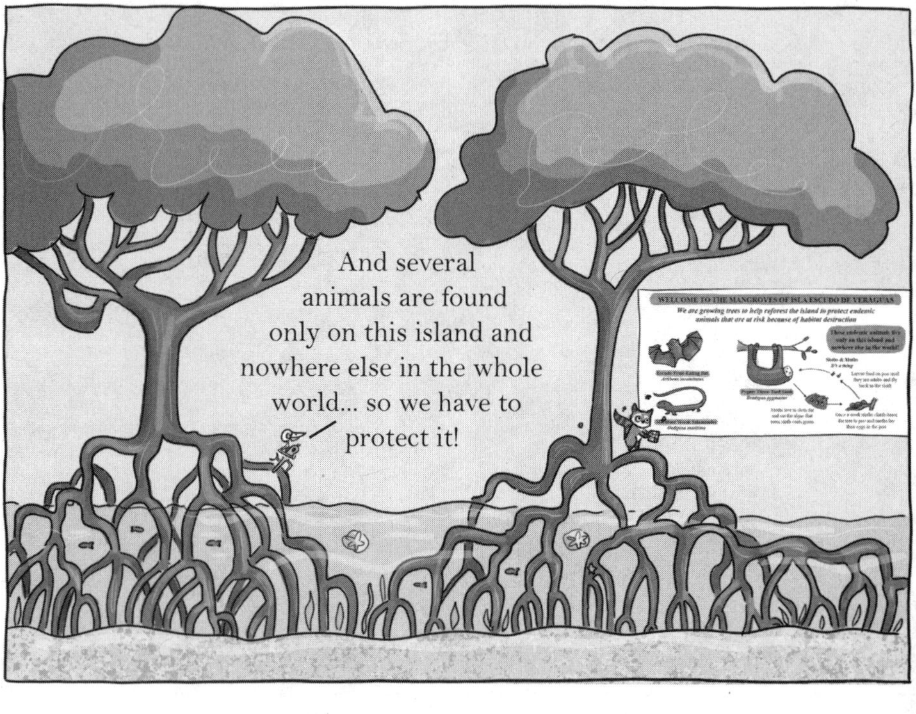
And several animals are found only on this island and nowhere else in the whole world... so we have to protect it!
WELCOME TO THE MANGROVES OF ISLA ESCUDO DE VERAGUAS
We are growing trees to help reforest the island to protect endemic animals that are at risk because of habitat destruction

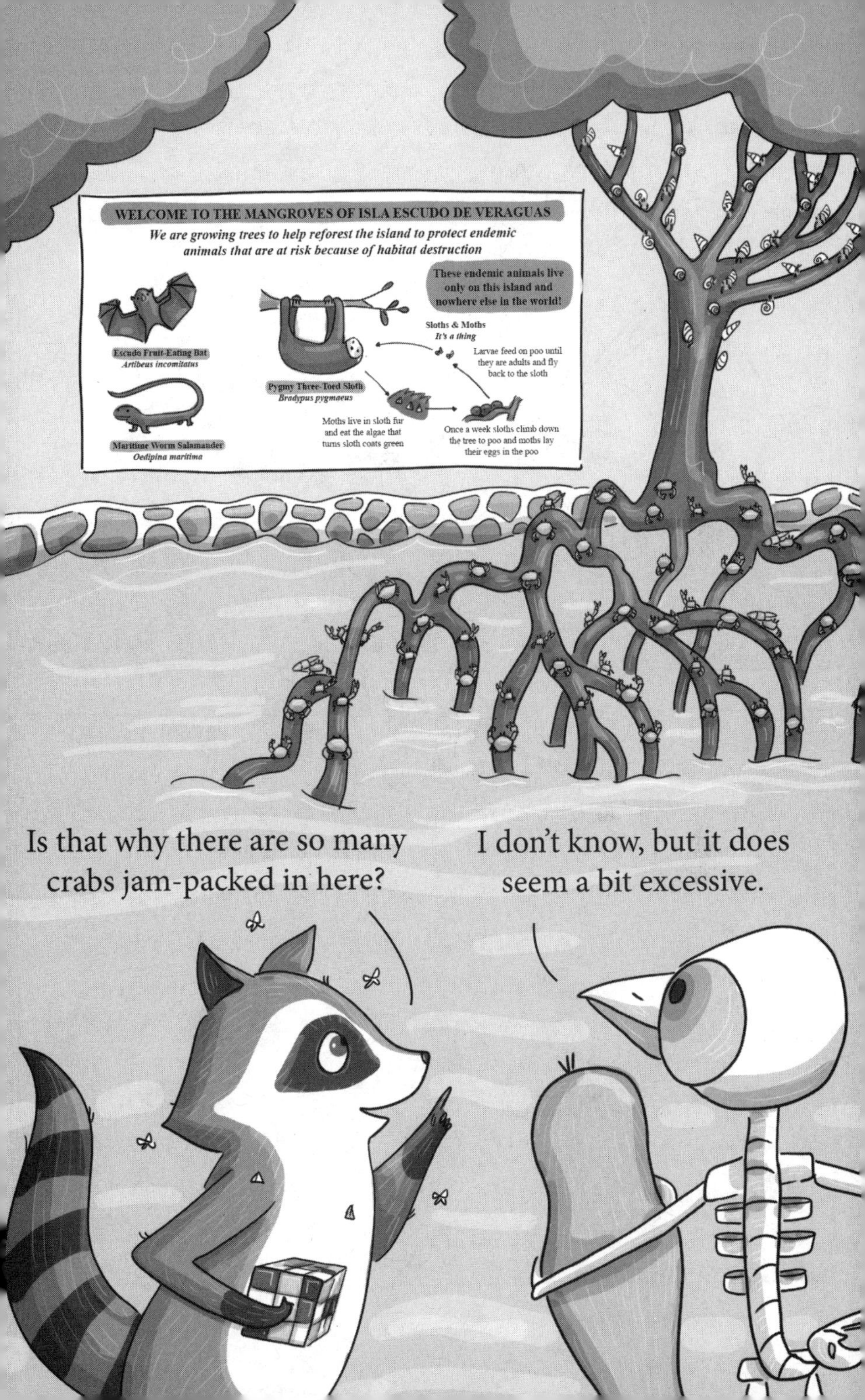

WELCOME TO THE MANGROVES OF ISLA ESCUDO DE VERAGUAS
We are growing trees to help reforest the island to protect endemic animals that are at risk because of habitat destruction
These endemic animals live only on this island and nowhere else in the world!
Escudo Fruit-Eating Bat
Artibeus incomitatus
Maritime Worm Salamander
Oedipina maritima
Pygmy Three-Toed Sloth
Bradypus pygmaeus
Sloths & Moths
It's a thing
Larvae feed on poo until they are adults and fly back to the sloth
Moths live in sloth fur and eat the algae that turns sloth coats green
Once a week sloths climb down the tree to poo and moths lay their eggs in the poo
Is that why there are so many crabs jam-packed in here?
I don't know, but it does seem a bit excessive.

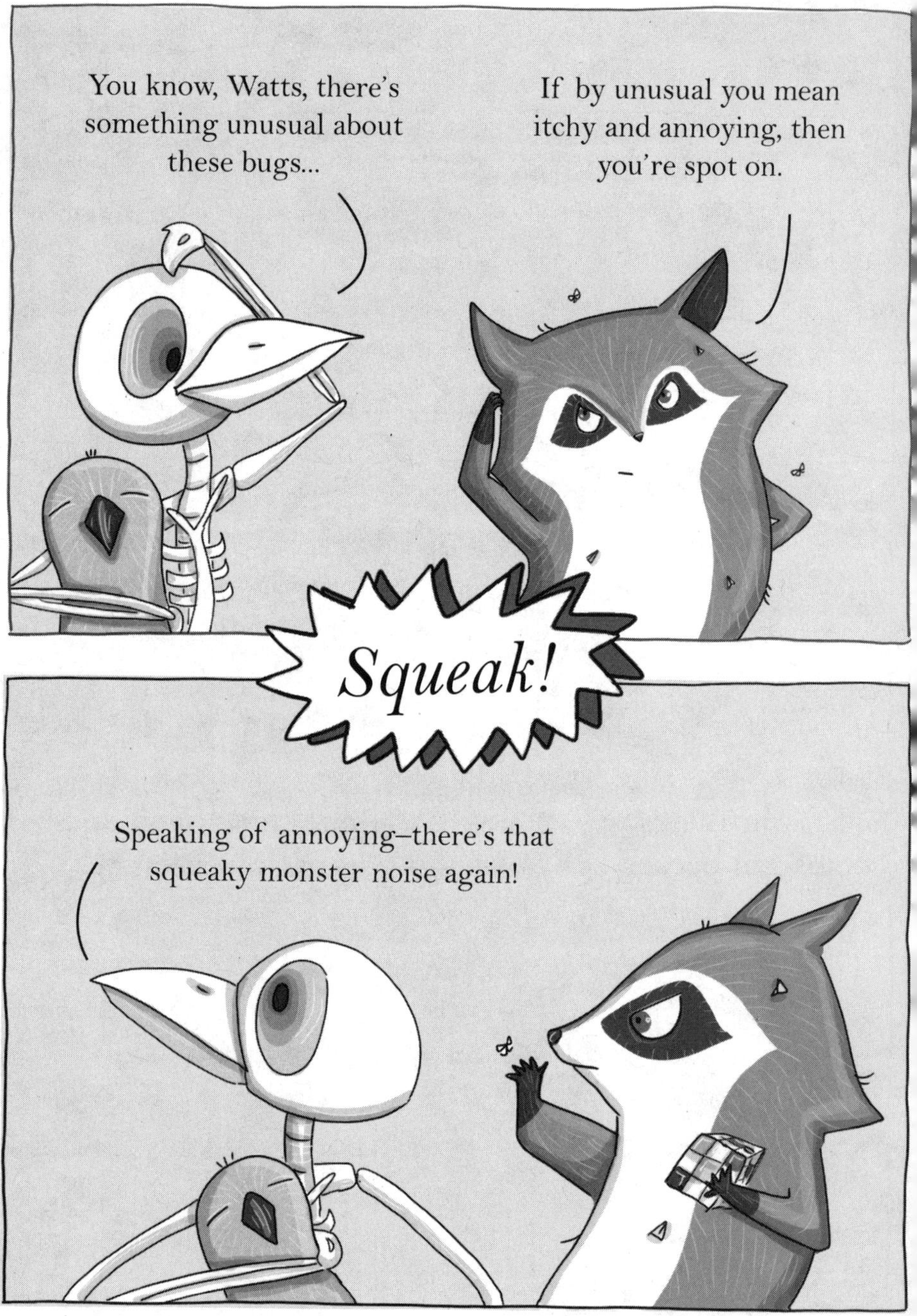
You know, Watts, there's something unusual about these bugs...
If by unusual you mean itchy and annoying, then you're spot on.
Squeak!
Speaking of annoying–there's that squeaky monster noise again!

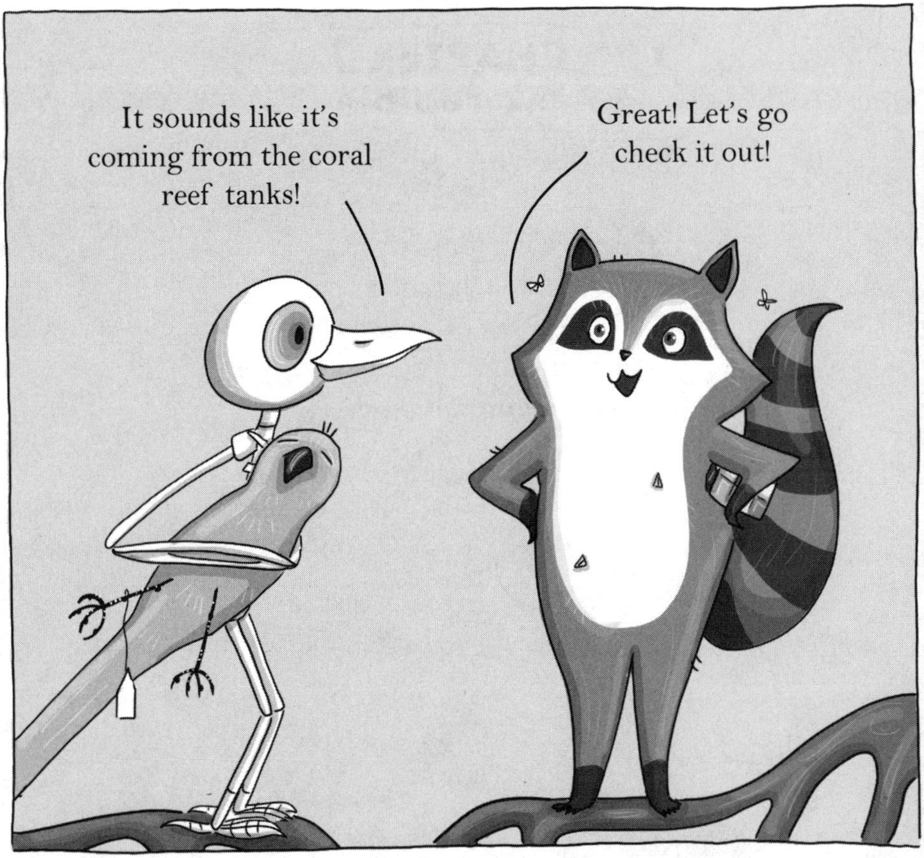
It sounds like it's coming from the coral reef tanks!
Great! Let's go check it out!

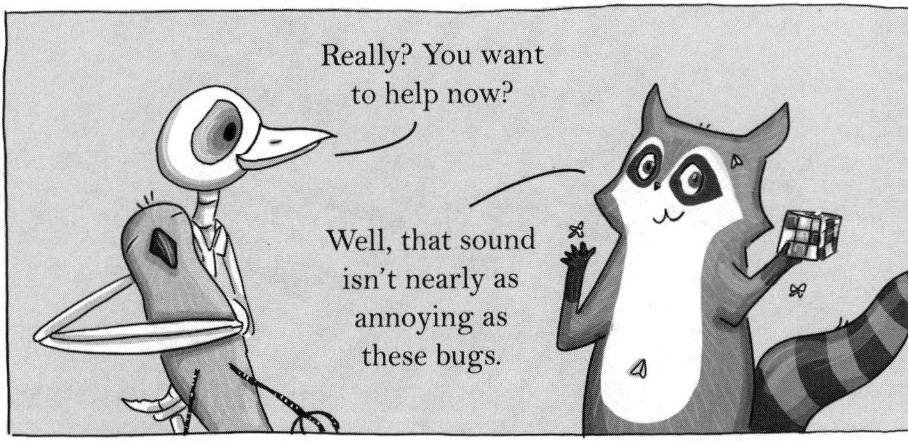
Really? You want to help now?
Well, that sound isn't nearly as annoying as these bugs.

CHAPTER 7
Ink-redible

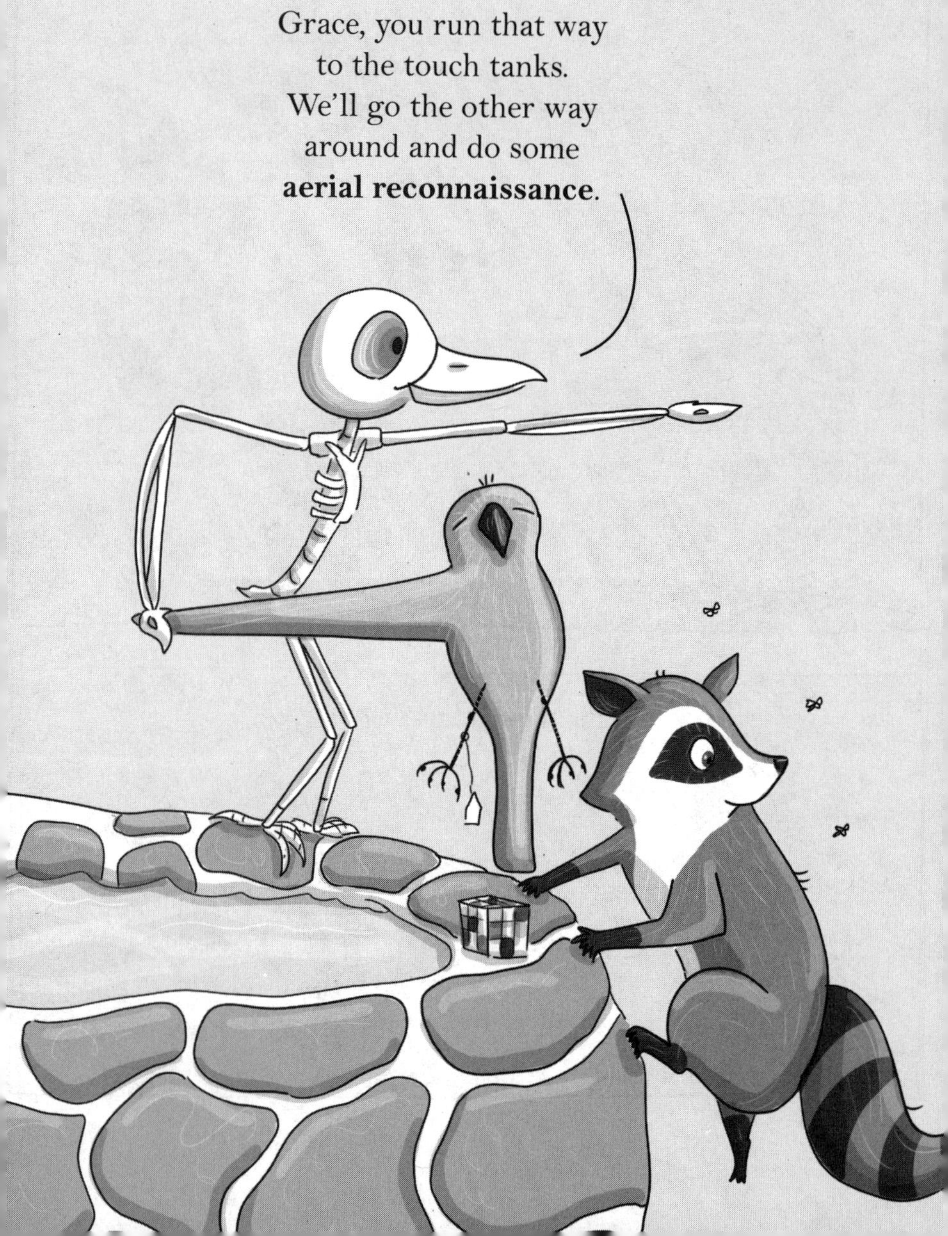
Grace, you run that way to the touch tanks. We'll go the other way around and do some **aerial reconnaissance**.

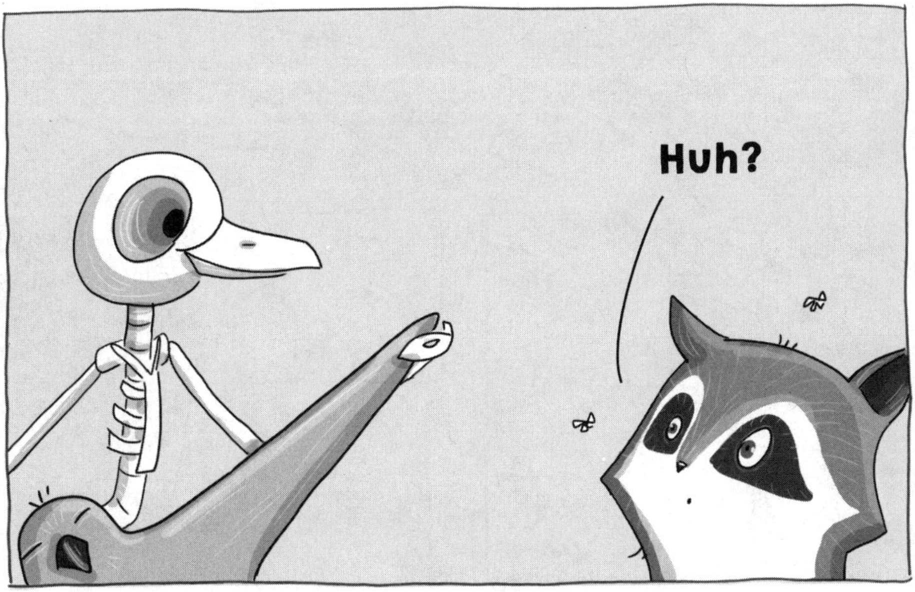
Huh?

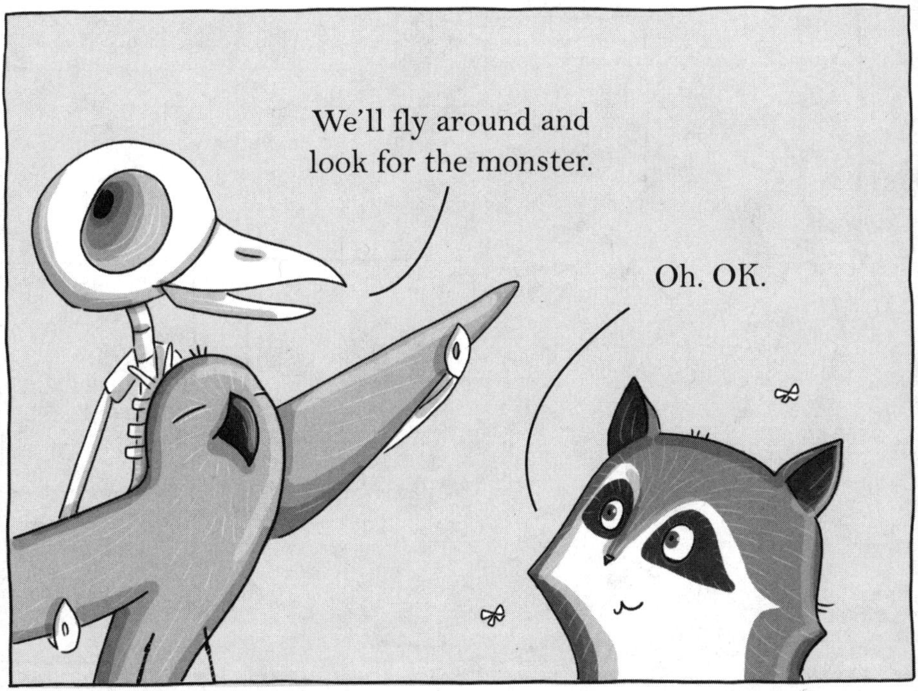
We'll fly around and
look for the monster.
Oh. OK.

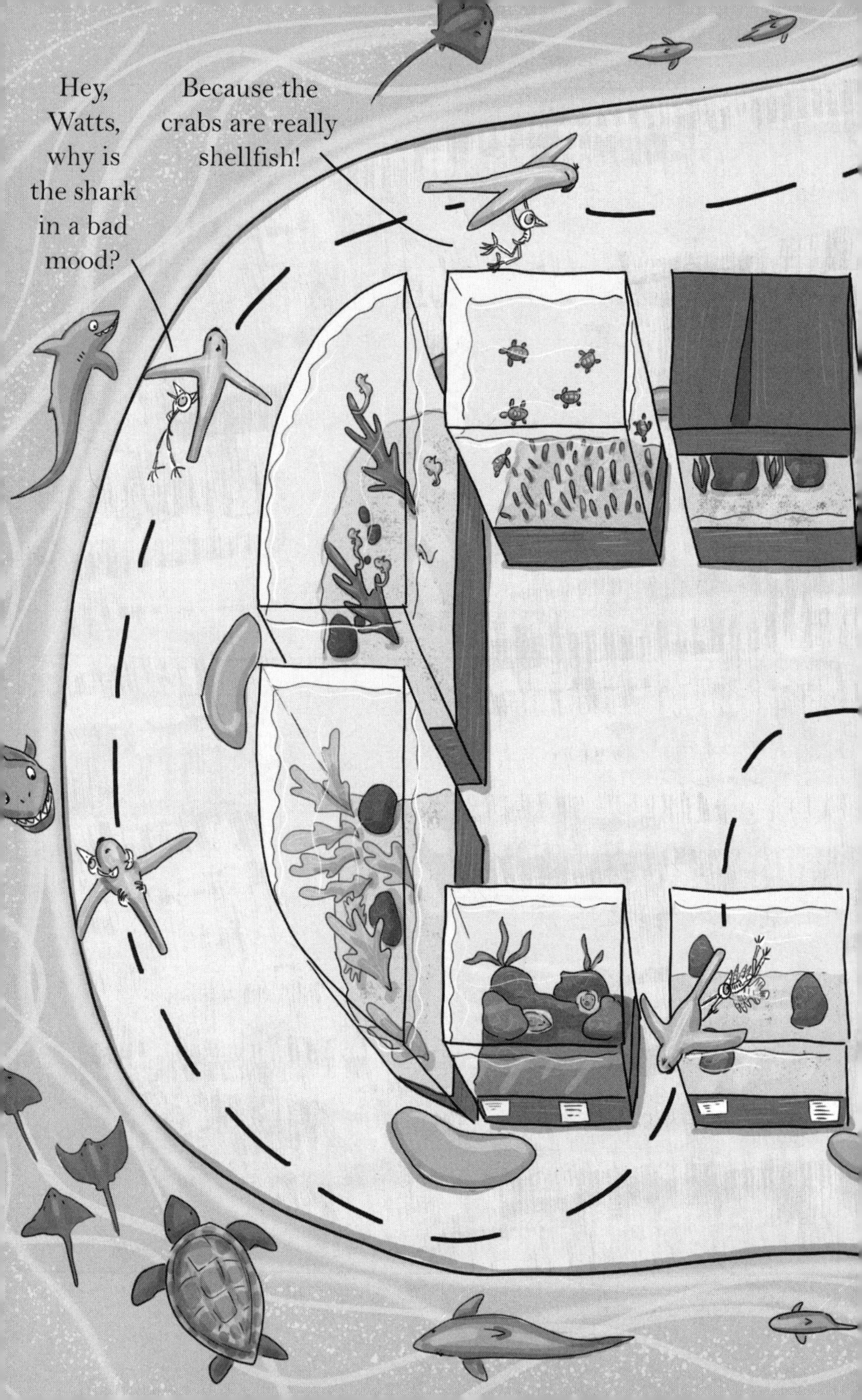
Hey, Watts, why is the shark in a bad mood?
Because the crabs are really shellfish!

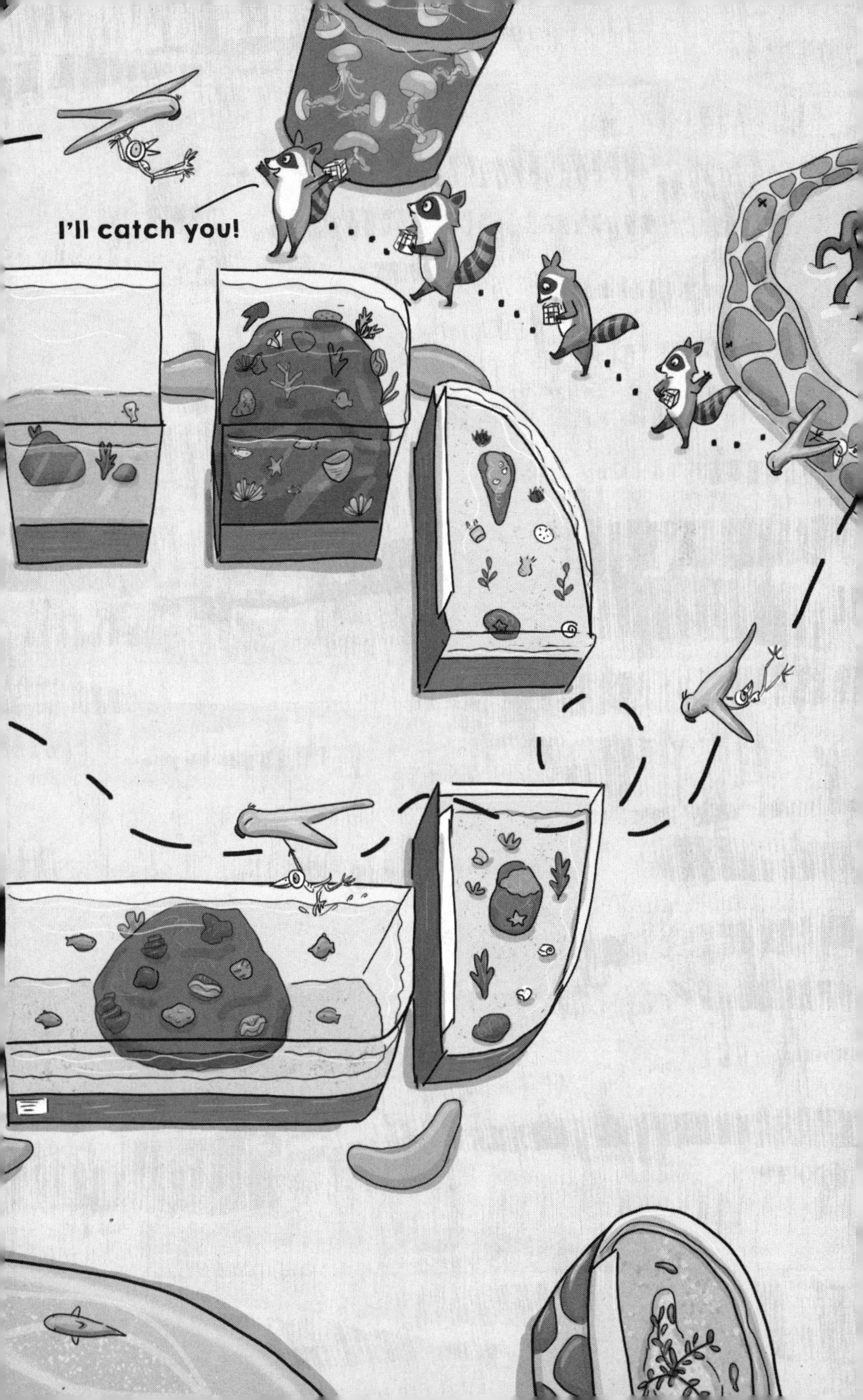
I'll catch you!

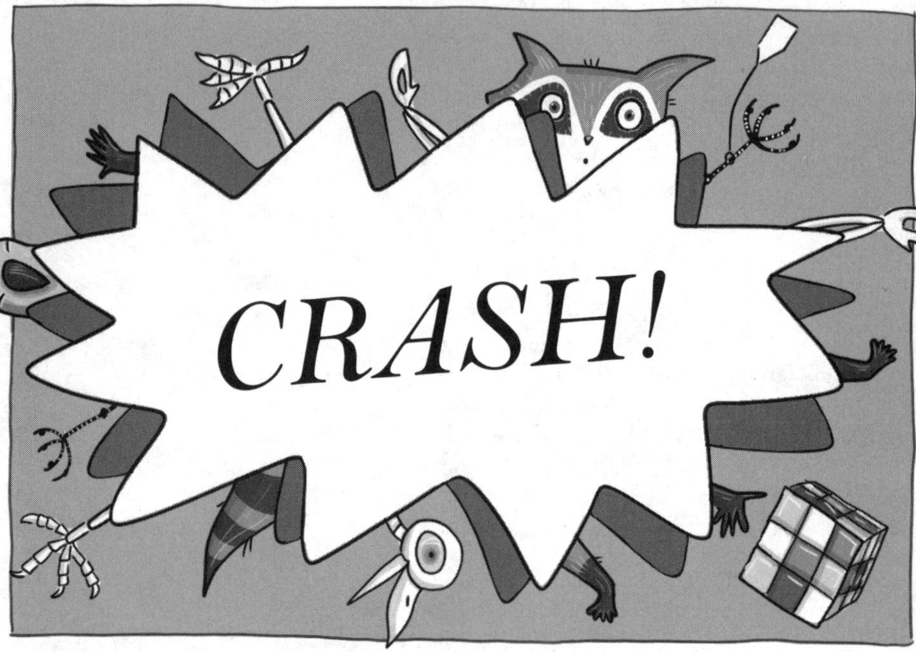
CRASH!

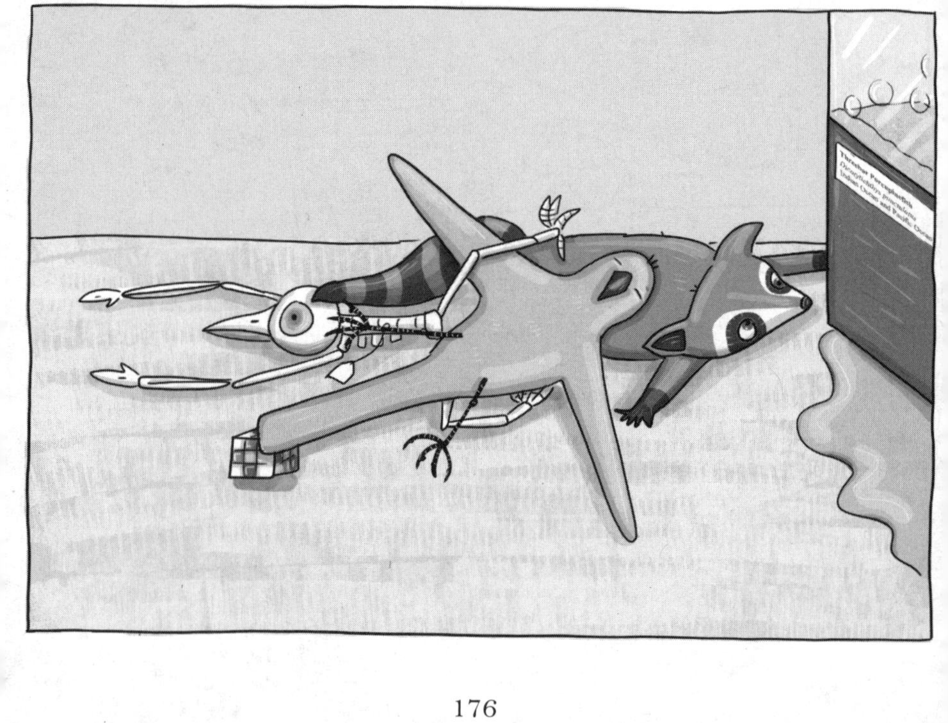
Thresher Porcupinefish

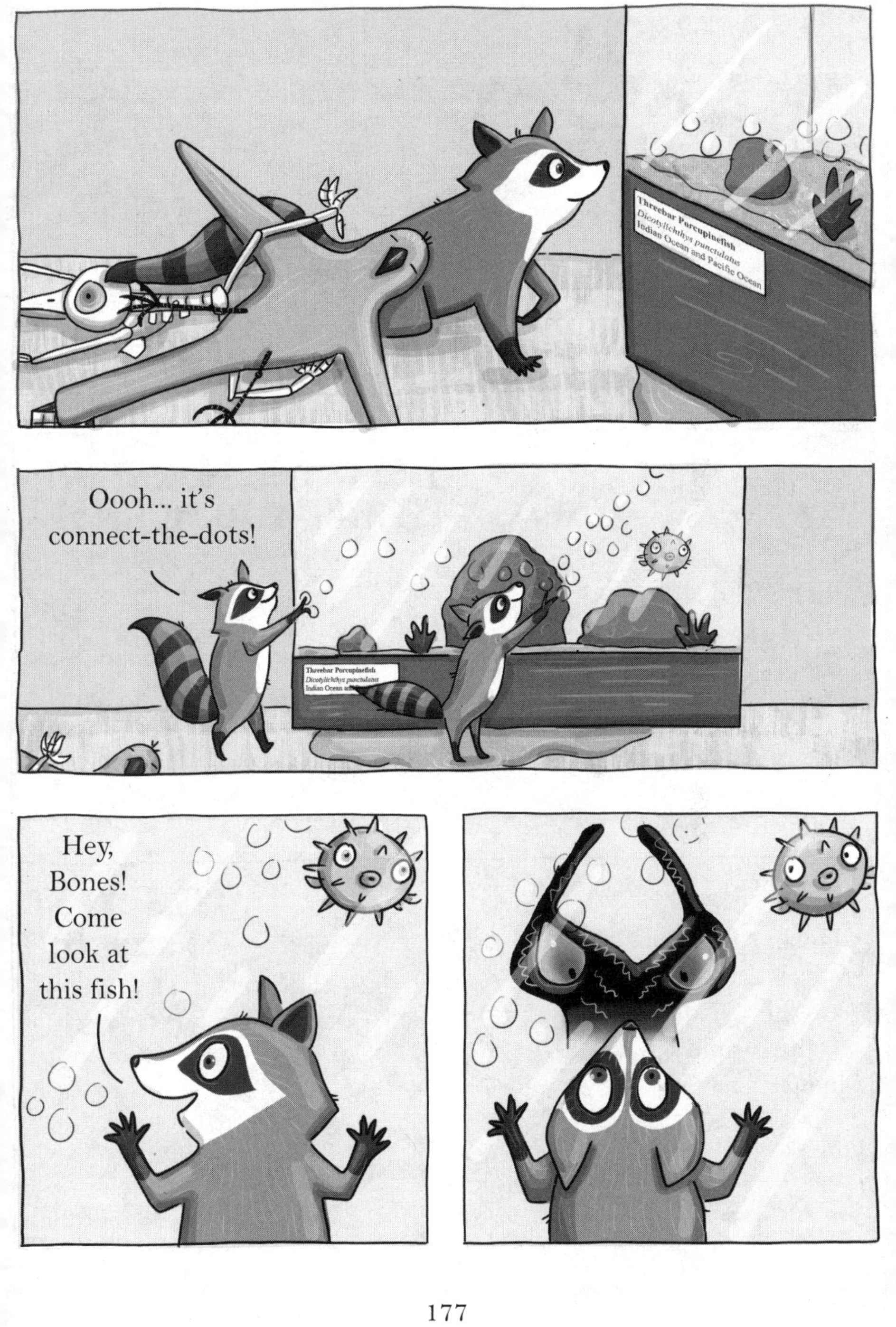
Threebar Porcupinefish
Dicotylichthys punctulatus
Indian Ocean and Pacific Ocean
Oooh... it's connect-the-dots!
Hey, Bones! Come look at this fish!

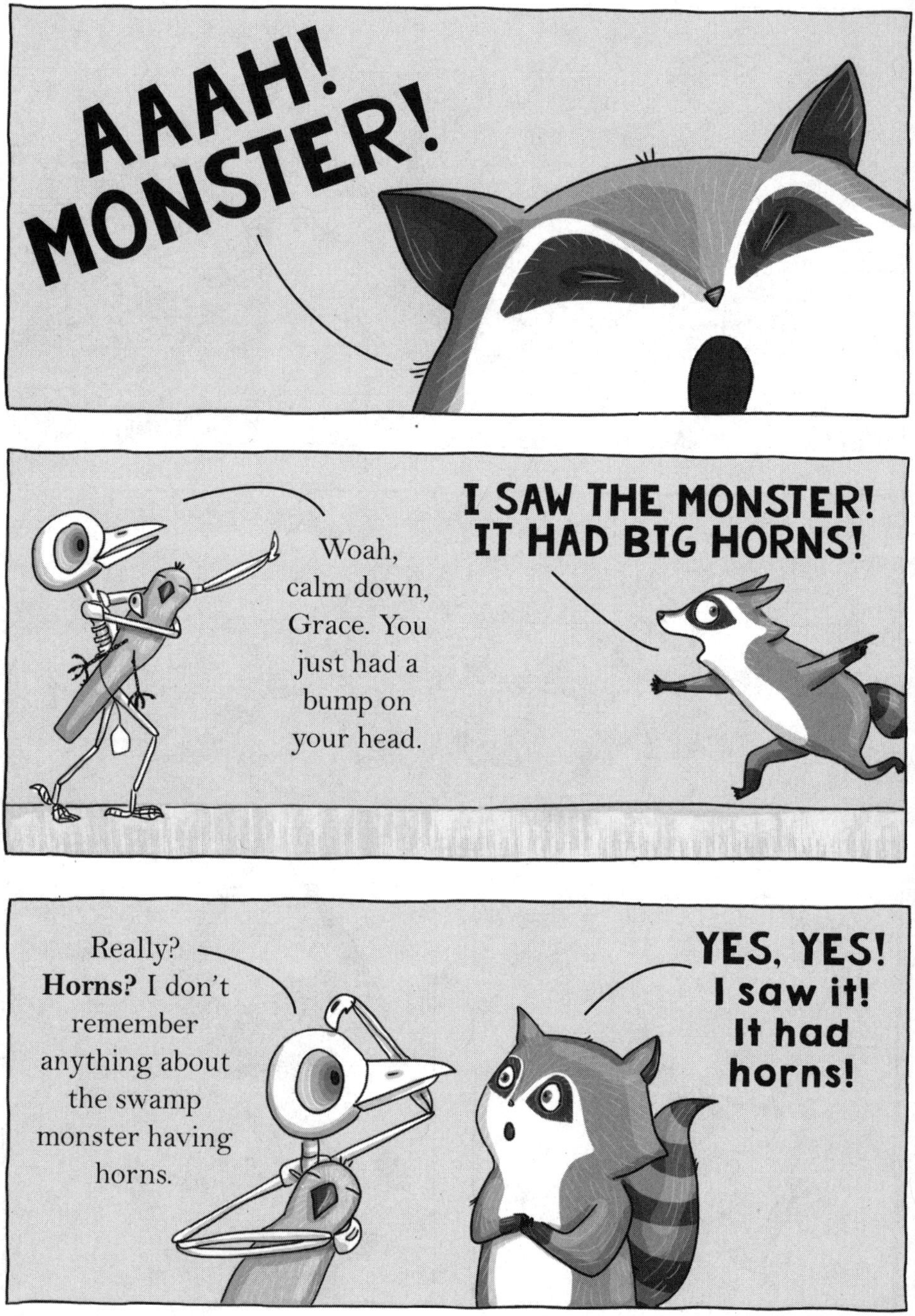
AAAH! MONSTER!
Woah, calm down, Grace. You just had a bump on your head.
I SAW THE MONSTER! IT HAD BIG HORNS!
Really? **Horns?** I don't remember anything about the swamp monster having horns.
YES, YES! I saw it! It had horns!

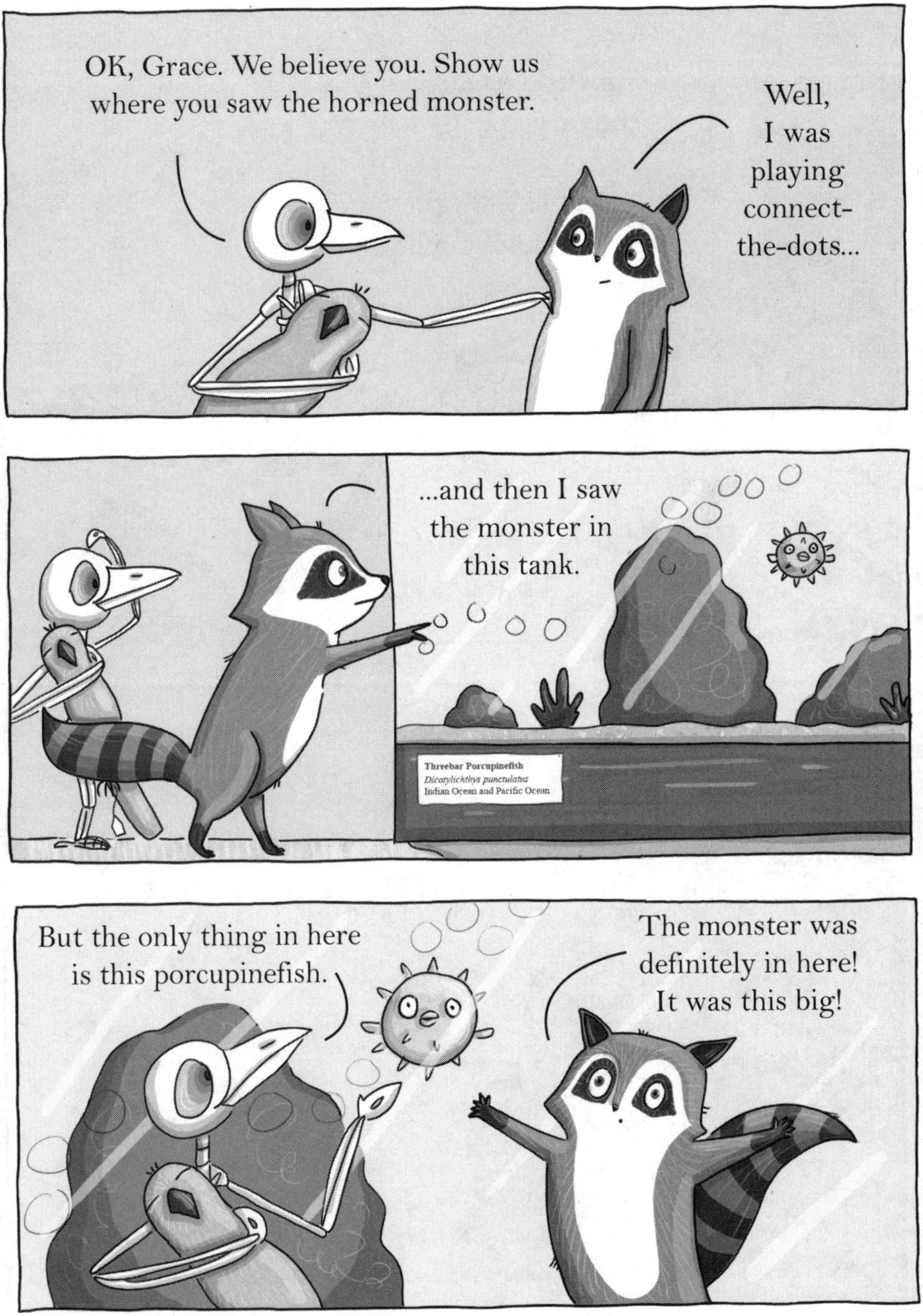
OK, Grace. We believe you. Show us where you saw the horned monster.
Well, I was playing connect-the-dots...
...and then I saw the monster in this tank.
Threebar Porcupinefish
Dicotylichthys punctulatus
Indian Ocean and Pacific Ocean
But the only thing in here is this porcupinefish.
The monster was definitely in here! It was this big!

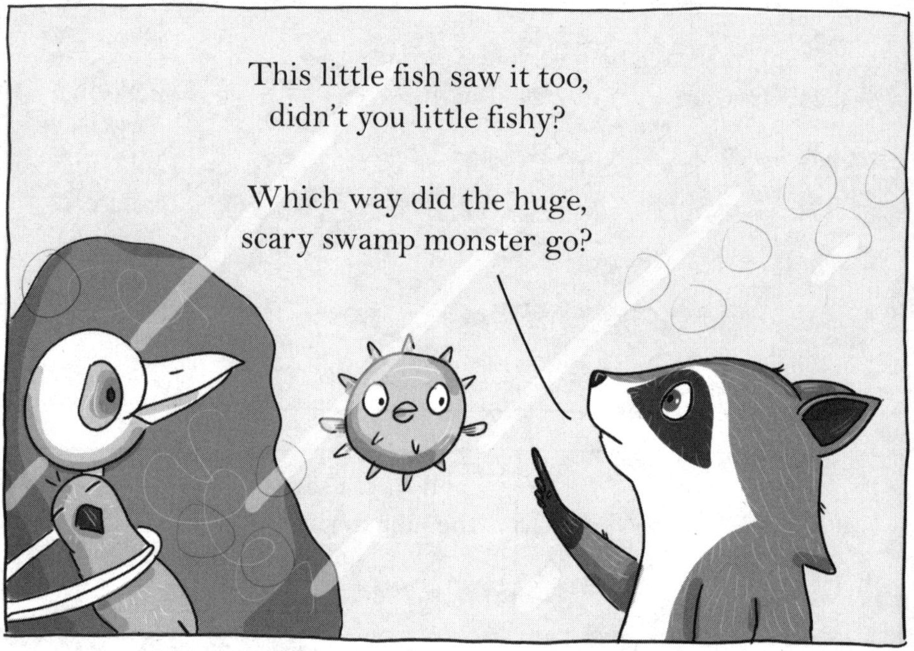
This little fish saw it too,
didn't you little fishy?
Which way did the huge,
scary swamp monster go?

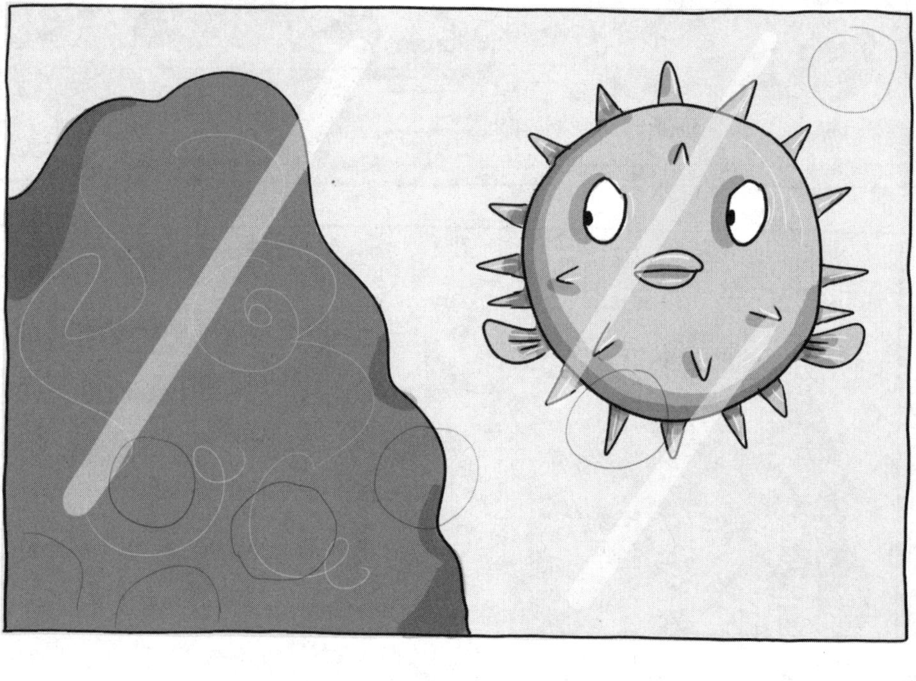

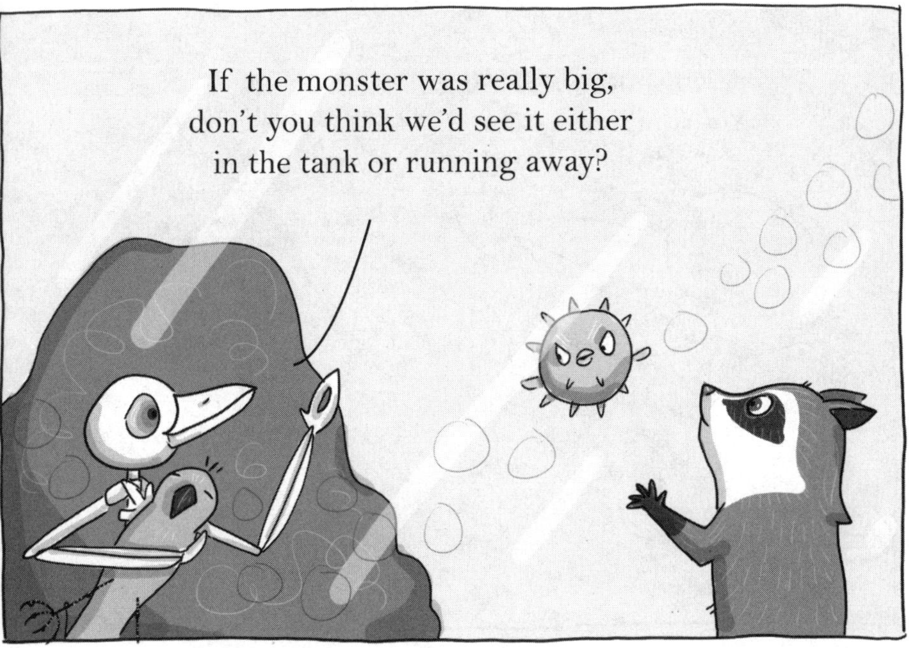
If the monster was really big, don't you think we'd see it either in the tank or running away?

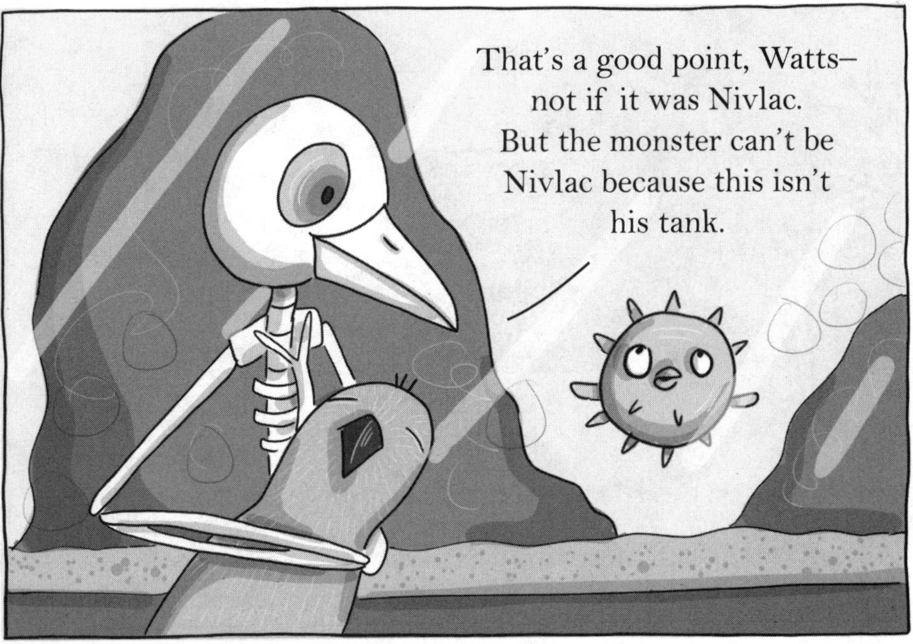
That's a good point, Watts– not if it was Nivlac. But the monster can't be Nivlac because this isn't his tank.

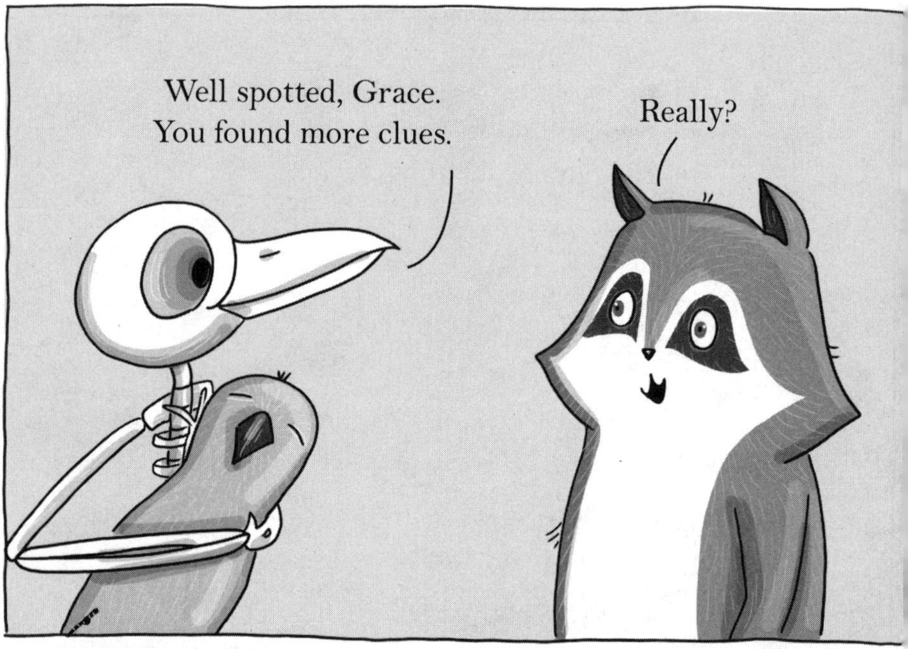
Well spotted, Grace. You found more clues.
Really?

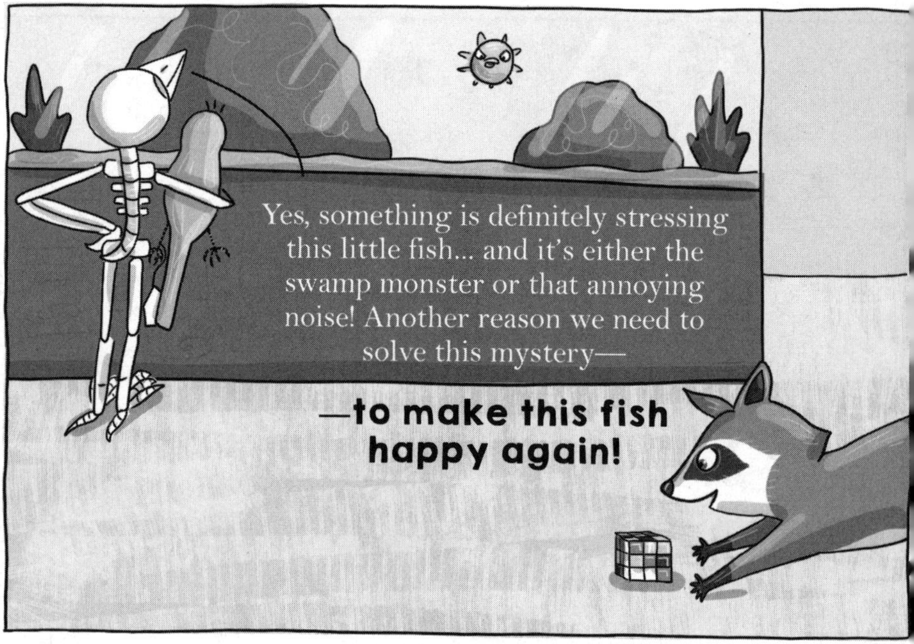
Yes, something is definitely stressing this little fish... and it's either the swamp monster or that annoying noise! Another reason we need to solve this mystery—
—to make this fish happy again!

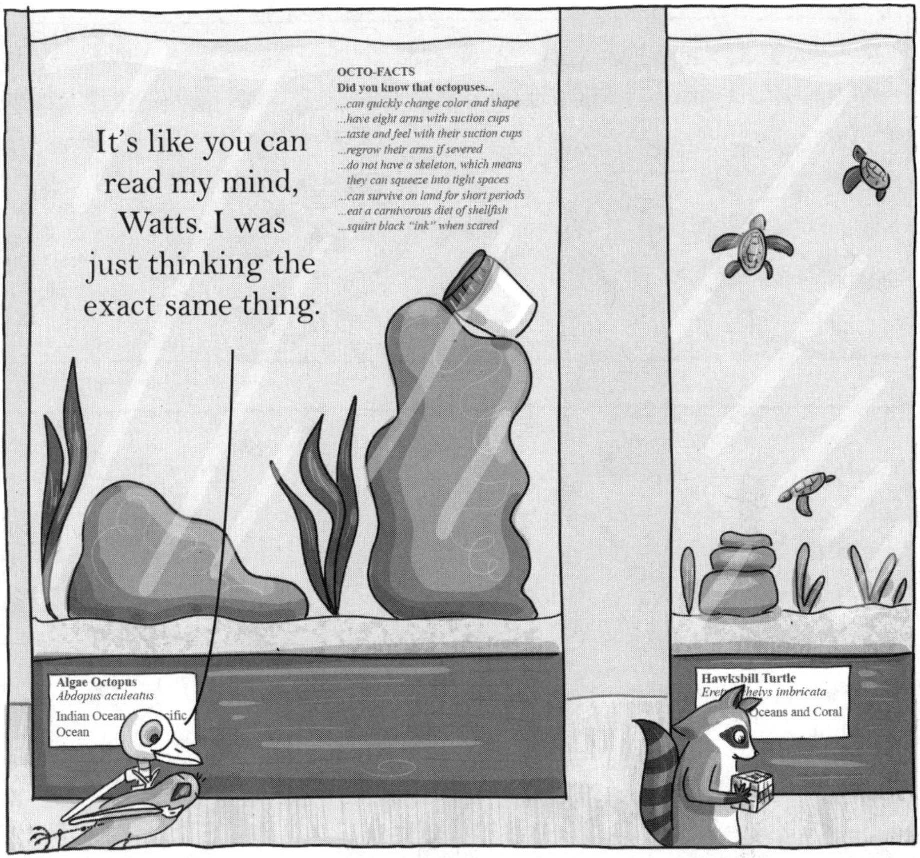
OCTO-FACTS
Did you know that octopuses...
...can quickly change color and shape
...have eight arms with suction cups
...taste and feel with their suction cups
...regrow their arms if severed
...do not have a skeleton, which means they can squeeze into tight spaces
...can survive on land for short periods
...eat a carnivorous diet of shellfish
...squirt black "ink" when scared
It's like you can read my mind, Watts. I was just thinking the exact same thing.
Algae Octopus
Abdopus aculeatus
Indian Ocean
Ocean
Hawksbill Turtle
helys imbricata
Oceans and Coral

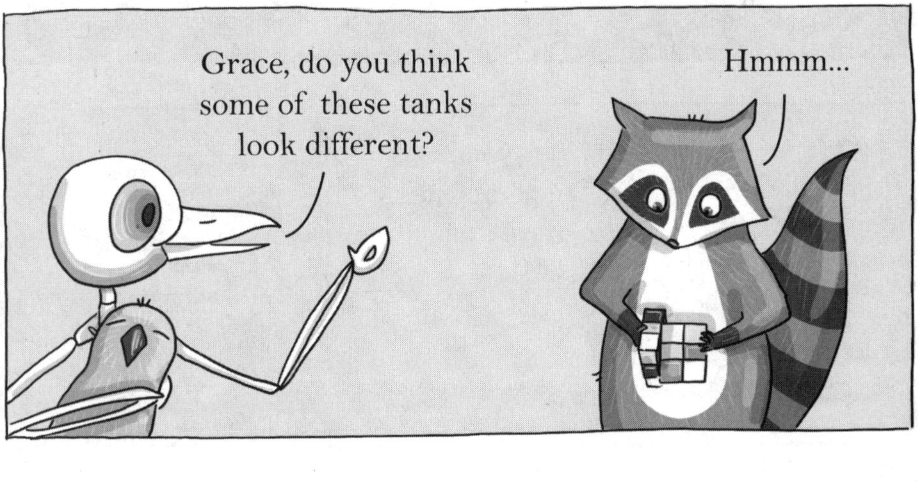
Grace, do you think some of these tanks look different?
Hmmm...

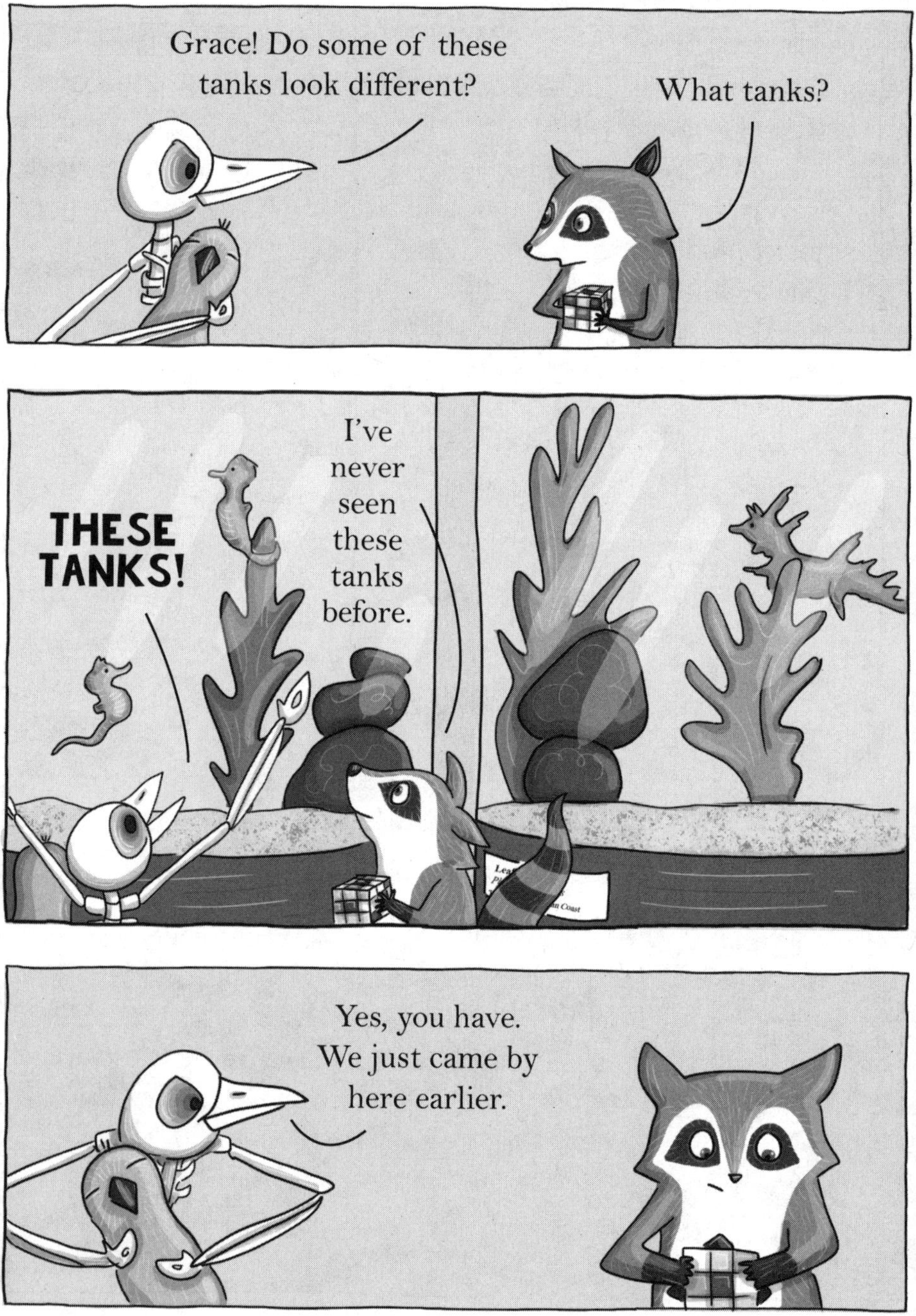
Grace! Do some of these tanks look different?
What tanks?
THESE TANKS!
I've never seen these tanks before.
Yes, you have. We just came by here earlier.

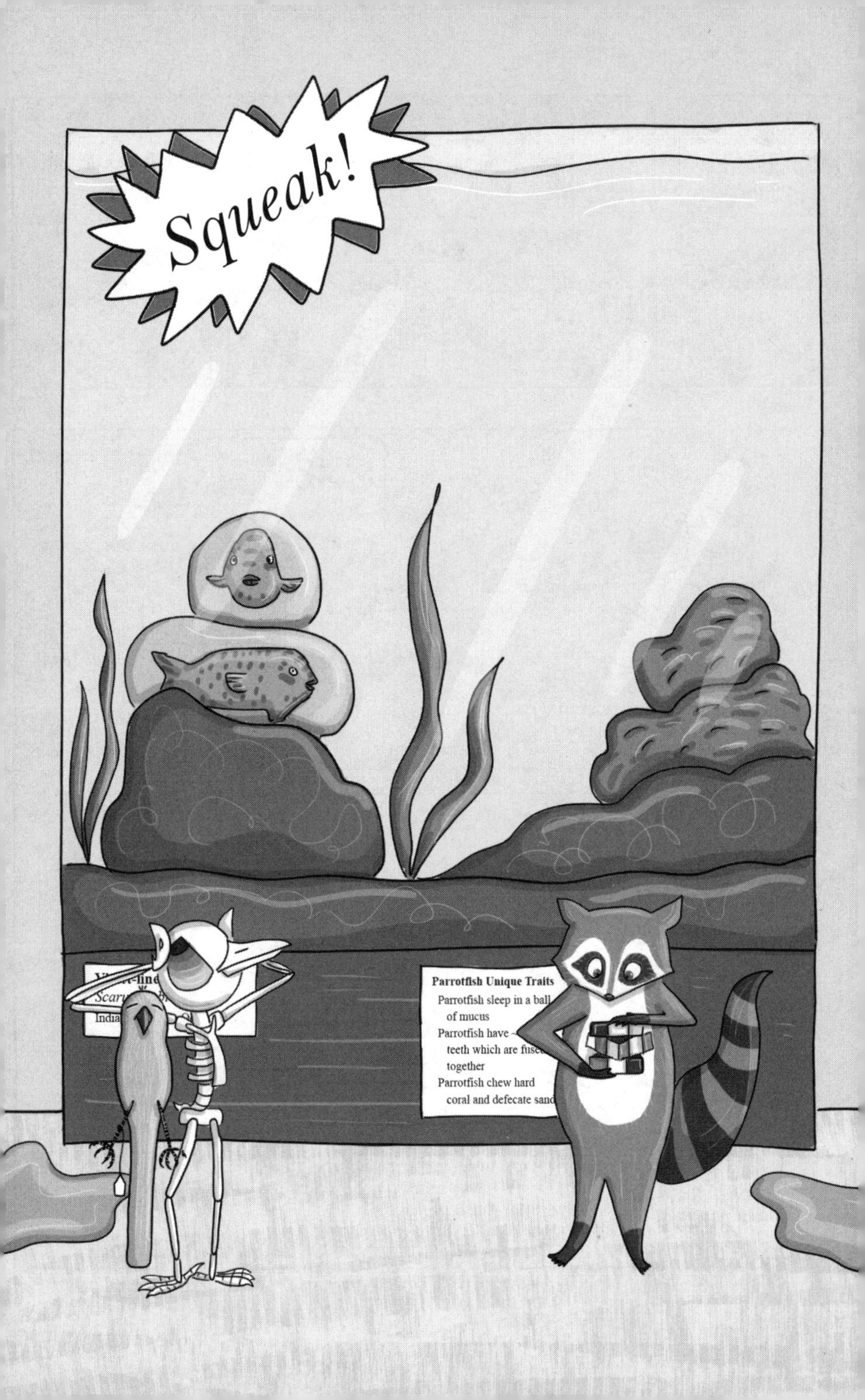
Squeak!
Parrotfish Unique Traits
Parrotfish sleep in a ball
of mucus
Parrotfish have
teeth which are fuse
together
Parrotfish chew hard
coral and defecate sand

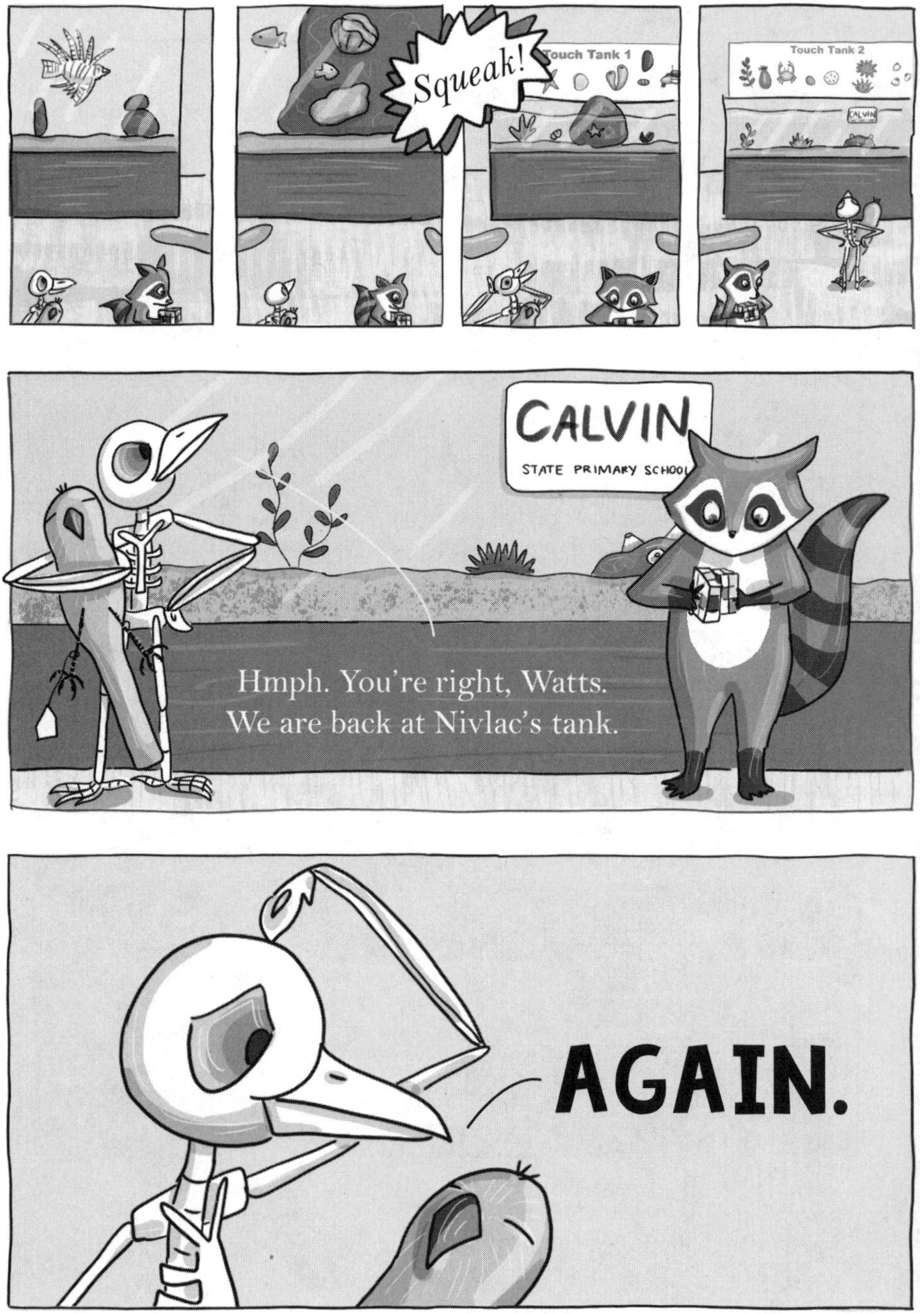
Squeak!
Touch Tank 1
Touch Tank 2
CALVIN
CALVIN
STATE PRIMARY SCHOOL
Hmph. You're right, Watts.
We are back at Nivlac's tank.
AGAIN.

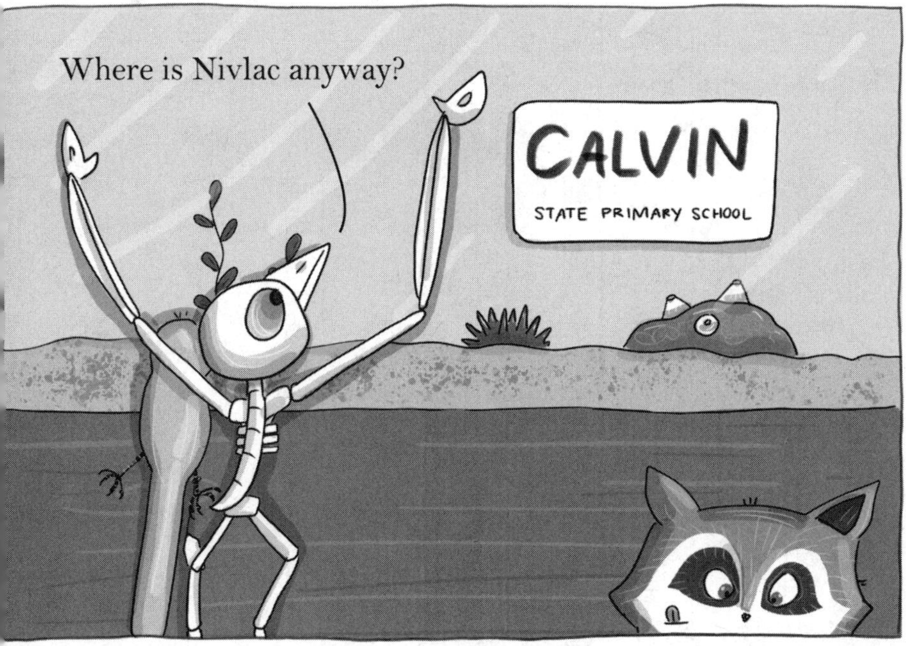
Where is Nivlac anyway?
CALVIN
STATE PRIMARY SCHOOL

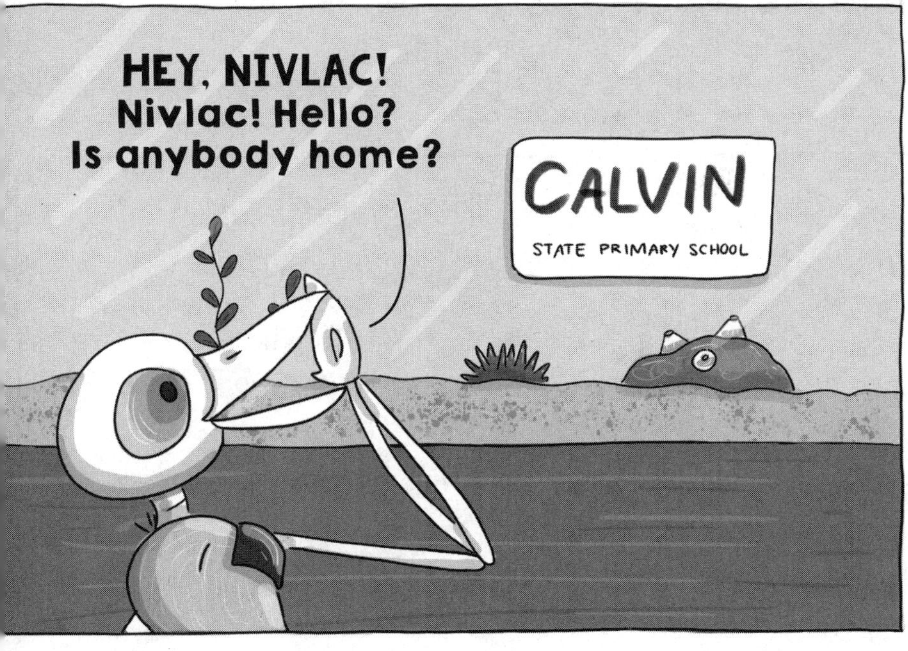
HEY, NIVLAC!
Nivlac! Hello?
Is anybody home?
CALVIN
STATE PRIMARY SCHOOL

Is he pretending to be this rock?

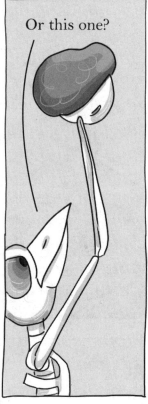

Or this one?

But I'm sure this is his tank, Watts.

Hmmm... you make a good point. None of these signs actually say "octopus."

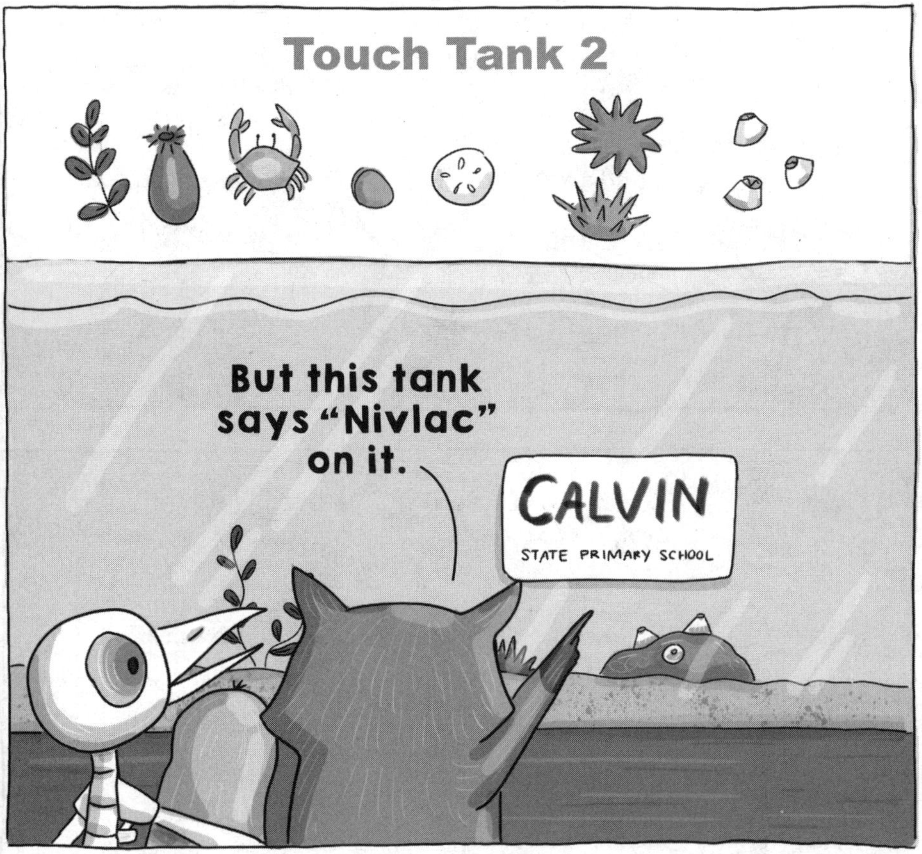
Touch Tank 2
But this tank says "Nivlac" on it.
CALVIN
STATE PRIMARY SCHOOL

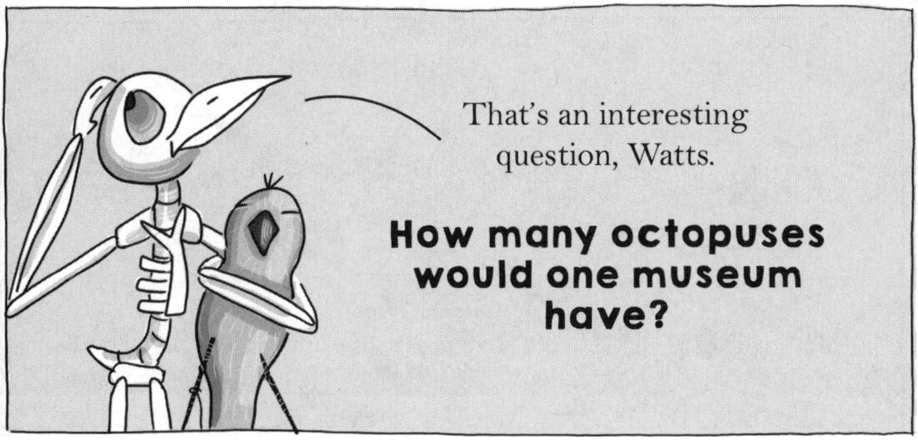
That's an interesting question, Watts.
How many octopuses would one museum have?

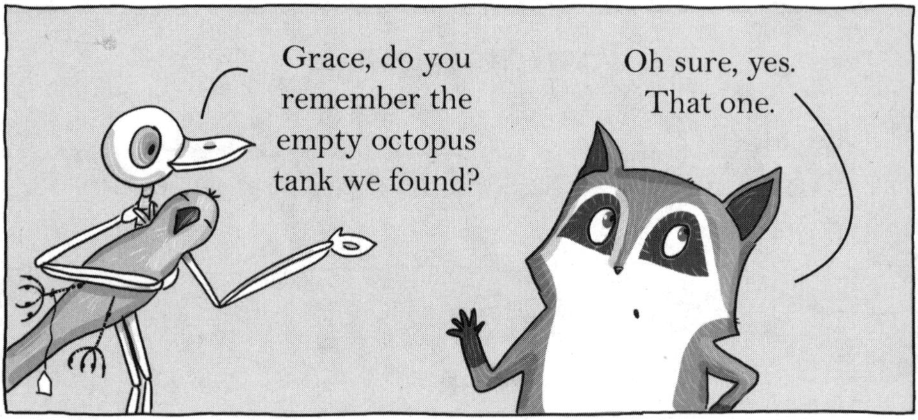
Grace, do you remember the empty octopus tank we found?
Oh sure, yes. That one.

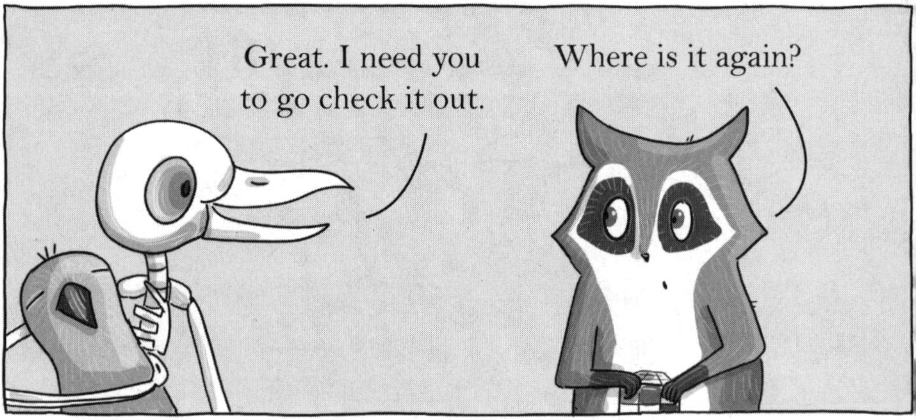
Great. I need you to go check it out.
Where is it again?

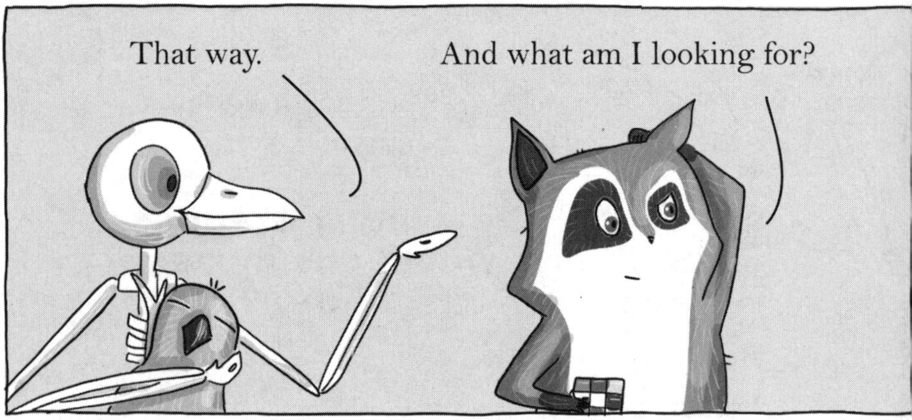
That way.
And what am I looking for?

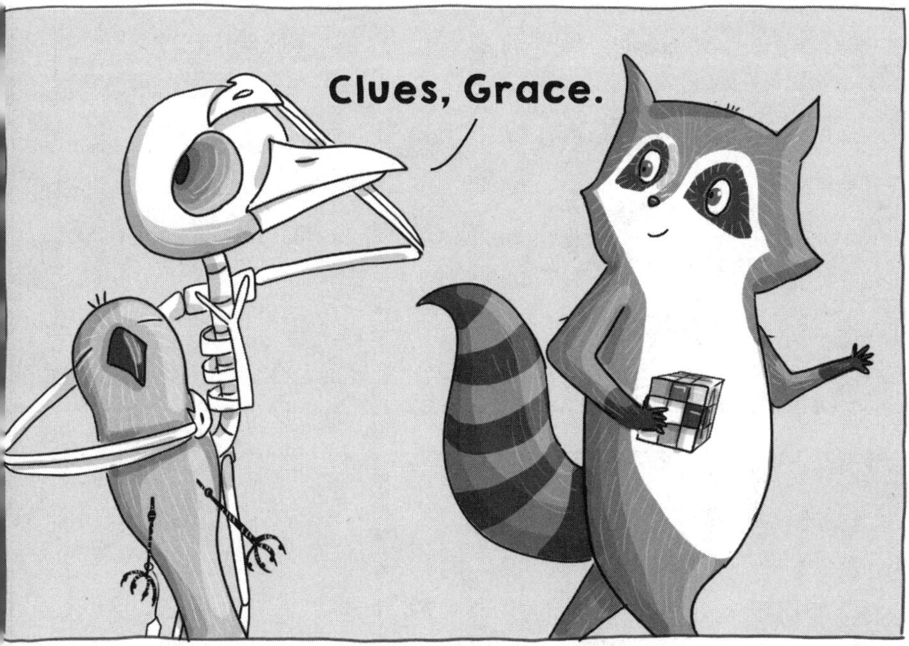
Clues, Grace.

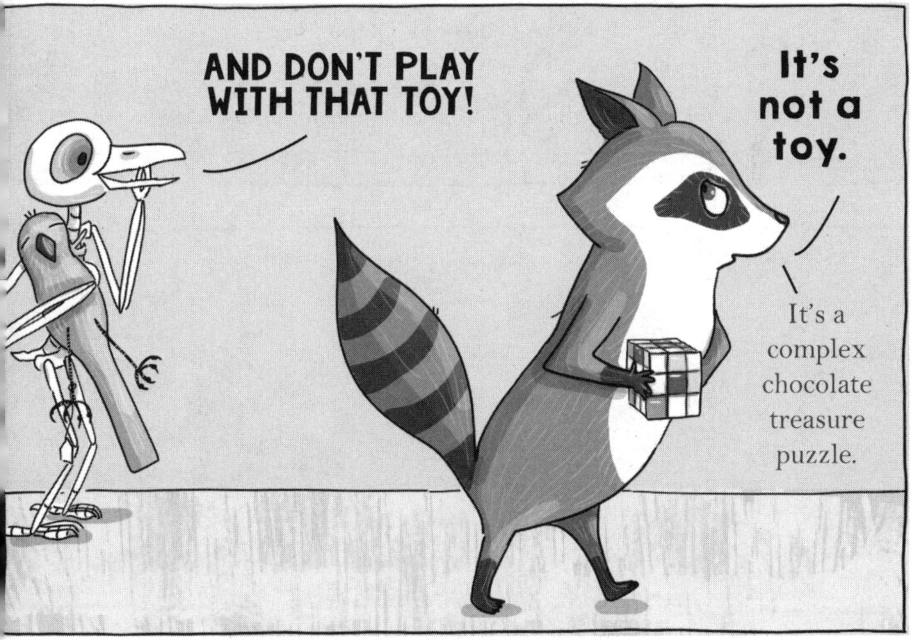
AND DON'T PLAY
WITH THAT TOY!
It's
not a
toy.
It's a
complex
chocolate
treasure
puzzle.

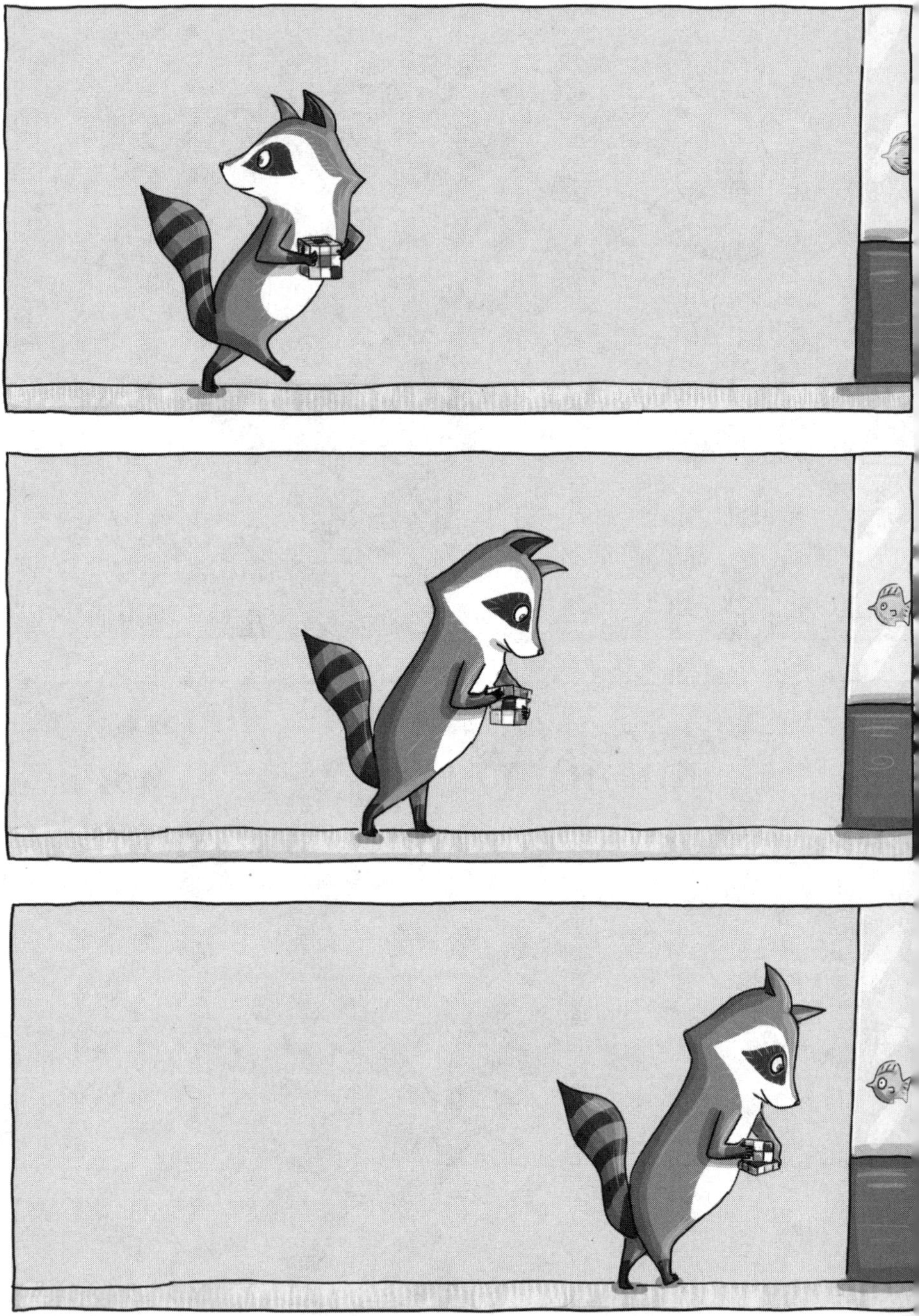

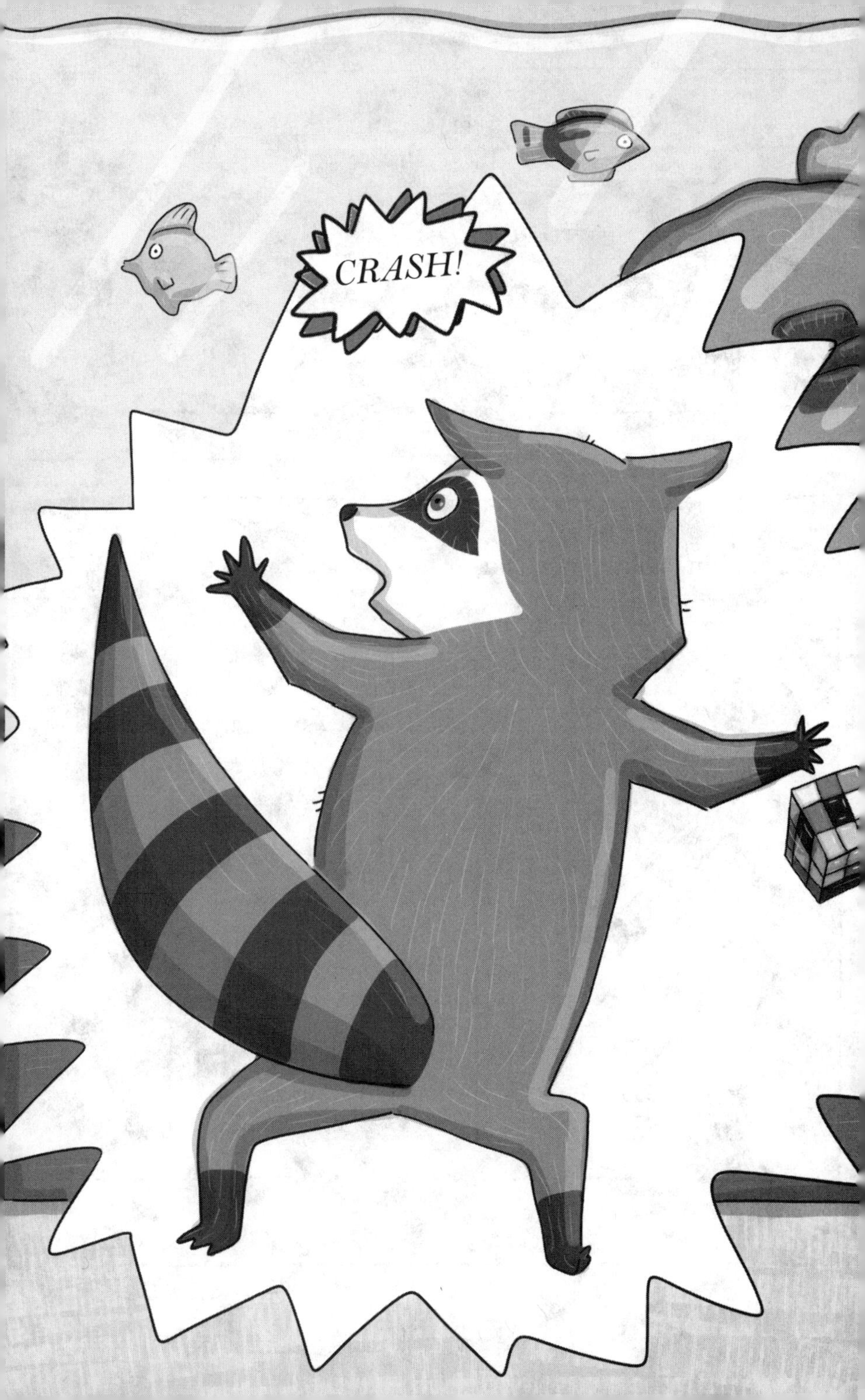
CRASH!

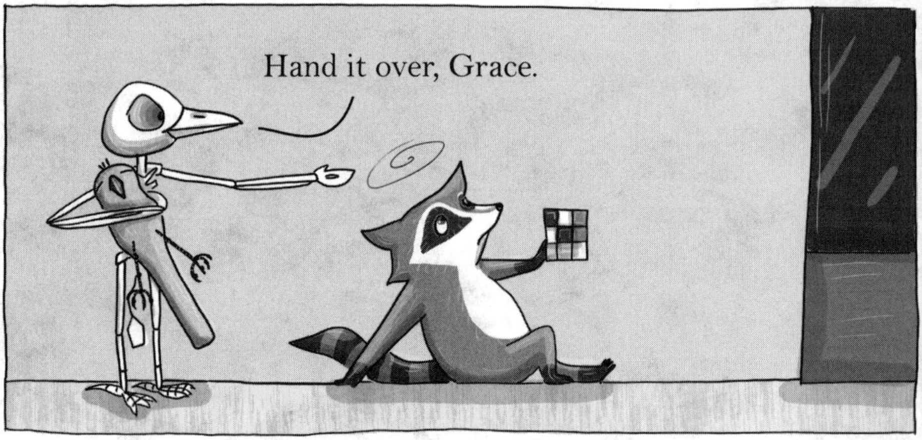
Hand it over, Grace.

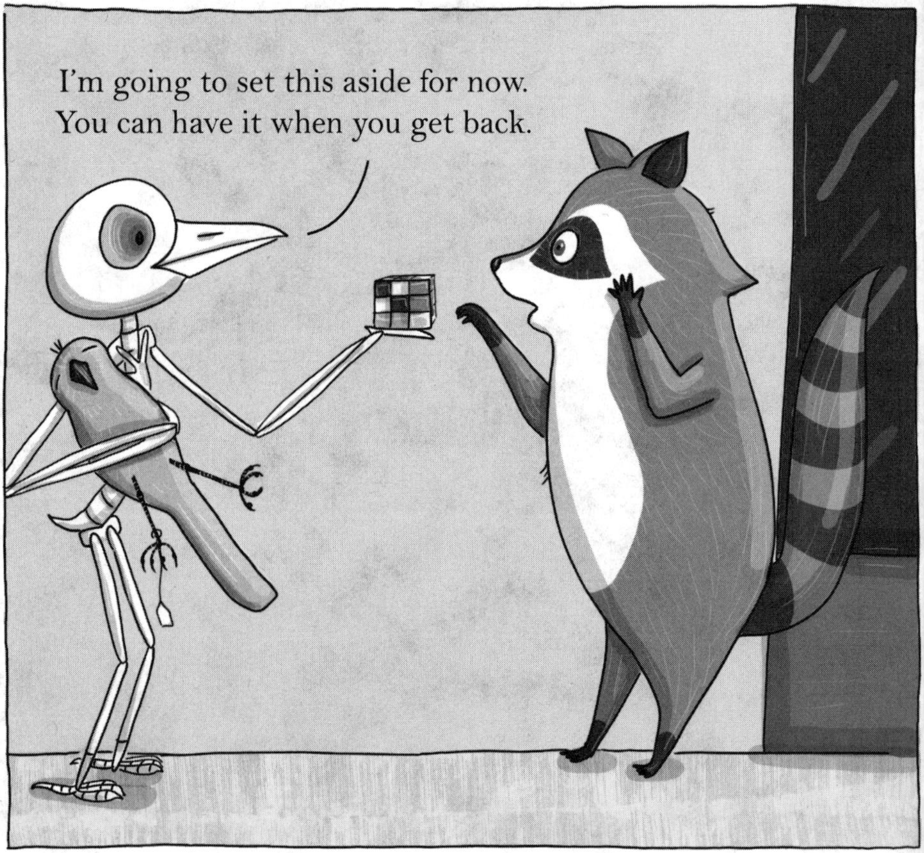
I'm going to set this aside for now. You can have it when you get back.

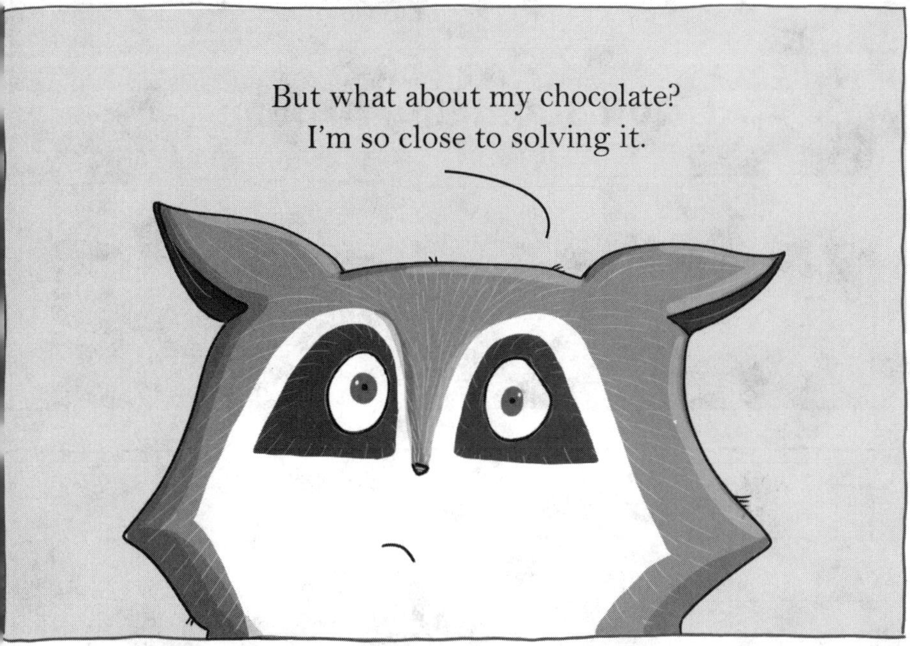
But what about my chocolate? I'm so close to solving it.

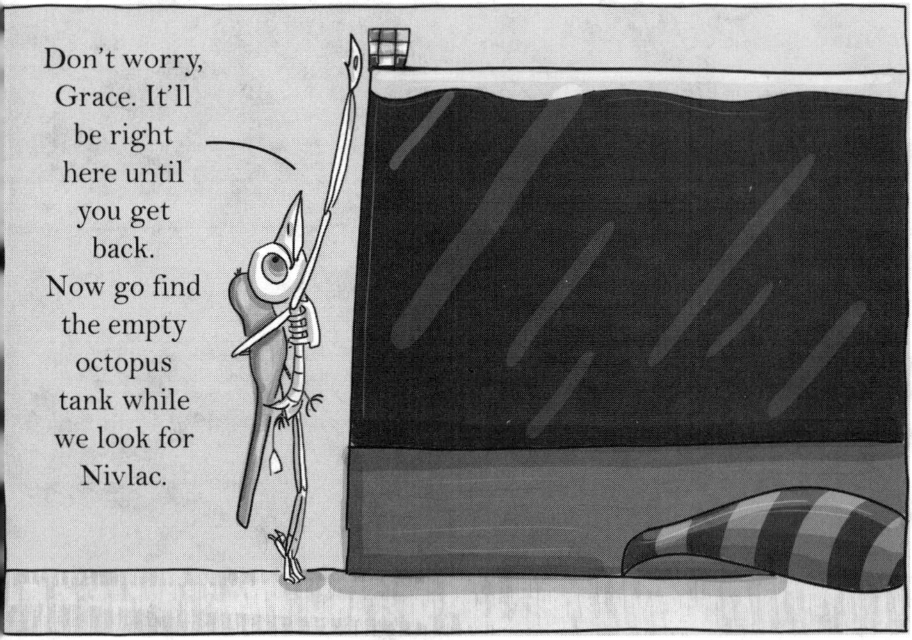
Don't worry, Grace. It'll be right here until you get back. Now go find the empty octopus tank while we look for Nivlac.

CHAPTER 8
Quit Squidding Around

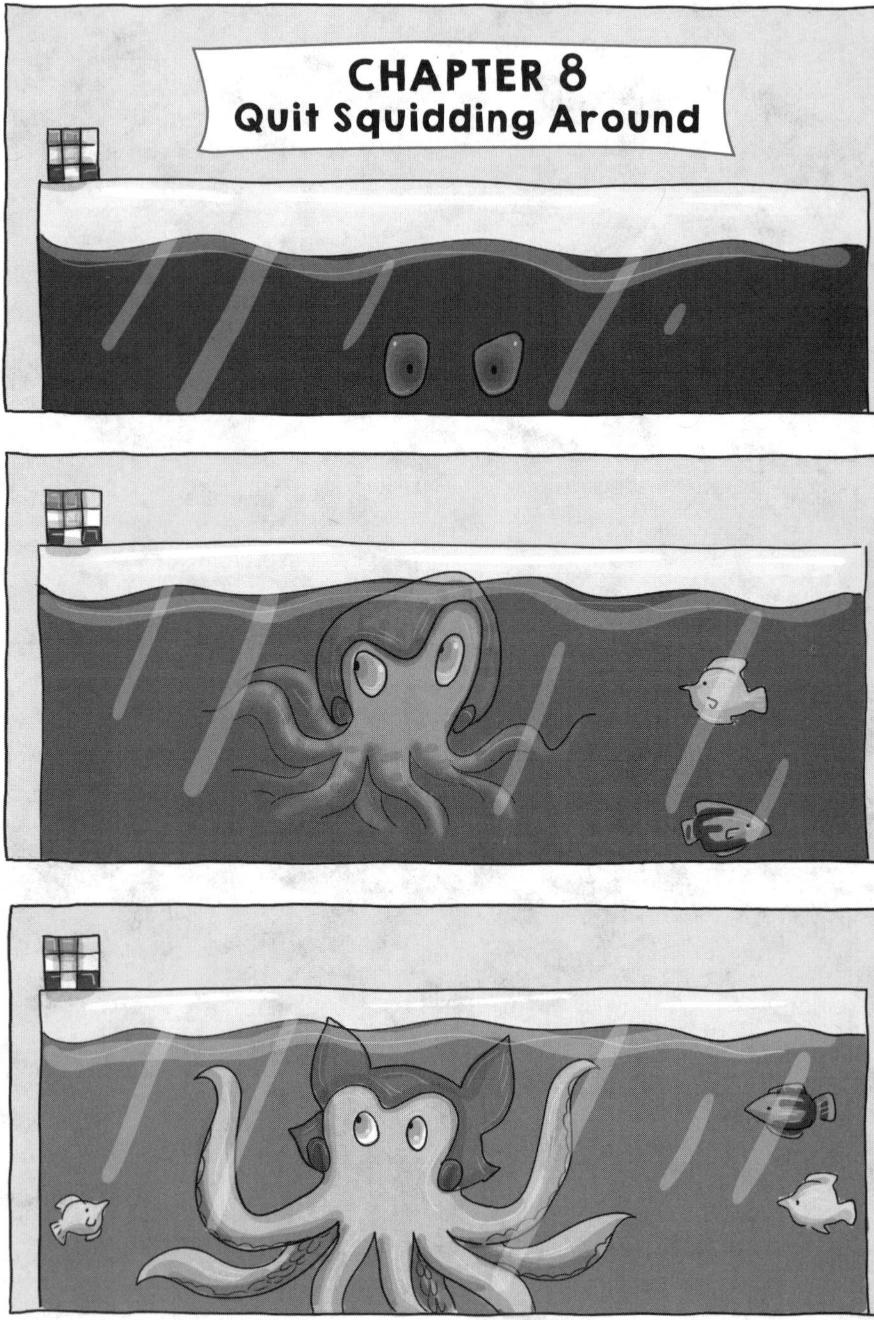

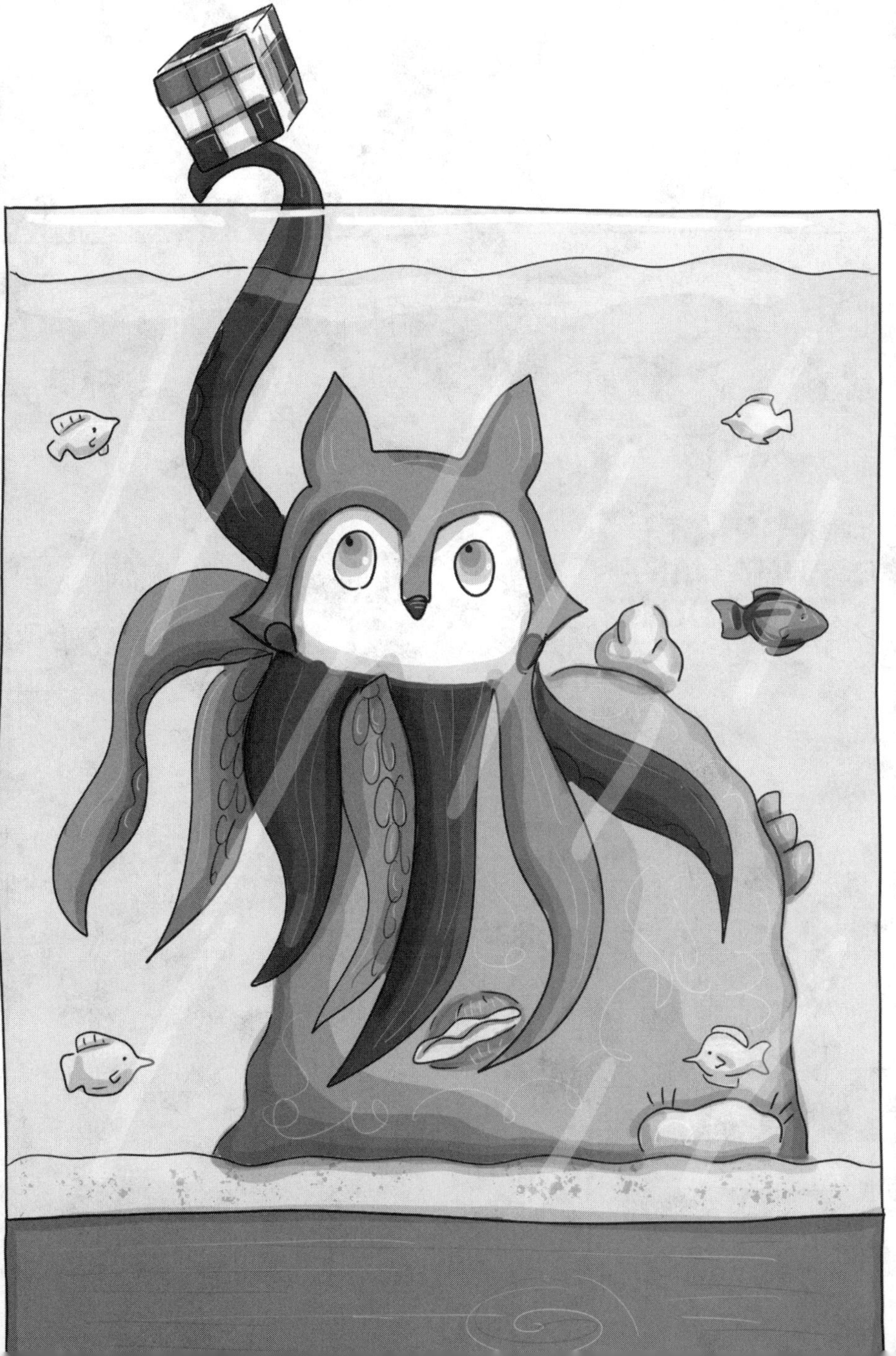

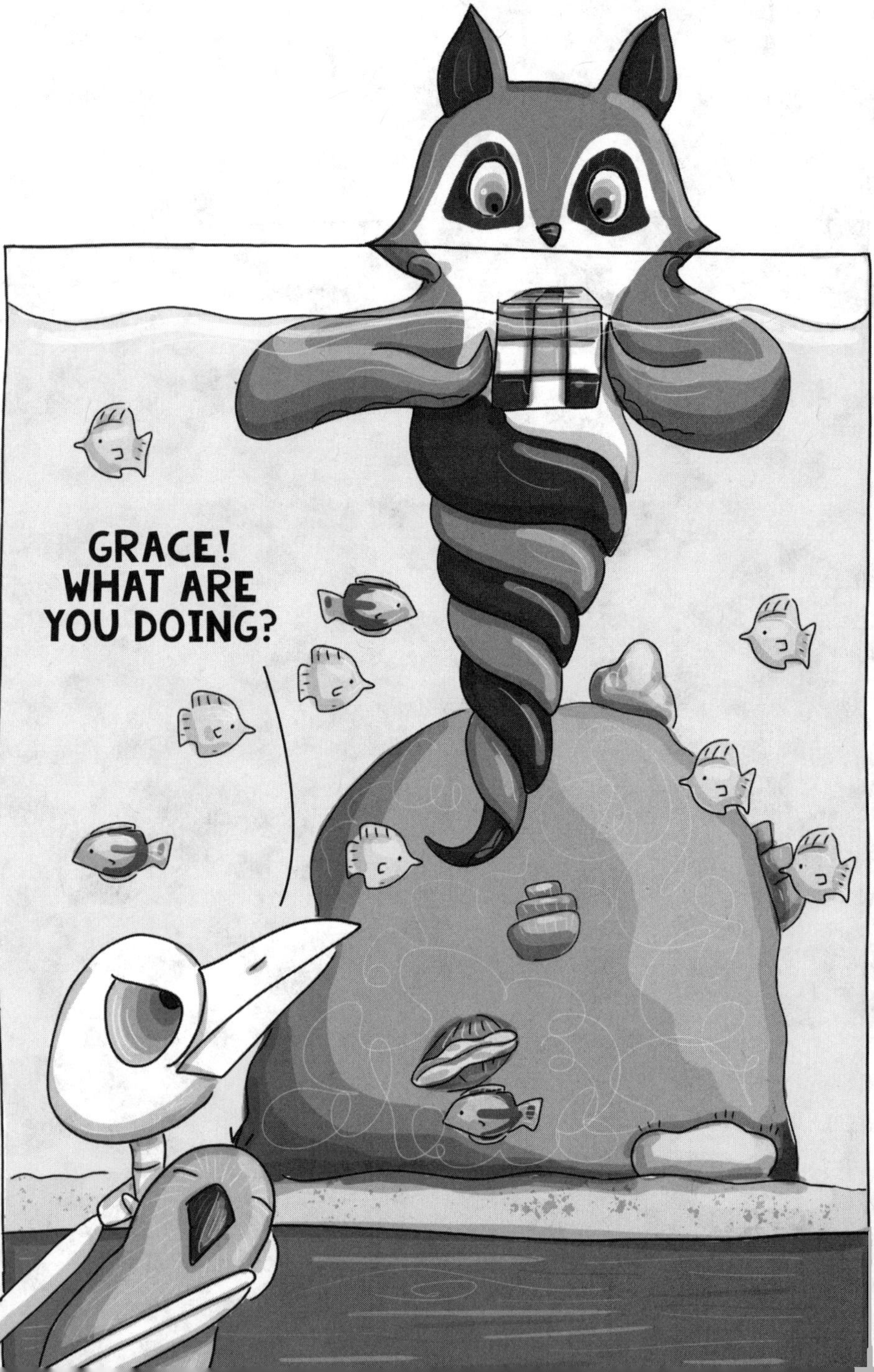
GRACE! WHAT ARE YOU DOING?

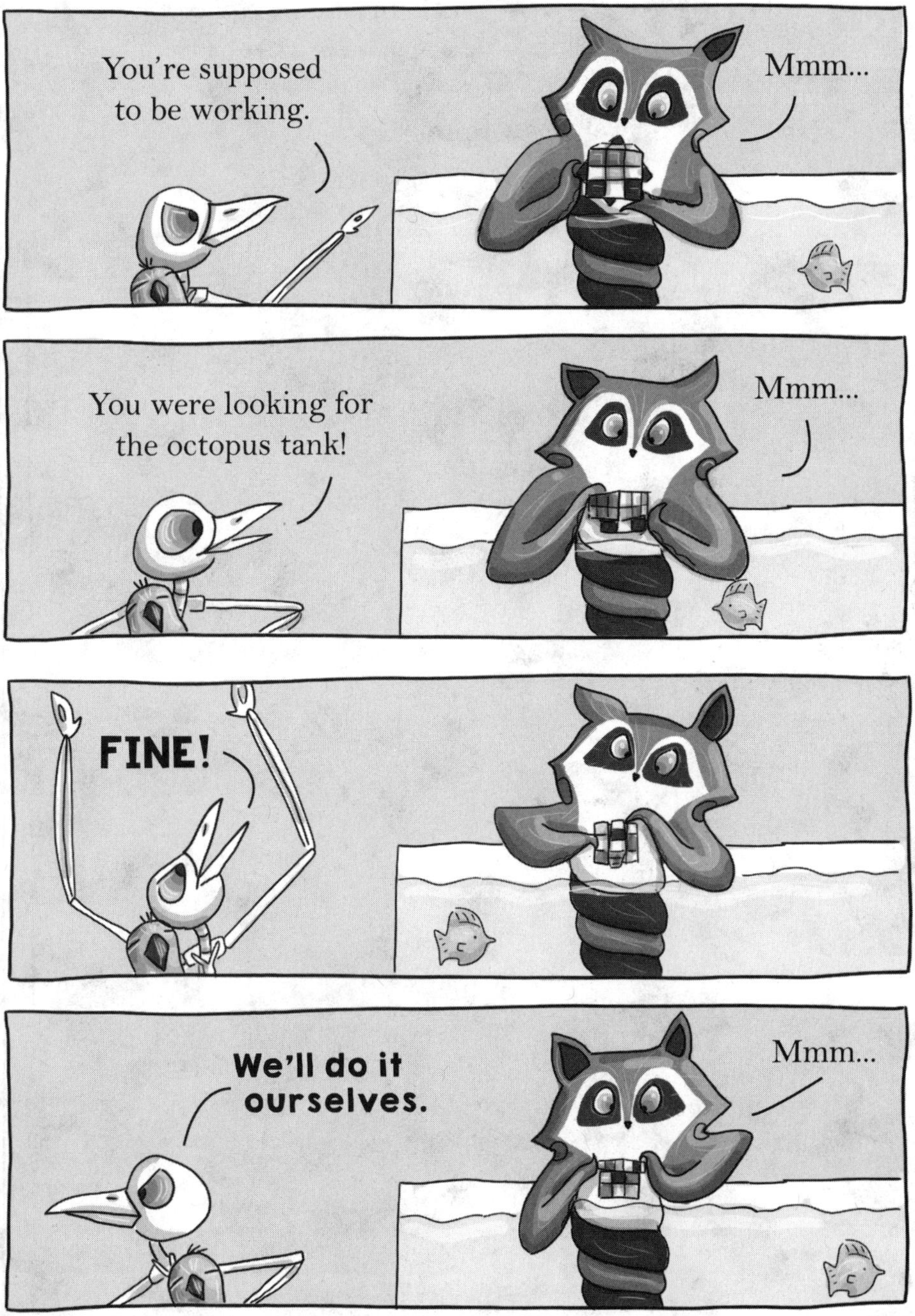
You're supposed to be working.
Mmm...
You were looking for the octopus tank!
Mmm...
FINE!
We'll do it ourselves.
Mmm...

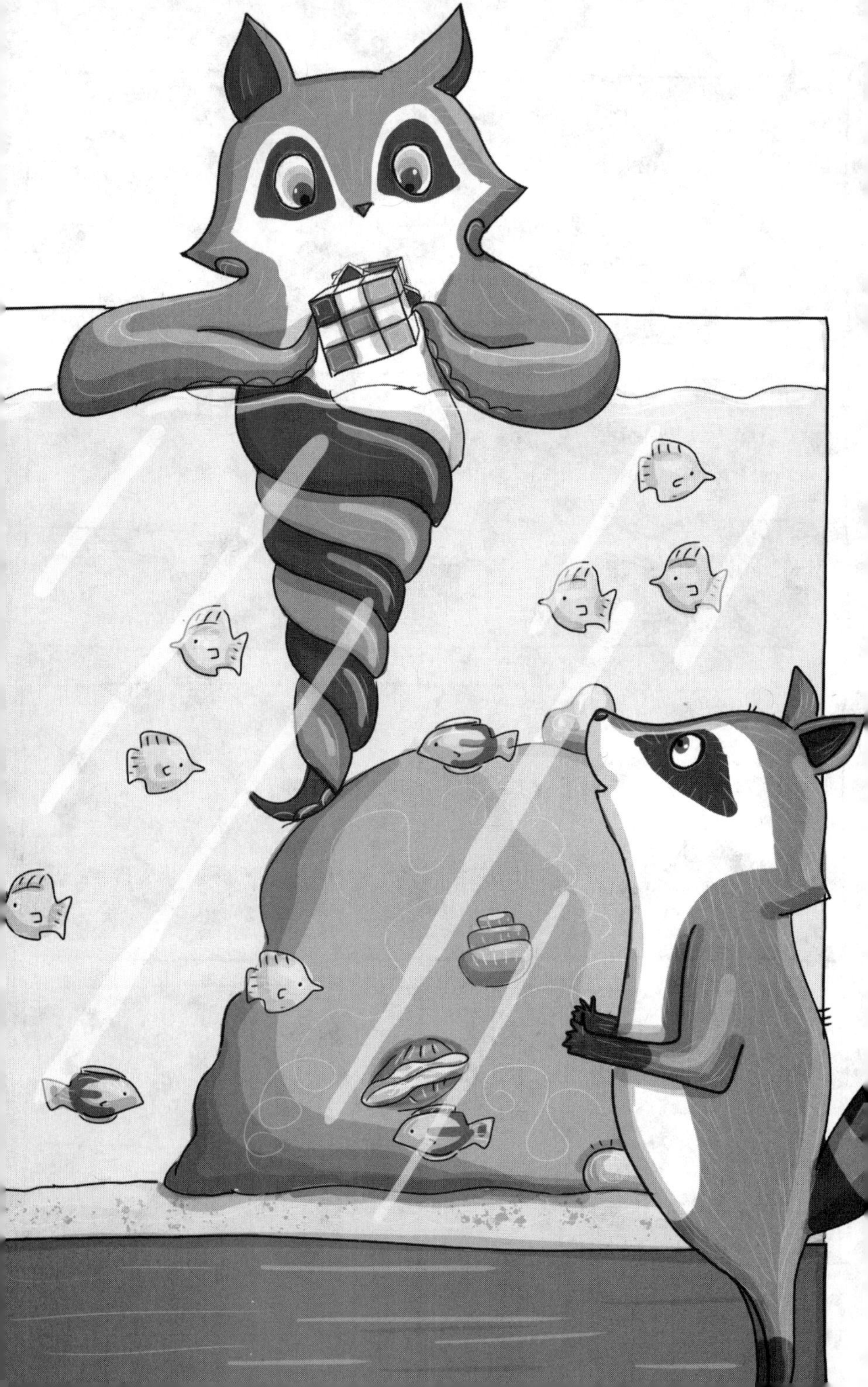

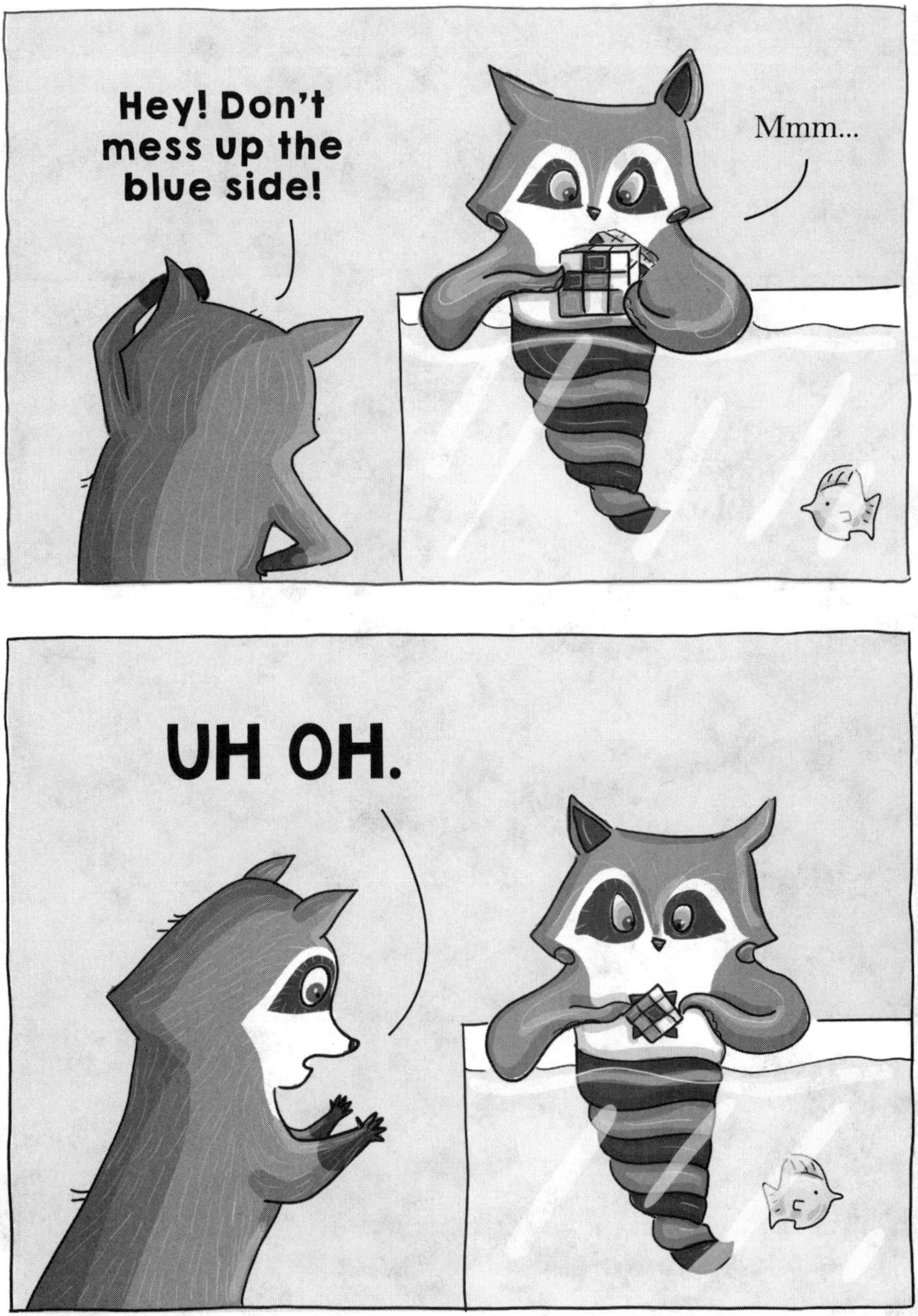
Hey! Don't mess up the blue side!
Mmm...
UH OH.

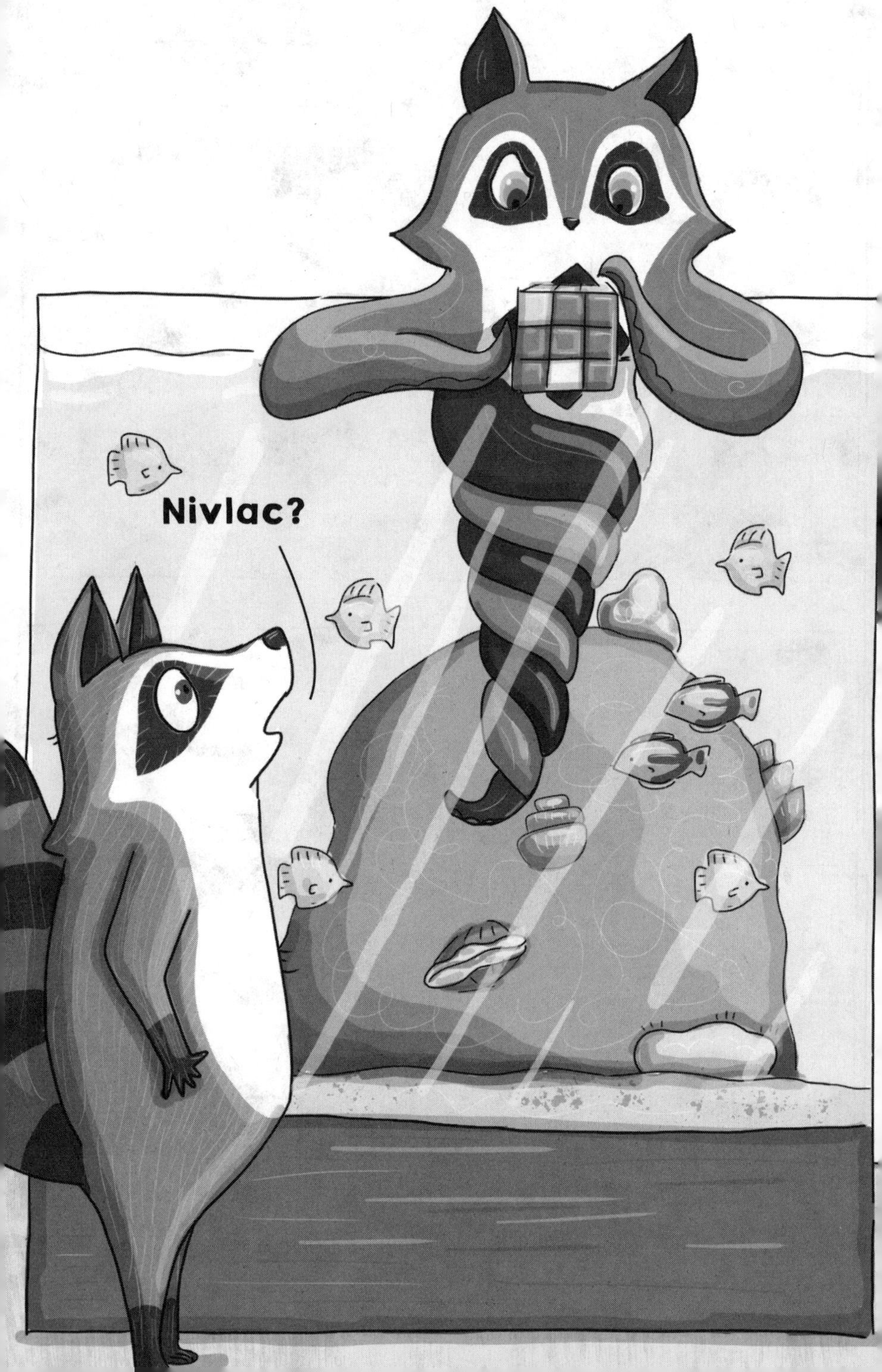
Nivlac?

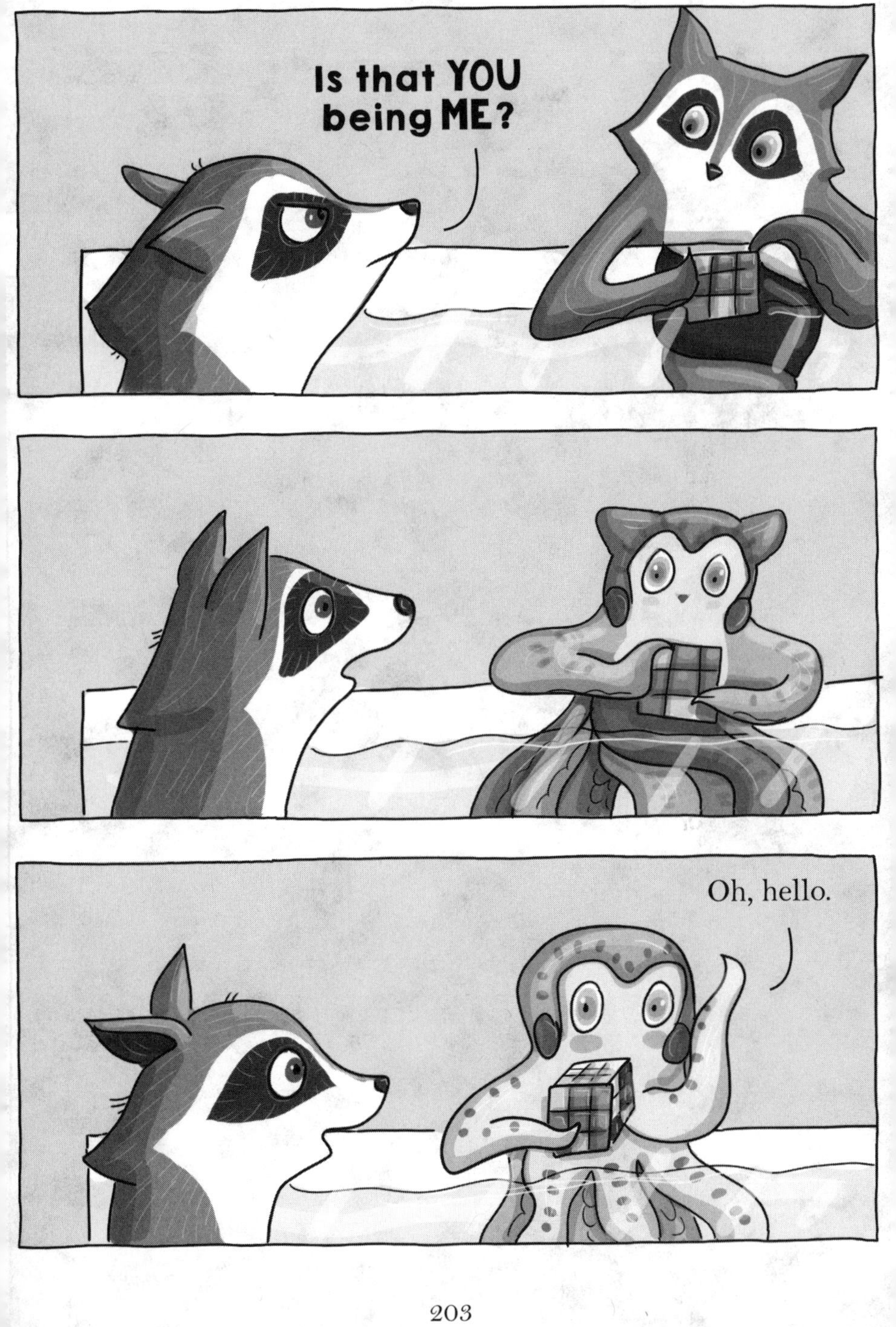
Is that YOU being ME?
Oh, hello.

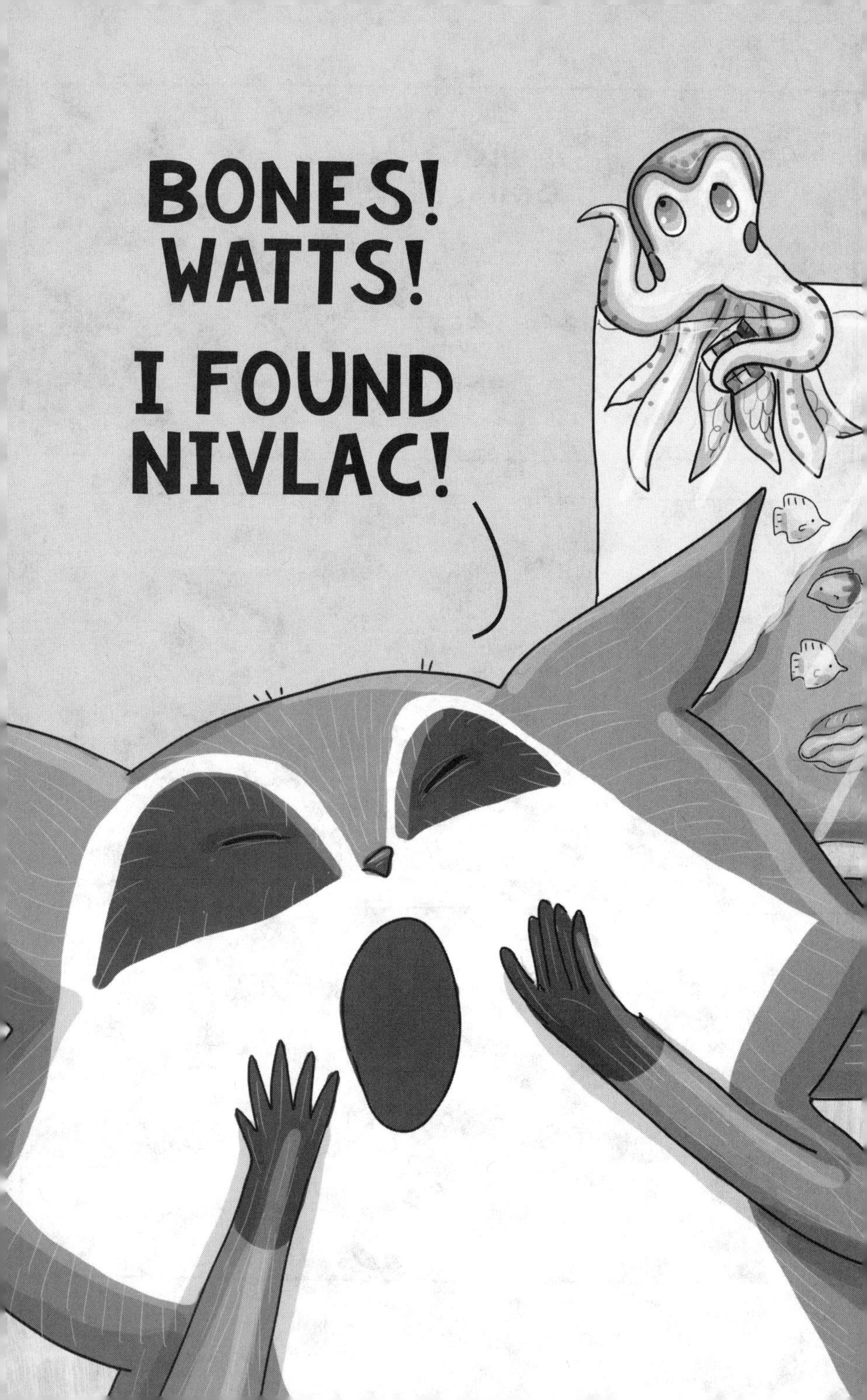
BONES! WATTS!
I FOUND NIVLAC!

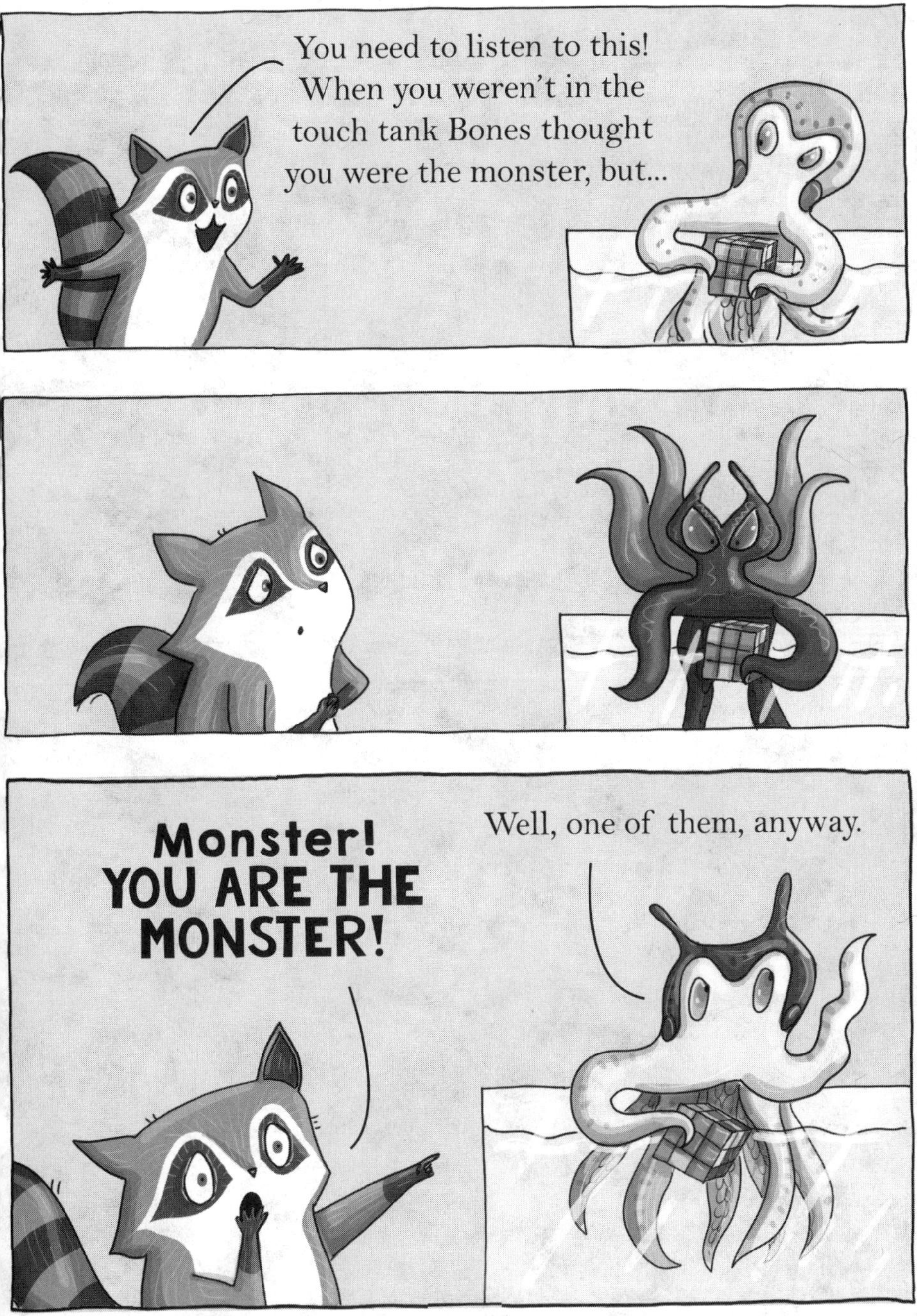
You need to listen to this! When you weren't in the touch tank Bones thought you were the monster, but...
Monster! YOU ARE THE MONSTER!
Well, one of them, anyway.

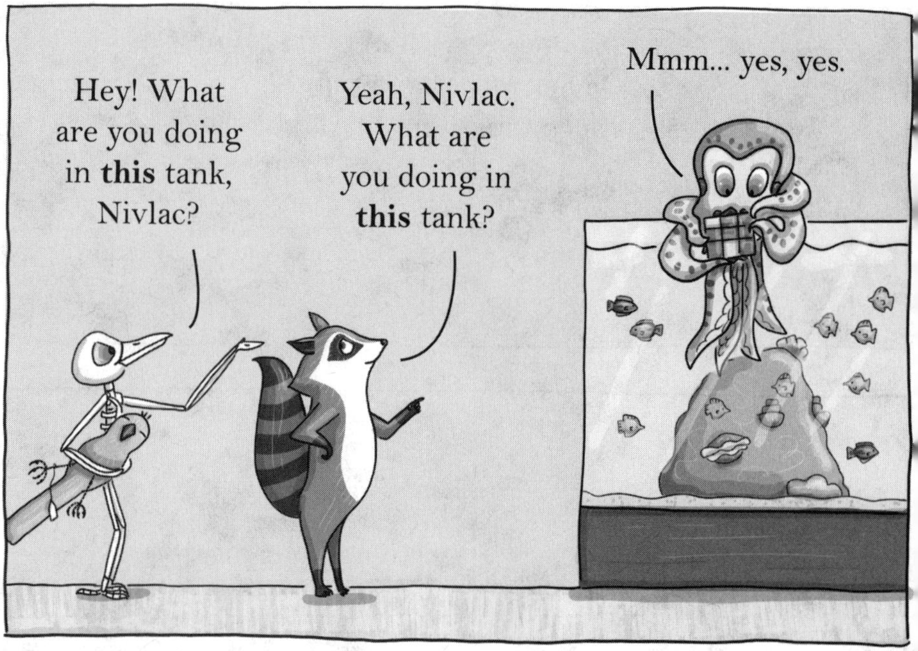
Hey! What are you doing in **this** tank, Nivlac?
Yeah, Nivlac. What are you doing in **this** tank?
Mmm... yes, yes.

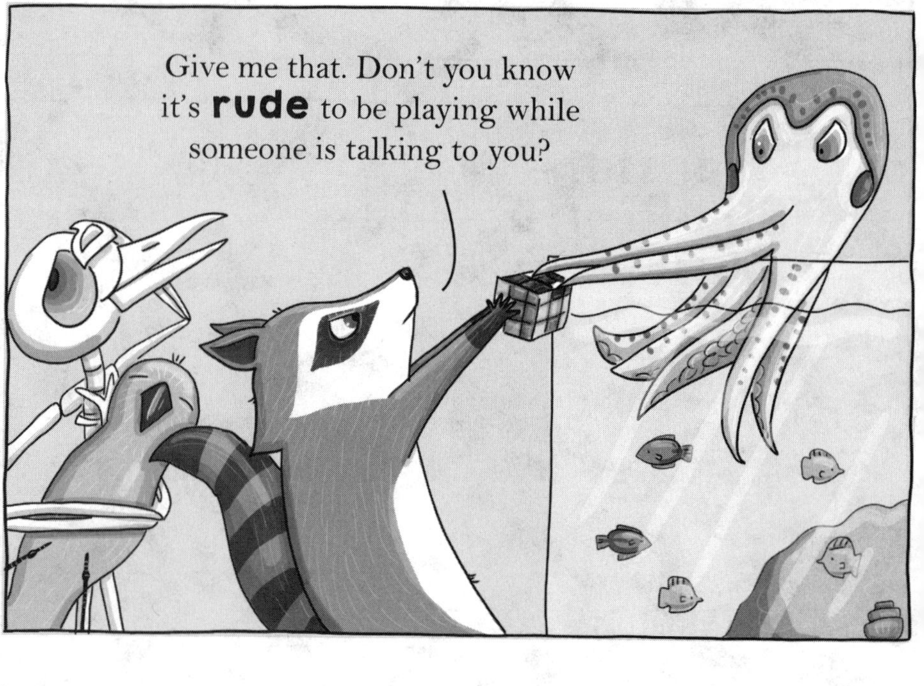
Give me that. Don't you know it's **rude** to be playing while someone is talking to you?

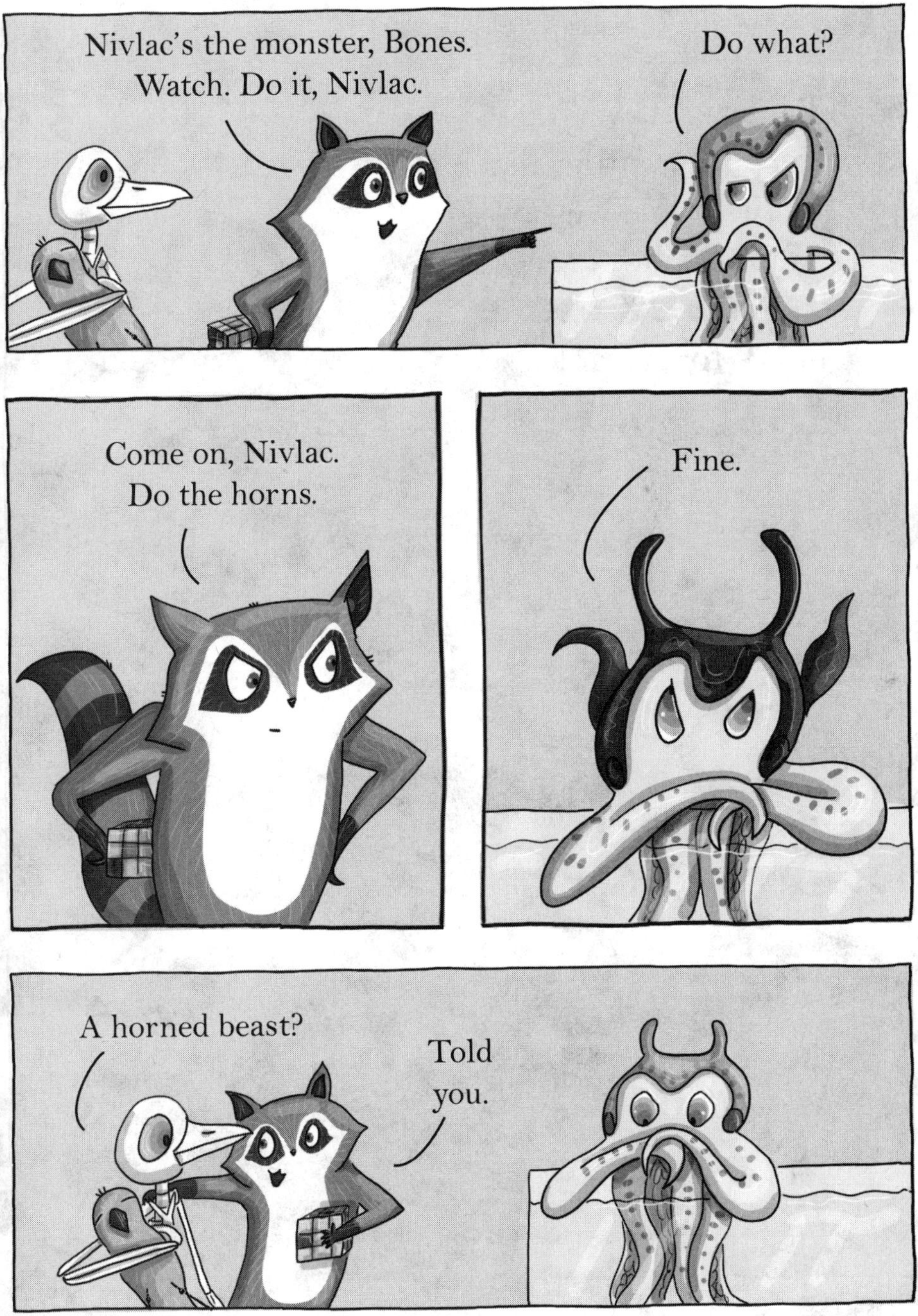
Nivlac's the monster, Bones.
Watch. Do it, Nivlac.
Do what?
Come on, Nivlac.
Do the horns.
Fine.
A horned beast?
Told
you.

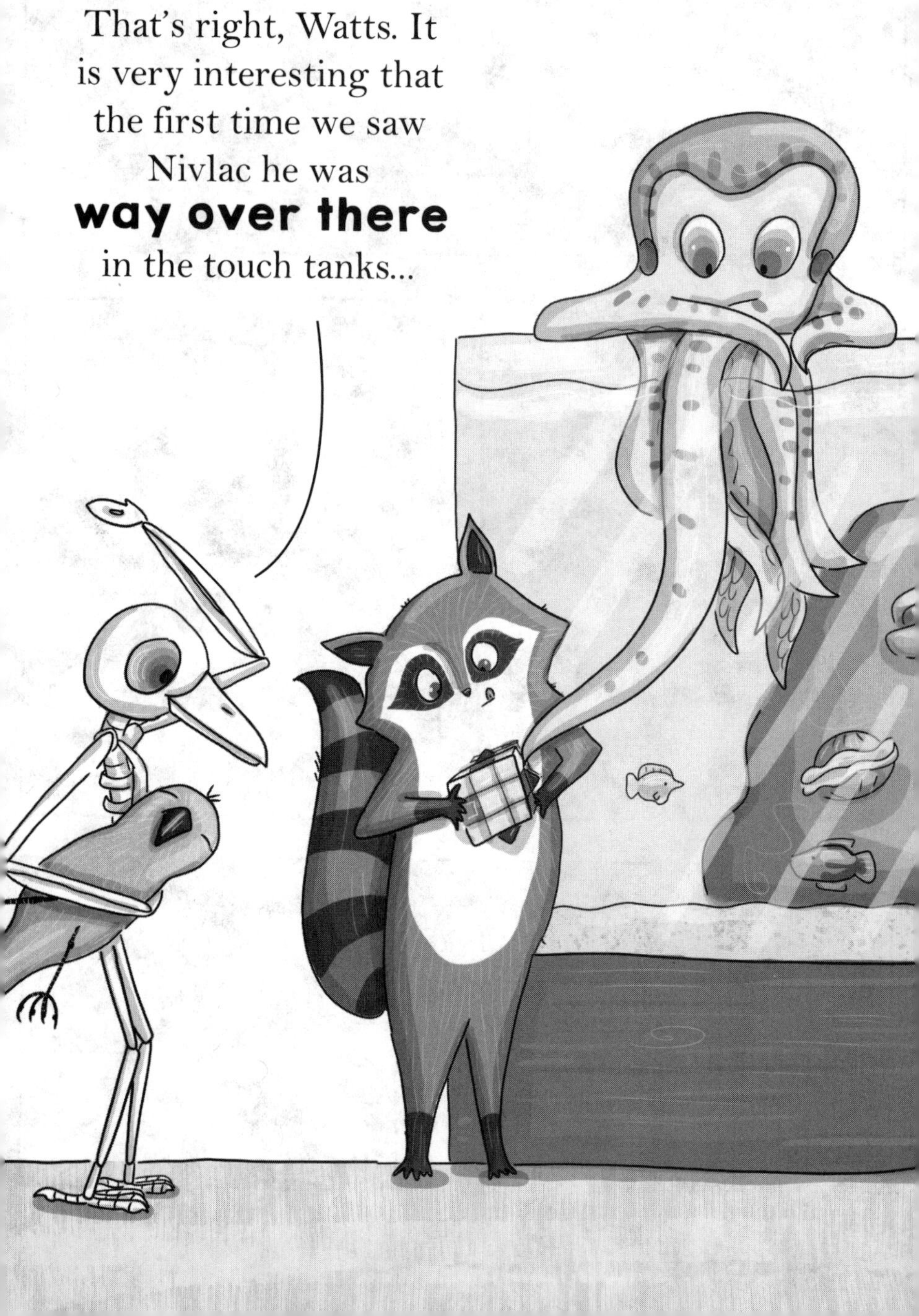
That's right, Watts. It is very interesting that the first time we saw Nivlac he was **way over there** in the touch tanks...

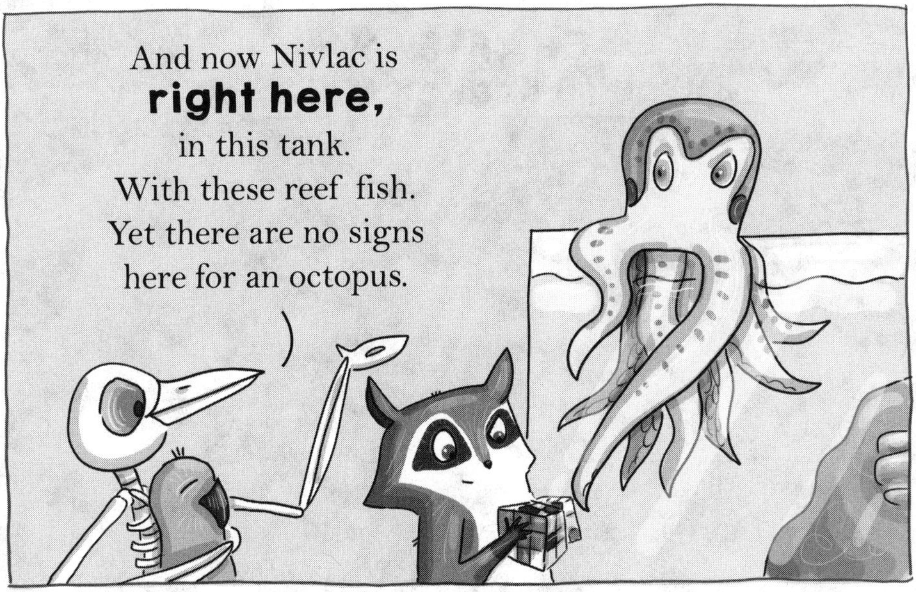
And now Nivlac is **right here,** in this tank. With these reef fish. Yet there are no signs here for an octopus.

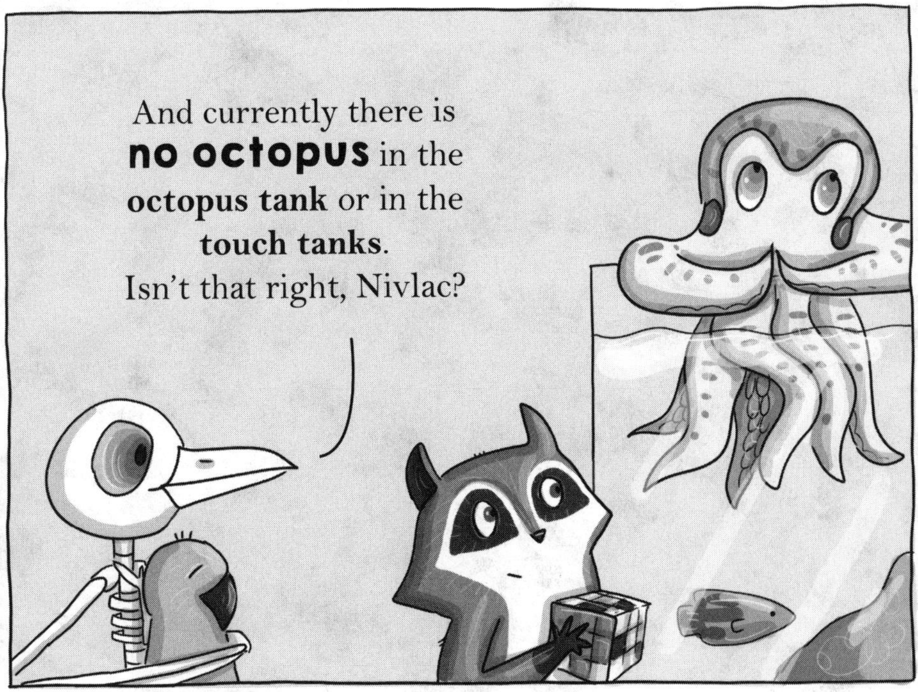
And currently there is **no octopus** in the **octopus tank** or in the **touch tanks**. Isn't that right, Nivlac?

CHAPTER 9
You're Kraken Me Up

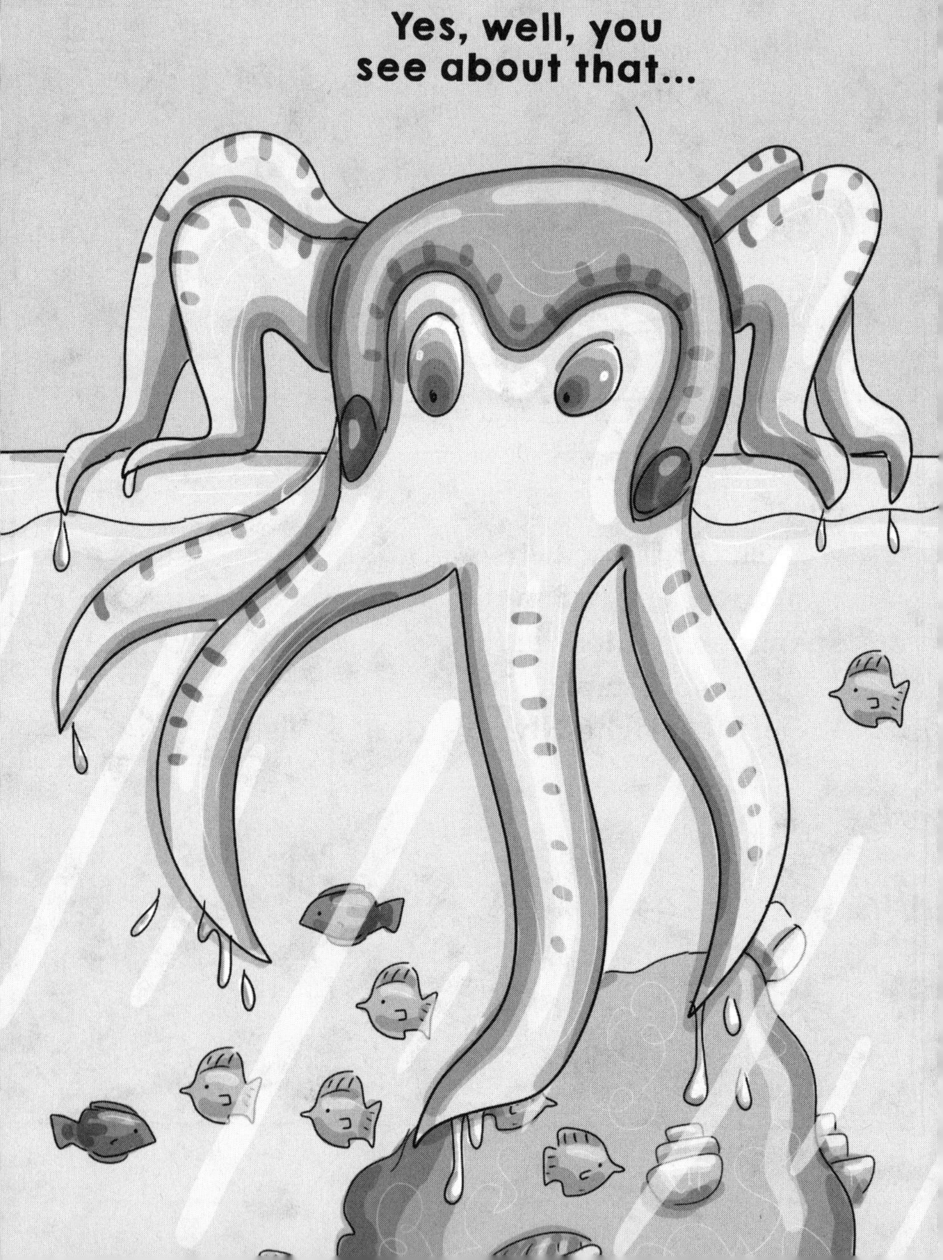
Yes, well, you see about that...

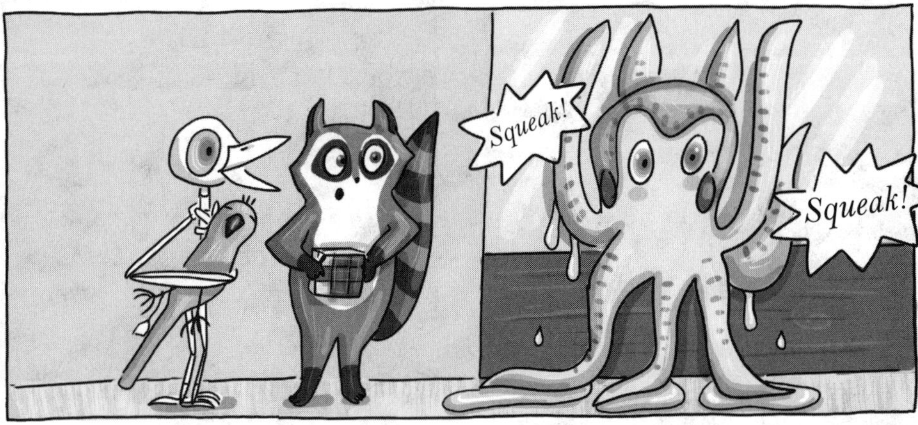
Squeak!
Squeak!

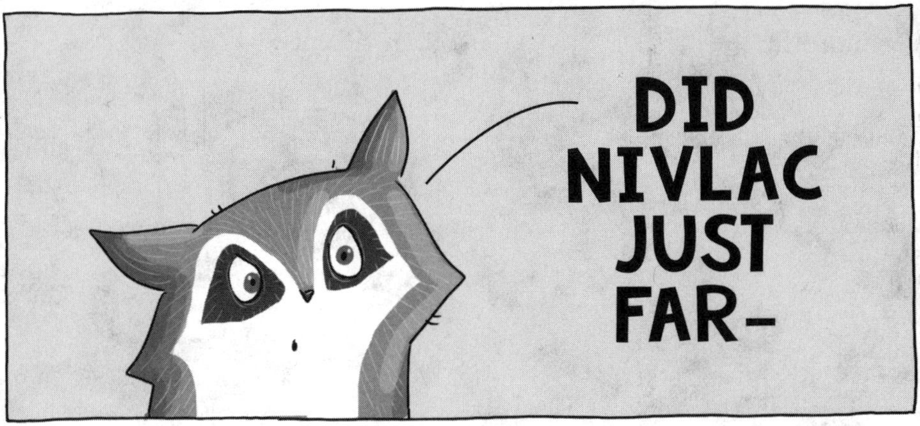
DID NIVLAC JUST FAR–

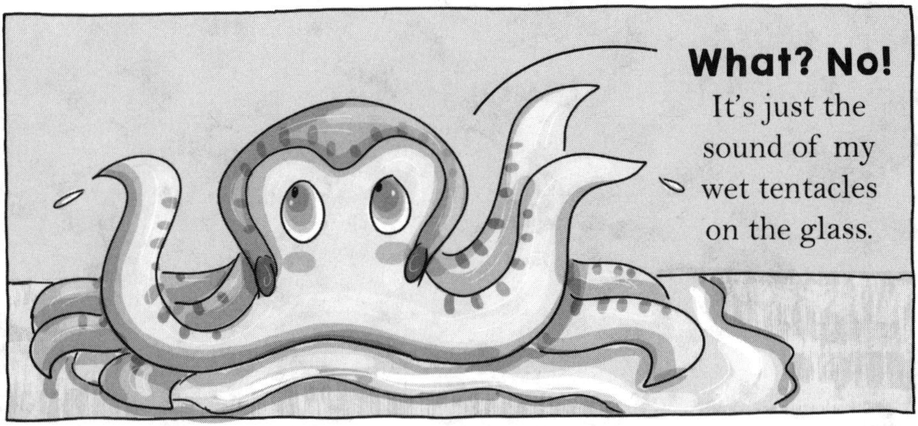
What? No!
It's just the sound of my wet tentacles on the glass.

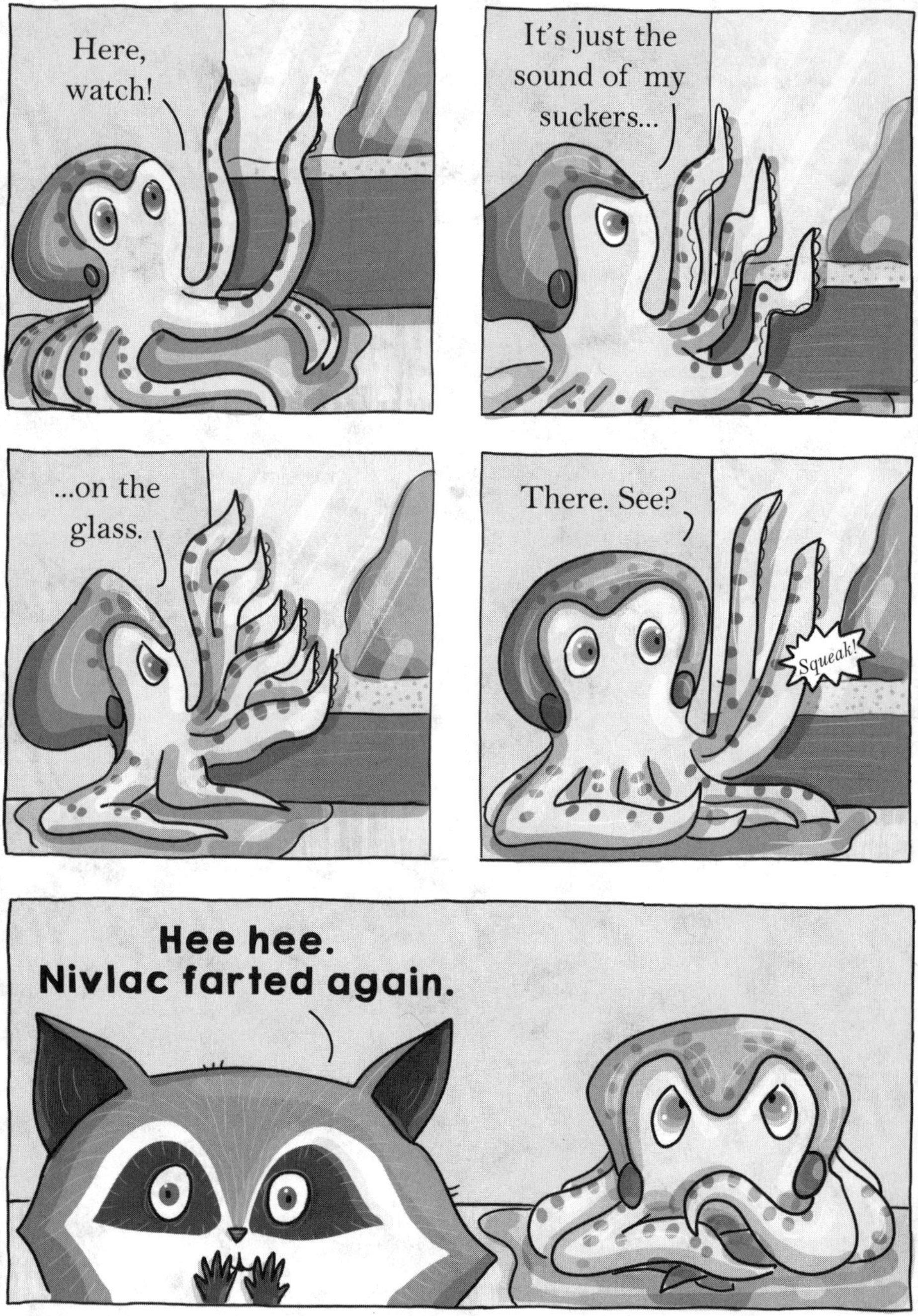
Here, watch!
It's just the sound of my suckers...
...on the glass.
There. See?
Squeak!
Hee hee. Nivlac farted again.

Look, it's really boring here!

I'm stuck in a tank all day and the only toy I've got is this jar.

Open the jar. Close the jar.

IT'S MAKING ME CRAZY!

I need to be out here, enjoying all the **wonderful** and **delicious** things this museum has to offer.

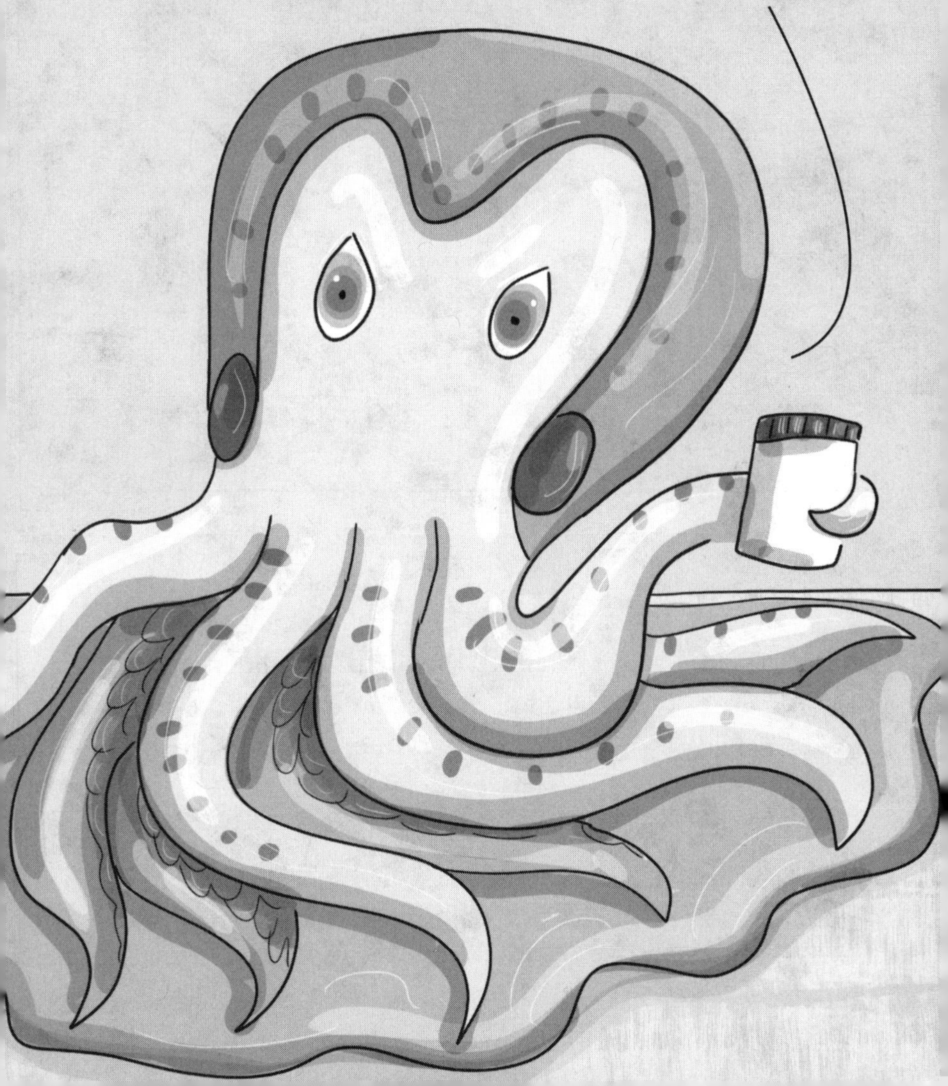

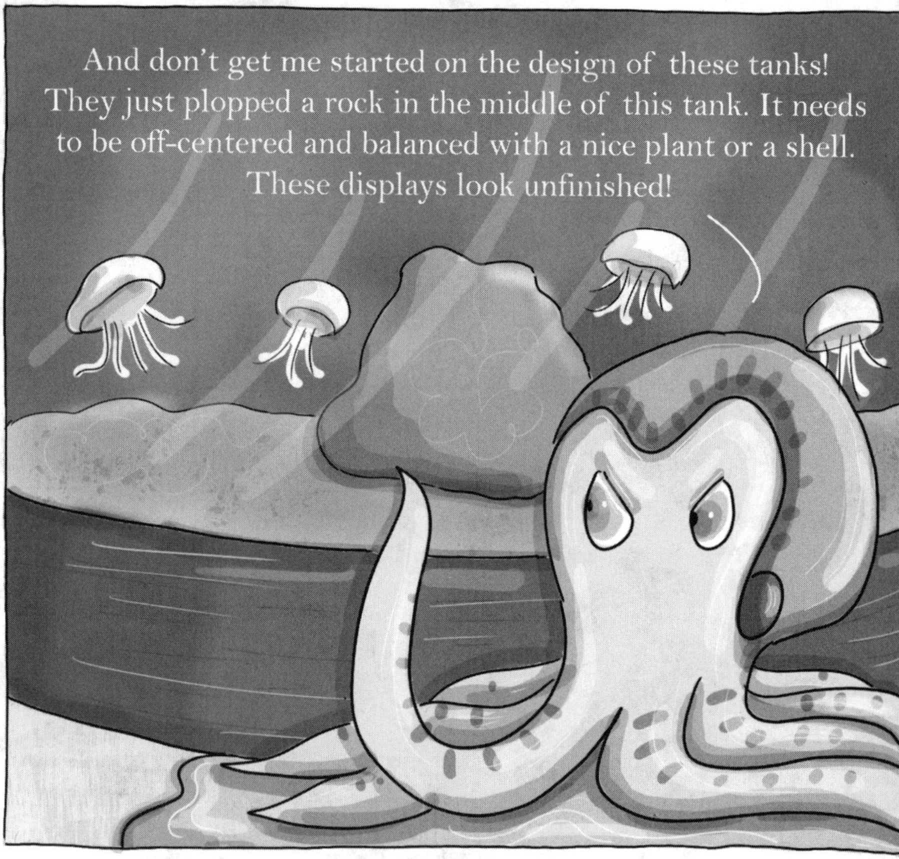
And don't get me started on the design of these tanks! They just plopped a rock in the middle of this tank. It needs to be off-centered and balanced with a nice plant or a shell. These displays look unfinished!

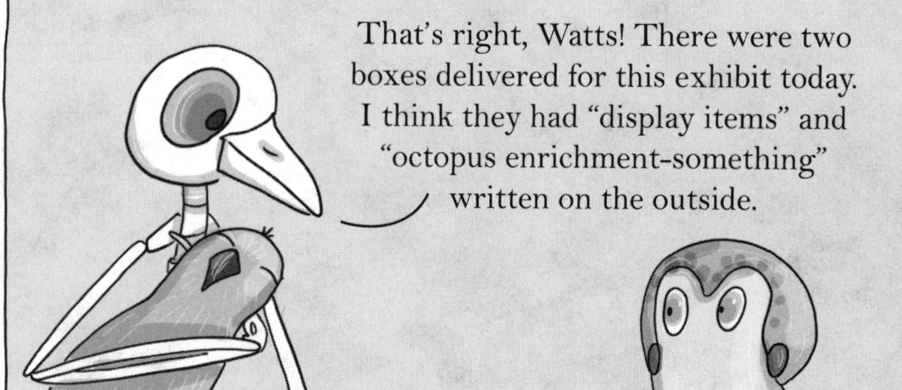
That's right, Watts! There were two boxes delivered for this exhibit today. I think they had "display items" and "octopus enrichment-something" written on the outside.

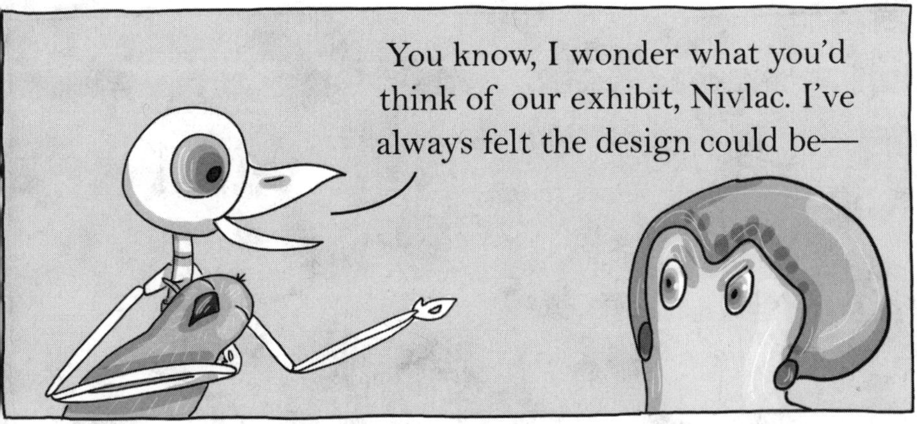
You know, I wonder what you'd think of our exhibit, Nivlac. I've always felt the design could be—

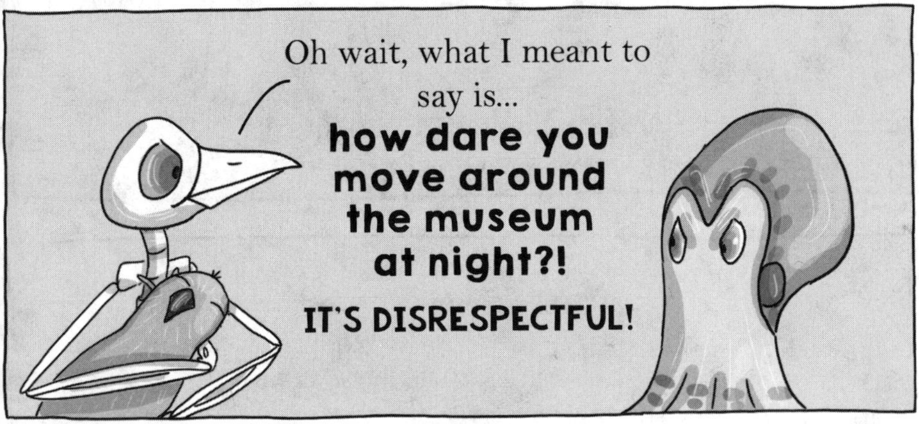
Oh wait, what I meant to say is...
how dare you move around the museum at night?!
IT'S DISRESPECTFUL!

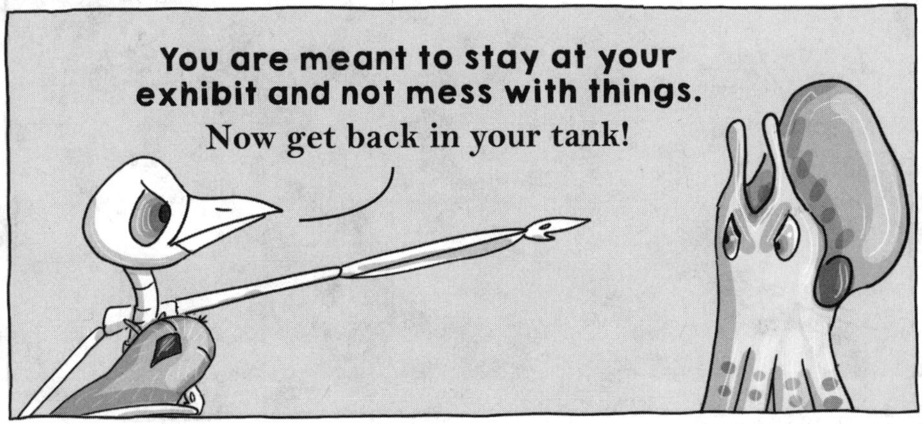
You are meant to stay at your exhibit and not mess with things.
Now get back in your tank!

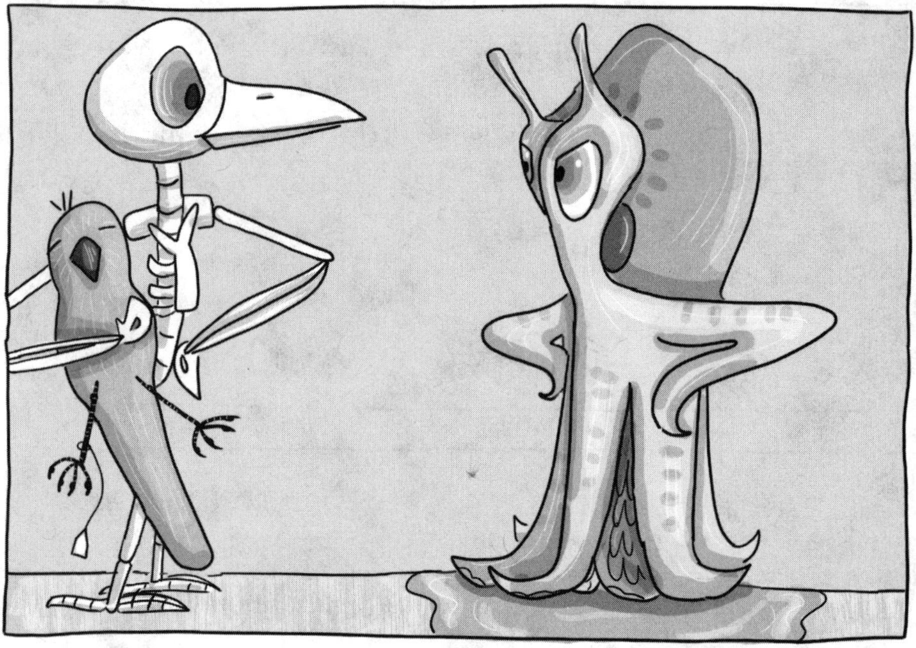

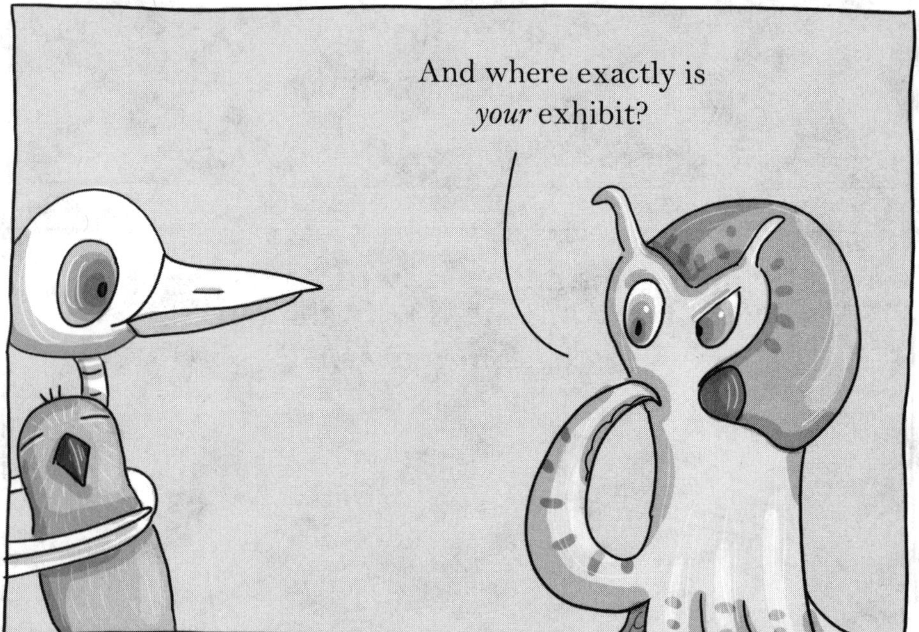
And where exactly is *your* exhibit?

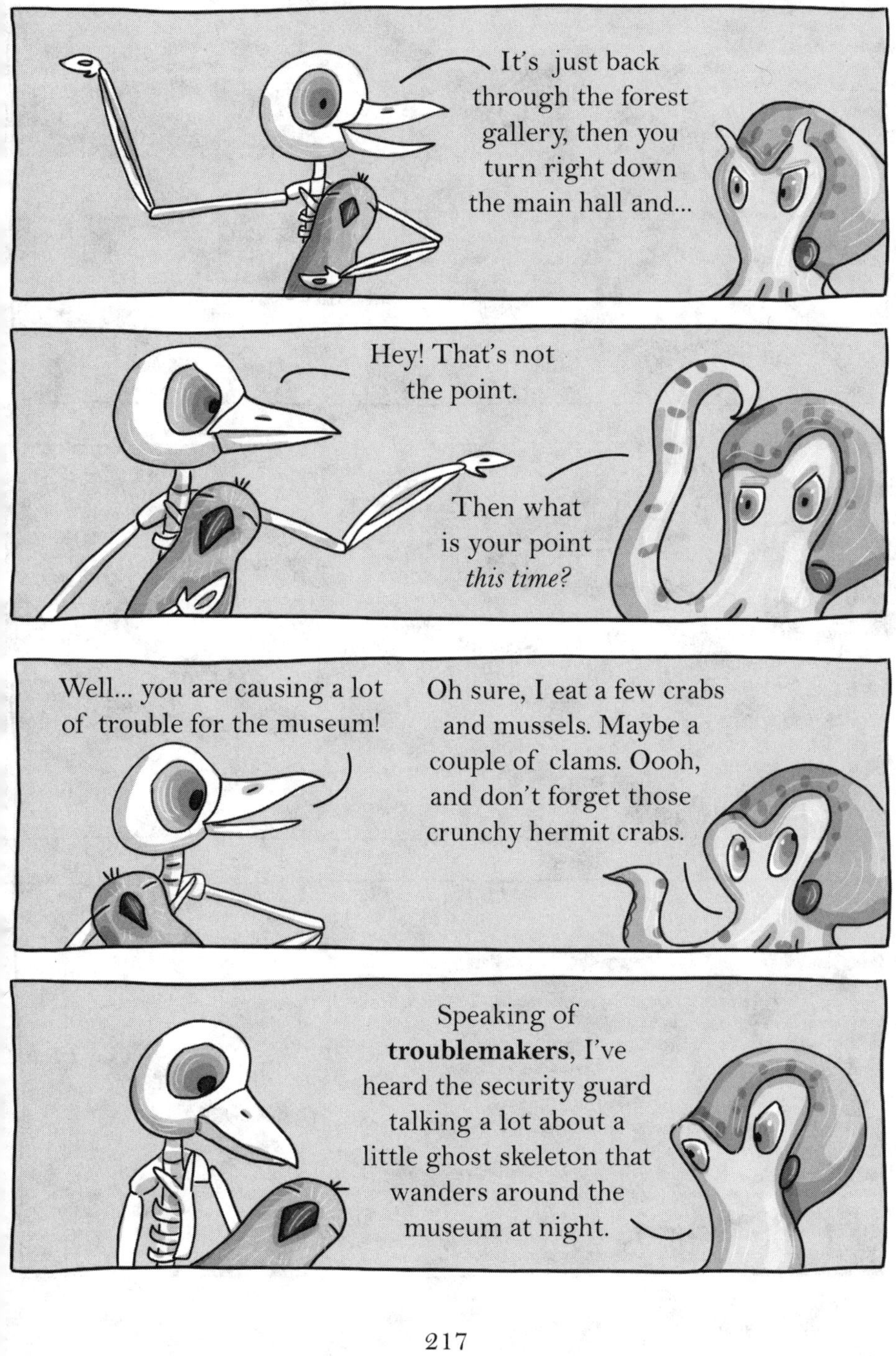
It's just back through the forest gallery, then you turn right down the main hall and...
Hey! That's not the point.
Then what is your point *this time?*
Well... you are causing a lot of trouble for the museum!
Oh sure, I eat a few crabs and mussels. Maybe a couple of clams. Oooh, and don't forget those crunchy hermit crabs.
Speaking of **troublemakers**, I've heard the security guard talking a lot about a little ghost skeleton that wanders around the museum at night.

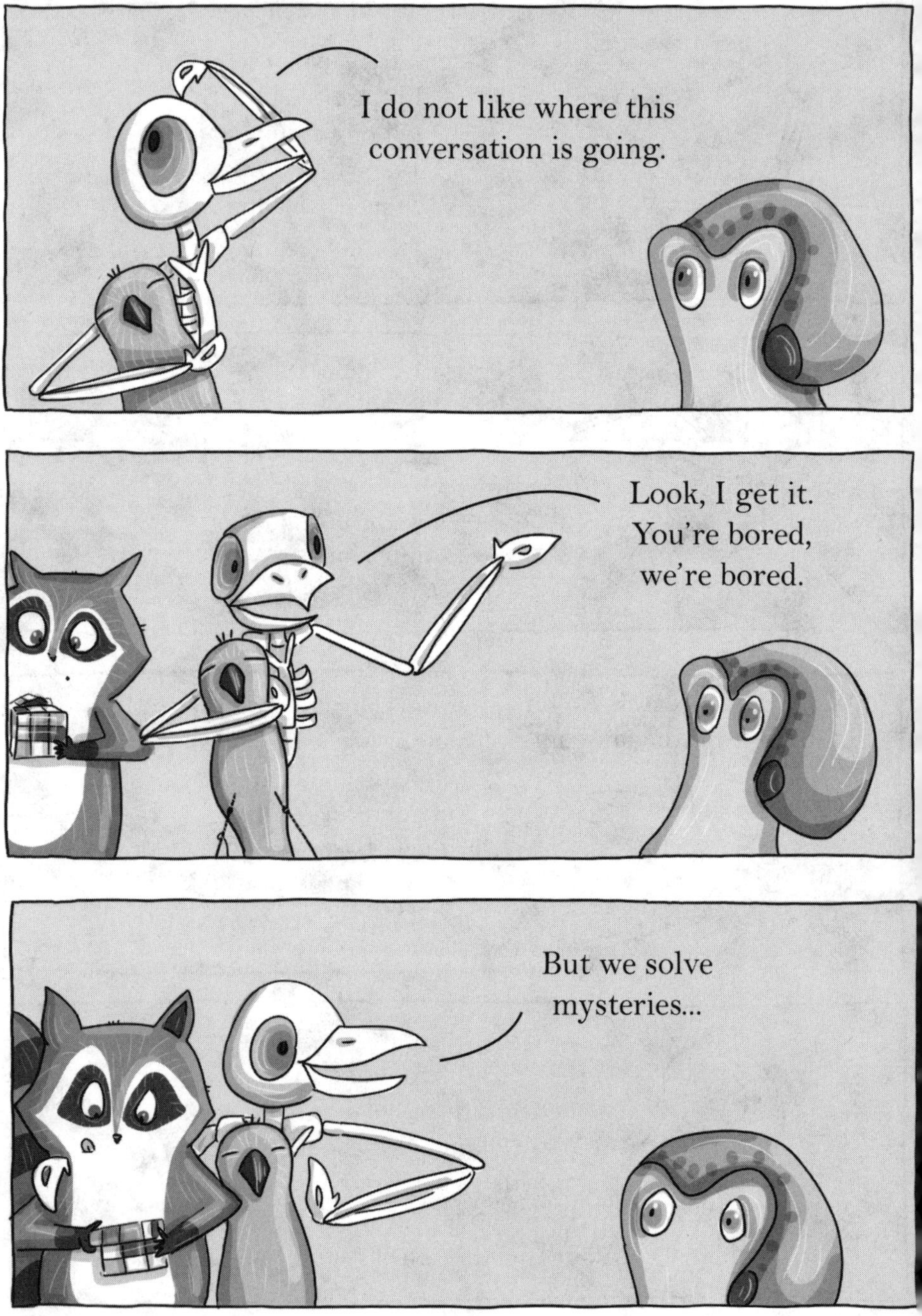
I do not like where this conversation is going.
Look, I get it. You're bored, we're bored.
But we solve mysteries...

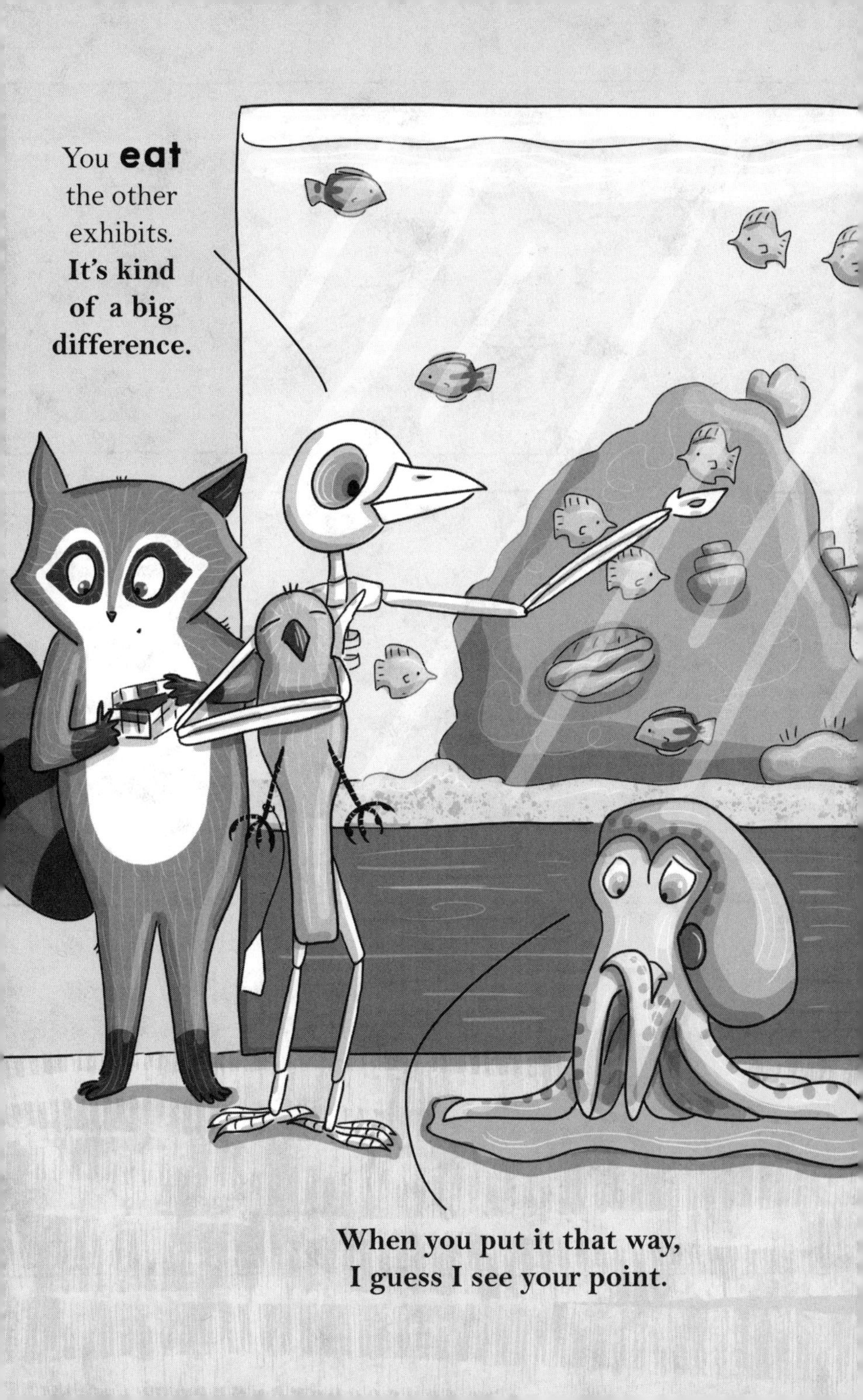
You **eat** the other exhibits. **It's kind of a big difference.**
When you put it that way, I guess I see your point.

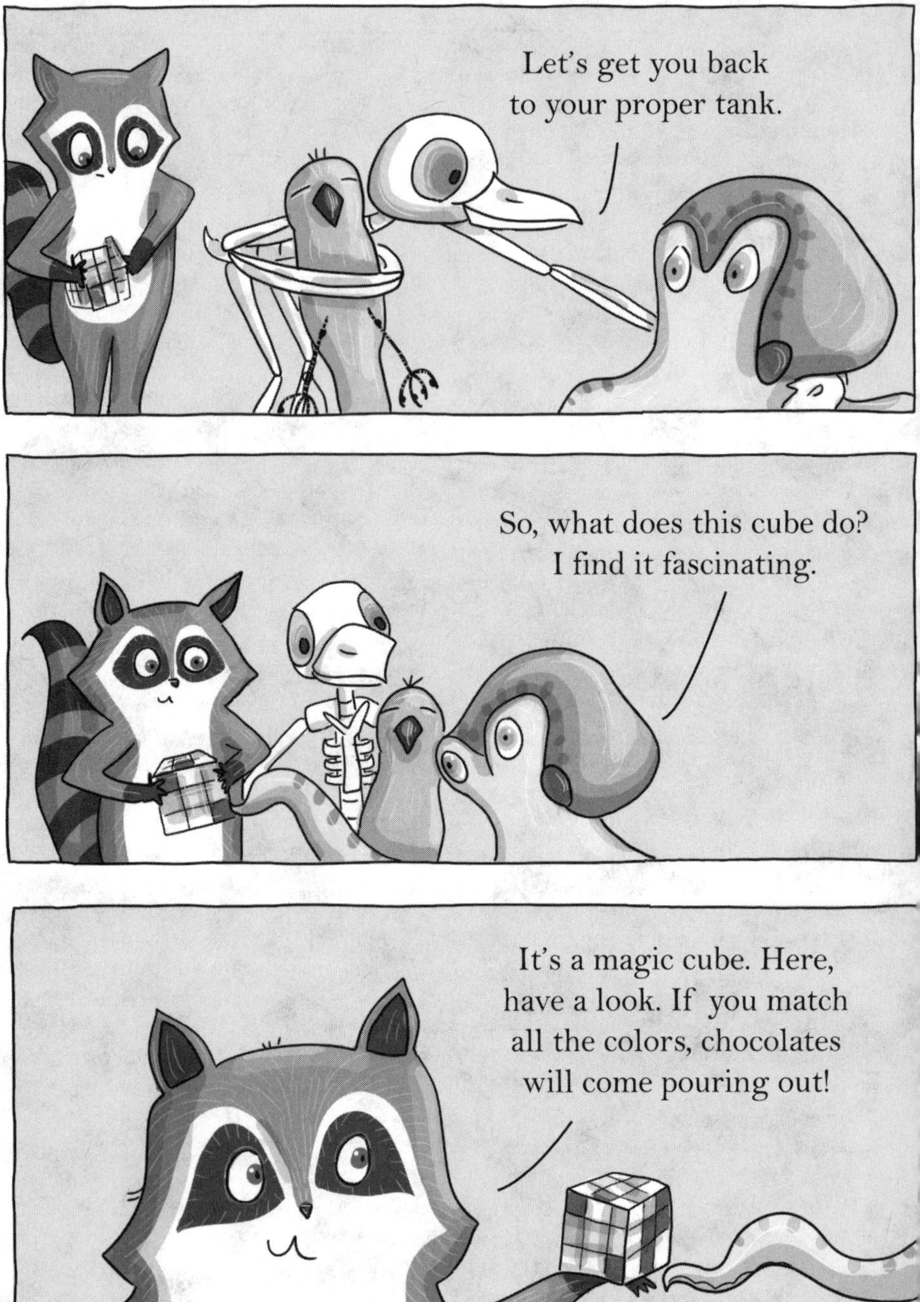
Let's get you back to your proper tank.
So, what does this cube do? I find it fascinating.
It's a magic cube. Here, have a look. If you match all the colors, chocolates will come pouring out!

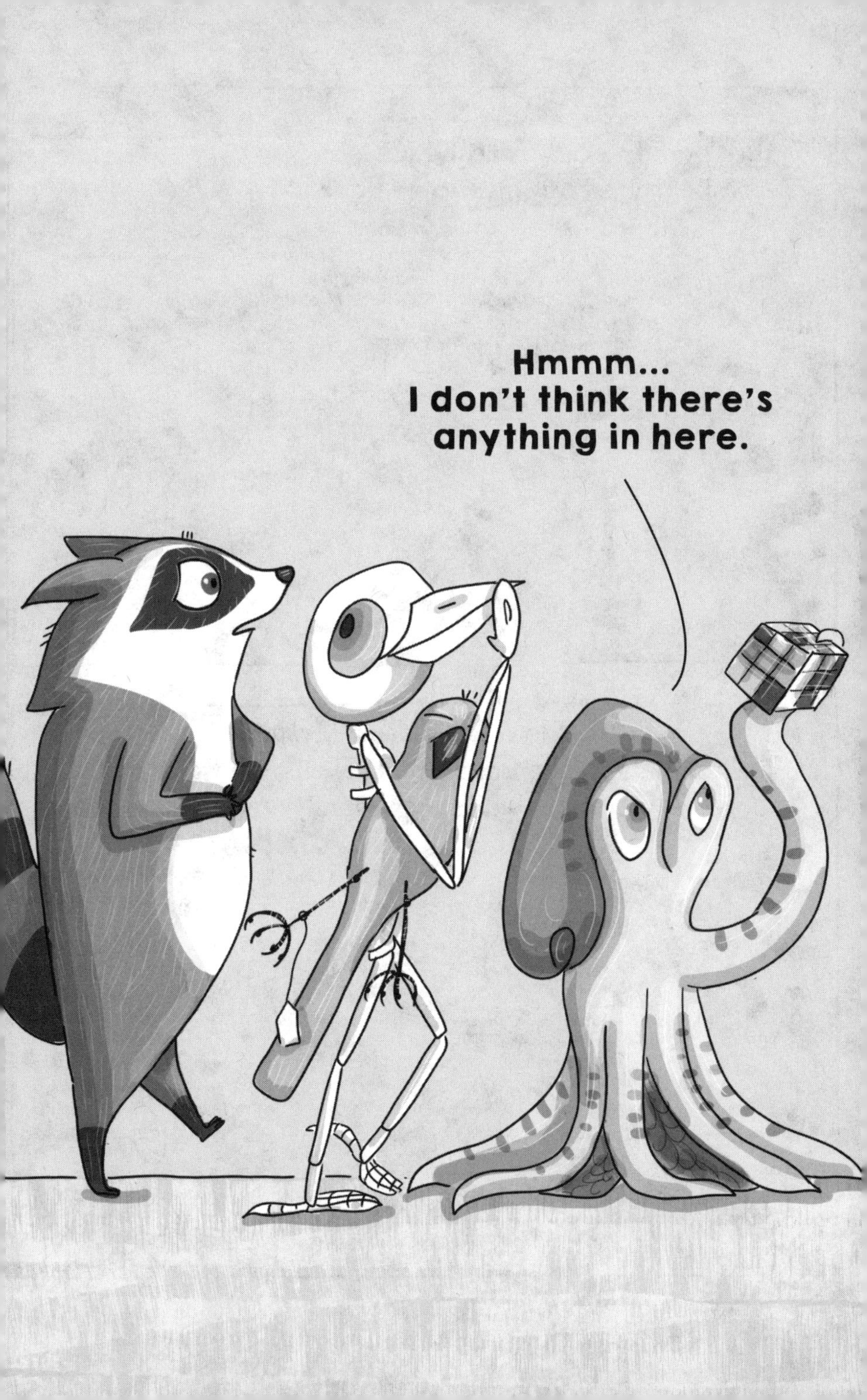
Hmmm...
I don't think there's
anything in here.

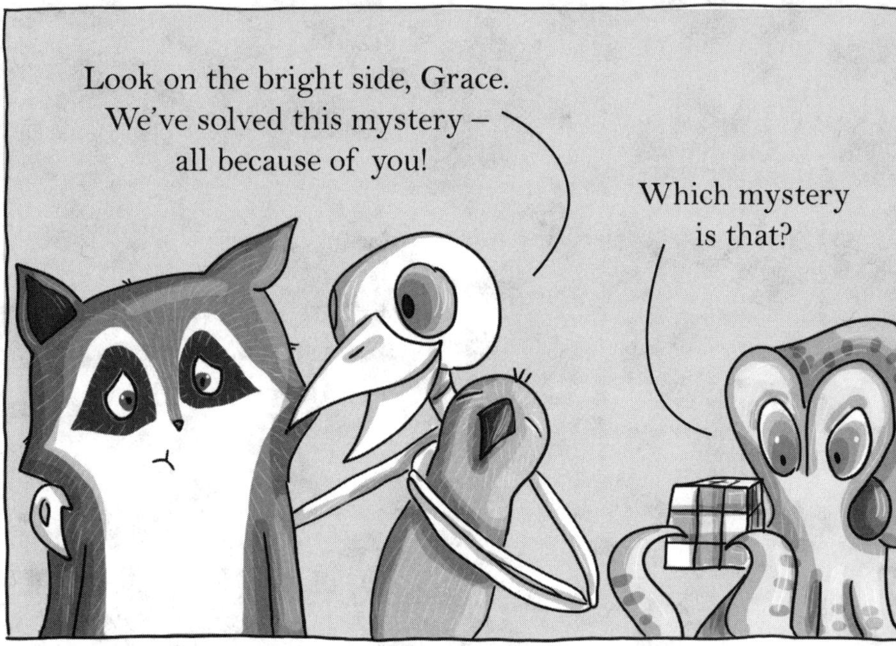
Look on the bright side, Grace. We've solved this mystery – all because of you!
Which mystery is that?

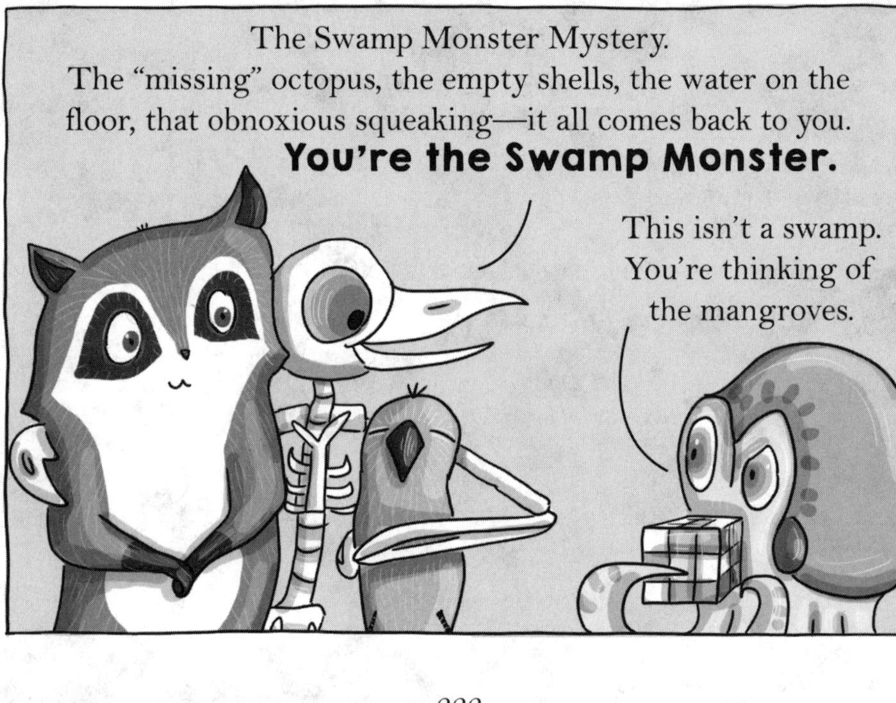
The Swamp Monster Mystery. The "missing" octopus, the empty shells, the water on the floor, that obnoxious squeaking—it all comes back to you.
You're the Swamp Monster.
This isn't a swamp. You're thinking of the mangroves.

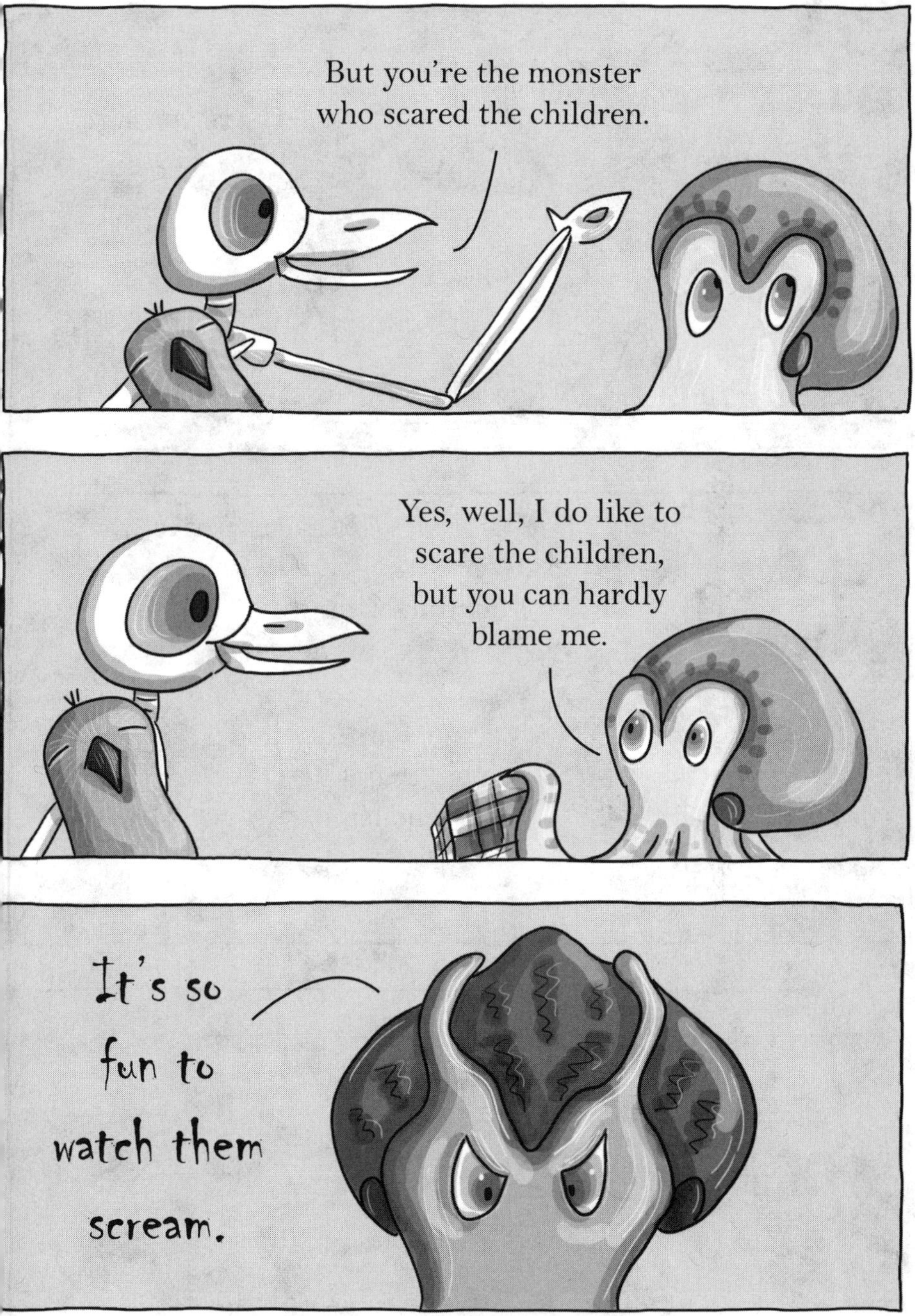
But you're the monster who scared the children.
Yes, well, I do like to scare the children, but you can hardly blame me.
It's so fun to watch them scream.

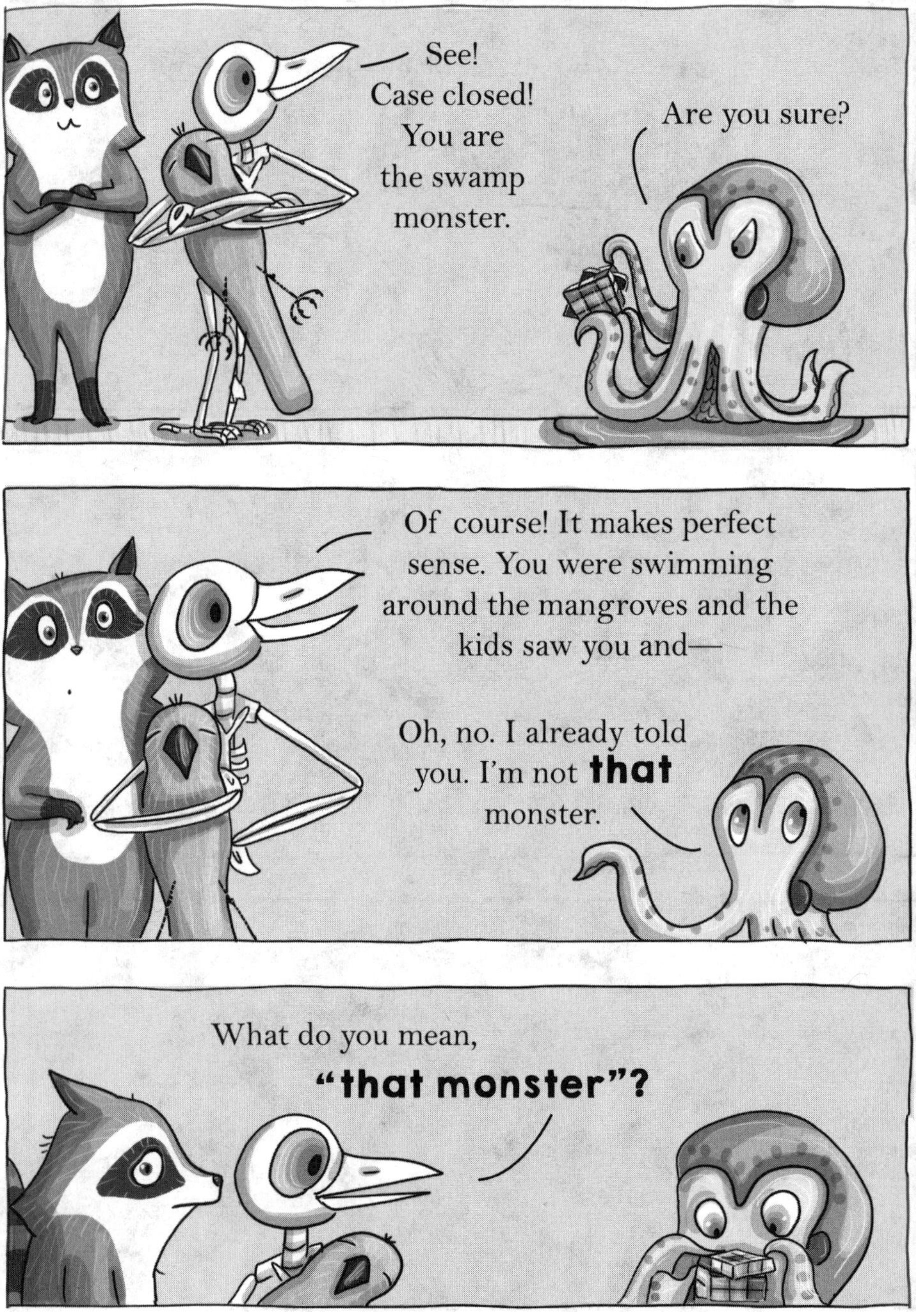
See! Case closed! You are the swamp monster.
Are you sure?
Of course! It makes perfect sense. You were swimming around the mangroves and the kids saw you and—
Oh, no. I already told you. I'm not **that** monster.
What do you mean, **"that monster"?**

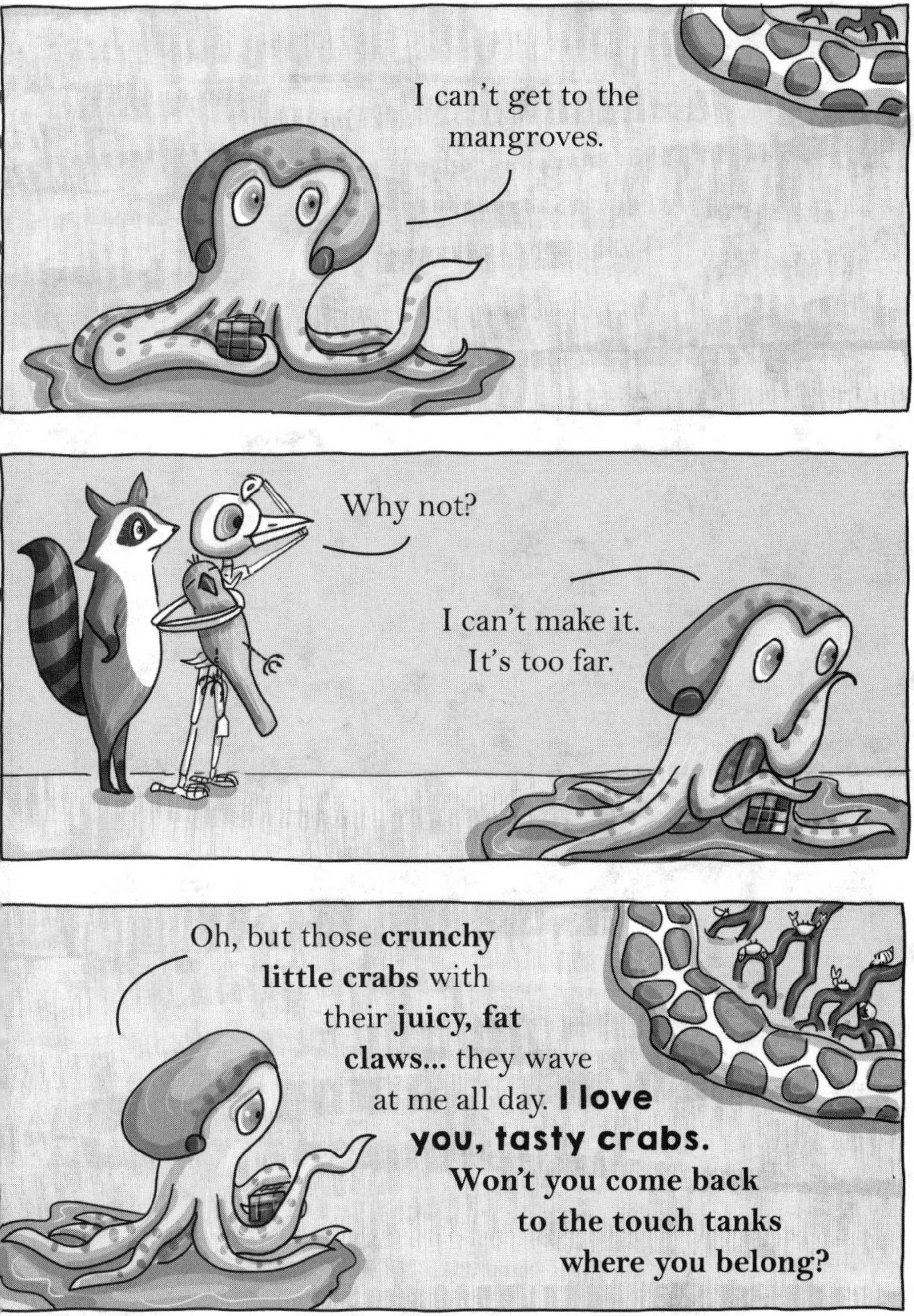

I can't get to the mangroves.
Why not?
I can't make it. It's too far.
Oh, but those **crunchy little crabs** with their **juicy, fat claws...** they wave at me all day. **I love you, tasty crabs. Won't you come back to the touch tanks where you belong?**

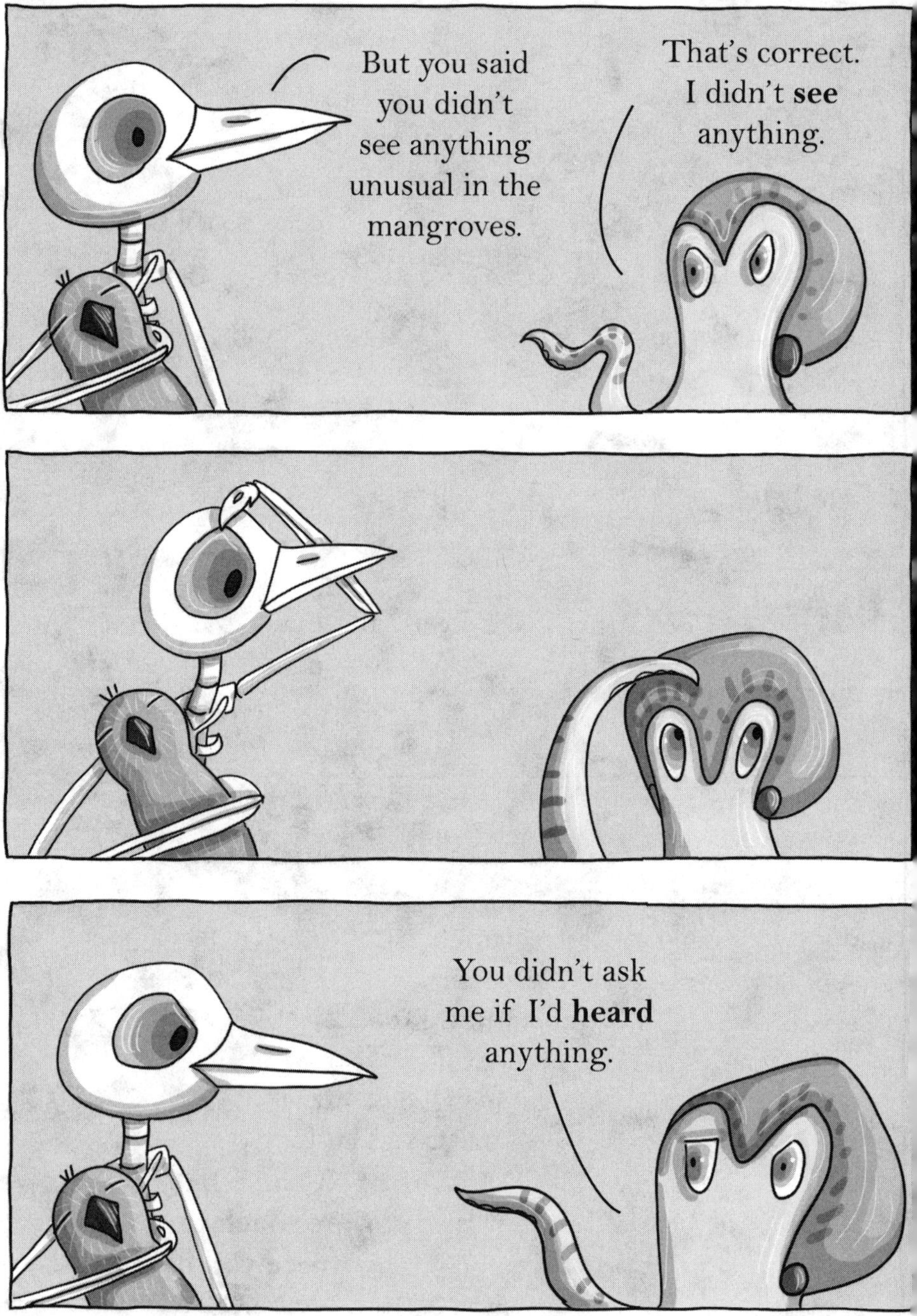
But you said you didn't see anything unusual in the mangroves.
That's correct. I didn't **see** anything.
You didn't ask me if I'd **heard** anything.

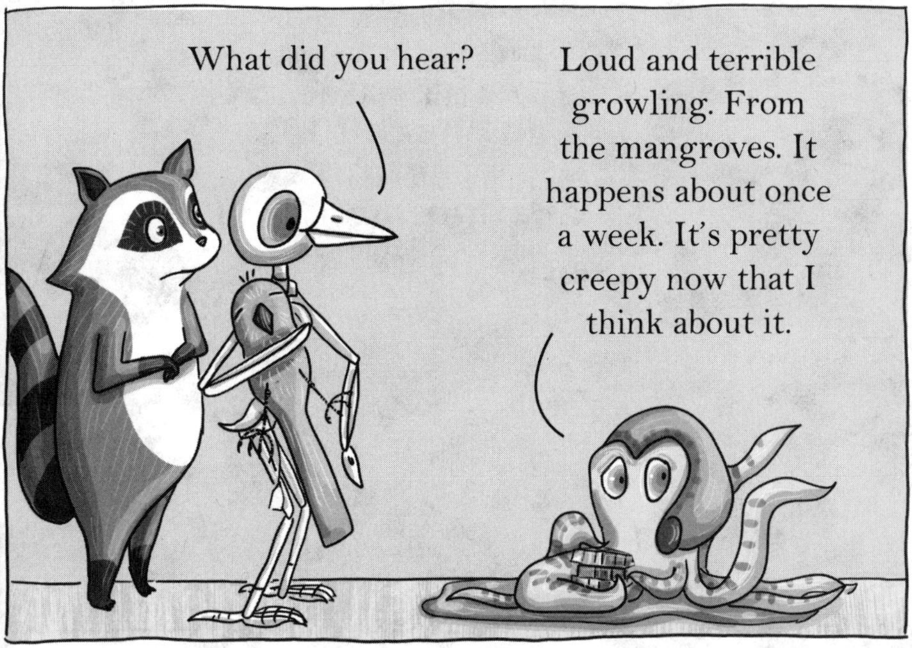
What did you hear?
Loud and terrible growling. From the mangroves. It happens about once a week. It's pretty creepy now that I think about it.

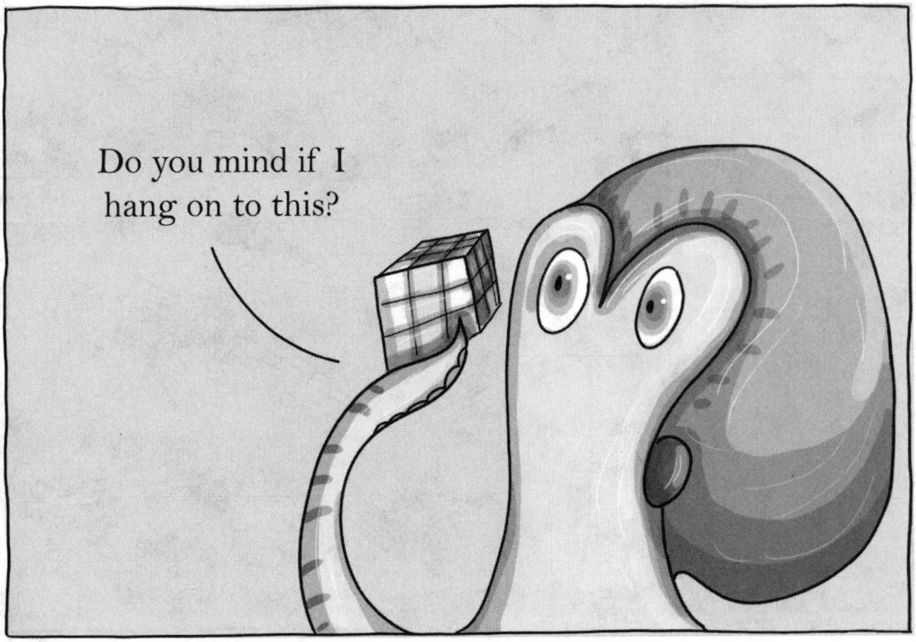
Do you mind if I hang on to this?

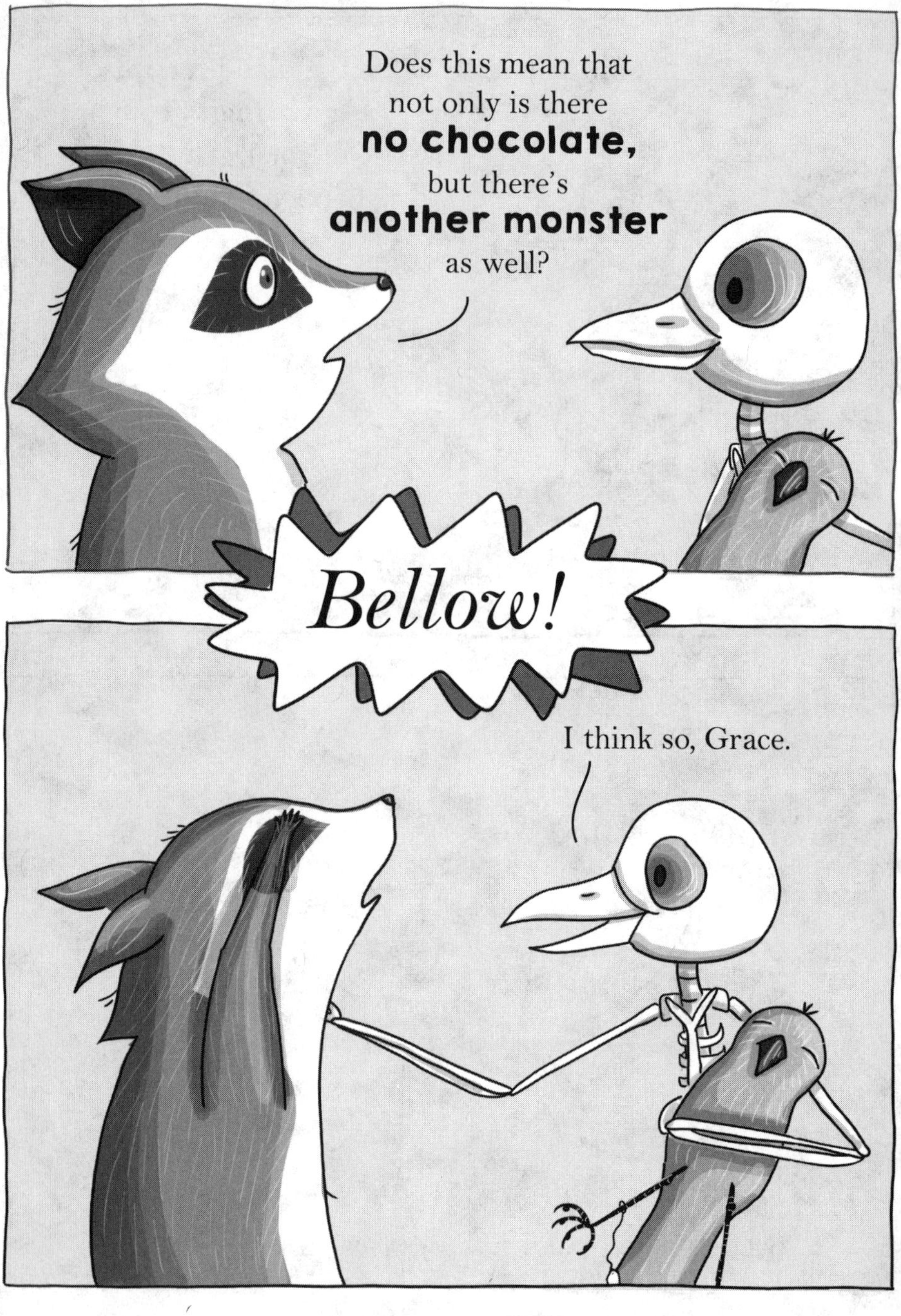
Does this mean that not only is there **no chocolate,** but there's **another monster** as well?
Bellow!
I think so, Grace.

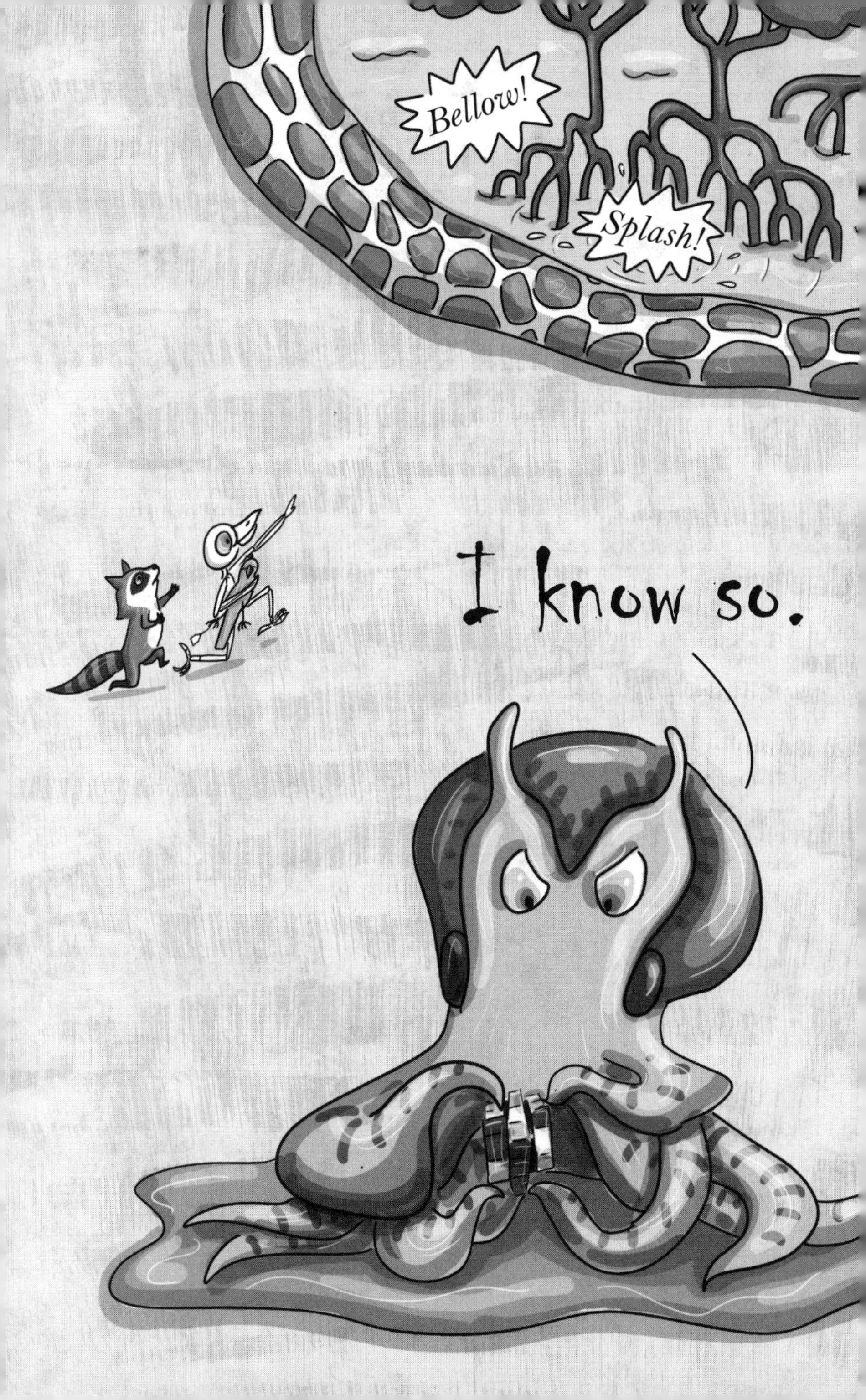
Bellow!
Splash!
I know so.

CHAPTER 10
You're Krilling Me

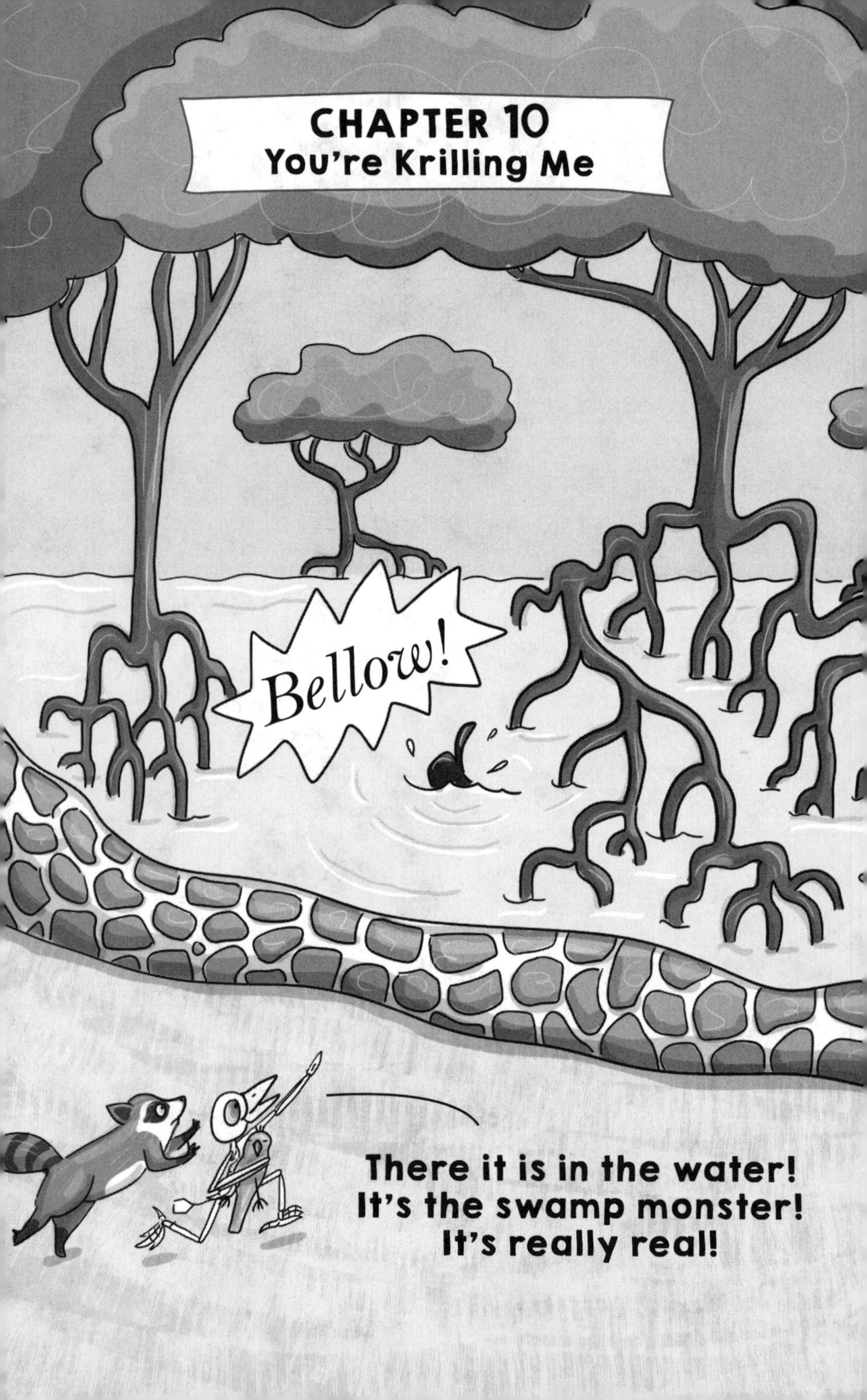
Bellow!
There it is in the water!
It's the swamp monster!
It's really real!

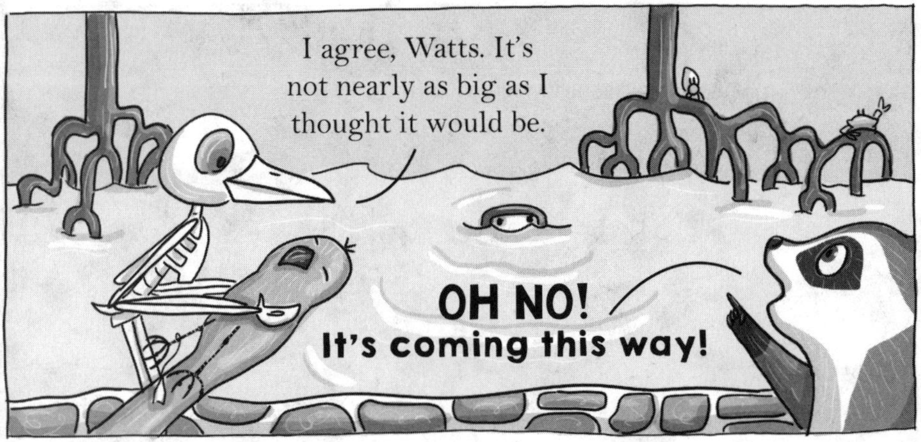
I agree, Watts. It's not nearly as big as I thought it would be.
OH NO!
It's coming this way!

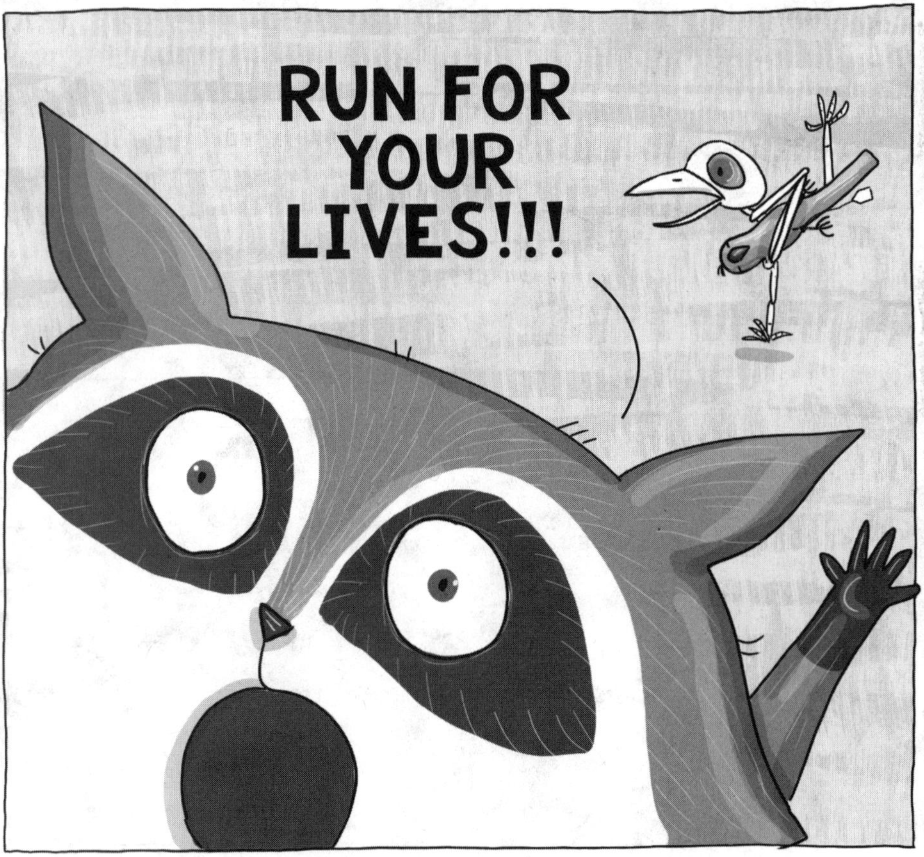
RUN FOR YOUR LIVES!!!

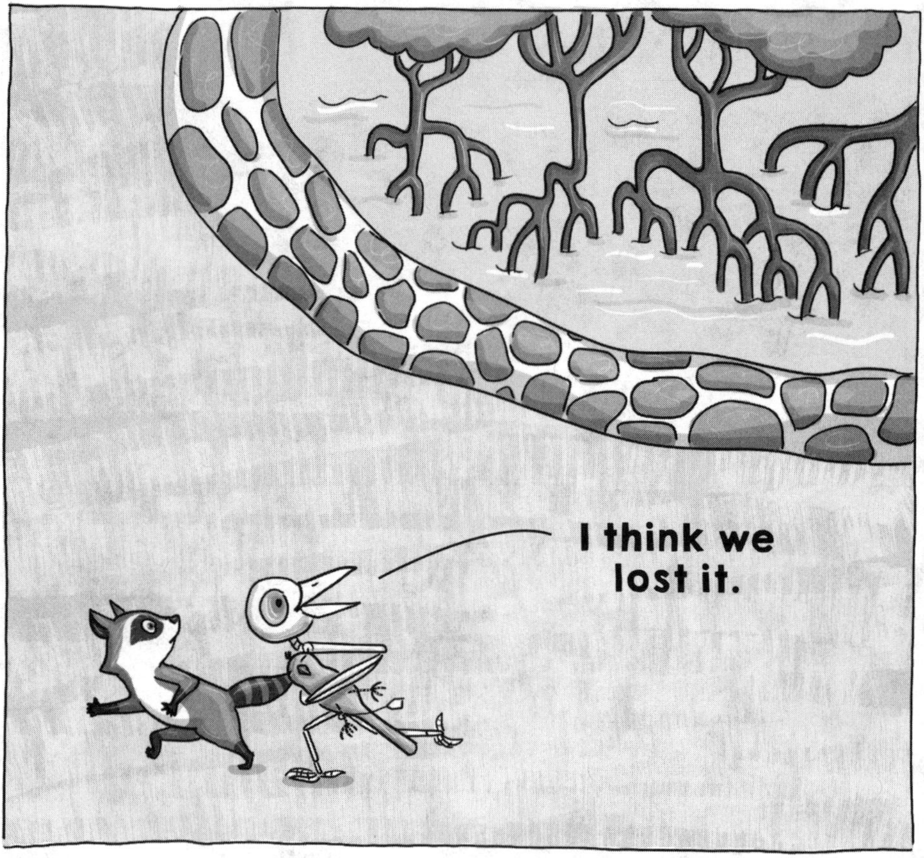
I think we lost it.

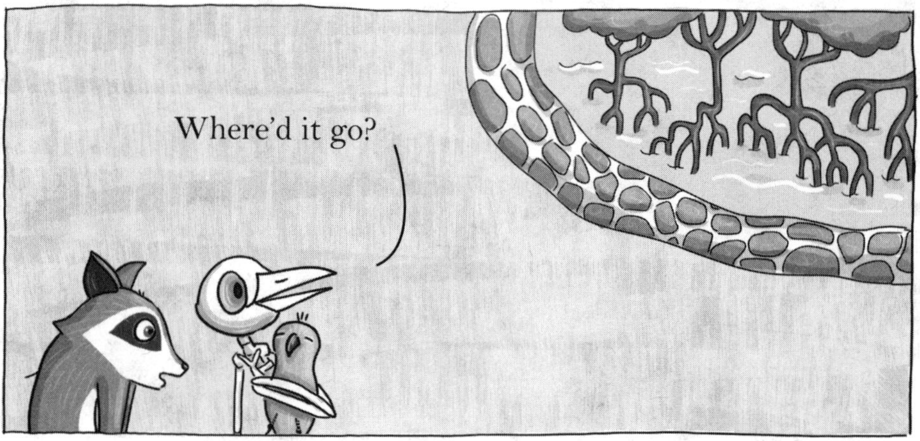
Where'd it go?

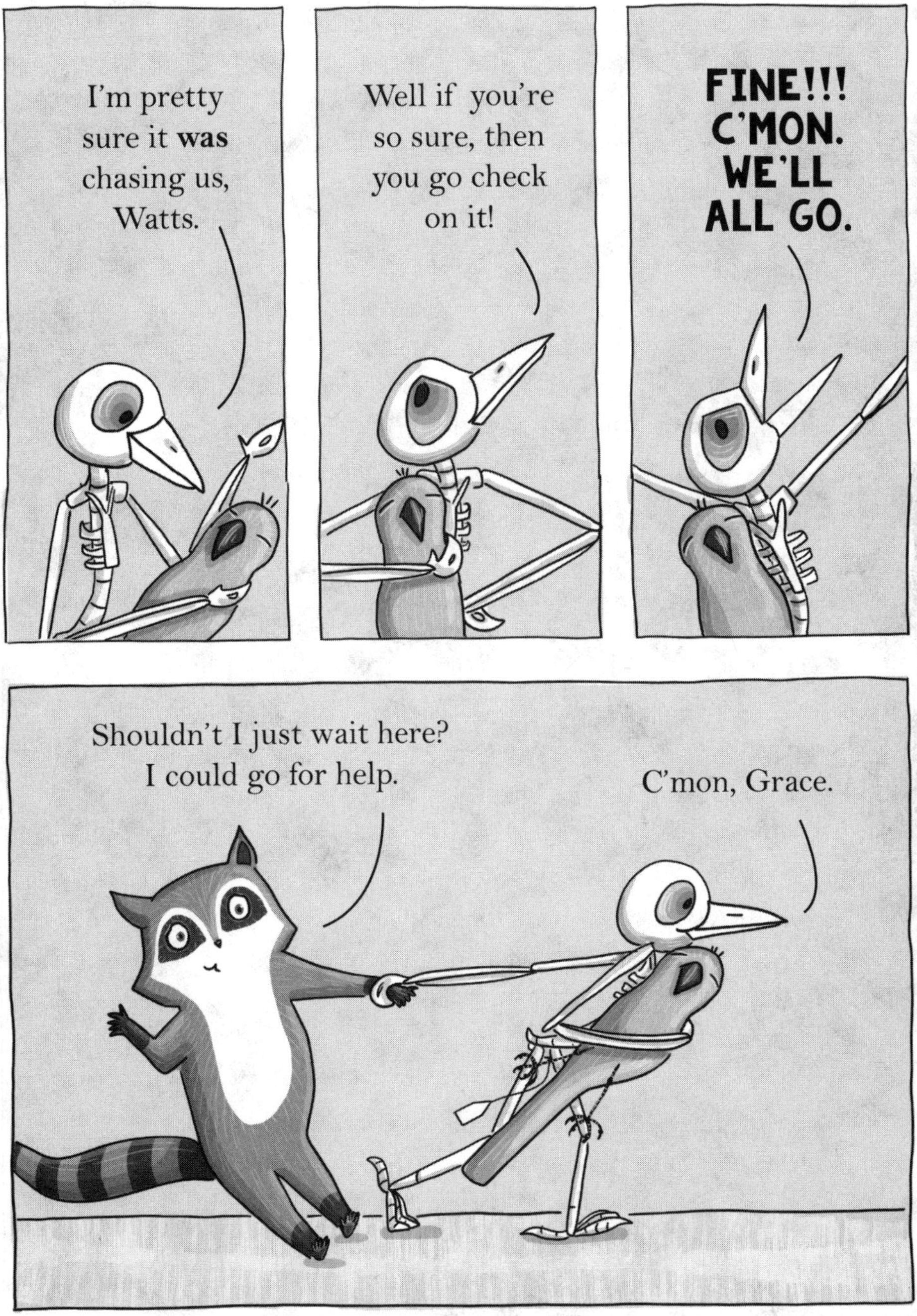
I'm pretty sure it **was** chasing us, Watts.
Well if you're so sure, then you go check on it!
FINE!!! C'MON. WE'LL ALL GO.
Shouldn't I just wait here? I could go for help.
C'mon, Grace.

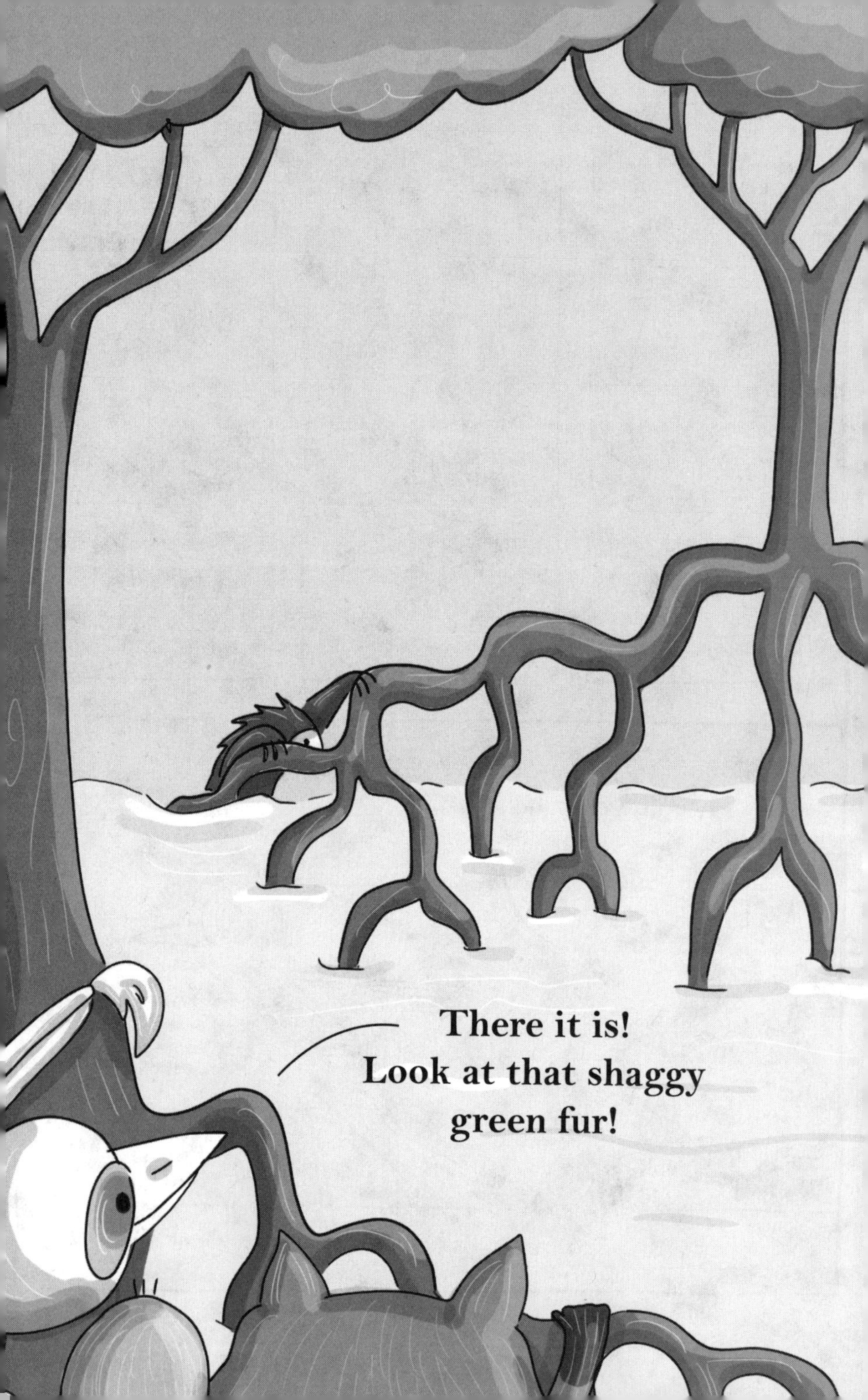
There it is!
Look at that shaggy
green fur!

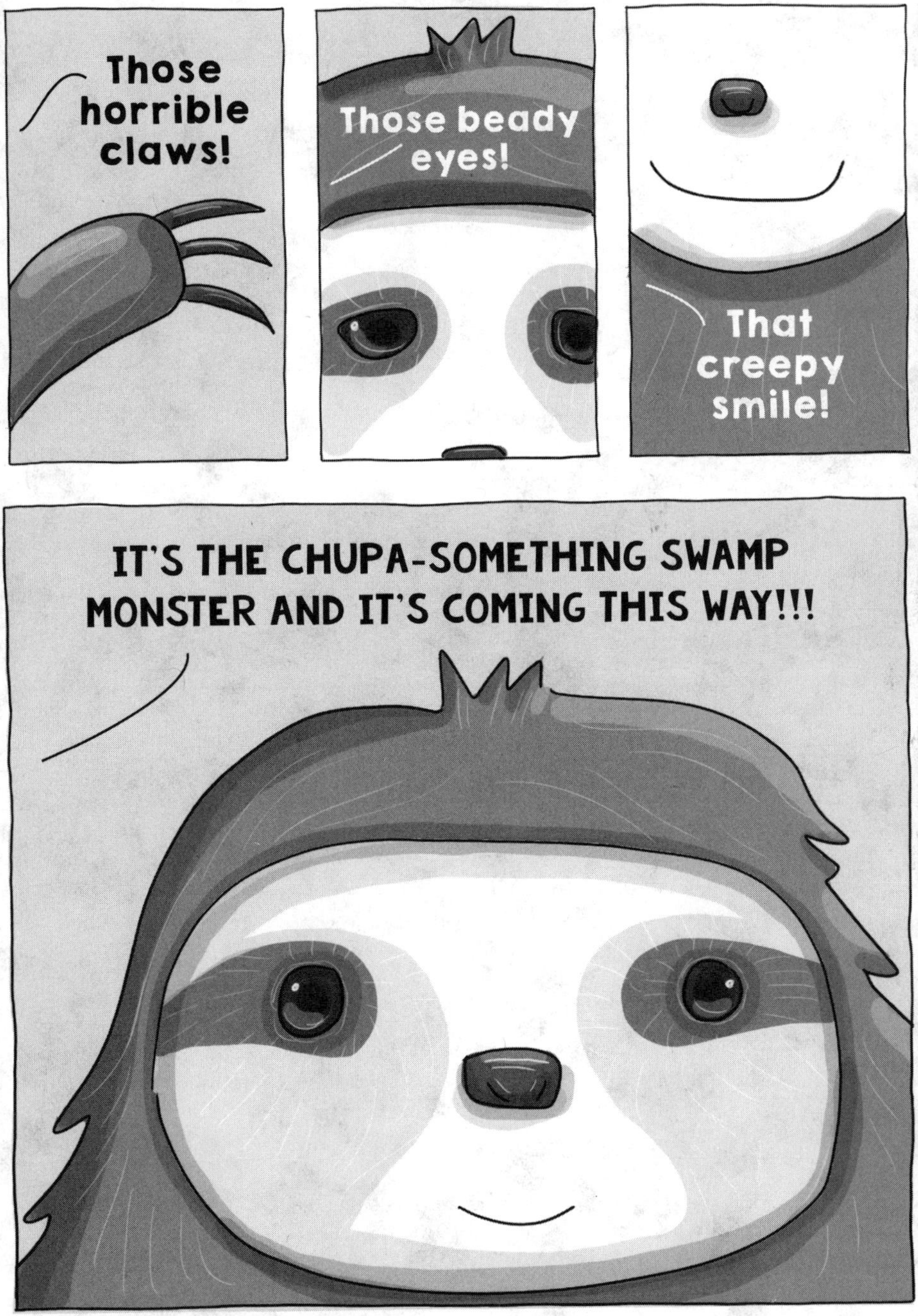
Those horrible claws!
Those beady eyes!
That creepy smile!
IT'S THE CHUPA-SOMETHING SWAMP MONSTER AND IT'S COMING THIS WAY!!!

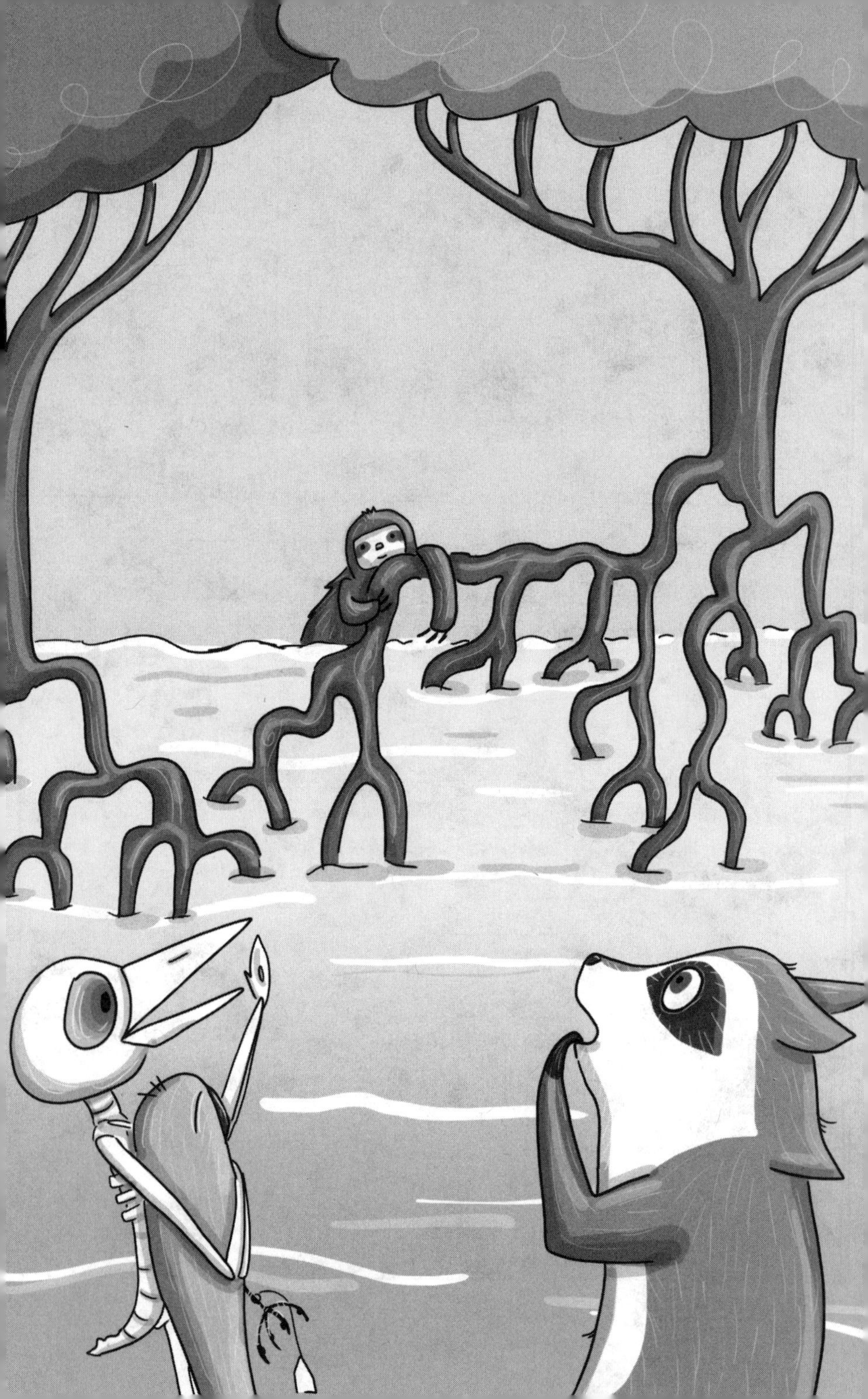

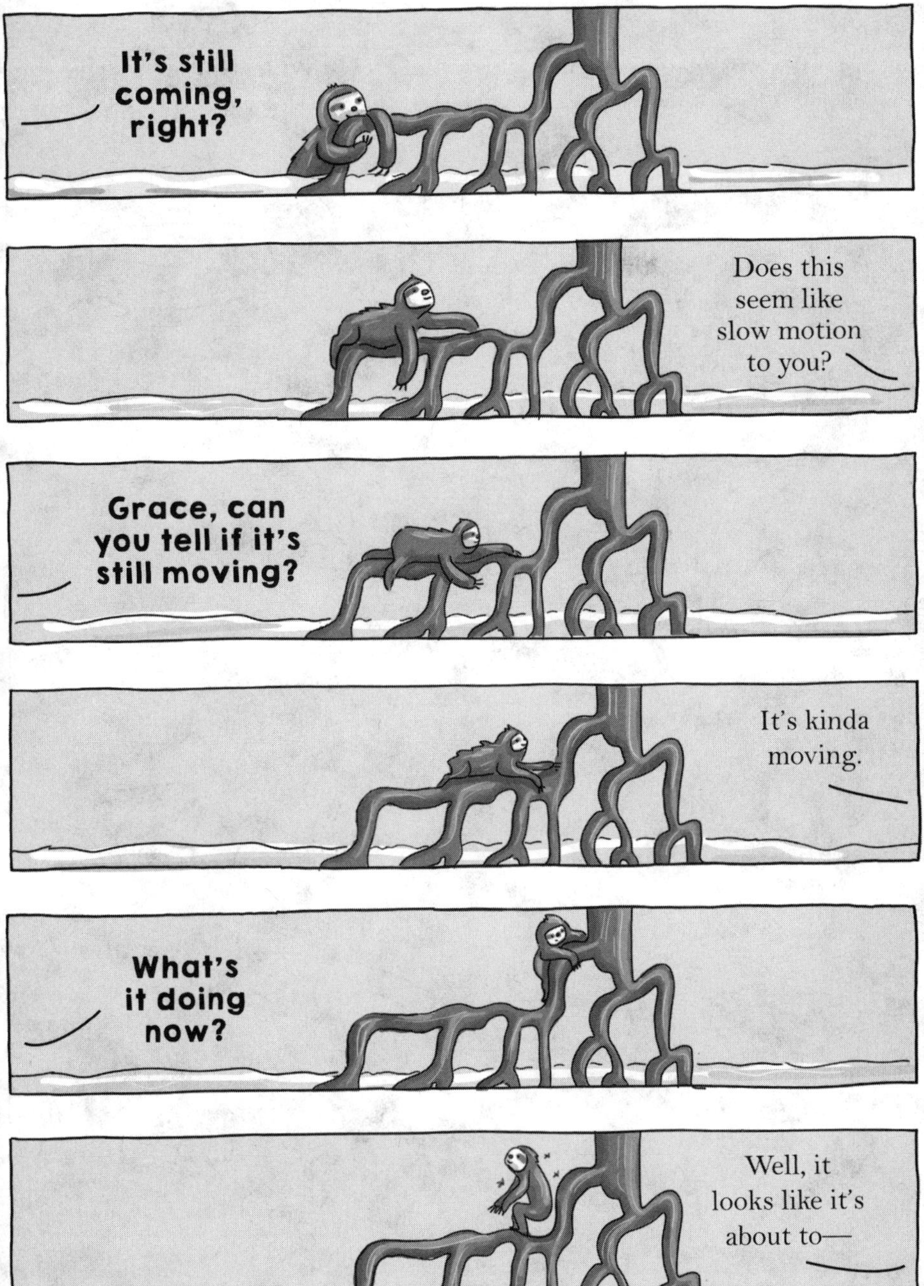
It's still coming, right?
Does this seem like slow motion to you?
Grace, can you tell if it's still moving?
It's kinda moving.
What's it doing now?
Well, it looks like it's about to—

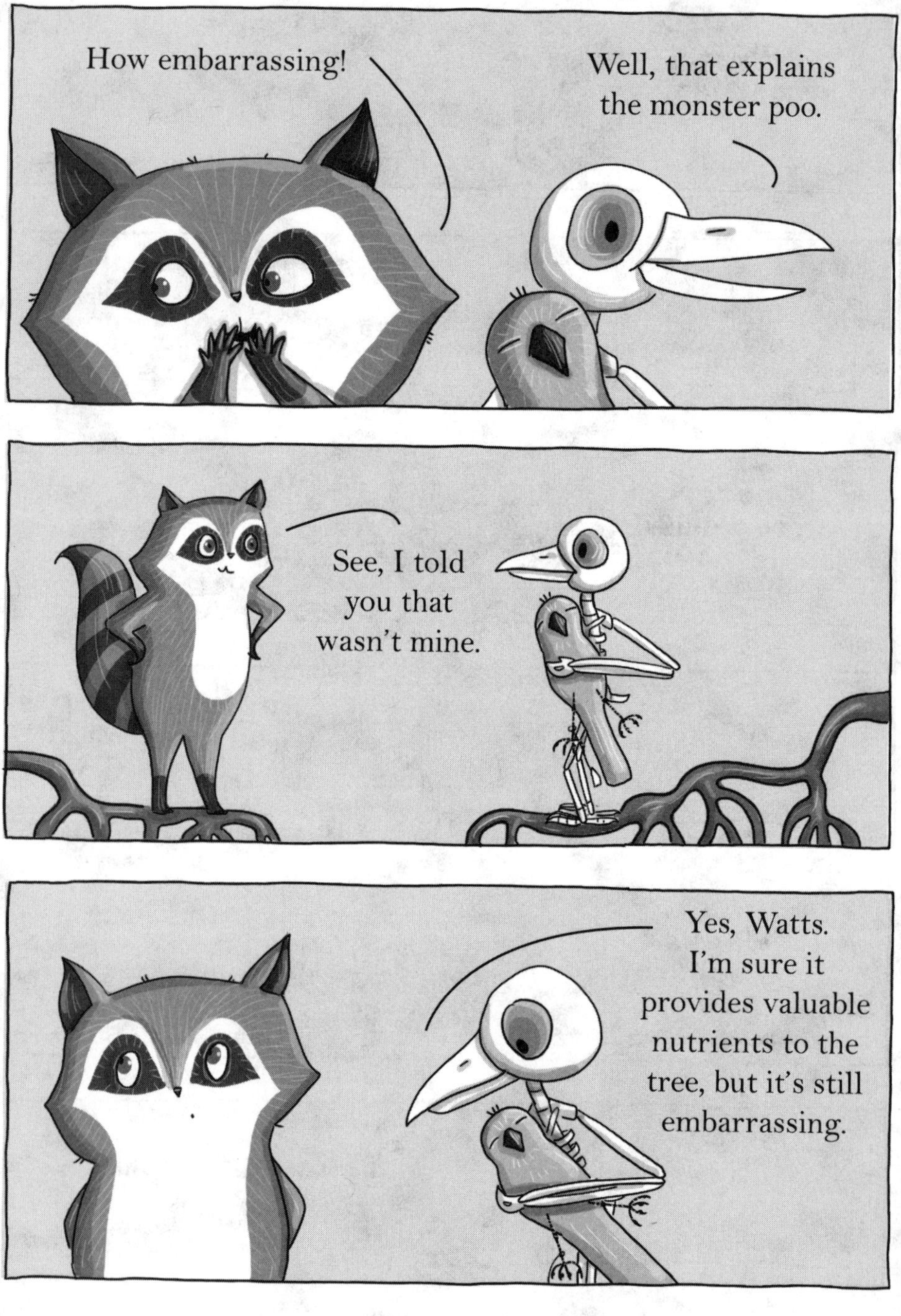
How embarrassing!
Well, that explains the monster poo.
See, I told you that wasn't mine.
Yes, Watts. I'm sure it provides valuable nutrients to the tree, but it's still embarrassing.

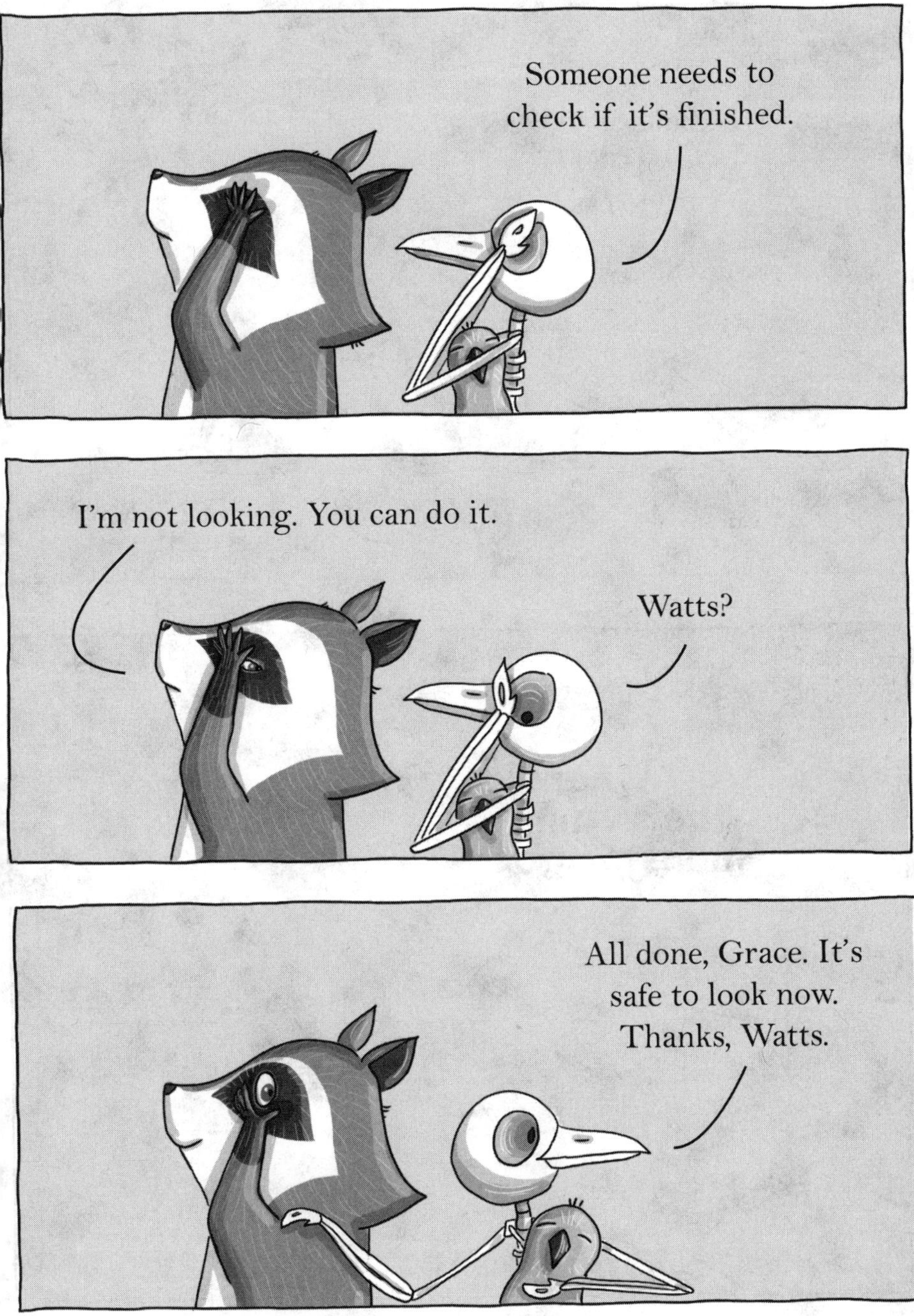
Someone needs to check if it's finished.
I'm not looking. You can do it.
Watts?
All done, Grace. It's safe to look now.
Thanks, Watts.

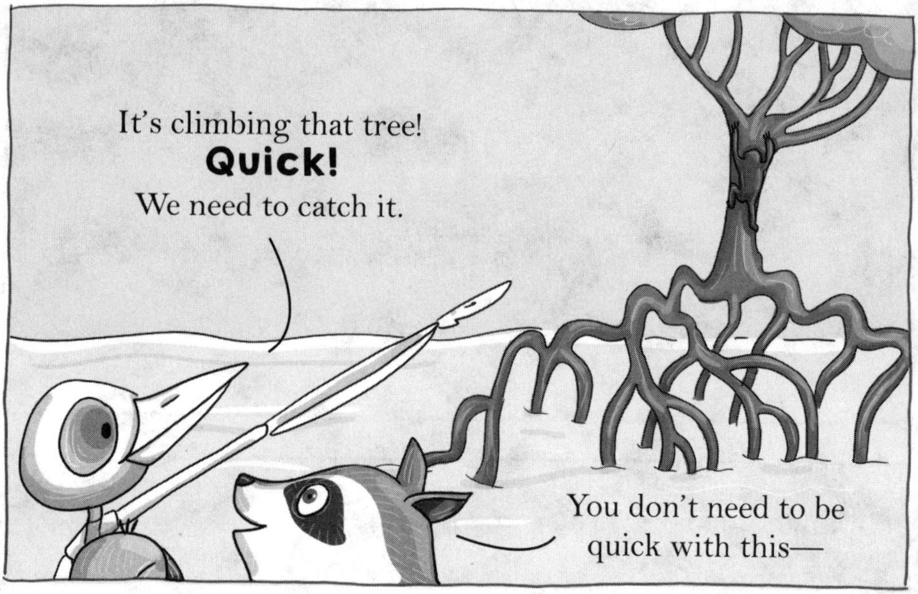
It's climbing that tree!
Quick!
We need to catch it.
You don't need to be quick with this—

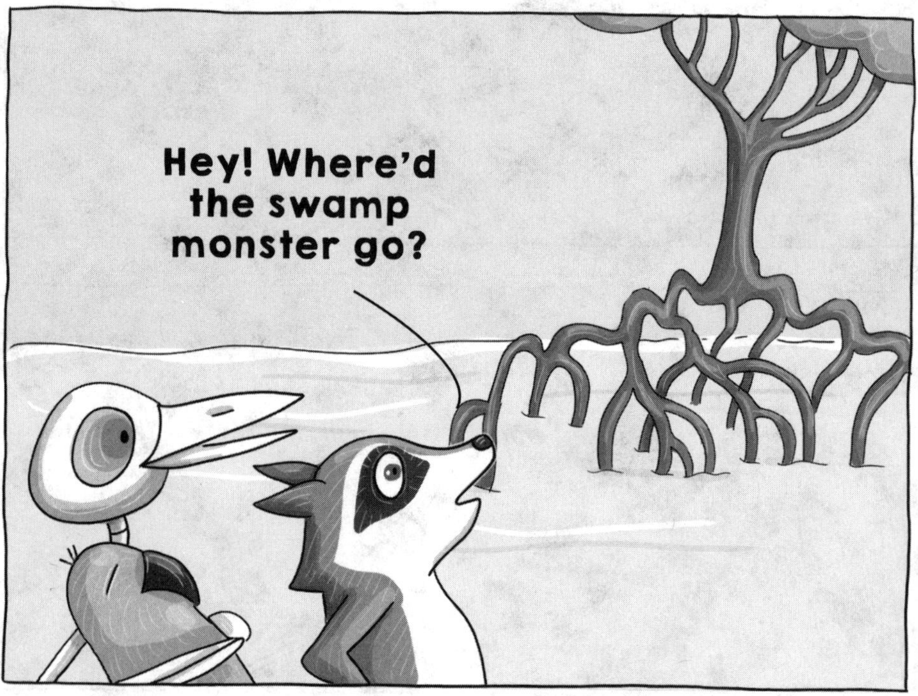
Hey! Where'd the swamp monster go?

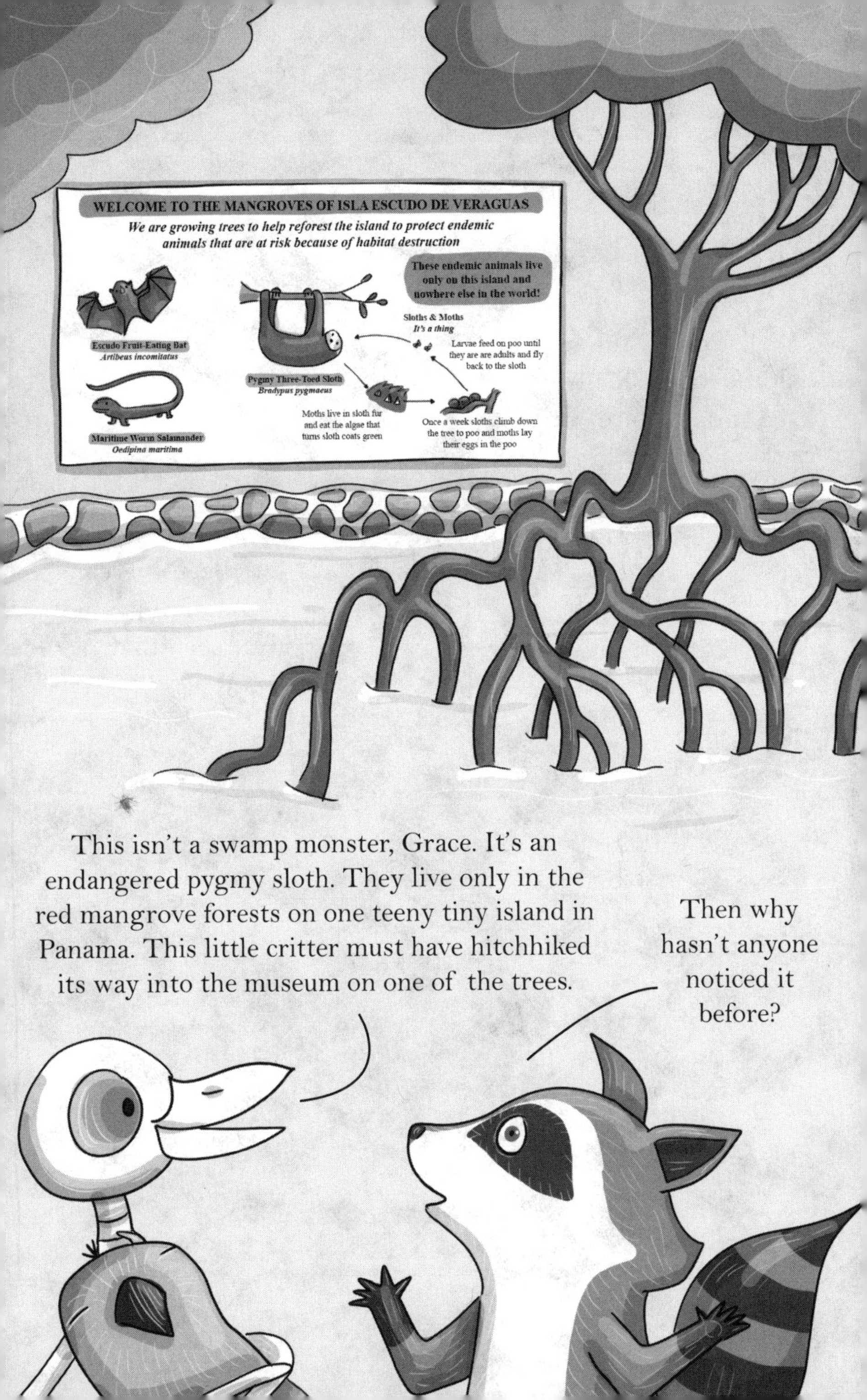
WELCOME TO THE MANGROVES OF ISLA ESCUDO DE VERAGUAS
We are growing trees to help reforest the island to protect endemic animals that are at risk because of habitat destruction
These endemic animals live only on this island and nowhere else in the world!
Escudo Fruit-Eating Bat
Artibeus incomitatus
Maritime Worm Salamander
Oedipina maritima
Pygmy Three-Toed Sloth
Bradypus pygmaeus
Sloths & Moths
It's a thing
Larvae feed on poo until they are are adults and fly back to the sloth
Moths live in sloth fur and eat the algae that turns sloth coats green
Once a week sloths climb down the tree to poo and moths lay their eggs in the poo
This isn't a swamp monster, Grace. It's an endangered pygmy sloth. They live only in the red mangrove forests on one teeny tiny island in Panama. This little critter must have hitchhiked its way into the museum on one of the trees.
Then why hasn't anyone noticed it before?

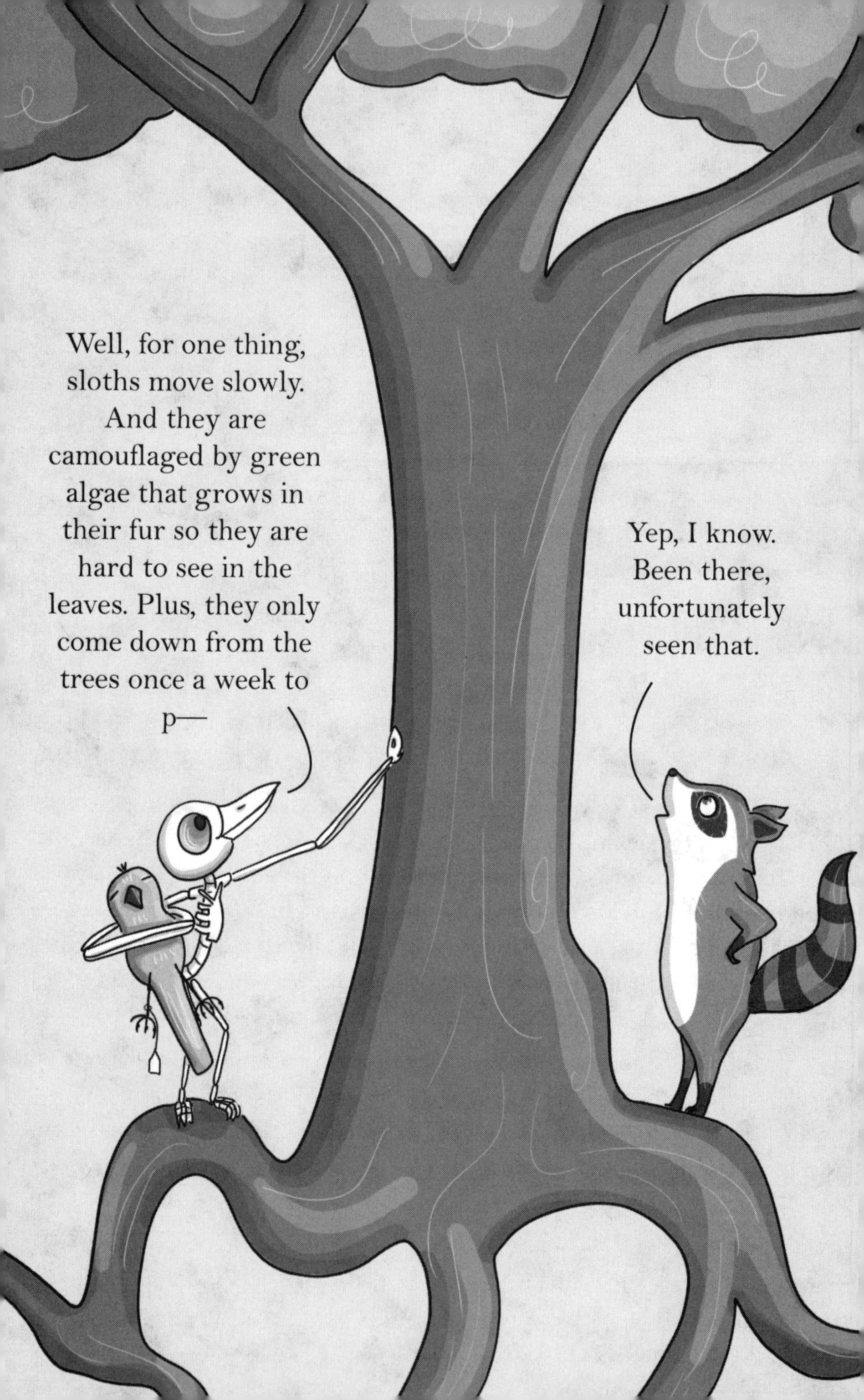
Well, for one thing, sloths move slowly. And they are camouflaged by green algae that grows in their fur so they are hard to see in the leaves. Plus, they only come down from the trees once a week to p—
Yep, I know. Been there, unfortunately seen that.

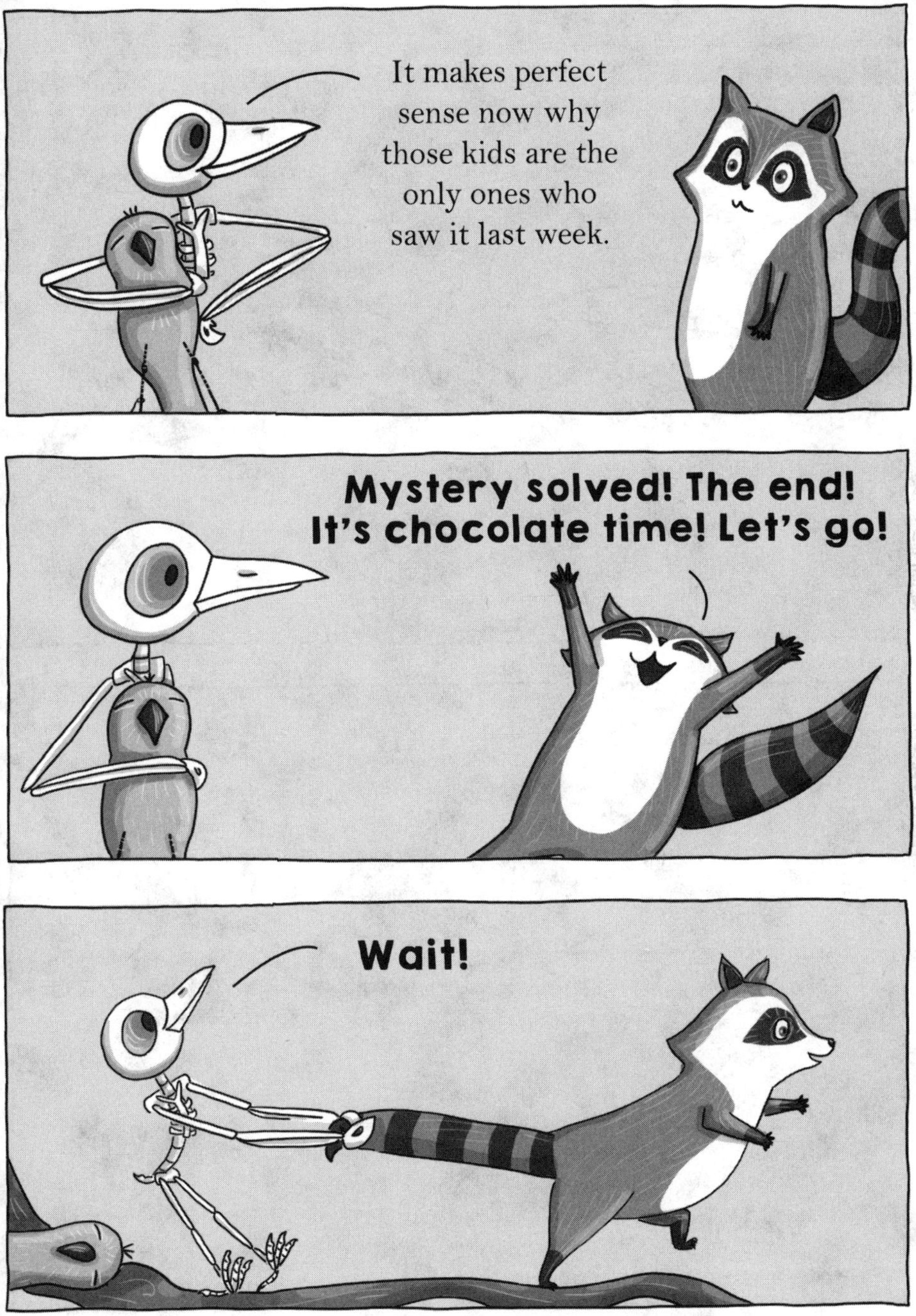
It makes perfect sense now why those kids are the only ones who saw it last week.
Mystery solved! The end! It's chocolate time! Let's go!
Wait!

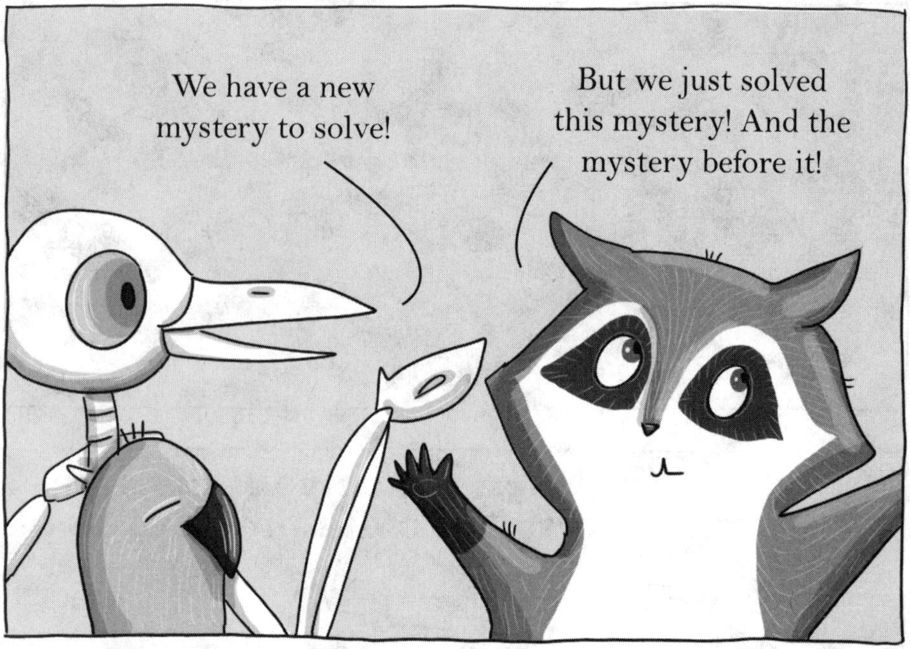
We have a new mystery to solve!
But we just solved this mystery! And the mystery before it!

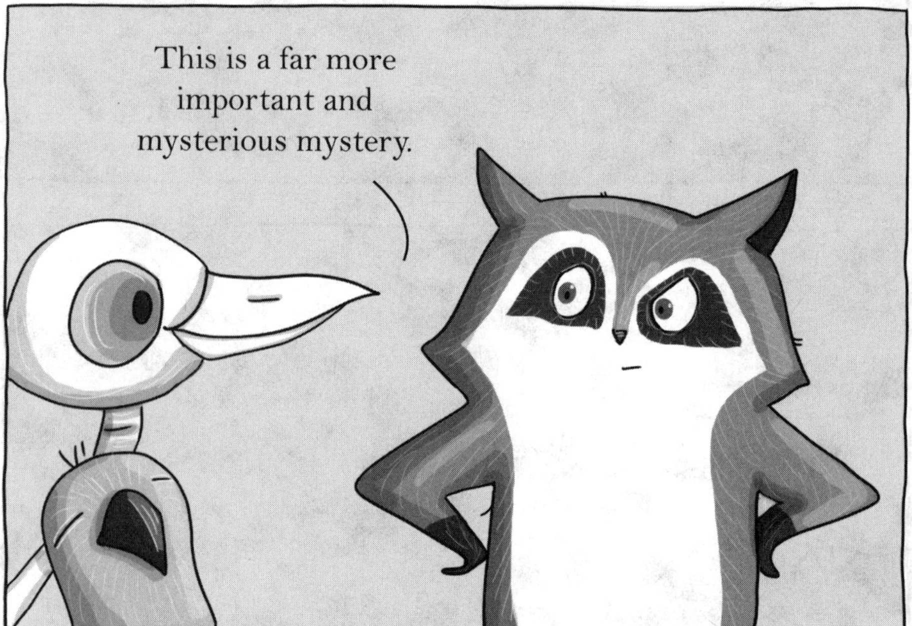
This is a far more important and mysterious mystery.

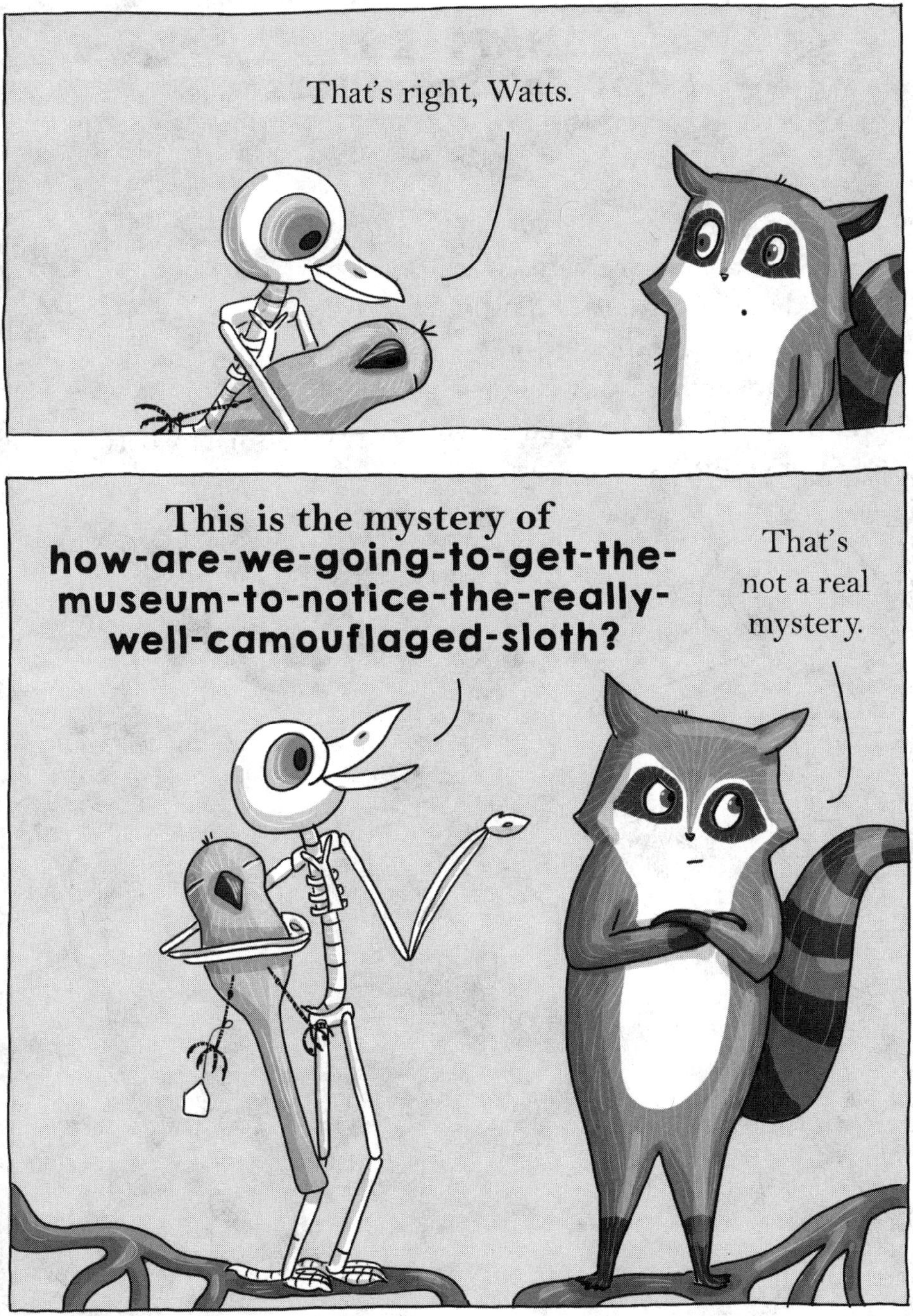
That's right, Watts.
This is the mystery of how-are-we-going-to-get-the-museum-to-notice-the-really-well-camouflaged-sloth?
That's not a real mystery.

CHAPTER 11
Couldn't Scare Less

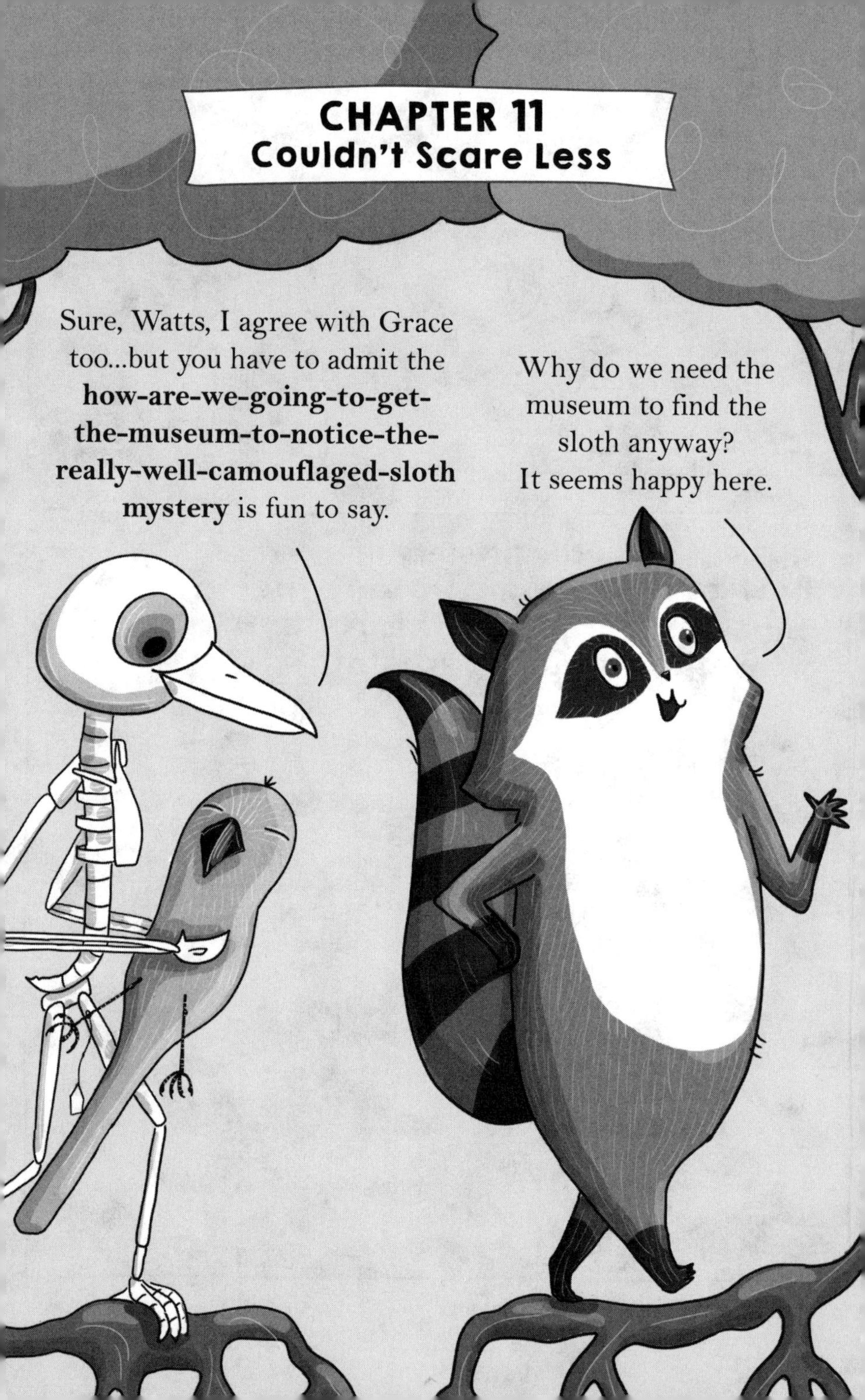
Sure, Watts, I agree with Grace too...but you have to admit the **how-are-we-going-to-get-the-museum-to-notice-the-really-well-camouflaged-sloth mystery** is fun to say.
Why do we need the museum to find the sloth anyway? It seems happy here.

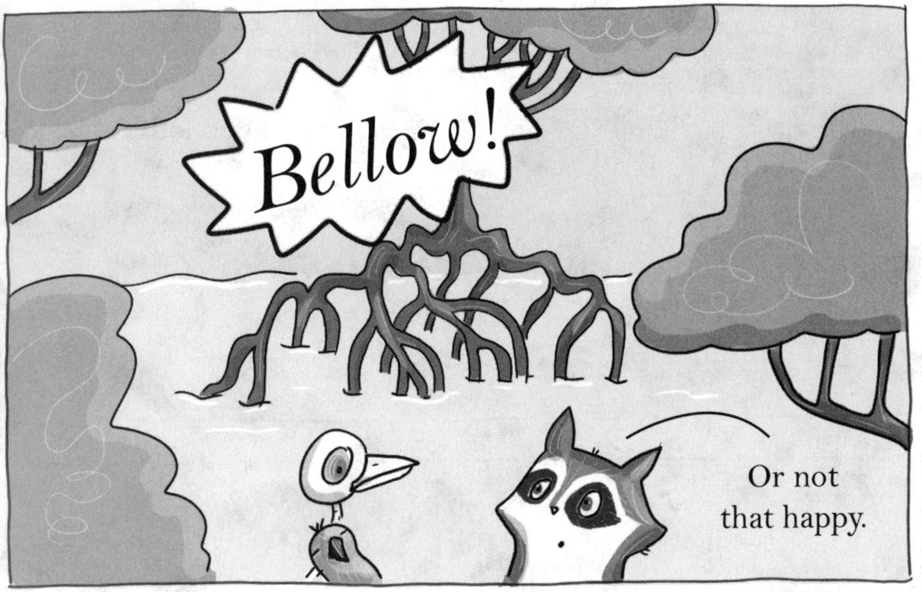
Bellow!
Or not that happy.

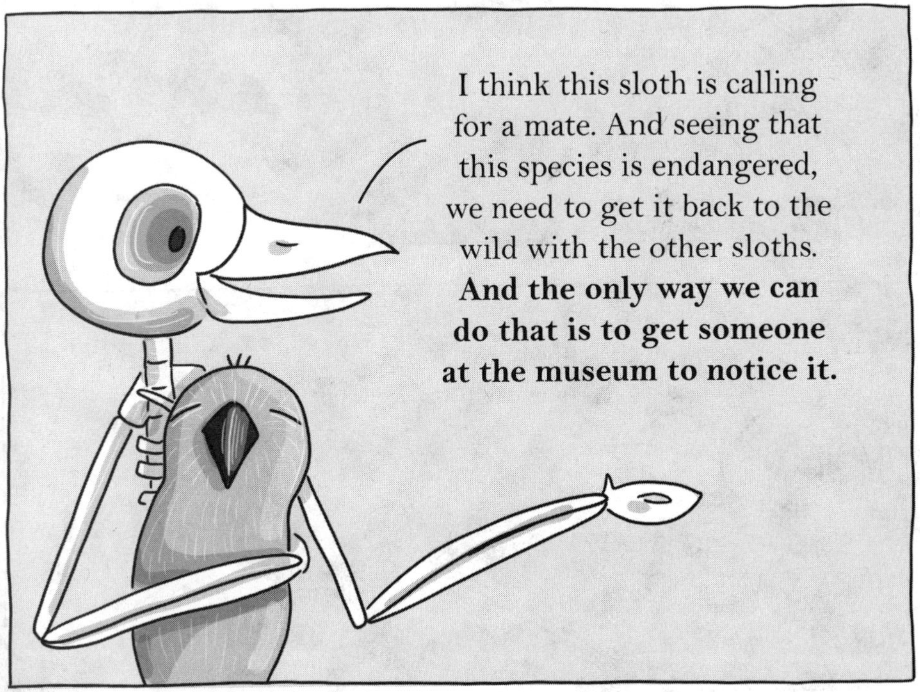
I think this sloth is calling for a mate. And seeing that this species is endangered, we need to get it back to the wild with the other sloths. **And the only way we can do that is to get someone at the museum to notice it.**

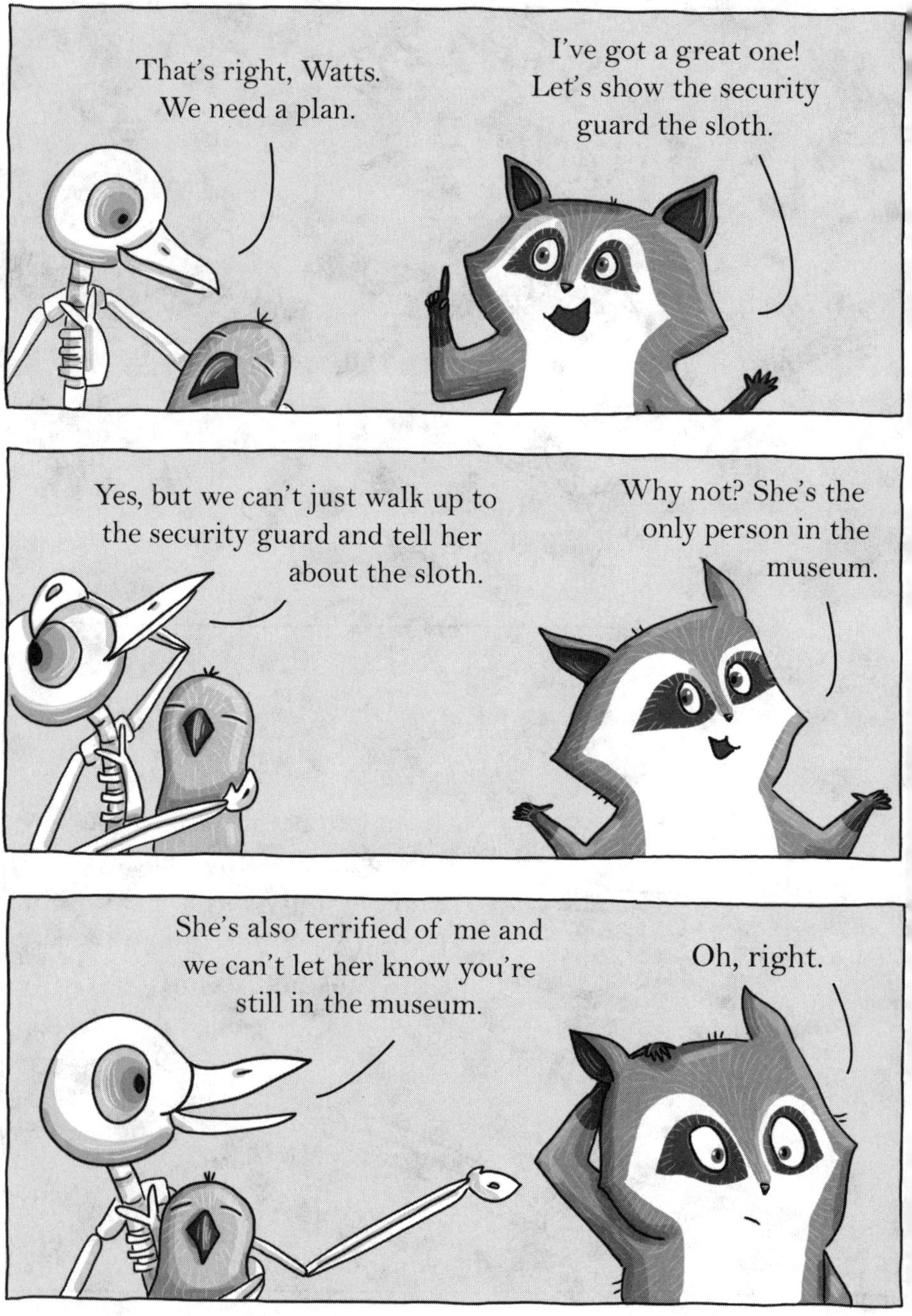
That's right, Watts. We need a plan.
I've got a great one! Let's show the security guard the sloth.
Yes, but we can't just walk up to the security guard and tell her about the sloth.
Why not? She's the only person in the museum.
She's also terrified of me and we can't let her know you're still in the museum.
Oh, right.

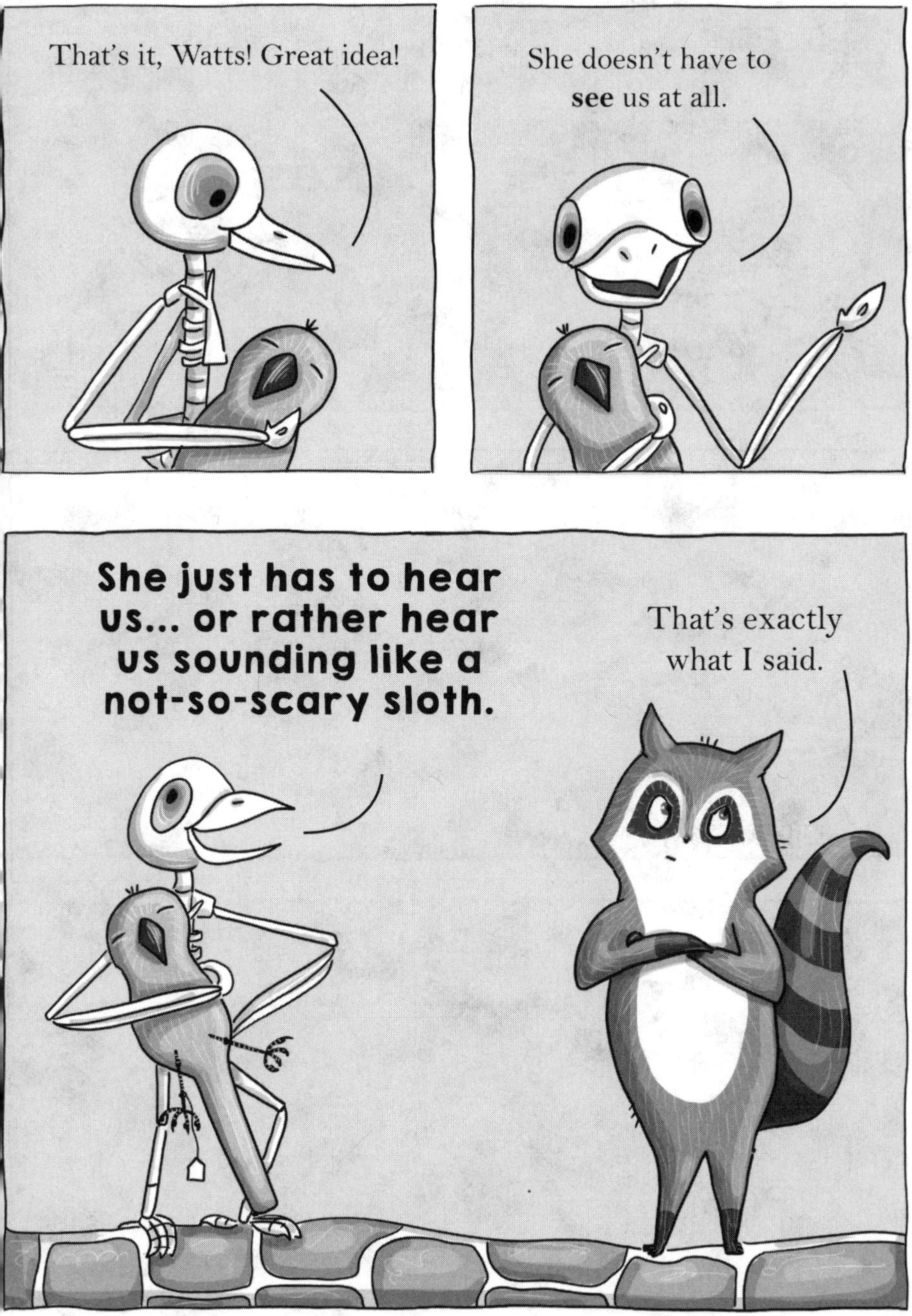
That's it, Watts! Great idea!
She doesn't have to **see** us at all.
She just has to hear us... or rather hear us sounding like a not-so-scary sloth.
That's exactly what I said.

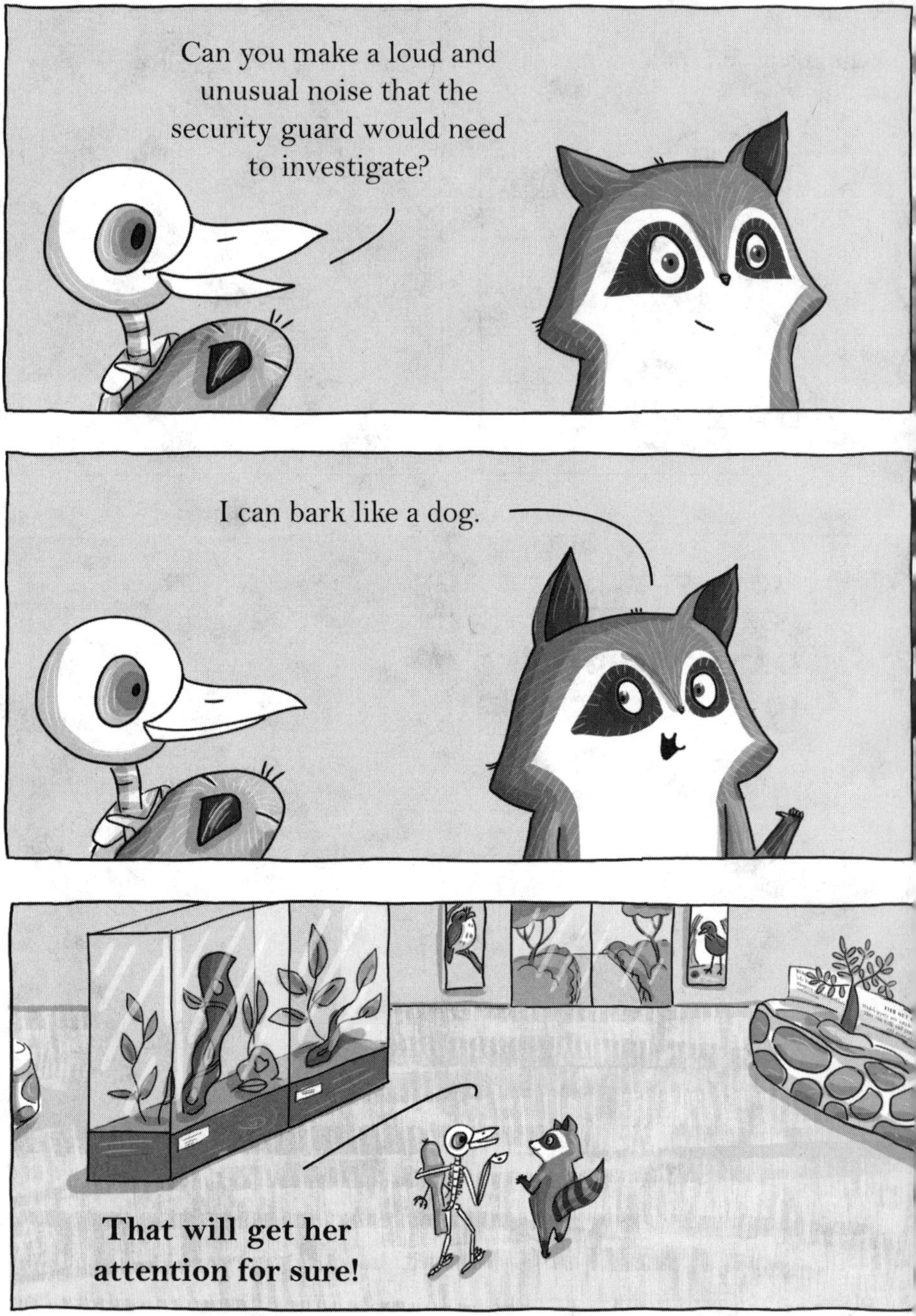
Can you make a loud and unusual noise that the security guard would need to investigate?
I can bark like a dog.
That will get her attention for sure!

LIVING RAINFOREST & MAIN HALL

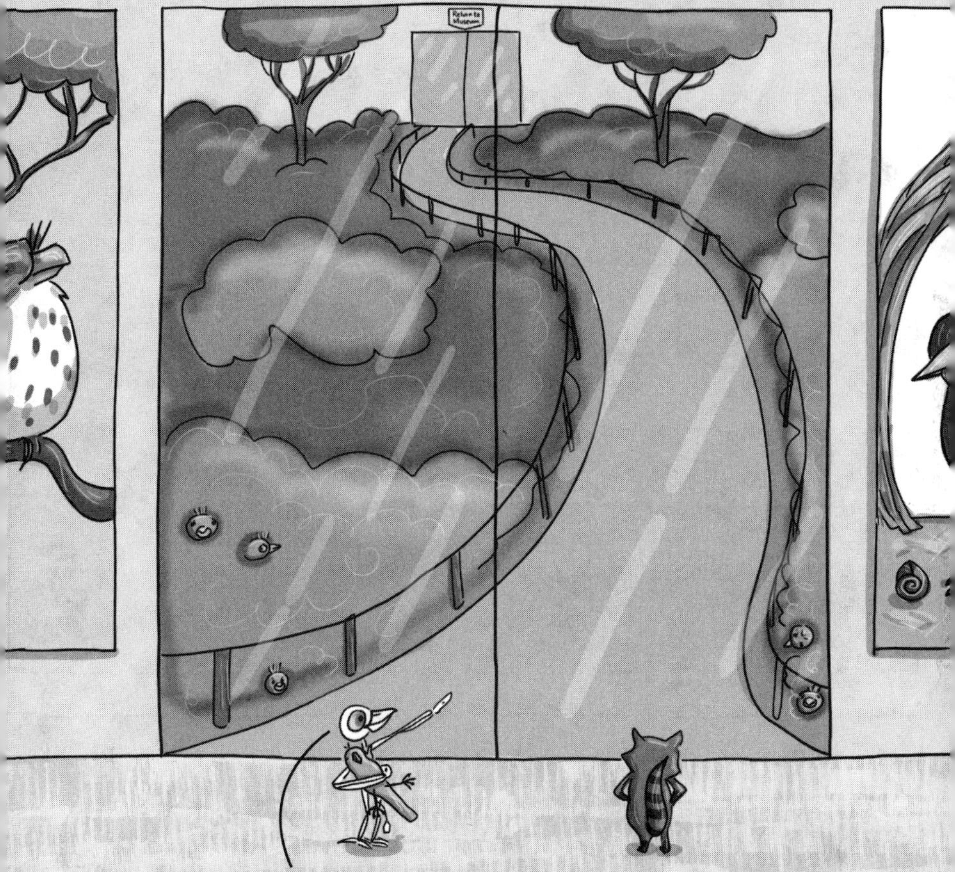

Here's the plan:
I'll distract the bowerbirds by waving Watts around on this side of the doors.

You run through the forest gallery, open the doors to the main hallway, find a good hiding spot, then bark loudly.

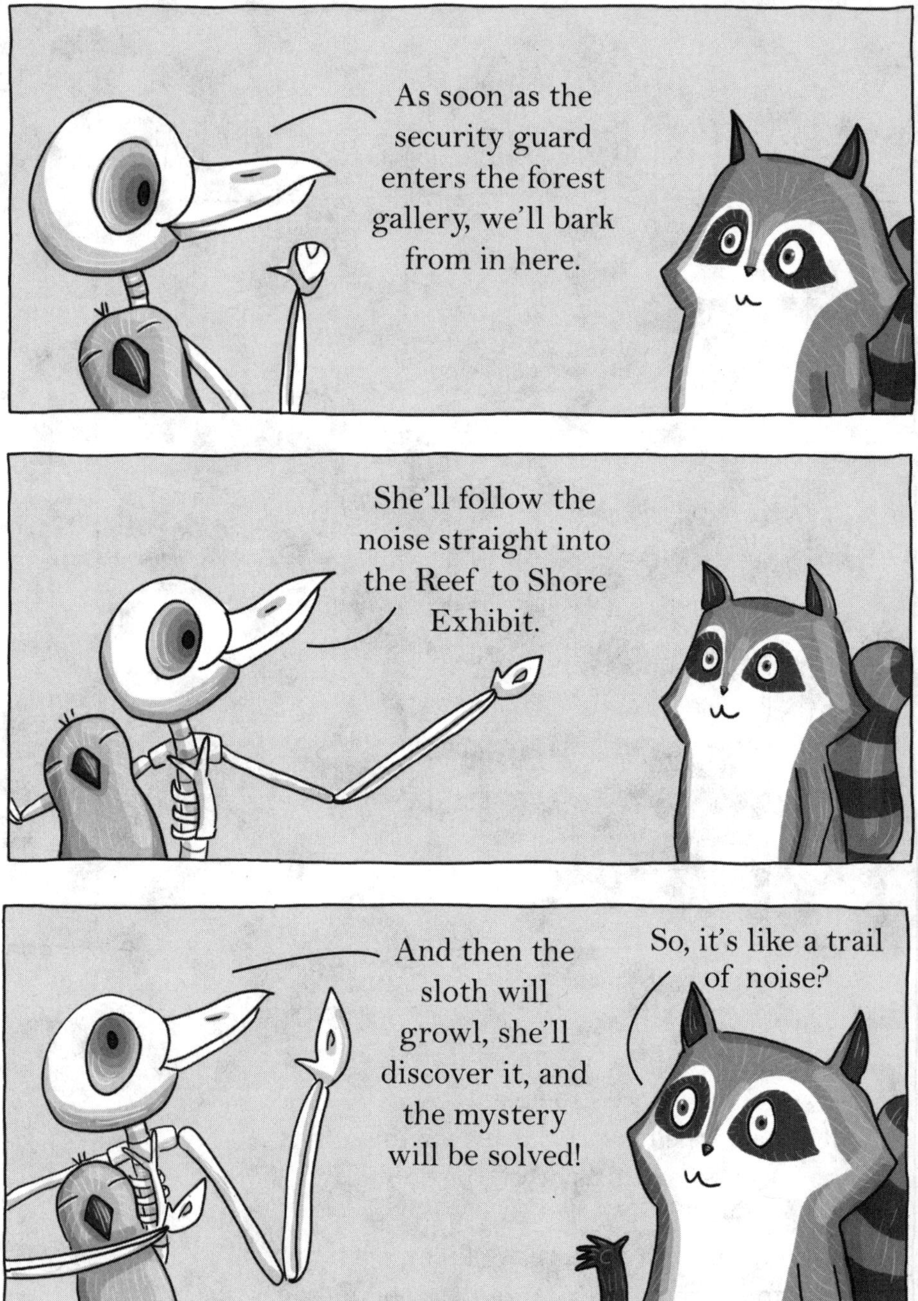
As soon as the security guard enters the forest gallery, we'll bark from in here.
She'll follow the noise straight into the Reef to Shore Exhibit.
And then the sloth will growl, she'll discover it, and the mystery will be solved!
So, it's like a trail of noise?

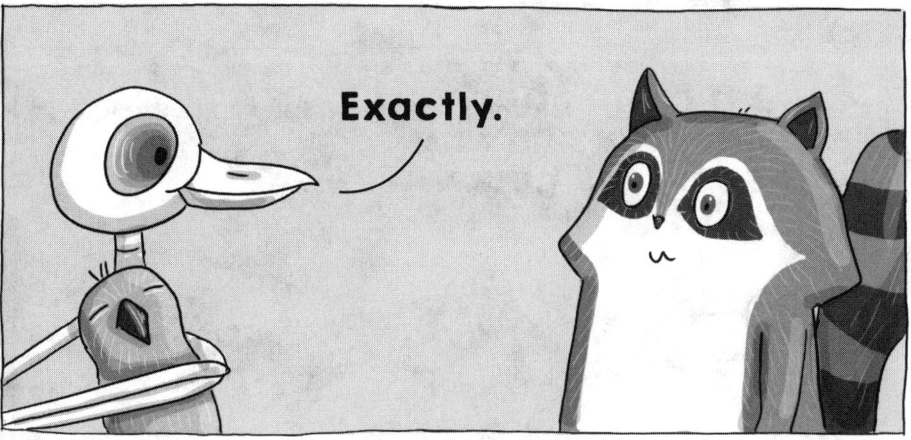
Exactly.

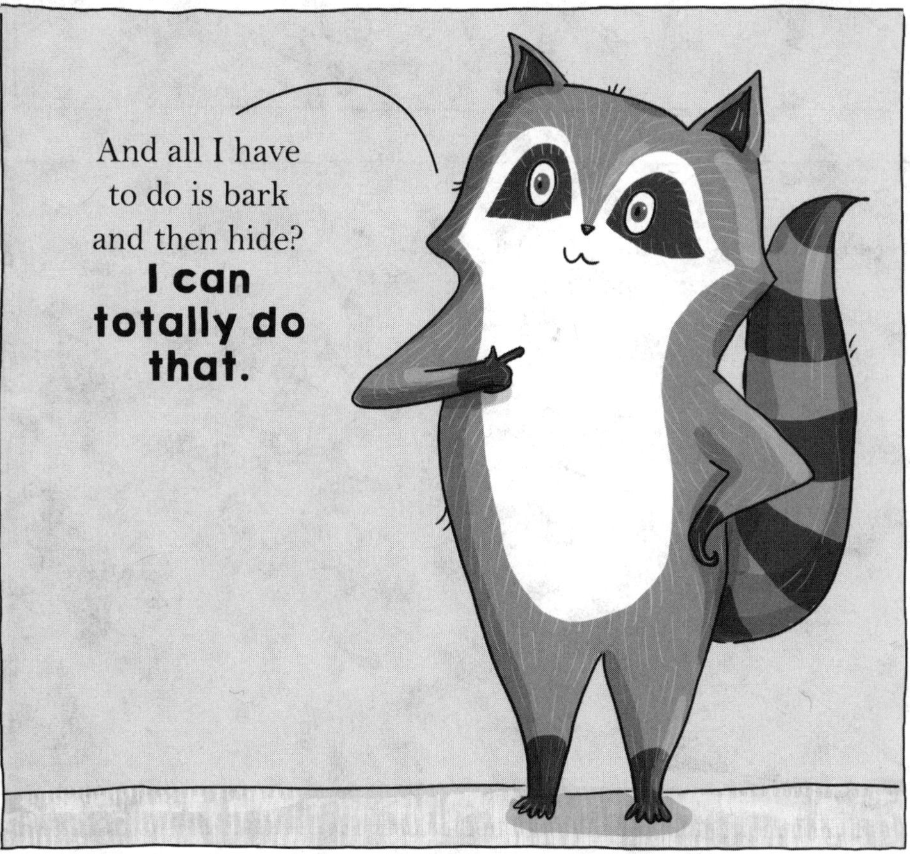
And all I have to do is bark and then hide?
I can totally do that.

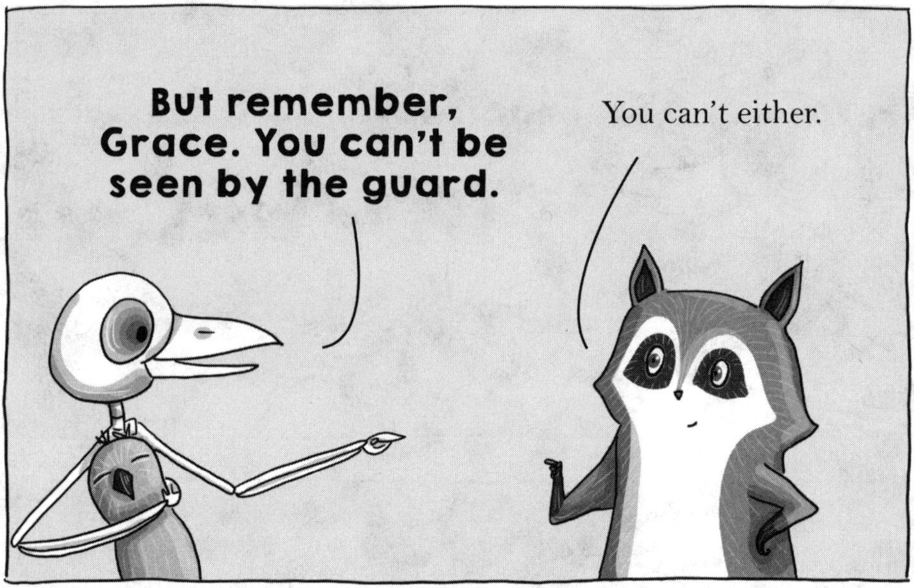
But remember, Grace. You can't be seen by the guard.
You can't either.

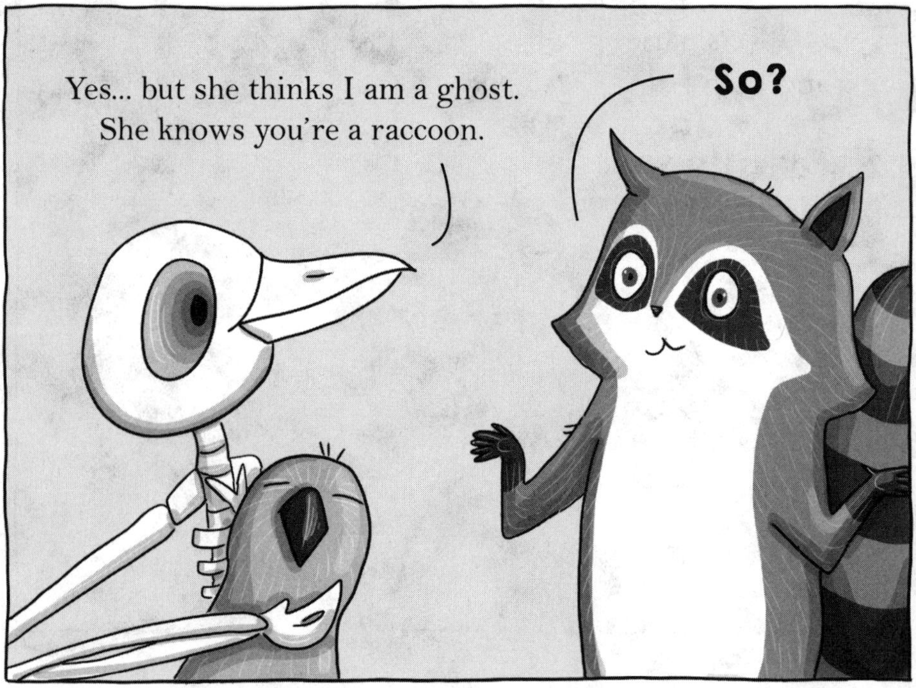
Yes... but she thinks I am a ghost. She knows you're a raccoon.
So?

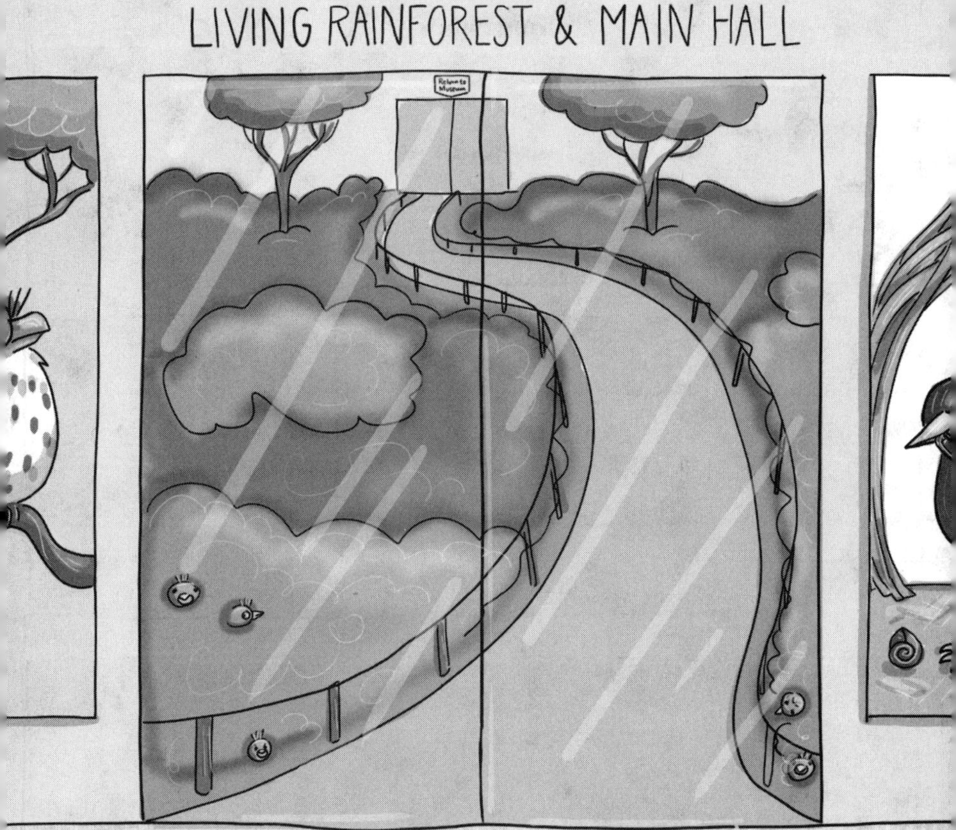
LIVING RAINFOREST & MAIN HALL

The museum can't get rid of a ghost...
but they can get rid of a raccoon.

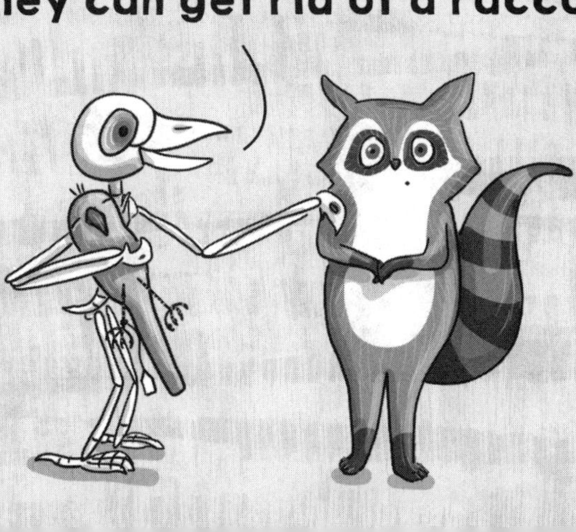

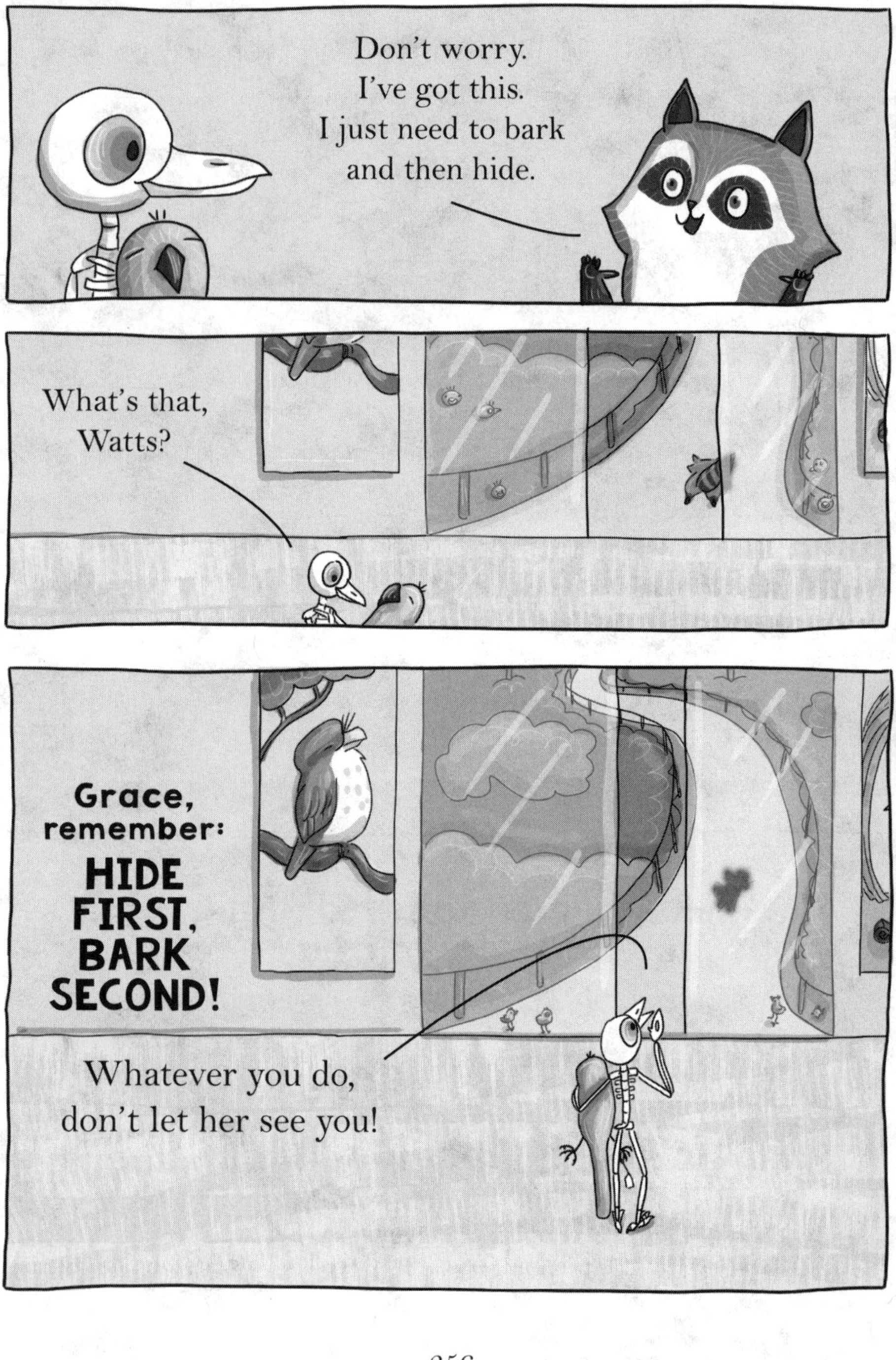
Don't worry. I've got this. I just need to bark and then hide.
What's that, Watts?
Grace, remember:
HIDE FIRST, BARK SECOND!
Whatever you do, don't let her see you!

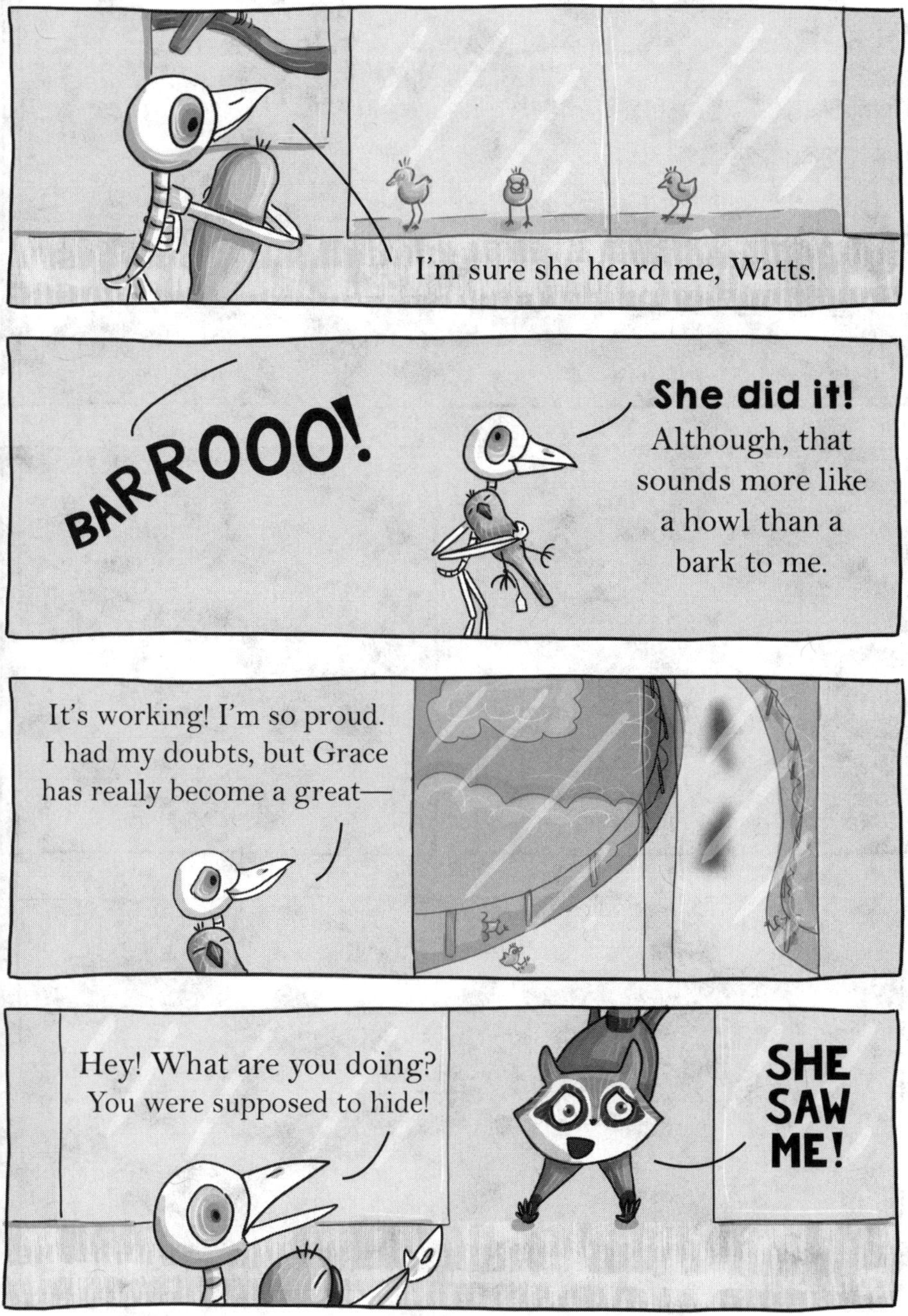
I'm sure she heard me, Watts.
BARROOO!
She did it! Although, that sounds more like a howl than a bark to me.
It's working! I'm so proud. I had my doubts, but Grace has really become a great—
Hey! What are you doing? You were supposed to hide!
SHE SAW ME!

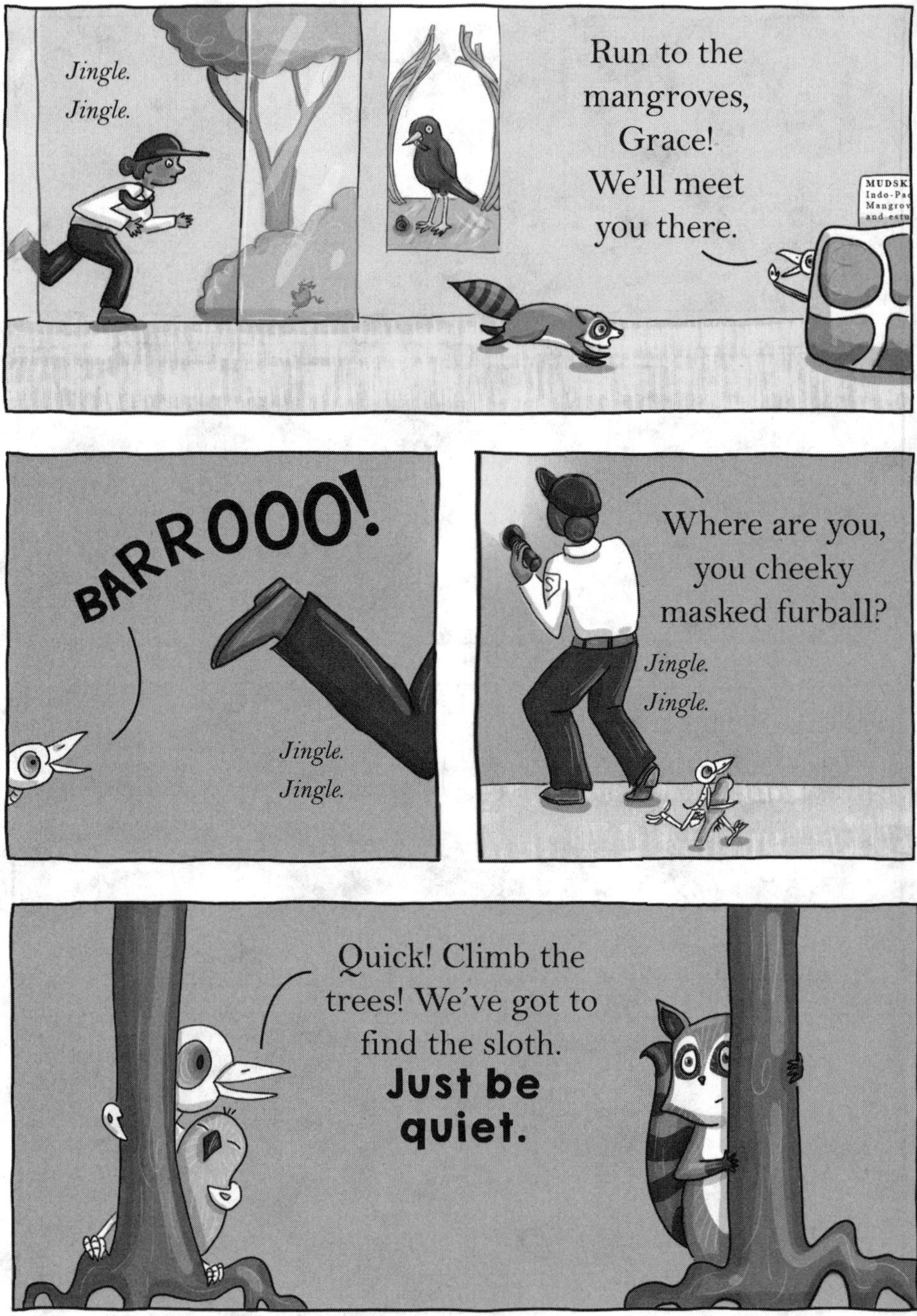
Jingle.
Jingle.
Run to the mangroves, Grace! We'll meet you there.
BARROOO!
Jingle.
Jingle.
Where are you, you cheeky masked furball?
Jingle.
Jingle.
Quick! Climb the trees! We've got to find the sloth.
Just be quiet.

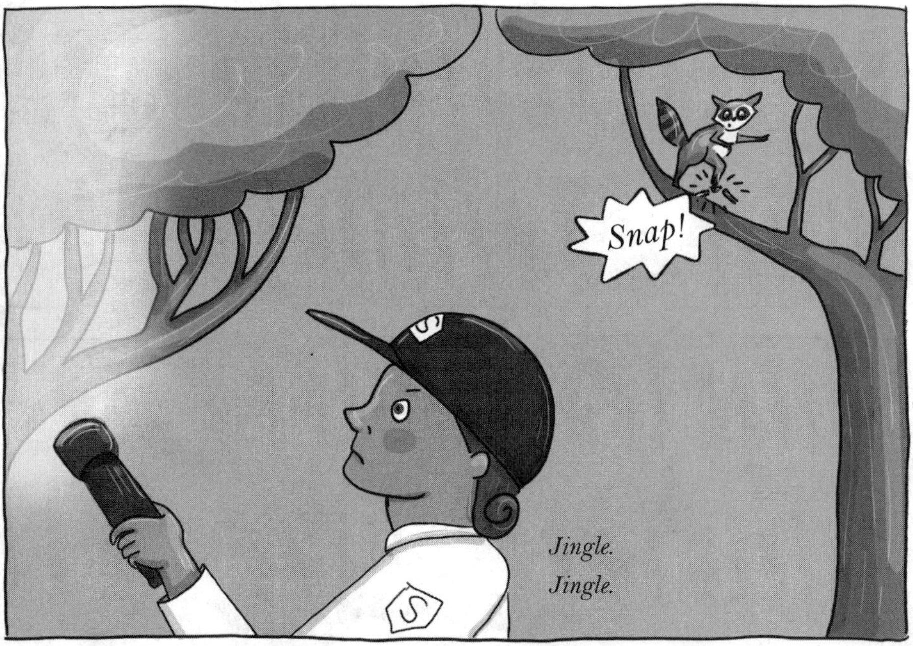
Snap!
Jingle.
Jingle.

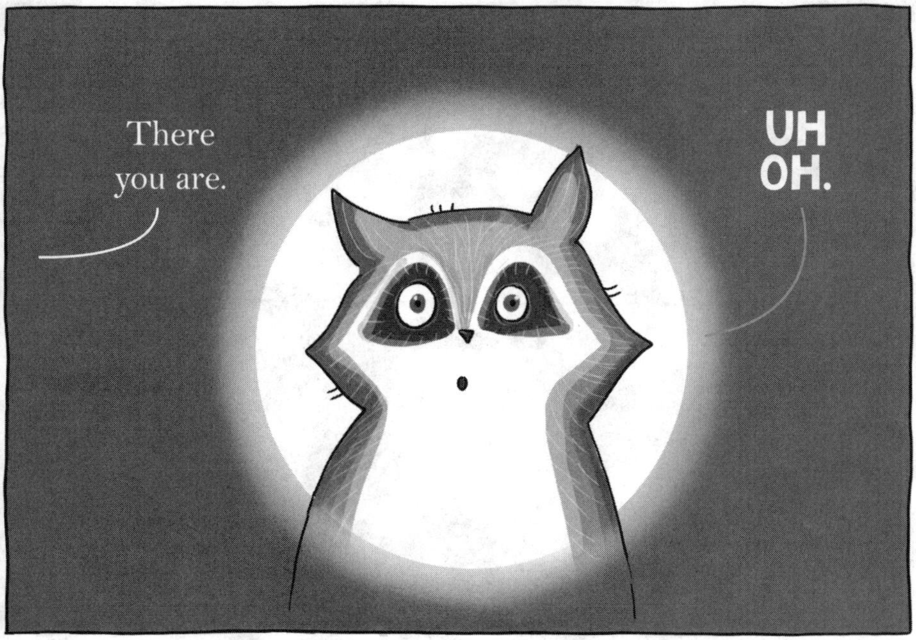
There you are.
UH OH.

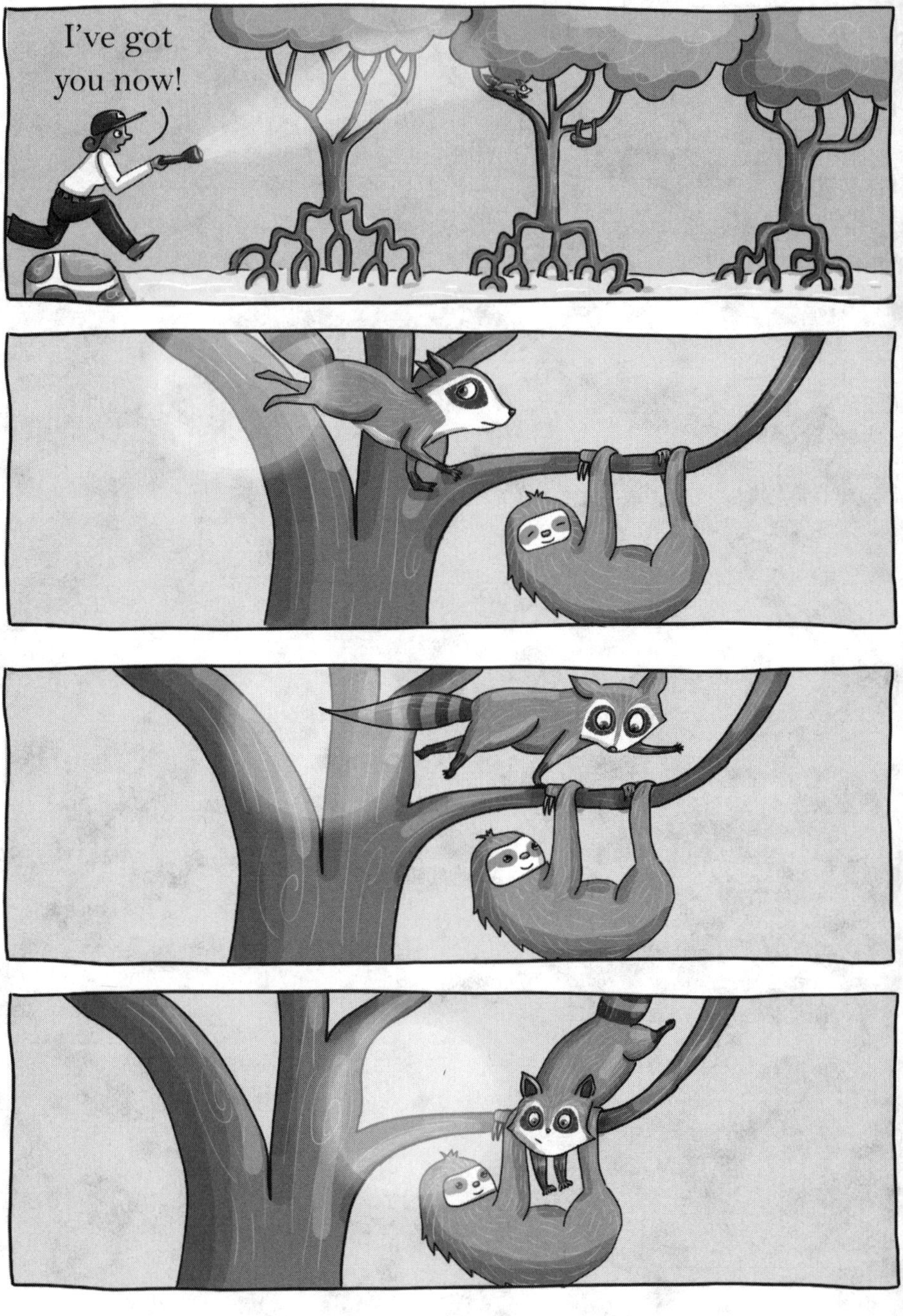
I've got you now!

AHHHHHH!!!

IT'S A MONSTER!

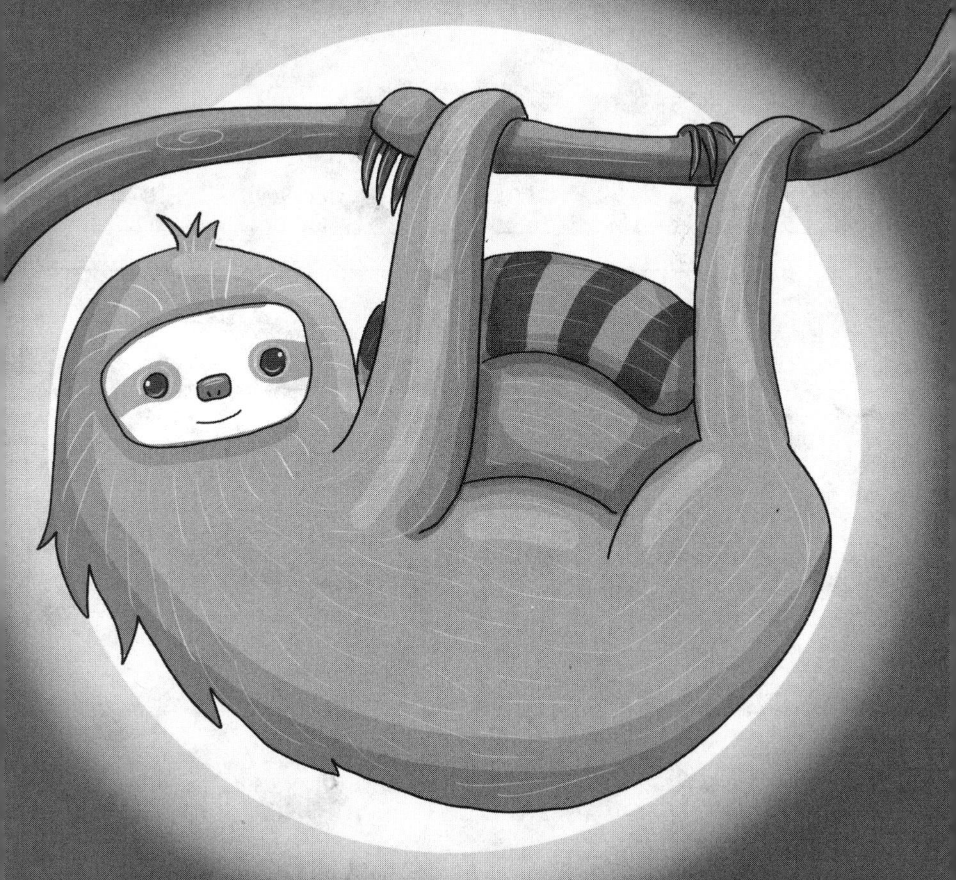

...a smiling cute monster...

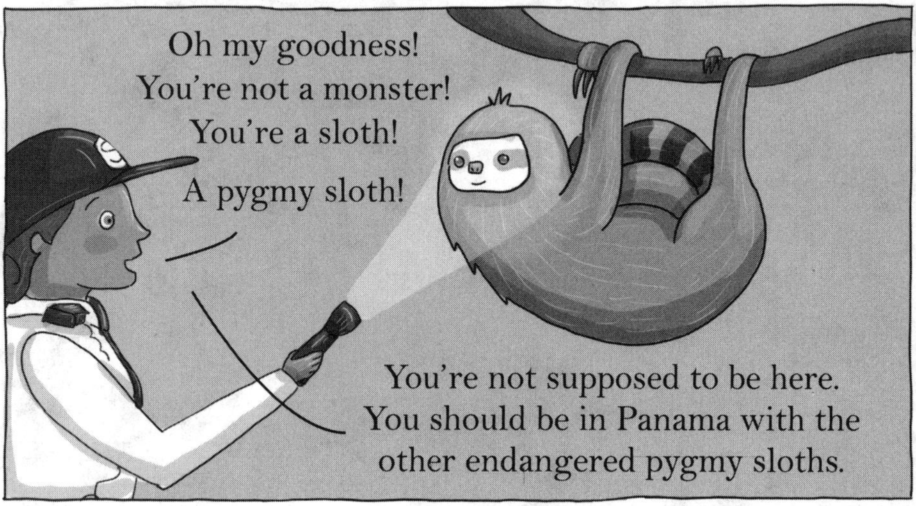
Oh my goodness! You're not a monster! You're a sloth!
A pygmy sloth!
You're not supposed to be here. You should be in Panama with the other endangered pygmy sloths.

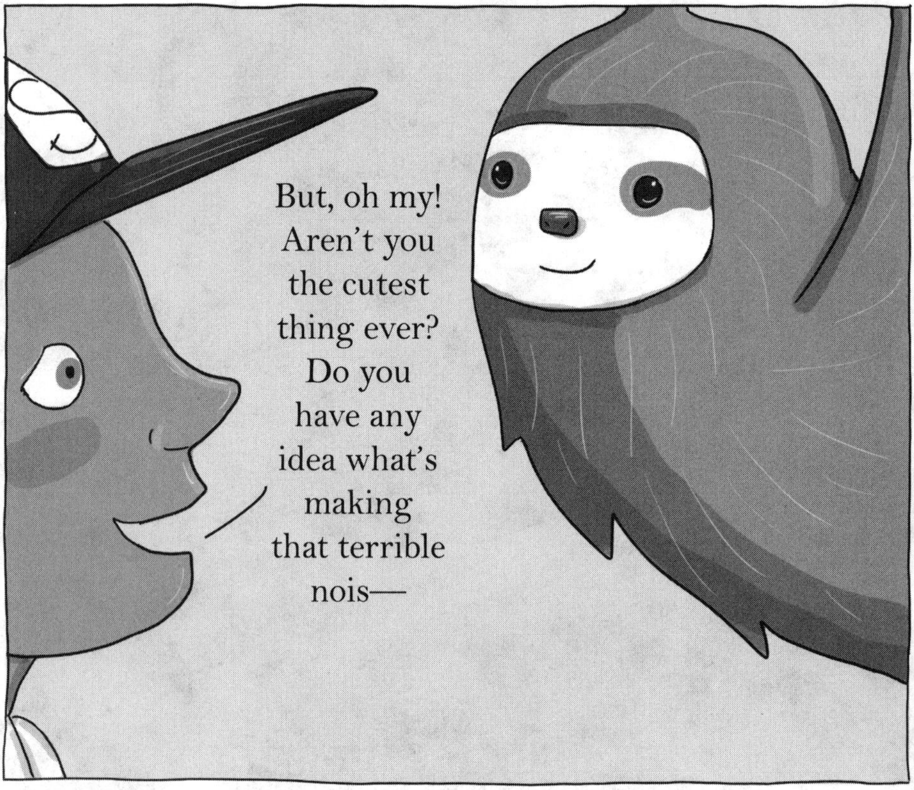
But, oh my! Aren't you the cutest thing ever? Do you have any idea what's making that terrible nois—

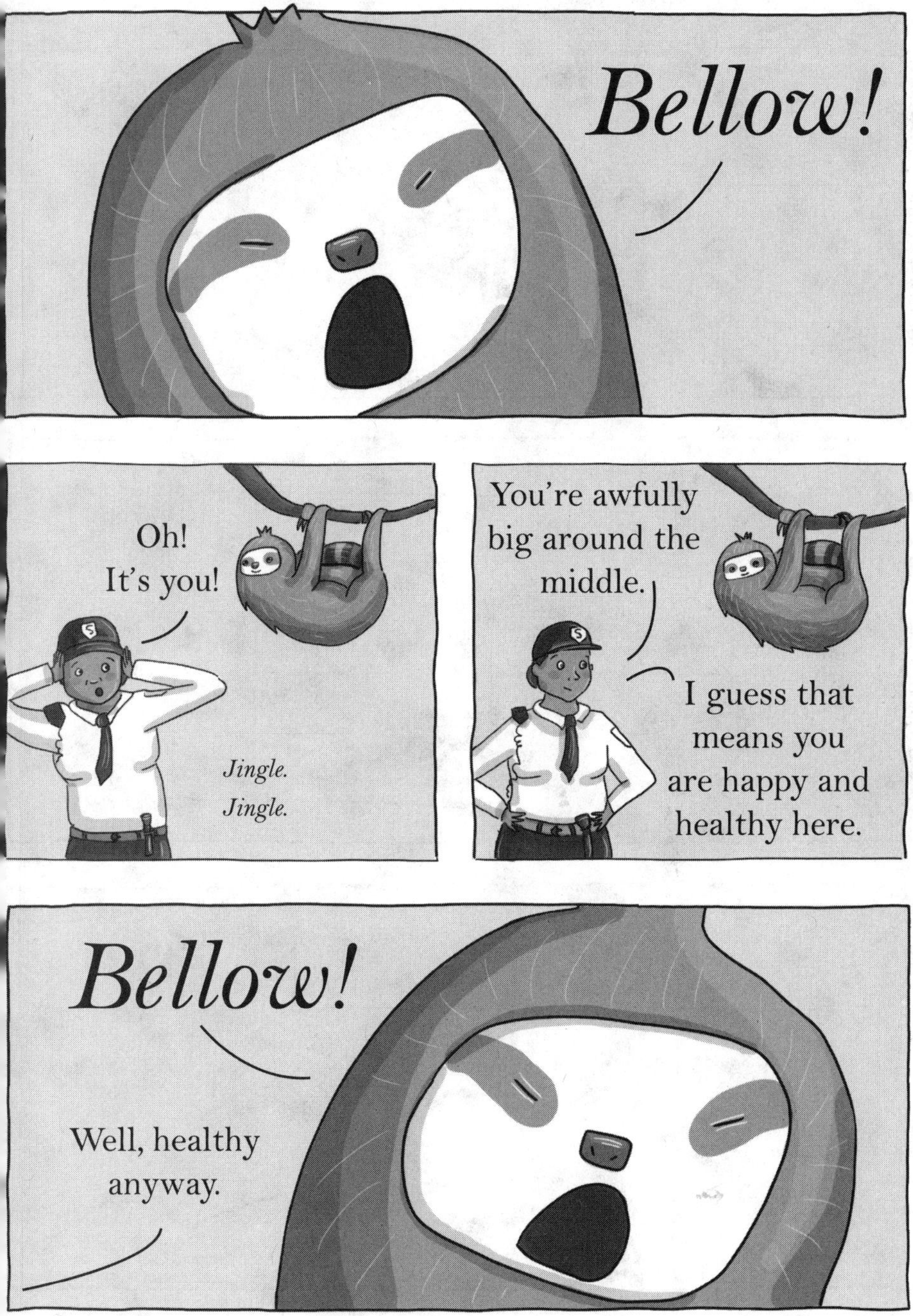
Bellow!
Oh! It's you!
Jingle. Jingle.
You're awfully big around the middle.
I guess that means you are happy and healthy here.
Bellow!
Well, healthy anyway.

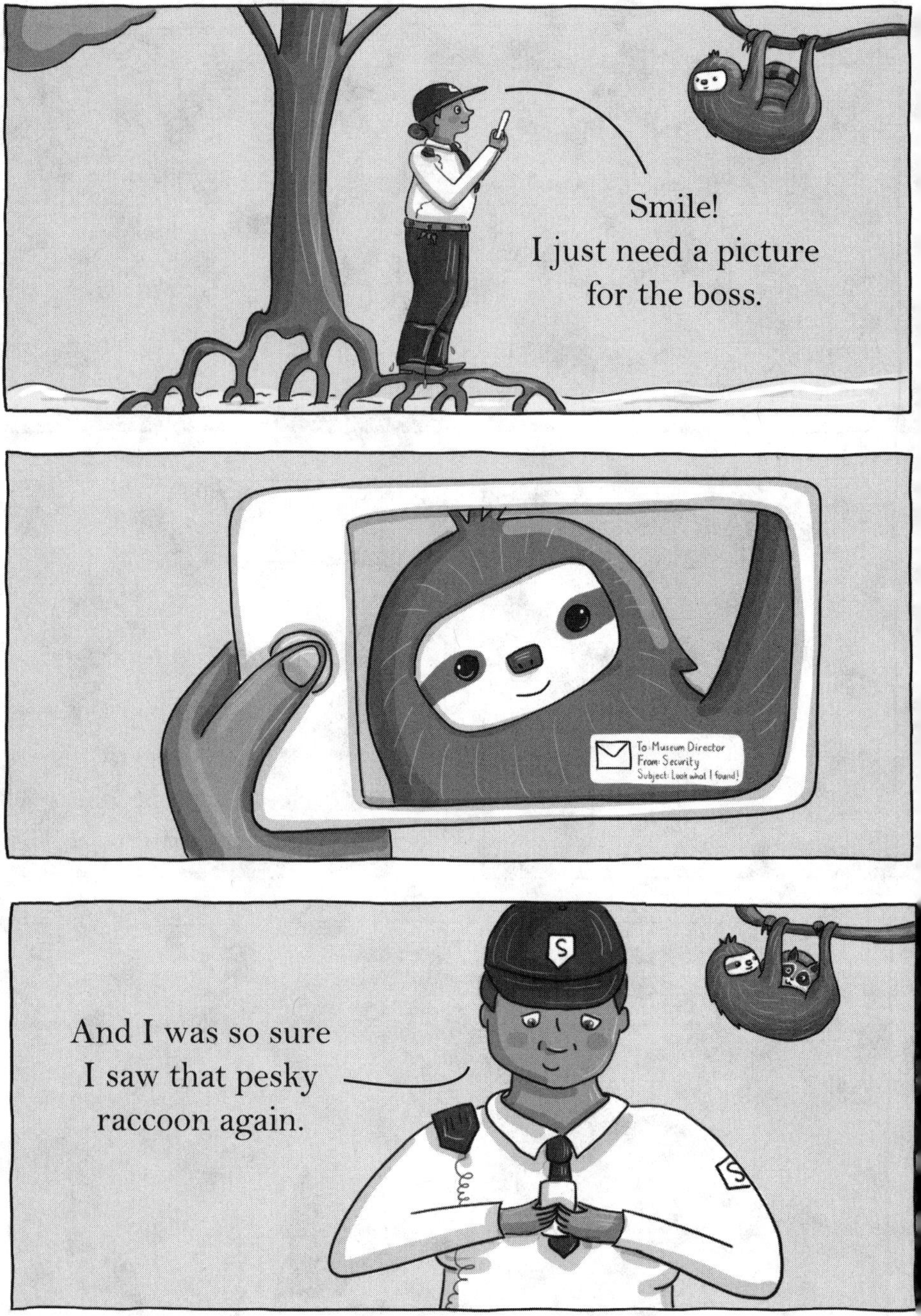
Smile!
I just need a picture
for the boss.
To: Museum Director
From: Security
Subject: Look what I found!
And I was so sure
I saw that pesky
raccoon again.

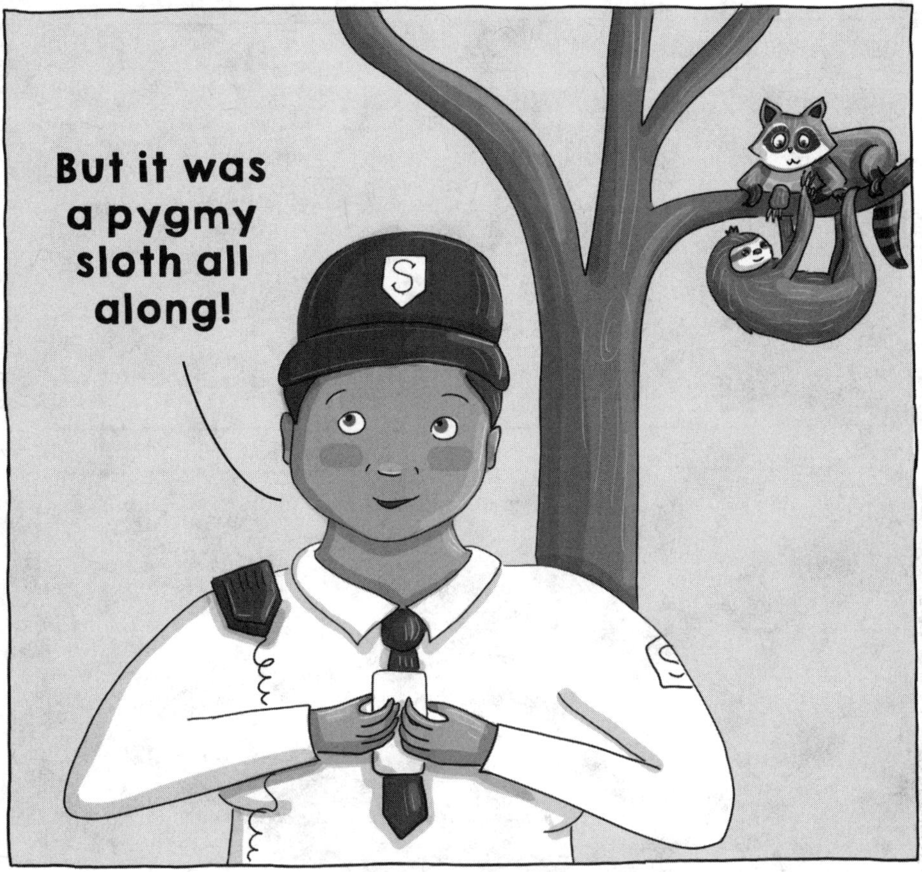
But it was a pygmy sloth all along!

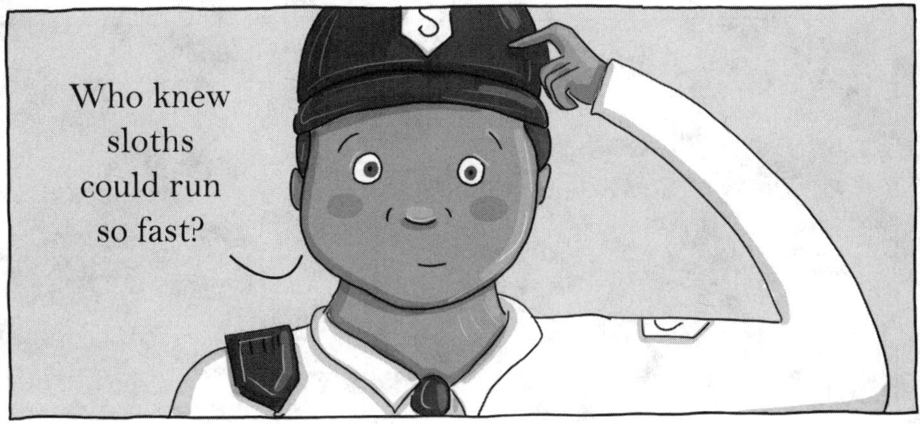
Who knew sloths could run so fast?

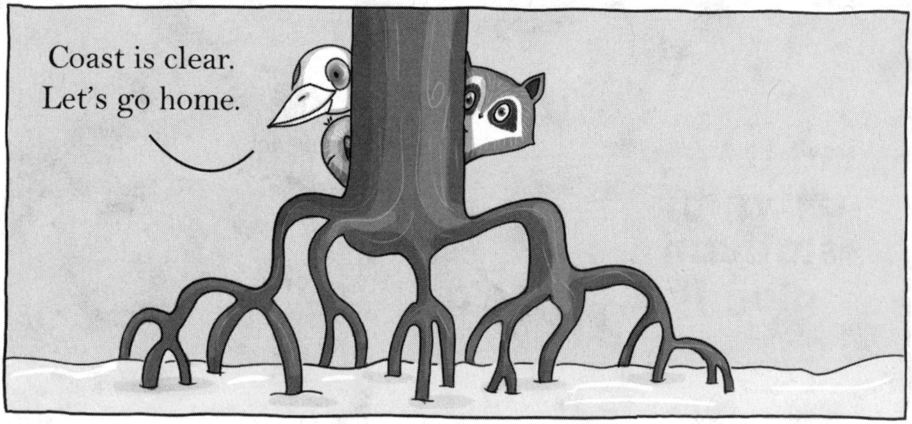
Coast is clear. Let's go home.

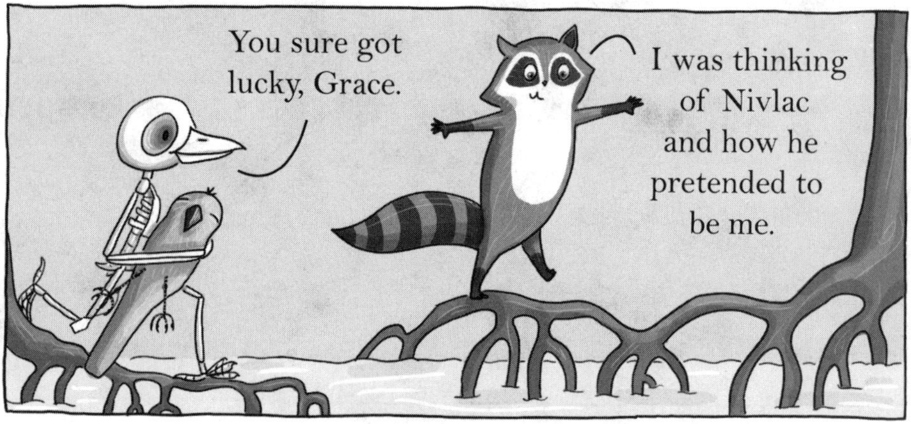
You sure got lucky, Grace.
I was thinking of Nivlac and how he pretended to be me.

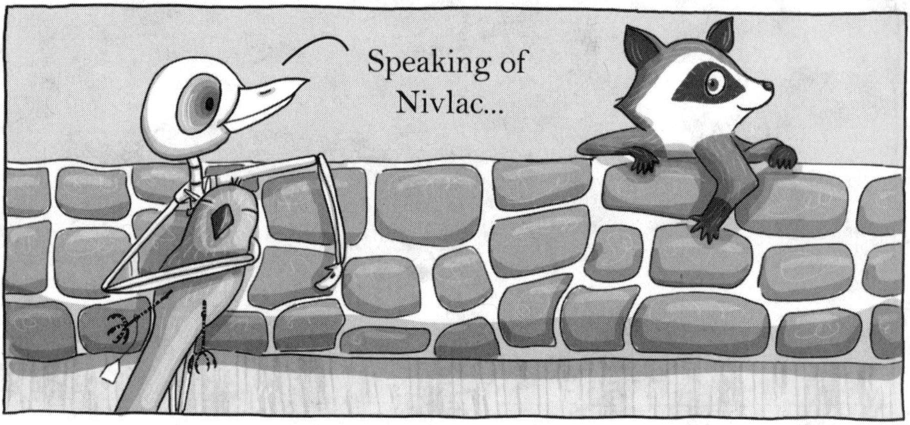
Speaking of Nivlac...

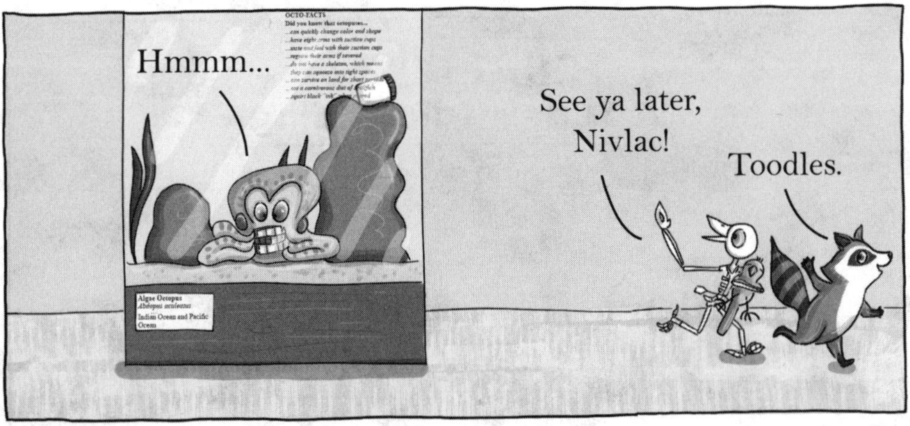
OCTO-FACTS
Did you know that octopuses...
...can quickly change color and shape
...have eight arms with suction cups
Hmmm...
Algae Octopus
Abdopus aculeatus
Indian Ocean and Pacific Ocean
See ya later, Nivlac!
Toodles.

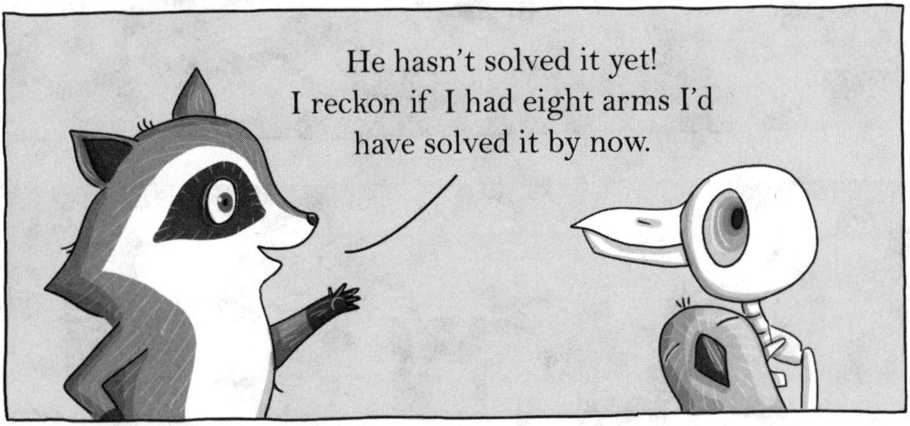
He hasn't solved it yet! I reckon if I had eight arms I'd have solved it by now.

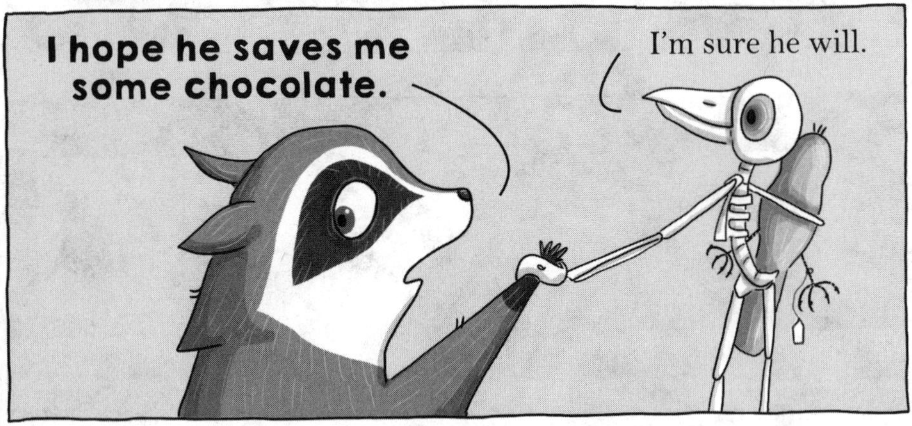
I hope he saves me some chocolate.
I'm sure he will.

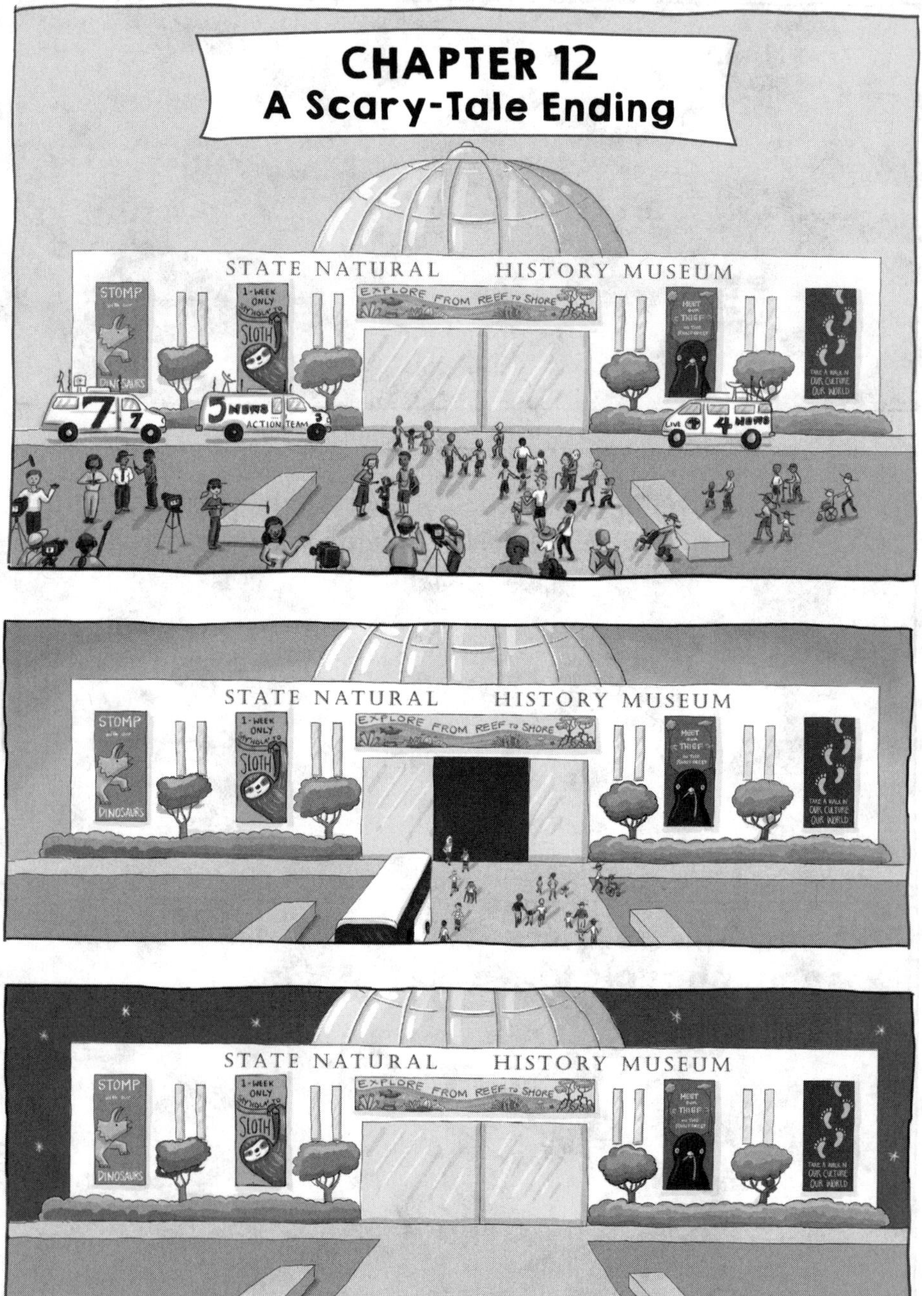
CHAPTER 12
A Scary-Tale Ending
STATE NATURAL HISTORY MUSEUM
STOMP
DINOSAURS
1-WEEK ONLY
SLOTH
EXPLORE FROM REEF TO SHORE
MEET OUR THIEF
TAKE A WALK IN OUR CULTURE OUR WORLD
7
5 NEWS ACTION TEAM
LIVE 4 NEWS
STATE NATURAL HISTORY MUSEUM
STATE NATURAL HISTORY MUSEUM

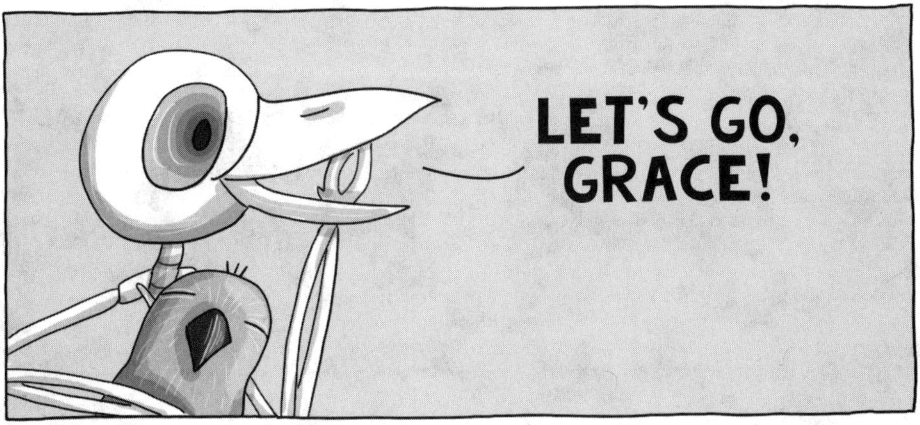
LET'S GO, GRACE!

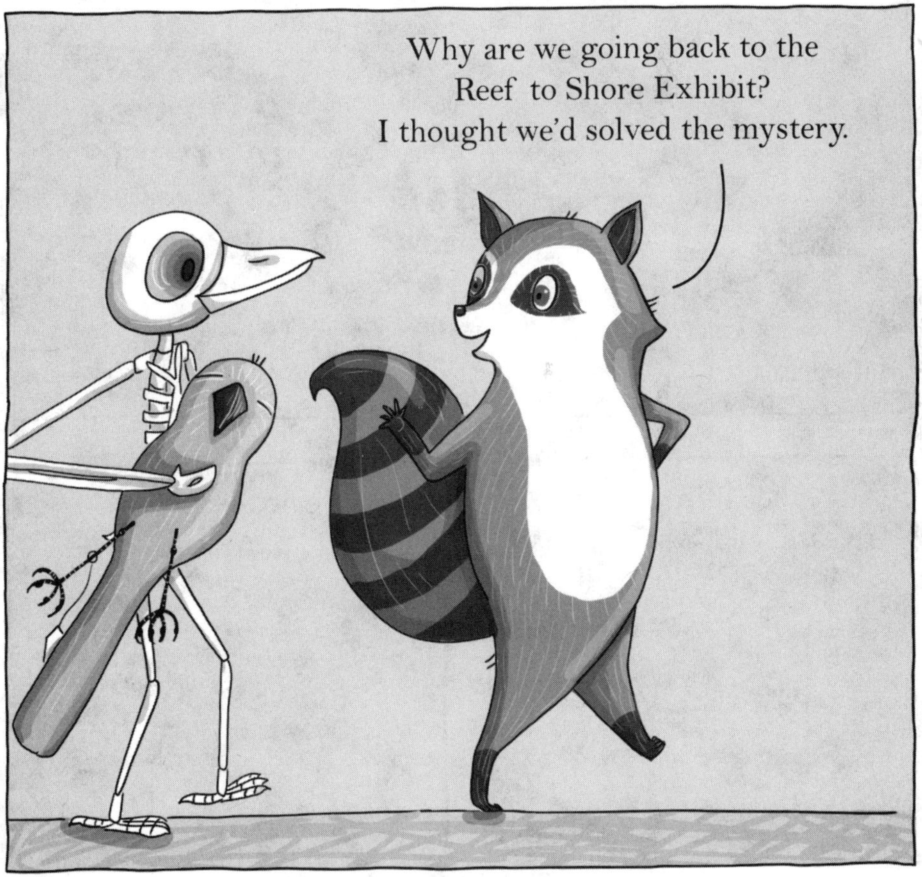
Why are we going back to the Reef to Shore Exhibit? I thought we'd solved the mystery.

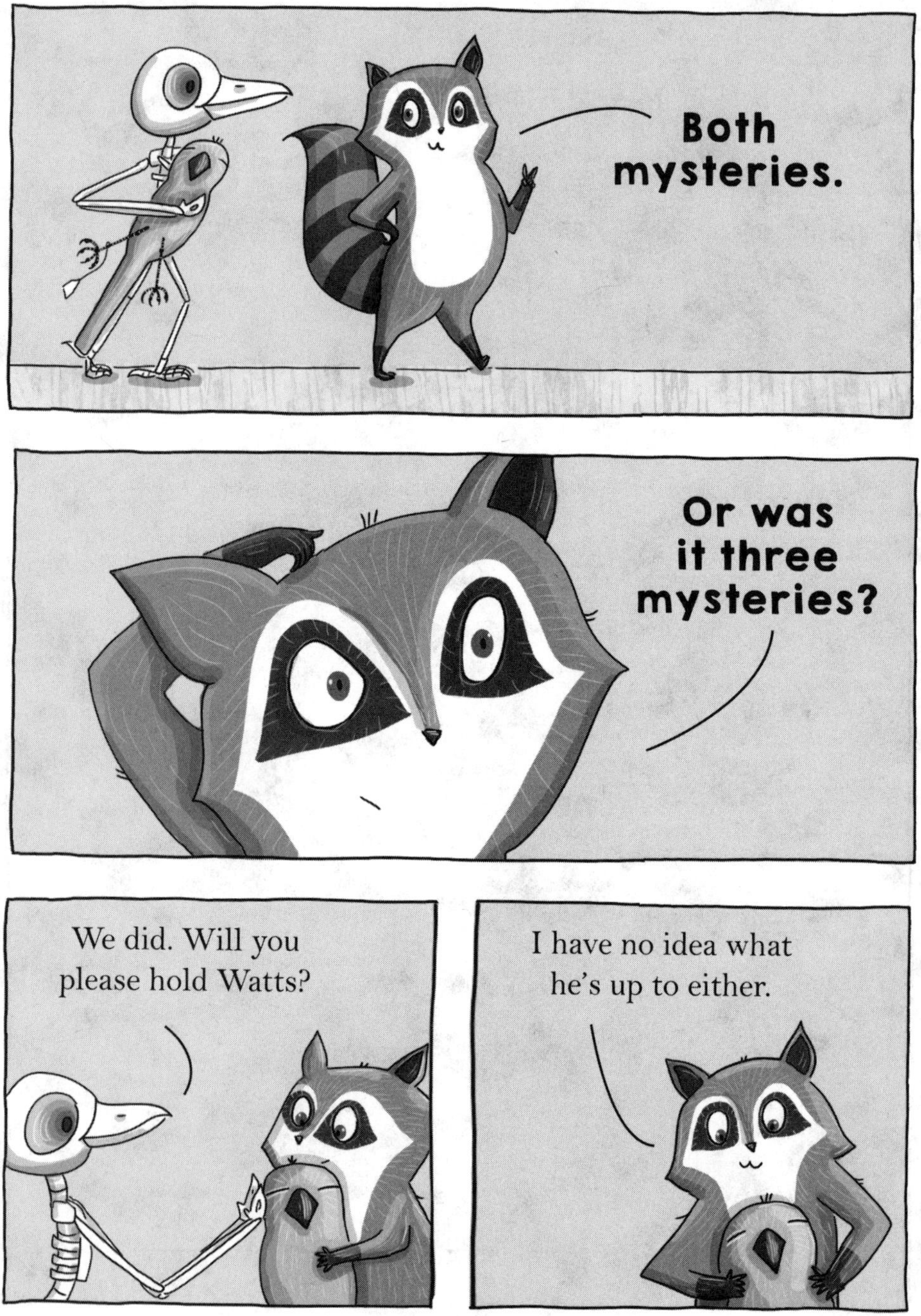
Both mysteries.
Or was it three mysteries?
We did. Will you please hold Watts?
I have no idea what he's up to either.

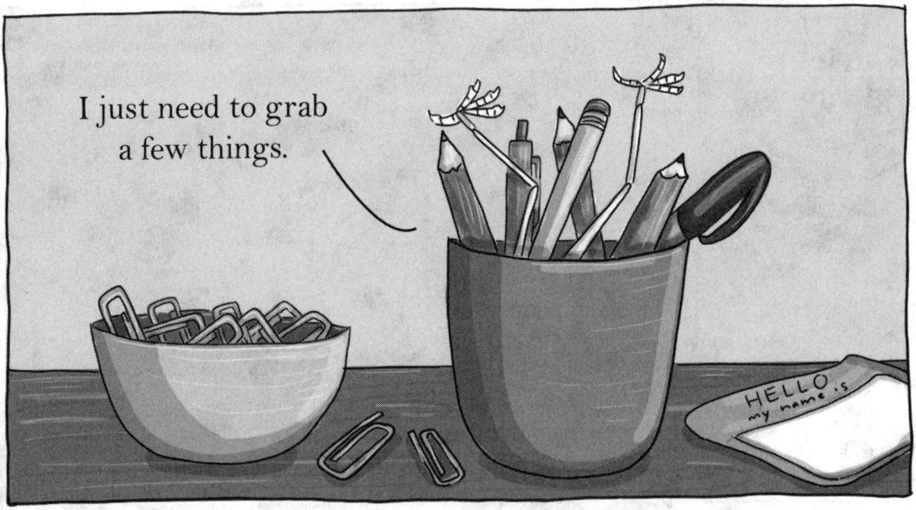
I just need to grab a few things.
HELLO my name is

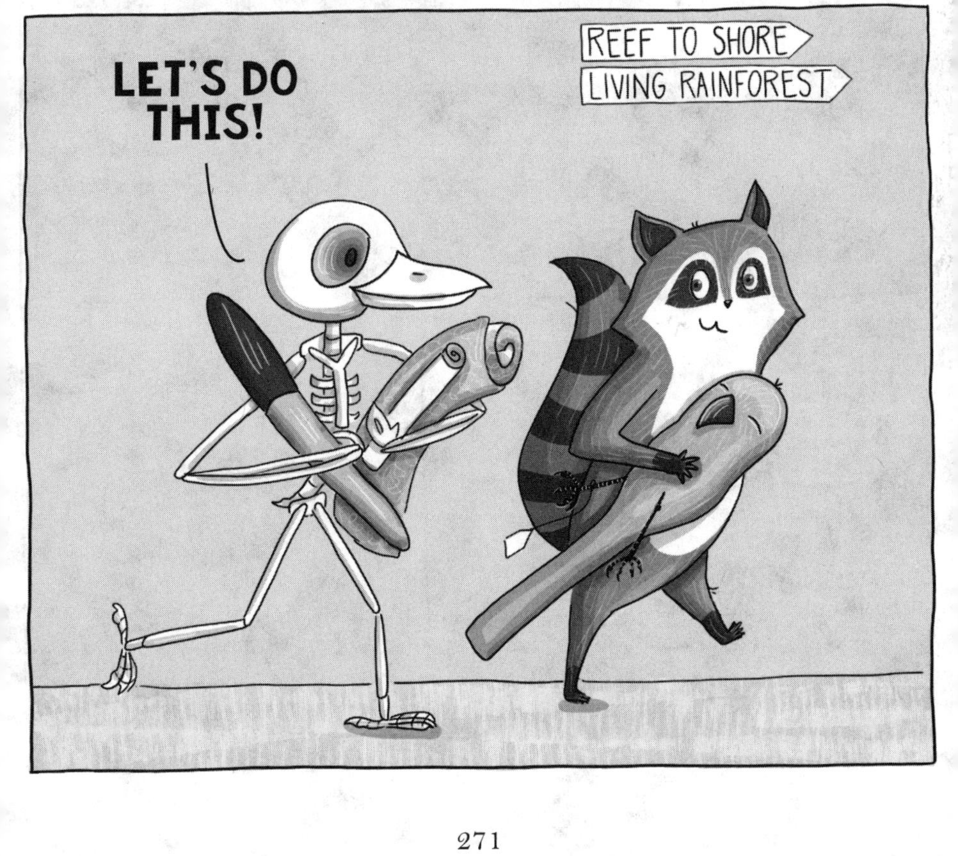
REEF TO SHORE
LIVING RAINFOREST
LET'S DO THIS!

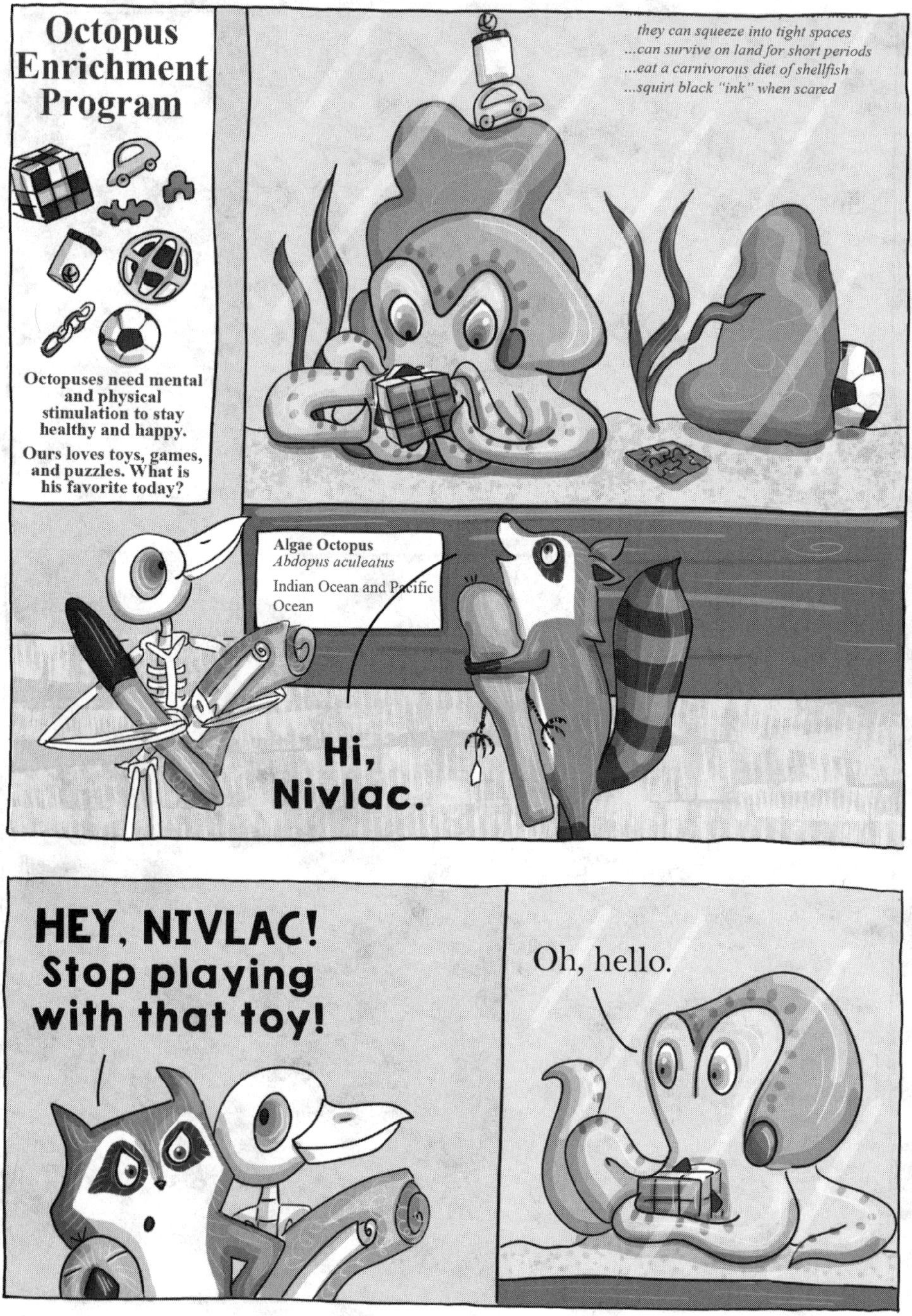
Octopus Enrichment Program
Octopuses need mental and physical stimulation to stay healthy and happy.
Ours loves toys, games, and puzzles. What is his favorite today?
they can squeeze into tight spaces
...can survive on land for short periods
...eat a carnivorous diet of shellfish
...squirt black "ink" when scared
Algae Octopus
Abdopus aculeatus
Indian Ocean and Pacific Ocean
Hi, Nivlac.
HEY, NIVLAC! Stop playing with that toy!
Oh, hello.

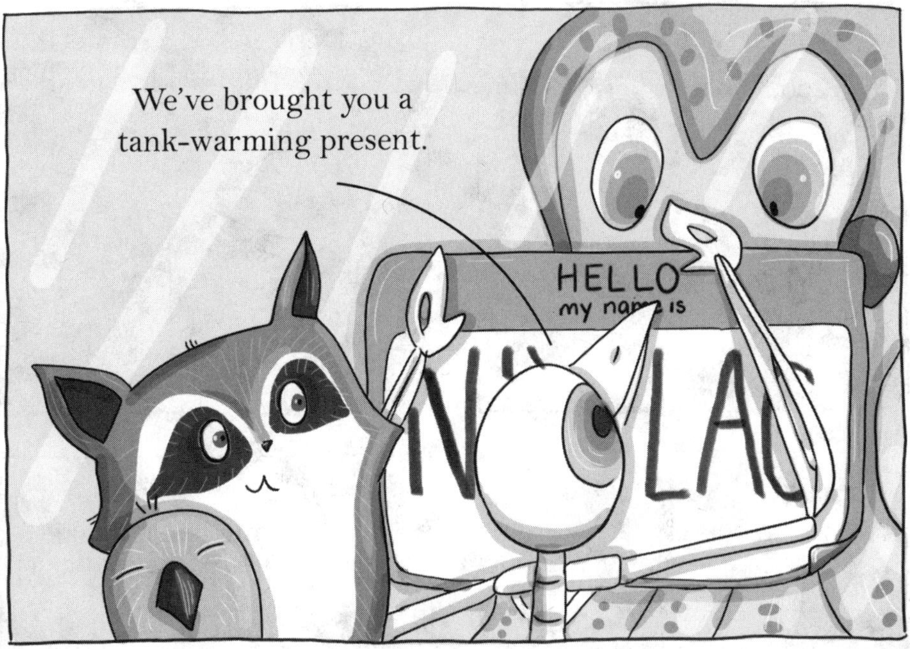
We've brought you a tank-warming present.
HELLO
my name is
NIVLAC

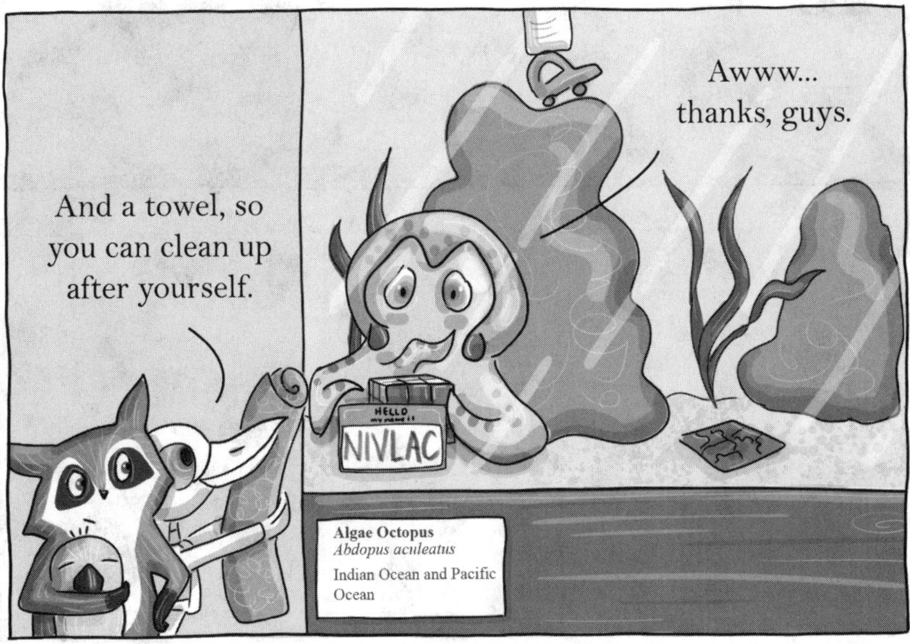
Awww... thanks, guys.
And a towel, so you can clean up after yourself.
HELLO
NIVLAC
Algae Octopus
Abdopus aculeatus
Indian Ocean and Pacific Ocean

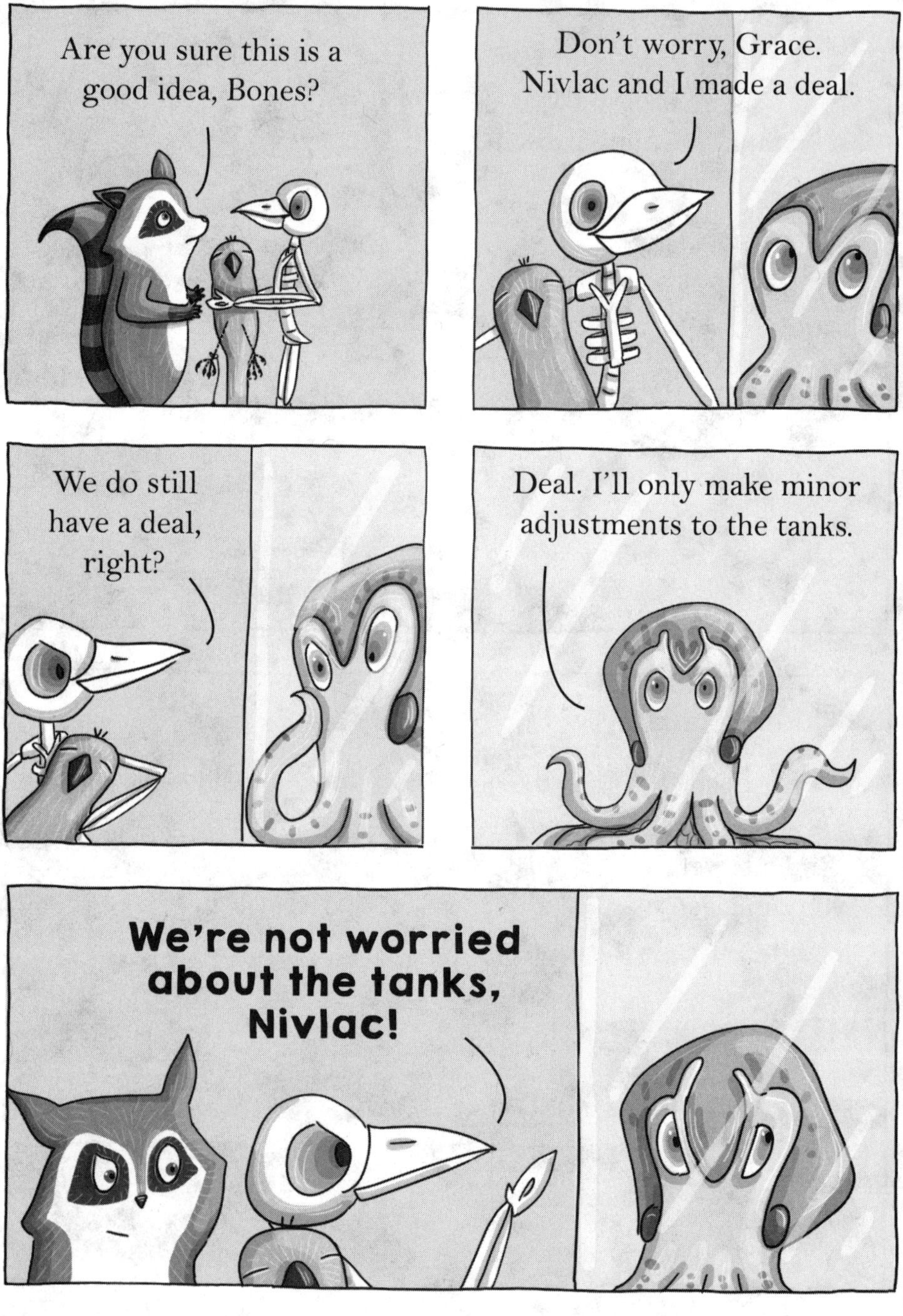
Are you sure this is a good idea, Bones?
Don't worry, Grace. Nivlac and I made a deal.
We do still have a deal, right?
Deal. I'll only make minor adjustments to the tanks.
We're not worried about the tanks, Nivlac!

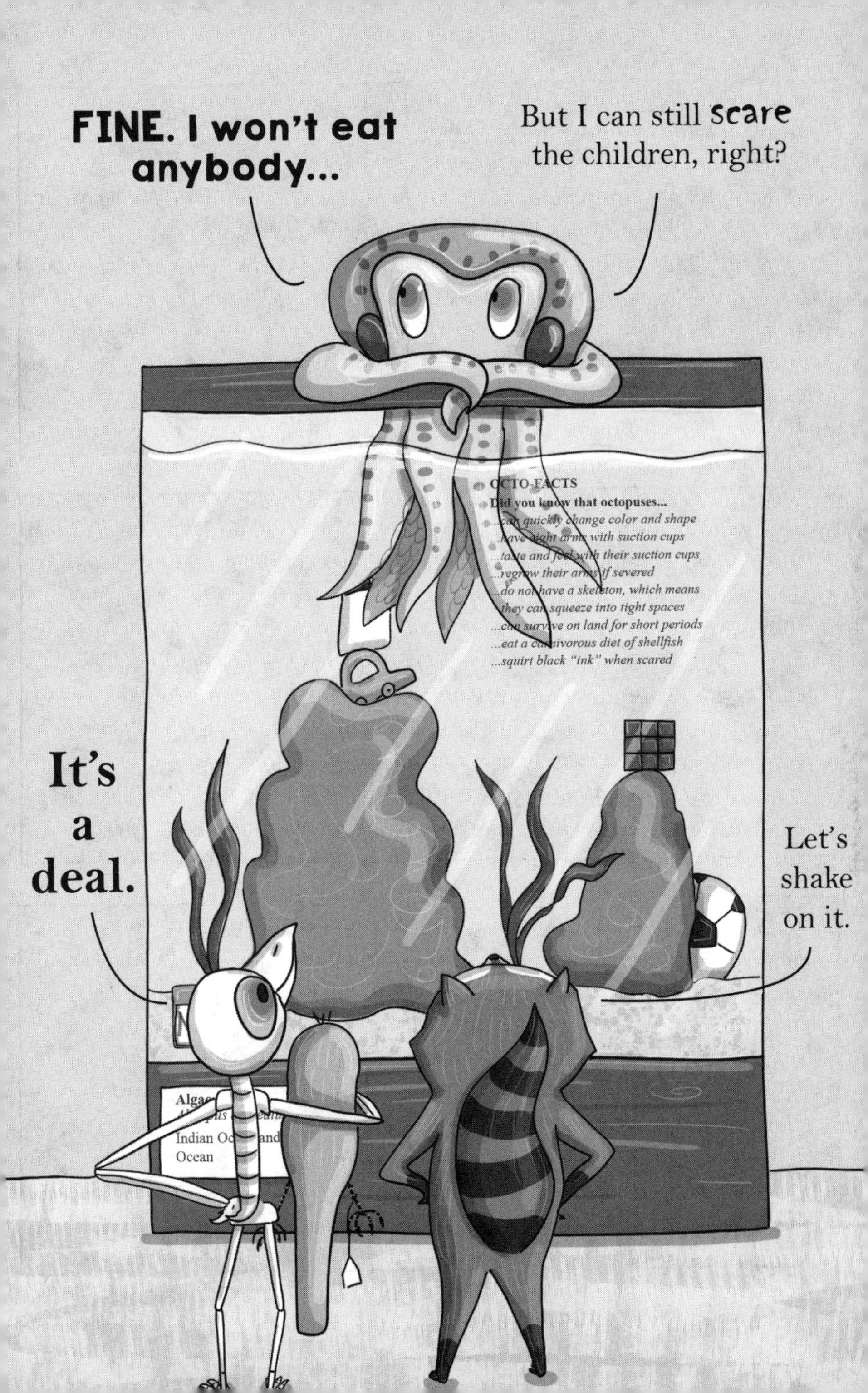
FINE. I won't eat anybody...
But I can still scare the children, right?
OCTO-FACTS
Did you know that octopuses...
...can quickly change color and shape
...have eight arms with suction cups
...taste and feel with their suction cups
...regrow their arms if severed
...do not have a skeleton, which means they can squeeze into tight spaces
...can survive on land for short periods
...eat a carnivorous diet of shellfish
...squirt black "ink" when scared
It's a deal.
Let's shake on it.

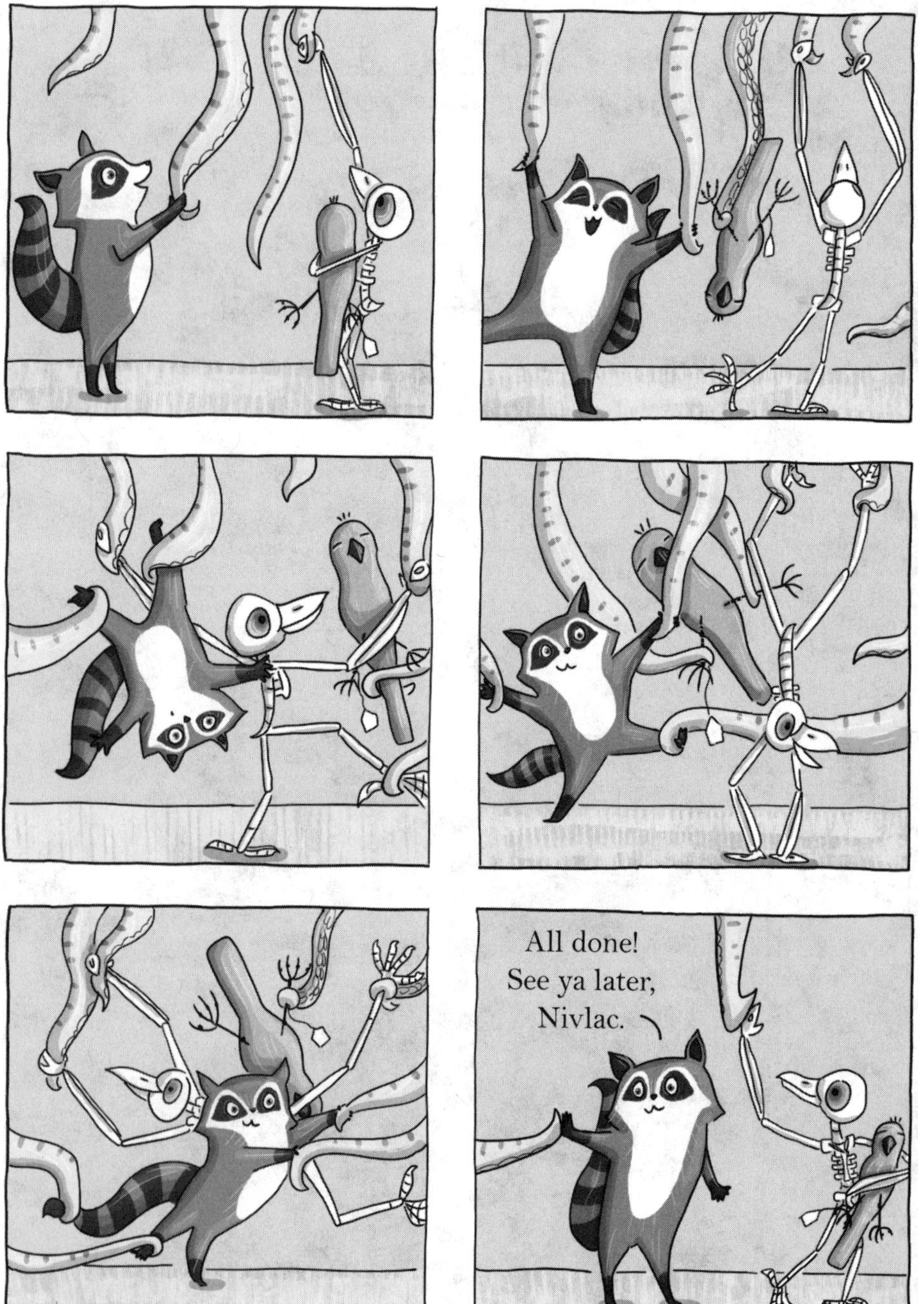
All done!
See ya later,
Nivlac.

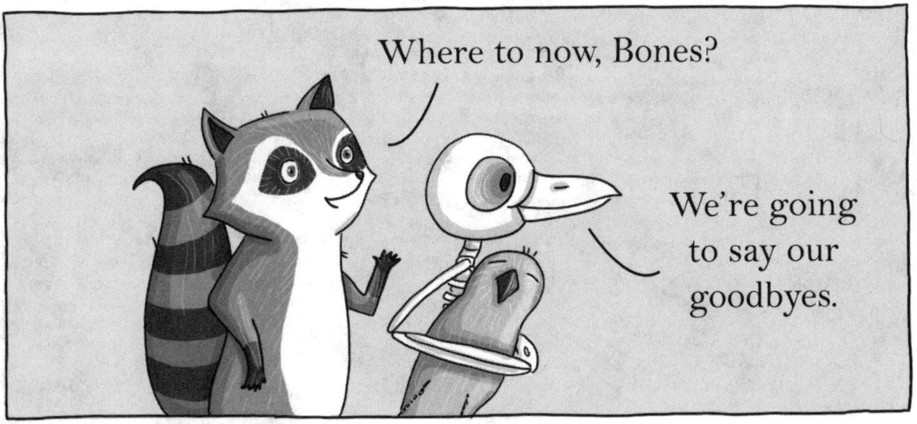
Where to now, Bones?
We're going to say our goodbyes.

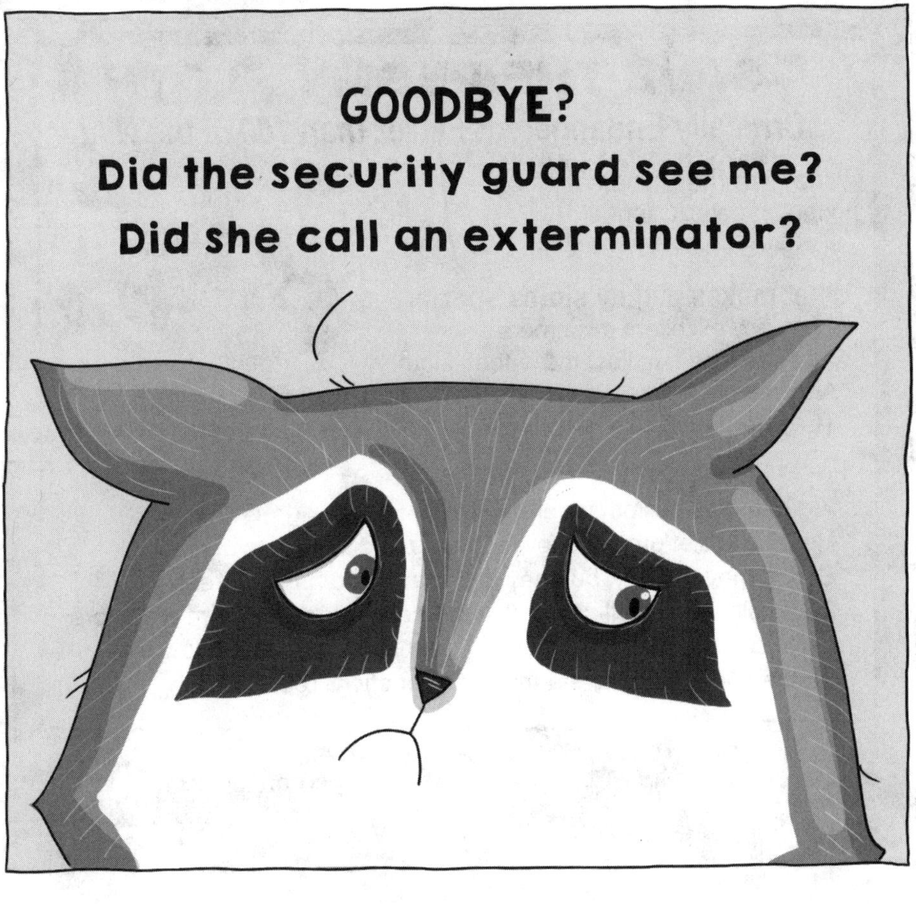
GOODBYE?
Did the security guard see me?
Did she call an exterminator?

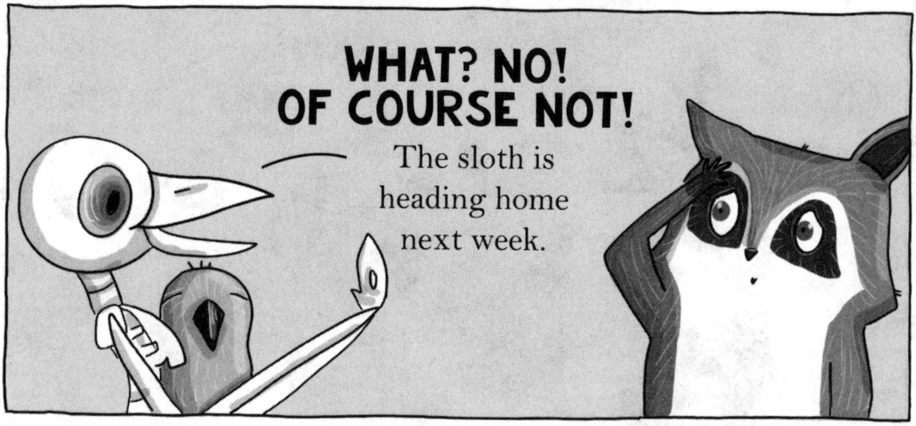
WHAT? NO!
OF COURSE NOT!
The sloth is heading home next week.

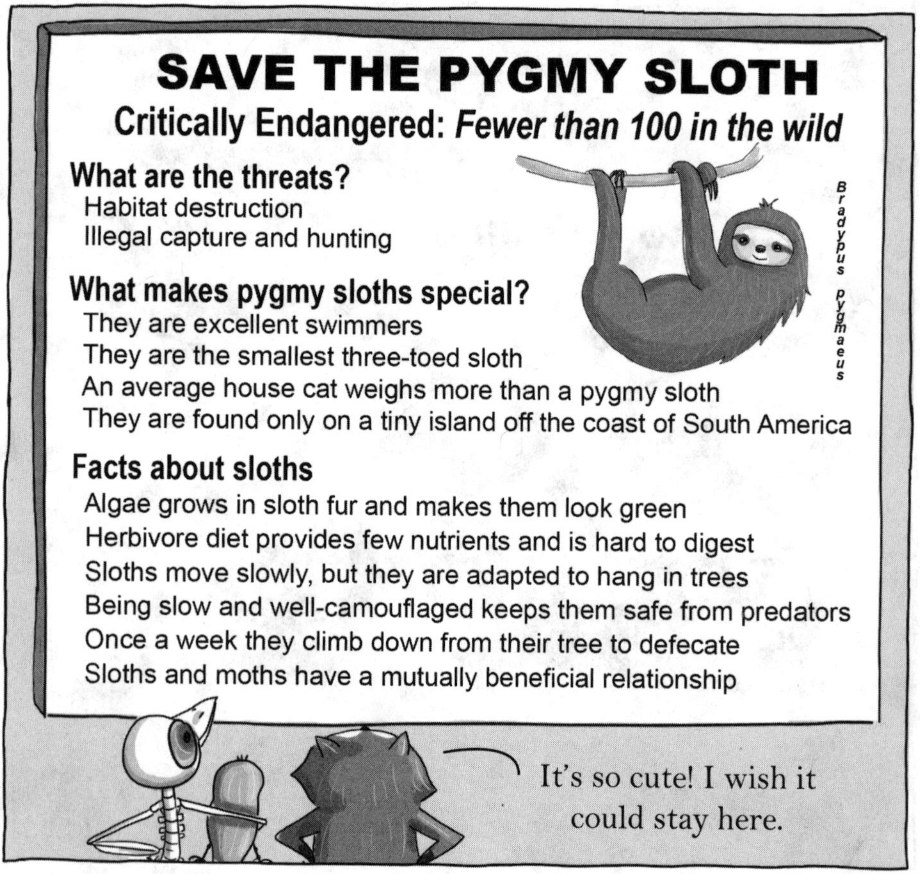
SAVE THE PYGMY SLOTH
Critically Endangered: Fewer than 100 in the wild
What are the threats?
Habitat destruction
Illegal capture and hunting
Bradypus pygmaeus
What makes pygmy sloths special?
They are excellent swimmers
They are the smallest three-toed sloth
An average house cat weighs more than a pygmy sloth
They are found only on a tiny island off the coast of South America
Facts about sloths
Algae grows in sloth fur and makes them look green
Herbivore diet provides few nutrients and is hard to digest
Sloths move slowly, but they are adapted to hang in trees
Being slow and well-camouflaged keeps them safe from predators
Once a week they climb down from their tree to defecate
Sloths and moths have a mutually beneficial relationship
It's so cute! I wish it could stay here.

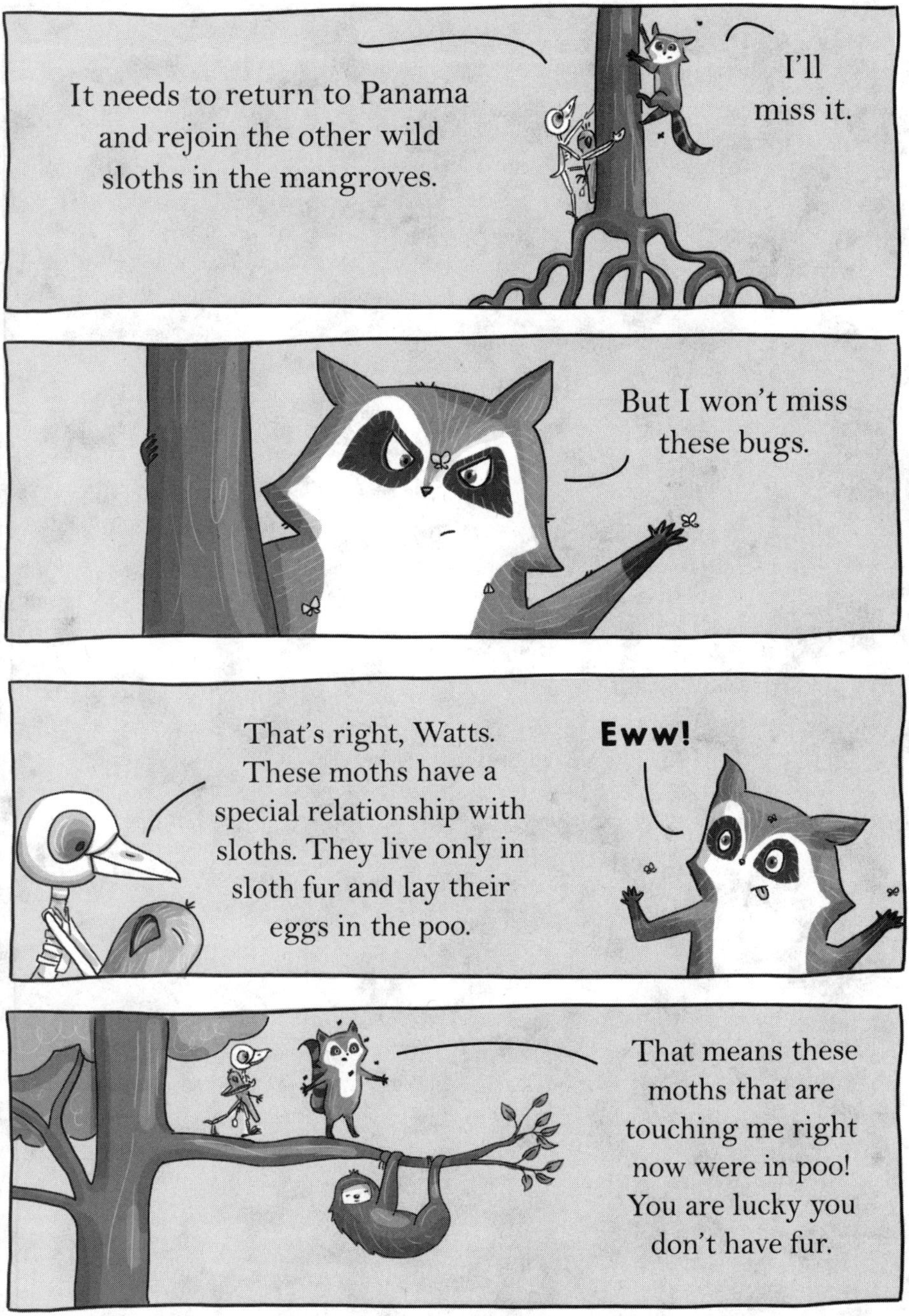
It needs to return to Panama and rejoin the other wild sloths in the mangroves.
I'll miss it.
But I won't miss these bugs.
That's right, Watts. These moths have a special relationship with sloths. They live only in sloth fur and lay their eggs in the poo.
Eww!
That means these moths that are touching me right now were in poo! You are lucky you don't have fur.

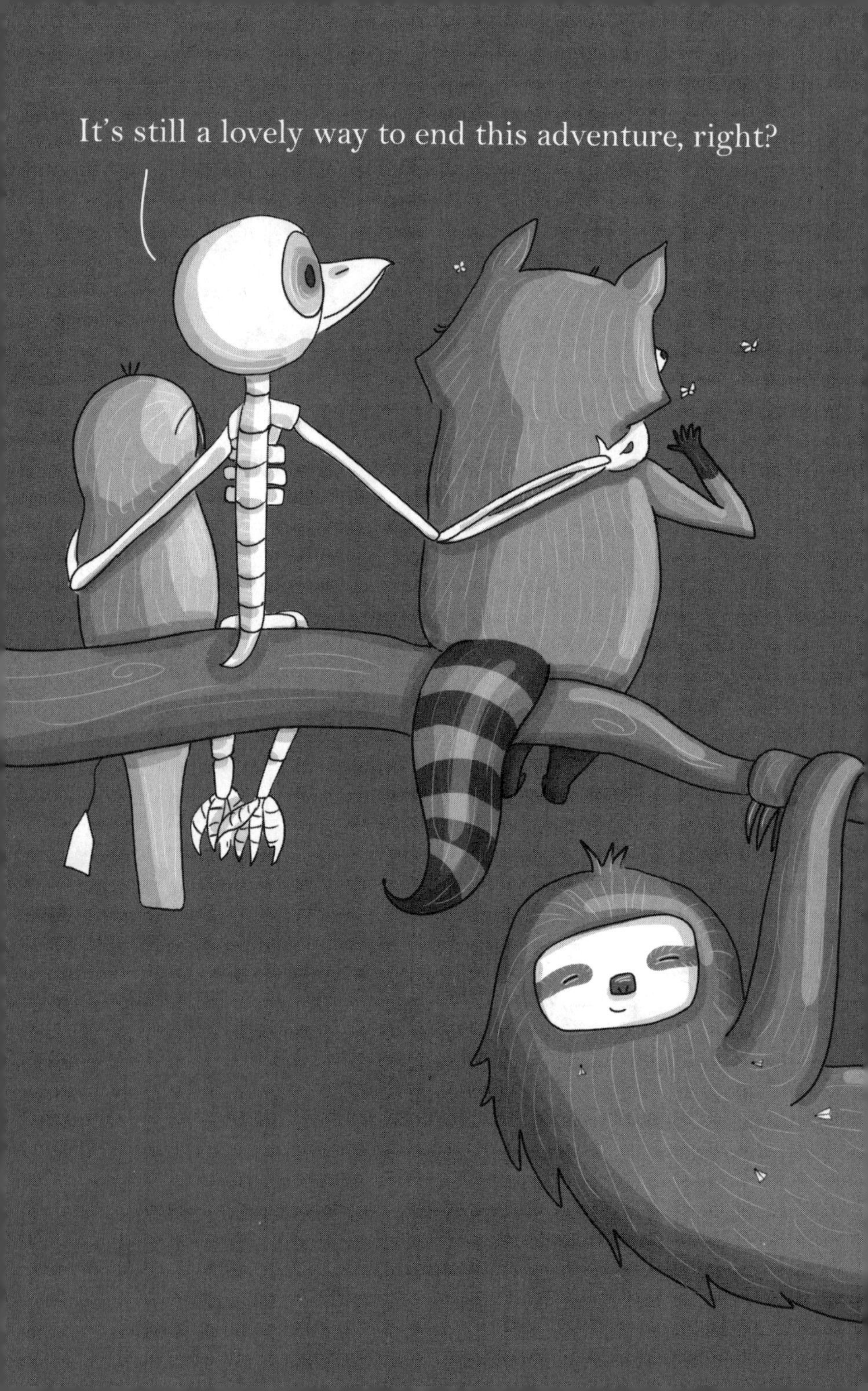
It's still a lovely way to end this adventure, right?

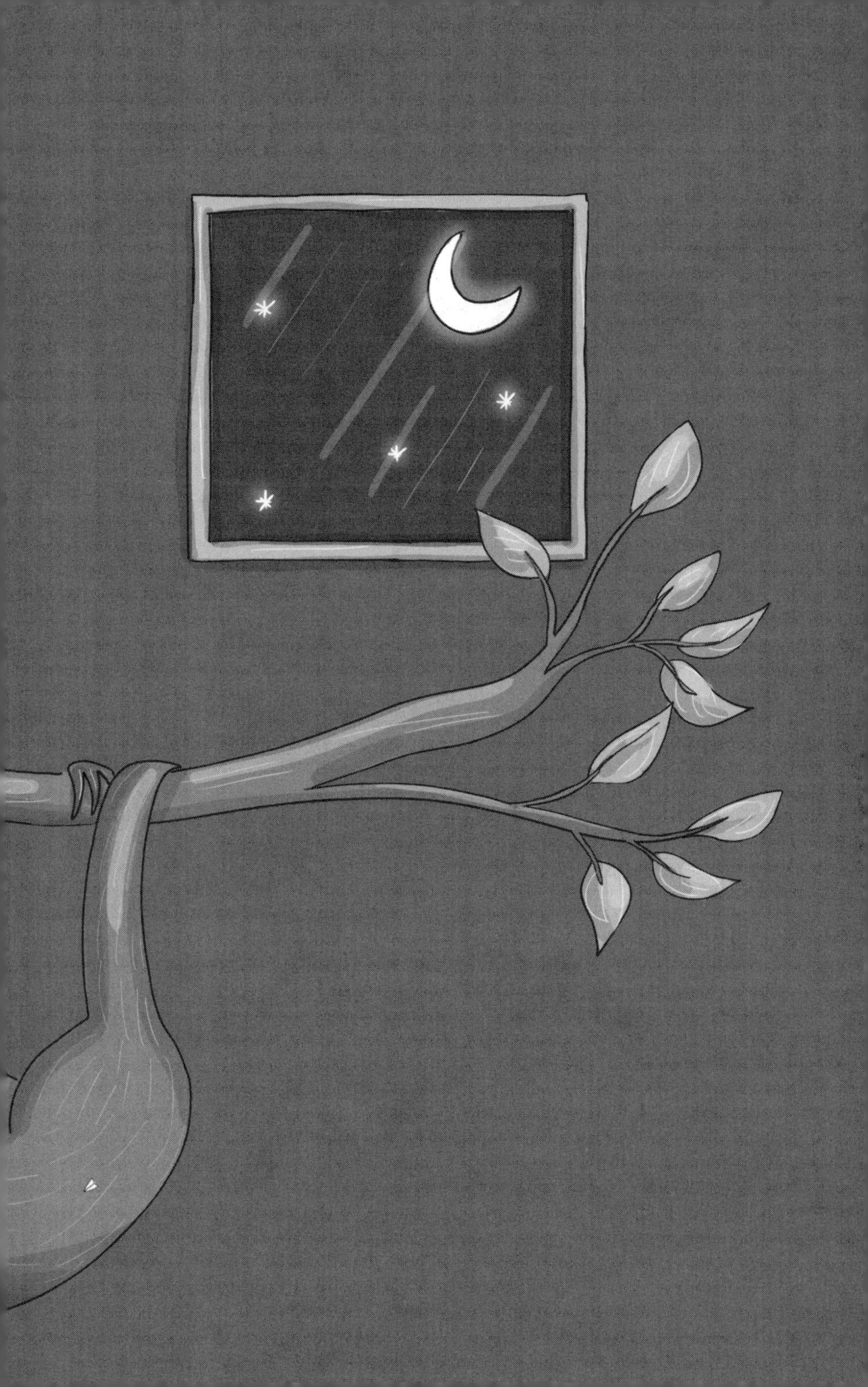

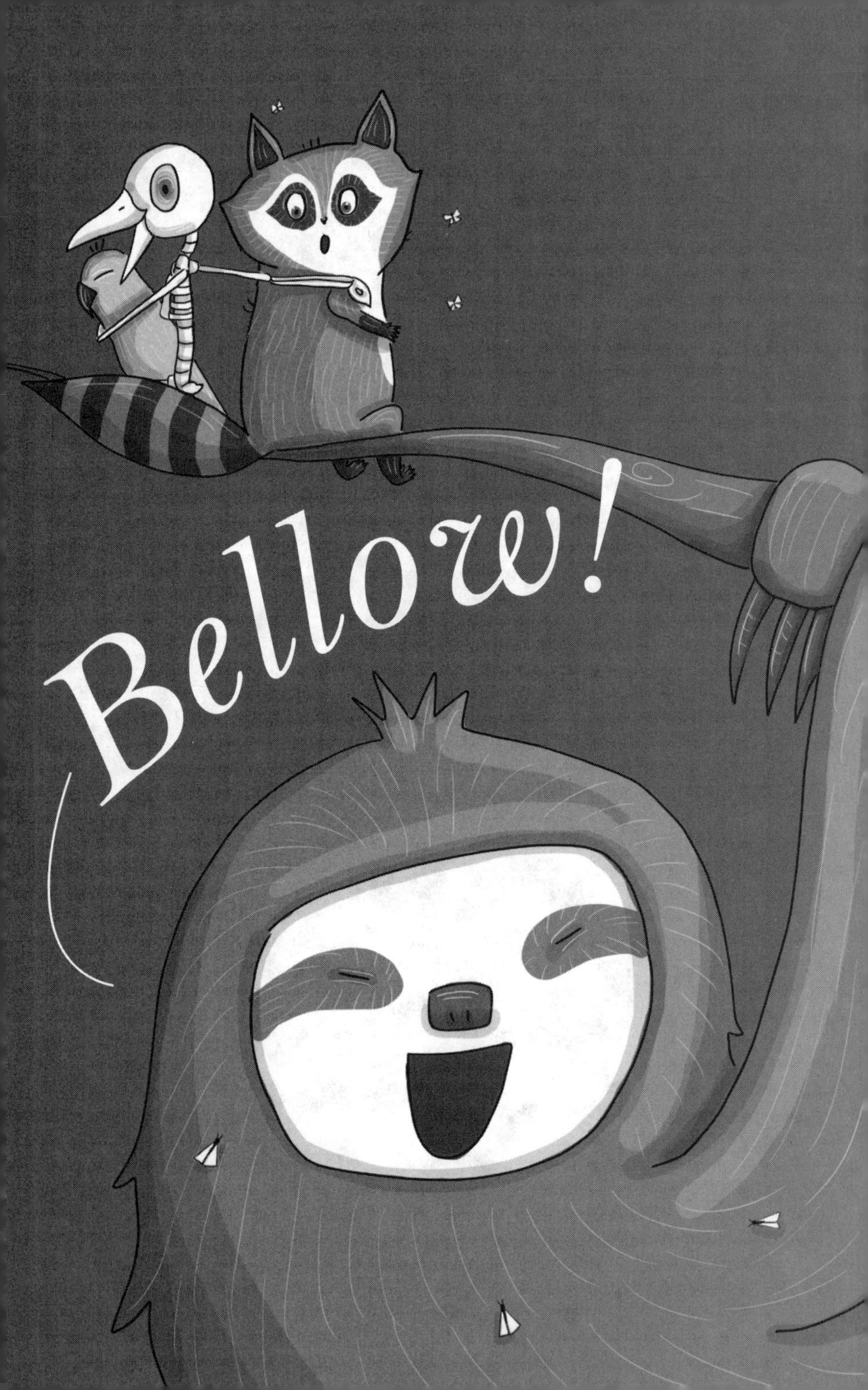
Bellow!

Etch is an imprint of Houghton Mifflin Harcourt Publishing Company.

First published by Allen & Unwin in 2019.

hmhbooks.com

The text was set in Bell MT, KG Happy Solid, and KG Summer Storm.

The Library of Congress Cataloging-in-Publication data is on file.
ISBN: 978-0-358-30933-8 hardcover
ISBN: 978-0-358-30939-0 paperback

Manufactured in the United States of America
DOC 10 9 8 7 6 5 4 3 2 1
4500818641

ACKNOWLEDGMENTS

I am grateful to all the amazing children, parents, teachers, and librarians who have written me messages, sent letters, or spoken with me at events. Your excitement helped me get through the hard parts of creating this book.

Thank you to all the booksellers for hosting me at events and selling my books—you are so important to our community and I appreciate your amazing support! Special thanks to Leesa at The Little Bookroom for her ongoing encouragement and energy . . . not just for me, but for all authors and illustrators.

Thank you to Dr. James Wood, an octopus expert who clarified a few of the finer details of octopus behavior for me. Thank you, Jodie and Sophie and the amazing team at Allen & Unwin, for creating this book with me! Thank you to Sadie and Tony for providing feedback on early (and messy) drafts of this story. Many thanks to my fellow writers and illustrators for all your wisdom and guidance, and many more to my friends for helping keep my life and family together while working on this book. And last but not least, thank you to Eric, Calvin, Tassie, and Moke for everything.

ABOUT THE AUTHOR

Renée Treml was born and raised in the United States and moved to Australia in 2007 so her husband could conduct research in the Coral Triangle. She first met Sherlock Bones shortly after arriving—he was posing in an exhibit of tawny frogmouth skeletons in the Queensland Museum in Brisbane.

Renée's stories and illustrations are inspired by nature and influenced by her background in environmental science. When Renée is not writing or illustrating, she can be found walking in the bush or on the beach and exploring museums, zoos, and aquariums with her family. She lives and works on the beautiful Surf Coast in Victoria with her husband, son, crazy little dog, and even crazier bearded dragon.

WANT MORE MYSTERY-SOLVING FUN?

Check out *Sherlock Bones and the Natural History Mystery*—available now!

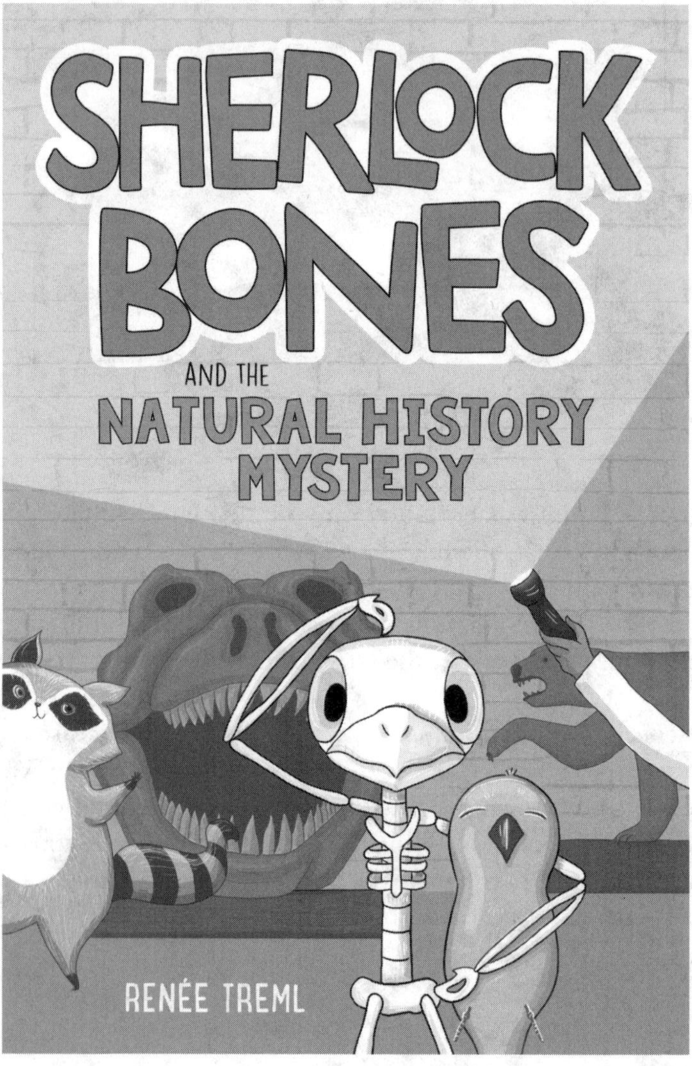
SHERLOCK BONES
AND THE
NATURAL HISTORY MYSTERY
RENÉE TREML